The Quivera Trail

by

Celia Hayes

*for Rosa —
who loves history!*

*Hayes
12/2014*

Geron **GA** *& Associates*

San Antonio, 2013

ISBN-13 978-0934955-32-4
ISBN-10 0-934955-32-8

Geron & Associates
A Division of Watercress Press.
2013

Notes from the Author

Thanks and acknowledgements are due to a great number of people who contributed advice and support to the writer of this novel. I should begin also with thanks to the San Antonio Conservation Society and the Steves Homestead Museum, for allowing me to photograph the hallway of the Steves mansion, which photograph was then used by my clever younger brother Alex of 3iii Graphics in designing the cover. I would also like to thank the extremely helpful docent volunteers of the Texas Transportation Museum, for information regarding the arrival of the railway in San Antonio, the care and storage of a privately-owned parlor car, and for their especially thorough website.

Thanks are also due to Alice Geron of Watercress Press, for editing and encouragement, and to long-time blog-fan Mary "Proud Veteran" Young for friendship and support in time of crisis. Thanks are always due to longtime fan Andrew Brooks of San Diego, California. Upon reading various early chapters of the *Adelsverein Trilogy* posted on online, he jestingly suggested the subtitle of *Barsetshire with Cypress Trees and Lots of Side-Arms,* which has since turned out as apt as it was foresighted, since the interlinked adventures of the Becker, Steinmetz, and Richter families on the Texas frontier has now gone into six volumes.

This book is dedicated with love to Mom and my daughter Jeanne, both of whom were supportive well and above the call of duty, and to the memory of Dad, the best alpha-reader ever.

Celia Hayes
San Antonio, Texas
July, 2013

The Quivera Trail

Entreat me not to leave thee,
Or to return from following after thee:
For whither thou goest, I will go;
And where thou lodgest, I will lodge:
Thy people shall be my people,
And thy God my God - Ruth 1:16

Prelude: Tired of London
October, 1875 – The Langham Hotel, London

On a dreary grey day, three men took their ease in the parlor of a quietly opulent hotel suite. Rather, two of them sat at ease by a glowing fire, while the third looked out of the elaborately silk-curtained window that overlooked Regent's Park, now half-hidden in a hazy veil of rain. The room was as luxurious as a place – which existed by appealing to the very wealthy – could possibly be in this year of our lord and the 39th year of the reign of Victoria, fitted with comfortable furniture and decorations in the very best and most expensive of tastes.

Nothing was too good for a wealthy man from a distant land, taking an extended suite of rooms at the Langham for many months, and Hans Gottfried Richter – Hansi to his friends – surveyed his temporary domain with a great deal of satisfaction, half asleep in the warmth of the room and the luxuriant comfort of a soft chair. He had spent many a night in his younger days in Texas sleeping on the ground and rolled in a blanket or two, underneath his freight wagon or along the cattle trails to the north – those very freight wagons and cattle trails which had made him a very rich and important man. In both the country of his birth and the country where he had made that fortune most folk called him a cattle baron, although those whose fortunes were old and ancestors long-ennobled usually murmured it scornfully from behind a raised hand and not to Hansi Richter's face. Hansi hardly bothered with responding to the scorn of those he did not respect. Those who had merely inherited position and wealth were in his mind the least worthy of any respect at all. For himself, he was a man of simple tastes and elementary comforts; a warm fire, a soft bed with his wife to warm it, and a fine pipe were good enough for him, and had satisfied him for the first decade or two of his adult life. But a new life in a new world, the far frontier of faraway Texas had afforded Hansi Richter many opportunities, all of which he had explored with increasing energy and delight, until he found himself in vigorous middle age, wealthy beyond any expectations of a poor German farmer's youngest son, the owner of more acres than he could count, cattle as many as there were grains of wheat in one of his father's fields, and the father of hard-working and ambitious sons.

Neither of the two younger men presently sharing the comfortable accommodations at the Langham were his sons, but he held both of them in considerable affection and listened to their conversation with mild interest.

The lads were of his kin, but not of blood, a thing which would have been plain to an observer. Hansi was a stocky, thick-shouldered man, dark-headed and dark likewise of eye, coffee-brown, one would have said – and the lads were both tall, lanky, and Saxon-fair, enough alike to be brothers. Their relationship to him was by marriage. Peter Vining was the husband of his oldest and favorite daughter. Peter's cousin, Rudolph Becker, was the son of Liesel Richter's older sister. Hansi put considerable value in family ties.

Peter, sitting opposite the fire from his father-in-law, took his pipe from his mouth and drawled, "Cuz, I would venture a guess that you were tired of life, in being tired of London. Doctor Johnson would not approve." He spoke in English. An old scar made by a sharp blade slashed through his left eyebrow and down the cheek; giving him an appearance of cynical amusement. Peter's left hand was encased in a fine leather glove and he held the pipe stem with it at a curious angle, as if his fingers were stiff. It was an artificial hand, made to replace the one amputated during the last days of the War in Virginia. Dolph, still staring out of the window, answered without turning his head.

"Doc Johnson – is he that drunk ol' sawbones in Elsworth that patched up Billy Inman that time he got into a fight over the pretty waiter girl? I tell you straight, if he likes London he can keep it."

"The immortal Doctor Johnson," answered Peter, a tone of faint exasperation somewhat tingeing his reply. Hansi listened, much amused. "Not, I assure you – a drunken incompetent quack in a trail town, but one of the geniuses of the ages."

"You're the one with all the education, so you would know," answered Dolph without any heat, and his cousin laughed.

"You've surely had an education one way or another, Cuz," he answered. "Now you can claim to be a man of the world, ever since Onkel took it into his head to improve our cattle and show us the Old Country."

Dolph Becker shook his head. "I'd go back to Texas in a heartbeat," he answered. "Nothin' much here I'd want myself. Now I know why Opa Steinmetz and Onkel left when they did."

"None of this – we still have work to do, lads." Hansi roused himself with a start at this, better to take part in the lazy conversation. "And Christmas in Italy – a holiday, eh? A little better weather in winter, so they say."

Dolph finally turned away from the window. He was as reserved as his cousin was outgoing and his smile did not come as easily, but he was as fond of his uncle as his uncle was of him. "They say that in England the roosters don't crow – they gargle. I can believe it. I don't know how you can endure staying in a city like this. The smoke, the noise, and all of the people rushing about."

"I endure," Hansi answered, with a flash of wry wit. "Under the hardship of such conditions as exist at the Langham. Besides, Anna and the boys are having such fun, no?"

"Such fun as is to be had when it's pissing down rain every single hour of every single day," Dolph answered and Peter protested.

"Not true, Cuz – it stopped for a little while last week. There was even a bit of blue sky to be seen."

"I made a note of that," Dolph nodded. "I nearly didn't recognize it for what it was – been so long since I saw it last." At that moment, the outer door to the suite opened and closed, admitting the sound of children's excited voices. In another moment two small boys rushed into the room, their voices excitedly vying with each other in two languages.

"Opa, there was a room, a special room with horrible things; Mama wouldn't let us see!"

"They brought her heads, and made her . . . Papa, can we go to the Baker Street exhibition again? Please?"

"Harry! Christian!" Peter barely made himself heard over the voices of his sons, rambunctious imps of three and four. His wife followed the boys into the room, commanding them briskly in German to be quiet and take turns in speaking. She was a dainty dark-haired woman with a fine creamy complexion, turned out in a walking costume of elegant simplicity, the style favored by a woman with sufficient confidence to insist on dressing to please herself rather than transient fashion and a pocketbook generous enough to afford an expert seamstress and the finest materials. She had already shed her damp mantle-coat in the suite anteroom and was removing the long pins which held her hat tip-tilted on the piled-up mass of her hair.

"I see that the boys loved the wax exhibition," Peter remarked, as Anna Richter Vining stooped to drop a brief but affectionate kiss on his lips. "It was all that I could do to drag them away," she answered. "So many questions! By the time I answer one they have three more."

"Our boys," Peter answered, returning the kiss, while Hansi took the youngest, Christian, onto his lap, listening to the boy's breathless recital with every evidence of fond interest. Harry, nearly five and possessed of single-minded determination, leaned against the arm of Peter's chair and began a similar account. From across the room, Dolph Becker observed this all, a faintly wistful expression on his face. Peter's glance met his from across the room.

"Dear Cuz," he drawled, "observe the fruits of connubial bliss. In the words of Benedict – 'Prince, thou art sad. Get thee a wife, get thee a wife.'"

"When I find a girl who likes dogs and cows," Dolph answered, almost automatically, as if in response to an old jest, "perhaps I will ask her to marry. But I don't think I'll find one such in London." As if he had suddenly come to a decision, he straightened from leaning against the window sill. "Onkel, I think I will go away to the country for a bit. This place chokes me. Too many people."

"Ah," Hansi Richter looked at him with shrewd understanding. He put Christian out of his lap, followed his nephew out of the parlor, and into that room which had been set aside for his use. Dolph took a small valise from under the bed. Open on the counterpane, he was already taking a few items from the wardrobe and tossing them into it. "The old world . . . it is not your place. You cannot be in two at a time, as some of us can. Take your holiday, lad. But don't forget we must depart next week, if we are to be in Italy for Christmas. Where do you think to go, Dolph?"

"Anywhere but here," his nephew answered. "Someplace empty and not too far away. I'll be back in a week, Onkel — don't worry about me."

"I wouldn't stay awake for a moment," Hansi smiled. Dolph was like his father, whom Hansi had considered a good friend, and known as well as one might ever know a silent and stoical man who had spent too many years alone under the blue sky, in the empty rolling miles of the Llano country. On the day this one was born, Hansi recalled, he had taken Dolph's father to Nimitz's tap-room in Fredrichsburg and drunk beer with him, waiting for word from the midwife. And then during the War . . . Hansi wrenched his mind from that particular memory. Events during that bitter War – now more than a decade past – had fired certain ambitions within him, as it had within his nephew. "What hazards could lay in wait for you, after trailing cattle in all weather for ten years, eh?"

"Can't picture any," Dolph answered, but Hansi noted that he had added a heavy Colt revolver to the items in the valise. No, Hansi had no fears for his nephew – not in the English countryside that the lad was heading towards. *What could happen to him, in the green and pleasant lands of the Old Country?*

Chapter 1 – *Enter a Lady, Pursued*

With her knees drawn up to her bosom, as close as her corset would allow, Isobel Lindsay-Groves huddled wretchedly in the window seat of her bedroom, and wondered – yet one more time – what was wrong with her. She leaned her flushed cheek against the cool glass, hardly seeing the winter-burnt park outside, the trees with either bare branches silvered with frost, or pine-green and glittering with frozen droplets, as cold and glittering as Mama's green-velvet afternoon dress. Isobel felt a sob rising into her throat, and forced it back down.

"You are the most awful crybaby, Isobel Lindsay-Groves," she told herself, trying to sound as stern as Nurse, but her voice wavered, as the sob rose up again. "What do you have to cry about then?" she continued, as first one tear and then another rolled down her cheeks. "You should be the happiest girl in England . . . you have a rich Papa who builds the most wonderful bridges, and a beautiful Mama who is very well-thought of at Court, all the pretty dresses you want, and live at Acton Hall," she smeared the back of her hand across one cheek, but the tear on the other fell onto the fuchsia-pink bodice of her gown and made a dark rose blotch. Seeing that, Isobel sobbed anew. Just another item on that long list of her imperfections; where was her handkerchief? Mama insisted that a lady should always have a handkerchief.

"I don't want to go to India!" Isobel wailed – but softly; a lady never raised her voice. "Why can't I ever do anything right, the way that Mama wants?" Not for the first time, the rebellious thought arose in her that maybe if she had been the perfect lady, perhaps then Mama might love her, or at least not be pick-pick-picking away at her always, the way that chickens pecked at each other. That brought a vision of Mama as a long-billed hen, splendid in shiny feathers, but with the same mercilessly beady eyes, always on the alert for the tiniest scrap. Isobel's brief giggle warred with the sobs and vanquished them momentarily. "Fa loves me the way I am!" Isobel told herself, triumphantly, but she was nearly done-in by the insistent sound of a bell ringing distantly within the great pile of building that was Acton Hall. Simultaneously, the little carriage clock on the mantelpiece of her bedroom chimed the quarter hour and someone tapped lightly on her bedroom door.

"Lady Isobel?" A woman's voice. "Lady Isobel, are you nearly ready? Your mother is expecting you downstairs. Her guests are already here. Mr. Spencer has already shown them into the Yellow Salon."

"I am, Kitty-Cat," Isobel answered. "I will be downstairs in a moment," but instead of being content with that answer and going to bear that message downstairs, Mrs. Kittredge the housekeeper opened the door and looked around it. Seeing Isobel's woeful face, Mrs. Kittredge clicked her tongue. She looked back over her shoulder, saying to someone in the corridor behind her,

"Jane, will you bring a jug of cool water to Lady Isobel's room, please? Quickly. Yes, I know that Havers looks after the young mistress as well as her Ladyship, but there is no time for that. Her Ladyship is downstairs this very moment and if Miss Isobel is not down there also in a very few moments . . ." Mrs. Kittredge closed the door softly, and advanced across the room, the keys which hung always from a long loop of heavy ribbon at her waist jingling pleasantly. "Now, you know how your lady mother will be, Miss Isobel," she said, fond but implacable. "You really should indulge her in some small ways. You would be a good bit happier if you did."

"And so would you all below stairs," Isobel answered, and sighed that little quavering sigh that meant the end of tears.

"Little Miss Pert," Mrs. Kittredge answered, but without heat. Unbidden, she sat beside Isobel and took her hand. "Now, tell me, child – whatever is the matter? You know I'll do whatever I may to sort it out. I've known you all your life, before you were ever born! Why such tears, then?"

"Because I am so dreadfully unhappy, Kitty-Cat, without any reason for it that I can tell myself!" If she had been nine years old, instead of nineteen, Isobel would have thrown herself into the housekeeper's matronly lap and begun crying again. And dear Kitty-Cat, as Isobel and her older brothers and sister had always called her when there was no one else around, would have held her comfortingly, wiped her face when she was done with tears, provided a bit of gingerbread or some other sweetmeat, and then given wise and gentle advice. "I thought that when I put up my hair and was presented and had a proper season, then I would be happy, that Mama would be pleased with me, I would have beaux and admirers, maybe even made a good match." Isobel hiccupped. "But I haven't, I am unhappier than ever, and Mama thinks it is my fault, even though I try and do everything just as she commands me, in every respect . . ."

"Your mother only wants what is best for you," Mrs. Kittredge answered calmly. "She wishes for you to make a good match with a worthy gentleman, a gentleman of property and position. Her Ladyship has such high expectations for you."

"I despair of meeting them, Kitty-Cat," Isobel said. "Just as I despair of ever meeting the high regard of all those gentleman which I have been paraded before during this last year. Do you know what it feels like? Like a prize cow at an agricultural fair, polished and groomed and led out to walk back and forth, while all the judges examine over strictly, looking for the tiniest flaw. Of course, they find them, for I am all flaws. I have no graces, no art, I can't dance or flirt or even play the pianoforte!"

"You can ride, Miss Isobel," Mrs. Kittredge answered robustly. "You have the finest seat and the best nerve of any woman in the field. Mr. Arkwright, he will say so to all that will listen in the servant's hall. You have a good heart and I've never seen a dog or a cat yet that didn't make up to you at once. They say that animals always know, and sometimes even better than humans." Someone tapped on the door; at Mrs. Kittredge's quiet command, one of the maids entered, a slender girl with a jug of water which looked almost too heavy for her hands. "Yes, Jane, is it cold water? Then put it on the washstand and bring me one of Lady Isobel's clean flannels, well-moistened in it and wrung out."

"Yes, Mrs. Kittredge," the young maid's voice quavered, as if she were almost too frightened to speak out loud. "Mrs. Kittredge. Marm. I also brought some lavender-flower-water."

"Excellent, Jane, "Mrs. Kittredge nodded, magisterially. "That was well-thought of. One should always anticipate the needs of the Family. There is no better way to advancement in service."

"Yes, Marm. Mrs. Kittredge, Marm." The girl blushed painfully. She looked very young; Isobel noted with a pang that the girl might be thought beautiful, even in a black afternoon dress two sizes too large for her and her dark hair scraped back underneath a prim and plain housemaid's cap. She had an oval face, with delicate features and eyes which were almost the color of pansies, a blue so dark they were nearly purple. How fair she might have looked in the plainest of the dresses that had been made for Isobel's season. Isobel considered how very unfair that was. The maid Jane brought the cool, lavender-scented flannel to Mrs. Kittredge, who accepted it with something of the air of a squire accepting something brought by a loyal young page.

"Thank you, Jane. Now, put this over your eyes, Miss Isobel. See if it will take down the swelling, somewhat. Her Ladyship will see that you have been distressed, and want to know the reason why."

"How can I explain the reason of that to her, when I don't even know myself?" Isobel answered.

"She will demand to know, regardless," Mrs. Kittredge replied. "I would advise you, Miss Isobel, to not even give her cause for inquiry." She placed the flannel over Isobel's eyes and forehead, and Isobel leaned back, allowing the cool weight and the soothing lavender scent to soak into her senses and her puffy eyes, while Kitty-Cat's calm, implacable voice continued. "You are a sensible person, Miss Isobel – think on the talents you possess, and consider how you might use them to obtain a favorable marriage and better than that, with a man who will think well of those qualities. I am sure you will soon meet such a man – perhaps there will be a gentleman following the Hunt, who will not care about any of those Society matters. A nice young country squire, with a fine stable and a well-established estate in Yorkshire or the West Country, who also loves horses and dogs and cats."

"Animals always know," added the hesitant voice of Jane, the maid. "Don't choose a man who's cruel to the beasties, Marm . . . Miss Isobel . . . your ladyship."

"Quite right, Jane," Mrs. Kittredge affirmed. "A man who would be cruel to a poor helpless animal is a man who would be cruel to a child, a woman, or any lesser person within his power. Someone who is kind to the least of His creatures is a man who is kind to all. What is written on their hearts is revealed for all to see. A man who is gentle with poor brute beasts? That makes it plain what is in his heart."

"M' stepfather killed our kitten," the little maid Jane quavered. "That was how we first knew how wicked he could be when crossed."

"Jane," Mrs. Kittredge voice had a faintly chiding tone to it. Isobel heard Jane whisper something apologetic.

Isobel replied firmly, "I would never encourage the attentions of a man who did anything as cruel as that." Her eyes already felt less swollen. "Nor do I think my father would permit me to so accept such advances, but I would so wish a household of my own, to manage as I saw fit and my husband preferred, rather than living under my mother's governance!" She put aside the cool flannel and smiled a little at Mrs. Kittredge and the little maid's concerned faces, to reassure them, but more to hearten herself. "Into the fray once more, Kitty-Cat. I promise, I am revived and ready to face our guests – but I so wish for assurance that your gentle country squire might be among them today!"

"There is a water-spot on your dress, Milady," Jane whispered. Mrs. Kittredge looked vexed. "So there is," she agreed, "And no time to summon Havers!"

"I know!" Jane's face lit with sudden inspiration. In that moment, Isobel noted that Jane and Mrs. Kittredge bore a certain resemblance, in the structure of their faces, particularly about the eyes. Jane hurried to Isobel's dressing table and rummaged in her jewel-case. She returned with a silver butterfly-shaped brooch of colored enamel and set with pearls. "This should cover the spot, Miss Isobel," she said, and then her face flamed pink with embarrassment. "Marm . . . beg pardon, Lady Isobel." Her pale features turned even redder, and those purple-pansy eyes turned pleadingly towards Mrs. Kittredge, as Isobel took the silver brooch from her fingers – fingers rough with needle-pricks and calluses.

"Don't fret, Jane," Isobel began to say, and Mrs. Kittredge interjected smoothly, "Thank you, Jane – I am sure Lady Isobel appreciates your quickness of thought. But do try to remember the proper way to address the Family and your superiors. You no longer live in a cottage, but are in service at Acton Hall, and if you take to heart all that I have taught, you may go higher than merely a sewing maid."

"Yes, Marm . . . Lady Isobel." Jane whispered, her face a bright crimson. She bobbed her head as Mrs. Kittredge added, "You may return to your duties, Jane." Jane dipped an awkward curtsy and fled the room. The door closed quietly, as Mrs. Kittredge opened the clasp of the butterfly brooch. "This will look very well, Lady Isobel," she said. Isobel reflected that Mrs. Kittredge spoke in the same soothing tone to herself as she did the little maid. On sober reflection, domestic servitude under Mrs. Kittredge's stern but kindly rule did not seem such a bad thing. Perhaps the little maid Jane would not have so many griefs and resentments stored up, under her plain black dress and housemaid's apron.

"She bears a resemblance to you, Kitty-Cat," Isobel remarked, as Mrs. Kittredge pinned the brooch over the water-spot on her bodice, "Is she a relation?"

"My oldest niece," Mrs. Kittredge replied. "This is her first position in service."

"Is it? She seems rather older, for a girl just starting out."

"My brother's wife needed Jane at home, to work in the shop after my brother died," Mrs. Kittredge answered. "And then she married again, just two years ago. It was providential that there was a position at the Hall, just at that moment."

"Was her new husband a cruel stepfather?" Isobel ventured idly. He must have been, from what Jane had said about the kitten, so Mrs. Kittredge's reaction was not altogether unexpected. Still, Isobel was taken a little aback by the flash of anger that crossed her face, quickly damped down.

"He cared more for his own, and for the boys," was all that Mrs. Kittredge would say, "and the quarters over the shop were very small. Jane is much happier, here at the Hall. Now, quickly, Lady Isobel – you should be downstairs."

Isobel stifled a tiny sigh: the Yellow Salon was a large room with an ornate plaster ceiling and walls hung with panels of yellow damask. The tall windows facing west were also hung with the same damask; in summer the afternoon sun made the room appear to glow, like a Chinese paper lantern, but in winter the room was garish and comfortless. A fire in the cavernous marble fireplace only heated the immediate area; the rest of the salon would be chilly and threaded with icy drafts. *Mama only favors it because of her Winterhalter portrait,* Isobel told herself. She straightened her back as she came down the staircase, the branching staircase that turned in noble, polished angles from the upper floors, all the way down into Acton's Jacobean-paneled Great Hall – an acre of polished wood floor, with a minstrel-gallery above, adorned with iron-work sconces filled with a constellation of wax candles on grand occasions, statues of gods, suits of armor, any number of splendid pictures of ancestors and scenery – but none as fine as the Winterhalter in the Yellow Salon, Isobel thought to herself. The entry hall was intended to overawe guests, even as they were being made welcome. Rooms like the Yellow Salon, the breakfast room, the dining room, the West Parlor, the Gallery and all the rest . . . those rooms were to make the guests feel slightly more welcome, perhaps even more comfortable. It came to Isobel – not for the first time – how like a railway station platform the public rooms at Acton felt. It was the same in the London house – the rooms were for entertaining in, to accommodate huge numbers of people for a great ball or a royal visit. The chairs and the divans in the drawing room were not truly to put guests at ease, or to make them feel at comfortable. They were stiff, fashionable, in the latest taste . . . not a bit like Fa's study, or Mama's little private sitting-room . . . nothing like the rooms and places that Isobel thought of when she thought of "home," nothing like what she thought of in a tiny corner of her heart, all during that exhausting season just past. Fa. The dogs. The stables. Riding out on a winter-crisp morning. None around her thinking of how a gawk she was, only welcoming and pleasant; Lady Isobel with the good seat and a hand with horseflesh, the younger daughter of Sir Robert. Nothing else demanded of her, save that she keep up with the Hunt, and it hardly mattered that she was what she was; plump and homely and awkward, save if she was on horseback.

My Season was an abject failure, Isobel said to herself, as she reached the bottom of that grand sweeping staircase. *So here am I – I must redeem some sort of success out of it. I simply must – else how will I ever escape Mama? She wishes me to go to India with Papa next year. To go out there – with all its diseases and snakes and awfulness – and if I don't make a good catch, oh the very horror of it! Martyn says his friends in the Regiment have a cruel name for it – they call such girls 'the fishing fleet' and at the end of the season, if they are not wed, they are the 'returned empties.'*

Isobel lifted her chin stubbornly. Such humiliation was unendurable, even more unbearable than the current humiliation, but in what direction lay escape? She could see no other path than the one which her mother had marked out for her, just as there was no permitted variance from her mother's implacable insistence on her presence at tea. *I know very little more about the world than I did before I made my debut into it,* Isobel thought. *Surely I should have enough knowledge by now to circumvent Mama's wishes and have a life for myself. If only Fa did not yield to her in every particular regarding my prospects!*

She walked across the vast, echoing space of the grand hallway, towards the tall pillar-guarded doors to the Statuary gallery, and through it into the Yellow Salon. The heels of her slippers pattered gently across the gleaming oak flooring. One of the junior footmen sprang out of the shadows and opened the door for her. Isobel nodded stiffly, precisely once. One was not supposed to notice the servants, insisted Mama – but Isobel had always vaguely thought it was rude not to make any notice at all. *Oh, one of the new ones. Tall, of course, but such a farm-boy. I think he has been fighting, for he has a graze on his cheek. He must be someone's nephew or cousin. I wish I could ask whose, and where he comes from, and if he misses the place he came from, and what he thinks of the Hall.*

She walked on through the gallery, a long room lit with tall French windows looking out into terrace above the formal gardens. Her shoes did not make quite such a noise here. The floor was of marble squares and angles, bisected by a long carpet runner woven in faded classical motifs. Each window was paired with a tall niche in the opposite wall which held a statue on a tall stone plinth, a work in bronze or marble. Isobel's great-grandfather had brought them back from his Grand Tour in Italy, many years before – Roman gods and goddesses, warriors and heroes – and had the gallery built to house them, as part of a splendid new addition to the Hall. It was still splendid, although Mama disliked the gallery, since it was in the old-fashioned Classical taste of a hundred and fifty years ago. But Fa would never allow her to redecorate, as he had a sentimental attachment to the gallery and accounts of his grandfather's travels and the statuary. At the end of the Gallery, another footman silently appeared; ready to open the doors for Isobel.

"Are there many guests – and am I terribly late, Horgan?" Isobel whispered to him, for the First Footman was an old friend, having served in the Hall since she was a small child.

"A fair number, Lady Isobel," he whispered, without moving the glacial expression of his face. "And not as such. They've just now brought in the cakes an' all."

Isobel stifled a tiny groan. She was late. "Just open it enough to let me slip inside," she begged. "With so many guests, perhaps my mother …"

Horgan winked at her in reassurance and opened one half of the great-double door into the drawing room just wide enough to allow her to squeeze through the gap. He closed it silently, imperceptibly behind her, and Isobel hurried across the floor towards the nearest welcoming sea of Axminster carpet. She kept a nervous eye on the gathering around the fireplace; oh, good – Mama was talking to her older brother, Robert whom everyone still called Robin, and his wife, Eleanor. Mama's head was turned away from the door. *Poor Eleanor*, Isobel thought, with sympathy – *she looks like a poor bird, hypnotized by a snake. I don't believe she really likes coming to Acton; three children and an establishment of her own and Mama still talks to her as if she were my age.* Isobel might have a chance of taking a place on one of the settees next to her brother Martyn. Fa was standing up, leaning against the fireplace. He looked across the room, and met her eye with a knowing look of conspirational sympathy – *dear Fa*, Isobel thought. *I should have been another son, since we are so alike, Fa and I. No doubt of my sire, as far as Robin and I are concerned – only Martyn and Victoria resemble Mama.*

Martyn, sitting with a cup of tea in one hand and a small plate of cake in the other, looked up at her as she slipped with a gentle rustle of skirts around the edge of the settee and obligingly shifted a little way to make room for her. He also winked, as he handed her the plate of cake, with a silver fork laid invitingly close to the sweet, and murmured, sotto-voice,

"Better late than never, Izzy."

Isobel made a face at him. They were barely three years apart in age. They had shared the nursery until Martyn was dispatched to boarding school and shared it again on his holidays. She settled onto the stiff-horsehair-stuffed cushions of the settee, which – now that she had achieved it, was a welcome refuge from which to look at the other guests; her sister Victoria and her husband, the Honorable Grenville Stanley, an older lady and gentleman who Isobel knew must be his aunt and uncle, and a dozen or so others besides her family, taking their ease with cups of tea out of delicate china, glazed in shades of yellow and trimmed with gold – Doulton to match the drawing-room. Now that she could draw an easy breath again, she could try and look as if she had been there for some few moments longer than she had. As always her eyes went to the Winterhalter portrait over the fireplace: Mama in her debut gown, a vision in white and lace, every stitch gloriously and gracefully detailed, from the curve of white feathers over her pale curls, down to the toes of her slippers, just peeking out from underneath the hem of her dress, with the court train falling in heavy velvet folds. *Caroline Mary de Brough in her presentation robes. Mama is beautiful,* Isobel acknowledged to herself – *and she is still beautiful. But as Mr. Winterhalter painted her – she looks so pleasant, as if she is about to laugh.* To drop her eyes from the lovely, laughing, hazel-eyed girl in the portrait, to Mama in the living flesh, on a winter afternoon almost thirty years after she had sat for Mr. Winterhalter was to experience a kind of shock. Isobel could not imagine Mama laughing, carefree as a girl, any more than she could imagine a warm look in her eyes – especially a warm look towards the least and youngest of her daughters. Victoria resembled Mama, as did Martyn, tall and slender, as graceful as a lily-stem, Isobel acknowledged this at least the thousandth time. She and Robin had the look of Fa about them; sturdy and square-shouldered, with round faces, snub noses, and light brown hair. At least her locks were as thick as fashion required – a bounty the color of demerara sugar, falling to her waist when unpinned. A parlor-maid deftly handed her a cup of tea, moving as a silent black and white ghost among Mama's guests, while talk washed back and forth like the last bit of a wave, reaching up through a rocky tidal pool before retreating again; talk of the Hunt tomorrow, of how Robin's eldest son had done at school, of the Court, and how Mama's precious palm-trees were passing the winter, tucked up with burlap comforters stuffed with straw around sewn around their leaves.

At her side, Martyn stretched out his legs and lounged against the armrest, and drawled, "Fa says you ain't so keen on this venture with the fishing fleet, little sis. Don't see why not – you should have a sparkling good season. I know plenty of upright sorts, out there. I'll be around, before I have to go up-country with the Regiment, I'll introduce you to them all. With Fa and I to look after you, out from under Mama's thumb, I think you might even make a very good catch on the voyage out." He winked at her broadly and Isobel's heart sank, under her fuchsia-pink bodice. Even Martyn accepted Mama's plan as a *fait accompli.* From beside the fireplace, leaning against the mantel, holding a teacup and saucer which looked absurdly small in his rugged hand, Fa smiled approvingly at her. Dear Fa, Isobel thought with deep affection; he always made her feel better, as if she were still a small girl, riding on his shoulders. Nothing bad could ever happen to her when she was with Fa, blunt-featured as a country farmer, stocky and broad-shouldered enough to strain the seams of his coats, however carefully tailored they were. He had been the youngest son of a younger son. In his youth, Sir Robert was not considered to be in the line of inheritance, and so he made his own way in the world, training as an engineer and builder of great works, until the death of first one childless kinsman and then two more had abruptly brought him home to do his duty for Acton and the family, to marry Mama, twenty years younger than himself, and bring forth heirs of his own. Fa, whose neck-cloth was always slightly awry, his hands roughened from the work that he loved; now he came around from the fireplace, and stood at the back of the settee.

"It will be a splendid adventure, Pet," he exclaimed, reaching down to pat her cheek. "Just think – we'll go on a tiger hunt, if you like, and I will show you both that great bridge that we built at Pures over the Soane River, Turnbull and I between us!"

"The longest bridge in India, so the chaps all say," Martyn answered; his and Fa's eyes were alike lit with the same exuberance.

"Dear Fa, you would make a walk through the garden into a grand adventure," Isobel answered and a little of her despair lightened. It wouldn't be quite so dreadful, with Fa. Both he and Martyn loved India, for all the heat and sickness and dreadful conditions, not to mention the ongoing unrest among the native tribes along the frontier. Fa had done the work there which he recalled most fondly. She took a drink of her tea, sweet and milky. Tea came from India, she marveled – perhaps she could see a tea plantation! *What did a tea bush look like,* she wondered; *did it truly have green leaves and of whatever shape?* With a part of her mind, she heard her mother's decisive voice, emerging from the sea-wash of conversation like a rock fang, one of those which wrecked the unwary.

". . . late summer of course. Sir Robert and our youngest son will accompany Lady Isobel, of course." At hearing her own name, Isobel had the sensation of being jerked back to earth. Shaken out of her contemplation of tea and wondering if tea leaves were aromatic like mint leaves and shaped similarly, she glanced up and met her mother's eye. For the first time, her mother was aware of her in the room. Now she bent the full severity of her regard upon her youngest daughter. "Isobel; so kind of you to join us at last."

Isobel's stomach cramped, with a sudden intensity that left her breathless. *No, Mama had not been fooled in the slightest. There was no way in the world to fool Mama.* Her stomach cramped again. Mama never took her eye off Isobel, not for a moment, not ever. There was no escape from that basilisk gaze and the merciless judgment that added up and ever found her wanting. Isobel tasted bile in the back of her throat. There was that peculiar hollow feeling in her chest and a lightness in her head; she was going to be sick, she was going to be sick, right in front of Mama's guests in the Yellow Salon.

"Pet?" That was Fa's voice, puzzled and concerned, and Martyn's face, so close to hers, echoing those feelings, assuring with blithe insouciance,

"Oh, but Mama – she's been here for simply ages. We've been talking about tomorrow's hunt. Fa says he will take the wolfhounds with us, in case we run into a wolf!"

"Indeed," Mama answered dryly. Isobel swallowed her nausea. Fa's hand was upon her shoulder, warm and reassuring. With fingers which she prided herself did not tremble, she raised a bite of cake on a silver fork to her lips. In that instant, Mama added, "Really, Isobel – you should not indulge yourself with sweets, like a greedy schoolgirl. The doctors now say it is not healthy to lace so tightly but what else can one can one do, against such an excess of flesh?"

"I am sorry, Mama," Isobel choked, as her stomach rebelled for once and all. She dropped the fork with a little ringing clatter and the bit of cake fell, shedding crumbs onto the floor at her feet as Martyn took the plate from her. "I . . . I do not feel well. Mama, Fa . . . please make my excuses."

She sprang to her feet and ran out of the room – barely aware of the exclamations rising behind her, of Fa's louder voice and Martyn's light footsteps. She was dimly aware of Horgan opening the door for her, of his great moon-face looking down at her as she ran past him, ran the length of the gallery and out into the hall. Up the stairs, as her stomach heaved, rebelliously. She fought to master that hollow feeling in her throat, and a buzzing in her ears, as if she would faint. She couldn't be sick in the corridor but she had no hope of reaching the safe refuge of her room. She clapped one hand over her mouth and wrenched at the doorknob of the nearest room at the top of the stairs, a little room tucked away beyond the angle of the stairs to the third floor – a little, odd-shaped room too small to be a bedroom, but which boasted a fine tall window and plenty of light. It had long since been fitted out as a workroom for a seamstress or the sewing maid to work, mending clothes and linens, fitted with cabinets, a table and a comfortable chair. As Isobel burst through the door, the little maid Jane started up from her chair, something white falling unnoticed from her lap.

"Oh, ma'am!" Jane cried at once. "Is there aught the matter?"

"I'm going to be sick," Isobel began. It was too late; vomit exploded from her mouth, into the hands clasped to her lips. She was very little aware of anything after that. She sank to her knees onto the floor, dimly grateful for the cool weight of an enamel basin in her hands, as she was sick into it, until there was nothing else to be sick with, nauseated anew with disgust from the smell of it. Someone held her shoulders, of that she was sure, someone with gentle authority. When she was done with being sick – although her stomach still roiled – that someone took the basin from her, lifted her forehead until she sat upright.

"Lady Isobel, do you want that I should send for the doctor?" Jane quavered. "Do you think you're going to be sick again?"

"I don't think so, Jane." Isobel answered, out of breath. "Just let me sit for a moment."

"You don't look well." Jane didn't move from where she knelt on the floor, regarding Isobel anxiously. "You should have something to drink. It'll settle things, like."

Isobel's stomach roiled again at the thought. "I couldn't possibly," she moaned. "I'd only bring it up again."

Jane answered, "If there's naught in you to be sick with, you might do yourself an injury."

"I'd rather go back to my room," Isobel answered. When Jane still looked dubious, she added, "I am sure I will be all right, as soon as I lay down. Oh," she looked down at herself. "There's some sick on my dress."

"I'll see to it, Lady Isobel," Jane replied. She stood and reached down to help Isobel from the floor. "Do you wish me to send for Havers?" she ventured, uncertainly. Isobel said, "No, just help me to my room, and assist me out of this dress."

Her own room was a refuge; she sighed with relief when the door closed behind the two of them, lady and maid. She couldn't hear anything from downstairs; perhaps no one had taken particular note of her hasty exit. Mama would not leave her guests and Fa would not think anything amiss for sometime. She sank unto the dressing table stool just in time, for her knees were wobbling and she felt the slightest bit faint. Someone did tap on her door, as Jane was divesting her of the spotted fuchsia dress; Mrs. Kittredge, who entered softly and sized up the situation at a glance.

"Havers is at tea in the servant's hall," she began, just as Jane had offered to send for Mama's personal maid.

Isobel answered, "No, Kitty-Cat. Jane has been – is being of very good service to me." She gasped, as Jane loosened her stays. "She is doing very well at taking care of me – no need to disturb Havers." Indeed, Jane was working deftly and with care with Isobel's garments, so absorbed in that task that she was biting on her lower lip – unfastening every button, cord or ribbon-tie, removing the pins from her hair, so that Isobel hardly needed to move in response. "I think I will lie down, Kitty-Cat."

"I will bring you some peppermint tea," Jane whispered. "I know where there is a spirit-stove in the still-room – I need never bother them as is downstairs."

"I would like that, very much," Isobel answered. Jane carried away her neatly-folded petticoats and the soiled dress. Mrs. Kittredge turned back the coverlet on Isobel's bed and thumped the pillows to fluff them up.

"Here is your nightgown, then, Miss Isobel," she offered. Isobel was more than grateful for Jane's silent return and her unobtrusive assistance with the buttons. Mrs. Kittredge watched the two of them, her concern quite evident on her pleasant countenance. Isobel could not be certain which of the two of them she worried the most over, herself or Jane. Isobel sank back onto the pillows with a sigh.

"Kitty-Cat," she said, as the door closed softly behind Jane. "There is a favor which I would ask of you . . ."

Jane Goodacre pattered silently down the hallway to the stillroom, in the oldest part of the hall, a tiny stone-walled room which smelt of herbs and cordials, faintly of medicine; she had no keys to unlock that particular cupboard, for that was Auntie Lydia's domain. No – Mrs. Kittredge, Jane reminded herself, although she had never called her Auntie anything else, not until the day when . . . Jane squeezed her eyes shut for a brief moment, a prayer of thanks for the day when Auntie Lydia came.

I knew what He was after, that dirty dog – what all men want, and once Mam began to wear her apron high – He had set his mind to having it, always trying to get me aside from Mam and the boys, and he was angry that he couldn't. No mistake, Him glaring at me, all the while. And the worst of it, I think Mam guessed, but yet didn't want to know. But Auntie Lydia, she knew very well, being mistress of a big house and all. Yes, her Ladyship may be the mistress of Acton, but Auntie Lydia, she has the management of it. She came to visit Mam and us in Didcot, and in the just in the space of an afternoon, Aunt Lydia knew exactly what He was after and the trouble it would make for me. She listened to Mam wittering about how I wouldn't go and help Him in the storehouse without one of the boys with us, and looked at Him, glowering over Mam's tea-table, and she came right out and said,

"Pack her things, this very afternoon. I'll be taking Jane back to Acton with me, Rose. There's a good place for her among the maids, at fifteen

*shillings a month and I'll see to it that some of her wages are sent to you.
Surely the boys are old enough now to help in the shop."*

*"But Lydia – she's so young, too young to be working so far away from
home!" Mam began to sniffle.*

*Aunt Lydia looked back at them both – such a meaning look she gave
Him, and she snapped, "My brother's daughter, god rest him, is sixteen years
of age this very month and I know very well what she might be old enough
for!" Then she turned to me and said, "Jane, would you like going into service
at Acton? The work is no harder than the shop, but you must always guard
your tongue and mind your manners."*

*"Oh, yes, Auntie Lydia!" I answered joyful-like, for it was like seeing a
prison door open and sunlight pouring in. "Please, Mam – may I?"*

*"You must remember to call me Mrs. Kittredge, after today," Auntie
Lydia said, something stern. "It is not your mam's decision, rather it is mine,
and yours." And then she looked at Mam and Him and I could see how she
could have the management of Acton, for she looked so hard and angry, any
fool could see it wouldn't do to cross her, not even the Queen herself. "My
brother James was dear to me, Rose: I will see his daughter safely on the way
towards bettering herself."*

*And at that, the both of them had nowt to say and I went back to Acton
that very day with my aunt, with my few things in a bundle like a beggar. But
now I have four dresses and a quiet place to work during the day – never
worrying about if Him should catch me. We maids have our own little rooms,
only two of us to share up under the eaves and the menservants have their
own separate stair to their rooms.*

Jane poured water from the kettle as soon as it began to purr: a tisane of
peppermint leaves, just the thing. *Poor Lady Isobel*, Jane thought, as she
looked for a tray with a proper little cloth to line it. *She looked that sick even
before she went downstairs.* Jane had ordinarily little to do with the Family
directly; they were as distant as figures on the stage at a theater-show that she
had been taken to, a long time ago. When she first came to Acton, they
appeared distant and glamorous. In the servants' hall they thrilled to read
about young Lady Isobel's debut. It seemed to Jane that an indefinable
glamour clung to Lady Caroline's garments, something that left traces on her
own hands, as a butterfly leaves a magical dust when one brushed against its
wings. The doings of the Family was as marvelous as watching an ongoing
stage-show to Jane; buff and down-to-earth Sir Robert, who never put on any
side with anyone, according to Mr. Spencer, the butler – and Lady Caroline,
once the acknowledged beauty of the Court and bridesmaid to Her Majesty.

Mr. Spencer approved of Lady Caroline without reserve. *She had high standards,* said Mr. Spencer, loftily. It was all, thought Jane, sitting with the other maids in the servants' hall and listening to the talk between the senior staff, as good as Punch and Judy – but she would never say so to anyone, except Auntie Lydia.

Jane regarded the tray. Yes, Auntie Lydia would approve: tray, cloth, delicate china cup and saucer, once of a fine but now unfashionable set, banished upstairs to the stillroom and for use of the upper servants, or the nursery. *Poor Lady Isobel, looking so miserable,* thought Jane – *like one of my little brothers, when they were ailing.* Queerly enough, Jane felt protective of Lady Isobel, as if someone had put her into Jane's care. She carried her tray from the stillroom, down the turning corridor in the old part of the Hall, up a half-flight to the new part, and down the wider corridor to Lady Isobel's room. She tapped twice, hearing voices within – and was momentarily startled at Sir Robert's voice bidding her to enter.

Aunt Lydia stood beyond the bed and Sir Robert sat in the chair next to it with Lady Isobel's hand in his. Jane's heart sank right down into her high-buttoned shoes; Sir Robert must be angry with her for some reason and she couldn't think what that reason might be. She had never spoken to Sir Robert. As far as she knew he had never taken notice of her, more than he had any of the maids, save in those absent-minded moments when one of them brought in the tea-tray or brought a message to his study. It took Jane some moments to realize that Aunt Lydia was beaming with quiet approval.

"Well, young Jane, is it?" Sir Robert asked. "And how long have you been working, at the Hall, hey?"

Jane flushed pink and answered, "Yes . . . yes, Sir Robert. Jane Goodacre. Since March this year, Sir Robert."

"Jane has been working upstairs as sewing-maid, Sir Robert," Aunt Lydia spoke as if she were tactfully reminding Sir Robert of something he had forgotten. "She has given every satisfaction with her work."

"Jolly good, then," Sir Robert beamed. "Jolly good. So, little miss Jane – are you happy with the mending and the ironing? Or are you ready to advance in service?"

"I . . ." Jane looked from face to face, looking for a clue to what she should say. She really quite liked the duties she had, the quiet solitude of the little sewing room – but one expected to advance.

"Lady Isobel has asked that you be given a position as her personal maid, Jane," Aunt Lydia explained. Even though she sounded as if she were issuing a warning, she still looked quite pleased. "It is, of course, quite an advance for one so young – and a great responsibility, as well as an increase in wages to twenty-five shillings monthly. Sir Robert and I wished that you be agreeable to this change in your duties. You will require instruction from Havers for a time, on certain elements such as hairdressing. As you will be in constant attendance on Lady Isobel, you need to keep in mind her best interest and her good name, always."

"No bullying the little maid into looking the other way, whilst you run away with some sponger," Sir Robert said, with bluff good humor to his daughter.

"Oh, Fa, I would never," Lady Isobel answered. "Bully Jane or run away." She turned her trusting hazel regard onto Jane. "I would like it so much. Havers is grim and ancient and grumbles under her breath that she must take time with me when she should be attending on Mama. Would you, Jane?"

Jane thought only momentarily of how long her days would be, attending on Lady Isobel from before the time she rose in the morning, to when she went to bed and all those duties in between, seeing to her clothes, her hair, her person, and her possessions, accompanying her when required, and waiting on her return when not. She considered only briefly her own inexperience and the high standards expected of a personal attendant. Lady Isobel had asked specifically for her – needed her, plain Jane Goodacre. Poor Lady Isobel, so unhappy and never daring to show it, just as Jane had been so unhappy, avoiding the malevolent attention of her stepfather, until Aunt Lydia came to her rescue. Jane's chin lifted.

"Yes, Milady, I shall."

Chapter 2 - *A Traveler from a New Land*

On the whole, Jane Goodacre reflected, the morning of her first day as personal maid to Lady Isobel, it was much more interesting – if a little more onerous – than her duties in the sewing room. Havers was torn between scorn, impatience and relief at having to hand over that portion of her duties as regards Lady Isobel to – as she said it, "A slip of a girl, with not even a year in service, and what were things coming to, then?" She had said that over supper in Mrs. Kittredge's parlor last night. Iris, the senior still-room maid had replied, "Well, Miss Havers, haven't you been complaining all year about having to look after both of their Ladyships? Strikes me your complaint now is having to address Jane as Miss Goodacre!" Whereupon Mr. Spencer, the butler had frowned magisterially upon them all and intoned, "Mrs. Kittredge and the Family have approved of Miss Goodacre, and Lady Isobel specifically requested her service. In my opinion, we should congratulate Miss Goodacre on her unexpected advancement. Her time in service at the Hall may have been brief, but such an honor bestowed upon her provides ample proof that she has not wasted a moment of those days and hours."

"Yes, Mr. Spencer," Jane had been emboldened to speak above a whisper. It had always been her mind since coming to the Hall that Mr. Spencer was really much more lordly, more intimidating than did his Lordship. More dignified, anyway; Sir Robert's cravat was often untied, the neck of his shirt unbuttoned, and the knees of his trousers in a disgraceful state from mud and dog-hair, and he certainly didn't bother with putting on airs, whereas Mr. Spencer was always impeccably turned out, eternally dignified, and never hesitated to remind all concerned of the required protocol. Now that she thought on it, Sir Robert minded her very much of jolly old Mr. Satterfield, who kept the pub in Upton; always interested in anyone's concern and more than happy to take off his coat and help out. She stifled a giggle, as she carefully pinned up Lady Isobel's heavy braid of hair into a knot, high on the back of her head. Lady Isobel met her mirrored eyes, and asked,

"Did you just think of something amusing, Jane?"

"I did," Jane answered, and daringly, enlarged on that answer. "It came to me, Milady, that Sir Robert reminds me of Mr. Satterfield at the Shepherd's Rest. Not so much in the looks, but the manner."

"Oh, my!" Isobel giggled, "I had never thought of that – but you are right. How very perceptive, Jane, and I had never seen it! Fa is very like Mine Host at the Shepherd's Rest. And do you know," she met Jane's eyes in the mirror again, "Martyn once told me there was an awful scandal, years and years ago. When Fa's grandfather was a young man, he fell in love with the daughter of Mr. Satterfield's ever-so-many-great-grandfather. The scandal is that Mr. Satterfield might yet be a sort of cousin to us, anyway."

"Indeed?" Jane answered, and thoughtfully inserted another hair pin. *Well, nothing new under the sun,* she said to herself, and regarded her handiwork with approval: Lady Isobel in her trimly-cut riding habit – a plain black skirt and jacket, over a white shirtwaist and stock and so much more flattering to her than her every-day dresses. Or perhaps it was because Lady Isobel preferred going out to the fields on horseback, so she radiated happiness rather than the misery of yesterday, bidden to tea in the Yellow Salon and sick with nerves and apprehension.

Lady Caroline does not care very much for her younger daughter, Jane realized. It was a heretical thought, but the more that Jane considered it, as she brought out Lady Isobel's hat – a man-style top-hat wound around with a long veil – the better that it fit. *Her Ladyship does not favor my ladyship. She cares not, nor does she think anything amiss when my ladyship runs upstairs, sicking up her very guts. She never came upstairs to see what was the matter, only Sir Robert did. Her mother cares nothing for her, just as Mam cared nothing much for me! Oh, poor Lady Isobel!* Upon that realization, Jane was won over, heart and soul, to be Lady Isobel's lowly but fierce champion, her squire and protector. Lady Isobel was a good lady, a considerate and soft-spoken mistress. It had not escaped Jane that all in the servant's hall spoke of her with affection in the same degree; she and Sir Robert alike. Her ladyship was kind, and fair, asking humbly for Jane to do things for her, as if she were friend or sister. In response, Jane had begun to feel as if Lady Isobel was – aside from the human consideration – a much-treasured doll or small sibling, whom it was Jane's duty and pleasure to dress and groom to best effect. And her clothes and things were all so fine! It was pure joy for Jane to have the responsibility for Lady Isobel's wardrobe, to be able to set those lovely dresses in order, the petticoats trimmed with deep lace flounces, the undergarments of lawn and linen, so finely woven they felt like cobwebs, to select for Lady Isobel what she would wear for every occasion, to lay out the dress and all the other garments – the mantle and her hat, the shoes and stockings – all the fashionable accoutrements suitable for a high-borne young lady.

Now she settled the riding hat on Lady Isobel's head – her hair smooth and gleaming like pale-brown silk from Jane's ministrations with the hairbrush – and arranged her veil over it, tying it carefully so that it would remain secure and their eyes met again in the mirror. Lady Isobel sighed, a happy and contented sigh, just as the tiny mantle-clock chimed.

Thank you Jane! Such a pleasure, after Havers' grumping at me under her breath. I must fly. Fa and my brothers will be waiting for me. If you have any power on earth, Jane, you must contrive somehow to keep me from always being late."

"I shall try my best, Lady Isobel," Jane answered, as Lady Isobel sprang up from the dressing-table bench, looping the sideways-train of her riding habit over one arm and taking up the slender riding-crop in her other hand. "The best of good luck this day, my lady."

"Thank you, Jane!" Lady Isobel flashed a smile over her shoulder as she hurried away. When the door closed behind her, Jane gathered up the clothing that Lady Isobel had shed – her morning dress and assembled petticoats – and sorted out what would need laundering and mending. When she went down the back stairs to the laundry, with a bundle of clothing to be washed in her arms, she paused at the landing, where a tall window gave light onto the flight. The window looked out onto the stable-yard, and there she caught a glimpse of Sir Robert, in his red hunt-coat, with his two sons and Lady Isobel clattering out of the cobbled yard, leaving only quiet behind them.

"Well, today should be a better day than yesterday, for herself!" Jane said to herself, and hitched up the bundle of laundry.

Isobel reveled in everything about this day day, the cold-washed pale blue sky arching overhead, the clean smell of outdoors, the chill breeze washing against her cheeks, and the feel of Thistle's disciplined strength under her. True to his name, he floated over a shallow trench and a low hedge between two fields, winter-ploughed and brown. What a wonderful beast! She reined him in as she caught up to her father, about midday; as powerful as a steam locomotive, yet as gentle as a kitten, perfectly mannered. *Why*, thought Isobel, *can't more people be as honest and straightforward as dogs or horses?* She gathered the reins into one hand, and patted Thistle's dapple-grey neck with the other. He tossed his head, and looked back at her, blowing out a faintly misty breath, and jingling his bridle impatiently as Luath – one of Fa's three wolfhounds walked under his nose. The wolfhounds were as silent as the hounds were noisy, three huge dogs and Luath the size of a small pony. At the edge of a leafless copse of trees lifting bare and shapely branches to the sky, the rabble of hounds went coursing back and forth,

"What a pity," Fa said at last. "Lost him – the Master says we'll try on the other side of Upton. Is it too early yet for a spot of cider, do you think?"

"Yes – especially if you wish to keep from breaking your neck," Isobel
replied and Fa laughed, uproariously.

"Very well then, Pet," he said, as the whole concourse of hounds and
riders crossed back across the field, flowing like water through an opened gate
into a narrow road leading towards the village. Tall bare hedges lined each
side of that road; in the deep shade, where the day's sunshine had not yet
fallen, a crust of ice lined each muddy puddle. Isobel took in a breath of the
air, fresh but with the tang of dead and damp grass, freshly trampled. What a
lovely morning, she thought – out in the open air. Why did she feel so at home
here, on the back of a horse, rather than in her mother's drawing-room? She
and the other hunt members followed after the piebald rabble of hounds, the
master of hounds and his assistants with their long whips containing them in
a compact mass of wriggling backs and tails and ears, until the lane opened
up into a cobbled street, and then another, with the patchwork common in
front of them, with Upton's tiny grey stone church punctuating the blue sky
with it's cross-crowned tower. Thistle shouldered next to Martyn's rangy
brown hunter. Her brother looked across at her and laughed.

"A wonderful morning, Izzy – believe me, I shall be remembering this,
next year, after I return to India. You should, likewise. I vow that you will be
married and have a roof of your own ere twelve months have passed!"

"Not a roof in India!" Isobel answered, determinedly. "Full of rats and
snakes! And I will not go to India. I shall beg Fa – I do not want to go, Martyn!
Can you picture me, being bound hand and foot and being carried on board
ship?"

"The Mater would do that, for your own particular good!" Martyn
laughed and his face sobered, "But you must be married, Izzy. Otherwise,
what is there for you? Be a governess, or a maiden aunt-companion, waiting
on Mama, as she grows ever older and more demanding?"

"Oh, horrors!" Isobel shuddered, contemplating that prospect. "I am at
her beck and call anyway. What would I have to loose?"

"A saddle on a fine horse, and riding out of a winter morning with the
Hunt!" Martyn answered. His gaze sharpened as he looked across towards the
stonework and iron enclosure around the churchyard. "Who is the stranger
that Fa is talking to? Luath has him cornered against the railings, but he
doesn't look the least put-out about it!"

"Anyone with any sense would know there is nothing to fear from Luath,"
Isobel answered, and followed her brother's eyes across the cobbled street, to
where a dog-cart with a pony in harness stood, tied to the railings. A tall and
fair-haired young man stood close by, one hand absently fondling Luath's

great shaggy head as he talked earnestly to Fa. The other two wolfhounds shouldered in for a caress, and yet the young man paid only absent attention to them. He was talking to Fa and Fa responded to him with great interest.

"Dressed like a navvy," Martyn remarked, "Or a student – looks German. Some kind of foreigner, I expect. Not a gentleman, at any rate."

At that same moment, the Master blew his horn and it was time to be away, after a pause in the street before the ancient stonework front of the Traveler's Rest, with the half-timber upper story leaning out above the street below.

"'Straordinary," remarked Fa, as he joined them, straggling out of Upton, at the back of the hounds and the other Hunt members. "Quite extraordinary – Luath and the fellows adored him, the beggars. But they say that dogs can always tell, what?"

"Who was that chap?" Martyn asked. Fa answered, cheerily, "An American, of all things; interesting chap – he owns property in Texas. He and his uncle are in England searching for good blood-stock. Horses and cattle both, but he was quite taken with Luath and the lads. I've invited him to come and see the puppies this afternoon. What a sight, eh? When your mother looks at him over the teacups? That would make a cat laugh, wouldn't it?" Sir Robert chuckled, while Martyn and Isobel exchanged glances.

"Well, Fa – it'll be your funeral if the Mater sets an eye on him, looking like that." Martyn said, "He looks like a tramp, fresh from a night spent under the nearest hedge. Don't they have decent tailors in America?"

"I imagine so," Fa answered, still chucking. "But perhaps not where he spends his time."

"Not even a gentleman," Martyn looked over his shoulder at the tall, fair-haired American, then faced front, dismissively. "I'd be laughed out of the Mess if I brought in a fellow like that as a guest!"

"He seemed a decent enough sort," Fa said once again.

Once out in the fields again, by mid-afternoon the hounds had picked up a fresh scent, setting up an excited chorus.

"That's more like it!" shouted Martyn. "And there old Reynard goes! Look at him run – now here's sport for a day!" A flash of rusty red through the trees at the bottom of the hill and the voices of the hounds reached a new peak. The pack spilled into the grove, and the horsemen followed after – spread out across the field like a flock of crows across the sky, but animated by the same instinct, the same excitement of pursuit.

Fa and Martyn plunged over the hedge at the bottom without a hesitation. Isobel followed after; Thistle tucked up his feet and landed as neatly as a bird on the far side. Isobel had a moment of cold apprehension as Thistle sailed up and over. "Too high!" she thought, the shock of landing on the other side jolted her spine. Then it was the cool wind rushing past her face and the winter-burnt pasture flashing under Thistle's thudding hoofs. Oh, he was a gentle-gaited beast, his gallop as smooth as silk, carrying her along on an endless ocean wave, the two of them – girl and horse – moving as one creature melded together. *Faster,* Isobel urged him silently, with her hands and knees, faster; *they're so far ahead of us!* To her fierce joy, Thistle's stride lengthened again . . . almost caught up to Fa and the others, spilling over a second hedge. Some of the bright-coated huntsmen and several ladies were coursing along the hedge-line, looking for a low place in it. There was a gate, but too far away. Thistle could make it easily, Isobel knew; it was not as high as the first one. Thistle was the grandest hunter of all in the field, he trusted her implicitly and she trusted him. There he was, adjusting his stride, just a little as he approached the hedge-line, so as to reach it with speed undiminished and his hoofs at the optimal place to begin that wonderful soaring . . .

She felt her mount gathering all that mighty strength together, beginning that spring up and up, as powerful as a bird in the first few moments of flight. Thistle launched himself up and over the hedge – and at the instant, Isobel realized with horror that there was a newly-dug ditch on the far side of the hedge. It was filled with water and Thistle would land short, land heavily in the mud. He came down with a jolt, up to his pasterns in the ditch, falling with his chest smashing heavily against the bank, a shock so abrupt that Isobel cried out, feeling poor Thistle's agony, even as the arrested momentum of his leap sent her flying forward, over his shoulder. In one tiny moment of awareness of danger to herself, she slipped her foot from the stirrup, as she felt her left leg dragged painfully over the leaping horn of her side-saddle. Then it was a blur and a rush of Thistle's neck and brown water, the muddy bank, and the ground beneath slamming into her body with a violence that expelled all the air from her lungs. She lay stunned on the ground for an endless minute, two minutes, her face half-buried in a patch of mud and straw-stubble, trying to catch her breath.

She hurt in every bone in her face, shoulder, and her knee. Painfully, she lifted herself off the ground, half-rolling until she sat, her skirts a-sprawl around her, taking inventory of her bruises and hurts. Her hat lay on the ground a little away, the veil torn and draggling in the dirt. She spat dirt out of her mouth and raised a shaking hand to her head, feeling her hair loosened from all the pins that Jane had so carefully set in place that morning; raw scrapes across her cheek, wet with something that wasn't mud. Thistle lurched and staggered, as he heaved himself up and out of the ditch, standing on level ground with head down and reins trailing. He was favoring his left front leg. Isobel thought that he looked on her reproachfully, white showing around his eyes with an expression of pain and bewilderment in them. Her heart was wrung. Poor Thistle! It was her fault. He trusted her and she made a bad decision, which might yet be the death of him.

"Lady Isobel! Be ye all right!" cried a voice, a male voice over her head. Painfully, she turned her head. It was Somers, one of the junior grooms. Somers had come along the safe way, well behind the Hunt, riding a replacement mount, a leggy beast who went by the stable-name of William the Conqueror. He swung hastily down from the saddle, and assisted her to stand with the clumsy courtesy of a boy hardly grown.

"I am," she gasped, "Thank you, Somers . . . but poor Thistle!"

"He don't look well, Milady," Somers answered, his concern seemingly divided between herself and her horse. "Poor lad! That was a wicked bad tumble." Isobel shook off Somers's hand on her arm and staggered the few steps towards her mount. She stood, supporting herself with an arm over his withers, taking the loose reins in one hand, seeing now that he stood with one hoof tipped up, barely touching the ground, as if he could not bear to put weight on it. Isobel momentarily buried her face against his neck – warm and damp with sweat and ditch-water.

"Milady," Somers cleared his throat. "Would you wish to rejoin the Hunt? It won't take a moment to put your saddle on Willie. You might catch up in a trice, while I take Thistle back to the Hall. It will be slow going, but I do not think he is so badly hurt as all that."

Isobel looked in the direction in which the Hunt had vanished, a few red coats visible over the next hill-crest, the sounds of horns and hounds faintly lingering on the air. Thistle laid his nose on her shoulder, as if he wished to lean on her. She reached up, absently stroking that velvet-soft muzzle.

"No, Somers – thank you. I will walk Thistle back to the Hall. It is but a short way and he is my own. Father and my brothers will need a replacement shortly. Now that Thistle is injured, I am out of all interest in hunting today."

"Very well, Milady," Somers answered reluctantly and swung up into the saddle again. William trotted obediently away, although Somers looked over his shoulder now and again as Isobel fondled Thistle's nose and whispered encouragement to him.

"Come on then, dear handsome lad," she urged, as he took one reluctant and quivering step, then another – and he followed as obedient to her command as he always had, although with evident pain. With soft words and encouragement, Isobel led him around by back ways and overgrown lanes, mapping in her head the shortest and easiest way, sternly forbidding her own aches and bruises to have mastery. She would recover from them in a fortnight or so – but Thistle! Damage to legs was a death-sentence for a hunter. He would be dispatched and his body cut up in collops to be fed to the hounds; all that fire and obedience and trust in her to be made into the dogs' meat. *I can't have that,* Isobel thought. *He was my present from Fa, my freedom from Mama. And he trusted me. I can't endure the thought that my carelessness condemned him. No. Mr. Arkwright will know what to do. He's a genius when it comes to caring for horses. Fa always said so. If I can just get Thistle back to the stables, Arkwright will know what to do. I will beg him to take every care – and of course, Arkwright will do it for me – he taught us all to ride. He will know what to do, once I get Thistle home.*

With considerable relief she returned to the Hall stables, leading her limping horse by the reins and limping no little herself: her head ached, and her poor bruised knee – only to find no Mr. Arkwright – kindly and competent and comforting. With a little part of her attention, Isobel thought that someone was coming around on the gravel drive from the front of the Hall. Would that it would be Mr. Arkwright!

"He's gone with the extra horses," Young Andrews the stable-lad answered. "I'm that sorry Milady. I'll do what I can, o'course, but it'll be only what I can do to make Thistle comfortable until Mr. Arkwright and them return. I don't know rightly what Mr. Arkwright will want to do, Milady."

At their backs, someone cleared a throat cautiously, as if wanting to give fair warning of another presence. Isobel and Andrews turned around. A modest dog-cart with a small pony in the shafts stood in the stable-yard, a tall, fair-haired young man at the reins. After a moment, Isobel recognized him: the man whom Fa had talked to, that morning in Upton.

"I was invited to come and look at the puppies," he ventured, diffidently. He was looking directly at Isobel, in a calm and mildly sympathetic way. He had light blue eyes, the color of a clear summer sky. Isobel realized what an absolute fright she must look. She pushed back at the hair hanging loose over her shoulders.

"Oh dear – the American gentleman. I saw you with Fa this morning. I'm afraid they're still out – they picked up a good scent and it was view-halloo and away." *Why was she babbling like this? He would think her a perfect idiot!* "Fa and the others will be almost to Harwell by now."

"I'm Rudolph Becker," the American gentleman answered. He had a nice voice, light but resolute. "Everyone calls me Dolph. What happened to you that you're not almost to Harwell, Miss . . . ?"

"Isobel," she sniffed, afraid that she would break out into tears. "Isobel Lindsay-Groves. Actually, it's Lady Isobel, but I don't care much for that. A ditch happened to me, a ditch on the far side of a hedge and poor Thistle tried his best but he landed short . . . and our head groom, Mr. Arkwright is off taking the spare horses to meet the Hunt."

"Ah," said Mr. Becker. He looked at Isobel again. Isobel had the feeling that he was really seeing her and understanding her concern over her horse. "I do know a bit about horses if you would like me to look at your poor old Thistle."

"Would you? I'd be so grateful. Fa bought him for me on my eighteenth birthday."

Mr. Becker solemnly tied up the dog-cart reins and jumped down. He was indeed a very a tall man, Isobel saw with a flicker of surprise. He towered over Young Andrews and herself alike. He gentled Thistle and stroked his nose; yes, he was a horseman. Isobel saw that at once, as he leaned into Thistle's shoulder, and deftly took up the injured foreleg.

"Miss Isobel, if you took a tumble yourself, shouldn't you . . ."

"Not until I am assured that Thistle is all right – and I came to no lasting harm, which is more than I can say of my riding habit. Mama will be distraught – which is as good a reason to remain here as any I can think of."

"Well, at least it looks like you landed in some nice soft mud," Mr. Becker observed. He felt along the bones with gentle fingers, and palpated the muscles, speaking softly to Thistle as he did so, "All right boy . . . let me have it . . . feels like he has torn a tendon. Not much you can do, except let him rest. A hot bran poultice might make him feel it a bit less." He let Thistle's hoof down and stood up. All Isobel could think of was how trusty he was, how direct, and how sympathetic. "I don't know that he'll be much good for jumping and all that after this. You'll want to go gently for a couple of months until it heals."

"At least it's nothing broken!" Isobel felt quite overtaken by relief, relief for Thistle's sake and gratitude to this tall, oddly reassuring stranger. "Thank you, thank you so much, Mr. Becker! I adore Thistle; he was a bribe to me, you should know. Fa promised me a horse of my very own if I should behave myself for the Season."

"The Season?" he asked, obviously puzzled. Isobel thought, *Oh, he is a stranger – from America, and he wouldn't know or care about the Season.*

"Oh, you know . . . being presented at Court . . . all the balls and events and that. Mama insisted." *And why,* thought Isobel helplessly, *am I nattering on about all that? Is it just because he seems so sympathetic and he listens? Most men, even my brothers – they hear, but they aren't really listening. They are just waiting for me to stop talking so they can say something clever.*

But Mr. Becker answered, very kindly, "It was that awful?"

In a rush, Isobel realized that yes, indeed it was that awful. It had been almost unendurably awful, paraded around, shown off to all those people that Lady Caroline wanted to impress, put in the way of all those gentleman of marriageable age.

"Picture me," she said, with sudden resentment. "In a white dress with three plumes on my head, being brought into Court before her Majesty. I endured for imagining coming home and Fa's promise of a horse of my own and being able to play with the dogs and go out among Fa's tenants. It almost made up for Mama not being able to marry me off and have a grand society wedding at the end of it."

"We don't do much of that where I come from. I have two sisters and I can't imagine my mother doing that to them."

"How lucky!" Isobel replied, at once and hopelessly envious. "Where is that – you must tell me more, Mr. Becker. It sounds like paradise!" Young Andrews led away the limping Thistle. The two of them were left momentarily alone. Isobel's hair fell across her shoulders again. *I must look a perfect fright,* she thought. *No wonder no eligible party wanted to marry me, the whole season long.* She pushed at her straggling hair again and nervously brushed at the mud on her skirt before blurting, "You've been very kind. Fa was fearfully impressed – the dogs usually don't take to people so readily. Quite honestly, they terrify most people. He so wanted to speak to you, you should know – he had ever so many questions!"

"Your butler didn't know that," Mr. Becker replied with a wry and amused look on his face. Isobel was horrified and understanding all at once. Spencer would have sent him away from the front door. He looked like an ordinary workman, in a plain jacket and collarless shirt, a calico kerchief tied around his neck. His hands were bare and Isobel saw that two fingers on his left hand were scarred and a little gnarled, as if they had once been broken and had never healed straight. But still – he had come at Fa's invitation. Spencer should be used to Fa's eccentric taste in friends by now.

Isobel exclaimed, "Oh! You went to the front door and Spencer sent . . ."

"He said that servants and trade went around to the back," Mr. Becker answered dryly. Isobel would have wept from vexation – that Fa would have asked him to come to the Hall, and then he would be so kind, after being turned away!

"I am so sorry," she blurted. "Sometimes, I think Spencer takes more care for propriety and the honor of the house than we do. Certainly more than Fa or I do. I am so sorry . . ." Mr. Becker did nothing more than smile, and take her hand with gentle grace.

"Think nothing of it, Miss Isobel. I didn't, except for the inconvenience." With unexpectedly courtly elegance, he kissed her hand and Isobel thought, *He is a gentleman after all. Martyn couldn't have bettered that gallantry!* Mr. Becker added, "Besides, I was promised another look at the dogs. Wolfhounds, your father said. I suppose they were used to hunt wolves with. Are there even wolves left in England?"

"Yes . . . and no," Isobel felt her cheeks flush and knew that she would look common and all pink with embarrassment. "They were once used so. They're an ancient breed, nearly extinct. The dogs, I mean. The wolves <u>are</u> extinct. Fa adores them – the dogs not the wolves! He and some of his friends are trying to revive the breed. I adore them because . . ."

"Because dogs are trustier than most people you know?" Mr. Becker answered unexpectedly.

"Exactly! Oh, you should come and see Deirdre's puppies! Deirdre's the dam, you know. They all have Irish names."

"Only logical," Mr. Becker observed. He had still not relinquished her hand. Isobel closed her fingers around his. Impulsively she tugged him after her, across the stable-yard and through another smaller gate into the farther and smaller enclosed courtyard, set aside for Fa's beloved wolfhounds, each with their own elevated little house. *He has come to see the dogs, so dogs he should see!* Isobel went directly to the one which housed Fa's prized bitch and her whelps and knelt on the ground – no worry for her riding habit, already torn and muddy to a fare-the-well.

"Deirdre," she called softly; as well as she knew all of Fa's wolfhounds, a sudden interference with a mother and her pups was not well-advised. She heard a scrabbling of claws on wood and Deirdre's shaggy grey head emerged from the doorway. "Come and pay your respects, dear pretty girl!" Isobel crooned encouragement and Deirdre emerged all at once. She licked Isobel's face and then her head went up alertly. Isobel could read Deirdre's thoughts as if the wolfhound bitch had the gift of speech and shouted them aloud. *Stranger. Not One I Know. But No Fear. Therefore, No Threat.* Deirdre sauntered over to sniff at Mr. Becker with regal dignity. Isobel's good opinion of Mr. Becker as a man well acquainted with and knowledgeable about dogs was instantly confirmed, as he dropped to one knee – dogs liked it, to be met by interest going down to their level. He fondled her ears and her muzzle. *Oh,* thought Isobel, *She likes him nearly as much as I do. Kitty-Cat and Jane said alike that animals always know.* Deirdre's puppies tumbled out of the kennel-house, a riot of eager curiosity; all grey and brindle, sand-colored and brown, falling and fawning upon the stranger.

"How old are they?" asked Mr. Becker, curiously.

"Six months," Isobel answered, "They really are not quite fully grown until over a year old. Fa says it's because they are so clever. I do so like dogs!" She sighed happily – on comfortable ground at last, with something of interest to talk about. She sat a little sideways and Deirdre nudged her shoulder. When Isobel embraced the dog, Deirdre settled with a soft 'woof' of affection into her lap. Isobel winced at the weight of the dog on her bruised knees, but the very size and solidity of the dog was a comfort. *I need no other chaperone*, Isobel thought, with an interior giggle. *The most determined blackguard in the land could get no more past Deirdre than he could past Mama, if she were present.* Meanwhile, the puppies were frolicking around Mr. Becker – indeed two of the pups were playing tug-of-war with the sleeve of his coat, which amused rather than annoyed him. He cleared his throat and asked a most diffident and curious question.

"Miss Isobel, if I might ask – how well do you like cows?"

"I don't know cows as well as I know dogs and horses, "Isobel answered, thoughtfully. " But I expect that I should like them as well as I like any other beast, once well and truly acquainted."

"That is good," Mr. Becker was quite cheerful. Isobel thought of how pleasant he was, handsome and good-natured, as open and wholesome as bread. "I happen to own an awful lot of cows in Texas – they're all around the place, as a matter of fact."

"I have not read very much about Texas – people have spoken of it as an awful sort of wilderness, full of Indians and bandits," Isobel ventured. "And that all the men go around armed to the teeth and ready to challenge each other to pistol-duels in the streets, but I cannot think that can be true. Is it?"

"Not so much," Mr. Becker's amusement was obvious.

"You must tell me more," Isobel said and inwardly wondered from where she had drawn such assurance. She had never been able to converse comfortably with the sort of men that she met at dances, the men introduced to her over Mama's silver teapot and fine porcelain cups, being either tongue-tied or given to blurt out irrelevancies. Talking with Mr. Becker, with his plain workman's clothes and battered hands, gentling the dogs as he had done with Thistle; that was as comfortable as talking to Martyn.

Now he smiled outright and answered, "It's somewhat like the land around here, Miss Isobel; green fields and groves of oak trees, with outcroppings of limestone. There are many rivers and creeks, in the Hills where my father's place is. My father built a stone house, which was the wonder of all the neighbors when it was first built."

"Why is that?" Isobel asked.

"Most settlers built in wood, out of cut timber. Papa meant to stay, and also he promised Mama a stone house. She lived in town with the German folk who settled there, you see. I think Papa was afraid she would not marry him and come out to the unsettled lands, unless she had a good stone house to live in."

"It sounds very romantic," Isobel said and could have bitten her own tongue. How very forward to mention romance to a man she had just met! Martyn claimed that his friends all fled from girls who said things like that. Husband-hunters, said Martyn.

"He planted an orchard on the hill below the house," Mr. Becker seemed hardly to have noticed her gaffe. "He farmed and ran some cattle for the lowland market, but it was my Uncle Hansi's notion to go into cattle in a bigger way."

"Does your father still tend his orchard and farm?" Isobel asked, and Mr. Becker shook his head, a momentary shadow over his face.

"No – he was a soldier. He was killed during the War."

"I am so sorry," the words of condolence came almost without thought to her lips, "I am sure that he died very bravely, a hero's death."

"Yes," answered Mr. Becker. Isobel dropped her eyes to that of the wolfhound, curling as much of her considerable length as possible in Isobel's lap. Deirdre's tail thumped gently on the cobbles. *Oh, what to say now?* Isobel wondered, and cast around for a safer topic.

"Is that where you learned so very much about horses?" she asked and he nodded. "In Texas we work cattle from horseback. The native breed has run wild for hundreds of years and they are fierce enough to see to their own welfare. We let them graze on the open range, no such paddocks and pastures as you have here. So I was on horseback and helping with spring round-up, even when I was barely stirrup-high. The vaqueros – the buckaroos, and some of Colonel Ford's rangers that I rode with, they know some right fine tricks, some of them learned from the Indians. The Comanche know riding stunts that you've never dreamed of, Miss Isobel."

"It sounds wonderfully exciting to live in Texas," Isobel hugged Deirdre closer to herself.

"More exciting than most folk would ever think," Mr. Becker agreed dryly.

"Did you serve in the War also?" Isobel asked, rather puzzled. He looked to be about Martyn's age. As nearly as Isobel could recollect, the great war between the Northern and Southern American states was over more than ten years ago.

"Towards the end, Miss Isobel, in Colonel Ford's cavalry." Mr. Becker absently tussled the belly of one of Deirdre's pups, who lay on its back wriggling in ecstasy. "Less'n you take care of your horses, cavalry and rangers ain't nothing but footsore infantry. A man without a horse is at a disadvantage in Texas and that's the truth."

"I should hate to be deprived of Thistle," Isobel confessed. "So I am doubly grateful to you, for relieving my mind, no less than something of his suffering. I had so feared that he had been so injured that he would be . . . do you know what they do with our hunters when they must be put down, Mr. Becker? They send them to the hounds, for their meat. I could not bear to think of that happening to Thistle. Have you ever heard the like in Texas?"

Mr. Becker nodded, "That is no surprise to me, Miss Isobel. The Comanche are commonly known for killing and eating horses, when the need strikes – raw and innards and all."

"Oh, surely not!" Isabel cried in horror, but Mr. Becker only nodded. "They do so indeed. I have seen it myself, when pursuing the war band that had taken . . ."

"Ah – so now you have seen the puppies, Mr. Becker!" Fa said, cheerfully, "Are they not splendid, more splendid than any other dog you have ever seen? And you have met m'daughter, Isobel!" Both Mr. Becker and Isobel started, slightly. There stood Fa, exuberant, and mud-splattered, beaming impartially upon them both. "And there is my darling Deirde, in the office of chaperone! Splendid, splendid! So Lady Isobel has been introducing you to Luath's get . . . oh, how marvelous. What a good, good girl!" Fa disposed an affectionate caress upon Deirdre and only at that moment noticed Isobel's disheveled condition. "That was a spectacular fall, Pet – yet you are blessedly unharmed, so Somers told us. I apologize, Mr. Becker, for my own failings as a host. But my daughter seems to have taken it upon herself when I was remiss."

"Miss Isobel has been very thoughtful," Mr. Becker shook off the puppies, rising with unconcerned grace and assurance from the cobbles of the dog-kennel yard. "I thank you, sir. You have been most hospitable and Miss Isobel has stood admirably in your stead. Your dogs are everything I would have expected from so splendid a sire."

"Ah . . . excellent, excellent." Fa shook the hand which Mr. Becker extended to him, and looked somewhat apologetic. "But, Mr. Becker, I would remind you that this is a noble house – my own dear wife would remind me constantly of the respect properly due to us . . . and to my daughter."

"Indeed." Mr. Becker had a particularly inscrutable look on his otherwise amiable countenance. He looked sideways at Isobel, and smiled – first at Isobel, and then with a somewhat blander expression at Fa. "But your daughter has expressed a desire to me that she wishes to be called merely Miss Isobel. I have been schooled to always do as a lady would command . . . Sir."

Chapter 3 – *A Man of Many Parts*

"I liked him extraordinarily well, Jane!" confessed Lady Isobel, as she settled in front of her dressing table that afternoon, while Jane – all the while trying to conceal her shock at her mistresses' appearance and the sad condition of her riding habit – began assisting her in removing those bedraggled garments. *Fortunately,* Jane silently consoled herself, *her coat is only ripped along the seams, and not in the fabric itself – quite within my own abilities to mend, and so well that it will look as good as new. I never thought Lady Isobel would be so very hard on her clothing!*

Out loud and meeting Lady Isobel's eyes in the mirror, she asked, "Does he make a fine and gentlemanly appearance, Milady?

"He is not unhandsome," Isobel's brow furrowed – not in a frown, but in a grimace of pain as Jane slid the unbuttoned habit coat from her shoulders. To Jane's relief the chemisette underneath was merely creased and smudged with mud at the point above the closing of the habit coat. "Oh, dear! That pains me now! I hardly felt it at the time."

"Shall we send for the doctor, Milady?" Jane asked anxiously. Isobel shook her head. "No, I think not – Fa asked, already." Unbidden, Isobel giggled as Jane continued unfastening and divesting her mistress of the remainder of her habit and the undergarments which underpinned that sadly muddy outer layer of coat and skirt. "I was so very stiff after sitting on the cobbles in the kennel-yard. Both Fa and Mr. Becker must assist me to rise and set me onto my feet. No, it is merely bruises and the usual aches and pains from a fall. I imagine Kitty-Cat has arnica and hot-water-bottles to hand; she always did after our childhood misadventures! Mr. Becker is a rough-hewn gentleman, Jane. He likes dogs, treats them gently and sensibly, and is terribly knowledgeable about horses, from having served in the cavalry, he said. Martyn will like that. Jane, he seemed truly different from any other gentleman of my acquaintance. He did not converse overmuch . . . but he listened. He pays little mind to convention, so Fa relishes his company. But I don't know what Mama will think. He is invited to tea tomorrow . . . oh!" she winced and attempted to stifle any sign of pain, as Jane eased the chemisette off her shoulder.

"I'm sorry Milady!" Jane exclaimed. Isobel attempted a reassuring smile. "It is not your fault, Jane – only my own haste and clumsiness. Do you think my poor habit may be rescued?"

"After a good sponging and a bit of mending," Jane answered, confidently, "I believe it will be as good as new. You should lie down, Milady, with a hot compress on your shoulder. You are coming out all in bruises." She eyed the bruises with concern. What was that straight pale mark; that silvery welt across Isobel's shoulder, running down under the ruffle of her chemise, faint marks only brought out by the livid bruising of the flesh underneath? It looked almost like an old scar. She looked closer as she untied Isobel's corset-lacings. Jane blinked in disbelief. There were several thin and arrow-straight marks; as if they had been laid on with a quirt or a willow-switch.

"They only appear frightful," Isobel giggled again, breathing deeply in and out again, as her corset-stays loosened, "I am like one of those delicate flowers; one merely brushes against their petals and they immediately turn brown. I do not feel much discomfort from them." Jane merely clicked her tongue against her teeth. "You sound like Kitty-Cat when you do that, Jane. I will retire early, now that I have the most perfect excuse for doing so. Mama has particularly tedious guests tonight. I think I should go mad, listening to their conversation and trying to keep my eyes open to all hours. Bear my excuses to Mama – don't look like that, Jane, all you need do is to relay them to Havers." She sighed involuntarily as Jane swathed her in her quilted silk wrapper and began plucking hairpins from the tangle that Isobel's hair had become in a few short hours, still wondering about the faint scars on her mistresses' back and shoulders. "I should like to look at my best for Mr. Becker's visit. That should be easy enough, now that he has seen me at worst! Anything will be an improvement, Jane. What do you think I should wear? I don't want to look too fine, as if I had made a great fuss over my toilette!"

"The princess-cut brown and black striped silk gown," Jane replied after some careful thought. "It is plainly cut, but the color sets off your hair very nicely. Perhaps a bow of Copenhagen-blue ribbon at the collar."

"I will leave it all to you, Jane," Lady Isobel smiled with cheerful relief and real affection, "You have the gift for such matters as what dress goes with what mantle and the color of flowers for a ball gown. I don't, no matter how much Mama and Havers hector me. It all looks the same to me, no matter how hard I would try! Tell Cook that I will have an invalid supper on a tray tonight and some more of your lovely peppermint tea, if you would be so kind."

"Yes, Milady," Jane answered. She pulled out the last of the pins, and left Lady Isobel looking dreamily into the mirror and pulling the hairbrush through her hair.

On Jane's return from her errand downstairs, she sought out her aunt's little private parlor-cum-office, to ask for the arnica and other remedies as the housekeeper might see fit to apply. Mrs. Kittredge sighed as she put aside a book of household accounts. "Fortunately, her ladyship usually recovers quite swiftly from these happenings. When she was a child, she always had some bruise or scrape about her person. The way that she went through stockings was the despair of her governesses!"

"I saw scars on her shoulders," Jane ventured, "They were very well healed, hardly a mark to be seen. Was that from some misadventure as well?"

Mrs. Kittredge frowned. "Indeed, Jane. That was quite some time ago. Her Ladyship had the governess sacked without a reference. She had a savage temper and as it turned out, she drank. His Lordship wished to have the matter hushed up entirely and I cannot criticize him in that regard. It's best forgotten about, Jane."

"Yes, Marm," Jane answered. She thought she could see at least a small corner of what had happened: a bad-tempered governess who drank and had undisputed authority over small children. Perhaps Aunt Lydia was correct: best forgotten. The scars were faded, almost to the point of invisibility save in clear light, and the person who bore them didn't seem to be bothered.

"Well, Jane?" Isobel asked, the following afternoon, to their reflections in the mirror; her own face pink-cheeked with suppressed excitement. "Am I presentable, at last?"

"Yes, Milady," Jane answered, her face puckered in concentration. "You look very fine. Do you feel well-recovered from yesterday?"

"I feel as if there are butterflies in my insides," Isobel laughed breathlessly. "As if I were looking a hedge so tall that Thistle must sprout wings." She did indeed feel quite breathless and not just from her corset. She looked at herself in the mirror and felt a small quiver of pleasure. "I hope that in my own mind I have not built up Mr. Becker into someone more marvelous than life. He is a mere man and quite ordinary, I am sure."

So she reminded herself, as she skimmed down the grand stairway, with her skirts rustling around her like rushes, whispering in the breeze at the river's edge. *I do like him*, she told herself obstinately. *I shouldn't be afraid to let him see that. He conversed with me as if he liked me as well and that must count for something. If he were truly a soldier and fought in a war, and if even the merest part of all those stories about Texas were true, then he should have no fears about facing Mama over the teacups. Oh, please god,*

Isobel paused momentarily in her haste, *let him have some kind of good manner. I couldn't bear to have Victoria and Mama laughing about him.*

Tea was served today in the Green Drawing Room, a cozy sitting room adjacent to the conservatory. Isobel preferred it; not as drafty as the Yellow Salon and the furniture was much more comfortable. Fa and Martyn were already lounging by the fire. Her sister Victoria sat with her skirts arrayed beautifully around her, while Robbie, the oldest of her sons, sat as mum as a mouse on the footstool by her feet. It was a very great privilege for Robbie to be allowed out of the nursery. The glass doors to the conservatory stood open, the greenery and the warmth of it within breathing a summer-like cheer into the Green Drawing Room. Alas, the parlor was so small that there was no hope of slipping in unnoticed by Mama, regally enthroned on the green-velvet divan.

"At last, Isobel," she remarked, with her usual touch of acid. "You shall have to forgive my daughter, Mr. Becker," she added to the man sitting on her right, teacup saucer balanced uneasily on his knee. "She is constitutionally incapable of being on time for anything."

"I don't pay any mind," Mr. Becker answered, as he rose, deftly placing the teacup on the edge of the tea-tray and bowing over Isobel's hand.

"I suppose your part of the world is devoid of clocks," Victoria purred, with mock-sympathy. Isobel's heart sank. She wished she were still enough of a little girl to make faces at Victoria, but Mr. Becker only clasped her hand in his and answered mildly, "No, ma'am, but there usually isn't much need to pay all that mind to them, ma'am."

Isobel thought Victoria was a trifle nonplussed. "My sister would find that a terribly convenient quality."

Isobel felt Mr. Becker gave her hand the tiniest, comforting squeeze before releasing it. Isobel settled herself on a ladies' chair opposite and looked at him, somewhat at a loss of what to say next. He had at least forsaken the rough working-man's jacket and collarless shirt of the day before in favor of a plain-cut suit of tweed and a collared shirt with a simple dark cravat; not quite up to the elegance and formality that Mama usually demanded, but apparently acceptable to Spencer. Isobel stifled an interior giggle; he did not appear to be put-out by Victoria's opportune malice or Mama's elaborate show of disapproval. If anything, he appeared secretly amused by them. Isobel wondered if Mama and Victoria found that disconcerting.

Now he smiled at her, saying, "I see that you are recovered from yesterday, Miss Isobel. That's good – falling from a horse at a dead gallop is a risky thing, most places."

"I am not a china doll, Mr. Becker," Isobel answered. "Which breaks into a thousand pieces after any little accident."

"That's good to know," he said. "The world is a tougher place than you might know, Miss Isobel . . . Marm." he nodded respectfully towards Lady Catherine, "It helps, bein' strong enough to handle it."

Mama set down her cup with a tiny fierce clink. "Fortunately, Mr. Becker, my daughter need never encounter any of that world, such as you describe, so she has no need of any other qualities beyond breeding and good manners."

Oh, dear, thought Isobel. *Mama does not approve of him at all. If it weren't for Fa, she would have Spencer show him the door.* Meanwhile, Fa chuckled, "Mr. Becker has something of the right of it, my dear. India mayn't be quite as unsettled as the far corners of America, but it may require more of our daughter than being a sheltered little Society flower."

"There is no comparison," Lady Catherine answered, in tones of finality. "India is managed by the best of our Island breed and defended by the finest soldiers in the world. Those far parts of America are . . ." her nostrils flared in distaste, "run by vulgar politicians, creatures of the basest degree selected by a mob."

"We like it, that way," Mr. Becker answered with serene assurance. Isobel thought she saw a glint of amusement in his eyes. Fa hastily interjected, "Mr. Becker has come to England, searching for fine blooded cattle and horses. His family possess substantial holdings and have extensive plans to improve them. Can you believe that the least of their properties is the size of Oxfordshire?"

"Indeed," Mama said dryly. Martyn brightened and addressed Mr. Becker directly, "Horses, you say? No better than good English bloodstock!"

Isobel sat quiet, while the men's conversation continued, although every now and again, Mr. Becker looked towards here with a private look of amusement, a smile just and only for her. Those glances were as heady as conversation would have been; although he did not have any chance for private words to be said – how could he, under Mama's basilisk gaze and on such short acquaintance? Isobel did not feel a need of such. It was enough to merely sit in the same parlor and look at him across the tea things, to listen to him speaking so quietly and modestly about his farm and horses, touching lightly upon his travels on the Continent.

"You must call on us again," Mama said, at last, with an air of finality, as the clock on the parlor mantel sweetly chimed the quarter-hour. "Ring for Spencer please, Victoria: We shall be at the Hall for Christmas, of course, but in London after the New Year."

Mr. Becker rose, and bowed very correctly over Mama's hand, "I'd be pleased, ma'am, but we are traveling to Italy to spend Christmas with a friend who has been hosting my mother and aunt on the Isle of Capri."

"How very delightful," Mama answered. "Although I don't imagine your friend is anyone we know. I do suppose there are some pleasing Christmas traditions observed there."

"I hope so," Mr. Becker answered, with bland assurance. "My mother writes that Princess Cherkevsky has turned her place upside down, anticipating so many guests. Miss Isobel . . ." again, he clasped Isobel's hand with much tenderness of feeling and looked at her face as if there was so much more that he wanted to say, "It was a pleasure."

"I hope we will meet again, before you depart our shores for Italy," Isobel stammered. To her inexpressible joy, he smiled very slightly and said, "We shall, Miss Isobel. On that you may depend."

As the door closed on Spencer's back, rigid with disapproval, Fa chuckled, "I say, Princess Cherkevsky? Young Becker flies in higher circles than one would think at first glance, eh, my dear?"

"Scandalous woman," Mama sighed. The slightest thread of a frown printed itself on her forehead. "Still, the Prince was once the Ambassador to France and she is received by the very best people and at court."

"And by more than one Prince," Martyn added with a chuckle. "Or so rumors have it."

"Don't be vulgar," Mama chided him, but as if her thoughts were elsewhere. "He is at least an eligible party." Her gaze fell speculatively on Isobel, who held her breath. "But a foreigner!" Mama added with a delicate shudder.

"Don't think that matters so much, if Izzy likes him," Martyn drawled provokingly, "Or if he favors her. If we receive him again, should I introduce him around?"

"Surely not, Martyn – you are jesting with us," Victoria protested. "We hardly know anything of him, of his family, his schooling. We could be so embarrassed, in picking up this . . . this nobody."

"That might be," Fa spoke up, unexpectedly. He shot a very a shrewd look at Mama. "He's a damned rich nobody and he knows horses. That uncle of his has been cutting a swath in the blood-stock market for the last six months. If he's all of what the City chaps tell me, he's as hardly a bludger. Young Becker doesn't strike me as a fortune hunter. And the dogs like him."

Isobel held her breath; if Mama forbade her to see Mr. Becker, or refused to receive his calls, she felt that her heart would be well broken. She would adore seeing him again. Already she looked forward to such visits with a longing she had never felt before.

At last, Mama replied, "It should do no harm to receive his calls, since he will remain only a little longer. I would warn you against forming any particular attachment to Mr. Becker, Isobel."

"Yes, Mama," Isobel answered obediently, but her heart was singing within her. In spite of Lady Caroline's commands, she had already formed an attachment. Something of it must have shown on her face, for Mama was less than pleased but Fa winked, conspiratorially, from behind Mama's back.

"We must hurry, Jane – I will be late again," Isobel gasped. "I must begin calling on Fa's tenants by half-past nine, or I will be late for everything else."

"I will tell Somers to hurry the dog-cart between," Jane said, comfortingly. She made haste to unfasten the buttons on Isobel's pale morning dress, which she had worn for breakfast the next day after Mr. Becker's visit. "Don't fidget, my lady. I have laid out the brown merino and I think you should wear the plain bonnet with the rose-pink lining."

"It's very old-fashioned," Isobel said dubiously. Jane shook her head. "It may be so, my lady, but the color flatters you and you do not want to appear too grand, going around to all the cottages with jars of calves-foot jelly and beef-tea for the invalids."

"Lady Bountiful!" Isobel met Jane's eyes in the mirror. "You are correct as always, Jane. Truly, I do relish these calls, so much more than my other duties. Tell me, where first? The Lattimore children at the Home Farm had the measles. Would they savor some fresh fruit from the hothouse? It would be such a treat. We have so much, I should think we can spare a little. Can you see to it, Jane, when you are finished with my buttons? I think I may cope with the onerous task of putting on my mantle and bonnet, if you can run down and beg it of Kitty-Cat."

"That would be a difficult bit of work," Jane answered drolly. Lady Isobel giggled. "It is, but I believe I am capable, just this once, dear Jane!"

Jane cast an approving eye over her mistress, as neat and plain as a school-girl in a brown merino walking-costume trimmed with darker brown ribbon. She and Isobel had their best conversations before the dressing table and Jane thought that Isobel took pleasure and comfort in Jane's company – a circumstance which pleased Jane very much.

They met downstairs, both robed for the out-of-doors; Jane swathed in a voluminous dark shawl, with her own plain black bonnet on her head. The dog-cart was drawn up, laden with one big hamper and a great many small baskets and bundles. Young Somers the groom handed up Isobel to sit next to him on the driver's seat, while Jane found a perch on top of the hamper in back. She hugged her shawl around herself; this was the first day since being promoted to ladies' maid that she had set foot farther than the winter-blasted gardens at the Hall. So many were the duties which kept her indoors, attending on Lady Isobel and her wardrobe and rooms! The weather being clear today and the sky a pale ice-blue scrubbed clean of clouds, she was accompanying Lady Isobel. Today, her ladyship was visiting wives and families of Sir Robert's tenants, with Jane to assist in carrying out the good works expected of a lady of wealth and high position, bringing delicacies and strengthening viands to the sick, and seeing to the welfare of the tenants. Those matters most affecting the families of Sir Robert's estate workers and tenants were often not those of which Sir Robert or Mr. Aubrey, his estate manager, would readily hear.

"You see, Jane," Lady Isobel explained over her shoulder, her cheeks pinker than usual from the brisk winter cold as the cart rattled down the narrow country lane toward the Home Farm. "Lattimore, or any of the other tenants might hesitate taking a complaint directly to Mr. Aubrey, or to Fa – even though it might be serious, something of which they should rightly be kept informed."

"Why, Milady?" Jane gasped, as the dog-cart jolted over a particularly deep cut. "Why would they not just speak to his Lordship?"

"Truly, Jane – I know not! It may have to do with pride and not wanting anyone to see their work and their care of their holding as anything less than perfection. The least wounding way for something to be done is for me to pay regular calls upon their wives." Lady Isobel straightened her bonnet with one hand. She sparkled with excitement, frankly relishing the tasks set before her on this day, "They will speak to me freely, of course. I think they would rather, for I have known most of them since I was a child. Mama used to take me calling, although I do not think she enjoyed it. I did; I would think of myself as Fa's secretary, taking note of all. Then I would tell Fa of what I had observed and very quietly, he would have Mr. Aubrey see that things were attended to, without injuring any feelings! They are my friends, Jane – besides being Fa's good and worthy yeomen. It is our duty to see to their welfare. Our duty," and her bright face dimmed. "I do not think Mama or Robin's wife take much pleasure in it. Rather a rather a pity, I think. They enjoy the privileges of position without undertaking the duties. Oh dear, I sound like a Jacobin."

"A what, Milady? Some kind of Frenchy?" Jane answered uncertainly. Isobel laughed again. "Oh Jane – I think your education has been neglected.

Mine, too," she added with candor. "Other people seem to know ever so much more. I meant a revolutionary, someone who believes in the brotherhood of all. Perhaps that is only because Mama would not approve. Mama has very definite ideas about our place and our obligation to lead."

"It is enough to appear at a grand London ball, dressed in the very latest fashion?" Jane said before she considered how blunt that sounded. "I am so sorry, Milady, I meant no disrespect," she added, to the back of Isobel's bonneted head.

Her voice must have sounded truly regretful. Isobel half-turned in the trap's spring seat and reached around to pat her hand. "Clever Jane; that is what I have often wondered and I think that Fa has said the same. Such thoughts you and I must rein in, for the sake of propriety . . . Somers, you must say nothing of our words to anyone!" Isobel added in sudden alarm. At the reins of the dog-cart, Somers looked straight ahead, answering blandly, "Of what, Milady? I heard nowt."

"Excellent, Somers." Lady Isobel sounded cheerful, as Somers chuckled to the pony and pulled on the reins. The pony turned at the lane leading towards the Home Farm and the first of their morning calls. Jane thought that he must be very new to service, answering Lady Isobel with such cheek.

Farmer Lattimore's wife received them in the farmyard, coming out from the door into the house while she made a half-hearted motion to untie her house-keeping apron, saying breathlessly, "Oh, my lady, we did not expect you so early! The parlor fire is not yet alight enough to warm it."

Lady Isobel hopped down from the dog-cart, without even waiting for assistance. "Dear Mrs. Lattimore, take no special care; I have been in and out of your kitchen since I was a child. Truly, I would rather visit with you there! I would be ashamed, knowing that my visit put such an additional burden upon you, with the children only lately recovered." She took Mrs. Lattimore's arm like an old friend, as Somers tied up the pony's reins and gravely assisted Jane to alight. "We have brought grapes for Thomas and Adeline . . . they are recovering well? I was so pleased to hear of this from Mrs. Kittredge. She says that the care of sick children is such an exacting task as to overwhelm the most careful of mothers."

Mrs. Lattimore's rosy face pinked with pleasure; Jane could not help noting that her mistress was someone who Mrs. Lattimore was pleased to see and welcomed into her house without any stiff standoffishness. Lady Isobel was chattering like a magpie.

"We must make ourselves useful then, Miss Goodacre," Somers said to Jane, in a low but cheerful voice, "What goes to the Lattimores, then. This basket?" He grinned at Jane, as he handed her the basket of grapes and delicate little cakes.

"Three jars of the calves-foot jelly," Jane answered sedately. She followed Lady Isobel through the farmhouse door into the kitchen, warm with firelight and the smell of bread baking. A ginger cat and her kittens basked on the hearthrug, close to the fire. Lady Isobel had settled herself on one of the comfortably shabby armchairs drawn up close to it. A small boy, his fair hair tousled and uncombed, was curled up in the other, wrapped in a blanket over his night-shirt.

"Hullo, Tommy," Lady Isobel was saying to him, "Are your spots all gone?" Jane set the basket on the kitchen table where the debris of bread-making was scattered over one end and a plate or two and a half-drunk mug of tea sat at the other. With a faint squeak of dismay, Mrs. Lattimore took up the plates, saying, "I've only just put the kettle on, my lady!"

"Let me help you with the tea," Jane offered timidly, while Mrs. Lattimore stood irresolute with a plate in each hand, "I've helped my mother in her kitchen and this is a little like coming home again."

"New in service, up t'the Hall?" Mrs. Lattimore seemed to see Jane for the first time and bobbed her head in distracted assent. "Himself's brother is junior gardener. He sleeps out, so you wouldn't know him, not unless you are from around the Hall."

"I'm very new, yes," Jane answered. "Mrs. Kittredge is my aunt and brought me from my home to work in the stillroom, but Lady Isobel asked for me to be her maid."

"Oh, she's a fine lady, Mrs. Kittredge is," Mrs. Lattimore beamed approval. "And Lady Isobel is another . . . the tea is on the dresser shelf there, in the black and gold tin."

By the fireside, Tommy was showing off the last of his faded pink measles-spots to Lady Isobel, who surveyed them with great interest. A friendly twenty minutes passed, while Lady Isobel chattered with Tommy and his mother, asked after his sister (still out in spots and confined upstairs) and promised to take Mrs. Lattimore's own mother's recipe for seed-cake back to Mrs. Kittredge. Jane took a mug of hot tea to Somers, waiting patiently in the dog-cart and upon her return, quietly pointed out to Lady Isobel that the hands of the clock on the kitchen mantel-piece now stood at half-past nine.

"We must fly," Lady Isobel stood up; she had not removed her bonnet or mantel, since they were paying so many brief calls. She must make no less than six more calls on outlaying farms and a visit to a very elderly lady who had been Sir Robert's nurse and lived in a tiny pension-cottage in Upton. She patted Tommy's cheek with great affection, thanked Mrs. Lattimore for her tea and hospitality, and effected a brisk leave-taking which curiously managed to appear as if she could not bear to tear herself from the Lattimore's company and hospitality and only departed with the greatest reluctance.

To Jane's amusement and delight, Lady Isobel repeated the visit at Home Farm three more times, at each place being welcomed with open affection. She knew the names of all the children, asked after absent family members, made herself perfectly at home in kitchens and humble parlors and dispensed what she had brought in so modest and an unaffected a manner as to make it seem that she was merely returning some small favor to a friend. Jane effaced herself as was expected, but observed much, especially at the smallest of Sir Robert's tenant farms.

"Dale Farm," Lady Isobel explained, as they departed. "They are new-married, and have only tenanted the place since last spring. Did not the room seem rather chill, to you, Jane?"

"The window in the kitchen did not fit properly into the frames," Jane ventured, after a moment of thought. Although the kitchen at Dale Farm was scoured clean, it was bare in comparison to the other kitchens where they had been hosted that morning. "And there was an awful draft through the room."

"No coal i'the shed," Somers spoke up, unexpectedly, "An' little wood, either, I'm bound." At Lady Isobel's look of astonishment, he added. "I looked, Milady. Curiosity killed the cat, but it never killed me, not yet."

"Ah," Lady Isobel thought deeply for a moment. "Do not let me forget, Jane – to ask Fa to authorize a cartload of coal for Dale Farm. And Mr. Aubrey to send the carpenter and glazier to mend the windows, so they might better keep out the cold. The property is Fa's after all and his obligation to keep in fit condition. And – I am correct, they are new married, just this year?"

"He's a son of Old Mr. Wright who has the freehold near Corsham and she's a cousin of the Wesley's out Hartlepool way," Somers answered, unbidden – for he was the one who had lived at the Hall for much longer than Jane's bare six months. "They married last January . . . in kind of a hurry, so the old biddies had it."

"I do know that we sent a christening-cup, at midsummer," Lady Isobel said with serene incomprehension, as Jane stifled a sudden giggle. "Somers, you are the most appalling gossip. But I think we neglected a proper wedding present, or if we did, then a gift for Christmas; a set of fine sheets and some lovely warm blankets. What do you think, Jane? Will that be suitable for a new-married couple?"

She looked over her shoulder at Jane who answered, "Very suitable and most likely to be very welcome, my lady – especially given that the rest of the farmhouse is likely to be even colder."

"At least someone did a season of sorts and got properly married!" Something of the bright pleasure in the day fled from Lady Isobel's pink face, "She may as well have some reward out of that accomplishment! A good man, a dear little baby, and her own establishment – even if it is cold and drafty. Do you not think her lucky among women, Jane?"

"Most lucky, my lady," Jane answered simply, ignoring Somers's slightly derisive and non-committal grunt. Young Mrs. Wright did seem content with her lot, only slightly more nervous with Lady Isobel's visitation than the wives of the other tenants, Jane judged, after fifteen minutes of standing at Lady Isobel's elbow in the small and chilly kitchen of Dale Farm.

"Make a note of it for me, Jane. I shall discuss this with Mrs. Kittredge. She always organizes Christmas presents for the tenants and the estate workers with Mr. Aubrey." Lady Isobel faced the front, again. So familiar was Jane becoming with her mistress and sensitive to Lady Isobel's very thoughts and moods that Jane knew she was dwelling once again on the silken and unyielding bars of the cage that her position imprisoned her in.

The dog-cart rattled along a lane where the temporary warmth of afternoon had softened some of the icy mud forming deep ruts, which would have made progress so much more painfully jolting. Jane wondered where they were. She thought they might be going towards Upton again, to complete the last of their rounds. If so, they were passing by the outer pastures of the Home Farm. At the turn of the lane, a gap in the hedgerow revealed a stone wall, waist-high to a man, with a couple of slabs of stone set into it for a stile and a widening verge, thatched with frost-killed grass. In that wide place stood a tall saddled riding horse and another dog-cart with a wiry pony in the shafts. Two men stood, leaning their elbows on the top of the wall, one short and another tall, looking at a small scattering of red cattle pastured within. A third man, the herdsman, stood unconcernedly among the cows.

"'tis old Willie," Somers remarked, "His Lordship was going to ride out today."

"Fa!" Lady Isobel exclaimed with delight, as the shorter and more elegantly dressed of the two men turned around, with a cheery smile. "Oh, stop the cart, Somers. I believe that is Mr. Becker with him. Jane, you have heard me speak of him, but had you ever set eyes on him before?"

"No, Milady," Jane studied the younger man with deep curiosity, attempting to fit what Lady Isobel had told her with the reality of a tall man, with broad shoulders in a rough canvas workman's jacket, who straightened unhurriedly from the wall and removed his hat. Underneath it, his hair was as pale as straw; he handed Lady Isobel down from the cart with every appearance of tender care.

"I thought Lattimore and I would show him some of our prize Durham heifers this morning," Sir Robert said, beaming impartially upon them all, "Some of old Comet's line; the finest beef cattle in the land, if I say so m'self."

"Good morning, Miss Isobel," Lady Isobel's gentleman said to her with apparent pleasure. Jane saw that Lady Isobel was blushing. "It's a real pleasure to see you again so soon. Your father's been right kindly, showing me around his place with Mr. Lattimore."

"Jane and I have been paying visits to the tenants," Lady Isobel explained. To Jane's consternation, before Somers could come around from tying up the pony's reins, Mr. Becker reached up to assist her down from the back of the dog-cart.

"If you'd allow me, Miss Jane," he said only, and lifted her effortlessly straight down to the ground, almost as if she were a small child. His hands were very strong; Jane gasped a little, out of surprise. Standing on the ground and looking up, he was very tall, indeed, as tall as her step-father, but Jane did not feel anything like the same threat, the menace from him that she felt from her step-father. Rather, Mr. Becker felt safe, sheltering, like a kindly tree. *If that is how he makes my lady feel*, Jane thought, *then that is a good thing.* And she saw that when he had reached up to her, his coat lifted with the movement of his arms: underneath it, she caught a glimpse of a heavy leather belt around his middle. A holster with a revolver in it hung from one side and from the other, a long coiled length of braided leather.

"Thank you," she gasped. He nodded acknowledgement and took Lady Isobel's arm, just as Lady Isobel asked, "What do you think of Farmer Lattimore's prize stock?"

"Very fine, Miss Isobel," he replied, with an amused half-smile, "Although I don't know how well they would do, out in the Llano for half a year eating buffalo grass."

"Is this so very different from your pastures?" Jane heard Lady Isobel ask with breathless interest. Yes, he was smiling outright as he answered her. "Yes, Miss Isobel, it is."

"Mr. Becker must return to London shortly," Sir Robert said. "So, I thought, best come out this morning, hey? Not waste any time – straight to the heart of the matter, eh, young fellow? Which do you like the looks of, most particularly?"

"The heifer with a blaze shaped like a star," Mr. Becker answered.

"Bring up young Rosebud," Sir Robert called. "It is young Rosebud, isn't it, it Lattimore? A fine three-year-old and a blue-ribbon winner to boot. Clever girl, she's the farthest away."

"Don't trouble yourself," Mr. Becker answered. Without any visible effort, he vaulted the stone wall and walked out a little way towards the cattle, with an easy lounging stride. As he walked, he was taking out the coil of leather from under his coat. Holding one long loop in one hand, he held the rest of the slender coil in the other.

"They're wary of those they don't know," Sir Robert called, but Mr. Becker only nodded. He was spinning a loop of the leather coil at his side, a loop that widened as he lifted an arm over his head. The loop spun ever wider and Jane blinked, as he threw it overhand like a cricket ball. The spinning loop shot out and fell neatly over the horns of the cow with the while blaze on her forehead. Mr. Becker tightened it with a snap of his arm. The cow tossed her head in surprise. "I say," Sir Robert exclaimed, in astonished admiration; even Somers whistled. "What a deucedly good trick! Is that something you have cause to use often, among your cattle? What do you call it, then?"

"Quite often," Mr. Becker deftly took up the excess, as he led Rosebud the cow towards the stile. She followed obediently. Farmer Lattimore hurried over to hold her headstall, while Mr. Becker removed his leather rope. "It's called a lariat – this is the old Mex style, of braided leather. *La reata*, that's Spanish for rope. Most of the hands and wranglers use grass-rope, for strength . . . but the old style is lighter and bein' longer, can be thrown farther." He held out the braided coil of leather out for Lady Isobel and Sir Robert to take and marvel over, adding, "My father's foreman taught me to use it, the old way – almost as soon as I was able to climb into a saddle. Now, let's see what your young Rosebud would offer to the R-B outfit." He looked over the young cow very carefully, her teeth and udder and all, and asked some very specific questions of Farmer Lattimore, in a voice so low that Jane guessed that ladies were not supposed to hear. Then he came back to the wall and vaulted over as easily as he had done before. "I like her, very much," he said earnestly to Sir Robert. "Much the best of the young heifers I have seen." It seemed to Jane that his glance slid obliquely toward Lady Isobel before he continued, "I will take careful note and commend this one or any other of yours to my uncle. He is an equal partner in all of our business to do with stock and our efforts to breed better. I would not embarrass him by committing our resources on my word alone. But he reposes considerable confidence in my judgment. May I call on you, after the New Year, to convey our final decision?"

"Of course, of course," Sir Robert answered, with an expansive gesture. "Consider yourself our welcome guest and your uncle, also. I have heard mention of him among the City chaps of my acquaintance. He sounds quite the rogue, one of those rough diamonds."

"*Mi casa, su casa?*" Mr. Becker smiled, very slightly. "He is. Princess Cherkevsky compared him to a buccaneer. You might enjoy his company; as folk say in Texas, there ain't no flies on him." Sir Robert looked blank for a moment, then let out a jovial chuckle, answering, "What a very singular expression! I assume that means he is of an active disposition? Never standing still long enough?"

"Something like that," Mr. Becker answered. "Uncle Hansi never stays in one place long enough to let the grass grow under his feet. He took a taste for traveling when he was a teamster for the Verein and then for the Confederate Army. One thing led to another. He has a hand in doing profitable business in just about every town in our part of Texas, through his sons, or nephews and in-laws. I shall call on you, after our return from Italy. Good day, sir . . . Ma'am . . . Miss Jane." He shook hands with Sir Robert, clasped Lady Isobel's lingeringly and nodded to Jane. He climbed into his dog-cart's seat with the grace of an athlete and taking up the reins, soon vanished along the lane, while Sir Robert chuckled again.

"I judge that young fellow has not let the flies settle, nor the grass grow, either." Jane thought that he looked upon his daughter with a peculiar and searching look. "I daresay he has taken a page from his uncle's book. A d'Medici of the western plains, I would venture; from humble beginnings into great riches, by dint of effort. A great enterprise, something to stir the heart; would he stir your heart, Pet?"

"I do like him, Fa," Lady Isobel answered, wistfully. "And the dogs like him, too." Jane thought she would have said more, but for Sir Robert taking up Willie the Conquerors' reins and swinging up into the saddle, "Duty calls, Pet – and so do yours, I expect. Convey my good wishes to Nanny Solomon. Tell her that I shall call upon her later in the week."

"I will, Fa. She will doubtless put on her best cap and make crumpets for you to toast before the fire," Lady Isobel replied. Sir Robert called over his shoulder, "Marvelous, Pet – tell Nanny I will look forward to them."

When he and Willie had vanished around the turn of the lane, Lady Isobel accepted Somers's hand, assisting her back into the dog-cart's seat. Jane scrambled into the back. They were late and no time to wait upon courtesies which would delay them further. As Somers took up the reins, Lady Isobel added, with an air of disconsolation, "I think I will have to ask my father, when he really does plan to visit Nanny Solomon. She will expect him every day from tomorrow on and forgive him when he does not appear. I shall have to speak to Fa about Dale Farm, anyway. Do you think that I may I plead tardiness at tea to my mother, Jane?"

"It's your father that you would be speaking to," Jane answered, with a robust sense of exasperation. *Lady Isobel was the apple of Sir Robert's eye, why should she so fear her termagant of a mother?* Then, she thought of her stepfather and her own mother; of how she mortally feared one, and was desperately disappointed by the other. Mayhap she should be more patient with Lady Isobel.

Still in her brown dress, but having gratefully shed her bonnet and other outer garments, Isobel crept down the main staircase into the Great Hall. In a few hours, the outdoor servants would bring in the Christmas tree, which would stand below the minstrel-gallery, laden with ornaments and gifts wrapped in pretty paper and tied with tinsel-ribbons. Mama had not come down to tea – it was to be in the Yellow Salon again, for houseguests had begun arriving, all the long morning that Isobel had been busy on her calls. Isobel heard her mother's voice coming from behind the closed door to her suite, low but insistent. Mama was dressing, for Isobel also heard Havers' voice, submissively responding. She crept past that door on silent feet. *If Mama did not see her, Mama could not issue orders.* Thus, Isobel did not feel bound to obey them, even though she knew very well what Mama would have told her.

Instead, she sought out her father's study and office at the other end of the Gallery from the Yellow Salon, an ordinary panel door half-hidden in the shadows. One might never know that it lead into Fa's study; a comfortable snuggery, lined with a jumble of books, some of them so old that the pages stuck together when first taken down from the shelf. The books opened with a faint creak of leather binding and the indefinable smell of old paper. Isobel loved Fa's study; the shabby divan and old-fashioned horse-hair upholstered wing-chairs drawn up before the polished brass fender, and books and the curling drawings laid out on Fa's vast morocco-leather-topped desk, the models of his great works lined up in miniature among the books. It smelled also of tobacco and the smoke from Fa's pipe, of damp leather boots and wet wool. The windows looked out towards the lake, with the woods beyond, bare-leafed trees lifting up their branches against a faint apricot-colored smear of the sunset beyond. Isobel tapped gently on the door and opened it, just as Sir Robert looked around the side of the biggest, most comfortable wing-chair.

"Oh, it's you, Pet. How went the calls? Close the door, come and sit down." She obeyed; Fa looked at her, with one eye-brow raised and rumbled. "Not changed for tea, yet? Just as well; your lady mother would smell the smoke of my pipe on your gown and know you have been wasting your time."

"I never consider it wasted time with you, Fa," Isobel answered.

Sir Robert grinned like a conspiring school-boy and coughed. "Of course not, Pet, but we both know, if you are not out with your fan and falderals while some likely young sprog is dancing attendance on you, it is time wasted as far as your mother is concerned."

"It's tiresome, Fa – and most tiresome this evening." Isobel settled herself onto the chair opposite her father: tobacco in the bowl of his pipe fitfully glowed cherry-red. He looked at her very shrewdly, through the cloud of pipe-smoke. "I see, Pet," he said, and waited for her to begin. That was one of the things she most loved about Fa: he waited for her to speak and honestly listened as if he wished to know what she thought.

"It went quite well, Fa. Tommy and Adeline Lattimore are recovered or recovering from the measles. I brought some hothouse grapes for them, now that they are in health enough to relish them. But I do not think all is well at Dale Farm, Fa. The kitchen was very cold. My dear Jane saw that the windows do not close all the way and so admit considerable of a draft."

Sir Robert grunted, "The house was empty a good few years. Thought Aubrey had seen to the repairs."

"I'm sure he did, Fa – but it might not have been so evident, in the spring. There was little wood in the shed and no coal, or so said Somers. Might we not send them a cart-load or two? I know they are new and unproved tenants, but they seem worthy and if they are of good repute . . ."

"Of course, Pet," Sir Robert puffed out another cloud of pipe-smoke. "You need no special pleading on their behalf. I'll tell Aubrey to see to it. What else, Pet?"

"I had some thoughts as to a special Christmas gift, for them," Isobel answered. "But I shall take that up with Kitty-Cat." She made as if to leave, but astonishingly, her father took the pipe from his mouth. "No, stay a moment, Pet. Stay and sit with your dear old Fa. I know you are in no hurry for tea with your mother's guests, so I plead for the pleasure of your companionship, while I may. Besides, I thought I would ask your opinion on a certain matter."

"Fa," Isobel ventured after a moment. "You sound as if you are up to something; something which concerns me."

"Something which concerns all of us," her father answered. "And young Mr. Becker, in particular."

"Mr. Becker?" Isobel, caught off-guard, felt a blush rising into her cheeks and hoped that in the dim firelight, the color in her face would not be so apparent. "We . . . he was with you this afternoon, at the Lattimores' field and he promised to call on us in London."

"So he did, Pet." Her father looked into the fire as if deep in thought. "So he did. I'm not blind, you know, Pet. Eyes to see, an' all that. Spoke to me, he did, this very afternoon. He's a gentleman, in his rough way and he wanted my permission. He's in a bit of a hurry, so I told him I'd give it, once I talked to you."

"Permission?" Isobel's breath caught in her throat. "Fa – permission for what?"

"To court you," Sir Robert answered. "I didn't say yes or no, Pet. I said I'd give it careful consideration, since he is asking so much. He's planning to sail back to Texas in the spring. April at the latest and for you to accompany him as his wife, if you are so inclined."

Isobel felt as if she had been rocked by a mighty explosion, an explosion of relief and joy. To marry Mr. Becker, stranger though he was and not have to go to India, a prospect which she dreaded so much as to feel ill even contemplating it? In the back of her mind, a wicked imp whispered, *You'd marry the Hunchback himself, if you could escape thereby*! She immediately felt ashamed. Mr. Becker was handsome, rich, and considerate, and the dogs liked him. Why should she not come to love him? Sir Robert sighed very deeply and when Isobel looked at his face, she thought there was a shine of unshed tears in his eyes. "I see, then . . . you would welcome his suit. No need for words, Pet. I will write to him, conveying my permission. I thought as much." Sir Robert made a sound rather like a cough, converted at the last minute into a laugh. "He does cut a dashing figure, doesn't he? And a man of considerable property as well. That will please your mother," Her father's voice was rough with barely-suppressed emotion. "Dear little Pet, can we endure seeing you go so far away from us?"

"It's not as far as India, Fa," Isobel said, her voice unsteady. "This was Mama's intent, all this Season; that I contract a good marriage. And I daresay

I shall be able to travel Home for visits, if I choose to acquiesce to Mr. Becker's honorable offer. I think he will be kind. He *is* kind, Fa. Very kind."

In her heart, Isobel was torn by indecision, as a prisoner in a dark dungeon, seeing the heavy doors flung open and the light of bright day light shining in. Would she dare set foot outside? *When he asks,* Isobel wondered *– and he will ask, no doubt on it – what shall I do? Should I go with him to a foreign place, even more alien than India? How far will I go to be married and escape Mama's authority for once and all? Would I go with him to his home in Texas and make Mama at last happy with me? I will be married and escaping her authority for once and all. But I would be going so far away. . .*

Chapter 4 – *Come a' Courting*

Keenly aware of Lady Isobel's moods, Jane did not at first notice any particular amendment to her mistresses' temperament, after the day-long excursion visiting Sir Robert's tenants, and she was not yet so bold as to ask about the young American, Mr. Becker. Jane sensed that Lady Isobel would unburden herself in her own good time. Jane had laid out her gown for dinner and was waiting with concealed impatience, her eye on the mantel clock, when Lady Isobel returned at last, a whiff of tobacco-smoke smell attending on her clothes. Jane sighed; the walking-costume would have to be brushed and aired for many days, then laid away with lavender-sachets in the folds, to eradicate the odor of Sir Robert's pipe-smoke. Lady Isobel smiled at Jane in the mirror, as Jane made adjustments to her hair, quickly tucking in stray wisps of pale brown hair back into the ornate braided knot and smoothing with a bit of scented pomade on her palms. She had concocted a hair-ornament of tiny hothouse flowers, some lace, and a ribbon-bow which exactly matched the color of Lady Isobel's ice-blue gown.

"Oh, how lovely, Jane," Lady Isobel exclaimed, as Jane carefully pinned it into the arrangement of her hair. The mantel clock chimed the quarter-hour. "How careful you are of me! I would have never thought of that. I am late!"

"Your gloves," Jane handed them to her. "And I thought the aquamarine and diamond choker. Nothing more."

"Elegant and simple," Lady Isobel drew on her long gloves, while Jane rummaged through Lady Isobel's jewel-case. "Fasten the clasp swiftly, Jane. Mama will be in a hasty temper with me, otherwise." She sprang up from the dressing-table stool, while Jane thought that her lady really did not seem so nervous at the thought of Lady Caroline's displeasure this evening. That must have been a good talk with Sir Robert.

Jane thought wistfully of how pleasant it must be to have a fond father. Her own father had been such and she missed him still. It was a mystery to Jane, how her mother had married again as soon as it was decent. A widow needed a man to be the head of the house and to keep the store, but to choose so recklessly! Jane shivered inwardly at the memory of her stepfather, of him leering at her from behind her mother's back, the murmured remarks that only her ears could hear, the unwanted touch, the caresses that sent her shuddering from the room. Aunt Lydia rescued her that, for which Jane said a prayer of thanks every day and especially whenever she looked at herself, reflected in the mirror over Lady Isobel's shoulder.

Now she was almost seventeen and pretty enough to be unwilling prey for any man the ilk of her stepfather. She would have looked even prettier, if she permitted it, dressed in the finer garments of a proper ladies' maid. Wisps of dark hair curled around her face, escaping the confines of a cap with more elaborate lace on it than she had ever before; no, that must not be allowed. There was still pomade on her hands; she captured the rebellious strands and smoothed them back. It would not do, to give any gentleman or upper servant improper ideas. Somers the groom acted as if he would have liked to flirt with her, but Jane knew that must never be allowed. She must seem older than she was, severe and prim like Miss Havers. Jane often felt worldlier and so much wiser – paradoxically like an older sister, though she was almost two years Lady Isobel's junior. Jane stood now as Lady Isobel's confident and even chaperone, her guardian and protector in all things. Jane sighed again; it was a great burden, but there were rewards for bearing it and being of a trustworthy and upright character. Auntie Lydia had it in mind that Jane would someday be the housekeeper in Lady Isobel's establishment – to whatever establishment an advantageous marriage took her. *Of course I will go with Lady Isobel; who else will take care of her, who shall she trust, otherwise?*

Christmas at the Hall passed, in lavish scenes of merriment and hospitality over the two weeks after the tenant-visitation day and the meeting in the lane by Farmer Lattimore's cow-pasture. Jane had never seen the like, from the tall pine-tree in the Great Hall, hung with marvelously delicate blown-glass ornaments, colored garlands of multi-colored tinsel-paper, and hundreds of tiny candles, the light of which cast the Great Hall in a mellow golden light, down to the gaily-wrapped parcels piled underneath. In the breath of air moving in the Great Hall, from the various drafts creeping under the doors and from the corridors, the ornaments and candles shimmered like a vision seen from afar. The children all clapped their hands with glee; Young Sir Robert and Lady Eleanor's little boys, the Stanley's son and little daughter, brought down from the Nursery in Nanny Porter's capable arms. There was a chorus of carolers at the door; local folk, carrying lanterns and all wrapped in coats and mufflers, singing on the doorstep of the Hall, while Auntie Lydia – Mrs. Kittredge sent to the kitchen for hot cider and cakes for the footmen to take around to the carolers.

The day before Christmas Eve, there was to be a grand ball, with all of the gentry from the county around invited, besides the Hall's houseguests. Below-stairs was as crammed as upstairs, as many guests were attended by their own servants. Jane saw little of the procession of the first local guests arriving. She was dressing Lady Isobel in a primrose-colored ball gown of delicate muslin and tulle made in the latest fashion, the overskirt looped up over the fullness in back, cascading in a froth of lace and ruching into a short train. They both could hear carriage-wheels crunching on the gravel forecourt and see the carriage-lamps bobbing and swaying all the way along the drive.

"If I can only keep from tripping over it," Lady Isobel lamented. "Or my dance partner from treading on it. I shall be afraid to sit down, lest I crush all the ruffles." Her cheeks were flushed; for once, Lady Isobel was looking forward to this ball. Much of what she had said to Jane before about such things had been mild complaint about the exhaustion of dancing, the tediousness of conversing with young men as they attempted not to step on her toes – shod in kid leather, dyed primrose to match her dress – and agonies of embarrassment at having no dances at all.

"There is a loop, here, to lift up the train," Jane answered. "If you must, contrive to sit a little sideways. And if you have an accident with your gown, send for me. I will come with a needle and thread or whatever is necessary."

There was a brief tap on the door. Before Jane or Lady Isobel could bid anyone enter, the door opened. Lady Caroline advanced, attended by Havers carrying her jewel-case. Lady Caroline was splendidly arrayed in a deep-green satin trimmed with gold, emeralds and pearls set in gold at her throat, her wrists and in her hair.

"I am nearly ready, Mama," Lady Isobel protested. Her mother summed up the state of her dress in one swift glance, a glance as keen and cutting as a surgeon's knife.

"I can see that, Isobel," Lady Caroline replied. "I confess it is such a pleasant change." She favored Jane with another one of those piercing looks. Jane thought it must have been the first time that Lady Caroline really looked at her, noticed her as she truly was – more than just another girl in a black maid's dress with a neat white cap, one of dozens or hundreds which had served her over the years, brought messages or the tea-tray, built a fire in the fireplace of a morning or made the bed. "I can see the chit of a maid has done well for you. She learns swiftly; a rough jewel among the mire of the commonality, Isobel. Make sure that she never learns ideas above her place, else you will be put to the chore of finding another of equal skill."

"Mama . . ." Lady Isobel's voice had a tone of hopeless pleading in it. She already looked diminished, over-plump and uncertain, dressed in clothes too fine for her. The contrast with her daughter was cruel. Lady Caroline would look queenly in rags. Lady Caroline commanded, "Stand up straight, and don't mumble; it's very missish. I hoped you had outgrown that. I have

decided that you should wear my wedding pearls tonight." At a nod from her
mistress, Havers set the jewel case on the dressing table and opened it.

Lady Isobel stammered, "Thank you, Mama. I thought Victoria –"

"Don't think, Isobel. You can't and the effort does not become you.
Victoria is wearing the Stanley sapphire choker tonight. You should have the
pearls. Your father tells me that he has given his permission to that young
American, to bring a suit of marriage to you. He is present tonight," Lady
Caroline added, with a touch of exasperation. "Most unexpectedly, it seems.
Do not bore him out of countenance, Isobel. As unprepossessing as he is, he
is heir to such a sufficient property that your father has been brought to
consider him seriously as a suitor."

"Mr. Becker is here tonight? But he told me . . . he told Fa that he was to
spend Christmas in Italy with his family and that Russian princess." Lady
Isobel's voice died away, as her mother shrugged indifferently.

"You were misinformed or did not hear truly. Which does not surprise me
in the least. Don't goggle at me like a moon-calf, Isobel, of course he is here
tonight." Lady Caroline clapped her gloved hands together sharply. "Havers
. . . the pearls. You too, girl – whatever your name is – assist her. I must lead
the first dance shortly. Hurry or I shall be late! Isobel, I presume that you wish
to have the first dance with your rough cavalier?"

Jane went to help the acid-tongued Miss Havers with the jewel-case,
setting the delicate and gleaming earrings into her ladyship's ears. Lady Isobel
mutely held up her gloved arms, so Jane and Miss Havers could close the
clasps of the bracelets on her wrists, with such an expression of apprehension
and resignation mixed that it felt to Jane as if she were fastening manacles on
the wrists of a prisoner or a slave. Yet her lady had such a look in her dark-
lashed hazel eyes – which if one looked at her with a cold and assessing
judgment – were her only claim to beauty, an expression of simmering
rebellion and hope all mixed together.

"Thank you for loan of your pearls, Mama," she said in a steady voice.
"Mr. Becker is a very pleasing gentleman to me. I should be able to hold his
attention, as we have many interests in common."

"See that you do," Lady Caroline looked her up and down, quite severely.
"As odd as he is, he appears to be about the best that you can get. Don't appear
to be too eager. That is even more poisonous to gentlemanly affections as a
display of complete disinterest would be."

"Mama, I am sure of Mr. Becker's interests," Lady Isobel replied, as Lady
Caroline turned and sailed towards the door. Havers trailed after, obedient as
a shadow. Jane hurried to close it after them. As she did, she heard Lady

Caroline speak to Miss Havers in a voice careless of being overheard in the long hallway, "What a waste of my pearls! Isobel looks like a cow adorned with Christmas garlands. With luck, she will marry this rough Cousin Jonathon and be off my hands entirely. All this year, I despaired of success attending on my endeavors with her. How fitting to be rewarded at the very last and at Christmas!"

Jane shut the door very firmly on Lady Caroline's spiteful voice. "So, he will be here, Milady," she said bravely. "That is good news, I would say. Do you wish to marry him?"

"Fa said that he had asked for permission to seek my hand," Lady Isobel answered distantly. She looked at herself in the mirror, but her eyes were far away, remote. "I don't know why his choice would settle on me, Jane. He is handsome and amiable and possessed of a fortune; all most attractive to females. I marvel that such a paragon has not already been engaged to marry."

"Perhaps he has been disappointed in love," Jane ventured. "His intended died tragically, or he did not feel that he could support a wife until now."

"He could be a fortune hunter," Lady Isobel said, fiddling with one of the earrings dripping down from her ears. "But I expect that Fa would have already considered that."

"What will you do, Milady?" Jane began gathering up Lady Isobel's discarded garments and the detritus from the effort to dress her fittingly for the evening, while Lady Isobel stared unseeingly into the mirror. "About Mr. Becker."

"I expect I will dance with him now and again. And perhaps have a few moments of conversation, as we nibble at the cold collation in the dining room. Fa says that he would wish me to accompany him to America in April, so I expect that he will propose without delay."

"And what will you say then?" Jane held her breath with anticipation.

"I will consider his proposal carefully," Lady Isobel answered. "Such a tangle, Jane! I barely know him, cannot even claim that I love him, but I must marry. Continuing as I am is unendurable, Jane. Completely unendurable. I would be driven mad, very shortly. I also dread the alternative that my mother insists that I accept, otherwise. India – the very thought makes my blood run cold. I cannot abide snakes and everyone says India is full of them. But," she added with an air of someone desperately hoping that it might be so. "I might come to love Mr. Becker. They say most husbands and wives do, even if they have not married for love to begin with. Would you wish well for me tonight, Jane? Wish me well and for me to be steadfast in purpose?"

"I will, Milady," Jane answered. Her heart felt as if it would overflow with pity and fear for Lady Isobel, bravely accepting the lesser evil of the unfortunate options set before her. *There are prisons and there are prisons. Aunt Lydia gave me an escape from mine, but there is only one escape for Milady!* Perhaps Mr. Becker would prove to be the best choice; he might come to appreciate Lady Isobel's good heart, her courage, and sense of obligation. "Here is your fan and the program of dances. I will bring another pair of gloves in the interval after the second set. If you have need of another pair, I will bring them as soon as you send for them. Do you want me to accompany you downstairs?"

Lady Isobel straightened her shoulders, looking away from the mirror. "Dear Jane – no, I don't think it necessary. I will send Horgan or one of the other footmen, should I need assistance during the evening."

"Good fortune, Milady," Jane said as Lady Isobel embraced her suddenly, with fierce affection. The fabulous pearls pressed against Jane's cheek and neck, as hard and unforgiving as pebbles. "I think he might come to love you, Milady. He seems a considerate gentleman."

"Thank you, Jane." Lady Isobel straightened her shoulders, holding her head as high as if she had a book balanced on it. The door opened and closed with a soft click of the latch, leaving Jane to finish sorting out the littered dressing table, and putting away the garments rejected – a task which Jane found oddly comforting, as she liked to see things tidy and neat.

Isobel felt as if she were floating, as if she moved in a surreal dream, detached from her own flesh. She marveled at how her customary nervous dread had vanished, dissolved as morning sunlight dissolved the frost. She moved down the main staircase in a rustle of muslin, as detached as if she were watching herself from inside her own head. She wondered if Martyn felt this extraordinary calm, preparing for some skirmish in the borderlands of India. The chatter of voices, the music floating in from the ballroom reminded her of the sea, the rhythmic rattle of pebbles in the wave-wash. She moved like an automaton through the crush of guests arriving in the main hall, each announced in a puff of frigid air from the front door opening and closing and Horgan's practiced bellow.

So many guests, so many people . . . again, she was reminded of how most of the public rooms of the Hall didn't not feel truly inhabited unless they were as crowded as a railway station in the City. *How wonderful it would be to spend an evening at the fireside of a cozy little cottage or a small house; just enough room for a handful of friends, children and a husband. To sit before the fire of an evening, without the agony of being forced to be charming to hostile strangers. Courage, Isobel Lindsay-Groves,* she whispered to herself. *Courage – endure this evening, these next few weeks.* She nodded mechanically, barely aware of those who spoke to her; distant friends and remote strangers. They passed in a dream; gentlemen in evening-dress, punctuated by colorful regimentals and gold braid, young ladies clad in dresses the color of spring flowers, of older ladies in more dramatic colors, sparkling in jewels, an Aladdin's cave of gold and gems. She was distantly aware of those who looked at her with derision and scorn, the cruel amusement in their eyes, derision so artfully veiled in honeyed malice that one could not show a reaction without being made the object of even more pointed malice! She hated that. *It's not fair! What did I ever do to you? Why do I merit this cruel scorn!*

There was an escape; from across the ballroom she saw him. Mr. Becker – so very tall, pale hair the color of ripe wheat. The orchestra had already begun the music for the first dance, the grand promenade. Isobel moved around the edge of the ballroom and the graceful procession of dancers, intensely aware of his eyes upon her. He stood next to Martyn, resplendent in scarlet regimentals, both of them by a range of chairs lined up against the ballroom wall. She felt a rush of confidence, when his eyes met hers and he smiled very slightly. Mama would have found nothing to criticize in his evening dress. It was impeccably tailored, nor would she have found a fault in the way that he bowed very over her hand.

She could think of nothing to say, but he spared her the trouble and agony. "Miss Isobel," he ventured, the corners of his eyes crinkling slightly with amusement. "I have been told wrong. Cap'n Lindsay-Groves says that you are always late. He said I might have to dance with another lady while I waited for you. I didn't think it right proper."

"Thank you for your patience, Mr. Becker," Isobel answered and that detached part of her was gratified that she wasn't stammering. "I was just told you were among the guests. I came downstairs straightaway. You had said you were traveling to Italy within days; his is most unexpected."

"My uncle's plans changed unexpectedly," Mr. Becker answered. "He and my aunt and all are returning to Texas as soon as it can be arranged. I stay on to finish up Uncle Hansi's errands."

"There has not been some awful tragedy?" Isobel ventured, with some apprehension. Mr. Becker gravely shook his head, answering, "No, quite the opposite. But my aunt wanted to return home at once. "

Martyn observed, "A bit of good luck for you then, Izzy; I'll take the quadrille. Fa would like to see that your dance card is full. Remember," he sounded as if he were half-warning, half-joking. "Never two dances in a row, with a lady, y'know, even the lady one is courting."

"I do know what custom demands," Mr. Becker answered mildly. "Though I might not want to pay much mind. Ma'am," he took her hand again. "May I have the pleasure of the dance with you?"

"The pleasure is mine," Isobel answered. He held out his elbow for her hand and led her onto the dance floor as carefully as if she were something delicate made of glass. As the quadrille began, Isobel set her mind on endurance, but discovered to her astonishment that Mr. Becker was an excellent dancer, confident and sure-footed. The only awkwardness came from the difference in height. She must tilt her head back so very far to see his face and converse with him as they whirled through the quadrille. That small discomfort was overshadowed by the wholly-unaccustomed assurance and grace, which she discovered with delight as they moved together; dancing with him was like riding Thistle. They moved together easily, sensing the shift and balance of each others' bodies as if they were twinned creatures, two halves sliding together to make one whole being.

"I . . . must compliment you, Mr. Becker," Isobel stammered at last. "You dance very well. My mother will be astonished to learn that Texas must have a sufficiency of dancing-masters."

"No, not that you'd notice," he replied agreeably and Isobel saw that he was smiling. "But like most things, Miss Isobel – if you do something a lot, you'll get good at it after a while."

"Do you often attend balls and dances?" Isobel was honestly intrigued; his smile widened, as he looked over her head at the ballroom, decorated with swags of holly and garlands of sweet-smelling pine, the golden chandeliers, glittering with crystal drops and lights, which bathed the vast room in mellow golden candlelight. "Not in so grand a hall as this. I reckon the biggest room that I ever danced with a lady in was a dance-hall in Abilene. A right nice place it was, too," he added, seemingly in response to her look of momentary bafflement. "Noisier, though. The boys was all dancing in their boots. And the ladies weren't near so pretty or as handsome-dressed."

"Thank you," Isobel accepted the compliment with as demure an expression as her mother had ever urged upon her. Mr. Becker's smile widened. "Truth to tell," he continued, as Isobel listened avidly, one corner of her mind astounded at how comfortable she felt, dancing with a man. Always before, she had been nervous, counting the steps and turns, miserably aware of her own awkwardness and inability at the flirtatious conversation which came so easily to other girls. "It was a right enjoyable fandango, until a drover from the Millett outfit took it into his head to ride his pony onto the dance floor." At Isobel's expression of disbelief, he added with a humorously solemn expression, "I swear to you, Miss Isobel – it did really happen. He insisted that his cow-pony had a neater foot than any of the ladies and was better able to turn and bow."

"I believe you are telling wild stories," Isobel answered. "And trying over-much to impress, with such improbable tales."

"Do you?" Mr. Becker's smile broadened to an outright grin. "I have an acquaintance present who can attest to the truth. He was trying to play a quiet game of whist in a far corner, but he was there."

"I still believe you are exaggerating, Mr. Becker." Isobel answered, "Surely this was a flight of fancy. Who among this company tonight was present in a . . . what do you call it . . . a dance-hall in Abilene?"

"We called him English Jack," Mr. Becker answered. "Jack Sutcliffe was his proper moniker but we never called him anything but English Jack, when he rode up the trail with us from Texas ten years ago." As they dipped and turned, he added, "He is standing next to your brother."

"Major Sutcliffe?" Isobel would have missed a step in her surprise but for Mr. Becker's relative strength. She looked past her partner – yes, another man in brilliant red regimentals and gold braid stood next to her brother. "He is a very distant connection. I used to think he was ever so gallant and handsome; I had a school-girl passion which I confess that I have long outgrown! Fa always liked him, although I should say that my mother does not approve. She says that he is a rake and a wastrel. I suppose he is Martyn's guest."

"He may be all that," Mr. Becker answered agreeably. "The fellows back home thought he was a good sort, even if they thought he talked a little funny."

"I suppose it is a very different sort of life," Isobel mused. "With men leading a different sort of life, apart from the ladies; I would not be surprised if you and Major Sutcliffe find Society rather boring."

"Not so far, Miss Isobel," he answered as the quadrille ended. He bowed as Isobel sank into a curtsey and offered his arm to escort her back to the chairs. As they approached Jack Sutcliffe straightened up from his usual languid posture, an expression of lively interest brightening his face.

"Lady Isobel," he drawled. "Martyn said you had been presented – so help me, I don't know where the time goes. I thought of you as still in the schoolroom. You must do me the honor of the next dance."

"Of course you may." Isobel marveled at herself, feeling so very composed and worldly, writing Jack Sutcliffe's name in her program with the tiny silver pencil, as Jack Sutcliffe's regard turned toward her escort.

"Ah, Becker – a long way from the trail, isn't it?" he said with a broad grin, echoed by Mr. Becker's own expression. "I see that dear old Uncle Hansi's venture in cattle went well!"

"It did, Jack," Mr. Becker answered with honest pleasure. "It did. I took your advice, too. I came to look at a white horse and got distracted by a promising young filly."

"I see that." Jack Sutcliffe's smile got even broader; Isobel wondered if he referred to herself. Martyn looked quite dour as he said, "I'll have the waltz, Izzy. That'll leave the varsovienne for you, Becker."

"If that is Miss Isobel's wish," Mr. Becker answered and bowed sedately over her hand. "Shall I bring you some little refreshment, before they begin the next dance?"

"No, thank you," Isobel answered. "But it is kind of you to offer."

"You should ask some other lady for a dance, Becker," Jack Sutcliffe drawled. "Give them a bit of a flutter, a turn around the ballroom with a wild American frontiersman. Ever consider painting yourself like a savage Indian?"

"I don't think Lady Caroline would be real amused," Mr. Becker answered, sounding equally unruffled, but Isobel saw that he silently formed a rude word with his lips, directed at Jack Sutcliffe as he straightened from another bow over Isobel's gloved hand. "I shall return for the var-varso-dance, whatever that is, Miss Isobel."

"Thank you, sir – it will be my pleasure to look forward to your company again," Isobel curtsied once more. As he sauntered away, Martyn asked with no little impatience, "The range of your friends and acquaintances never ceases to amaze me, Jack! However did you fetch up with Becker and his lot?"

"Ah," Jack Sutcliffe answered, with perfect assurance. "Officially, a spot of leave and travel to exotic lands, don't you know. Unofficially, let's just not say. I was temporarily embarrassed with regard to funds and desirous of traveling north. An opportunity presented itself, with Becker, his uncle and some other stout fellows with a large quantity of beef cattle."

"How extraordinary," Isobel could think of nothing else say.

"I recall the experience with considerable relish whenever I sit down to an excellent roast-beef dinner," Jack assured them. "The journey proved rather tedious in the main, but the company was quite jolly, if rather rough-hewn. Stout fellows, those chaps of Beckers'. Cousin Isobel, I believe it is time to take to the dance floor."

"It is my pleasure, sir." Isobel took the arm that he proffered, as Martyn said, "Stay a moment, Jack; there is a question I would have an answer to. Is he – this Becker – a gentleman? Fa has given his permission for him to court Isobel. I like to think that Fa has made his own estimation of his worth, but I should like to know for myself of what manner of man he is."

Jack half-turned with Isobel on his arm to answer; Isobel thought that his reply was as much for her as for Martyn. "I would say that he is," Jack Sutcliffe's expression, usually one of cynical good cheer, seemed somehow softened with thought. "A rough diamond, but a gentleman nonetheless."

"And his family?" Martyn persisted, as the orchestra in the ballroom took up their instruments for the next dance. "What of his family?"

"Among the very finest, in that part of the world," Jack answered. "Well-thought of and received in every parlor, up to the highest. Which," he added with something of his customary tone to Isobel, as they stepped onto the dancing floor and took their places, "Is only as high as a provincial governor, but still; the backbone of the country. Salt of the earth, as they say. You look very smart tonight, Cousin Isobel. Is that true, what Martyn told me about you coming out to India in the spring?"

"It is," Isobel admitted, honestly. "Mama says that I have made a terrible botch of my Season. She insists that I marry well."

"Marry well, or marry to please Mama?" Jack asked shrewdly. Isobel was just enough vexed that she answered, "Marry to please myself!" as the orchestra leader lifted his little baton for attention from the musicians.

"Rather than gamble a throw with the fishing fleet?" Jack had his customary cynical expression back. So he knew about that; Isobel's heart felt as if it sank down to the toes of her primrose-kid slippers. "Oh, little cousin, life is one long game of chance. Toss the dice and be done. Chin up and accept the results. I presume that if you choose instead to marry that worthy young Jonathon, he will take you to Texas with him."

"I am certain of that, yes," Isobel answered. "Fa has said as much." Dancing with Jack was not as comfortable as it was with Mr. Becker, although Jack was accomplished and masterful. There was not the feeling of being tuned perfectly to another, moving as one and yet separate, like two birds soaring together. "I dread the thought of India – all the stories that I have heard from Fa and Martyn of the snakes and wild animals, the heat and the dust and the strange ways of the natives."

"I will admit," Jack grinned, broadly. "The heat and dust of Texas, and the strange ways of the natives have not a patch on those of India; though some are passing curious."

"You have been to both places," Isobel ventured. "What do you think?"

"Of India and Texas? Oh, different from here and very different from each other, although honesty compels me to admit they are both very hot, with strange religions and violence sometimes simmering in odd corners. One's full of dusky-skinned natives and the other of Jonathans; pretty dusky-skinned themselves after long months on the cattle-trail. At least most of them speak some kind of English, barbarous though it might sound at times. One needn't study half a dozen languages; one or two will do – or send for an interpreter when it comes to the aboriginal natives. Another kettle entirely, little cousin."

"Do you think that I could make a home there?" Isobel was nearly breathless from the exertions of the waltz. How vexing, when it had felt so effortless, dancing far more energetically in Mr. Becker's arms!

"You are entirely serious, little cousin?" For the long breath of several measures of the waltz, Jack Sutcliffe remained silent. At last he continued. "The sky is such a clear blue – it appears endless, all the way around, to every horizon. No scrap of smoke, no haze upon the horizon; the very clouds float in it and vanish, save those occasions when they gather. Flat grey at the bottom, towering up and up into pure white mounds, lit from within like a paper lantern from the lightening. And the land ... also endless; nothing but rolling waves of grass, like the sea or the deserts of Arabia – nothing like what we have on our little safe island. Now and again, the crumbling skull of a buffalo crunches under the hoofs of your horse. There is nothing, as far as you can see, the sky and the waves of grass. I rather liked it," Jack continued with a half-laugh. "It would drive some mad, out in the middle of all that emptiness, unless you had something in your soul that would answer to it."

"It sounds ... quite delightful," Isobel gasped. In the midst of the waltz, Jack Sutcliffe was half a world away, his expression distant and absorbed in his recollections.

"Would your soul answer to it, little cousin? To an empty prairie, half the size of England? No village, no church spire to be seen, no fences and crumbled towers, as you travel for days and days? The immensity drives men mad sometimes, especially those who come from our little islands and face that emptiness all alone. At night there is nothing but one's own pitiful campfire, and an ocean of stars overhead. Ah, the stars in the prairie sky, little cousin Isobel!"

"Are they a pretty sight?" Isobel asked breathlessly and Jack laughed. "Pretty? My dear, they are magnificent! Imagine, as you prepare to sleep on a pallet laid out on the ground, you look up to see thousands of diamonds, all lit from within, and strewn by handfuls as if they were grain, on dark-blue velvet and seeming to be as close overhead that you could reach up and touch them, but it is a rare traveler, newly-come to that country who arrives with a soul fully open to such wonders."

"Have I such a soul, do you think?" Isobel ventured. Jack Sutcliffe spun her in the waltz so that her primrose skirts flared gracefully.

"I would not venture to say, little cousin – but of you, I do know this for a certainly; that you have no fear of the highest fence or the deepest ditch that the Hunt ever crosses and that bodes exceedingly well. Alas, "Jack swept her in one last whirl, as the music ended. "I do not think they hunt to hounds in America, yet. But I think you will find enough other amusements, should you choose to marry young Becker."

In the dark twilight hour of the morning, after the ball had ended, Isobel sat in the window embrasure of her room, having danced for most of the night – and for nearly the first time in a year, without complaint. She had breakfasted with Mr. Becker, attended by Jack and Martyn, making polite conversation. She had not danced every dance with him, but more often throughout the Christmas ball than with any other man who requested the pleasure of her company. Each time, she went to his arms with a sense of joyous relief. They had not conversed much, but his silences were restful, even comforting. Finally, she had been undressed by Jane, sleepy-eyed and smothering yawns all the while. Gratefully, she dismissed Jane to her own bed, but went to sit a little while, looking out at the winter-blasted park down below, and the sky just beginning to pale. In her hand, she held the little dance program, the tiny silver pencil dangling from it, but she saw neither the pages of it, scribbled with names, or the eastern sky, now pink with sunrise. In her mind, she was seeing stars, glittering stars on a velvet sky, or an endless grassy prairie, unrolling like ocean waves, as far as could be seen – and thinking how it had been, dancing wordlessly with a man, how they moved like birds in the sky, together and yet separate.

If he asks me, Isobel thought, *I think I will say yes. I am almost certain that I will say yes.*

Chapter 5 – *A Decent Proposal*

Late in January, the Family moved to their London establishment, after a brief visit to the Stanley estate in Kent. The London house was situated on Wilton Crescent, at a corner opposite the Belgrave Square garden; an imposing pale stone mansion trimmed with a modest amount of classical ornaments and iron lace with a tiny strip of palisaded area before it. Jane was agog with excitement, although she did her best to conceal it. She would go to London, in her capacity of ladies' maid to Lady Isobel! She had never been to a larger city than Abingdon, although she knew some of their neighbors had been as far as Bristol. To travel on the train! And to see the City in company with Lady Isobel. Jane was inexpressibly thrilled, although Aunt Lydia did offer a number of gravely worded warnings, when she was summoned to the housekeeper's private parlor after supper on the evening before departure. Jane listened with careful attention; Aunt Lydia did know much of the world and the ways of the Family, although she would remain at the Hall. The Belgravia mansion had a regular housekeeper who looked after it when the Family was not in residence, just as Aunt Lydia looked after the Hall.

"It is a large city," Aunt Lydia intoned solemnly. "And some aspects of it as barbaric as any savage place in India, or the Americas. You must always be careful of your lady's reputation – although, I have never thought Lady Isobel was reckless of her own, only her neck in the Hunt. You must always go with her, lest she is un-chaperoned. You should ensure that whenever she goes to the shops that you both are accompanied by at least one trusty footman. When you have your afternoons off, Jane, take care that you frequent only respectable places and choose your friends and companions wisely."

"Yes, Mrs. Kittredge," Jane answered obediently. Her aunt was both fond and exasperated.

"Jane, dear child, I know that you are being amiable and respectful to those in authority over you, but I also know that you are young. The young are heedless of hazards and dangers, thinking that by their very youth they are magically impervious to all harm."

"But I will be careful," Jane regarded her aunt with affection. "And you know that the City is not nearly so far as Texas . . ." she stopped, abruptly aware that she might have betrayed Lady Isobel's confidences. "I have heard it said that there is a place to seek hazard and adventure," she added awkwardly, but her aunt only looked thoughtful, quite unsurprised.

"Jane, I know of Lady Isobel's suitor and of his intentions, as I am in the confidence of the Family. I have observed that Lady Isobel is inclined to look upon him with favor; rightfully so, in my opinion. Would that he were only a north-country squire, or perhaps endowed with an Irish estate! He would be perfection as far as the Family is concerned! It is very well for young men, particularly younger sons, to go seek adventure and fortune in far distant lands, but when did it become acceptable for young women of good family to do the same? Modern times, Jane – they bring as many trials as they do blessings. He must make his proposal soon – within the month, I think."

"Why would that be?" Her aunt's certainty startled Jane. Lady Isobel had drifted in a misty cloud of happiness ever since Christmas. Although Mr. Becker had not called upon her in person, pleading urgent family matters taking him to Germany, he had written several times. Lady Isobel had tied the letters into a neat stack with a length of yellow ribbon and kept them secreted in her jewel case.

"Because the young man wishes to return to America no later than mid-April," Mrs. Kittredge answered, patiently as if to a child. "With Lady Isobel as his wife; they must marry therefore by the first of that month. Your lady must have sufficient time to prepare her trousseau, and for Lady Caroline to plan a wedding of such magnificence that gossipy tongues will be immediately stilled – that must likewise take time, at least six weeks. It is now nearly February. As he has given assurance to Sir Robert that his intentions are serious, I conclude that Mr. Becker will formally ask for her hand in the next few weeks."

"So soon?" Jane sat back into comfortable chair in the housekeeper's parlor. "How can you can be certain of this? I had not thought . . ."

"Experience, dear child," Mrs. Kittredge answered her. Jane thought that her aunt was very pleased, almost smug. "Coupled with logic, observation, and consideration of the Family's needs – in that way, one may always be prepared for any eventuality which may arise. That is the means by which one cultivates a reputation for the management of an establishment such as this and increases one's value to an employer. As for yourself, and Lady Isobel," Mrs. Kittredge frowned, thoughtfully. "Lady Caroline will doubtless wish to have her way in everything, whether it be Lady Isobel's wish or not. You might – without being too forward, Jane dear – encourage Lady Isobel in expressing her own desires and wishes. She will soon have the governing of her own establishment, so it would be a salutary experience for her to exercise independence in small matters, And also, Jane" she added, in deeply practical tones. "You might wish to take some instruction from Miss Havers on the art of packing steamer trucks for a long voyage. As I understand, a large stock of tissue paper is an absolute necessity. I assume Lady Isobel wishes you to continue attending upon her after her marriage?"

"Yes, Mrs. Kittredge," Jane answered, demurely. "She has spoken often of married life as if I shall continue in her service, wherever a marriage shall take her." Her aunt looked at her and unexpectedly laughed.

"Dear Jane, I have no doubt that you and Lady Isobel are also anticipating a degree of freedom in the far corners of Texas from an onerous existence in Society – a lessening of the burden of constantly being observed and judged. But do take care, child; freedom comes at a price. One of those prices is a separation from those whom you love and who love you in return."

Jane's eyes filled; that sounded like a rebuke, or at least a chiding, even though her aunt sounded as if she were in sympathy. "Should I accompany Lady Isobel to Texas," she answered, "I would miss you very much. And my mother – just a little, as well as my brothers. But as for my step-father? Not at all; indeed, I rejoice at anything which puts half the world between us!"

"Jane dear," Mrs. Kittredge looked searchingly at Jane's face. "I would not ask, save for that I hold you in such fondness . . . but it is my perception that your stepfather might have made unsuitable advances towards you; advances that were improper in the extreme, especially towards a young girl."

"He said things," Jane answered. "And he leered – and if I could not avoid him, he . . . touched me as if he wished to do more than just that. I think he spied on me, when I was undressing for bed at night." Jane shuddered and her aunt took up her hand.

"But did he do any more than that, child?" Jane shook her head. "That relieves my mind! Your stepfather is a wicked man – wicked and disgusting and unnatural. That your mother chose to marry him, rather than remain a respectable widow as I did is a disgrace to our sex and to your dear father's memory! She put you in danger; how could she have done so! It passes belief, Jane! She risked your virtue and future happiness, marrying that man out of her own base desires! I did not fear that he had succeeded in forcing himself upon you, but that he had poisoned your thoughts against all men. The honest love of a good man is a wondrous thing, Jane. If such could come your way, I pray that you not have any apprehensions in reciprocating such affections."

"I am duty-bound to Lady Isobel," Jane answered. "I would never think of leaving her. I do not fear the general nature of men or their regard; it's just in my position, I must not be seen to welcome their attentions." Her aunt smiled, with a touch of sadness to her,

"But you are pretty, Jane, and amiable of disposition. If Mr. Becker is a fair indication of the manner of men in Texas – and I am sure there are more men than women in such a place – you may have many admirers. You might even find yourself inclined to marriage, being offered a much better match than any you might attain here. Would you prefer to have the governance of your own establishment, rather than Lady Isobel's? I have often read that the spirit of rebellion and independence attends on those who choose a life on the ungoverned frontier."

"I don't know what you mean, Auntie," Jane answered, in such puzzlement that she addressed her aunt as she did of old, without the careful strictures upon her tongue that a year of service at the Hall had imposed upon her. "Do you think that I would leave milady, just like that? I like her very much and she treats me well. What better respectable position could I be offered? I am not a lady; I am just a lady's maid."

"I do not know for certain, Jane," her aunt answered. "But you might be offered a respectable marriage and position, regardless. These American men strike me as being very forward. Consider carefully – choose wisely."

"I cannot think that I would be so charmed by one that I would consider leaving my lady," Jane answered sturdily. Her aunt laughed, with indulgent fondness. "Wait and see, dear Jane, wait and see."

Jane did puzzle briefly over her aunt's words; Aunt Lydia might be correct in judging Mr. Becker to be a fair example of the manner of men to be seen in far America. But Jane had never observed any other such but him and Aunt Lydia herself had never traveled farther than Yorkshire. There might be something in her words, but in the labor of preparing for the Family's departure she had little time to think about them. The excitement of their arrival in London left her with even less time for private thoughts. She was hard-put to conceal her wonder and unseemly curiosity from Miss Havers, when they arrived at Waterloo Bridge Station, demurely following their ladies along the crowded platform.

So many people, of every rank and condition, so much noise, with the shriek and clatter of the engines and cars, of plumes of steam and smoke writhing around the ornate metal columns holding up the roof – a roof as seemingly high above their heads as the sky. A cold gale blew through the station and the very air smelt of coal-soot and garbage. Jane clutched Lady Isobel's jewel-case and an armful of traveling rugs to her, as Miss Havers directed a porter with a huge barrow to load such luggage as they had brought with them, although most of the heavier trunks had gone days before, to be unpacked and arranged as suitable in the London house by the household staff. Sir Robert's manservant and Mr. Asbury, his secretary had already gone to locate their carriage, which had been arranged to meet them.

"You look quite dazed, Jane," Lady Isobel said with a quiet laugh. "It is always such a tangle at Waterloo! They say that not even the stationmaster knows what train is going where and from what platform and when."

"I have never seen so many people at one time," Jane answered, "Not even at race-day. And so noisy," she added, as a train rumbled through, several platforms away. "However do folk sleep at night in the city, my lady?"

"I expect they manage," Lady Isobel answered. "If they are accustomed to it. Have no fear; Belgravia is in the center of the City but beautifully quiet, always – mostly because of the parks. If one must live in a city, then Fa's house is much the best situation imaginable. When I feel that I simply must go riding, there is Hyde Park. I can endure the city for a season, I think."

"Isobel," Lady Caroline commanded. "Come along. Havers, my coat, please. This cold is merciless!" Havers draped a fur-lined mantle around Lady Caroline's shoulders and they all followed obediently after her. Jane thought that Lady Caroline never looked as imperious as she did now; she strode along the platform as if she owned it, freehold and all, hardly looking left or right. Everyone made way for her, from the prosperous appearing gentlemen in tall silk hats, down to the boys begging for pennies by carrying bags and running errands. So many men doffed their hats, or bowed, even if only slightly. *I don't think even the queen herself would have so many gentlemen paying her a courtesy*, Jane thought.

Sir Robert's black-covered landau waited for them in the station forecourt, with a plain dray for hire behind for their luggage. Once out in the open street, Jane shivered. The cold bit more acutely once they moved from the shelter of the station, as drafty as it was. The sky was cast over with drear, smoke-colored clouds. Although it was only afternoon, it felt to Jane as if it were already early evening. She and Miss Havers sat together on the backwards-facing seat with Lady Isobel, while Sir Robert and Lady Caroline shared the more comfortable, front-facing seat. Mr. Alsbury sat with the coachman, up on the box. Lady Caroline asked for her smelling salts, complaining of feeling faint: Jane could hardly blame her. She also felt a little light-headed, as the tall, soot-darkened buildings closed in around them – so many other carriages, coaches, hackney-cabs and drays! The traffic and the mud, the filth in the streets! Jane found it all quite overwhelming. Without warning, everything seemed to open up around the landau's glass windows. They were crossing a long bridge, over a river whose reaches gleamed dull-silver.

Jane gasped involuntarily; across from her in the landau, Sir Robert chuckled, "Ah, Miss Goodacre – it is a sight, isn't it? Turn and look, for there is Westminster! If ever there is a heart to our Empire, it is here – the Thames and the Houses of our Parliament!" Jane half-turned, looking out the glass window at her back, at the rank of gray walls rising up and up and up on the bank opposite; gray walls trimmed with elaborate stone lace, topped with crenels, all along the roof-edge and punctuated with tall spires. The nearest tower housed a great clock at the top. As they approached the middle of the bridge, the clock began chiming the half hour. At the sound, birds flew up in a flock from the roof of the clock-tower. In the distance, they appeared as tiny as motes of dust floating in a sunbeam. Jane drank in the sight. Although she had seen pictures of this place now and again, crudely printed in the newspapers and broadsheets, or painted on a china plate which her Aunt Lydia most particularly cherished; those images were nothing like contemplating it from below, as the landau drew closer and closer.

Since Sir Robert had spoken to her, she could surely answer; Jane said, "Yes, Milord, it is a sight!" Sir Robert laughed, "That it is, little miss. There have been times when it offered a mighty stench, as well."

"Oh, Robert, really!" admonished Lady Caroline, fanning herself with her hand, "Not politics again!"

"I wasn't speaking of Gladstone and his infernally long nose, m'dear." Sir Robert answered as Lady Isobel whispered to her, "Fa abominates Mr. Gladstone; he'd rather associate with a clever chap from nowhere, who has the right sort of ideas about our obligations to our people, than a pious hypocrite who runs around claiming we should mind everyone else's affairs."

This meant a little less than nothing to Jane, but her already high opinion of Sir Robert increased. He spoke of nobles and important folk as if they were as familiar to him as the ordinary folk around the Hall were to her. Now the landau bowled along a wide avenue, with open parkland along one side and railed gardens with fine tall mansions behind them. The parkland gave way now and again to tall walls of pale brick, topped with ornamental urns and a gateway, down the length of which Jane briefly glimpsed a very grand mansion. The landau threaded a crossroads, with a triangle of green parkland touching upon one corner.

Sir Robert patted Lady Caroline's hand, with the bottle of smelling-salts in it, and said, "Cheer up, m'dear, we've just crossed Grosvenor Place – we'll be there in a trice."

Jane looked over her shoulder again. The coachman had just turned a corner and they were coming up on building with a tower on top and a porch with tall columns with what looked like two bolster-pillows at the top of each. Looking ahead, she could see more parkland at the end of the street, trees just faintly touched with faint green and squeezed in between the buildings. Yes, it would soon be spring. If her aunt was correct, she and her lady would very well be gone from this place, by the time they were fully out in leaf.

Isobel smiled to see Jane's face, as they drew up before the Lindsay-Groves' mansion, with its tall windows and welcoming portico. Her eyes had been as huge as saucers, all the way from Waterloo Bridge station. She looked a perfect child, looking upon the city around them with astonished wonderment, yet she kept herself contained and deliberately copied Miss Havers' bearing and air. Even before the landau stopped moving, the front door opened. There was Spencer, who had traveled in advance, in order to ensure that everything in the London house was prepared for their arrival; this was the comfortable and familiar routine, the cycle of their year – every event an ornate jewel in Society's ever-moving calendar. Several tall footmen sprang out to unfold the landau's step and assist their lord and lady to the pavement.

"I shall go upstairs directly," Isobel whispered to Jane, as she joined her parents. "Best to follow after me. This house is not so much a maze as the Hall. You will have a little room next to mine, so it will be easier for you to attend upon me."

"Yes, Milady," Jane answered. Isobel stepped down from the coach and drew a deep breath. The indoor servants were already lined up on the stairs, to welcome the master and mistress back to London. Isobel looked at them quickly. Oh, yes, several new housemaids hardly older than Jane and now the Lindsay-Groves kitchen boasted a very superior sort of chef. Mama was speaking to him in French. Isobel smiled at Mrs. Pitts, the housekeeper – as old and as dear a friend as Kitty-Cat.

In response to her curtsey and words of welcome, Isobel replied gaily, "Hullo, Mrs. Pitts! Yes, I am so glad to return and this time I have my own ladies' maid, for there was simply too much for Havers to do, attending on both of us. I hope there will be no trouble making room for one more in the household."

"Mrs. Kittredge's Jane," Mrs. Pitts replied instantly. Of course, the servants knew simply everything. "She will be no trouble at all, not like Monsewer Duquesne, I am sure." It sounded like Mrs. Pitts was ready for a good gossip, "He's a foreigner, you know," Mrs. Pitts added in a confidential whisper.

"Indeed, Mrs. Pitts." Isobel kept a straight face with an effort and went up into the house. The entry-way, tiled in alternating black and white squares, was full of hothouse flowers – a breath of early spring. Spencer gravely proffered his silver salver towards her, as the front door closed behind her and Jane. There was an envelope on it, an envelope of heavy cream-colored paper

"This was delivered personally for you this morning, Lady Isobel."

"Thank you, Spencer," Isobel had already recognized the handwriting and her heart fair leapt into her throat. Delivered personally? It must mean that Mr. Becker was returned from Germany and his various errands for his uncle. She took the envelope and did not break the seal until she had climbed the stairs to her room.

I will pay a visit upon you tomorrow morning – most respectfully, RB

"Are you terribly excited, Milady?" Jane asked her, the next day. Isobel had changed her mind three times regarding a dress to wear for receiving morning calls.

"I don't want to look as if I had taken so much mind!" she wailed to Jane, sitting all indecisive among her dress-strewn bedroom, a corner room with a pair of windows overlooking the Gardens.

"But you have taken much mind," Jane answered.

"Well, I want to take some consideration!" Isobel felt as if she would weep with despair. "I want him to think that I thought of him, but not so much! I want to look pretty but not as if I had thought of him desperately for every day and night since I last spoke to him and considered the arrangement of my toilette for half the morning! I want to feel as if I were not about to be sick, every time Mama chides me for not having made a good marriage!"

"You're not feeling ill, are you, Milady?" Jane asked swiftly. Isobel looked upon her concerned face and brought her own to smile.

"No, Jane. I daresay I do not feel that ill; not as of yet, anyway." She sank onto the edge of her bed, still clad in her simple combinations and underpetticoat. Her hair fell loose around her shoulders. "I just don't know what to do!"

"Then," Jane answered, "Let me guide you, Milady – if you would permit. I think I know what would suit you best and allow you to regain your confidence. He was a man who did not look at you as if summing up all your faults in dress and deportment, was he?"

"No," Isobel answered, hiccupping slightly. "In truth, Jane, I think he barely noticed articles of dress – other than noting in passing that I had donned garments appropriate to the occasion. I truly think he did not see anything more than that."

"Then he does not see your clothing, Milady, or any such superficial thing; he sees your essential person," Jane answered firmly. "He is a good and kind gentleman. Sir Robert said the same, has he not? In permitting him to court you, he has expressed every confidence in him as a gentleman of honor and good character. Let me sort out what you shall wear, Milady. You do trust me?" She looked anxiously at Isobel. Isobel reflected momentarily upon how odd it was, that she might depend so much on a simple little village girl – that this same girl might be her only true friend of her own age in all the world. Yes, Jane was the only one that she could depend upon, who had never proven false, sniggering behind her hand, the only one besides Fa, Kitty-Cat, and Martyn who had never laughed at her for being gauche and clumsy. Her heart overflowed with gratitude. How could anything unfortunate happen to her, when Jane stood guard, in all those moments before she sallied out into the brutal arena that was Society?

"Yes, dear Jane – I trust you. Chose what I should wear and I promise my implicit trust in this regard. I am in your hands."

"Thank you, Milady." Before her eyes, Jane's countenance turned thoughtful – almost calculating. She surveyed Isobel keenly, as if she had not ever contemplated her person before. "The bronze taffeta. There is some lace that I can sew along the neckline and some other things that I can do for the look of it."

"It is a dress from last year," Isobel answered, quailing at the thought of what Lady Caroline would say. Jane answered with utmost confidence, "The color of it suits your hair, Milady. It is a plain-cut dress, which makes you appear taller and thinner. Did you not feel most comfortable in that costume, knowing that it made you appear in your best aspect? It mayn't be the fashion of the moment – but isn't there something to be said in knowing that you are arrayed in a gown which flatters your person and is colored to suit you to best advantage?"

"You win, dear Jane," Isobel answered. "I am utterly in your hands."

Some forty minutes later, she came down the stairs from the upper floor where her own chamber was; Jane had swiftly amended the neckline and the sleeves of the bronze-taffeta day dress with a quantity of lace conjured from some private store. She worked a similar miracle with Isobel's hair; looking into the mirror of her dressing-table Isobel felt inordinately pleased with what she saw there. Her hair picked up the rich color and Jane was right; she looked taller, even slimmer. *I look very well indeed,* Isobel thought and confidence came out in her face and in the sparkle of her eyes.

Even Mama's swiftly-raised eyebrow could not entirely dash her spirits. That was all that Lady Caroline could venture, as there were already guests in the parlor; some political connections of Fa's and friends of Mama's, guests for whom she had the usual polite and empty greetings. Her eyes were on the one gentleman who was already standing when she came into the room, smiling that reserved smile for only her. He bowed over her hand; she took cheer from his presence and came very close to laughing, when Lady Lynley, Mama's friend who lived just across Belgrave Square, looked at him very severely through her lorgnette and asked,

"Do tell us, Mr. Becker – how did you find London, upon your first visit?" Lady Lynley was tiny and imperturbable, always dressed in black, and noted for her devotion to the Belgrave Square Garden, and the practice of improving one's mind. She was an elderly widow, the relict of a gentleman who had made no small name for himself in India, searching out plants and learning odd languages. Isobel considered Lady Lynley to be the only person in their circle whose disapproval her mother feared.

"I assure you, without difficulty, ma'am," he answered solemnly. "I got off the train, and there it was."

"A singular experience, I daresay," Lady Lynley pronounced and Mr. Becker shook his head, "It was, ma'am – but I must assure you, I don't usually have trouble finding a town, being that I have some fair tracking skills. The smoke in the sky from a distance is something in the way of a hint and then there are all the folk around, once you get there."

"Mr. Becker has interests in cattle-ranching," Lady Caroline explained. Those gentleman friends of Fa's immediately appeared more interested, or if not, they at least put on a convincing impression of interest. Mr. Becker answered their questions with a becoming air of modesty, although Isobel had the distinct impression that he was privately amused by it all; the parlor, the elaborate courtesy, and Mama's friends. At the end of half an hour – the correct length of a visit – he rose and took his farewells, asking modestly if he could pay another visit the following day.

"You are most welcome, although I must confess we have no cattle, to divert you with, Mr. Becker," Lady Caroline answered.

"A walk in the garden would suit, ma'am." He nodded towards the windows, where the trees in Belgrave Square had not even begun to show a slight mist of green. "If Miss Isobel would be among the company . . . "

"You have an interest in gardens?" Lady Caroline sounded skeptical. Mr. Becker answered, "My grandfather was a good friend of the naturalist, Mr. Lindheimer. He took an interest in his work in Texas, an interest so deep that Mr. Lindheimer named one of his plant discoveries after my grandfather. My cousins and I didn't have that great an interest, but my grandfather's enthusiasm surrounded us."

"I know of Mr. Lindheimer's extraordinary collection of plants in the Museum." Lady Lynley's interest also had been piqued. To Isobel's amusement, she offered to accompany them on the following day, having more interest in what Mr. Becker might have known regarding the plants of his native soil, than in fulfilling her intended purpose as a chaperone.

Over the next fortnight, Isobel felt as if she were living in the center of a whirlwind. Visitors came and went, and the intricately meshed gears of the world of Society turned and turned again. The only constant was the presence of the man who was paying quiet court to her, under the eyes of her parents, or Lady Lynley, or even just Havers and Jane, walking a respectful distance behind, through the garden in Belgrave Square. At the end of that time, she knew little more about him than she had when they first met, for he was a soft-spoken cipher, always polite and attentive. Isobel soon realized that even though he was open to answering questions about Texas, and cattle and a hundred other things, he vouchsafed very little about himself. She gathered that he spoke German well enough to pass as a native – and astonishingly, Spanish also, but little else of his personal qualities were immediately evident. The only unsettling incident came one afternoon, as she and Mr. Becker returned from a walk in the Garden with Lady Lynley and attended by Jane. As they emerged from the garden, Mr. Becker assisted Lady Lynley with locking the gate behind them. Of all Mama's friends, Isobel thought that Lady Lynley had warmed to Mr. Becker; perhaps her late husband's many adventures had transferred a taste for eccentric company to her. Mr. Becker likewise appeared to enjoy Lady Lynley's company and conversation. There was a crowd in front of one of the houses on the square, gathered around a barouche lavishly ornamented with white ribbons and flowers. Someone was being married; Isobel's heart beat a little faster.

"I think they must be going to St. Peters," Isobel ventured. "It's only a short way away." The assembled crowd was of common folk and servants, by their dress; not residents of the Square. Something must have been published in the lower sort of newssheet to draw them, the spectacle of the daughter of a notable man, sallying forth in a white dress and veil to meet her destiny at the marital altar. Isobel could not conceive of why anyone, especially strangers should care, but apparently people did. A scuffle erupted at the edge of the crowd between two well-dressed men and a slender youth, whose clothing was obviously shabbier, even at a little distance.

"We should go around the other way to avoid the rabble," Lady Lynley insisted. "It looks like there is trouble already."

"Not to my way of seeing," Mr. Becker observed confidently. Isobel saw he was watching the crowd with great interest. Now one of the men had the youth by the collar, although the lad struggled considerably. "Thief! Thief!" shouted the man. "Call a constable – I've caught this 'un picking pockets!"

"I didn'!" screeched his prisoner. "I wis only lookin' at them 'orses!" The boy was a skinny, feral youth and his coat was too large for him. Like an eel, he swiftly turned and wriggled free, leaving the coat hanging in the hands of the man who held him, but the other man was at least as quick. He caught the boy by his matchstick arm, twisting it swiftly behind his back so that the boy cried out in pain.

"I'll 'ave you!" the first man shouted and lifted a heavy walking-stick, "Teach you scum of the gutters to thieve from your betters!"

"Lemme go!" the boy cried in desperation. At Isobel's side, Mr. Becker murmured, "If you would pardon me for a moment, ladies. I don't hold with that kind of thing."

"Let them be," Lady Lynley sniffed. "The patrolling constables will see to the whole wretched situation."

"But they ain't here," returned Mr. Becker. "And I am. If you will wait for me here, ladies." He solemnly touched the brim of his hat to them both and nodded to Jane. Then he strode purposefully across the street towards the crowd, some of whom had coalesced around the doorway while others gathered around the decorated barouche. Two or three more scattered at a deliberate pace along the wide sidewalks along the row of neo-classical houses which edged Belgrave Square. Isobel looked around for the constable. No, no blue coat and tall helmet in sight. Across the road, the man with the cane raised it and brought it down on the boy's back, the crack of it meeting flesh and the boy's involuntary cry of pain almost simultaneous. Isobel felt an up-rush of bile into the back of her throat and a peculiar high-pitched buzzing in her ears.

"Isobel, dear, are you unwell?" Lady Lynley asked anxiously, although it was difficult for Isobel to attend to her voice. Jane – trusty Jane – pressed an opened smelling-salts bottle into her hand.

"Breathe, Milady, breathe." Jane urged her. Isobel obeyed. The pungent odor of the salts rushed into her senses and she found herself leaning on Jane. Across the avenue, the man with the cane raised it again, but when it fell, it was arrested by Mr. Becker's firm grip.

"'Ere!" shouted the man with the cane, "'Let be – 'ose business is it of yours, then?"

"I'm making it mine," Mr. Becker answered, in a firm voice that Isobel could hear clearly from across the street. "I don't hold with grown men beating children."

"By 'ose right . . ." the first man thrust his chin pugnaciously forward. He was still gripping the boy's matchstick-thin arms. In response, Mr. Becker moved to open the front of his coat, holding it a little aside. At that both the men's expressions changed from red-faced anger to something warier.

"'E's a thief," insisted the man with the club. "'E nicked me watch an' 'o knows wot else!"

Mr. Becker shook his head again, "No. There was a thief but not this boy. Just as he said, he was standing apart from the crowd, looking at the horses. Search his pockets if you like. Your thief is one of those who walked away, just now. Now," he looked at the two of them and his voice dropped, just as the door to the mansion opened above them. A rustle of exclamations and cheers in the crowd on the sidewalk drowned out whatever he was saying. When he had done saying it, the man holding the boy by the arm had relinquished his grip. The other man had picked up the boy's ragged coat and handed it to him, with something of shame in his expression. They melted into the crowd, for the wedding party had emerged from the house.

To Isobel's astonishment, the boy and Mr. Becker remained, engaging in some quiet conversation. The boy accompanied Mr. Becker upon his return to where he had left the three women, half trotting to keep pace with him, instead of vanishing likewise.

"Good heavens," Lady Lynley exclaimed, "The man has an affinity for strays. I wonder what he said; he seems quite forceful, in a quiet way."

"All settled," Mr. Becker touched the brim of his hat, and then noted Isobel's pale face. "You did not have cause for alarm, Miss Isobel," he added, with quick concern.

"I do not like to see such a cruel thing as a flogging," Isobel answered. She was rewarded with a flash of a smile.

"Nor do I. Lady Lynley, Miss Isobel – this is Alf, Alfred Thomas Trotter – he also is fond of horses. Miss Isobel is my particular friend. Alf, you should always take off your hat to ladies," he added as an aside.

The boy Alf looked boldly at Isobel. "Oh-er!" he exclaimed, "G'day, miss! Pleased to meetcher!" and shot out his dirty hand, as if to shake hers. Close up, he was an unprepossessing specimen of humanity, a grimy London street urchin, appearing to be ten years or so, stunted by the bad air of the city and not enough wholesome food. Lady Lynley sniffed and contented herself with nodding briskly, but Isobel shook his dirty little paw, feeling some relief that she was wearing gloves. Alf was such a pitiful little scrap; for all that he was as cheeky as a sparrow.

"I am considering offering young Alf a position," Mr. Becker explained. "I always have need of another good hand."

"Good heavens!" Lady Lynley exclaimed again. "My dear Isobel, I thought I was merely being humorous, remarking on your admirer's affinity for strays."

"He likes horses, Lady Lynley," Mr. Becker did not appear to have taken offense. "Horses like him as well, if he tells me true." *Dogs and horses liked him*, Isobel reminded herself – *so, no wonder that a grubby little street urchin would*. Alf followed after them all, to Lady Lynley and Jane's obvious horror, crouching on the bottommost step of the Lindsay-Groves villa, as patient as a gargoyle waiting for his master, as she and Jane and Lady Lynley were conducted inside. As Spenser closed the door behind them, Isobel saw that Alf went trotting after Mr. Becker, like the tail following after a kite. When next Mr. Becker came to call, Isobel asked after him, fully expecting that he had run away, but Alf was now in Mr. Becker's employ as a kind of errand-boy and valet. What the management of the Langham Hotel, where Mr. Becker was keeping rooms, thought of that, Isobel could hardly fathom.

"Everyone was always asking me why I did not keep a manservant," Mr. Becker allowed by way of explanation. "I got tired of explaining why – it was less trouble to hire Alf."

On several occasions, Mr. Becker rode with Isobel and Fa in Rotten Row; to her secret relief, he rode extraordinarily well, although his riding attire left much to be desired. Over an open-collared shirt, he wore a loose coat of tan buckskin leather, belted around his waist and a plain wide-brimmed felt hat, although everything else about his person and his equipage and mount were all above reproach.

"They are staring at you," Isobel remarked, one sunny afternoon in mid-February, after having held her tongue on previous occasions. "Don't you mind?"

"No," he answered, after a moment's consideration. "Not much."

"Why ever not?" Isobel would not have ventured so bold a question, but that she felt the discreet horror, quickly hidden, in the gaze of every rider they passed along the wide avenue underneath the trees at the edge of Hyde Park.

"They don't matter to me, Miss Isobel," he replied serenely. "I do not know them an' I do not look for their respect. What they think is of no concern to me. Besides," he added, flashing a quick smile at her. "In two months and a bit, me and Alf will take ship from Southampton and never see any of these again, less'n they want to invest in Texas cattle."

"Are you departing from us so soon?" Isobel felt the tiniest unease in the pit of her stomach. They rode almost knee to knee, the closest they had come to being alone and to speak privately although Fa was cantering ahead at some distance and the row was crowded with horses, promenading their riders. It was nothing like the Hunt – not the pell-mell rush across field and hedge, but rather a stately pavane the length of the Park and back again.

"I can't stay here forever," Mr. Becker answered, as if it were so casual a matter that it hardly brooked comment. "I must return to Texas for this year's trail season. Do you want to come with me, Miss Isobel?"

"I beg your pardon?" Isobel was not entirely sure that she had heard correctly. If that were a proposal of marriage, then it was such a modest and understated one as to be all but invisible. She reined in her horse, still in the center of the Row and he did also.

"D'you want to come with me?" he repeated. "I thought you might. Your pa said that maybe you'd like to and he thought I would suit. I've got all the horses and dogs you would like, back home. Cows, too. We'd have to get married beforehand, though."

Isobel thought of all the things she had been told were proper in accepting a proposal, most of which flew out of her mind immediately. It felt rather silly to say anything more complicated than the simple and obvious. He waited as patient as a monument in the Row, knee to knee as their horses shifted restlessly.

"Yes, I'd like to go with you," she answered. That quick smile flashed across his face. He took the reins of his horse in one hand and reached into the breast of his coat with the other.

"Oh, good. M'cousin Anna reminded me to buy a ring. She picked out one she thought you would like. If you don't care for it, I'll return it and buy another." He handed her a little velvet-covered box and watched as she opened it: nested in a bed of satin was a ring of rose gold, a vivid cerulean stone in the center with a constellation of small diamonds set around it. "She said the stone was the color of the sky at home."

"It's perfect," Isobel answered, with all her heart. "I expect I should put it on, right away, shouldn't I?"

"I think so," Mr. Becker agreeably took back the little box, while she removed her riding glove from her hand. The ring slid easily onto her finger. For one moment, she and he looked at it; aware that something momentous might have happened. But there were no crescendos of music, no choruses of angels – nothing much other than other riders moving impatiently around them and Fa looking down at them both.

"Dear little Pet," he said at last. Isobel wondered why he sounded as if he might be close to weeping. "I imagine we'd best go and tell your mother." He coughed and looked at Mr. Becker with his sternest expression, usually reserved for unsatisfactory tenants, the accused before the bar, and Mr. Gladstone. "Congratulations, m'boy. Dearest to my heart and now you've won her. Take care of her, you hear?"

"Always," Mr. Becker answered with serene composure. Fa coughed again. "See that you do – or else I'll come to Texas and give you a sound thrashing!"

"Fa!" Isobel expostulated and Mr. Becker smiled sideways at her. He reached out, and covered her hand – the one with the ring on it – with his.

"Not to worry, Miss Isobel . . . sir. Not to worry in the least."

Chapter 6 - *Wedding Day*

The day of her wedding passed like an eternal waking dream to Isobel. All through it she held on to one thought; escape lay at the end, escape from all of the strictures laid upon her life, from Mama's impossibly high standards and strict governance, the horror of going to India with the 'fishing fleet' – but a departure from all dear and familiar. The regular rounds of visiting tenants and the Hunt, of everything moving like clockwork in it's appointed time and place, the frost on the trees in the Park at mid-winter and the bounty of flowers in the garden in summer, all the comfortable goings-on in the neighborhood of the Hall – from the moment she said the words of the vows, accepted the ring on her hand and the kiss of a man whom she barely knew, her parents would no longer have the governing of her life. Her husband would; a diffident and soft-spoken stranger, with so many mysteries about him, mysteries that she would never begin to fathom until she had joined her life to his. What would he expect of her? Surely, in Texas her household duties would not be anything like what would have been expected of her if she had married as her mother had wished and expected.

She and Jane had studied the pages of *Mrs. Beetons' Book of Household Management*, and dear Kitty-Cat allowed them to experiment with cooking an omelet and other modest delights over the little spirit-stove in the still-room. She had even spent several awkward afternoons below-stairs in the kitchen, where Mrs. Huckaby the cook had vouchsafed some of her secrets with regard to roasts, pies, and pastries. Jane had taken careful notes, always hovering at Isobel's elbow, but Isobel did not believe she would ever have need of Mrs. Huckaby's expertise in organizing fifteen courses for a formal dinner party for two hundred, including royalty. Or at least, she hoped that she never would. Perhaps, as Jack Sutcliffe had jestingly allowed, her husbands' family did not have to cope with anything higher in society than a provincial governor. Still, she was grateful for the carefully hand-written recipes for game pie and a particular sort of fruitcake which Mrs. Huckaby had pressed upon her, along with her best wishes.

Other than those experimental essays in household matters, everything about her wedding was firmly taken in hand by Mama, just as everything to do with her debut had been. Isobel needed do nothing other than stand still for endless dress fittings, and passively agree with Mama about her attendants, the trousseau, the flowers and decoration of the church, and the menu for the wedding breakfast. Everything was decided by Mama. All that was required of her was to be a life-sized doll. Sometimes Isobel entertained the rebellious notion that Mama had even selected all the wedding presents and the household items deemed suitable for her to take with her to Texas. She had only spoken once in opposition to Mama's plans, the afternoon when she and Fa and Mr. Becker had returned from riding in Rotten Row to inform Mama of their engagement.

"St. Peter's Church, of course," Mama said decidedly. Isobel had quailed and ventured, "Mama, I always wanted to be married in the church in Upton."

"A country wedding? Really, Isobel, what with the trouble of arranging the house for guests . . ." At Isobel's side, Mr. Becker took her hand in his and squeezed her fingers encouragingly.

"What do you really prefer, Miss Isobel?" he asked, as seriously as if it was something which mattered to him After a moment, she realized with a little shock of joyful discovery that yes – what she wanted did matter very much to him.

"I should prefer to be married in Upton," Isobel answered. "All my friends are in the country and I would rather spend my last night as a daughter under the roof of the Hall." Across the room, Fa looked at them both and winked – from that, Isobel knew that he agreed. It did amuse her faintly when Mama detailed Jack Sutcliffe to be the best man for her husband.

"After all," Mama had said grandly. "He has no other acceptable friends or kin in England. Of course Jack Sutcliffe should stand up with him. At the very least, he will not disgrace us. Perhaps it was best for you both to insist on a country wedding, Isobel. Any embarrassment may thus be minimized."

"Yes, Mama," Isobel had answered meekly, having won on the important point. From beside the parlor fireplace, Fa had smiled, a secret and encouraging smile, just for Isobel. Fa knew very well that Mama should be given free rein in those matters considered a woman's sphere, but at least he was assured of Mr. Becker's honesty and true worth. Next to that assurance, whatever Mama felt meant very little to Isobel.

Nonetheless, the night before her wedding day, just when Isobel was beginning to feel a mild state of panic, Mrs. Kittredge tapped on her door. Isobel had eaten sparely of a supper sent on a tray, since Mama had ruled that she must retire early. Jane had already undressed her for the night: she sat curled up in the armchair by the window, looking around her room and not quite recognizing it as hers.

Mrs. Kittredge appeared around the door, bearing a silver salver covered with a napkin. "I have brought a hot drink for both of you," she said.

"Tomorrow will be a long day and with the start of an even longer journey at the end of it. You should get a good night's rest."

Mrs. Kittredge looked very searchingly at Jane, still fussing about the white bridal dress and veil, the petticoats and accessories carefully laid out across the chaise-lounge, in order for the bridesmaids to come and perform the ritual of dressing the bride. Jane privately thought it rather pointless for several of Isobel's cousins to pretend to do what she did, every morning and at stated times during the day. The bridesmaids were but children and nobly-born ladies, so of course she and Miss Havers should have everything at hand and lurk unobtrusively to assist. Still, Jane felt obliged to see that everything was perfect, for her own ladyship's day and also to escape the acidulous judgments of Miss Havers. Never was a lady more prominent than on that day when she performed the duty expected of her since the day she was born; to make an advantageous marriage. On the other hand, once the events of the following day were negotiated, Jane would no longer have to concern herself with Miss Havers and her opinions – or anyone's opinions than her ladyships'. This pleased Jane no end. Now she bobbed a quick curtsy to her aunt, who added, "And you should rest also, Jane. I take it that you are prepared for the journey as well?"

"Yes, Mrs. Kittredge – my trunk went with milady's, in the van this afternoon."

"Very well," her aunt nodded magisterially. "This is yours, Miss Isobel – I suggest that you drink it now and then go to bed. There is a little sleeping tonic in it, so you should feel sleepy almost at once."

"Thank you, Kitty-Cat," Isobel said, over a sudden lump in her throat. "That is so very kind of you. I so wish it were over, already."

"I am sure that you do, Miss Isobel." Mrs. Kittredge hesitated. "If I may ask something of a personal nature . . . has Lady Caroline spoken to you, about the duties of a wife? That is, those intimate duties between a husband and wife, shared after the wedding." Her voice trailed off, as if she were reluctant to venture any farther.

"Mama did not," Isobel answered. "But Victoria did, so you should be relieved on that score. It all sounded rather grotesque, Kitty-Cat, but I am assured that such congress is necessary. I must have observed it often among the farm animals and Fa's dogs, as much as our governess didn't wish me to see."

"Very good, Miss Isobel." Mrs. Kittredge did appear to be immensely relieved. "Your intended strikes me as a kindly-intentioned young man. Good night, then. Sleep well. And you too, Jane."

Isobel was already yawning; the sleeping tonic must have been a powerful one, for she fell into a deep and dreamless sleep as soon as she laid her head on the pillow.

It was the next morning which passed more like a dream, with Jane combing out her hair, while Miss Havers handed her the pins and paddings. Underneath her wrapper, she already had on her combinations and corset. Jane had assisted her with her stockings. Across the room, three young cousins and the youngest sister of Victoria's husband whispered to each other and vied for a place in front of the tall pier-glass which had been brought in, as Victoria and her own maid primped and chided them. Isobel's mind wandered. How very odd to be attended on her wedding day by four girls that she barely knew, let alone liked very much. Mama had seen it all, just as she had seen to her dress – which Isobel liked hardly better than her bridesmaids.

Now her hair was done; all but the wreath of sweet-smelling orange blossoms and the veil. Obediently she slid her feet into the slippers that the youngest bridesmaid had knelt and placed beside her feet. Jane took her wrapper off her shoulders. Isobel shivered in spite of the warmth of the room. Miss Havers tightened her corset-lacings,

"Breath in, my lady – now out!" and tightened them again. Isobel thought that Miss Havers' face looked a little less cross than usual, reflected in the dressing-table mirror. She supposed that while she might not miss her mother's lady's maid very much, Havers had been with her mother as long as she could remember, a part of Isobel's life left behind after today.

Corset cover, trimmed with embroidered rosebuds and cob-web fine lace – under-petticoat and *tournere* – all solemnly handed by Havers and Jane to the bridesmaids, who held them up for Isobel to put her arms into, or tied around her waist.

"Now I know what the Christmas tree feels like," she observed, once. The other girls looked at her as if they did not understand, while Jane stifled a small giggle as hers and Isobel's eyes met. She bent her knees so they could lift the over-petticoat over her head, careful not to disturb the careful handiwork that Jane and Havers had made of her hair. The bedroom door opened and closed; Mama in pale grey satin, a princess-cut gown, trimmed with darker grey embroidered lace and Lady Eleanor in primrose yellow.

"Nearly ready, my lady." Havers lifted up the wedding dress skirt, looking from it to the bridesmaids as if she were already assuming they would make a hash of assisting Isobel in putting it on. A complicated array of tapes and buttons on the inside drew the skirt back to fall in graceful loops and folds into a long train. Isobel bent her knees again and the nervously giggling bridesmaids guided it carefully over her head.

"What an effort it is, to ensure that my daughter is on time," Lady Caroline remarked. "The carriages are already waiting downstairs."

"It's not as if they can start without you," Jane whispered, as she knelt to adjust the fall of the skirt. Isobel would have laughed out loud but for the eyes upon her. There was a front apron-overskirt with a separate waistband; this tied at the back with an even more ornamented bow and then the bodice, buttoned up the front to a high collar which ended just below Isobel's chin. Then her jewelry – the gift of her husband-to-be, a gold chain of pale blue enameled flowers and leaves, trimmed with pearls and very tiny diamonds. Mama had brought out her own pearl earrings.

"Mr. Becker has provided the blue," she allowed, and remarkably sounded rather kindly. "And your grandmother's French-lace veil the old, so I shall provide the borrowed. Don't fidget, Isobel." Lady Caroline removed her gloves. To Isobel's surprise, her mother fastened the fabulous earrings in her ears with her own hands. To her further surprise, Lady Caroline kissed her cheek, saying, "There. I do not think we have forgotten anything of importance, have we?"

"No, Mama . . . thank you, Mama." Isobel stammered. She didn't really recognize herself, especially after the silken veil was dropped over her head – just a blur of white. She did not know who pinned the circlet of orange-blossoms over the veil, or put her gloves on her hands, handed her a bouquet of roses and more orange-blossoms. Another tap at the door and she heard Fa's voice. The carriage for Mama and Lady Eleanor and the second for the bridesmaids waited downstairs – they must leave now. In a rustle of skirts and whispered excitement, the other women emptied out of Isobel's room as swiftly as water escaping a broken pot. She stood alone in the middle of the room, a living statue of flesh and silk, instead of marble. She thought that Jane must now be laying out her going-away costume, which she would wear for the start of the wedding journey – the dress she would change into, as soon as the wedding breakfast was over. For Isobel that felt like an age away, as far away as Christmas to an anxious child.

"Five minutes," Fa sounded as if he were trying to be hearty. "When the clock strikes a quarter past. You look lovely, Pet. If you weren't m'daughter and I were thirty years younger, I'd want to marry you m'self."

"Oh, Fa!" Isobel gulped, as a feeling of desolation washed over her. To her horror, a fat tear spilled out of each eye and trickled down her cheeks. "If I had a suitor such as you, with a princely estate and a kennel of dogs and a stable of horses – I would give your proposal consideration, I would!"

"You're not crying, Pet?" Fa asked, anxiously. He took her hands, regardless of the bouquet. "You should not be crying on your wedding day. What is the matter? Dearest little Pet, if you don't want to go through with it, if you don't want to marry, then you need not! We'll sort it out, eh? What do you say – you need not marry, count on your old Fa to fix it up!"

"No, Fa," Isobel hiccupped. "I have given my promise to marry and I will, but that promise will take me so far away! It grieves me so to think on it."

"Well, never you mind, Pet." Fa squeezed her hands, intending to be comforting. "As long as you love him – that's the thing, eh? You love him, and he's a good sort. He is a good sort, isn't he? You may return to visit whenever you wish, I am certain. It's only a week or so, on the Atlantic crossing these days, not eight or nine as it was when I was a lad. You may marry but he won't keep you from us, of that I am certain. It's an adventure, Pet – like building the bridge at Pures!"

"I know, Fa. I take him to be a trustworthy man." Isobel sobbed again.

"Dear Pet – you mustn't cry." Her father embraced her very gently, taking care not to crush the folds of her dress, "It must be nerves eh? Now – there's the quarter-past, we must leave now. Miss Goodacre, do you have a handkerchief handy? Help m'daughter pull herself together; bad omen for you to walk into church with tear-tracks down your cheeks."

"Here, Sir Robert," Jane's voice sounded as calm as ever. She lifted up the veil which turned everything around Isobel into a fog, swiftly blotting up the tears on Isobel's face with a careful handkerchief. "There, my lady – you're not going to cry any more, are you? Keep this. Let me put a little pearl-powder on your face, just the thing to mend little accidents with one's complexion. This is the happiest day of your life, remember? You are to marry a good man of property who loves dogs. He owns a fine stable and an orchard, and his family is well-thought of. Isn't that what you told me? Here, my lady; think of this as a tall fence and a deep ditch to be gotten over, mounted on Thistle." Jane smiled into Isobel's eyes. Marvelously Isobel felt steadied and reassured almost at once, as Jane patted her cheeks with a tiny powder-puff.

The urge for tears vanished; Jane quickly arranged her veil as it was before and Fa took her arm.

"I'm ready now, Fa - as ready as I will ever be."

Jane drew on her own best bonnet and mantle and followed after, stooping swiftly now and again to rescue the train of Isobel's dress, as her lady and Sir Robert made a stately procession down the grand staircase. She had a needle and a spool of white thread, and a miniscule pair of scissors in her reticule, along with some spare handkerchiefs. A number of the lower servants watched from the back of the Great Hall with undisguised fascination, calling out their best wishes. Somers the groom helped Jane up into the first carriage, full of the bridesmaids and those small attendants, the Stanley boys, all got up in velveteen knickerbockers suits with wide lace collars.

"How is her Ladyship bearing up?" he whispered to Jane, who answered calmly, "Only the usual bride's nerves."

"Hope she doesn't bolt at the church door," Somers latched the carriage door. Jane sniffed disdainfully – such cheek! She sat mum in the corner of the carriage, trying to be at once invisible to the two little boys and the bridesmaids and a quelling influence on them. What with seeing them lined up on the steps of the church, with the spring breeze blowing their skirts and the ribbons at their waists and in their hair this way and that, and ensuring that Lady Isobel and the train of her dress emerged from the open coach without incident or damage, Jane had no thought to spare for much else. She slipped into the back of the church, squeezed into a space behind the last pew where many of the upper servants from the Hall were standing, as the church organ triumphantly blared the first notes of the Processional. From there she could hear a little, but see rather less: the Vicar and Sir Robert's voices boomed, but Lady Isobel's and Mr. Becker's were just barely audible. For most of the day, Jane felt that she was watching from the edge, at once alert for any sign that her ladyship needed her, but with most of her mind running ahead to the next step, the next stage of the journey and the preparations necessary for it.

The carriages of the Family, with the open barouche carrying the bridal couple and Sir Robert and Lady Caroline led the grand procession to the Hall. Sir Roberts' tenants and their families lined the streets of Upton, all the way to the Gatehouse, cheering the wedding party. Jane made a mental note to see that the last of Lady Isobel's trunks would be packed as soon as she had changed into her travel costume. *Did she have enough tissue paper?* She must see to the last of her own things, too. She had already bid her own farewell to Mam and to *Him,* as well as her brothers and little half-brother, taking a half-day the week before. Lady Isobel sent Somers to drive her to Didcot and back. Reflecting now, Jane did not think she would miss Mam very much – she certainly had not, in year she had spent at the Hall. *Him*, of course, had glared at her sullenly, the whole of her visit. If going to Texas meant that she would never have to see *Him* again, Jane considered that a very fair trade.

Jane only felt a twinge of melancholy at the very last, as they were about to depart. She stood on the front steps, waiting with her own small bag at her feet and Lady Isobel's jewel-case in her hand. Lady Isobel – now Mrs. Becker stood in the midst of a crush of servants and staff who had come around to the drive where the closed carriage which waited to take the newlyweds, Jane and the boy Alf, who attended on Mr. Becker to the railway station. It gratified Jane that so many of the house servants took pleasure in Isobel's marriage day, wished her well, and seemed genuinely grieved at her imminent departure. She was just noting with mild approval that Mr. Becker himself stood back a little from the throng, yet near enough to be protective of her lady, when someone at her side cleared a masculine throat and coughed, as if to gain her own attention.

"Miss Goodacre," Sir Robert said, huskily. "Little miss Jane – I see that you are prepared well for departure? Hah! Good, good. I think it is well that you accompany my daughter. I haven't missed much, you know. You have taken good care of her, better than any choice of maid that I or Lady Caroline would have made for her. So, it's only fitting that I be grateful, eh? There is a gift that I have for you." Sir Robert winked in the most avuncular fashion, and took a small pasteboard box out of his coat-pocket. "Had it engraved especially – so many wedding gifts and falderals – well, it seemed most fitting, Miss Goodacre, and a way to best express our gratitude with a gift that you will find good use for."

He pressed the little box into her hand and Jane accepted it, noting only that his face had the slightly anxious expression of a man unsure of his own facility for selecting gifts. Sir Robert had always been good to her – a bluff but slightly distant figure. To relieve his anxiety, Jane opened the box – which to her surprise bore the name of a very fashionable and expensive London jeweler. Inside was a fine gold ladies' pocket watch, depending from a dainty pin in the shape of a ribbon bow set with miniscule seed pearls.

"Oh!" Jane explained, with involuntary surprise and pleasure. Sir Robert appeared immediately more relived. "Thank you, sir – it is a lovely gift and it is for me, truly?"

"So it is!" Sir Robert laughed, more heartily for the relief. "And we had the jeweler-chappie put your name on it, in the cover y'see. It is for you, Miss

Goodacre, so that you may continue to see that m'daughter is on time for things. Y'see," He winked broadly again, "I hoped that this will be of help in seeing that she becomes more punctual. Our hopes in this regard depend upon you, so of course you should have the very best time-piece to assist you. May I suggest that you begin using it at once? I fear you will have need of it, since Isobel's chosen appears to have the same casual regard for time as she does."

"Thank you, Sir Robert," Jane bobbed a careful courtesy. Beaming happily, Sir Robert took the ladies' watch from its nest of cotton-wool and brought out his own massy gold one, as heavy as a goose-egg.

"There, you see? Perfect time . . . you'll have to keep it carefully wound, o'course," Jane pinned Sir Robert's gift to the front of her dark travel-dress. "Ah – they are ready at last." Sir Robert's voice cracked on the rocks of some deep emotion. "Take care of her, Jane. She will be so far from us and alone among strangers!"

"I will, Sir Robert, I promise." Jane took up her bag and the jewel-case once again, realizing with some astonishment that Sir Robert's eyes were near to overflowing, bright with tears.

"Thank you, little Miss – good in name, good in nature!" He would have said more, Jane thought, but Mr. Becker had unobtrusively taken Lady Isobel's arm. Their departure could not be put off any longer. She bobbed another curtsy to Sir Robert, and followed her lady.

The end of that interminable day finally arrived. A mere twenty-four hours ago dear Kitty-Cat had brought her a hot drink, gently advising her to rest well, for it would be a long day. Only now did Isobel feel entirely awake. She sat in front of another dressing table – but not her own, at the Hall. This dressing table and mirror was in a suite of rooms in the Langham Hotel with windows that looked toward Regent's Park. Here they would spend the night, a night together, as Isobel had been told to expect. Tomorrow, they would rise very early, to catch the train for Southampton and take ship for America.

She could not bring herself to think any farther than that. Poor Jane, so weary there were dark shadows under her eyes, had laid out her clothes for the next day and prepared her for the night. Isobel had dismissed her, feeling rather guilty. Jane's day must have been even wearier than hers and certainly longer. Isobel could see to the rest of her person for the night. She drew her hairbrush through her hair; it felt like the brush was almost too heavy to hold. At her back, an ornate archway opened into the bedroom, where the covers had already been turned invitingly down. The hotel staff at the Langham had taken every care. There were fresh flowers everywhere and a little tray on the bedside table with some oranges, a plate of water-crackers, two glasses, and a decanter of brandy on it. She could hear the voice of Alf and Mr. Becker, from behind a closed door beyond the bedroom. *I suppose I should think of him as my husband, now*, Isobel told herself. Alf, as little as her husband had need of one, served as his manservant. It sounded as if he were also dismissing Alf for the night. The door opened and shut. She knew he was in the room, although he moved as quietly as a ghost. She was still startled, though, to look up into the mirror and see him standing behind her, peeling one of the oranges with a silver pocket-knife.

"Do you know," he remarked, cheerfully. "This will be the very first time since we met that we will be completely alone together? It seems very odd to me."

"It wasn't proper," Isobel answered. "For us to be un-chaperoned, at any time until we were married."

"Sometimes it seemed awful silly. They've left us something for us to eat. Would you like to share an orange?"

"Yes, thank you." *What a very odd conversation for a wedding night!* Very odd, too – considering what she had been led to expect – it felt for the two of them to sit in the middle of the bed in their nightclothes, while her husband finished peeling the orange and broke it into segments. "This is rather like our nursery days," she remarked. "Or nights. Martyn and I would share something that he had sneaked from downstairs tea, after Nurse had sent us to bed early for being bad."

"I can't believe that you were ever bad," he handed her an orange slice. "The Cap'n? Oh, yes. I could see him being a bit of a hell-raiser. I'd take a bet," he added. "That he would do things that you would be blamed for and then feel awful sorry when you were punished."

"How did you know?" Isobel asked in delight.

"I have sisters and a brother – and many cousins. Would you like me to peel another orange?"

"No, I'm not hungry," Isobel answered, although she had barely eaten anything, not even at the wedding breakfast so many hours ago.

"You're not? I am," her husband answered with feeling. "I couldn't take a bite; I was afraid it would fall off my fork or dribble down my chin with everyone watching." He reached out for another orange, and peeled it as deftly as he had the first. Isobel realized that yes, indeed, she was still hungry. The orange tasted good, as good as anything she had eaten in days. The last segment oozed juice onto her hand and fingers.

"Now that you mention dribbling . . ." Isobel sighed. She made as if to reach for the napkin in which the oranges had been nestled, but he caught her hand, grinning impishly.

"Allow me, Miss Isobel." He licked the juice from her fingers, all the while as if daring her to object. He did not let go her hand when he was finished but kissed her palm and fingers, once and again. When he had done, he looked at her again, newly solemn. "You do know about . . . well, what married folk do in bed. They tell me that the proper young miss isn't supposed to know about any of it."

"Oh, I know," Isobel answered. "My sister and Kitty-Cat – Mrs. Kittredge told me."

"And what you think of it?" He asked, with genuine curiosity.

"As if I were on Thistle, facing the tallest fence in England and the deepest ditch on the other side," she said. Unexpectedly, he began to laugh. He pulled her towards him, still laughing and Isobel decided that she liked the sound and the feel of him laughing and also being held, closer than ever he had held her in the dance.

And it – that other thing – wasn't at all like the tallest fence and the deepest ditch, but it <u>was</u> like dancing, two birds soaring into the sky and then dipping close, close and even closer, but maybe a bit like riding Thistle, sensing the fiery heartbeat, the breathing of that other person, a safe shelter in the dark. Afterwards, they lay curled together, and Isobel held his left hand between hers, the hand with the two fingers a little bent and scarred. They had shed their nightclothes. Somewhat to her astonishment, she felt perfectly at ease in nakedness. She could see all of him and he all of her; nothing hidden.

She had always wondered about the fingers, since she had noticed it during his first visit to the Hall. Now she asked, sleepily, "What did that come from?"

"What?" he answered sleepily, "Oh . . . putting up fence-rails to enclose one of Uncle Hansi's pastures – ten, twelve years ago when we first went into cattle in a big way. I was holding a fence-post steady, while one of the hands pounded it home with a twenty-pound sledge. I thought I had the easy part, until he missed."

"Oh, dear." Isobel said. He laughed again. "That's not what I said to him, the clumsy oaf."

"And this?" she traced her fingers along his upper arm, where an arrow-straight length of discolored flesh slashed straight across, a dark mark the length of her hand.

"Grazed by a Yankee bullet in the Palmito Ranch fight, down on the Rio Grande. Last fight in the war that was. Even General Lee had given up, by then. But our commander, Colonel Ford – he was a stubborn man."

"It looks awful," Isobel said, for it truly did.

"It wasn't the bullet that hurt so much," her husband answered dryly. "But the red-hot iron they put to it to stop the bleeding and keep from going septic. You could have heard me yelling all the way to Brownsville." He pulled her closer to him and with contentment, she listened to the regular thud of his heart, next to her ear. "I got one more scar," he said, into her hair, the wealth of it spread all across the pillow like a silken shawl. "Not one I can rightly show in public – from when I was eight-nine years old. My cousins and I were playing Indians and Rangers in the woods by Uncle Hansi's place on Baron's Creek and my cousin Jacob shot me in the backside with a willow-stem arrow. You should have seen it when we got back to Opa's house; blood all over the both of us, the willow-stem still stuck in me and my Aunt Liesel having the hysterics. My father, he was doubled over laughing; he said in all of his life he'd never heard of a Comanche struck in the arse with an arrow." As they lay, his hand rested on her back, his fingers moving as if he were inventorying the bones of her spine. Isobel thought how Martyn would have enjoyed playing with other boys in the woods with bows and arrows. When her husband spoke again, the tone of his voice had changed. "I've told you about mine," he said. "Now, you should tell me about yours."

"Mine?" She was honestly puzzled. He answered, patiently, "I've a right to know how your back came to be all scarred up like a flogged nigra slave. I've seen marks like that before and I know what makes them. I wondered why you were so distressed the day that I stopped those men from beating Alf. I never thought you had been mistreated so." Isobel was startled first into silence. How had she forgotten that he would have seen the marks on her back, once she had shed her nightgown?

"It was the governess that we had," she began tremulously. "Martyn and I. They're on my back, so I don't see them. I forget, since no one ever dared speak of it. I don't suppose anyone but Jane has ever seen them of late and she is discreet. She has never asked me . . . I suppose Kitty-Cat told her. She's her aunt, you know. Jane's aunt. Mrs. Kittredge, the housekeeper."

"Isobel . . ." his embrace of her tightened, as one would comfort a child. "Go on. Were you punished for something your brother did? Is that how it happened?"

Isobel nodded. "Miss Barnwell had an awful temper . . . and she was a secret tippler which made her temper even worse. Mama didn't know any of this. She gave Miss Barnwell leave to punish us as she thought fit, when we were bad. Martyn played a trick on her. He put an emetic in her secret gin-bottle the night before he left to return to school. She thought I had done it.

"How old were you?"

"Six or seven." Isobel gulped. "She was shaking me by the shoulders and everything I said made her angrier. Finally she said that I should be birched soundly. I should take off my dress and petticoat combinations and . . . she made me kneel in front of a foot-stool. She used a willow-switch but it broke. Then she used Martyn's riding whip. It was as if she couldn't stop and wouldn't stop . . . it hurt dreadfully and there was blood everywhere. Finally she came to her senses. I think she knew that she had gone too far. She made me keep it a secret. The nursery-maid would never dare say anything against her and Mama would never believe me."

"What happened then?" Isobel felt the anger rising in her husband, an anger like a slow, unstoppable tide, but not directed against her – oh, never against her. He held her closer still, as if he could shelter her from that ghastly memory.

"She had some nursery remedies – but some of the wounds bled and bled, and broke open and bled some more. One of the laundry-maids began to wonder, seeing blood stains on my shifts and things. She went to Kitty-Cat and she came to the nursery one evening. Miss Barnwell could not stand against her, not once she saw my back. Mrs. Kittredge wrapped me in a blanket and carried me to Fa's study at once. Fa had Miss Barnwell sacked without a reference within the hour. He was furious with Mama for allowing Miss Barnwell free rein with us, even for hiring her to begin with . . ." Isobel sighed, a quick and shuddering little sigh, almost as if she had been weeping and now was done. "Fa would not even allow me to return to the nursery until she had left the Hall. He had them bring blankets and pillows and make a bed out of the chair in his study. I slept there the night, and several nights after. I had dreadful nightmares for years afterwards. I still can't bear to look at a picture of someone being flogged."

"Isobel," he answered. "Don't cry. That is a thing that I would never do; lift a hand against a child, a woman, even an animal, or permit anyone who works for me to do so. I will promise you this; no one will ever strike you again and I will never put our children in the care of someone who even considers that as a proper punishment. To allow it is as much of a wrong as doing the deed yourself. Do you understand, Isobel? You are safe now. I will promise on my own life that I will keep you so."

"I understand," Isobel answered and her own arms went around him, as if she clung to a sheltering tree. She believed him, unswervingly – for he had already rescued her once.

Chapter 7 – *The Voyage*

"'Ere's the last of the Big Smoke, then!" exclaimed Alf Trotter with an enormously satisfied air, as he and Jane followed their employers onto the boat train at Waterloo Station early the next morning. The boat-train platform was crowded thick with departing passengers, many of them bidding such tearful farewells, and burdened with so many trunks and carpet-bags that it was clear to Jane that they were immigrants. Now she sniffed and Alf added, "Say, Miss G – ain't you happy, too? The Missus looks like a cat who been at a bowl o'cream this morning!" He nudged Jane with his elbow and leered suggestively; an expression which set very oddly on his thin little face. "Marriage agree wiv'er, wot say?"

"You are a disgusting little guttersnipe, Alf," Jane returned, equably. She had come to know Alf rather better than she would have liked to, alternately horrified yet grudgingly sympathetic to the plight of a boy only a little older than her brothers, who seemed never to have had a proper bath, slept in a bed or sat at a table for a good meal until Mr. Becker took him into employment. "And you would never have been allowed to polish the boots in a good household. The only reason the Master hired you is that we're going to Texas where it doesn't matter."

"'E promised horses," Alf answered. Very little of what Jane said to him had the capacity to dent his scrappy self-possession. "Good 'ousehold, Miss G? I don't care none for a good 'ousehold. Wotever the Sir says, that'll do for Alf Trotter." His countenance practically glowed, the face of a worshipper at a shrine. Jane reflected that of all Alf's qualities, the only remotely endearing one was that his adoration of Mr. Becker was absolute and unswerving. Of all the adults who had passed through Alf's grubby and chaotic world, Mr. Becker was the only one ever to have been kind and generous. Now Alf repaid that kindness tenfold with dogged and dog-like devotion.

"To the ends of the earth," Jane remarked, almost to herself. "He and milady have seats in First Class, Alf. We'll be in Second. When we reach Southampton Station, you must fetch a porter. Most of the luggage has already been sent ahead to the *Wieland*. I wish they had chosen a British ship, but passage was booked months ago on Hamburg-America. Try and behave like a proper servant, Alf. Keep your hands clean; don't blow your nose on your shirt-sleeve and only speak when you are spoken to."

"'Ere, Miss G – is that wot a proper servant does?" Alf looked as if that question had never before occurred to him. "Yes, Alf," Jane answered, with sudden insight and calculation. "That's what the Master wants; for you to be a credit to him and reflect well on his household and milady."

Up ahead, Jane could see Mr. Becker's wide-brimmed hat and fair hair, bending attentively towards Lady Isobel's plain brown traveling bonnet. Jane's heart lifted. Her ladyship was happy this morning, as if she had returned from a good day in the hunting field. They had not talked much, as Jane ministered to her. Lady Isobel was rosy and flushed and she looked at her husband much as Alf did. Mr. Becker had rescued Lady Isobel just as surely as he had rescued Alf. This had first contented Jane. But now that her ladyship had a strong protector, Jane wondered with a twinge of unease, would she still continue to rely on herself so much?

Jane took a deep breath, upon realizing that it was really happening. She, her lady, and Alf were going from England and traveling far. Like so many other passengers on that platform, it was possible they would never return. Never return to the land of their birth . . . Jane hesitated. The enormity of it yawned before her like an open pit, but then she straightened shoulders. The steamship ticket had already been paid for, her trunk sent ahead, the farewells made – and where would Lady Isobel be, without Jane to rely on? Now there was a train-conductor, showing the newlyweds towards their compartment. Jane quickened her footsteps. The crowd lessened slightly around the first class carriages. As the conductor made as if to close the door, Jane darted forward. She held Lady Isobel's jewel-case in one hand, her own small carry-all in the other. Lady Isobel was just settling herself on the horse-hair padded seat, looking starry-eyed at Mr. Becker, as he courteously took her fur-lined mantel from around her shoulders.

"Your jewel-case, Milady," Jane set the case on the seat and Isobel took Jane's hand in hers. "Are you excited, Jane?" she asked, "It doesn't quite seem real, doesn't it – and yet it is! We are on our way at last!"

"Yes, Milady," Jane answered. Mr. Becker smiled at them both, "You'll believe it, once the ship is well enough out in the open sea."

"Surely we will not feel the motion too badly?" Lady Isobel looked anxious. Her husband reassured her. "The First Class staterooms are towards the middle of the ship. Coming over, we found such to be very comfortable. The steamship only seems to roll a little with the motion of the waves."

The slamming of compartment doors, farther down the train recalled Jane to the present. "I will join you on the platform, as soon as we arrive in Southampton, Milady," she said hastily. "Alf will fetch a porter to the van for your luggage – I have already told him so."

"Thank you, Jane," Lady Isobel released Jane's hand and Mr. Becker smiled also. "A clever woman who thinks ahead," he remarked approvingly, as Jane bobbed a curtsey to them both and fled. It was curious, she thought, as she settled herself into a Second-Class compartment, how Mr. Becker saw her – not as some kind of automaton in a black maid's dress and white cap. He noticed her as a person, in a way that the gentry who had been guests at the Hall or at the Belgravia house did not. Jane wondered if she would be seen in the same way by Americans, or was this just peculiar to Mr. Becker.

"Sit down!" She reproved Alf, who fidgeted restlessly in his own seat before getting up and standing before the carriage window. The train lurched once, twice, and the platform slid past, gradually faster and faster. "We'll be there soon enough."

"I ain't never bin out o' Lunnen." Alf replied. He did not sound regretful. He sat down, though he still looked rather peaked and pale. "Wot's Texas like, Miss G? Sir tole me it were like a bit o' garden."

"I don't know, Alf," Jane answered. "I've never been there either."

Platform and columns holding up the glass canopy overhead went by, followed by the tangle of the rail-yard, under a cloud-speckled blue sky. Close-crowded terraces of soot-stained red-brick houses gave way to villas standing in tree-shaded gardens, then to hedgerow-surrounded fields and pastures dotted with slow-moving cows. Now and again a church spire rose from a huddle of slate or thatched roofs, there and gone in a minute: the train seemed to advance speed. *Goodbye to England*, Jane thought with just a tinge of sorrow. *I shall try very hard to remember the look of all this. I don't know if I will ever return; somehow, I think not.*

"Think on how this will appear all in reverse, when we return!" Isobel said merrily to her husband. They stood side by side on the First Class promenade, watching the last of the *Wieland's* immigrant passengers board below. She was glad of the warmth of her furs against the crisp, salt-smelling breeze, and the shelter of him with his arm possessively around her waist, standing close beside. Even if she was venturing into the unknown – that starkly beautiful and violent land on the other side of the ocean, Isobel could have shouted aloud for sheer joy. She was out from under Mama's inflexibly iron rule; never again to fear her curt displeasure or crueler indifference. She had escaped, as free as any of the sea-birds, wheeling overhead. Behind them, the ships' steam-whistle shrieked, once and once again. *Free.* Isobel savored the word, as sweet as honey on her lips. She looked sideways at him, also savoring the quiet satisfaction of possessing such a man for herself and herself alone. It did not escape Isobel's notice that other women looked upon him with covert admiration, so tall and well-formed, confident but gentle-mannered. He had chosen her and she him! In one night, she had learned more about him than she had during all the weeks of their courtship. He was that much less a stranger now. Isobel had confidence that every passing day would reveal more. So much for the terrors of the marriage bed – how very wise Fa had proved to be in his judgment, in permitting his courtship of her!

"Bell," he said in reply. His eyes crinkled at the corners as he smiled at her. Isobel felt as if her heart become as malleable as warm butter. *Last night he had announced, sleepily, "The Cap'n called you Izzy – I don't like that for you. It's an ugly sounding name. I'd rather nip a bit off'n the other end, and call you Bell." "Of course you may," Isobel had answered, "But then, what shall I call you, when we are alone?" "Most folk call me Dolph," he replied. Isobel had turned that over in her mind. Dolph. She expected that she would get used to it.* Now he said, "It'll be a bit, before we see this again. My life is in Texas and my business in cattle. It was just a fancy of my Uncle Hansi, to come traveling. I'll need to get back to work for a good few seasons. Years, mebbe."

"We'll bring our children, then!" Isobel exclaimed. Her exuberance was a little dimmed by the fact that he hesitated for a moment, before his embrace of her tightened a little.

"We'll do that, Bell darlin'," he answered at last. Isobel thought no more about it, for the ship-whistle blew again. There was a clanging, as of great iron doors closing within the ship. On the dock, a handful of sweating men pulled away the gang-way and let it drop with a clatter. The deck beneath their feet trembled slightly but regularly. The motion intensified; the mooring lines holding the *Wieland* to the dock loosened and dropped. The band of open water between the *Wieland's* dark-painted hull and the dockside widened and widened again. "We're away," Dolph Becker said. "We're away home, Bell."

By evening, the *Wieland* had left Southampton Water far behind. After supper, Isobel and Dolph took a walk around the deck, watching the faint lights from land fade and drop away. The rolling of the ship did not particularly affect them – although Jane looked white-faced, when she attended Isobel that evening.

"You are feeling the motion?" Isobel asked with concern. "Dear Jane, just unbutton my dress and loosen my corset. I can see myself into my night things just as easily. I fear that it may take a few days for you to become accustomed to it."

"Thank you, Milady," Jane answered. She unfastened Isobel's dress, and suddenly made the most extraordinary gagging sound. "I am sorry, Milady, I am unwell!" She fled in haste, gasping out an apology to Isobel and to Mr. Becker – to Dolph as she ran past him, just come from smoking a last cigar in the First Class salon. Even a First Class Cabin – a sitting room and sleeping room together – left little privacy. He had settled onto one of the comfortable chairs, with a German newspaper in his lap, courteously waiting for Isobel. Poor Jane, Isobel thought with just a touch of smugness. Even her lips looked grey from the *mal-de-mer*. A paragon, as a ladies' maid, at least there was some small weakness in her – but now she would have to cope with her corset herself. Isobel twisted, reaching up her back with one arm, trying to reach around for the ends of the corset-ties. She could not; her fingertips brushed the ends of the strings. Her husband – Dolph – appeared in the tiny dressing-table mirror.

"May I be of assistance to a lady?" He drawled. Isobel met his mirrored amusement with her own. "Yes please, untie my corset. Loosen the strings for me, I am perishing for not being able to take a breath. Poor Jane is feeling the first effects of a sea journey."

"My pleasure, Bell," he answered. Provokingly, he kissed her bare shoulder first. Isobel shivered at the touch of his lips on her skin. *Why, oh, why had no one ever told her how delightful it was to be married, to enjoy such intimacies freely, without censure or limitation?* Gravely, he untied the knots which kept her so tightly laced and Isobel gasped at the loosening of those stiff and unyielding bonds. She could breathe deep once again. In the release of that, she did not notice at first that her husband – that Dolph, as she reminded herself was the name that he liked to be called by – was looking speculatively at her hair. "Would you like me to find your hairpins, too?" he offered, as she unhooked the now-loosened front of her corset. "I don't think Miss G will be any good to you for a couple of days, at least. Not if Alf is any indication. I left him with a chamber-pot in his arms, swearing that Texas had better be worth such a considerable misery. I assured him on that account." He smiled at her again, in the mirror. "The trouble with sea-sickness is that first you are afraid you are going to die and then that you will not. My Ma and uncles told us how miserable it was when they came over from Germany on a sailing ship. It is good that you have a stout stomach for this, Bell."

"My good fortune," Isobel breathed deeply once and again. She set the corset aside, taking up the wrapper that Jane had brought, and laid close at hand, "Yes, you would be welcome to venture on an expedition for my hairpins. Jane is a marvel. I can hardly think how she does it, hairdressing is a mystery to me."

"To myself, also," her husband answered with dry good humor. "I confess, all of women's dress is a mystery. What you wear and why you do it, was always perfectly impenetrable to me and I speak as a man with sisters and female cousins. Still, Bell," he flashed a smile at her in the mirror, as he began search out hairpins. "It's better fun than I first imagined, finding out!"

"La, my dear . . . husband." To her surprise, Isobel felt such flirtatious words now come easily to her lips. *Why had she never been able to jest with such confidence, ever before?* Mama had been so severe on this lack and now it came so easily! "Do you speak as one with many adventures in the lists of deep affections?"

"No," her husband replied. "No, not many at all."

"How drear. Were you never in love at all? Was there ever anyone of the fair sex who had engaged your interest?" Isobel spoke in light tones but watched her husband in the mirror, as he studiously plucked hairpins from the wealth of her hair and laid them one by one on the dressing-table. Soon the wavy length of it lay around her shoulders, while Isobel listened with breathless attention.

"Fleeting things; a little flirting at a dance and my uncles now and again telling me that I should settle down with one girl or another. I have another uncle, not of blood, but who was a particular friend of my father's – who counseled me to have particular care, in selecting the woman whom I should honor with my name, the care of my household, and the upbringing of my sons. I must have taken his advice. There <u>was</u> one woman, but she was cruel."

"La belle dam sans merci?" Isobel's interest was piqued. She knew her husband hated cruelty of any kind. It would have killed any interest on his part. "Who was she? If chance should take us into the same circles, I would like to have some subtle revenge in showing that we are happily matched."

"Oh, you'll meet her," Dolph replied. "She's a connection by marriage; her husband was a cousin of ours and died in the War. She has gone about ever since, beautifully in mourning, and making cow-eyes at every single man of riches. When I Alf's age, I thought her as one of the two most beautiful women I had ever seen. Your mother reminded me of her. But she never had any interest in me – not until Uncle Hansi and Uncle Freddy and Cuz and I made a fortune in trailing cattle to the North."

"Such is the way of the world," Isobel replied and almost choked on the words. "A substantial income makes the meanest of men appear to best advantage." *How many times had Mama pushed her in front of this or the*

other, who had nothing in charm, wit, or ability – no other quality than their
wealth or ancestry to recommend them!

"Uncle Hansi used to say that it was gold-plating on a pile of cattle-turds"
her husband replied wryly and Isobel laughed.

"I will like your Uncle Hansi," she said, as he picked up her hairbrush
unbidden and began to brush her hair. "You have a gentle hand, my love."

"Years of experience with horses," he answered, with such a droll
expression that Isobel laughed again. She turned to throw herself into his
embrace, confidant of her affection being welcomed and returned tenfold.

Jane continued to be wretchedly sick for the first two days and nights of
their voyage, tended in her misery by her cabin-mate, a robust Irishwoman in
her forties who was traveling to America to live with her brother's family in
Boston. Bridget O'Malley was a well-traveled woman. She had gone to India
and back on a troop-ship, having followed her soldier husband there, but he
died and his widow declined to marry another soldier.

"I was only sick once, on the first time out," Bridget said comfortingly,
as she held a basin for Jane to be sick into. "An' then niver again. Which is
well, because there was a storm the like of which I had niver seen, it fair made
all but mysel' an' the sailors unwell. I think the captain of the ship, he was a
fair green color. Y'll be as right as rain in a day or so, niver ye worry about
yer lady."

Jane, sunk deep in misery for two days, had no energy for any worries
outside the confines of the cramped second-class cabin, but she did wonder
how Lady Isobel was managing. Mr. Becker was kind to her and loving, too.
Her ladyship glowed with happiness during the brief journey from London to
Southampton. But the uncomfortable thought did intrude on Jane's mind:
Texas was a new land, a far land – very different from Acton Hall. In the
sunshine and shelter of her husband's regard, would Lady Isobel still have
such need of Jane's unstinting support and companionship?

That very day, she was able to drink a cup of broth and nibble on a dry
biscuits which the cheerful Widow O'Malley urged upon her, and keep them
where they belonged after passing through her teeth and over her tongue. The
very next morning, she rose from her bed, dressed herself in her plain
respectable travel dress, put up her hair, and hastened to the First Class suite
which the Beckers had for themselves. She let herself in without knocking,
for that was the purview of a trusted servant. She found Lady Isobel and Mr.
Becker at a private breakfast in their stateroom, her ladyship in dishabille, a

dressing-gown over her nightdress and Mr. Becker in his shirtsleeves and waistcoat.

As Jane came in through the door, he pulled out his pocket watch and opened it, observing as he did so, "Eight-twenty, Bell darlin'. You owe me a forfeit."

"You are a horrible man," Lady Isobel flashed a fond and bright smile at them both. "Jane, you were so ill with the *mal-de-mer,* I was afraid you would be indisposed for days! My wicked husband engaged in a wager that you would be fit for duty before we had been three days abroad on the breast of the ocean. His manservant is still indisposed, so we have been looking after each other." Lady Isobel smiled again at her husband. Jane reflected that there was something of the adoration of a dog in it, a dog adoring a pleasant and indulgent master and she chided herself for yet another unworthy thought. Lady Isobel was a good and considerate mistress; Mr. Becker was the husband who had rescued her from an intolerable situation. Jane should rejoice in her good fortune and accommodate herself to whatever Lady Isobel should require in her new life. It would be a new life, far from the cramped confines of what Jane had known in her parent's little village store, and even in the wider realms of Acton Hall. Lady Isobel seemed to have gotten along very well in Jane's absence, even if it were only for the space of two days . . . two days without being cosseted, dressed, and reassured, two days without evidence of being cherished and cared for by any other than her wedded husband. *She is going so far from us*; the words of Sir Robert whispered in Jane's memory, *take care of her. Now,* Jane thought – *She may go so far enough that she will not need care. And what of me – shall I be free to sort out a life for myself? A life without my lady – but I cannot. I am bound to look after her; she will be alone in a far land*. But the rebellious thought whispered in the back of her mind. *I am alone, too – who shall look after me?*

Resolutely, Jane put those disloyal thoughts aside; she was cheered through having passed through the dreadful wretchedness of seasickness at least as much as she was cheered by the evident happiness of her mistress. They whispered and giggled together that evening like a pair of giddy schoolgirls, as Jane brushed her hair and arranged it in a simple style before the tiny mirror in the stateroom, while Mr. Becker interjected remarks from the parlor, sounding – so Jane whispered to her mistress – just like an elder brother or a schoolmaster. The Beckers were to sit at the captain's table in the main salon for supper, a supper held in as much state as could be achieved on a packet-steamer in the mid-Atlantic.

"It's all very quaint and very cozy," Lady Isobel giggled. "With a white cloth and silver candlesticks and all, but in a heavy sea, they bolt a gallery-railing around the edge of the table so that the plates and wineglasses don't fall off and the steward who serves us! Oh, my – to watch him move across the salon with a full tray as the ship rolls in an especially heavy sea! It is like watching the most marvelously comic ballet. He goes on his tip-toes and positively swoops across the room, while the tray seems to float across the salon, and his feet! Dear Jane, his feet are positively everywhere and in every attitude imaginable!" she burst into a peal of giggles.

Mr. Becker called from the sitting room, "We'll be late, Bell – the two of you sound as silly as my sisters, dressing for one of Auntie Liesel's parties."

"We're nearly ready!" Lady Isobel answered, then frowned briefly in concentration, holding her head nearly still as Jane fastened in her hair ornament – a modest jeweled agliette. "Your sisters; Lottie is the youngest – fourteen and very pretty and Anna is married to your cousin Peter."

"Hannah," Mr. Becker corrected, from the next room. "Hannah is my other sister. She's the one married to Christ and the care of the orphans of Galveston. Anna is my cousin; Uncle Hansi's daughter. She has two little boys and may have another one by now, for all I know. She was in foal when they all sailed home after Christmas."

"Dearest, don't be so agricultural!" Lady Isobel answered. In a softer tone, she continued, "Jane, can you have thought it? My husband has a sister who converted and took the veil! What would my parents have thought of that, if they had known! Perhaps she was," Lady Isobel paused as she searched for a word, "unfortunate in her looks."

"Perhaps a harelip, Milady," Jane whispered and Lady Isobel laughed merrily. "If women are as short in number as my husband tells me – perhaps it is a worse disfiguration than a harelip, so that she must take refuge in the life of a religious."

"No," said Mr. Becker mildly. Both of them jumped for surprise: he had come up behind them so very quietly, on near-silent feet from the other room. "My sister Hannah is not unlovely. She is merely very . . . very good," he added, as he took Lady Isobel's lace evening wrap from where Jane had let it lie across the foot of the bed. "You would like her, I think." He looked in the mirror, in a way that met both Isobel's and Jane's eyes and held a mild reproof in his own. "She has a way of knowing her own mind and being resolved to follow a path of her own choosing."

"I am sure that I will, dearest." Lady Isobel answered, while Jane kept silent. "I so want them all to think well of me; your sisters, cousins, and your aunt. Especially your mother; she must be such a formidable woman. I would like to think that I know them well, even before we meet, so that we will be at ease when we reach your home . . . that is, our home. I expect that as a stranger," she added and Jane thought the old unhappiness and dread showed in Lady Isobel's face. "I will be the object of much curiosity."

"Not to worry," Mr. Becker assured her, with an easy smile. "Mama is very down-to-earth. She accepts folk as they are at face value. She will consider you another daughter, without a second thought. Auntie Liesel Richter will be in a twitter, telling all her friends that I have married a lord's daughter. She's an awful snob, but a silly one. She could not say a hurtful word to anyone even if you held a six-shooter at her head. Cousin Anna might be called formidable, but she is a one like Lady Lynley; a woman with a man's way of seeing things. She says things straight and honest to your face. She doesn't go in for . . ." and he stopped and thought for the right word, "Malice dipped in honey. That's Cousin Amelia's line, but she's only a Vining by marriage and you might go for years without meeting her."

"It sounds like a terribly large family," Lady Isobel mused. Her husband laughed. "No, not really. Onkel Hansi and Aunt Liesel are the largest part. They have – had nine children. Cousin Anna is their oldest."

"Like Her Majesty?" Lady Isobel wondered, while Jane attended. During the long months when her ladyship had been courted by Mr. Becker, they had often discussed what little Mr. Becker had vouchsafed about himself and wondered about his family, his connections, and his life in Texas. Now their mutual curiosities were about to be rewarded, as Mr. Becker nodded.

"I have only one brother; Sam. He's younger than me by four years. My father's sister Margaret married twice; she had four sons by her first husband but all save Cousin Peter Vining were killed in the Gettysburg fight. Cuz Peter was the only man around with nerve enough to marry Cousin Anna. You'll like Sam. He's good at the business, good with cattle, and good at managing the hands, but he's not interested in it. He'd rather be daubing little bits of paint around with brushes. Sends Mama and Onkel Fredi into conniption fits when he talks about how he's like to be a proper artist. Onkel Fredi Steinmetz is Mama's brother. He manages one of our biggest properties. He's the best herd-boss there is; the first long drive we did north to Kansas, he was the only one among us who had ever done the like before. He went out to California with a big herd once before the war, stayed to look at the gold-mines and came back, shaking his head. Said after that, he'd just as soon stay in Texas. You sure you can keep this all straight in your head, Bell?" Jane adjusted the final strands of Lady Isobel's coiffure and stood back, mutely awaiting approval. It was not long forthcoming, for Lady Isobel smiled at her in the tiny mirror and said,

"Perfection, Jane – I am fortunate indeed that you are recovered! I could put myself together with my husband's assistance just well enough that I could step outside this cabin, but your skills lend me strength sufficient to face dining at the Captain's table." Lady Isobel flashed another confident smile over her shoulder at her husband. "I can, indeed, dearest Dolph. I was made to study and recite the smallest details of *Burke's Peerage*. Names of those titled families, their properties, titles and heirs, their connections, and strengths of their breeding. My recitations on the subject were the only aspect of my debut which pleased my mother."

"It's not a thing you'll have much use for in Texas," Mr. Becker said, with a grave face and an eyebrow quirked in amusement, as he draped Lady Isobel's lace wrapper around her shoulders and dropped a brief kiss on her forehead. "But if you can be brought to pay mind to the breeding qualities of cattle and horses, there might be a use for it!"

"You are awful!" Lady Isobel's face sparkled with laughter and affection. In a moment the outer cabin door fell to, leaving Jane by herself in the suddenly quiet stateroom. She tidied away Lady Isobel's day dress, the shoes and underthings she had worn with it, feeling a little as if her life had returned to something like normal, within the confines of the *Wieland* . . . of course, nothing like the Hall, or the Lindsey-Groves' London house. But Jane had every confidence that Mr. Becker's home, where her ladyship would have authority over her own establishment, would be ordered much along the same comfortable lines. Her ladyship had said so often enough; it would just be a smaller establishment and not so rigidly ordered. How often had Lady Isobel sighed and told Jane that she would love a cozy little house of her very own, no larger than Dale Farm, not a great echoing barrack like Acton. But in a new country, which Jane had been led to believe was far from entirely settled and civilized ... *'Well, then,'* Jane told herself, *'It will be an adventure, at least.'* Having laid out Lady Isobel's nightgown across the foot of the stateroom bed and turned the covers invitingly down, Jane went to seek her own supper in the 2nd Class Dining room, aware of a pleasant sense of anticipation.

That was what she said to Alf, five days later, as the *Wieland* approached the port of New York City. It was mid-morning, and the light of the sun crept in golden fingers between the clouds, touching now and again on the prospect before them, as they stood at the rail of the 2nd Class promenade deck. The coastline was nothing but low-lying islets of sand, yet there was a smudge of smoke on the horizon. Little white triangles and oblongs of white sails dotted the blue-grey breast of the sea.

"It will be an adventure," Jane said confidently.

Alf answered, "Hit don' look like much at all, Miss G."

"Our ship is still far from land, Alf." Jane observed. For a time they both were silent, as the *Wieland's* great steam engine belched clouds of coal smoke into the air at their backs. The vibration of it under their feet lessened slightly. Now Jane perceived that they were actually in a great bay of water; there was land on either side of the *Wieland*, that to their right being closer and more distinct. That to their left was barely visible, a dark-blue shadow lining the horizon. The sky was alive with sea-birds, swooping down to the waves and spiraling upwards again. "It looks very green, there," Jane added, casting her mind back to everything she had heard or read about America, which was not all that much. "Not like a city at all, more like the Island of Wight, I think."

"Is it true that the streets are really paved w' gold, Miss G?" Alf craned his neck and stood on tiptoes, as if that would aid him in getting a clearer view of the near shore, lined with a promenade, and many gaily-painted buildings.

"No, I don't think that is true," Jane said.

Alf persisted. "But it is true, Miss G – that summon can get as rich as a lord, just by working hard in America? Sir, he says his uncle hadn't nothin' much when 'e came from Germany; now 'e's a baron."

"A cattle baron," Jane explained. "Not a real baron."

"But 'e is as rich as a baron, innt 'e?"

"Yes, I expect so." Jane looked out at the landscape slipping past the *Wieland's* bows. Now the great ship was turning, the shadows cast by her stacks and rigging sweeping across the deck. "We're going north, now . . . New York is supposed to be the largest city in America, but it's odd that we can't see anything yet."

The waterway narrowed presently, hemmed in on either side by wharves and lines of ships tied up to them, buildings that loomed up, closer and closer, interspersed with parks of trees and grass and crowned with ornate spires and towers. The fresh salt-sea smell of the air was mixed with less-pleasant odors – of sewage and wood-smoke, of wood rotting at the edge of the water. Flags fluttered everywhere in the light breeze, from the masts of ships at anchor or under way, making splashes of bright color against the cloud-curdled sky and the blue-gray water. The *Wieland* slowly approached a narrow point of land where the buildings were the most closely huddled together. Above their heads, the great steam whistle shrieked, once, and once again. The *Wieland's* railings were crowded with her passengers, silent with apprehension or cheering lustily.

Jane took in a deep breath. "I believe we are arrived in America, Alf."

Alf's pinched little street-urchin face was pale and thoughtful, as he surveyed the docks, the wharves and the ships, with the city looming beyond them. Finally he said, "Ain't a patch on Lunnon, Miss G."

Chapter 8 – *The Cattle Baroness*

When the *Wieland* docked, and the 1st Class passengers were allowed to leave, Jane and Alf followed Mr. Becker and Lady Isobel down the passenger gangway. Jane dared not admit that she followed her employer especially close. Here was a foreign country, full of strange, jostling people, officials who commanded in preemptory voices, odd people and odder smells. Lady Isobel was her lifeline to safety. She did not dare let go, not in this place, even though the 1st Class on the *Wieland* were treated with an appropriate degree of courtesy.

"We have rooms for ourselves at the Gilsey Hotel," Jane heard Mr. Becker say to Lady Isobel, hanging on his arm. Jane was reassured at hearing this. They had a place to go to, in this strange city, this alien land. Alf followed, chivvying a porter with a barrow, piled with all their cabin-luggage. From the words which Jane caught, Alf reveled in his brief authority, telling the porter how important the Beckers were. It didn't sound as if the porter was particularly impressed with Alf's recitation; possibly he couldn't understand Alf anyway. It did not escape Jane's attention that Mr. Becker was looking around for someone in the crowd below, as they had come down the passenger gangway. She could not think who, unless he was looking for the nearest cab-rank. Now they were well among the crowd; Jane followed after, short of breath from lugging her own bag and Lady Isobel's jewel-case.

Already the stevedores were hard at work, unloading baggage and cargo from the *Wieland's* hold; muscular men of all colors, in drab work clothing and shouting in a strange argot to each other. She gasped as a policeman in a blue coat and tall helmet collared a pickpocket – right in front of them! She clutched Lady Isobel's jewel-case in a tighter grip. All these people formed a motley and noisy crowd; the 3rd Class immigrants being directed towards a tall round building, the clamor of a hundred languages . . . a newsboy, with a sheaf of newspapers under his arms, whose shrill voice punctuated the clamor around them. Jane turned her head momentarily, to stare at the spectacle of a tall black woman clad in gaudy calico and balancing a heavy basket on her head, from which she was selling fruits and vegetables that Jane didn't recognize. She had been accustomed to the swaying of the *Wieland's* deck for the last week but now the solid wharf under her feet swayed as well. How peculiar! Distracted, she nearly ran into Lady Isobel, who had stopped short.

Mr. Becker was looking down at her ladyship with a smile on his face. "Bell, I confess to a conspiracy with your Pa. He arranged for one of your wedding presents to be sent ahead as a surprise."

"Fa did? I thought that Mama had seen to everything?" Lady Isobel sounded puzzled, as well she might. Everything about her marriage: trousseau, gifts, and household fittings thought suitable for her new home had been overseen by Lady Caroline. Sir Robert loudly declaimed his disinterest in every aspect of the wedding, save to escort Lady Isobel down the aisle. Now Jane looked between them, seeing a young man with hair nearly as fair as Mr. Becker's own – a young man who must be an Englishman, by his bearing and his clothes, in marked contrast to all around him. The young Englishman held the leashes of two enormous shaggy dogs. Jane caught her breath; why, the dogs looked like some of Sir Robert's half-grown wolfhounds. From Lady Isobel's involuntary cry of joy and the way that the two dogs surged towards her, towing the young man at the end of their leashes, they were and recognized her as well. They fawned adoringly on Lady Isobel, licking her hands and her face when she bent down towards them, calling them by name, "Sorsha – and Gawain! Oh, you dear things! Fa told me only that you were sent to a kennel in the Highlands! Wicked Fa! He must have planned this, and you connived with him, Dolph!" She struck her husband's arm in mock-anger and he grinned broadly.

"That we did, Bell. I knew of a trusty party heading across the big pond who would get to New York before we did. Bell, this is Mr. Bertrand – Sebastian Bertrand."

"Marm," Sebastian Bertrand bowed over Lady Isobel's hand. Now that Jane saw him nearer, she realized that he was very young; hardly older than herself and flushed pink with embarrassment.

Mr. Becker continued, "He wishes to invest a large inheritance in Texas cattle. My mother is acquainted with some of his kin, so she promised them I would take him in and teach him everything he need know. In return for that, Seb's been making himself right useful."

"It was my pleasure," Seb Bertrand said, blushing even deeper. He let the dog's leashes pass to Lady Isobel and took a place at Mr. Becker's side. Obviously, he had matters of import to share and Jane listened with heightened interest. She couldn't help but notice that the presence of the dogs kept the dockyard crowd from pressing too close to their party, although certain men looked at them with envious calculation, mixed with a healthy dose of apprehension. The dogs paced next to Lady Isobel, now and again turning to look at her adoringly.

"Our passage is booked for Wednesday on the Morgan steamer to Galveston," Young Seb Bertrand was saying. "I've already arranged for your hold luggage to be transferred to the Morgan Company's dock. I sent a telegraph to your cousin Jacob in Galveston and another to Mr. Richter, letting him know of the date that you would arrive, although no one could say with certainty whether he was in Austin or in San Antonio. He seems to be an active man, moving among his various properties."

"He is. Thanks, Seb; you done good. So what do you think of New York?" Mr. Becker asked. "Compared to the great cities of Europe?"

"It's interesting," Seb Bertrand replied, with what sounded to Jane like an effort to be tactful. She also noted that he was pleased with Mr. Becker's approval. "New and modern, but somewhat raw, in places."

"Like Five Points?" Mr. Becker was grinning. Lady Isobel's attention was on the dogs. Jane wondered if Mr. Becker had forgotten that she was listening. That sounded like men's talk, unsuited to women's ears. "There are some places so raw, the boldest cow-poke wouldn't be advised to venture into them, not even to get his horn scraped. But," he added hastily, "Texas isn't that raw, less'n you get caught up in a feud, or make yourself dangerous friends or a dangerous enemy. By the way, Seb; you don't want to ask too many questions of a feller out west. It's considered unseemly."

"Not the done thing?" Seb ventured. The brim of Mr. Becker's wide-brimmed hat bobbed as he nodded. "Commonly, a man will tell just enough as he thinks you need to know. Any further questions are rude. Besides," Mr. Becker added, with a chuckle. "Should you later be asked questions in a court of law, you can rightly swear to knowing nothing else."

"How very singular," Seb observed after a moment. Jane wondered if the young gentleman wasn't re-thinking his ambition to invest in Texas cattle, but she also noted that Seb Bertrand squared his narrow, boyish shoulders and straightened his back, as if he wished to take on a little of Mr. Beckers' confidence, as he strolled along the dockland, past the Holland-America offices.

There was a hired coach waiting, of course; one with generous space for all, including the dogs, and the luggage and a cheery cab-man who got down from his box to admire Sorcha and Gawain – who fawned upon him as if he was an old and dear friend. Which he probably was, Jane recollected, if he had been the one to transport them and Seb Bertrand from where they had been domiciled down to the Battery docks – knowing the indiscriminate tastes of dogs towards anyone who had been kindly and affectionate towards them.

Jane was impressed by the Gilsey Hotel; new and modern, gleaming in pure marble-white on a corner of a grand avenue that Seb Bertrand explained was called the Broadway. Their rooms did not overlook a quiet park, as the Langham did, but the noise of the street below was diminished to a quiet night-time murmur. The rooms themselves were splendidly adorned with tapestries and beautifully carved rosewood furnishings. The management even provided a pair of suitably-sized quilted pallet-beds for Sorsha and Gawain, who from they way they quietly settled down on them with muffled sighs of doggy pleasure, seemed already quite at home.

"We'll have five days wait in New York, 'afore we catch the Morgan steamer to Galveston." Mr. Becker hardly noticed the lavish comfort of the sitting room, as Lady Isobel shed her travel bonnet and mantle and Jane took them away. "We can go to the theater – this place is right handy to the best of them."

"I'd love that," Isobel answered. "But I would better love to catch my breath, first. Might we dine in tonight and see the sights tomorrow? Some aspects of the city seem very fine and I should love to explore them farther."

"As you like," Mr. Becker answered, "I will have business to conduct for my uncle . . . and there are investors that Seb and I have to meet, so I will not be able to spend every day, all day with you."

"I will be able to amuse myself," Lady Isobel answered. "And there are a number of calling cards and notes left for me. I am sure that those ladies who have left them will be able to advise me."

"Good." Mr. Becker sounded relieved.

"Still," Lady Isobel sighed, just a little. "It seems that we have been traveling and traveling forever. I will be so very glad to reach Texas and our new home at last."

"When we get to Texas, we still won't be home, yet." Mr. Becker warned. "It's a big place – takes a long journey to get anywhere."

Late that night, as the lights from the street below shifted like willow-the-wisps across the high ceiling of the bedchamber, Isobel lay in her husbands' arms, grateful for his embrace and for the generous size of the bed that they shared. She was pleasantly weary from the journey and her husband had not been averse to exploring the mutual pleasures of marriage. Isobel felt sometimes as if she were a bird who had just managed to break the hard confines of a shell. Now she could stretch her wings and fly. Perhaps this was what a prisoner felt like, upon release, but she had merely a dim sense that she was a prisoner. Only now was it clear. She felt as if she only had to take flight, to take up the reins of as fine a horse as Thistle and fly, and fly and fly, forever and as fast as she could.

"I wish we could stay longer in the city," she murmured. "It seems such a pleasant place, with so much to see and do. Mr. Bertrand told me of the Philadelphia Exposition. Fa talked to me of the fantastic engine that will be exhibited there . . . surely we can stay a few weeks more, and have a properly honeymoon journey? I should so like to see some of the marvels that people have spoken of. That very nice couple from Hartford who shared our supper one night on the *Wieland*; she told me so very much. Could we not see such wonders for ourselves?"

"We can't, Bell." Her husband answered. "Why not?" Isobel felt unreasonably rebuked. "Surely we can take time?"

"I cannot," he answered, a thread of impatience in his voice. "I have already taken more than a year from the ranch and our businesses. I cannot remain away any longer. Uncle Hansi has plans. I'll need to be there."

"But we are new-married; surely he will not take it amiss?" Isobel hated that she sounded so childish. Dolph replied curtly, "Uncle Hansi might not but I would not ask for special consideration. He has particular confidence in me, almost more than he does in his own sons. I will not let him down, as I owe him much." He did not pull away from her, as they lay so close-entangled, but Isobel keenly felt the sting of rebuke. In a moment they had gone from heart-close to an impossible distance apart.

"As you would have it," Isobel answered, after some moment. "Then I will not mention this matter again."

"Thank you." Her husband said, with dry courtesy which stung as much as his impatience did. Isobel lay awake for a long while, staring at the reflected lights on the ceiling above, wondering why his consideration for her was now so limited. The thought intruded that perhaps she had been hasty, rash even – in agreeing to marry him.

Six days later, Isobel still wondered about her decision to marry and go to Texas with Dolph Becker, as the Harris & Morgan steamship bore them out of New York's harbor; a smaller ship than the *Wieland* and consequently more cramped. The steamship also rolled more, sitting lower in the water, but Isobel assured Jane that the journey would be broken at Charleston and at New Orleans before delivering them to Galveston.

"I am glad that you are not so indisposed, Jane." Isobel added. "I expect you had not become unfamiliar with the motion in the time that we spent in New York. You know, I could very easily become accustomed to living in

America. The city was quite homelike. I had expected something rather different." She smiled affectionately at Jane – dear little mouse of a maid, trying with every fiber of her being to be at once housekeeper and chaperone, as prim as a spinster twice her age! *No*, thought Isobel – *I may yet travel very far from Acton, but as long as Jane remains with me, she is an assurance that I am as much Fa's daughter as I am my husband's wife. And she is my only trusted friend in this place.* Noting that young Mr. Bertrand was deep in conversation with Dolph, farther along the railing and with Alf lurking close at hand, she asked, "Jane, what do you think of Mr. Bertrand?"

"He's a gentleman," Jane answered carefully. "And Sir trusts him very much, for someone just-met."

"So I thought," Isobel frowned – a slight frown which barely wrinkled her forehead. Sorsha the wolfhound leaned her great shaggy head against Isobel's skirt and looked up at her in adoration. "I think it must be a family connection of some sort – else why he would take such trouble."

"Have you asked him?" Jane mused. Isobel shook her head. Although she had enjoyed the short days spent in New York which measured a bare third of her marriage, she also felt a niggling sense of unease and discontent, since Dolph had refused to consider an extended honeymoon journey. It had been all very romantic to become engaged to him and escape the twin horrors of Mama's authority and a voyage to India in one. He was handsome, rich and obliging, but only to a point. While Isobel had little to complain of, now she had begun to consider those worries and fears she had set aside, in the hustle of a hurried wedding to a stranger and a stranger from a far land. Returned to the every-day company of his countrymen, Isobel noted that his speech had subtly become less formal; unguarded, even. She wondered what this presaged.

"I wondered if I should. Then I recollect what he said about it being rude to ask too many questions. Mr. Bertrand is an investor, so my husband said. If he wanted to tell me more of such matters, he would freely do so, but it is a puzzle, Jane. What connection can he have, when my husband's ancestral family ties lie all on the Continent?"

"The Sir keeps his own counsel," Jane observed.

"So he does," Isobel agreed, wondering if such reserve would ever melt entirely. "I did not think that I would never be consulted regarding matters like this. I would have liked to remain in New York, to spend some weeks at Newport, perhaps make a leisurely journey to see wonders such as the great Niagara Falls, or take in the Centennial Exhibition. I wished to see more! To travel by railroad could not have been any great inconvenience! I should like to have been asked, Jane!" The more she thought on this, the more that Isobel's mild annoyance simmered into resentment. "He . . . my husband seemed at first to think my preference in certain matters were of importance. But I cannot help seeing that he decides all, and I must perforce acquiesce."

"It's what married folk do," Jane answered. Suddenly Isobel was overtaken by a tide of annoyance at the smug expression on her face, with its well-schooled blandness of expression. *She was a servant – what could she truly know of my predicament?* For the space of a few moments, Isobel fought the urge to slap her, an angry impulse immediately governed. No – she was here on a paddle-wheel steamer carrying her to Texas and to the property owned by her husband and his family; her doing and hers alone. Jane had nothing to do with her decision. If it turned out to be an unwise choice born of desperation, it was no one's fault but her own.

The steamer rounded the end of the Florida peninsula after a journey of some days on a southerly heading. To Isobel the air felt as warm as a heavy blanket, as warm as blood, only cooled briefly by a spray of salt-mist, scooped from the crest of a wave by an errant breeze. Jane and Isobel strolled on the deck together, or sometimes Isobel walked with her husband, who appeared to be even more distant as they approached New Orleans, although as courteous as ever. The steamer stopped there for a day and a night, for passengers and to take on a load of fuel. Jane and Isobel watched the jungly banks of the river-passage slip past; grown with tall trees which settled half in the water and half out. Masses of grey moss hung from the lower branches, like tangled grey rags. Humidity hung thick in the air and the cries of strange birds echoed from the banks. Dolph had business to conduct in New Orleans, but he did offer to hire a carriage and show Isobel some of the sights of the town, but the time was too short for them to see very much more than the old French Quarter of town. Isobel marveled at the look of the streets and the people.

"How extraordinary! It's as if parts of Africa were transported to France and then a portion of it sliced off and planted here. It's as unlike New York as it could possibly be, yet still be in the same country."

"It wasn't the same country," Dolph answered with a faint smile. "It was French for a long while and Spanish for a bit. Yankee for a while, then not . . . and then again."

"Is Texas anything like New Orleans?" Isobel asked. Her husband's smile broadened. "New Orleans ain't like anything but New Orleans, Bell darlin'!" You'll see for yourself, when we get to Galveston." With that, Isobel must be content.

As the steamer approached Galveston, it first appeared there was no change in the coast at all; low-lying, fringed with a sandy shore and edged with green, lighter with meadows star-scattered with wildflowers, darker where tall marsh-grasses waved and rippled like a green mirror of the sea itself. Presently, Isobel discerned the shapes of buildings; white and regular as cubes of fine sugar, an occasional church spire rising up like an explanation point. The steamer passed through one of those wide sea-passages into an open bay. There was the city, on the inland side of an island shaped like a crescent-moon; a Venetian city built of wood, sprawling generously among brilliant-flowered shrubs and trees, with verandas and balconies facing the sea or the bay between it and the mainland. It was a tropical place, set about with tall palm-trees like huge green feather-dusters set on end. Late-afternoon sun lay golden across the roofs and the streets and gardens below. She and Jane, with her husband, Seb Bertrand and Alf Tanner looked from the railings as the steamer was made fast to the dock. It felt as if she looked down from a good height on the city below.

When she said as much to Dolph, he nodded. "It's built on a sand island, Bell – there is not a place on the Island more than fifteen feet above sea level. That is why most of the houses are on tall foundations. One of Uncle's businesses was in Indianola, farther along the coast, but there was a huge storm last fall and half the town was swept away. Jacob and Uncle Hansi didn't want to take a chance of that happening again, so they relocated here."

"Wouldn't Galveston be in the same danger?" Isobel asked. Dolph shrugged. "Uncle Hansi doesn't think so. There's never been a storm bad enough to do more than flood the lower streets a little and blow some tiles off the roofs. Galveston is in a fortunate situation. The storms always go one way or the other; into the west, or turn and veer north. There's nothing to worry about, Bell." He sent her a quick, reassuring smile. "It ain't the storm season yet." He looked down onto the scattering of men and a few women on the dock, obviously awaiting the arrival of the steamer's passengers and waved his arm. "See? There's my brother Sam and Cuz Peter. Everyone else is at Cousin Jacob's house."

"Everyone?" Isobel was afraid her voice trembled. She knew that some of her husband's family would meet them in Galveston. This was worse than her court presentation; brought out like a prize mare, decked out in white with three plumes in her hair and everyone in the world looking at her! Isobel was certain that she would disgrace herself by being sick, in spite of Dolph's comforting presence. Two young men stood side by side on the dock; one tall and fair, the other a mere stripling beside him. The younger took off his hat, waving it like a semaphore signal, while the other man cupped his hands and shouted over the clamor of docking, "Welcome home, Cuz!"

Dolph Becker took off his own hat and waved it in return. He turned to Isobel, his arm around her shoulders. "Not everyone; Auntie Liesel's megrims keep her close to home and I doubt Hannah has been let out of the convent. You'll like Mama. Cousin Anna approved of you, sight unseen. It won't be too much of a shock, Bell." He kissed her very briefly on her forehead a mark of affection rarely done in public. "Heart up, Bell, darlin'. It's only the second biggest fence and deepest ditch."

"St. George for England, hurrah, hurrah, hurrah!" Isobel whispered in response. The deckhands down below had set the gangplank ramp in place. The other passengers were beginning to surge towards it. She lifted her chin, took her husband's arm; Jane followed as an obedient shadow and Alf with his own two shadows, Sorsha and Gawain pacing with regal dignity on their leads. Seb Bertrand went ahead. Isobel wondered again, when and why had be become so much of their party.

The tall, fair-haired cousin met them at the bottom of the gangplank; he and her husband clapped each other on the shoulders. Cuz Peter whipped off his hat and bowed very gallantly over her hand, as Dolph said with tremulous pride, "Bell, my cousin, Peter Vining. Cuz – this is Isobel, my wife."

"Welcome to Texas, Cuz's bride!" Cousin Peter exclaimed. He kissed her hand, very gallantly. Dolph and the younger man embraced – a silent and fierce embrace; the two brothers saying only a few words to each other, in voices so quiet that Isobel didn't hear what was said. "You are kin to us now, will you permit?" Cousin Peter stooped from his considerable height and kissed her with cordial respect on her cheek. He still held her hand in his. Isobel noticed with some shock that his gloved left hand was hard, unyielding as if it were not flesh and then she saw the white scar that slashed across his brow and cheek.

"I will," Isobel answered; Dolph's scars were hidden on his body, but his cousin's were otherwise. That war they had both fought in had been brutal, bruising and very long. She had already noted so many men – in New York and New Orleans alike, men with missing arms, and sleeves pinned up, or who walked on crutches with a limp and a lurch, men with scars on their faces – and that they were many women wearing black, although the war was ten years and more gone in the past. "He has often and fondly spoken of you as fond as if a brother from birth."

"I only came late to the family. Cousin Isobel," Peter Vining chuckled. He looked at her with a friendly concern which melted some of Isobel's reserve. "But they were kind, to me, a stranger and made me a warm and enduring welcome. For you, it will be even warmer." His voice lowered, confidentially. "Dear Cuz has been harried for years over the matter of his marrying. He had high standards, he claimed; now they have been met in you." Such reassurance and approval calmed Isobel's apprehensions. Now the younger man was bowing over her hand; his sandy hair fell over his forehead. He smiled, a happy and open smile, without guile or reservation.

"Welcome home, Sister Isobel," he said. "I'm Samuel – Sam for short. We didn't know what to think when Dolph wrote that he would bring home an English filly. Usually, he just brings more dogs."

"We've brought dogs, too," Isobel answered, unaccountably cheered by the humorous affection shining from his face. Sam reminded her of Martyn, though Sam was not handsome in the way that Martyn was. Sam cast a glance at the dogs, their leashes held by an unusually silent Alf, who was staring around at everyone and everything, his eyes wider than saucers.

"They look like splendid critters," Sam snapped his fingers. Gawain advanced cautiously to sniff at him, allowing Sam to tousle his ears and the long shaggy fur on his head. "I've never seen the like in Texas, or Kansas neither. Let me do a sketch of them; they'll be famous."

"I would be most pleased for you to draw them," Isobel answered. "My husband said that you were a most accomplished artist."

"I don't know about that," Sam allowed generously. He had already taken a battered little sketchpad from inside the front of his coat. "I get along all right."

"Not right here and now," Peter Vining interjected. "Put the pencil away – they must be tired from a long journey and Ma'am Becker and Uncle Hansi are waiting."

"We've got a mud-wagon waiting and Jacob said he'd send a wagon later for the heavy baggage," In good humor, Sam put his notebook away.

Jane lurked unobtrusively at Isobel's side. The Galveston docks were much less crowded than those in New York, or even New Orleans. The passengers from the steamer quickly dispersed in all directions. Dolph handed Isobel into a tall coach with a square canvas top that must be the mud-wagon and boosted Jane up to follow. Jane's eyes were also as wide as saucers. Isobel whispered, "So, Jane – what to you think so far?"

"I don't know, Milady," Jane replied. "It's all so very big." The mud-wagon lurched on its metal springs as the men followed, with Alf and the two dogs. Sam scrambled up into the driver's bench and snapped the reins over the backs of the horse team which pulled it.

"I'll take the long way," he called over his shoulder, "So that Seb and the ladies may see the sights of Galveston!"

"There's been a lot new-built a year," Cousin Peter explained. "It's a growing town since Morgan decided not to rebuild their dock at Indianola. The railway is within twenty miles of San Antonio now. Uncle Hansi is beside himself with impatience for the connection to be completed."

The iron wagon wheels clattered hollowly over a street paved with wooden cobbles, lined on either side with wide raised sidewalks – many of them shaded with a gallery or a long balcony overhead. For all that Isobel could see, there were only a dozen or so city blocks, tightly packed with shops, public houses, and places of business. All were new and modern; wooden walls and trim painted with fresh white paint or in pastel colors as neat as a new bandbox. Even the brick buildings looked as fresh as if they had been finished the day before. The paving gave way to hard-packed gravel and sand and the city businesses were replaced by houses; cottages and villas, large and small, all of them with neatly fenced gardens spreading out, gardens full of bright-colored flowers. Banners of brilliant magenta and red bougainvillea vines hung from balconies and loggias, and climbed up porch posts, while a light sea-breeze brought the salt-smell of the ocean and sent the palm-tree leaves to moving with a dry, leathery rustle. Isobel marveled at how exotically tropical it was. There were shrubs and flowers growing here in the open air which she had heretofore only seen in hothouses and conservatories. Although it was only April, it was summer-hot already.

"I will need only the lightest of summer dresses," she murmured to Jane, who nodded silently. Of the houses they passed, most had tall windows, standing open to the fresh breeze and shade was dearly courted. Children played in gardens of the houses as the mud-wagon rolled by, girls with jump-ropes and barefoot boys rolling hoops. One of the largest houses sat a little above a curve of white-sand beach, two stories and a mansard roof adorned with iron-lacework such as Isobel had seen in New Orleans. A deep veranda surrounded the entire ground floor. Covered balconies thrust out here and there on the second. It sat in an extensive garden, as did all the others nearby. Much care had been taken with it and of late. The paths were freshly graveled; around a tree hung with yellow globes of heavy citrus fruit, someone had marked out a new flower bed, edged with sea-weathered white pebbles.

At this house, the mud-wagon turned from the road into the gravel drive which let towards it in a gentle loop. Sam Becker called, "We're here! Mama, Onkel Hansi, Dolph and his missus are here!"

Not only had their party been expected, but they were watched for by people gathered on the verandah at the side of the house, a sort of outdoor parlor overlooking the sea. This outdoor room was comfortably set with cushioned wicker chairs and tables, hung with ferns in baskets and adorned with larger plants in pots. Isobel saw, with a sinking heart, that the outdoor parlor was full of men and women, a small piebald lapdog and children – two small boys who came shrieking with excitement as the mud-wagon halted at the foot of wide stairs leading up to the house.

Saint George for England, Isobel thought. *Hurrah, hurrah, hurrah . . . What was I thinking, Fa? Why didn't I let you talk me out of this?*

Too late now. She went to her husband's arms, as he lifted her down. Perhaps he sensed her thoughts; he whispered, "Highest fence, deepest ditch, Bell." She took his elbow as he offered it, straightened her back and forced a brave smile onto her lips. Jane and Alf Trotter followed with the dogs and Seb Bertrand at her other elbow – *what was Seb Bertrand doing here, still?* She wondered with part of her mind, as Dolph led her towards the steps. They had arrived during afternoon tea. There was a tray on a low table, with a pot and plates of cake and biscuits on it. Part of her mind was frozen in a mild panic, but the other part observed and tallied, matching what she had been told, sorting out the multiplicity of family assembled there; three men, one older and two young. The older man and one of the younger held a family resemblance, of stocky build and dark hair. Uncle Hansi Richter, the rich cattle baron and one of his sons, no doubt of that. Three women also sat there; one barely more than a girl, tall and fair and so like Dolph that Isobel knew without a doubt that she would be Lottie. The second woman, tiny and elegant as a pedigree cat, must be Cousin Anna, the formidable wife of Cousin Peter. That older woman in a black dress at the edge of the family circle must be a governess. The girl sprang from where she had been sitting with the little dog at her feet and ran to meet them, the dog barking in a shrill soprano as she flung her arms around Seb Bertrand, crying, "Oh, Seb – I never thought I would see you, it seems like forever!"

"Steady on," Seb answered, blushing like a girl himself, although quite moved. "Everybody's watching us, Lottie!"

"Oh, don't be such a cold fish!" Lottie answered. She kissed Seb on either cheek, as Dolph said with dry amusement, "Let the poor chap catch his breath, Lottchen."

"Oh, pooh! He's my sweetheart, we haven't seen each other in simply months and I'll kiss him in the middle of the Strand, if I like. Welcome home, big brother!" Lottie flung herself exuberantly at Dolph, whose hug in return lifted her off her feet in a rustle of lacey petticoats. Then it was Isobel's turn, enveloped in a fiercely affectionate embrace, as the two boys and the small dog danced around their feet like a wind-up toy. "Welcome to Texas! You're a Becker now, so you'll have to love it!" Lottie whispered. She was looking into Isobel's face with with eyes the same blue as her brothers', set widely in a fair oval countenance, slightly marred with a scattering of pale freckles across her nose. Isobel was startled and unaccountably warmed by the open friendliness, just as she had been with Sam. "Dolph, the beast, he only told us a little about you – that you're a lord's daughter and you love horses! I have so wanted another sister! You must tell me everything! Dolph wrote us that you had been presented at Court, he said you thought it tiresome, but . . . Mauschen – behave, boy! " At that moment, the little dog discovered Sorsha and Gawain, as Alf led them from the mud-wagon. He darted across the drive like a small furry thunderbolt, still in a fury of high-pitched barking and the two little boys shouted in excited glee.

"Papa, Mauschen is going to fight!" Sorsha's ears pricked upwards in puzzlement but Gawain put his back and growled, a deep and menacing growl – which sent the smaller dog into an even deeper frenzy, although he did not advance.

Lottie cried out in dismay, "Don't hurt him!" while Alf hastily wrapped the ends of the leashes around his fists and held tight against the weight of the two wolfhounds, crying, "Be' ave, you buggers!"

"Nothing of the sort!" Cousin Peter roared, in a voice barely equal to the bedlam of excited children and frantic dogs.

"They're perfectly well-mannered," Isobel protested, over a rising cavalcade of barking dogs. Lottie scooped small Mauschen into her arms. "Sorsha! Gawain! Quiet!" Isobel begged, scarlet with embarrassment. "Alf, make them hush, at once!" This was hardly a dignified arrival; now the governess came hurrying down the stairs in a rustle of skirts. Isobel hardly glanced at her, as she chided the excited boys in German and took the still-excited Mauschen into her arms. That's what well-trained servants were for, of course. But instead of withdrawing unobtrusively, the woman simply stood there, gentling the little dog into silence and studying Isobel with open and unseemly curiosity. The governess was plain-faced and over-tall, her near-black hair threaded with grey under a plain house-bonnet of an old-fashioned style. Isobel realized, with a horrifying sense of even deeper embarrassment, that this supposed governesses' cap was trimmed with a deep fringe of cob-web fine lace and her black dress was of rich fabric, well-cut in a way that no mere governess could afford, even dressed in her mistresses' cast-offs.

At her side, Dolph cleared his throat; even so, he sounded as if he were overcome with emotions alien to him. "H'lo, Mama. This is Isobel. I married her in England. She likes dogs, too – and horses and cows. I hope you like her – I do, fine."

Isobel wished that the earth would open right that very moment and take her down.

Chapter 9 – *A Sky Full of Stars*

"So, what did you think of her?" Hansi Richter asked his sister-in-law late that evening. The tall windows on either side of the study stood opened to the breeze which wandered through, bearing with it the smell of the salt-sea and night-blooming jasmine planted under the windows of the house which overlooked West Bay. The faint sounds of laughter and piano music came from the parlor at the other side of the house, where the younger element had rolled back the parlor carpet and brought out the latest sheet music from the east. Hansi uncorked the decanter which sat on a silver tray on the sideboard, and Magda Vogel Becker sniffed in disapproval. "She is now Dolphchen's wife," she answered. "I had best think well of her."

They had known each other all their lives; born in the same little Bavarian village of Albeck, where Hansi had once courted her, the stepdaughter of Christian Steinmetz, whose ancestral acres were adjacent to those few owned by Hansi's father. Thirty years and a lifetime ago, they came to Texas, following the promises of the Mainzer Adelsverein; Vati Steinmetz, his wife, sons, stepdaughter Magda, daughter Liesel and her husband. Years and lives ago; now Hansi chuckled and drew on his pipe, which glowed briefly in the twilight. Beyond the tall windows, with their blowing muslin curtains, the sky in the west still held the pale golden flush of a departing sunset.

"But what were your first thoughts, eh?" Hansi persisted. Magda's strong-featured, intelligent countenance bore on it an expression of fond exasperation. "I thought *'God in Heaven, he has not brought a wife, he has found three sad little orphans, gathered them up and brought them home, just as he has always had with those poor starving dogs!'* Where did he find that skinny little lad, Hansi? In an English gutter, I am assured. Of course he felt sorry for him! They all looked so terribly frightened, even my new daughter. Am I that fearsome in aspect, Hansi?"

"You have your moments, Magda," Hansi answered, vastly amused.

Magda snorted. "Why did he do this, Hansi; do you have any idea? The daughter of a First? I cannot see what my son saw in her, or any advantage in marrying a woman so far outside of what we know. He had his pick of the daughters of our friends. I wish he had married one of our own kind, like Charley Nimitz's Bertha."

Hansi grinned. "He's a man, Magda, and a damned good-looking one. The daughter of a First or a peasant-farmer are all the same in their shifts and between the sheets. Perhaps she's uncommonly lively in that respect."

"You're disgusting, Hansi," Magda answered, without any particular heat. Truthfully she felt oddly honored that Hansi conversed with her without reservation or guard upon his tongue, as if she was one of his men friends or associates, or as Dolph's father would have done, in the privacy of the marriage bed. Yes, she could imagine Carl Becker – fifteen years buried in a grave in a corner of the orchard that he had planted and cherished – saying something of the sort. She could almost hear his voice, see him in candlelight with the bedding fallen to his naked waist . . . No. Magda wrenched her thoughts from that image. "A ladies' maid! What earthly use will she have for a ladies' maid, in our summer in the hills. To assist her in dressing for a day of weeding the garden, or put her apron on her, when we retire to the kitchen to skim cream and make cheese?"

Hansi chuckled again and drew on his pipe. "The maid? She's a pretty little thing. If I noticed it, so will the lads. I don't think she'll be a maid for long! Lise will be thrilled no end. There will be many occasions for your new daughter to dress in all her furbelows and fashions. Every woman of good family in San Antonio will be calling, just to see the daughter of a real First. My wife is probably already planning a whole series of parties and balls. As if she needs an excuse, eh?" He puffed on his pipe and the embers glowed briefly red. The door to his study opened, admitting his daughter Anna.

"The boys are in bed at last," she dropped gracefully onto the leather-upholstered sofa. "Peter is finishing with their nightly bedtime story. Such a day! What do you think of Dolphchen's wife, Auntie? They were made for each other, since each thinks of little besides horses and dogs. They have gone upstairs, pleading the exhaustion of the journey as an excuse to retire early. A good sign – even if they have been married only a short time. I think they are fond. The young ones are in the parlor, dancing to the latest music-hall songs. The prospect exhausts me. Also, Horrie plays the piano abominably."

"I do not pretend to know if that is a basis for a marriage," Magda answered, austerely. "But I would hope so.

"A Lucifer, Papa, if you would be so kind." Anna opened the beaded reticule in her lap and took out a small leather tobacco pouch and a roll of cigarette papers. She deftly rolled one for herself, and held it out towards Hansi, who struck a patent match. When it was well alight, Anna blew a trickle of smoke out of her mouth and Magda observed, "I wish you had not taken up that habit, Annchen – it's very unseemly."

"Papa and the other men love their pipes," Anna drawled. "It is a very small and pleasurable vice, after all. The doctors say it is soothing for the lungs. Why should women not indulge in the same pleasures?" The study door opened and closed softly, admitting her husband. "Miss Lizzie Johnson is a bad influence on you," Peter Vining observed. He leaned down from his considerable height to kiss Magda's cheek and even farther to kiss his wife's, before setting onto the other half of the sofa, with a sigh that mixed pleasant exhaustion with plain affection. "What are we planning? Lottchen and Mr. Bertrand, I know . . ."

"She may marry when she is eighteen," Magda interjected, with a severe expression which brooked no argument. That youngest and most precious of her children had formed an attachment to this English foreigner, who to the best of her knowledge was of an upright nature, with an inheritance to invest in American cattle. The uncle who made Sebastian Bertrand his heir had personally appealed to Magda that his nephew be looked after. He was a good and well-spoken lad, yet this was Lottie whom he wished to marry. And Lottie wished to marry him and had moped after him for months, until Magda was out of all patience with her normally sweet-tempered and affectionate daughter.

"That is three years from now," Hansi chuckled. "Time enough for him to set himself up in the cattle business, not so? And take his time building a house for your dearest Lottie in the wild country of the Palo Duro."

"At least as good a house as my husband built for me," Magda answered; again, that never-vanished twist of grief in her heart. "Of stone, even if it has to be hauled from Fort Belknap and a stone-mason sent from Friedrichsburg. That is my final word," she added as Anna laughed indulgently.

"Auntie, the Indians are vanquished and confined to their reserves in Oklahoma! There is no need for a house to be built as stoutly as a fortress! This summer, Mr. Goodnight is taking his own wife – and his investor, Mr. Adair, and Mrs. Adair, too – to make their establishment there."

"This is what I wish for my daughter," Magda answered. "And Dolphchen will train him up in the proper way of managing cattle and the ranch."

"And so," Hansi surveyed the company gathered in his study through a cloud of pipe-smoke. "Will your new daughter accompany Dolphchen on his excursion to the Palo Duro and establish a new fashion for a honey-moon journey? The daughter of a First following the trail of cattle!"

"I have done so, Papa." Anna blew a mouthful of smoke in her father's direction as her husband chuckled, reminiscently. "It was a most splendid experience; there is nothing for establishing a basis for a good marriage like seeing one's husband, hatless and cursing, as he attempts to coax a cow knee-deep from a pool of mud."

"You were up to your knees in the mud, too," Peter added. "And saying words that I was glad the hands didn't understand."

"It was a cow worth nearly fifty dollars to the brokers in Dodge City," Anna's face held the same austere expression that it did when she did accounts. "We did not get to where we are by being careless about such things. I think our new cousin will expect to go with Dolphchen. When we withdrew after supper, she said something about wishing to see more of this America. Dolphchen rushed them here so fast that she hardly had a chance to see anything, not even the Philadelphia Exposition."

"This will be her chance," Hansi chuckled again. "You must take her in hand, Annchen – let her know what to expect."

"When are they leaving for the Palo Duro?" Magda asked, with mild curiosity.

Peter answered, "Onkel Fredi wrote that the cattle will be ready by the first week in July. The trail will only be half the length that it is to Kansas in any case. He still made up a list of necessities – you know Fredi and his lists of necessary things."

"Besides moving the herd, your son and young Bertrand must also set up the new ranch headquarters before winter," Hansi rumbled. "You know what that means; a year and more of supplies, a couple of wagons full of sawn lumber, all that is the needful for building a house, a barn for the horses, and quarters for the hands. Young Dolph will see that he has everything in hand by the time winter sets in. By next summer, when the cows have calved, we'll know if young Bertrand has the skills and earned the respect of the hands."

"All winter, in that wild place," Anna shuddered delicately. "I would go mad, with nothing but the wind in the grass. And cold . . . it is cold beyond words. The snow comes down so thick and the wind blows it like sand. In twenty minutes everything is frozen hard, where it was as mild as spring not an hour before. You are setting Mr. Bertrand a hard test, Papa. And your cows, too."

"Young men need hard testing," Hansi answered. "As for the welfare of the cattle, I have consulted with Mr. Goodnight. The canyons of the Palo Duro provide shelter, even in the worst winter. They will thrive and so will young Bertrand, I believe. In any case, we will leave him with some experienced hands and a good foreman, too." He drew on his pipe and added. "We have our own investment in this to consider – not so?"

They spent a week in Galveston, for which Isobel was grateful. During the day, her husband and the men of the family had business matters to attend, of which they explained very little. It did pique Isobel's curiosity that both the acerbic Anna and Dolph's formidable mother were much caught up in whatever business it was. She hesitated to ask very much about it and no one seemed much inclined to tell her of those concerns. Isobel was left to the company of Lottie; quite enjoyable, although the girl was but four years younger than Isobel. Dolph's sister was so forward in her address and spirit that she appeared to be much older.

"La!" Isobel exclaimed, several mornings after their arrival, as Jane buttoned the back of her day-dress. "It seems as if I have been traveling for months, if not years! When shall we arrive at home, Lottie? Your family home, the stone house in the hills that my husband told me of?"

"Not for another while," Lottie answered. She was sitting on the edge of the bed in the suite of rooms set aside for guests, examining the contents of Isobel's jewel-case. "We shall have to go to San Antonio, to Onkel Hansi's house and only then home for the summer. Everyone will want to meet you, you see – before Dolph and Cuz go north with the cattle to Seb's ranch in the Palo Duro. This is lovely! Opals – Auntie Liesel has a wonderful parure of opals and diamonds set in gold that Uncle Hansi gave her. The necklace comes apart to make two bracelets, a brooch and a hair ornament. This is much more elegant. And such enormous pearls. Mama does not think I should wear any jewelry but plain little pearls."

"My mother has a magnificent set of them," Isobel smiled into the mirror. Lottie was sitting with her legs carelessly drawn up under her, like a schoolchild. "They came down through her family – and are famous. They were said to be a gift from Queen Elizabeth. Mama lent them to me to wear at the ball where I first danced with your brother."

"I haven't danced yet with Sebastian at a ball," Lottie ventured wistfully. "I suppose I shall, once we arrive in San Antonio. Auntie Liesel lives for a party. I suppose that she has already engaged an orchestra for dancing and sent out invitations. But Mama will not let me wear any pearls but a simple necklace or stay up past midnight! I wish that she would. Cousin Anna says that when she and Auntie Rosalie were girls, Mama and Papa would dance through the night at the grand Fourth of July celebrations. They used to have a whole day of parades, and competitions, then dancing until morning, and my Papa was so handsome and gallant that Mama was quite envied."

"It sounds quite wonderful," Isobel answered. Secretly she could not imagine that gaunt, plain woman who was her mother-in-law dancing through the night with anyone, let alone a well-favored man. "What was your father like, Lottie? Your brother says very little about him. He talks rather to me of Uncle Hansi."

"I never knew him," Lottie replied wistfully. "He died before I was born. All I know was what my sister and brothers and Cuz say: he looked like Cuz. but more like Dolph in manner. I wish more than anything that I did know him. A father is a wonderful thing to have, Bell. You must love yours very well."

"I do," Isobel answered. Her own expression in the mirror was also wistful. "Mine own father was my most faithful champion in all the world . . . before I married your brother, of course. I wish still that he were closer to me. He would like Texas. Given any opportunity, he would design and undertake to build a better bridge to the mainland and any number of railways. Papa likes to build things."

"I miss my own father," Jane remarked, unexpectedly. "He died of the flux when I was ten, but I recall him very well. I wish that he had lived." Jane's pale face blushed a deep red. Isobel wondered absently what had gotten into her; Jane who was usually as mum as a mouse, when she and Isobel were not alone.

"So do I," Lottie sighed. "Everyone remembers him, but me. I make up stories in my head about him, which I am sure are far from the truth that everyone else recalls. You are both fortunate in having memories to treasure." Lottie's face reflected a moment of melancholy, then brightened. "Shall we go for a walk along the shore this afternoon with your wolf-dogs? Cousin Horrie can come with us; we'll walk as far as we may and carry a picnic with us! Jane can come, too. There is a place I know where we can gather the loveliest shells and sea-glass."

"I would so enjoy that," Isobel answered, even if she thought it sounded rather like a nursery excursion. She would rather have gone for a ride, but when she had asked about that possibility the night before, her husband had chuckled and explained that the only horses in the stable were those trained for the carriage, or to haul freight wagons. The family's saddle horses were all on the mainland. "We do business here in Galveston, Bell," he explained. To Isobel it sounded patronizing. "Not pleasure. A day in the saddle is nearly always work to us – not pleasure."

"I see." Isobel felt a niggling sense of disappointment. She had expected rather more of Texas, although she wasn't quite sure what it was that she had expected.

At the end of the week, the whole family packed up and entrained for Houston; not just Isobel and Dolph and their party, but Lottie and her mother, Mr. Vining – whom everyone called Cuz – his family, and the man whom Jane thought of as the cattle baron, but whom everyone else called Uncle Hansi. The ride from Galveston to Houston was mercifully short; the passenger car was devoid of luxury – indeed, of every scrap of comfort itself. It was one long open car, not divided into separate compartments with padded seats – merely hard wooden benches. The sun beat down outside, and now and again a cloud of smoke from the engine blew into the open car.

"I feel like we are one of the wandering tribes of Israel," Isobel whispered to Jane, as they waited in the First Class waiting room for the train to the west. Cousin Peter told them cheerily that the train would be on time, with a private parlor car for their party hitched to it.

"All we are lacking are a herd of goats, Milady," Jane whispered back. Jane looked wistfully at the gentlemen; they stood at ease, attended by a worshipful Alf and the other boy, Mr. Vining's ward Horrie. The men looked cooler, in their shirts and dark coats, more comfortable than Jane and the other ladies, in their shifts and corsets, and layers of petticoats and dresses. Jane scratched surreptitiously at an insect bite on her wrist. She had a number of them on her hands and neck, from those night-time flying insects that Isobel had told her were called mosquitos. Those nasty things were the reason that all the beds in Cousin Jacob Richter's house were hung with filmy white nets. Jane had forgotten most nights to pull the net closed and suffered the bites as a consequence. Mercifully, the waiting room was cooler. Tall doors and windows stood open to catch the vagrant breeze, although this also allowed flies and other insects. Dolph's mother sat across from them, fanning herself with a palm-leaf fan, a small valise in her lap which Jane had offered to carry for her, feeling that she ought to extend that courtesy to her ladyship's mother. But the elder Mrs. Becker shook her head and thanked Jane in harshly-accented English. Jane looked around, thoughtfully. There were not nearly as many servants in attendance as there would have been in England on a similar party. She and Alf were the only ones; not even a nanny for Anna Vining's small sons, or a nurse for her infant daughter, asleep in a nest of ruffles and lace in the wicker pram, which her mother absently rolled back and forth with one hand while keeping a sharp eye on her romping sons. The boys occupied themselves with sending a spinning top along the not-quite-level floor of the waiting room, to the hazard of another passenger, a slight and well-dressed young gentleman who paused just inside the door, letting his eyes adjust to the relative dimness within.

Jane did not see anything alarming about the gentlemen, other than the fact that he had two long pistols in holsters at his waist. It had seemed to her quite peculiar at first; men of every age and degree wearing such weaponry openly or barely veiled by the skirts of a long frock coat. It was, she decided after some consideration, a customary accessory in Texas. Men thought of them as an adornment, donned as casually as they put on their cuff-links, pocket-watch, fobs, and chain. This man's left hand rested easily on the butt of the revolver at his waist and his eyes quickly scanned the room. Jane thought at once that he did not except to find the waiting room so crowded. His first impulse, quickly squelched, was to turn and go outside onto the platform again.

But his pale blue eyes brightened with recognition and an expression that Jane couldn't fathom, just as Isobel asked, "Jane, I am perishing of thirst – is there a place here where you might find a glass of water for me?"

"I will ask the gentlemen, Milady," Jane answered, rising from her seat. As she did, the stranger tipped his hat respectfully to them both, saying, "There is no call to trouble yourself, ma'am." His voice was husky but light. "There is a place serving libations across the way. I am certain they have water for a lady an' with ice in it, too. If you would permit me, I would be honored to fetch some for you."

"I . . ." Jane began a mild protest, but the stranger said, "It is not a suitable place for ladies, although the refreshments are of the finest. I will return momentarily, ladies." He nodded to Mr. Becker and Mr. Vining, who had stopped their conversation in mid-sentence.

Mr. Becker spoke first, saying, "Why, if it isn't Wes . . . ."

"Swain," smoothly interjected the young man. "James Swain. The boys called me Little Arkansas, when we all met up in Abilene in '71. I'd 'mire to swap yarns with you all, as soon as I have fetched these ladies some iced water from across the way. Gentlemen," he nodded politely and withdrew. Jane spared a glance at the gentlemen. The Baron, Mr. Becker, and Mr. Vining were exchanging significant looks. Jane divined that they knew something about Mr. Swain from the wariness in their expressions when he returned bearing a cut-glass pitcher full of water and a number of glass tumblers. Jane took them from him with shy gratitude, at which he removed his hat again and smiled at her.

"My pleasure, ma'am," before he looked straight at Mr. Becker and grinned. "The RB outfit's got nice taste in womenfolk, Becker."

Jane poured out a glass of water, clinking with ice, for Isobel, and another for Anna Vining, who's sharp, coffee-dark eyes were roving between her sons and her husband. She offered another to the elder Mrs. Becker, unlatching the straps that held her little valise closed, but the older lady shook her head in dismissal. Irresolute, Jane set the pitcher down and took the glass herself. She was thirsty; the room was suddenly very hot.

"This lady is my wife," Mr. Becker said, his face as dark as if a storm-cloud had passed over it. "Isobel, I must introduce you to Mr. Swain, of Gonzales and thereabouts. He's kin to the Taylors, a prominent family in these parts. Swain; my wife, Isobel. She's from England; we were just married last month. Miss Goodacre is her personal attendant."

"Indeed," Mr. Swain grinned again, bowing very gallantly over the gloved hand that Isobel extended towards him. "I am honored. All the way from England. Amazed you didn't turn Mormon, Becker, so you could marry the both of them."

"Swain, you go too far," Mr. Becker snapped. Mr. Swain grinned again, as if he didn't care that he was being insulting. "My apologies to the ladies," he drawled. He didn't sound apologetic at all. Barely noticed by anyone but Jane, old Mrs. Becker had opened her valise and dipped one hand deep inside. "So, Becker – you're on the trail again? So am I; just returning from a visit."

"We're returning from our honeymoon journey," Mr. Becker explained, an unaccustomed scowl on his face. "You're a little out of your home pasture, aren't you, Swain? Planning devilment with your Taylor kin?"

Mr. Swain shook his head. "I dassn't say, Becker. The answer might be bad for my health."

"Understand," Mr. Becker answered, evenly. "I ain't looking for trouble, this trip. You ever come on to the SB range, though, I guarantee a wagon-load of it, Swain. Just so's you know that." Very ostentatiously he swept his own coat aside and rested his hand on the butt of the long revolver strapped to his own belt. Just for that moment, the atmosphere in the waiting room was heavy with tension. Jane could hardly breathe, it was so thick in the air, like one of those winter fogs in London, when the soot-smoke hung heavy against the windows of the Belgrave Square mansion. She was not the only one to feel it. Even the sunny-natured Sam Becker had a grim expression on his countenance. In the heavy silence, a distant train whistle blew. Mr. Swain let his coat skirts fall to. He nodded to the men, still a broad grin across his face, and touched the brim of his hat as he nodded towards the ladies.

"Alas, fair ladies, I must bid you adieu, as that is my train. You're a lucky man, Becker – in love as in most other matters." Swain was gone, still with a mocking grin on his face. A train rumbled into the station, with a roar and a crash, a screech of metal against metal, and the hiss of steam escaping. The tension in the waiting room eased perceptibly on his departure, and there was a restful quiet for some minutes. Jane noticed that the elder Mrs. Becker was still intent on the contents of her valise. Jane looked – and blinked in astonishment; was that the long, matte-metal thing a pistol barrel? She had only that momentary glimpse of the object before it was hidden underneath old Mrs. Becker's knitting, as she turned towards her son and asked a question in German, a language that Jane couldn't begin to understand. Out on the platform, more steam escaped from the train engine with a deep hiss and a distant voice called for passengers to board, and listing a handful of cities where that particular train was destined – to the east, Jane assumed.

"You can put it away, Mama," Mr. Becker said while Mr. Vining looked very amused. "He's gone."

Lady Isobel asked, deeply curious, "Is this Mr. Swain a desperado of some kind?"

Her husband answered with care. "Afraid so, darlin'. His name sure wasn't Swain when Cuz and I first met him. He went by the moniker Wesley Clemmons then. Some say his real name is Hardin. Whatever he goes by, he has a reputation for being handy with a shooting-iron and a little too eager to show off with it."

"He has that look!" old Mrs. Becker exclaimed indignantly. "I know that kind of man. He has killed before, Dolphchen, has he not?"

Mr. Becker and Mr. Vining exchanged a look before Mr. Becker answered, "I can't say I ever personally saw him kill anyone, Mama, but the stories about him have it that he has killed a man – black, white and Mex – for every year since he was born and he's no older n' Sam. Even lawmen walked warily about him. My guess is he's probably on the run from the law, in some jurisdiction or other – for rustling cattle, or murder, an' likely both."

"The city marshal in Abilene allowed him to wear his pocket-cannons into town during the trail season," Mr. Vining added. "There wasn't another man-jack around who was that privileged, otherwise and nobody save Ben Thompson ever claimed that Marshal Hickok was a coward."

"If he is a wanted man," Isobel exclaimed, looking from her husband to his cousin and the other men. "Shouldn't you inform the magistrate, or the police, someone – anyone?"

Her mother-in-law made a derisive sound somewhere between a snort and a chuckle and Mr. Becker explained indulgently, "We don't know nothin' for sure, Bell. We don't even know which is his real name; Swain, Clemmons, or mebbe something else; what he might have done, or even where. There'd be no good to it. Just let it slide. Besides," he added, in a more practical sounding voice. "He's gone on the train east. Whoever he might be, he ain't Texas' problem any longer." He consulted his own pocket watch and snapped it shut. "Our own train will be along any moment. As soon as they get Onkel Hansi's palace car attached to it, we'll board and get settled. Bell, darlin', you didn't think we were going all the way to San Antone the same way we came up from Galveston?"

"I didn't know what to think," Lady Isobel still looked puzzled. Jane didn't blame her in the least. *A palace car?* She had never heard of any such thing and was certain that her ladyship hadn't, either.

Sam Becker chuckled at their obvious mystification. "Onkel Hansi spent too many nights, sleeping on the ground, not to travel in style – Mama says that this is his one indulgence."

"I travel for my business," the cattle baron growled, although his eyes twinkled. "I may as well be comfortable, hey? I do not own so much property scattered here and there that I might spend every night at a place I own. This is next best."

"Not arguing with you, Onkel," Mr. Becker answered and took Lady Isobel's hand. "I've slept on the ground too many nights myself."

Jane followed the party out of the waiting room. At the last instant a breathless boy with a white waiter's apron wrapped around his waist ran into the waiting room and took up the empty water pitcher and the tumblers. Jane thanked him, and took out her own reticule, in order to pass him some coins in gratitude, but the boy blushed as red as a beet and mumbled something she couldn't quite hear, before trotting away. Jane sighed. Really, sometimes she couldn't fathom Americans.

The dazzle of full daylight outside momentarily blinded her, even under the wide roof which overhung part of the platform. The great black steam engine, adorned with gold and red trim panted like an overheated dog, expressing steam from every aperture. It was a much larger engine than Jane had ever seen in England and there was a fair crowd of people waiting to climb into the passenger cars. To her mystification, the Baron and his family proceeded along the platform towards the end of the train, towards an especially ornate car, painted deep green with gold trim, and adorned with a lot of brass so highly polished it gleamed like gold. The end of the car was open, like a generous balcony, with a pair of wicker armchairs set in it. The brass railing had an ornate logo set in it; the letters R and B, with a lot of curlicues surrounding them. A side gate was open to the platform. Jane hastened her steps; there was a uniformed porter already taking up the Baron's grip, another rushing to assist Anna Vining with the perambulator.

She caught up to her mistress, just as the porter turned towards Mr. Becker, his dark African face beaming with good cheer, "Welcome, seh! You have had a pleasant journey, Mistah Becker? They brought your luggage around half an hour ago – James and I put your things and Missus Becker's in the blue stateroom, since Mistah Vining and the fambly have the the yellow."

"It's good to be almost home, Absalom," Mr. Becker answered. The porter looked even more cheerful than he had before. "This is my wife . . . and Miss Goodacre, her personal maid. I trust that you have a place for Miss Goodacre, for the two nights to Seguin – and my wife depends upon Miss Goodacre for everything."

"We have arranged everything, Mistah Becker," Absalom replied, with a tone of slight reproof. "Mistah Richter sent us a telly-gram, a week ago."

"No flies on you and James," Mr. Becker approved as he and Lady Isobel stepped from the platform onto the train. Absalom turned to Jane, the very last of their party, and courteously took her elbow. Jane was in need of it for her eyes were so drawn to that which surrounded her that she might very easily have missed her footing entirely, out of awe and wonder.

So this was a palace car! She could scarcely believe her eyes. Absalom closed the brass gate after her and leaned out over it, waving toward the front of the train. "May I take that fo' you, Miss Goodacre?" He offered. Jane let him take her own bag, but clutched Lady Isobel's jewel case to her chest, as Absalom solicitously led Jane through the door into the main part of the car. Here she stopped again to marvel. How splendid was the room before her, a long parlor room the width of a rail car, lined on each side with glass windows, paneled with richly varnished woods and set about with comfortable furniture. There was a thick carpet underneath her feet, brilliantly colored in shades of green, red and gold – again the R and B initials intertwined woven into it. The windows were curtained in matching colors, and brass and glass lamps depended from the ceiling overhead, although they were not lit. The light from narrow windows set under a higher, central roof shed enough light into the parlor – for that is what it was, comfortably arranged, with chairs and divans, centered on marble-topped tables. There were also Gawain and Sorsha's thick-padded beds, laid tidily in a corner.

The dogs were settling onto them, tended by Alf, for once stricken to silence from sheer awe. But not for long. "Oh, Miss G!" Alf whispered, "What do you think o' this! Is this the way to travel in Texas – Does 'er Maj' go in style like this?"

Jane hardly knew what to say, but Absalom's uniformed chest swelled with pride. "There ain't no private car anywhere in the worl' as fine as Mistah Richter's!" He assured them. "Them crowned heads, they ain't got nothin' better. Heated w' steam, an' with runnin' water, an' a kitchen, too! Mistah Richter, he can allus pack up an' go, t' where he needs to be an' stay as long as he like! There ain't no one in the worl' take better care o' dis here car, an' Mistah Richter than James an' I, between us." He lowered his voice to a confidential rumble. "Mistah Richter, he tell me dey wanted to display this car at dat Philadelphia Exposition! Because dey built it so fine! But Mr. Richter, he say no, he need dis car now and he need here. He got business to do, an' so on."

From outside on the station platform came the whistle of the station master, and one last cry of "All aboard! All ab-o-o-ard!" Beneath Jane's feet, the parlor car jerked slightly. Outside of the polished glass windows, the station building appeared to startle and then glide smoothly past. Absalom explained, "Dere's Mistah Richter's office, here . . . the dining room . . . an' three staterooms . . . course, dey ain't big. Two lil' cabins, an' den de kitchen, wid de cabin foah James an' me." Jane obediently followed him down the narrow corridor which opened off the end of the parlor, windowed all along one side, paneled with richly varnished wood all along the other and intermittently broken by narrow sliding doors. This was tight quarters, almost as tight as those on the paddle steamer which had carried them from New York to Galveston, yet every inch was ornamented. As tiny as the little space beyond the door which Absalom opened for her, it was outfitted with every luxury. The folding bed was drawn down, and made up with crisp white sheets and a fat down pillow. There was barely enough room to walk in and stand next to it. "Yo' Miss Isabel, she an' Mistah Dolph are in the next room," Absalom explained, setting down Jane's bag. He showed her how there was a little washbasin, which opened out of a cabinet set in the wall, with a mirror over it, and a clean white towel. Then he courteously withdrew, leaving Jane to sit on her narrow bed and wonder if she were dreaming all this.

Chapter 10 – *The Palace Car*

Isobel silently removed her bonnet and gloves in the privacy of the little stateroom to which she had been led by her husband, who appeared perfectly at home. He hung up his own hat and turned towards her with one eyebrow lifted and a smile just quirking at the corners of his mouth. The green countryside unfurled through the window to the outside; flower-starred meadows and woods broken now and again by a reach of placid green water.

"Well?" he said at last, and Isobel replied, "It's a marvel, really it is. However did he come to want something so princely? Uncle Richter seems otherwise rather modest in his tastes."

"Two things, really," Dolph explained. There was no room in the narrow corridor for her to take his elbow; instead, he let his hand on her corseted waist steer her back to the large parlor section. "The old boy really does travel a lot; besides the ranches, there are the freighting interests, and the general stores, and they are spread out all over. With the railways making traveling easier, it makes sense for him to have an office that can go nearly anywhere. Onkel read about a railway company owner who had his own private car and he decided it would be just the the thing – never another night in a noisy flea-bag flop house, or a bad meal, either. To him, having money means that you can arrange things in your life to suit yourself, rather than other folk. A home on wheels suits him very well. He's talked about going all the way to California. That would be an adventure! I think he hopes that he might get Auntie Liesel to go with him sometimes. Auntie Liesel's always been a bit nervous about leaving her house, but if she had a little tidy place that she didn't have to set foot out of if she didn't want to . . ."

"Has it worked for Aunt Richter?" Isobel asked, and her husband shook his head. "She hasn't yet agreed to go very far, Onkel says – but he hopes. Let's sit on the platform. You can say that you have seen something of the country. Myself, I'd sooner see Texas again than any old Philadelphia Exposition." He led her to the wicker chairs on the observation platform, where the fresh air cooled the heat of the day somewhat, and the long shining steel rails unrolled like a metallic ribbon behind them. The lands around them were mostly flat, and studded with towering trees – cypress with feathery green leaves and stately grey trunks which rose directly from the banks of the rivers they fringed, oaks as large and old as anything that Isobel had ever seen in England, and other trees with long clusters of leaves which her husband said were pecan trees. To Isobel it looked more like England than anything she had so far seen, but the towns that the rails passed through were nothing like England. They were all American; like Galveston, the buildings all band-box new and constructed principally of wood. There were new-ploughed fields here and there, some with crops already grown tall; sugar cane and cotton, her husband told her.

"This is the way to travel, indeed!" she finally exclaimed, as the sun set in a ruddy smear of red, gold and purple. Absalom appeared, resplendent in his brass-buttoned uniform to say that supper would be served shortly in the dining room.

"Don't become too used to it," her husband advised in dry tones. "When we take Seb's cattle up to the new place on the Palo Duro, we'll travel the old way; on horseback, driving a wagon, sleeping on the ground and getting our supper from the chuck wagon."

"So," Isobel mused. "You have already decided that I will accompany you. I presume that at some moment, you were going to ask if I cared to join the excursion?"

"You did want to see the countryside," Dolph answered, with a broad grin. Isobel laughed, her heart melting reluctantly. "I suppose Jane won't mind such an adventure. After all, I can't imagine going anywhere without a maid. What is so funny?" she added, as Dolph began to laugh, outright.

"Bell, darlin' – I'm seeing you getting dressed for a morning on the trail, and the faces of the hands when I tell them that my wife needs the help of Miss Jane every morning without fail."

"But I do," Isobel insisted. Dolph dropped an affectionate kiss on the back of her hand. "No, you don't, Bell – you just think you do."

The dining room part of Uncle Hansi's palace on wheels was smaller than the parlor, just barely large enough to seat ten at the table, with the two little Vining boys sharing one chair. Hansi Richter presided over the head of the table, with Magda Becker at the foot. The table was as finely set with fine silverware, china and crystal arrayed on crisp white linen, all gleaming under the lamplight. Only the movement of the railway carriage and the flickering of the lights suspended from the car's ornate ceiling betrayed the fact that they were not sitting down to dine in some elegant establishment. Absalom brought out each course from the tiny galley kitchen; simply cooked but delicious, and poured wine with the ceremony of a maître d' hotel of a much larger establishment. Isobel thought that she had never eaten so well while traveling – certainly never while traveling on a train, not even on those occasions when the kitchen at Acton had provided a picnic hamper for the journey. The conversation was general and animated. Seb Bertrand and Horrie Vining were to accompany the cattle drive and were excited beyond all words; boy-like, they did their best to conceal it, while Peter Vining and Dolph looked on with expressions of amused toleration and Uncle Richter beamed indulgently on all. When the last course was finished, Isobel and Anna, with Lottie and her mother withdrew to the parlor to leave the men and the two boys to their cigars and port. The little Vining boys and the baby had been put to bed under the supervision of Jane, who had gratified Isobel by offering her services. Now Isobel followed Anna onto the observation deck; the evening was cool, the sky above sprinkled with stars. Anna settled onto one of the wicker chairs and rolled herself a cigarette

"They seem so very excited over the drive to . . . where is this Palo Duro place?" Isobel asked of Anna, somewhat nervously. Anna, effortlessly chic and slender, competent in the ways of the world, was everything that Isobel wanted in herself, but despaired of ever attaining.

"It's away to the north in the Llano country, nearly five hundred miles from our established interests, or any interests until a few years ago. It's nearly all prairie grassland, open plains . . . rich grass and good for grazing cattle. The Palo Duro is a great canyon in the middle of it, where the Comanche had their winter camps, once. You know about the Comanche Indians, of course."

"Yes, I had heard much of them," Isobel answered. For a brief moment, a tiny frown line appeared between Anna's brows and her expression darkened. "Ah. You have heard, which is different from experiencing the threat they posed to us all. They raided often, from the earliest years of settlements here. They were murderous and cruel, crueler to the innocent and helpless than you can imagine in your worst dreams, but the Army finally put a stop to them. I was glad of that and I am not in the least ashamed to say so to such fools who wring their hands over the poor misunderstood Indians. They are shut up on their Reservation in the Territory; now we can go about our business without fear . . . of the Comanche, although there are still too many cattle thieves. Dolphchen says that you will go with him to help establish the new ranch."

"I like horses and cows," Isobel answered. She was taken back at the bitter passion in Anna's voice when she spoke of the Comanche, but it only distracted her briefly. "Some have spoken of the beauty of the country and the stars at night. There is much that I wish to see for myself. I have never cared for the social round and the seasons of Society. It would be a great adventure, beginning a new venture with my husband."

"Adventure is what it will be . . . maybe," Anna's expression softened into wry laughter. "You have no idea of how much trouble the cattle can be and how slowly they move along the trail. It may take as long as two months to reach the Palo Duro. You will be quite thoroughly bored of it by the time you reach there . . . and then, to establish the ranch. You will live under canvas for a time, I think." For the first time, she looked at Isobel with intense interest. "What then, can you do? Have you any skills of use in this venture?"

"I can ride any horse ever foaled," Isobel answered. "Over practically any country, no matter how rough. I know some useful medical remedies for animals. I can cook, a little. I can read and write, and I know . . ." Her voice died away. It was s sadly limited collection of talents. "That doesn't sound very promising. But I am not afraid."

Anna did not look as if she disparaged Isobel's meager skills. "Good. Good that you fear little. There are many hands who can neither read nor write and know only enough numbers to make tally marks, so you might be at least a little ahead. You should study a brand book. Can you shoot?"

"Of course. My father is a keen hunter and my brother taught me how to use a pistol."

"Excellent," Anna blew out a cloud of smoke and the end of the cigarette glowed briefly red-gold in the twilight. "I will make a list of what you should bring." She laid her head against the chair back and surveyed Isobel, her eyes half closed and a trickle of smoke rising up from her cigarette. Abruptly she said, "There are two kinds of wives here, you know. Which kind do you want to be, dear little English Isobel?"

"I don't know what you mean," Isobel replied. Anna drew deep on her cigarette before she answered. "Yes, you do. You were, I think – trained to be the ornamental wife; to bear children and keep the household. The angel of the house, they call such wives. Do not think I scorn them. I do not. My mother is one. She dotes on Papa, spends his money, makes the house pleasant for him, loves pretty dresses and parties, and tended devotedly to all their children. All but one of my brothers and sisters who are of age are happy, settled in marriage or a trade of their own; Mama's doing, as much as Papa's. But she took no interest in his business affairs; that was my concern and Auntie Magda's. The other kind of wife – and there are many out here, as you may yet discover – is a partner in whatever business their husband pursues. They keep the books and accounts, they manage whatever establishment their man owns, they supervise the workers and they have their husband's trust in such matters to do with the conduct of it. It can be no other way, especially in a place like the Palo Duro. There will be a foreman, wranglers, and hands.

When your husband is not there, they will look to his wife to use his authority. Are you ready for that, little English Isobel?"

"I expect that I must," Isobel answered, putting as brave a face upon it as she could, although her heart sank. She knew next to nothing about this place. Much of what she had been schooled in – Society, Court decorum, and the endless rules for propter behavior – would be perfectly useless. "I will try, at least – to be a partner in my husband's business. I don't know if I shall be any good at it, though."

"But you will try," Anna blew out a cloud of smoke. "With that, you may be well on the way to being that which you wish to be. Cheer up, English Isobel; you met my dear cousin's requirements for a wife, so he may repose great trust in you already."

For another day and night Isobel, her husband's family, and Seb Bertrand reveled in the comfort of Hansi Richter's palace car, as it rolled at a brisk twenty or thirty miles every hour, only slowing down for a stop at each town. In some places, they interrupted the journey for as much as half an hour, so that regular passengers could get a meal from whatever restaurant or boarding house was nearby. Isobel did not grudge the delay. It was a chance for her to take Gawain and Sorsha on their leashes for a walk and obey such calls of nature as affected them. Quite often old Mrs. Becker and Lottie accompanied her with Mouse the lapdog, for the same purpose. Oftentimes there were those on the platform who gawked openly at the enormous dogs or at the splendor of the palace car. To Isobel's amusement, Alf Trotter styled his skinny twelve-year-old self as their official protector. Such seemed hardly necessary, especially as she and Jane, Lottie and Mrs. Becker were treated with extraordinary deference and courtesy by the ordinary run of men, even the youngest.

"It is the custom of this country," Old Mrs. Becker explained, in her thick German accent, as she and Lottie and Jane walked the length of the platform with the dogs, at midday of the second day. "The men are schooled to be perfect paladins, even if they dress in rags and live in a hovel. From earliest childhood, they are told that to be a proper gallant gentleman is the ideal for which they must aspire. Sometimes the semblance of a prince in manners is all the riches they have."

"That, and a large hat and a couple of revolvers," Isobel answered. Her mother-in-law chuckled in wry amusement, rather to Isobel's surprise. She had not believed herself capable of saying anything that would amuse or entertain the elder Mrs. Becker, so severe and serious. In her way, Dolph's mother was as terrifying as Lady Caroline.

"Also!" Mrs. Becker agreed. "It was so, when I first arrived in this country." She nodded in acknowledgement to a gentleman with a cane, who doffed his own hat, as the women passed. Isobel asked, "Dear Mother Becker . . . how long was it since you arrived in this country?"

"Thirty years," Mrs. Becker answered. "We also came first to Galveston and I marveled even then. The war was about to begin; a war between Mexico and the United States. There were uniforms everywhere, but I thought nothing of it. I did wonder at the courtly manners of even the meanest and lowest. My father wrote in a letter to his friend back in Ulm that it was as if each man were a nobleman, disguised in the rags of a beggar. Such are also quick to anger at an affront to honor. With each man thinking he is the equal of any other and quick to take anger at an insult." She turned to look at Isobel, and smiled in a reassuring way. Just then, Mouse snarled at Gawain, who had walked too close and sniffed at the smaller dog in a manner which Mouse clearly saw as overfamiliarity. Gawain immediately veered away, and Mouse stalked on his way, all fifteen pounds of fluff and importance. "Sometimes," Mrs. Becker added, "It is enough to look like one is eager to defend the rights one has. Do you recollect that Mr. Swain, in the station at Houston? He was one of those. To appear as if one is ready to fight is often enough to win it, before ever being fought. So my husband said. He was one who came to Texas in the earliest days. He was a small child then. His father was one of the first Americans come to settle on lands that the Mexicans offered, you see. A difficult man, I have heard; and quarrelsome in the extreme. But many others followed over the path they wore smooth."

"To have seen such marvelous enterprises as a town or a farm . . . even a railway, all built in a single lifetime still seems extraordinary to me." Isobel remarked, as they reached the very end of the platform. This town, where the train had paused was one of the more long-established, so the train station was itself on the outskirts. From the end of the platform, Isobel and her mother-in-law gazed out at an open prairie, an endless sweep of grasslands, dotted here and there with massive dark green oaks. The most distant hills faded to shades of blue and lavender. The sky arched overhead, a clear and pure blue, unsullied by smoke from coal fires and industry, marred only by clouds floating serenely in it. "There is nothing of great antiquity here. It lends to the feeling of emptiness about these lands." Isobel ventured. Mrs. Becker nodded in agreement.

"Such marvels here are constructed by nature," she answered. "When we first came from Germany, there was less than this, not even a road. There were the trees, and the stones, those few Indians who passed over – they left their shadows, little more. Perhaps the flints where they made arrow-heads and the bones of the deer and bison that they hunted. We came from Bavaria, where the newest house in our village was built in the time of my father's grandfather! This is our home, now . . . and will be yours. This place will claim you, although it may not seem so yet."

"I do so hope," Isobel agreed, warmed by the older woman's sensitivity. At that moment, the steam whistle on the train blew a warning of departure. They must turn around and hurry with the dogs to the palace car, where Absalom watched for them with impatience.

The railroad's steel rails had not yet reached San Antonio, as Hansi Richter had complained at breakfast on the second day. They must break their journey at the busy town of Seguin and continue on by carriage. Isobel was not surprised in the least to find two equipages and a wagon for the luggage waiting for them.

"Uncle Hansi believes that the telegram is an even greater invention than the steam engine," Dolph observed, as he handed Isobel into the first carriage. "We'll be in San Antonio in time for dinner."

"Is San Antonio as modern as Galveston?" Isobel settled herself, as Lottie and Jane followed her, assisted by Dolph and Sam's strong hands. Dolph laughed at that. "No, Bell, darlin' – San Antonio is ancient, as things here go. You'll see."

Excitement buoyed Isobel, so close to the end of that journey, although she noticed that Jane looked quite drained and tired, sharing little of Isobel's interest in the passing scenery. Again, it recalled to her the parklands around Acton Hall. In late afternoon, she noticed substantial stone buildings scattered amongst the trees and gardens, and a cluster of taller structures ahead. There were a great many with roofs of faded rust-red or rose-colored tiles, surrounding several tall spires and domes. As they drew closer, more and more of it appeared, modestly veiled in tall trees. Lottie chattered, excitedly pointing out this landmark or that – a tall mill building of honey-colored brick, an ancient cross-topped church dome. Everything in field and grove was green, nearly as green as those eastern parts of Texas where their journey had begun. The countryside became laced with small rivers – or perhaps it was the same river, looping back and forth under the road, which crossed it on a succession of narrow stone bridges – and netted with the straight lines of small stone-lined channels. Isobel looked back at the carriage following. Hansi Richter had settled onto the coach box next to the driver and was at the reins. She recollected that her husband had told her that his uncle had begun as a wagoneer; he drove with considerable skill and very little use of the whip.

"The old Spanish friars, they designed irrigation ditches to water the fields," Dolph explained over his shoulder, from where he sat with the driver. "There is water everywhere around here. It springs up from the ground in fountains. There was not any other place like it for hundreds of miles, so this is where the built their missions. Then they brought in settlers to make a town and made the oldest mission into the presidio – a military fort to defend these parts. It's pretty tumbledown these days. The Army is planning to move their wagon yard and barracks out to a new fort north of town. Uncle Hansi's house is this way. All the German merchants built their houses on the south side of town."

A side road, another turning, and the two carriages with the wagon lumbering a fair distance after, came to an avenue lined with tall, spreading oaks. That road, paved in crushed pale stone, ended at the river bank, where deep clear water was shaded by yet more tall trees. Before they came that far, though, there was a drive and a tall and gaily-painted house, adorned with quantities of wooden fretwork lace and surrounded by an apron of carefully tended lawns and gardens – gardens planted with bright pink and yellow roses. Isobel stifled a small and dolorous sigh; yet another arrival and more of her husband's wide-spread family. This would not be quite as daunting as the first and by way of consolation, she already had come to an amiable acquaintance – nay, even friendship with Anna, Lottie and her mother-in-law. But this was the one arena where more would be expected of her in a society setting, even if she couldn't possibly be judged as harshly as she had been over the previous year. Isobel sensed that she was suspended somewhat uncomfortably between what she had been and what she might be, if she truly became a partner to her husband, that soft-spoken stranger she had wed in desperation. That he was kind and had rescued her from an intolerable situation would only take her so far along that road. *Heart up, Bell*, his voice whispered in her ears; *the tallest fence and deepest ditch.*

Well, this was only a low fence and a small ditch, and Jane was with her. Isobel could not think of anyone of significance left for her to meet, save his sister in her convent – and Auntie Liesel Richter, the doyenne of such local society as would exist in this place. *How formidable could the wife of such a bourgeoisie be?*

Not formidable at all; she was a plump fussy woman, somewhat over-dressed and with her hair in elaborate curls. She came running down the front stairs of the bright-painted mansion, gasping endearments and throwing herself into the arms of Uncle Richter with exuberant affection. She chattered in a garble of German and such deeply accented English that Isobel could not make out a single word, embraced her daughter, and – Isobel could not mistake the chiding tone of voice – dispatched the Vining boys into the house. Then it was Isobel's turn to be enveloped in too many lacy ruffles and the scent of rosewater. Isobel still couldn't understand a single word Aunt Liesel said. She looked despairingly at her husband.

"I don't know what she is saying!" She whispered.

"Auntie always forgets her English when she is excited," Dolph whispered back and then he addressed Auntie Liesel, who covered her mouth with her hands and laughed, exclaiming breathlessly, "Oh-oh, I am sorry!" Then she was off again, in her mix of garbled English and German. Dolph looked sideways at Isobel. "She is thrilled beyond words to welcome you to hers and Onkel Hansi's house. There was a mention in the newspaper, so she has been receiving callers asking after us for weeks. She is thrilled beyond words that I am married at last . . . and she ventured something indelicate about our first child."

"What?" Isobel exclaimed. "What did she say about a first child?"

"She wondered if we had started one yet," Dolph answered, looking studiously over their heads. "Auntie Liesel dearly loves babies and always thought it no end of fun in starting them, you see."

Isobel didn't know whether to be shocked or amused. She knew for a certainty that Lady Caroline would have been appalled and Jane, now being assisted down from the carriage by Sam Becker, would be shocked to the depths of her prim and working-class soul to hear this peasant crudity. "Say to your aunt whatever is polite . . . and I don't think there is, of yet. A child," Isobel finally brought herself to answer. She was certain of this; her monthly course had occurred during the journey to Galveston."

"I will tell her that we are trying – most enjoyably," Dolph whispered, his lips very close to her ear.

"Don't you dare!" Isobel hissed. From the way that Aunt Liesel was looking at their faces, Isobel feared that she had understood every word.

A few afternoons after their arrival, Isobel invited Anna to her room, asking for advice on what clothing she ought to take with her on the long drive north with the cattle to the new ranch on the Palo Duro. This was all that her

husband and his uncle talked of and everyone accepted that Isobel would
accompany her husband. Anna spent some minutes, looking over the clothing
that Isobel had Jane bring out from out of her trunks, which she thought might
be suitable for the overland journey by horseback and wagon.

"This, this, and maybe the riding habit, for after the journey. Plain linen
petticoats and drawers. Skirts in plain heavy cloth and bodices of dark cloth,
to wear with them. Loose; you will not want to lace so tightly. You will need
to dress as plainly as your maid. Do not forget the wash-tub. Whatever you
wear, be assured you will be washing it yourself. Do you have any plain hats
with a wide brim?"

"No," Isobel answered, horrified at the thought of having to do washing.
Anna sighed, kindly but exasperated. "I will call for the carriage. We must
then go to town."

Anna directed her firmly into one of the largest mercantile establishments
in San Antonio. Once there, she marched Isobel into the gentlemen's
haberdashery section. There she selected two hats for her, one of felt, the other
of straw, a number of large calico kerchiefs, and several pair of heavy leather
gloves.

"You will be driving a wagon," Anna explained. "The wagon that will be
your home for the journey. My husband always had me to follow the cook-
wagon, ahead of the herd and the dust. I am reminded; there is a Parker shotgun which goes with the wagon. Under the seat is best. It is simple to use.
You can shoot a pistol? Do you have one of your own?"

"It wasn't thought to be a necessary wedding gift," Isobel answered. Her
attempt at humor went straight past Anna. "It is when on a trail drive," Anna
replied. She led Isobel to a display case full of pistols, some as fine as anything
seen in England, studying them with the considered air of a connoisseur of
the gun-making profession. To the evident surprise of the young man
attending on them, Anna passed over the various fancy nickel and silver-
plated sidearms in favor of a long-barreled model with plain polished walnut
grips and a dull, matte metal finish.

"It is the very newest model Colt," she explained, indicating to the young
counterman to take it from the case. "This is the one approved for the Army
– should it be too heavy for you, they make several smaller versions. Here,"
she handed it to Isobel. "Good that you have strong hands. I think this will
suit." She nodded at the counterman, "This and six boxes of cartridges. You'll
want to carry it in a belt-holster, I think. It may not be the latest fashion in
London and Paris but better to have and not need, then need and not have at

hand. There are no constables on the cattle trail. Sometimes rattlesnakes, though."

"Do you carry a pistol, Anna?" Isobel demanded in mild horror. The mention of snakes made her skin crawl. Anna nodded, crisply. "Not ordinarily. When I accompanied my husband on the trail – of course. At home and here, there is no need. It is quite civilized. But once there was a need." She looked sideways at Isobel, and hesitated. "Auntie Magda has a pistol with her, always when she travels."

"Good heavens!" Isobel gasped. "Has she ever had cause to use it?"

Anna hesitated again, considering her answer carefully. "Once. Just after the war, in Fredericksburg. She and I kept a store there, for Papa and our Opa. One day, there was a dangerous criminal come to town, a man who was being hunted by the Sheriff and everyone. I do not know what happened, exactly. Auntie and Lottie were returning from an errand, not knowing of this . . . what do they call – hue and cry? Lottie was a child the age of Harry. What I heard was that the man tried to take Lottie as a hostage from Auntie Magda – to use to escape from town. Auntie Magda shot him with her pistol. It is not a thing well-known, even in the family. We do not speak of it even now. That man had friends. For all they know, he fell dead in the middle of the street and no one knows who killed him. But we know that Auntie Magda did, protecting Lottie."

Isobel recalled that young man – *Swain; was that his name?* The man who had bought her iced water, as she and the others waited for their train. Her husband and the others had looked at and spoken to him warily, as if he was one of those dangerous men. Certainly to have a pistol near at hand, might very well be a reassurance in such a wild and lawless country as this, where dangerous criminals did as they pleased.

Barely a week after their arrival, Jane dressed her lady for another grand ball. It was queerly reminiscent of the Christmas ball at Acton. *Was that only been six months ago?* The whole affair was otherwise as different as it could possibly be. Mrs. Liesel Richter had been buzzing about the house like a fat and exotically-dressed bee for the week since their arrival; now there was a dance floor laid on the lawn nearest the house and a band already playing popular music in the garden pavilion. The whole was lit by strings of exotic Japanese-style paper lanterns, which bobbed gently in the light evening breeze. Carriages and been arriving and depositing guests in the porte-cochère for the last hour or so. Jane shook her head and then wished she hadn't for she had such an awful headache. She had been feeling achy and unwell for some days, but nothing could have forced a complaint past her lips – not when her lady was about to enter into the lists of this Society. Jane regarded Lady Isobel's reflection in the tall dressing-table mirror with approval. She was laced into a low-cut ball-gown from her trousseau, a confection of up-to-the-minute London fashion from the atelier which Lady Caroline favored. As befitted a married woman, this dress was dark blue and cut in flattering lines, although Isobel laughed and said that her corset was laced so tightly that she would be entirely breathless after a single dance. She wore her wedding-present necklace of gold and blue enameled flowers, and Jane was just now piling up the bountiful waves of her hair, and adorning it with a simple agliette of gold lace and deep blue peacock feathers.

"You do not want to outdo your hostess," Jane observed. Isobel pealed with laughter. "She is kindness itself, but everything that my mother and her circle warned against; provincial newly-rich, with pretentions and ambition to take Society by storm. Crass and crude, not to mention vulgar . . ."

"It offers an easier situation for her than virtuous poverty." Jane was stung enough to venture that opinion in defense of the cattle baron and his lady. In those moments when they took note of her at all, they had been unfailingly kind and considerate, as if there were no gulf at all between her station and theirs save a temporary embarrassment on her part of not having an income greater than twenty-five shillings a month. "And the railway coach was very comfortable."

"I am reproved, Jane." Isobel met her eyes in the mirror. "Aunt Richter is generous with her house and her hospitality, but I wish that she was not such a fright! I am certain that she was pretty when young, but now she is so like a comic image of an American millionairess!"

"She seems very well-liked," Jane observed. Isobel nodded. This was self-evidently true; there had been a constant stream of visitors to the painted mansion, partaking of the generous hospitality extended by the cattle baron and baroness. While Isobel suspected that most of Liesel Richter's callers were motivated by curiosity regarding herself, most appeared to hold her hostess in fond affection. She had detected none of that veiled malice which made Lady Caroline's at-home afternoons and her debut year such a trial. "On the other hand," Isobel said out loud. "Perhaps I do not know Americans well enough yet to detect any save what is on the surface. Am I ready for the evening, Jane?"

"Yes, Milady," Jane handed her the long gloves and the dance-card, hanging from a loop of silken cord. Her head felt like it was splitting, and perhaps it showed on her face, for Isobel paused and said, with sudden concern, "Are you unwell, Jane? You should go and lie down. My husband says that these parties last until dawn – if I need assistance during the evening, then I shall ask one of Aunt Richter's maids for it."

"I should stay in readiness, Milady," Jane insisted bravely, but Isobel demurred. "No, Jane, I insist. I could not enjoy myself, knowing that you were waiting on me and feeling ill. Besides," she added, as she collected the loop that discretely held up the train of her dress, in a rustle of silk. "We will embark on another journey soon – just think of what an adventure it will be, Jane – north with the cattle herd. That will be taxing enough, I am certain!'

"Yes, Milady," Jane yielded gratefully; her head really did ache. She lingered a moment in the suite of rooms that Mr. Becker and Lady Isobel shared, for the largest window overlooked the terrace and the lawn where the ball was taking place. Such a lovely sight; the lights and the gorgeously colored gowns of the ladies, and the music; already some couples were dancing. Jane leaned her aching head against the glass; yes, there was Miss Lottie Becker, with young Mr. Bertrand. To her vague astonishment, the older Mrs. Becker was dancing, too – her partner a stout mustachioed gentlemen in black, his short jacket trimmed with many silver buttons that flashed briefly in the light, as he turned with his partner in the steps of a lively schottische. So very many guests, Jane thought; some plainly dressed, and yet others as elegant as any who joined in the revels last Christmas at Acton. There was Mr. Becker down below on the edge of the terrace, standing with a tall man whose shock of white hair contrasted oddly with his ginger-red beard, deep in conversation. Now there was a stirring among those on the terrace below, as if in a disturbance among a bevy of hens in the farmyard. They were turning to see someone emerge from the house; Lady Isobel. It gratified Jane that her lady was the cynosure of all eyes, as her husband took her arm with his usual courtesy. She lingered for a moment, seeing Mr. Becker introduce his wife to the gentlemen whom he had been in such close conversation. It all looked as if it were going well, so Jane abandoned her post at the window, gathered up some small things at the dressing table and saw that her ladyship's nightgown was laid out. The ache in her head redoubled, so she took herself off to her own room and went to bed, soothed by the faint strains of music that came drifting on on the night's cool breeze.

Chapter 11 – *Trailing North*

A week after the grand ball at the Richter mansion, Mr. Becker and his party commenced the next leg of their journey. Jane felt little better – in fact, appreciably worse, but it relieved her no end to know that Lady Isobel's turn through the social whirl of San Antonio society was completed. She could relax her guard and care of her lady for at least a little bit. It had proved to be a bad week for Jane. None of those nostrums and remedies which Aunt Lydia had schooled her in provided any relief and neither did a covert consultation of Lady Isobel's cobble-stone thick edition of *Mrs. Beeton's Guide to Household Management.* Besides the headaches and bouts of chills and fever, Jane increasingly felt listless and tired. For all that her lady was excited about seeing the home that her husband's father had built and which would be her own, Jane couldn't share those feelings. All that she wished most sincerely to do was to lie down and sleep. Her body ached with exhaustion. She thought longingly of the cool and misty greenness of England and the little dormitory under the eaves of Acton Hall where the maids slept.

Today was set for their departure to the headquarters ranch, on the upper reaches of the Guadalupe River. To her ladyship's infinite joy, her husband had procured a proper saddle horse for her and the cattle baron's groom and man of all work had managed to search out Lady Isobel's side saddle from among the trunks and crates of her baggage. There was a horse for Alf Trotter, which rendered that young man speechless with awe and gratitude. Jane was only grateful that she was not expected to ride. For her, old Mrs. Becker, and Miss Lottie there was an odd-looking spring conveyance with a canvas top and sides which rolled neatly up.

"It's the old ambulance," Lottie explained, with happy excitement. "Onkel Hansi bought it to use as a cook-wagon once, but we have used it ever since, because it is so comfortable for a long journey."

"How far is it to the ranch?" Jane asked, as a sudden wave of faintness overtook her. She fought it back, just as Sam Becker took her arm to help her up through the door at the back of the wagon.

"Sixty miles, more or less," he answered cheerily. "We'll be there by suppertime, as long as we don't press the horses too hard." He was again to be their coachman. Jane still found it disquieting how much these people preferred to do for themselves, rather than hire servants. Sam handed up his sister and closed the door on them. In a minute, the wagon jostled on its springs. They were off, following after the mounted members of the party;

Mr. Becker, her lady, Seb Bertrand and Alf, with the wolfhounds loping after them as the cattle baron, Mrs. Liesel, and the Vinings waved their farewells from the shaded front porch of the painted mansion.

Jane found the inside of the ambulance comfortable enough. A pair of long padded seats the length of the wagon bed faced each other. With the canvas sides rolled up, there was nothing to impede the view, or the light spring breeze that cooled her cheeks. She was not particularly interested in the sights of the bustling town of San Antonio, such as they were; muddy streets lined with thick-walled, ancient-looking buildings plastered with stucco, alternating now and again with larger frame-built ones. The streets were busy at this hour of the morning, and the wide plaza that opened at the top of the main street was busiest of all. The scent of roasting meats and scented wood smoke wafted towards them briefly, from a row of little booths and trestle-tables set up at the edge of the next plaza. Even at mid-morning, the tables groaned with bowls of the peppery-red meat stew, and the benches were close-packed with hungry customers. It was all very alien, very colorful, but Jane had no particular interest in it for her misery. Sitting wedged into the back corner of the ambulance, she let her throbbing head rest against the padded seatback. Soothed by the gentle rocking of the metal springs, she supposed that she fell asleep. The last thing that she recalled was that the pace of the horses drawing it had increased to a lively trot and she thought they must now be leaving town.

Jane woke from that doze when the wagon stopped and sat up blinking. The sides of the wagon were still rolled up; beyond them she could see only trees and an inviting meadow of grass, with the sky beyond. They must have stopped for a picnic luncheon at the side of the road which led up into the hills, for all the horses were set out at the ends of ropes to graze in the grass at some distance.

Old Mrs. Becker was looking quizzically down at her, saying, *"Was ist los?"* Jane looked at her, not understanding. "What is the matter?" the older woman repeated, patiently. "Are you ailing?"

"I have a headache," Jane answered. "And I feel sometimes hot, then cold, as if I can never get warm again." Mrs. Becker looked at her thoughtfully. She had taken off her gloves. Now she touched Jane's forehead lightly with the inside of her wrist, and drew back her hand with a hiss of astonishment. "A fever, too. A very high fever; you are burning up. You should lie down, rest now. I will tell the others. We are close to Comfort now, farther from the city. Otherwise I would tell my sons to return there at once."

She withdrew from the wagon. Jane, feeling very much as if the world had gone slightly fuzzy around her, took off her bonnet and lay at full length on the narrow bench. That was a little better. She heard voices; Mrs. Becker, Lottie, her ladyship, and a more distant sound of Mr. Becker's voice issuing crisp orders. There came a scrape of wood on wood, and the wagon jostled a little.

Now it was Mrs. Becker's mild voice, seasoned with that harsh-sounding accent. "Drink this; it is a tincture of quinine. I fear that you have the malaria, what they call the ague." She lifted Jane's head, and held a tin cup to her lips. The liquid in it was bitter. Jane didn't want to drink, but Mrs. Becker was relentless. When Jane had swallowed the last vile-tasting drop, the older woman wrapped a heavy travel-rug around her. Paradoxically, now she was shivering with the phantom cold and was grateful for the warmth of the rough wool. Between the gentle rocking of the ambulance and the heat of her own fever, she fell into a troubled sleep. She remained aware of Mrs. Becker's hovering presence, all that long afternoon and the motherly hands which now and again wiped her face and hands with a damp verbena-scented cloth. This kindness brought a brief coolness to her fever and a respite to those dreams which now and again troubled her sleep.

Once, when she swam up to the surface of consciousness, it was Lady Isobel holding her hands, while bright tears trickled down her cheeks. "Jane, dear – I am so sorry, I ought to have known! You should have said something. I knew you had headaches, but I didn't think it was anything like this."

"I couldn't," Jane whispered. "You depend so on me. I couldn't leave you alone."

"Then don't, dear Jane." Isobel blotted Jane's face with a handkerchief. "My husband has ridden ahead to fetch a doctor from Comfort. And we will be at the ranch very shortly – you will be well and we will go to the new ranch together. And do you know? We might ride together in a wagon very like this!" She went on talking, while Jane drifted away into slumber, oddly comforted by the sound of her lady's voice. Sometime – perhaps a brief, or maybe a long time later, she was aware that she was being carried in a man's arms. She thought it was her father and she a small child again, safe in the strong arms of someone who loved her. The easy rocking movement of the carriage had ceased.

"To the small bedchamber, Sam." That was the voice of the older Mrs. Becker, decisive and also oddly comforting. There was another voice, a woman speaking in a quick percussive rattle of Spanish. The last thing that Jane was aware of for quite some time was that someone was helping her remove her dress, petticoats, and shoes. She shivered so hard in the sudden chill that her teeth chattered together, and gratefully sank down into the bed under blankets they piled on her, as thick as the snow around Acton Hall in the winter.

Isobel adored the Becker home-place at once, a tall house set on a knoll above the lazy bends of the cypress-lined Guadalupe River. As soon as she walked into the stone-built house, surrounded by meadows and the walled orchard of apple trees, she felt oddly at home. It took her but a short time to reason out why; it reminded her of the Home Farm at Acton. There was solidity and an agelessness to the Becker's home, with the apple branch and bird in the nest carved over the front door, the tall shutters that stood open to the light spring breeze. The outside walls had weathered to the color of old ivory. Inside, they were whitewashed. The rooms upstairs had their walls pleasingly tinted in pastel colors. All was plainly and comfortably furnished with furniture of agreeably ageless design; sturdy chairs and chests, spotlessly clean and polished. Pots of violets sat on many of the windowsills, perfuming the air with sweetness. To her vague astonishment, the Beckers had a housekeeper in residence, a quick-moving little Mexican woman about Mrs. Becker's age, whom they addressed as Tia Leticia. Sam, Lottie, and her husband chatted easily with her in Spanish, when they had arrived that afternoon. Isobel had not seen her since, as she took ready charge of the sickroom, rattling off brisk orders in her own language.

"I have dreamed of a home like this," Isobel said to her husband that evening, inexpressibly happy at the end of this journey. They sat in the parlor, where a tripartite window offered a view of the orchard on the slope below the house and the meadows beyond, all the way down to the river – marked by the line of tall green trees and shrubs, and the fading purple and blue outlines of distant hills. Lottie was showing Seb Bertrand around the ranch headquarters; Isobel heard their voices from the walled orchard below. Now Sam sat on the hearthrug, absorbed in a sketch of Sorsha and Gawain that he was drawing, in quick strokes of his pencil, while the dogs lay tranquilly sleeping. "In my deepest heart, I did not want a grand mansion! I loved the Hall but I always longed for a cozy little cottage. To return to a place like this will be a joy. It will be hard to tear myself away for the cattle drive; I think I love your house almost as much as yourself."

"That is a good thing to know," Dolph replied. He looked pleased also. "I promised you that there were dogs and horses about, as well as cows."

The one dark marring of Isobel's pleasure was worry and guilt over Jane. How could she have not seen that Jane was truly ill? Of course, Mrs. Becker assured her that such an affliction as the ague came on almost without warning. Even so, Jane had lately complained of a headaches, she who had otherwise enjoyed robust good health in all the time that she had been Isobel's personal attendant. Isobel should have noticed how wan and feverish Jane had been, but the excitement of the journey and the merry whirl of hospitality in San Antonio had distracted her, and poor Jane was too much of a stoic to complain.

Now there came a step on the stairs in the hallway outside the parlor. Mrs. Becker came into the parlor, setting aside a large apron as she did so. She appeared more gaunt than usual. Before Isobel could get the words from her mouth, her mother-in-law said, "She is resting comfortably, your Miss Jane. The doctor says that it is the malaria. He has doubled the dose of quinine. She will not recover complete health for some weeks, perhaps months. The ague reoccurs, you know."

"There is no danger of death, is there?" Isobel asked, piteously. Mrs. Becker shook her head. "No, but I do not think you will have a maid for some time. There is no question of Miss Jane going with you to the Palo Duro in two weeks. The doctor forbids it. So do I."

"But surely, we can delay departing, if it a matter of her health," Isobel suggested. "Jane is at least as much my friend as my maid. I did not consider going anywhere without her."

"You will have to consider it, Bell, darlin'," Dolph answered with blunt directness. "We are already set to depart with the cattle in fourteen days. There's too much already put into motion. We can't delay by as much as another week. Come with me to the Palo Duro, or stay here with your Miss Jane until we meet again at Christmastime in Austin with Cuz and his tribe. That's six months from now; your choice, Bell." Isobel looked between her husband, and his mother, stricken to silence by the enormity of the decision before her.

Sam lifted his head from his sketching, his usual merry expression dimmed and somber. "Mama and I can see to Isobel and Miss Jane both, if they stay here," he ventured and Mrs. Becker looked stern. "A wife's place should be with her husband," she said only.

"Then I should go with you," Isobel answered, though she felt wretchedly torn. "If Jane cannot be moved . . . is there a means for us to stay until she is well, then both of us follow after?" Her voice died away, as Dolph's expression turned thunderous.

"This matter is complicated enough as it is, Bell. You are not accustomed to our ways – for you and Miss Jane to journey alone, or in a wagon with a few of the hands? I won't even consider it. Come with me in two weeks, or not at all."

"Then I will go with you," Isobel answered. Having made the decision gave her no comfort at all. Remaining with her loyal servant Jane or going with her lawfully-wedded husband? There was no good solution to this dilemma. If she stayed at the Becker ranch for the remainder of the year, she was disloyal to the husband she barely knew. If she went with him, she was abandoning poor Jane to the care of strangers. As she mused upon this bitter situation, Sam finished his sketch with a few deft strokes of his pencil, and came to sit beside her. Dolph had been called into the next room, a study which served as his office.

"It's only proper that you go with Dolph," he reassured her. "Mama and Tia Leticia will see to Jane. You shouldn't worry; Tia Leticia knows all about nursing folk with the ague and shivers. After supper, maybe you can sit up with Jane for a while."

"Thank you," Isobel quavered. Sam was so kind. So was Dolph, of course; but as brothers they could not have been less alike. Sam was cheerful, as transparent as water, his every thought an open book, while Dolph kept his his private feelings on most matters always to himself. In one way they were similar; they were both gallant, perfect knights. The courtly manners of this rough country had schooled them both in rustic chivalry.

"With Tia Leticia and her girls to look after them all, Jane will have all the rest she needs, and the time to get well," Sam said again. "Although I don't know that Mama and Lottie have need of a ladies' maid. Summer here is a rest from Auntie Liesel and her society friends and Onkel Hansi's businesses. Mama puts on her plainest gown, works in her garden, and teaches Lottie to make cheese and apple pie."

"It sounds very bucolic," Isobel offered, dubiously. Sam laughed.

"Yes it is – but it's usually a lot of work for me . . . especially this last year. I had the whole responsibility of it and a long road to Kansas and back. Now it's Dolph's turn. Still, we love this place. We had to leave it during the War, you know. The Army burned most of the old buildings down. It was Dolph and Cuz and Onkel Fredi who rebuilt it all, and Onkel Hansi who decided that we should get into cattle in a big way."

"You are fortunate to be born into a family with such advantages," Isobel observed. "You have been raised in a particular industry – and poor Mr. Bertrand must be schooled in it now from the beginning."

Sam shrugged. "Truth to tell, I work at it for the good of the family . . . but I'm not so much interested in it, the way Dolph, or Seb is. My brother is a good cattleman because he was born to it, and he loves every bit of the business. Seb wants to be a good cattleman because he also loves every bit. So does Onkel Fredi. Me, I am just born to it." This was curious. Isobel would have asked more, but for a breathless Lottie coming into the parlor, trailing Seb Bertrand after her, like the tail on a particularly exuberant kite.

"So, what do you think, Sister Isobel!" she exclaimed. "Is it not the most perfect house that you have ever seen?"

"It is," Isobel agreed, and in the chatter as one of the Mexican girls came into the parlor to say that supper was ready, she lost the opportunity of asking Sam what he might rather have been doing.

After supper, Isobel climbed the stairs, and found her way to the little room where Jane lay. The door to it stood open and a small lamp burned inside. The chair next to the bed was empty. Mrs. Becker and Tia Leticia were for the moment, not watching over their patient, although Mrs. Becker's tiny wooden sewing box stood on the bedside table next to the lamp and a basket of mending sat on the floor beside the chair. Isobel's throat felt as if it would close for tears – how very plain, and simple. No minute went past, without that her mother-in-laws' hands were not taken up with some useful work.

She down, overcome by a feeling that she was useless, as useless and inept as Lady Caroline thought she was and implied so with every slighting word and gesture. Jane was her friend, her only friend. In two weeks she would have to depart with her husband and leave Jane here. Jane was sleeping now, although she did so restlessly. Jane took the hand that lay slack outside the blankets that covered her, and was stuck again at how young Jane looked, how small that hand was, cradled in hers. That face on the pillow looked to be little more than than a child. Jane had such determination, such presence that she usually seemed older. So confident, so capable; all the qualities that Isobel lacked. Isobel wondered what she should say and concluded after some moments that anything she could think of would be inadequate, and also would further disturb Jane's unquiet slumber. So, Isobel sat there for some time, slowly realizing that this plain room was as comfortable and pleasant as any of the others. The pastel plaster walls caught the last umber lights of the sunset, through the tall window that looked to the west. The light wind which also found an errant way into the room was cool, bringing with it the sweet scent of apple cider, of spring flowers and turned earth. It relieved Isobel immensely to think that Jane would have such a pleasant, homey place for her convalescence. Perhaps she should not torment herself with guilt and depart with a cheerful mind.

On the whole, Isobel was glad of the trunk of practical clothes and bedding that Anna had assembled for her during their brief stay in San Antonio, as well as a selection of simples and remedies: "Sage tea," Anna had advised, providing her with a large tin full of it. "Good for fevers; also to wash small wounds in." When it became clear that Jane would not accompany her, Isobel did seek out her mother-in-law. There was one last thing that she would have to do for herself now and she was afraid that the redoubtable Mrs. Becker might laugh.

"I need to learn how to do laundry," Isobel admitted. "I have never had to do any such thing as wash my own linens. This is not something I may ask a manservant . . . one of the hands to do."

"Of a certainty," Mrs. Becker agreed, although with a glint of amusement. Her face remained utterly solemn, as she showed Isobel the wash-tub, the scrubber and the bucket of soft soap and directed her in filling the first with hot water from the kitchen stove reservoir. It appeared a relatively simple process, though rather awkward. Isobel rather hoped that she would not have to wash anything more than her own clothing.

"To do by a stream, with the water running clear – is easiest for rinsing," Mrs. Becker added, as a final piece of useful advice. Isobel tucked it away in her memory against future needs.

Before dawn, on the morning of the day chosen for departure, Isobel dressed herself in one of those simple skirts and bodices which Anna had recommended. Her husband had already risen, dressed, and gone to the yard with Sam and Sebastian Bertrand. Lanterns cast blobs of pale yellow light in the foggy dawn. Two wagons stood waiting; horse teams already hitched up. From the barn came the disconsolate howling of Sorsha, Gawain, and several ranch dogs, who had been shut up there to prevent them following after. Dolph had absolutely forbidden the dogs to accompany the herd, saying they might panic the wilder of the cows and set then to stampede. Isobel combed out her hair and wove it into a single long braid that hung down her back nearly to her waist. Sitting before the simple dressing table, she felt as if there were another person looking back at her from the mirror. A calico kerchief went about her throat, as she had observed the men wearing them, ready to serve as a mask against dust rising from the tracks of the cattle. She buckled the belt at her waist, with the weight of the long pistol hanging heavy in it, and added the wide-brimmed felt hat, which sat straight on her head. She hardly needed to secure it with a long hatpin or two, but she did anyway, and looked at herself again.

This was another Isobel looking back at her, not the fashionable Isobel clad in bright colors and fine fabrics, but a harder, braver, stronger-looking Isobel. She was still too plump, Isobel realized; but she had assurance, clad in these rough and drab garments. She looked capable, the equal of her husband. She wondered, as she left the room, what Fa would think, if he could see her at this moment.

There was no doubt of what her husband thought when he saw her dressed for the trail. His own countenance lit with that brief smile that was hers and hers only. "You look good, Bell darlin'," he said. She was reassured in the warmth of his approval the thought that maybe, just maybe she could be a part of all this. The wife of a cattle rancher in the west was something that was in her reach. He handed her up to the wagon seat. She took the reins in her hands; this light wagon was drawn by a single team, which she could easily manage. The other wagon, with a tall wooden tail-gate and a large barrel for a water-butt lashed to one side like some kind of wooden carbuncle was pulled by two horse teams. The driver was an elderly Negro man, who had been briefly introduced to her as Daddy Hurst, the trail-cook.

"You'll follow his wagon," her husband told her. "And don't wander far from camp once we're over the Llano or very far from his sight. The two of you will be moving ahead of the herd – that's just the way it is."

"How far are we going today?" she asked.

Dolph answered, "Up the river to Onkel Hansi's old place in Live Oak. We'll sleep rough tonight, but under a roof tomorrow – likely that will be the last one until we get the new ranch headquarters built. You can't hurry cows."

He turned away, to untie the reins of his own horse from around the top fence rail of the the corral by the barn. Two shadowy figures joined him; Seb Bertrand, and Alf Trotter, whose thin face was pale with excitement now that he had a duty to perform involving horses. They had already eaten a hasty breakfast and said their goodbyes. Tia Leticia, Mrs. Becker, and Lottie stood on the porch with Sam, waving a last farewell. Isobel quailed for a moment, thinking once again of poor Jane. *Shouldn't I be standing with the other women, waving a white handkerchief?* The moment passed; she slapped the reins and chirruped to the horses.

The two wagons slowly lumbered out of the farmyard and down the hill, down the little road which led to a larger one. The sun peeped over the range of low hills, sending their shadows stretching long into the grass. Behind them followed her husband and the other horse-mounted drovers, urging along a herd of cattle, which multiplied as they passed pasture and paddock. She looked back at them, as the road bent back and forth along the river and she could see beyond the wagon. They were rangy, slab-sided beasts, dappled and spotted, of every color and combination imaginable – all boasting an immense spread of horns, so unlike the gentle red cows of Lattimore farm. Now Isobel realized the import of what her husband had said about how they worked their cattle from horseback. These were not the tame and agreeable cattle that she was accustomed to, but more like the legendary wild aurochs, hunted long ago by primitive tribes across Europe. These were hardy beasts and such horns defended them well against wolves. Dolph had talked to her of their plans to breed the best of the strong young bulls with the best of the heifers they had bought last summer in England. For now these hardy native cattle were the best suited for conditions on the new grassland range. It made a stirring procession, this mighty cavalcade heading north; the two wagons in the lead, the stream of cattle pouring after, although as the horses moved a trifle faster than the cattle, the wagons increasingly drew ahead.

As the sun rose towards zenith, her husband and Seb Bertrand passed the wagons. "We'll noon, about a mile or two ahead," Dolph drew rein and rode alongside for a moment. "Daddy's got cold chow for the boys. We'll water the cows and let them rest for a bit." He looked very seriously at Isobel. "It's the first couple days, set the pace. It ain't too late for you to turn this wagon around and go home, Bell darlin'."

"No, my place is here," Isobel answered, although she was sorely tempted. Sleeping on a thin mattress laid on the ground or in the wagon had very little appeal, but this was her duty, plain and clear; go with her husband. Turning back because she feared hardship or the very strangeness of this country and what might be demanded of her; that would have been like turning back on her wedding-day, when Fa told her that he would sort it out if she changed her mind. Dolph nodded, and rode ahead to speak a few words to Daddy Hurst.

In time, they came to a wide meadow, sheltered in a wide bend of the river, a meadow fringed with a stand of tall nut trees. The grass underneath was mined with rotting husks and pieces of shell. Dolph had already marked the tallest tree with a bright calico kerchief that Isobel recognized as his tied to a lower branch. He waved towards the wagons, and turned back to ride the way they had come. Seb slid down from his mount, and came to assist Isobel, who wondered if she had to see to the team horses herself, too. No, it appeared not. Nosebags part-filled with grain would suit them very well for several hours.

She looked around, wondering what she might do for herself. As a picnic on the grass, it fell rather short. She found a thick blanket folded up under the wagon seat. Taking it down, she spread it in the shade near to where Daddy Hurst was clearing a circle in the grass down to bare soil, chopping at it with deft blows of a shovel blade.

"Dem han's, dey want coffee an' plenty hot," he explained when Isobel asked what he was doing.

"Is there anything I can do to be of assistance?" Isobel offered. This was practically the first time she had conversation with him. Although his countenance was as dark as a piece of carved walnut wood, he did not otherwise appear particularly African. Save for the color of his skin, he might have been taken for a white man, for his features were fine, but he was older than she first thought, Isobel realized. He moved spryly enough, but he had the fragility of the aged showing in his bones and the tonsure of hair gone entirely white. "No, ma'am, Miz Becker," he returned courteously enough. Isobel insisted, "Surely there must be something. I would like that my husband think me to be useful on this journey."

Daddy Hurst relented. "Well, iff'n dat be de case, Miz Becker, when I get dis fire goin' you can see to grinding beans foh coffee. I surely would appreciate dat, even if de han's don't."

"If you can show me how to make it," Isobel offered, feeling greatly daring. *Mrs. Beeton's Guide* had noted that in American housewives must do much for themselves that in England was done by others. It would embarrass her deeply, after the example of her mother-in-law, to sit quietly with her hands in her lap when everyone else, even her husband had duties to perform. Daddy Hurst acquiesced, and taking down the tall tailgate at the back of his wagon, revealed a whole cabinet of little cubby shelves and drawers. The tailgate itself sat level, braced on a single hinged leg, making a wide table, and Isobel clapped her hands and marveled.

"How very clever!" she exclaimed. Each shelf and cubby above the tailgate table was filled with kitchen implements, all secured in place: stacks of tin cups and plates, heavy lidded kettles of dark-burnished cast iron, long cooking forks and spoons, bowls, and a rolling-pin such as she had seen in the kitchen at the Hall, when Mrs. Huckaby attempted to teach her a little of the housewifely arts. Daddy Hurst took down a coffee-grinder; a square wooden cabinet with a single drawer and a brass funnel topped with a handle. From one of the larger drawers, he removed a square package wrapped in heavy paper printed in bright yellow and red. 'Arbuckle's Ariosa Coffee' read the label. He poured a measure of dark brown beans into the brass funnel.

"Jes' turn that handle at the top, Miz Becker," he urged her. "Them's come already roasted. If'n we finish this package, then you get the stick o' peppermint, 'cause you did the work." He chuckled and Isobel felt pleased by his approval.

While she turned the coffee grinder slowly, the old man built up a fire, kneeling slowly and painfully at the edge of the ground he had prepared. Isobel watched as he carved small slivers from a length of dry wood, each sliver curling under his knife – a long hunting knife such as many men wore at their belt or in their boot-top. The coffee smelt deliciously aromatic, as she worked the grinder, and faintly of peppermint candy. Overhead, the leaves of the nut trees rustled in a light breeze. The shade and the rest would be welcome for a few hours, Isobel thought. Her hands were aching and cramped from the leather reins, and she was stiff from sitting on the hard plank seat. That discomfort, she knew, would be nothing compared to the weariness of the men who had spent five or six hours in the saddle already, especially those like Seb Bertrand and Alf Trotter, who wouldn't have been used to it at all.

Now Daddy Hurst stacked together several of the feathered sticks that he had carved, struck a match and lit the finest of them. It caught, spitting sparks and sending up the merest thread of smoke. From the distance came faint sounds of the moving cattle; a shout from a man or boy, a sudden querulous bawling. A few puffy white clouds sailed overhead, the only marring of a sky of such a clear and pure blue that Isobel wondered if she had ever really seen the sky before. Among the necessities stored under the wagon-seat with the Parker shotgun was a small case with a telescope in it; a single brass tube covered with red Morocco leather which had long since darkened to the color of oxblood. Isobel took it from the battered leather-covered case, and held it to her eye.

Through it, she saw the leading edge of the cattle came into view, three and four abreast, snorting as the dust rose up in their nostrils, chivvied by men and boys on their spry, quick-moving ponies. Not a single one of them had anything like the elegant form or color of Thistle, but even after a morning of disciplining the cattle to move and in an organized body, the horses still moved with lively energy, the men on their backs sending them darting here and there, with short cries and whistles. They moved the cattle in a wide circle, around the perimeter of the meadow, a circle that widened and spread and gradually slowed, hemmed on one side by the river, into which many of the cows dipped their muzzles to drink and on the other by two or three alert horsemen. One by one, the other drovers came to the cook-wagon and the now-smoldering fire, dismounted and tied their horses by the reins to a rope strung between two trees. The last riders brought in the loose herd – those mounts which Isobel understood to be the spare horses. Working cattle was nearly as exhausting for a horse as a few hours in the hunting field. Three more ropes made a rough corral to pen in the horses, who were nearly as many-colored as the cattle.

Just as Daddy Hurst poured freshly ground coffee into three tall enameled tin beakers filled with water from the wooden butt appended to the wagon and set them by the fire, there came a shout from one of those herders still mounted. Isobel, as well as everyone else turned to look; his voice sounded alarmed. He pointed at something still invisible among the low thickets interspersed between the trees. Something was there, moving fast and disturbing the bushes; a flash of brindle hide. Both the watching drovers drew their own pistols, one of them shouting, "Look out! It's a wolf!"

"No!" Isobel screamed, just as the first drover fired. That single shot crashed the pastoral vista spread before her like a brick shivering a glass mirror. The horrified silence that followed was broken by a dog's agonized yelping.

Chapter 12 – *The Home Place*

The dreams tormented Jane, although in her moments of waking she could not remember what it was that terrified her so, other than an oppressive sense of being watched and pursued by her stepfather down the endless halls and staircases of Acton. She dreamed of Lady Caroline dancing in the ballroom; her person and her gown curiously transformed into glass and shattering into a thousand animated pieces on the hard floor, while Jane herself attempted to sweep up every particle, chasing the moving pieces of Lady Caroline with a broom and dustpan and Auntie Lydia looked down at her from an enormous height, chiding her, and saying, "Oh, dear – that will never do, child. You must try harder if you want to advance in service." Sometimes she dreamed that she was buried in snow, shivering so violently that she thought her own bones would break with the force of it; then she was hot, and so thirsty, but the water often tasted so bitter that she thought it must be poison and wanted to spit it out, but someone made her drink it.

At the end of that interminable period of torment and fever, the nightmares dissolved, like the ice melting at the end of winter. One early morning, Jane opened her eyes and looked up at the ceiling over her head, the ceiling of a room she didn't recognize. Not the servant's quarters at Acton Hall, or the rooms over the shop in Didcot, or any of the various small chambers she had slept in since her ladyship married. The last coherent memory she had was of her lady, Mr. Becker, and their party leaving San Antonio. *Ah,* she thought. *This must be their house in the hills . . . but how long have I been here? Where was her ladyship? Surely, they would not have gone to the new ranch? How will her ladyship manage without me?* Suddenly apprehensive, Jane levered herself to sit up, pushing the bedcovers from her. Her head spun; she held still until it steadied. She swung her feet to the floor and sat for a moment on the edge of the bedstead to catch her breath. There was her own little trunk at the foot of the bed, her carpetbag sitting on top of it. Someone had thought to hang two or three of her dresses from the pegs in a little niche beside the tall window which served as a wardrobe, so that the wrinkles would not be so marked. She was even wearing her own nightgown.

She should get dressed and find her ladyship and Mr. Becker's room. It was past dawn; the sky outside the window slowed clear and blue, unmasked by any cloud or fog. Jane set her bare feet to the floor; there was a rug at the bedside, made of braided cloth scraps sewn together to make a circular mat. She felt a little faint for a moment, but it passed. The long rest – *how long had she been ill* – must have done her good. She did feel weak, but well again. Before she could move any farther from the bed, there was a rattle of the doorknob and a short, dark woman in her middle years entered, bearing a cloth-covered tray in her hands.

When she caught sight of Jane, she exclaimed, *"Por dios! Qué estás haciendo? Vuelve a la cama!"* She set the tray on the bedside table and pushed Jane back towards the bed. Jane sat down on it abruptly and the woman shouted, *"Actualmente! Señora Becker, ven pronto!"* Mumbling under her breath, the woman lifted Jane's feet from the floor, tucking them forcefully back underneath the covers. Jane's strength could not withstand against such masterful determination. It was easier to submit.

"What is it, Leticia?" Mrs. Becker appeared in the open doorway, as neat as always, but her black dress was plain, gone rusty with age and unfashionable, without any bustle under it. Leticia answered in a flood of Spanish, of which Mrs. Becker apparently divined some meaning, for she gently chided Jane. "Miss Goodacre, you should not be venturing from your bed just yet." She felt Jane's forehead with her wrist, just as she had before. "You have no fever, which is good, but you should not over-exert yourself."

"Where is Lady Isobel?" Jane asked. Leticia, still grumbling under her breath, placed two or three pillows at her back so that she might sit up in bed.

Mrs. Becker placed the tray on her knees. "She and my son, and young Bertrand departed for the north a fortnight ago. They could not delay their departure. I am sorry, Miss Goodacre. My son's wife was distraught that you could not accompany them. She sat with you many evenings and begged my son to wait upon your return to health. But the business of the ranches could not be put off. I fear that my son's reasons for doing things are often matters which he does not care to share with anyone, even his mother or his wife."

Leticia's eyes were on Jane's face as Mrs. Becker relayed this news; Jane felt as if she had been struck breathless, as if she had been hit by a runaway carriage, left crumpled on the pavement, gasping for breath and hardly able to move. *Lady Isobel had abandoned her in this foreign country and gone off with her husband.* That was all she could take in. Leticia instantly began upbraiding Mrs. Becker in emphatic Spanish.

"What will happen to me now?" To her own ears, Jane's voice came out in a pathetic squeak. "What will I do?"

"You will get better," Mrs. Becker answered, as if it were a perfectly natural question. "Then what you wish. Your wages are paid until the end of the year. The Palo Duro ranch will be established; we will meet with my son and his wife again at Christmas. All will go on then as it has before. Of a certainty, she said she would always need you. For now, this is Leticia's best beef tea which you will drink. Perhaps she will make you some bread and milk, since you are awake." She patted Jane's shoulder, comfortingly. "Miss Goodacre, there is no need for tears, not so? I will write a letter to say that you are recovering and send it with a messenger. Drink your beef tea. For the moment, consider this your home."

Dazed with weakness and a lingering sense of having been betrayed, Jane obeyed. The beef tea was hot and good. Leticia watched her drink it, beaming approval, and took away the cup when she was finished. Later she brought up a dish of bread and milk, the eating of which so exhausted Jane that she lay back and fell asleep almost as soon as Leticia took away the empty tray.

Within a few days, she felt strong enough to dress herself and put up her hair, but then was confronted with what to do with the long hours of the day. The tall stone house was an oasis of quiet, at the center of a hub of activity, even if most of the hands and nearly all the horses were gone north. Everyone, even Lottie and Mrs. Becker had work enough and if Sam was not in the office, he was out on horseback, among the pastures of the property which sprawled the length of the valley along the river as far as she could see, and to the hills on either side. She wrote a long letter to Auntie Lydia, enclosing another, singularly brief and unspecific single-page letter for her mother and brothers. Then Jane busied herself unpacking those trunks of Lady Isobel's clothes left behind in the bedroom she had shared with Mr. Becker, setting their contents to air, before laying them away in the large wardrobe which took up almost all of one wall. After spinning out that task for as long as possible, she attempted to make herself useful to Lottie and Mrs. Becker, by offering her services as a seamstress and ladies' maid.

Lottie pealed with laughter. "But we have no use for that here! If it would amuse you, you can play at putting my hair in fancy rolls, and I am certain Mama can find some mending . . . if she can wrest it away from Tia Leticia!" Lottie's face sobered. "What I would like best would be if you just kept us company. There are so very few women. It is very lonely here, especially after last year! Our nearest neighbor is crazy old Mr. Berg. Leticia has the house to keep, but Mama has the garden, and the orchard and the bees. We would love to have your company. Would it be untoward if I just called you Jane, and you called me Lottie?"

"Not at all," Jane answered, a little nonplussed at the informality of it all, even if she and Lottie were not far apart in age. But everything here was so very different, less rigidly bound by proper courtesies and formality. It was ridiculous to expect to carry on as if this were anything like the Hall, but she was taken back upon discovering that she would take meals with Mrs. Becker, Lottie, and Sam.

"Of course you will," Lottie said briskly when Jane protested. "Otherwise, you'd be in the kitchen with Leticia and the girls. You don't understand Spanish and they would think that you were imposing on them. Jane, you aren't in England any more!"

"Apparently not," Jane answered, shaken at the prospect. *What would Lady Caroline, Mr. Spencer, and Aunt Lydia think of all this?* Mr. Spencer, she was certain, would expire in a fit of spectacular apoplexy, and Lady Caroline . . . Jane recollected her dream of trying to sweep up animated glass fragments of Lady Caroline and stifled a giggle. She might have felt much more awkward about it, but everyone else accepted her dining with them quite matter-of-factly, although it was at least a week before she could bring herself to do anything more than answer a direct question. On that particular evening, Sam Becker lay down his knife and fork.

"Miss Jane," he ventured, as if he had given the question a great deal of care. "Have you ever given thought to teaching school?"

Jane, utterly floored, simply stared at him for a few moments before shaking her head. "No, I have not. I only went to the village school until I was twelve and then I had to help my mother in the shop."

"But you can read, and write, and do sums?" Sam persisted and Jane answered, "Of course I can. I won a school prize for geography when I was ten and another for history, the next year. I had very high marks. If I had been a boy and they didn't need me in the shop, they said I might have gone to the university on scholarship."

"If you can do all that," Sam answered, "you can teach someone else from what you know, especially if you know more than they do." He sat a little forward in his chair, and leaned on his elbows as he fixed Jane with a look of willful intensity. Jane thought that his brother might be the tall and handsome gentleman, but Sam had a special quality about him. Sam made anyone whom he fixed his attention on to believe themselves the most fascinating person in the world.

"Elbows off the table, Samuel," Mrs. Becker chided him while Lottie demanded, "You're not looking to open a school, are you?"

"I am," Sam answered. "Here at the ranch. I know there is a perfectly good schoolhouse in Comfort but that's miles away and it's all German. See," he addressed his mother and sister, as well as Jane. "Bill Inman – that's our foreman at this ranch, Jane – he just this last year married a widow from someplace near Huntsville, a widow-woman with four little children and brought them up here to live."

"As is right," Mrs. Becker said. Sam continued, his attention focused most particularly on Jane.

"She don't much like it. She wants her children to go to school and there isn't a proper school any closer than Comfort. She and her kinder don't speak German, so that's a problem right there. Bill doesn't earn enough to send them all to boarding school in San Antonio and she wouldn't have that, anyway. She's not happy and so Bill's not happy. We'd not like to lose him as foreman, so as I see it, the best way is to start a school right here, on the ranch, with Miss Jane here teaching it."

"But I can't teach!" Jane protested. Sam replied with great assurance, "Yes you can, Miss Jane. I listened to you, that afternoon when you were amusing Cuz Peter's and Cousin Anna's little sprats on the train. You were teaching them their letters an' telling them all about Madagascar or some such place, just to pass the time. Harry and Christian don't commonly pay attention to anybody, outside of Peter and Anna, an' maybe Mama. They're willful, but they were listening to you! I know you can do it, Miss Jane." His blue-grey eyes fixed upon Jane's, filled with confidence. "If you can make those two imps pay mind, you sure can school Bill Inman's. Say that you will, Miss Jane. We have that little cabin between the bunkhouse and the stable that used to be for storing hay and corn. It's not much but we can move in some tables and benches. We can get some *McGuffey's Readers*, an' Lottie has her school-books an' we have a bunch of our Opa's old books in English, so that you can study ahead. They're only children; they don't know nothin' at all. All you need do is teach them what you know. Say you will do it, Miss Jane. It will give you something to do, you'll be giving Bill Inman's children a little schooling, and helping us keep a good foreman. And we can rustle up two dollars a week for you, as long as you're teaching. What do you say, Miss Jane? Will you?"

"I think I will," Jane answered, with a tremor in her voice that she couldn't quite conceal, but also a sense of a grand and glorious opportunity opening in front of her. It would be something to take the sting away from knowing that her ladyship had left her. There was otherwise nothing else for her to do to fill in the next six long months.

The following morning, she and Lottie went down to the little cabin; a windowless little shed made of inexpertly fitted logs. With so much clay chinking between the logs had fallen out, there was as much air and light within as if there had been windows. The rough plank floor was scattered with the detritus of its former function; wisps of dried grass, husks, and grains of yellow maize. The place was dusty, yet otherwise clean, and pleasantly imbued with the lingering odor of its previous use.

Lottie was ecstatic, like a child given a new dollhouse. "Oh, it's perfect!" she cried. "You should have your desk here, of course – and a blackboard behind it. And a globe – you should have a globe. Opa had a splendid one that Onkel Johann sent from Germany. I am sure Mama will let you make use of it. I do not think Sam will approve the expense of proper schoolroom desks, but surely Mr. Inman can make some simple tables and benches. Let's go find Mr. Inman, and tell him what we need . . . I am certain that he will be most helpful. When shall we tell them that school can begin?"

"A week?" Jane ventured and Lottie agreed. Before Jane had a moment to reconsider the whole project, Lottie had spun like a whirlwind, back to the house, trailing Jane in her wake.

"Mama is going to Comfort tomorrow to oversee inventory in the store," Lottie assured her. "Make a list, for whatever we do not have here . . . you may go with her and bring back on account. Chalk! You need chalk! I daresay the Inman children will have their own slates, but they may not. A set of *McGuffey Readers*, of course. Do you know *McGuffey Readers*, Jane? It is, I think, what they will expect to be taught from. Our Opa had many books and those in English might be of use to you."

Sam Becker was run to ground in the shed which housed the smithy. Apparently pleased by Lottie's enthusiasm for the project at least as much as he was by Jane's acquiescence, he agreed to contribute the globe to the nascent school, a small table to serve as a teacher's desk, and a plain wooden chair. That very afternoon the sound of a saw and hammer being vigorously wielded drifted through the windows of the office, where Jane sat on her heels before the twin bookcases. It was not a splendid library like the grand, book-lined shelves at the Hall. That was a room as large as this entire house, shelves so tall that one needed a long ladder to reach the topmost shelves. Grand paintings of improbable gods, goddesses and figures from history lined the ceiling and upper walls of Sir Robert's library, but the Becker's few shelves offered a satisfactory collection, and larger than Jane had expected. There were a great many books in foreign languages, some of them filled also with the most wonderfully delicate illustrations of plants and animals. She was supposed to be setting aside a handful of books of use to her in teaching Mr. Inman's children. She was distracted by a thin volume; a pamphlet crudely stitched together of letter-paper folded in half and bound in in a roughly-cut square of rawhide leather. The pages were filled with lively pen and watercolor and pencil sketches; Indians in brilliantly-colored blankets and feathers, soldiers clad in improbably ornate and detailed uniforms. There were landscapes and portraits of people scattered among them, animals and more soldiers on horseback. Jane turned a page; here was a sketch of a house which looked like this one even to the shape of the hills behind it, but smaller; only the one L-shaped wing. She frowned, briefly puzzled. *Why did it look as if it were on fire?* She turned to the first page, and there was the answer, written in childish square letters: *Samuel Houston Becker –1862– This is my book so keep out – This means YOU Elias!*

Jane hastily folded the little book together and replaced it on the shelf where she had found it, reminded with a pang of her little brothers. Just so they had marked their own dearest belongings. This little book must be the property of Sam Becker. If she recalled Lady Isobel's quizzings on board the *Wieland* about the complicated family of her lady's husband, one of the cattle baron's many sons was named Elias. Mr. Becker had mentioned something to her ladyship about his brother wishing to be an artist. Even if done by a child, the drawings were very fine, drawn with verve and an eye for detail. Jane continued searching the books, distracted yet again and again, until the moment when the clock in the next room chimed the five o'clock hour. She realized that the entire day had passed and late afternoon sun was painting the room in pale golden light. Where had the time gone, so sweetly had it passed?

The outside door to the office from the deep verandah swung open and there was Samuel Houston Becker himself, although after some weeks, Jane's first impulse was to call him Sam, as if he were one of her own kin and she were fond of him. There was not that deep gulf that society demanded between those served and the servant. This utterly baffled Jane at first. She thought that there ought to be, when it came to the older Mrs. Becker, and Lottie and Sam. But there wasn't, no matter how firmly she tried to draw that understanding. She ate at the table with them and the line became increasingly harder to hold onto; especially when Sam beamed upon her cheerfully and remarked, "Miss Jane – have you selected your books? Bill is nearly done with outfitting your school. Will you walk with me and have a look?"

"Of course I will," Jane replied and he answered, "Bring your books and I have my contribution. I think we shall have a very nice little school." He added, in a confining tone of voice, "I might just very well keep it up, you know. You will have several more pupils besides Bill's step-children before next Monday, Miss Jane."

"I will?" Jane replied, in complete bafflement. Sam took down a large framed map in pastels and sepia colors, which hung upon the wall of the office; a map of Texas and the territories surrounding. "Won't you need that? It leaves an empty space on the wall."

"I think your pupils will need it more, Miss Jane," he answered. "I already know this silly ol' map very well – but they will not. In the long run, won't it be more use in a school-room?"

With his other hand, he took her elbow and they walked down to the little hay-barn. To Jane's utter amazement, it was transformed. Now there was a window cut in the space opposite the doorway. Although there was no glass in it, there was already a set of shutters hinged within the frame. All had been swept clean; a large kerosene lantern hung from the center beam, just above head-height. At the gable end of the small barn, a blackboard had been hung; three or four boards cunningly smoothed and fitted together, and painted with black paint which was still shiny and damp. The small table and chair were placed before the blackboard with care for symmetry – and there, in the main part of the barn were two rows of rough-hewn plank benches with tables set before them to serve in the office of student desks.

"There is a shelf for those books," Sam pointed out the narrow plank, resting upon long pegs set into the wall below the new window. "With space for more, as soon as Bill finishes it; he even worked up a school bell for you – not much for looks, but it makes a noise." By that, Jane assumed that he meant the metal barrel hoop, hanging from the edge of the roof by the door, with a length of metal rod attached to it with a length of twine. There was already a nail pounded into the wall on either side of the new blackboard. Sam hung the Texas map from one of them and stood back to admire the look. "Bill says that his wife's children all have school slates, but his boy doesn't. Neither do Tia Leticia's granddaughters. Did I tell you that she wants Conchita and Adeliza to come to school too? Young Bill, he's eleven or so and never went to school. And there's one of the hands, too. He told me that he wants to learn to write his name proper, so I said he could come to school in the mornings." Sam allowed all this with an air of perfect confidence and good cheer. Jane stared at him in horror, her heart sinking.

"A school of eight pupils," she stammered. "I don't believe that I can teach as many as eight. I thought it was just to be the four children."

"It was at first," Sam agreed. "But the more I talked about it with Mama, and Bill, and Tia Leticia, the better idea they thought it was. Mama thinks it is awful that children are left to grow up without any schooling at all. Me, I think that something ought to be done here and now. Sometimes, Miss Jane, just what you can do even if you think it isn't very much – is still the best thing that you could ever do. I know you can teach, Miss Jane. If you can school Harry and Christian, you can teach. This very day, we have a school, right here on the RB ranch home place, where we never had one before. And that's something to boast about, Miss Jane. You spending the day teaching those children is lot more important than spending that very same day fiddling about with Sister Isobel's wardrobe, so don't you dare loose heart and think you can't do it. If you think you can't, and never try, then you are beaten before you ever start."

"I'll try my best," Jane answered with a small sigh. "Sometimes I think you and my Auntie Lydia have more faith in me than I do."

"You'll do fine, Miss Jane." Sam took her elbow to assist her down the two steps from the doorway and she thought again how very comforting was his assurance and belief in her. He was not like his older brother, who for all his handsome looks Jane found to be rather forbidding. The heretical thought that it might be very pleasant to be courted by Sam Becker arrived unbidden and was just as swiftly banished from Jane's mind, although for a moment, she lost track of what Sam was saying. "Mama is going to take the trap and spend the day in Comfort, at the store," he said. "We thought you should go with her to keep her company and to see what there is in Comfort that you might use for the school. Mama can charge it to the ranch account."

"That is very generous," Jane said, but Sam only shrugged. "If it's worth doing, it's worth doing well."

After an early breakfast the next morning, Mrs. Becker and Jane set off in the light two-horse trap for what Jane understood was the nearest town of any substance, some seven or eight miles distant. At the last minute, Lottie declared that she would also come, so the three women squeezed together on the single seat. Lottie brought out her parasol, for the day was very warm and the shade of the parasol was welcome. Part of the lane between the RB ranch and the main road was shaded by a row of young trees, planted on either side. When Jane remarked on it, Mrs. Becker nodded.

"My son's idea," she said. "It was the wish of my husband to make this a show-place but Dolphchen thought of searching out young trees and transplanting them to line the road." The lane dropped down from the low eminence on which the ranch buildings sprawled, with the crown of it being the tall stone main house, passing meadows and pastures, some of them randomly dotted with more trees. At the bottom of the lane, where it opened to the road which paralleled the river, the entrance to the ranch was marked by a pair of gateposts make from blocks of roughly-squared limestone which had weathered to the same dark ivory color as the house.

"When I first came this way, nearly thirty years ago," Mrs. Becker remarked, deftly twitching the reins, "there was no road. Only a track in the grass. My husband's men marked the way to our house with a bull-skull hung in a tree. Our nearest neighbors were three or four miles distant – there was no town, only a place where the Indians camped among the trees. In those days, three women would not dare travel alone on this road because of the Comanche or the worst kind of banditry. Now we may go about our business without fear."

"I am glad of that," Jane answered with a shiver. Such things were too awful to contemplate on a spring morning with fields of wildflowers unfurling on either side of the river; a dark green torrent between steep banks. Tall trees with feathery green and pine-like foliage lined the banks. Now and again the scent of fresh water wafted up towards them. It was as green as England, but there was a difference in the feel of the air, the look of the sky, even the untamed look of the land. How terrifying it must have been, for those who came here, all those years ago.

Lottie laughed, and the parasol bobbed. "This is the first time you have seen the Hills, Jane. You were so very sick when we came this way before. Comfort is a dear, sweet little place. Everyone there is related to everyone else and everyone knows us. We could spend the day making calls and still not meet every one of our friends!"

"It sounds very like Didcot, where I was born," Jane said, stuck by a feeling of nostalgia. "My father kept the village shop there. My mother kept on when he died. I was raised there and we knew everyone, too."

"You see?" Lottie promised extravagantly. "You will feel quite at home!"

Curiously enough, Jane did. From the outside, the general store on Comfort's High Street did not have much in common with the cramped little shop premise which had been her home until Auntie Lydia brought her to the Hall. Was that just a year ago? This store had two fine sixteen-pane windows on either side of the door, whereas the shop in Didcot had only the one tiny bow window, displaying a selection of goods to the passersby on Station Street, but inside – that caught at her heart and memory. Dim in the further recesses of the shop and far from the windows, the shop smelled so very much like home. Jane closed her eyes and drank in the familiar commingled scent of ripening cheeses, the dusty milled-grain odor of flour, of sugar still retaining the lingering richness of molasses that it had been refined from, of camphor, and kerosene, and a hundred other commodities; fine perfumed soap, bolts of calico fabric with the odor of the dye-vats still clinging faintly to it, the medicinal smell of whiskey and herbal concoctions, of salt-cod and crackers. All those goods, piled on shelves reaching nearly to the ceiling, lent each of their own peculiarity to the atmosphere. Jane felt herself nearly overcome with nostalgia and sorrow. From her earliest childhood he loved helping in the shop; she learned her numbers from her father's account-ledgers even before she learned them from the village schoolmistress. Of all the places she had seen in America, this caught at her heart and memory, the one place where she felt instantly at home.

She followed Mrs. Becker and Lottie to the back, where they were greeted warmly by the proprietor, a stout and broad-shouldered man in his thirties, who was introduced to her as Cousin George Richter – another one of the cattle baron's sons. George Richter was what the baron would have looked like at that age, Jane thought. He conversed with them in lively German, offered them all coffee and some tasty little pastries adorned with a dollop of jam and slivered almonds. Then Mrs. Becker removed her bonnet and gloves, put on an all-enveloping apron which she took from her valise, and she and George set to work.

"This store does very well," Lottie explained to Jane. "Onkel Hansi always said that the family businesses were a three-legged stool; the stores, the freighting concern, and the cattle. All of his sons and his son-in-law have a part in it. When I marry Seb, he will have a part in it, also, through the new ranch in the Palo Duro. You will never imagine how it all began, though."

"Tell me," Jane asked. She and Lottie perched on tall stools at the back of the shop. They were deputized to assist George Richter's single young store clerk with customers, although Jane was hampered by knowing any German, the language of this region. Even so, she reveled in the very familiarity of it, the careful order of merchandise on the shelves, the tidy ordering of drawers neatly labeled with the small things they contained, the way that the little bell on a spring on the front door chimed whenever anyone came and went.

"Two wagons of goods," Lottie explained. "And four teams of horses. Onkel Hansi and Cousin Jacob did not want to serve in the Confederate Army, so they were made to be teamsters instead. We were all for the Union, you know. When word came that the war was over and the Confederates had surrendered, Onkel Hansi and Jacob were in Galveston, ready to take two wagonloads from the Army warehouses. Onkel Hansi said that a mob of ordinary people began loot the goods within them, so he and Jacob came away at once, with their wagons loaded to bursting."

"But wasn't that like looting as well?" Jane asked. Lottie frowned, admitting, "I suppose it was, a little. But you see . . . during the war, the Confederates confiscated ever so much from us; all of Papa's cattle, his wagons, and the food that Papa and Mama had stored up. They took all of Onkel Hansi's horses and the wagon that he had at his farm at Live Oak. For the war effort, you see. They even confiscated Papa's land – they said he was a traitor. We had to live with Opa in Fredericksburg. We were very poor, then. I don't remember much of that, since I was just a baby. Onkel Hansi told us those two wagons and the goods in them were a fair repayment for what had been taken and we had a perfect right to keep them. He and Mama used the goods to set up a general store in the place where Opa had his clock-making shop, and the wagons and horses to begin freighting goods for it." Lottie waved her hand around at the shop. "All of this . . . came from that. When the Federal Army came back and we had a Reconstruction government again, they returned Papa's land to us, so we had that to raise cattle on once more."

"It sounds like a story," Jane said, "Like Dick Whittington and his cat . . . from rags to splendid riches and Lord Mayor of London."

"I suppose it does," Lottie answered, carelessly. "It was fortunate for Onkel Hansi, being in Galveston at that very moment, with the wagons just loaded, but if he had been elsewhere, I am certain he would have taken advantage just as readily."

At that moment, Mrs. Becker called from the office; a matter of numbers in the inventory not agreeing with that had been consigned to the storeroom or to the shelves. Lottie obediently hopped down from the stool and threaded her way across the room to count up the bolts of calico cloth neatly stacked on an upper shelf. Jane considered what she had just been told, and recollecting the splendors of the cattle baron's parlor car. This was a new thought to her; great riches such as the parlor car represented had not always been there, as permanent and enduring as the foursquare edifice of Acton Hall. They had, in fact, come from two wagons of goods rescued from the wreck of a failed rebellion, enlarged by a stubborn and far-seeing man into a not inconsiderable fortune. This was something for Jane to consider, a great and serious matter. Plain poor Dick Whittington had parlayed a cat into a fortune and Hansi Richter had wrung a fortune from goods that chance had placed in his hand. Jane was aware of a breathless sense of hope and possibility. Alf Trotter thought the streets of New York were paved in gold; which wasn't true, Jane knew very well. But maybe the streets of America were paved with something better; opportunity.

Chapter 13 – *Into the Wild Country*

Heedless of shouts from the drovers, Isobel plunged into the scrub-brush lining the pasture where the cows now circled uneasily, and fought her way through it, against twigs that clawed at her hair and her skirts. She followed that agonized yelping by ear, crying out for Gawain and Sorsha. The dogs must have escaped the barn and followed them all this way, only to be met with gunfire from a drover thinking they were some kind of wolf! Isobel was slightly reassured, hearing the dog carry on so noisily – whichever one it was could not be much harmed, not if it could continue making such a fuss. Something heavy crashed through the bushes, something running towards her, and she was nearly bowled over by the sudden weight of first one and then the second; a pair of frantic, bridle dogs trying to leap into her arms. She sank to her knees, breathless with relief, while the two of them licked at her face.

"Sit!" she commanded. "Behave!" They obeyed instantly, still whining in piteous entreaty. Isobel gathered them to her, whispering endearments and reassurance. Her hand found a patch of sodden, matted fur on Gawain's shoulder. He whined as she touched it again, with purpose. "Shush, my sugar-plum, my poppet, my dear . . . there, there . . . you're safe now." He yelped as her fingers explored the bloody gash across his shoulder and back. There was no bullet embedded in the flesh – no hard unyielding lump, for which she was grateful. Now Sorsha wriggled free of her grasp. Dolph looked down at her from horseback, with another three concerned faces – Seb, Alf, and the drover who had fired unseeing at the two dogs. That last looked especially worried.

"How bad is it?" Dolph came off the back of his horse in a rush and he was at her side, soothing Gawain. Isobel was reminded piercingly of how he had gentled Thistle, so calm and assured. Gawain winced from his hands and moaned again, deep in his throat, as the drover with the too-quick pistol asked urgently, "I didn't know it were one o' yours, Mister Becker, I'm sorry! I thought it were a wolf or or something!"

"You only grazed him, Johnny," Dolph replied. "You ride drag for two weeks for shooting at m'wife's dog – and another week for just wounding him." He assisted Isobel to stand. Sorsha pressed very close to her skirts and her husband lifted Gawain awkwardly. In a low voice, just loud enough for Isobel's hearing, he added. "Daddy will fix him right up, but I'm afraid the whiskey is gonna sting. I was afraid of something like this, Bell. I have half a mind to send them back to the ranch. Dogs and cattle on the trail are a dangerous mix."

"I'll keep them close to me," Isobel pleaded. "Away from the cattle. They'll be better guardians for me than anyone else." They had disputed about this, in the days before departure, Dolph insisting that there was no place for dogs on a long-trail drive, as they were apt to spook the cows through being mistaken for wolves or coyotes.

The old cook whistled in brief astonishment when he got a good look at Sorsha and Gawain. "Don't you be too hard, Mistah Becker – dis ol' nigra would have thought it was a wolf for sure an' let loose both barrels." From a drawer near to the top of his wagon-kitchen, he took town a bottle of whiskey and three cloths. While Gawain whined and thrashed in the firm grip of Dolph and Alf Trotter and the rest of the hands looked on in fascination, Daddy Hurst clipped hair away from the wound with the same shears that Isobel would later see him use to barber the hands. He roughly scoured the long, oozing graze with a cloth soaked in the harsh spirits. Then he tore the second into narrow strips and used them to secure the third, rolled into a narrow pad, over the wound. Dolph and Alf warily relaxed their grip. Gawain wobbled to all four feet, looking at them all with an expression of bewildered hurt. Sorsha whined and began licking his ears. After a time, Gawain curled up on the blanket which Isobel spread for him, in the shade of her wagon.

"See that he don't chew on that bandage none," advised Daddy Hurst. He wiped off his own hands, and put away the whiskey bottle.

Isobel had lost her own appetite for the cold biscuits and bacon which was all that Hurst provided for the midday meal for the hands – although they all were pleased enough with that fare. She nibbled a stale biscuit with honey spread on it and kept a wary eye on the dogs. Poor Gawain; what an unpropitious start to the journey! She had best not include mention of the incident in her next letter to Fa and the family. Fa would be incensed at the accidental wounding of one of his cherished wolfhounds.

She sat with the sleeping dogs a little apart from the drovers and wranglers; they extended a delicate kind of deference to her, as a woman and wife of the rancher who was their boss, just as Anna Vining said that they would. Dolph sat beside her, although not before he had gone and talked to all the hands as they came to the kitchen wagon to get their meal, after unsaddling their horses and turning them into the rope corral for the moment. Her husband ate sparingly of his own share of the meal, patted Sorsha and Gawain and fell promptly asleep. Under the cool shade and fluttering leaves of the trees, soothed by the burble of the river close by, the nooning passed as pleasantly as a country picnic for Isobel.

The men and boys ate their poor fare with relish and some chaffering of Daddy Hurst, which he returned with interest. They respected him for his age and office, which his color did not diminish in the slightest. He held authority among them, Isobel noted with interest; naturally, as he commanded the food stocks. Most of the hands and wranglers were very young and not all white, which vaguely surprised Isobel. Some five of six of the twenty were dark Mexicans or even darker Negroes. They dressed alike, in dark-blue canvas work-pants battened into tall leather boots and collarless calico shirts with vast neckerchiefs instead of a cravat. It amused her to observe Alf Trotter conscientiously aping their manner of speech. He already looked quite like his fellow drovers, although still not as sun-kippered as they were, or so assured in manner. Unasked, one of the wranglers brought to her a canteen full of water from the river and poured it out into a tin basin for the dogs. Gawain lapped it eagerly and returned to sleep, but Sorsha sat with her head raised.

"Thank you, Mister . . . May I know your name?" she was honestly grateful; this was one of the men who had come up with the horse herd some time after the wounding of poor Gawain; a Negro nearly as dark as Daddy Hurst. His hair hung down to his shoulders in a thick curly mop, under a wide-brimmed sombrero turned rakishly back at the front. He was lean-hipped and graceful, walking with an easy slouch and an air of complete assurance. He smiled at Isobel, his teeth a slash of white in his dark face.

"I'm Wash – short for Washington – Charpentier. An' you're mos' welcome, Miz Becker," he answered. Unbidden, he hunkered down to extend a tentative hand towards Sorsha. She sniffed at it in a regal manner; thus reassured, he petted her and tousled her long ears. "Dat's some dawg you got there, Mistah Becker, he got dogs, but dis dawg takes de prize. Dey gwine go all de way wid you?"

"They most certainly shall," Isobel answered.

"I reckon dey will be de bes' pertection for you, than dis ol' shootin' iron." Wash Charpentier rose to his feet, with another smile and sauntered away to where the horses were temporarily corralled. Beside her, Dolph opened his eyes with a yawn and observed, "Now, if Wash had been fool enough to shoot, instead of Johnny Benbow, we'd have been burying a dog. He's a crack shot and a champion roper . . . a top hand and the RB is lucky to have him. He gets into scrapes now and again, but he always talks his way out, and the other hands think he walks on water, even bein' a nigra." Dolph propped himself on an elbow and continued. "There was the time he rode onto the parade ground at Fort Dodge and lassoed himself one of the Army cannons. The soldiers caught up to him as he was dragging it away; they yelled at him, 'What do you want that thing for, boy?'"

"What did he say?" Isobel asked and her husband grinned. "Said he wanted to take it back to fight the Indians with!" Dolph shook his head. "Uncle Fredi had to talk something fast to get him out of the guardhouse. I just hope Wash can behave himself once we get to the Palo Duro, else he may be too much for Seb to handle." He stood and stretched, adding, "We'll get moving now, Bell – we want to make it to Live Oak by sundown tomorrow."

It took only a little time to reassemble the cavalcade after their meal break and rest. It amazed Isobel, as no one appeared in much of a hurry, but in the space of a few minutes, Daddy Hurst had folded up his camp kitchen and doused the fire while the drovers saddled fresh horses. She called the dogs to ride with her, not wanting to risk any more hurt to them until they and the drovers were more accustomed to each other. Gawain obeyed with a stiffness in his forelegs which was painful to observe. She bought the light wagon to follow Daddy Hursts' as they had in the morning. Two months, Anna Vining had told her that this journey would take.

"Oh, sugar-plum, I hope tomorrow will not be any more interesting," she murmured to Sorsha. The dog had her considerable length curled on the wagon-seat next to her, and dropped her long nose across Isobel's lap.

As hoped, they reached the Live Oak establishment the following afternoon; a small square stone house shaded by a single ancient oak tree and surrounded by trampled fields and pastures. Unlike the the Becker home place, this house had a faint air of neglect about it. It was plain to Isobel that no woman lived there – or had for years. It served now as a staging area for assembling RB herds for the long trail north; only a handful of hired men lived there regularly, to include the ranch foreman, Dolph's Uncle Fredi. He was Mrs. Becker's younger brother, Isobel was given to understand. He proved to be a man verging on middle years, wiry of build and very weathered, distractible in his attention, but kindly for that. He had something of the same features and coloring as Sam, so it was clear they were kin. He waved his hand towards the upstairs of the house, admired the dogs, and was then called outside to oversee some matter in the farmyard, where a whole beef was roasting on a spit and tables with white cloths were laid out among the trees. There was supposed to be a grand communal supper, to mark the departure of the herd.

Isobel sneezed, as she shook out the bedclothes in the largest upstairs room. They were clean enough, but a great cloud of dust rose and dissipated as she shook them out. "I thought I might like sleeping indoors, since this will be the last time in several months. But I do wish that your uncle kept a proper house, with a proper housekeeper.

"Onkel Fredi can't be bothered," Dolph answered, dropping the carpetbag with their scanty luggage brought from the wagon. "He spends so little time under a roof that I don't think it occurs to him. Where ever he hangs his hat, that's his home for the night."

"A pity," Isobel walked to the window and unfastened the shutters with some difficulty, for they were almost corroded shut. "It has a very pleasant aspect, and is a well-built house, otherwise."

"It was where Onkel Hansi and Aunt Liesel first lived," her husband explained. "And then things happened. During the War there was a great danger in living out here. Onkel Hansi took to the bush. Auntie Liesel and the children went to live in Fredericksburg. She couldn't bear to return afterwards, so Onkel's farm went to wrack and ruin – no matter, since the land is better put to grazing. And it's too small for anything other than a rendezvous for the herds." He dropped a somewhat distracted kiss on her lips adding, "There will be some folk – family friends come out from Fredericksburg tonight. A bit of a send-off for us . . . you needn't fret about putting on a fancy dress and all. They will not expect that. I expect that Cuz will be here as well – he will bring up the second herd, two or three days behind us. You might," he added fairly, "write letters to your family, and send them back with our friends to be mailed."

"I shall," Isobel answered, with a sudden feeling of her stomach falling to the level of her sturdy, high-laced boots. Tomorrow, they would head into the wilderness, towards that endless, rolling country that Jack Sutcliffe had spoken of to her, where the stars hung so thick in the sky at night and the desert emptiness of it called to the spirits of men. She sat down and scribbled some hurried pages to Jane, and to Fa and Martyn, as dusk fell. Down below the opened window, lighted lanterns hung in the lower bough of the oak tree, as several wagons full of men and families arrived. The evening filled with music, of men's voices singing in chorus, a concertina and fiddle scraping out a merry tune. She sealed the last of her letters and looked out the window once more; a few darker shadows flashed across the sky – swifts and perhaps bats going about their own business. An odd feeling of contentment filled her; although she had no idea why it would be so at this time. She savored that view and that odd feeling for some moments, before recalling herself to the present and an evening which passed like a brief dream. In the morning, just as dawn began to flush the eastern sky, and paint the edges of a few scanty purple clouds with the color of molten gold – they were off again.

If it were not for the dust, and the jolting of wagon-wheels rolling over another rock or into a deep rut – a jolting barely mitigated by the springs – Isobel often thought the journey passed in a particularly vivid waking dream, which never ended, repeating itself day after day, each with a slight variation to distinguish it from the rest. One day, as she sat with the reins carelessly loose in her hands, she realized they had passed out of the gentle, rounded hills, the flowered meadows threaded with cool green streams of water and stitched together with tall trees. She could not even be sure when this had happened. Now, she and Daddy Hurst traveled over terrain nearly as flat as the top of a baked crumpet, occasionally seamed with dry creek beds, and the distant horizon punctuated by oddly flat-topped hills. They made a curious sight, as neatly leveled as if they had been sliced off by an immense knife. The only trees of any height to be seen were those near running water – very few and far between. The vegetation was colored in shades of dull grey-green, frequently punctuated with a strange spiky plant, a cluster of long, spine-tipped leaves. From the center, a single tall stem shot up, ten or twelve feet in the air, the tip of it thickly festooned with of creamy white flowers. Isobel openly marveled at them. If Seb and Alf Trotter did so, they wisely kept such wonder to themselves, for the other hands and wranglers paid them no attention at all.

"The name of it in Spanish means 'Candles of the Lord' or sometimes they call it 'Spanish bayonet,'" Dolph explained to her, one evening after they had eaten with a good appetite of Daddy Hurst's plain workman's suppers, as the skies overhead darkened to velvet-black. "They say that is how the Staked Plain – the Llano Estacado – got the name. The old conquistadors and explorers looking out from the top of one of those bluffs saw nothing but a long flat desert marked with old yucca stems."

"It sounds quite fitting," Isobel answered. "And so very empty!"

"Not all that empty," her husband pointed out. "They came here looking for something; Quivera, the City of Gold. The old tales say there were seven cities, all full of gold and jewels and riches out here – somewhere away to the north."

"Did they ever find those cities?" Isobel asked breathlessly. She had spread out the large striped blanket in the area by her wagon – not quite removed from the campfire circle, around which the hands and wranglers had placed their bedrolls – but close enough that she and most especially Dolph could partake a little in the conversation that took place around the portion reasonably close to them. She was certain that all improper conversations among the hands were whispered at the far side of the campfire, safely out of her hearing. The hired men were painfully delicate in conversation with a lady listening. Anna had warned her about that.

"No, I don't b'lieve they did," Dolph answered, with that slight smile which warmed her heart. "Not a golden city, anyway. Quivera turned out to be jus' another Indian village, so Opa said. He also said that maybe it's the looking for, an' the trail in front of them that men like to seek. If they find it or not, the true aim is in the journey . . . not gold at the end of it."

"I hope that it was so for them," Isobel stretched her cramped arms and legs with a sigh; how blissful, this rest after a day on the trail. As blissful after a day with the hunt, but at that moment she would not have traded one for the other, even if she sat on the ground, instead of in a soft chair in a comfortable room. She was free of cruel Society, of Lady Caroline's viciously expressed judgement and expectations, free of it all. The journey for her was worth at least as much as whatever would come at the end of it. The drovers and the wranglers didn't give a fig that she was plump and awkward, and couldn't match one color to another or judge the cut of a fashionable ensemble to save her life. Her husband didn't give a fig either. Cows, and horses and dogs; that's what he cared for and so did she. This was the country that he loved. She could see that clearly; Dolph moved with assurance in English society, but he had never been been at home there as he was here and now.

Beyond the campfire, the cattle moved quietly, settling down for the night, with an occasional querulous moo. Now and again the voices of one of the drovers standing watch and guard over the cattle drifted on the evening air, singing to lull and reassure them to sleep. A log in the fire crumbled, sending up a shower of tiny sparks, briefly lighting the faces of those still awake. Isobel caught her breath. There was one of the cows, standing just outside the firelight; a long-legged and massive creature, whose horns would have spread to the height of a man, save that one was broken off short and capped with a metal sleeve. As she watched, the cow ambled into the light, the large bell hanging from a leather collar chiming gently and approached Daddy Hurst, sloshing the last of the tin plates through a bucket of soapy water. Daddy Hurst dried his hands and opened the tucker-box which held the leftover bread from supper. Daddy cut off a slice, while her husband chuckled at the expression on Isobel's face.

"That's Old Blue," he explained. "He's the RB's lead cow. That's why we hung a bell on him. He's been up the trail to Kansas more times than most of the hands and oftener than most cows – for them, it's a one-direction journey Onkel Hansi took a liking to him. Old Blue would step out in front and all the others would follow him. That's too good a cow to make supper from. He's about as tame as one of the dogs and he sure 'nuff knows that the boys are going to give him a treat or two. He likes cornbread and hot peppers and sugar, if there is some to spare."

"Extraordinary," Isobel breathed. Dolph whistled invitingly. "Here, Blue!" he called and the animal lumbered over towards where they sat, leaning up against the wheel of Isobel's wagon. Dolph patted his vest-pocket and pulled out a small piece of lump sugar. Blue took it delicately from his fingers, crunched it with apparent enjoyment and looked expectantly at them for a moment. Receiving nothing more, he ambled away content. Dolph looked at her and grinned. "'Member when I tol' you once, there were cows all about the place, Bell darlin'?"

"So you did," Isobel admitted.

The next morning Isobel discovered another matter regarding cows; as they prepared to break camp, her husband called over the young drover, Johnny Benbow – he who had shot at Gawain.

"One of the heifers dropped a calf last night," Dolph said, without preamble. "As soon as we get the herd moving, you know what to do. Try and shoot straight this time, Johnny."

"I don't like to do that, Mister Becker," Johnny shook his head, mutinously. Dolph looked exasperated. "I don't like it any better, but it's got to be done. A newborn calf can't keep up with the herd. The coyotes an' crows will eat the poor little thing alive, otherwise."

"Do what?" Isobel demanded. Both men turned to look at her. Johnny blurted, "Shoot the calf, ma'am. I don't like shooting those li'l babies. The mama cow carries on somethin' awful, it's like doing murder, right in front of her."

"Surely not!" Isobel gasped, horrified. "Dolph – aren't we moving this herd to the new ranch in order that they may thrive and multiply? That is the whole purpose, isn't it – to stock this property with cattle? Why should we begin by disposing of the first fruits of this enterprise?"

"It's too little to walk after the mama cow," Dolph answered patiently. Isobel regarded him with equal exasperation. "But I have a wagon and there's enough room in it for a calf, surely. I can transport the calf easily enough – it is not so very large, is it? In the evenings, it can feed from its mother. You can see the sense of this? And it's only for a little time, until it is strong enough to keep up during the day." She fixed her husband with a pleading look. "Dogs, and horses, and cows, you said."

He yielded as she thought he would. Obviously, he had no better liking for killing the calves than Johnny did. "All right then, Bell; Johnny, you get a gunny-sack from Hurst – when the herd moves out, you wrangle that calf into the sack and bring it to my wife's wagon. You do that every day, until that calf is big enough to keep up with the herd."

"Yes, Mister Becker," Johnny exclaimed, brightening with relief. Isobel was cheered, thinking that Johnny Benbow would be happy enough with the opportunity to make up for his carelessness in wounding poor Gawain. Sure enough, some twenty minutes into the morning march, Johnny Benbow rode alongside Isobel's wagon, with a small, bawling white and red calf draped across his saddle-bow. Even new-born, it was still nearly the size of the dogs and it took an effort to boost the little calf into the back of the wagon. Baffled and obviously unhappy, it made a constant complaint for a few minutes, but after that, only when jolted by the wagon going over a sudden rock or rut.

When they stopped that night, Johnny Benbow came unbidden for the calf, lifting it down from the wagon. It scampered away, soon lost among the herd and Isobel felt ridiculously pleased at the sight. Every day, the calf traveled in her wagon. It was joined by three more, as the days passed. Although she swept out the daily evidence of the calves being in excellent health and their bowels in good working order, the effluvia began to perfume the wagon to the point where Isobel and Dolph soon preferred to sleep on a thick cotton-stuffed pallet laid on the ground outside, under the web of stars. The weather was most often mild, so this was no particular hardship. Every night, Isobel looked up at the velvet-dark sky arched overhead, sequined with brilliant stars and the Milky Way twisted through it like an immense gauzy scarf, and thought of how Jack Sutcliffe had described them . . . Jack had been wrong. The stars each night were even more magnificent than words could describe.

"You see, the herd is increasing!" Isobel pointed out merrily to her amused husband, over a chorus of bawling caves, late one afternoon, as they assembled their evening camp.

"In noise, and numbers," Dolph answered. She had taken to halting the wagon at the edge of the nightly bedding ground and allowing the calves to leap down and run to join their mothers. "Still, Bell darlin' – that was a good notion of yours."

"You did promise me cows," Isobel answered. Dolph put his arm around her shoulders and gave them a brief, affectionate squeeze. "I did – but I never said nothin' about polecat-kittens!"

"You're horrid! Daddy Hurst is a tattle-tale of the worst kind," Isobel exclaimed indignantly. "He wasn't supposed to tell."

"Too good a story, Bell darlin'," Dolph answered, but relented. "I won't tell anyone but Cuz."

"You may as well tell the rest of the world!" Isobel still simmered with embarrassment over the incident. Several days before, she had gone a short way from their nooning camp for a bucket of fresh water before the cattle muddied and fouled the little trickling creek. It was only herself and Daddy Hurst, the dogs, and the temporarily orphaned calves, bawling disconsolately in the back of the wagon. Returning with the water, she had found what she thought were three tiny black and white kittens, their eyes barely open. How had they come to be abandoned on the prairie, miles from any habitation – three helpless kittens? Full of indignation, she set down the bucket and gathered up the kittens in a fold of her skirt. They nuzzled her fingers and squeaked pathetically – they must be so hungry! They must be able to work out something to feed them with, from the stores in the cook-wagon.

When she showed them to the old cook, he gaped at her in horror and exclaimed, "Miz Isobel, they ain't kittens! They is some nasty li'l polecat babies – you take them right back where you foun' dem, afore they lay some stink on you that you won't nebber forget!"

"But they look like kittens!" Isobel stammered and Daddy Hurst came as close to being un-deferential with her as he had ever been in their short acquaintance. "Miz Isobel, they ain't kittens an' you don't know nothin' 'bout this country! I know a damned pole-cat skunk when I see one – you put them back ezactly where yo' foun' dem this very minute!"

Isobel obeyed, crushed and discomfited. She retraced her steps to where she had found the kittens and put them down, hoping that their mother would find them, just as the mother cows had found their calves every evening. They were wild animals, if what Daddy Hurst said was true – and it probably was. When she returned to the wagons, it appeared Daddy Hurst regretted speaking so bluntly. He paused from chopping onions on the wagon-tailboard table and allowed, in a mollifying tone of voice, "Miz Isobel, I shouldn't have spoke so harsh. I am mos' particular sorry . . . dose li'l things, they look so sad an' helpless, o'course you would think about rescuin' dem, like dose li'l cows. But dose pole-cats. . . ."

"I understand completely," Isobel called upon every resource that she had to be gracious, although his previous words still stung. "They were wild things and it would have been wrong to take them from their mother. You were right in saying this is a country that I do not know. But I do wish to know and sometimes knowledge is gained with pain."

"You got dat right," Daddy Hurst chuckled. Isobel was struck with a sudden fancy. "Hurst," she said, wanting to act on the impulse before she talked herself out of it. "Would you show me how you cook those dried beans? I am sure you must add something special since they are so very flavorful. Yet you have to cook them very simply on a fire in the open air and the men say there are no other trail-cooks your equal. I would like to learn to cook. Until now, it was not a skill that I had any need for, but when everyone else is working so very hard I would like to think that I could be of use. And," she added, so that it would seem as if she did have more than just good intentions, "I have a marvelously savory recipe for game pie. It was often served at my family's home; everyone enjoyed it very much."

"Game pie?" Hurst looked interested. "What kind o'game, then?"

"Venison, and rabbit . . . duck or partridge. Perhaps when we reach the end of this journey, the men will have time to go hunting."

"Dat is a good thought, Miz Isobel," Daddy Hurst agreed. "Back in the day when my mama was the cook for ol' Massa Burnett's family, I b'lieve she baked game pies, but it's been a long time. Miz Isobel, I surely will show you how I cook dem beans. Biscuits, too – there ain't no way, no-how a good wife can get by wid-out knowin' how to make biscuits."

"That will certainly please my husband," Isobel agreed.

From that day on, Isobel assisted the old cook with preparing the evening meal, although at some cost in burnt fingers, scorched skirts and food spilled on her garments. Even though Isobel often felt that she was as clumsy as ever and something of a trial for Daddy Hurst, she suspected that he was otherwise grateful for her sturdy assistance and strong hands. When alone together, he was deferential to her in the manner that she had been accustomed to at home in England. Mr. Arkwright and Kitty-Cat might have been severe with her sometimes but respect for her position always softened adult exasperation. In turn, she came to feel quite fond and protective of him. He was spry enough and uncomplaining, but more and more of those labors which required a degree of physical strength fell to her, to the point where she began to worry.

One night, as she and Dolph lay close together, on the far side of her wagon, she asked him, "How old is Hurst?"

"I don't know," Dolph confessed, after a moment of thought. "Why do you want to know, Bell?"

"I think that he is often very tired. I wonder if he is older than everyone assumes. How long has he been in service to your family?"

"Cuz's family," Dolph corrected. "He hired out to Aunt Margaret around the time Texas was annexed. He belonged to a family she knew. I don't know how old he is, exactly. He was born a slave and came to Texas with his old master."

"Hmm," Isobel mused. "How long ago was that?"

"I never thought about it. Before we broke from Mexico, I guess."

"The other day, he began telling me about a battle with British soldiers near New Orleans. He says that he and his master were both there. They must have been well-grown enough to be soldiers. He talked about ranks of bright red coats and glittery bayonets. When was that?"

"Not all that well-grown," her husband pointed out. He turned in the bed, to lie on his side with his arm around her. "I enlisted with Colonel Ford when I was fifteen. My father was in the militia by the time he was a year older."

"But the battle," Isobel nestled closer to him, relishing the warmth and the solid feel of him, and his embrace of her. "What year was it?"

"Do I look like a schoolmaster?" He answered with some indignation. "Sam would know the answer to that. 1814, 1815 – around then, I think."

Isobel rapidly made some mathematical calculations, the final answer of which proved not reassuring. "That was sixty years ago! If he were fifteen or older then, that would now make Hurst at least seventy – maybe even eighty!"

"That may be so," Dolph agreed. "But he's a working man – even if Aunt Margaret left him a life pension. To a man like Daddy, living is their work! Building things, slinging beans for the hands, driving a wagon . . . Working keeps a man fit for life, otherwise he's just a lump on a log. Onkel Hansi, Daddy Hurst – if they stopped doing what they do and just sat around on the porch in a rocking-chair, they would purely up and die. Your Pa is a man like that. Mebbe it's why I like him so much. Young Seb has the makings of that. If ol' Daddy wants to come up the trail with us one more time, I reckon that he's earned that right. Don't fret, Bell. He'll be all right. In any case," he added, a whisper in her ear, as they lay under the blankets and quilts piled over them. "Daddy ain't been a slave for ten years. If he didn't want to go up the trail with us, wanted to sit on the porch of his little place at Aunt Margaret's house and smoke his pipe all the day, there was no one to make him do otherwise."

"As you say," Isobel agreed, with reluctance. It was true about the work that a man did. But Daddy Hurst was undoubtedly beginning to show his considerable age and too proud to admit to frailty. She moved closer to Dolph; agreeable to putting the days' worries aside, in the bliss of sleeping in his arms. But there remained a single small discomfort. There was a marked lump in the straw-stuffed pallet on which they lay, a long lump which lay between them. "Didn't you see the root?" she asked.

"What root?" he asked, reasonably enough. Isobel replied, "There is a huge tree root under this mattress. I can feel it quite plainly."

"There's not a tree big enough this far north of the Llano to make that much of a bump," Dolph yawned. "Don't pay it any mind, Bell – I don't think we'll be spending any time in the middle of the bed tonight. Go to sleep." And Isobel embraced him again, still annoyed at the presence of the long ridge though the center of their bed. No, all she wanted tonight was sleep, and the refuge of his arms about her.

Chapter 14 – *Schoolhouse*

On the Monday morning that had been decreed by a committee composed of Sam and Lottie Becker to be the first day of school, Jane Goodacre gathered up her courage, several more books which she had thought might be profitably added to the tiny library shelf, and briskly walked the short way down the hill to the former hay-shed. She dressed herself with considerable care that morning; the same care with which she attended Lady Isobel's daily toilette. She pinned the gold watch to the shoulder of her dress; a simple brown poplin walking dress of two seasons ago which Lady Isobel had gifted her. She piled up her hair to make herself seem taller, and pinned a plain hat over it. Now Jane looked into the mirror and was pleased at what she saw – a young woman who looked as stern and commanding as Aunt Lydia.

A handful of children played at a game with a ball in the yard before the school-building; three girls and three boys. They were all barefoot, but otherwise cleanly and plainly dressed. Jane's footsteps hesitated only for a moment; she walked on, acutely aware by the sudden silence that the game had ceased as soon as they caught sight of her. The hands of the watch pointed at three minutes of eight – she was early.

There were a row of pegs new-driven into the wall just inside the door, which now stood open. Jane added the books to those already on the shelf and straightened them with care. She took off her hat and hung it on the first peg with the air of someone establishing the first steps of a new ritual. She brushed a bit of invisible lint from her sleeve, consulted her watch again – it was time. The children were still quiet outside, although she heard a muffled giggle and the thump of a ball against the side of the schoolhouse. Time for the new school day, time for the new teacher. A deep breath; she willed her hands to be steady, her voice confident. She grasped the metal rod that hung from a length of twine, and struck it against the barrel-hoop, struck it hard enough that it rang like a bell, again and again. She looked out at the children lining up below the single step upon which she stood, now joined by two bashful older boys, the oldest of whom was nearly as tall as herself. They were not barefoot; they wore the same kind of boots that the men working on the ranch did.

"Good morning, children," Jane said in voice made firm with some effort. "I am Miss Goodacre. I am to be your teacher. If you will come inside and find a place to sit, then we will begin." She stood aside from the door while the children and boys filed in. The two youngest girls held hands and sat close together; they both had long black hair and eyes as dark as molasses syrup. When they had all taken a seat, Jane stood beside her desk and continued. "This is how we will begin every day. I will say, 'Good morning, children.' and then you will say all together, 'Good morning, Miss Goodacre.'"

"Good morning, Miss Goodacre!" they chorused obediently. Jane was gratified – they obeyed, the first time she asked it.

"Very good; now, I want each of you to tell me your name, how old you are, and how far you have gone in school or if you can write your name. beginning with the youngest."

The two smallest girls simply stared at her, owl-eyed. The slightly older boy sitting next to them answered in their stead. "That's Adeliza an' Conception Menchaca. 'Liza is seven, an' Chita is six. They ain't never been to school. I'm Andrew Sibley – I'm seven. I can write my name, and I'm in the Second Reader." Andrew had a gap between his front teeth which showed when he smiled and hair obviously newly bowl-cut around his head.

"Thank you, Andrew. It's better to say, 'They have never been' – not 'ain't'. Try to remember this. Using correct grammar is the sign of a good education." As a rebuke, it did not seem to sting Andrew overly. Jane made a mental note to encourage him in eschewing grammatical heresies as 'ain't' and in dropping certain letters at the ends of words.

"I'm Emma Sibley," whispered the third girl. She was pretty, and her light brown hair hung down in two braided loops tied with ribbon bows. Her dress was ruffled and obviously new. "I'm nine. I was almost to the Fourth Reader. At school in Huntsville, they let me study ahead."

"Very good, Emma," Jane said, with mixed relief and apprehension. From what she had reviewed in *McGuffey's Readers* this meant that Emma could read, write and do arithmetic reasonably well. Perhaps Jane might call on Emma to help those pupils farther behind in their skills, but Jane had only three years more in her own education. How much could a teacher struggle and still remain ahead of a pupil? She nodded at the next boy, who also had the gap in his teeth and the same unfortunate bowl-shaped haircut.

"I'm Corcoran Sibley," he answered confidently. "I'm ten-and-a-half – I was in the Fourth Reader, until I had to quit school."

"Austin Sibley," The next boy was a little taller than his brothers, and had taken a place on the second row of benches. "You sound funny when you talk. Miss Goodacre. You ain't from around here, are you?"

"I am not from around here," Jane answered. "I will tell you a little about where I am from, later. It will be today's geography lesson. How old are you, Austin?"

"Almos' thirteen, Miss Goodacre. I was in the Fourth Reader, too. It was the only one our last school had," he added with a touch of confiding honesty.

"Jeff Inman." The next boy spoke up, unbidden; he had an earnest face, sprinkled with freckles and unruly ginger-red hair which stuck out at all angles. "I'm thirteen. My pa married their ma, Miz Sibley, so we're family, now. I can write my name, but I cain't read none."

"Can not read anything," Jane corrected him automatically. This was one of those matters that Aunt Lydia insisted upon; that upstairs servants at the Hall all be well-spoken. Her mind was already running ahead; Tia Leticia's granddaughters and the Inman boy were all unlettered, but the Sibley children had advanced in in their schooling more or less fitting to their ages,

The last pupil – hardly a boy – must be the ranch hand which Sam Becker had mentioned. When she looked towards him, he half-rose from the bench and bowed awkwardly. "Ma'am, I'm Cody Weeks, I'm sixteen years old, I b'lieve, and I ain't never been to school."

"You haven't ever been to school," Jane corrected him and he answered, unruffled. "Yes ma'am, that's what I said. I ain't never been to school, but Mister Sam Becker, he says knowing my numbers and bein' able to write my name will help me get ahead in the world."

"So they would," Jane answered, with feeling. Her own education, as truncated as it was, had certainly helped her advance, at least temporarily. "You may sit down, Cody. Well, then . . . I think we shall begin with geography, today. I came from a country called England, which is a part of a large island off the coast of Europe." She had the children gather around the globe on her desk and moved the globe to show them where England was. She was able to fill in the next hours very comfortably with a lecture on the geography of her homeland, chief cities, and industry, and concluded by writing a short poem by William Blake on the blackboard, which she had intended that they all memorize. She set the Sibley children to that duty and drew the other four to sit close with their slates and chalk at the ready. For each, she spelled out their names in simple chalk letters and gradually realized that the Menchaca girls barely understood English. She bravely carried on, explaining the sounds that the various letters made and how they were strung together to make words. Before she realized how much time had passed, the sun stood high in the sky and the gold hands of her pocket watch pointed at noon. *Some small learning has been achieved*, she thought. Time for an hour recess; she dismissed the boys and girls. They scattered as she walked in a daze up to the ranch house and wondered where the morning had gone.

Sam met her in the front hallway, with a smile. "How went the first day of school, Miss Jane?"

Jane took a deep breath; "Marvelously well. After dinner, we shall have mathematics, grammar and natural science; grammar for the Sibley children, diagramming sentences, practicing making letters for the others."

"It would be good to teach Cody Weeks how to figure." Sam took her arm and led her into the dining room, where she could barely fit in answers to the questions from Mrs. Becker and an excited Lottie in between bites of her meal. By then she had a solution to one of her minor dilemmas; the Menchaca girls and their imperfect grasp of English.

"If you are at liberty," she suggested to Lottie. "Might you come every afternoon for an hour and assist me with Adeliza and Conchita, since you do understand Spanish? I do not think they understand English at all well. They are also embarrassed to speak the little they do know in front of me. They make themselves understood to Andrew and I am certain they are very clever girls but I know nothing of Spanish at all."

"Of course!" Lottie beamed good-will and excitation. "They are sweet children! Leticia wishes so much for them and so does their Uncle Porfirio. There is a connection between our family and theirs, you know. Porfirio was an excellent friend to our father and *his* father an intimate of Cuz Peter's father. Mister Vining was a schoolteacher, too. He had three bookshelves full of books; in the early days that made the largest library in Austin. I will be happy to help school Liza and 'Chita." She looked between her brother and Jane, with her sky-blue eyes sparkling with enthusiasm. "It is splendid, to have a school here, Jane – I am so glad that Sam thought of it and you consented to teach, since it will mean so very much to the children! I daresay we will never know how much it will mean, for we cannot see into the future, can we?"

For Jane, the afternoon and the days and weeks of work in the little schoolhouse which followed were fuller of excitement and happiness than she had ever imagined. She ate her meals at the family table in haste, her mind already running ahead with a plan of lessons, with a strategy to make Cody Weeks understand the place value of numbers, for Liza and 'Chita to realize that the same letters meant differing sounds, depending on the language, and a means of keeping Emma – whose intellect was ravenously curious – supplied with enough material to keep that appetite satiated. Her own evenings were spent in reading ahead, in enlarging on her own capacities. Now and again she wakened in the midnight hours to find that she had fallen asleep with a book lying across her chest and the flame in the lamp at her bedside having burned low and guttered out. All of her interest revolved around the little schoolroom, bent upon those eight pupils who were her daily care and concern.

One of the books that she found on the Becker's bookshelf was a well-thumbed copy of the complete *Pickwick Papers. S*he read aloud from it for the children during the last forty minutes of the school-day, as a reward for them having been obedient and diligent at their lessons during the day. This enchanted them all and offered many opportunities to expand on other subjects – notably geography. She did worry that if she finished that book too soon, she would have to find another which would work quite the same spell. Often, when the schoolhouse became too hot from the sun beating down on the split-shake roof for the entire day, she would take the children and the *Pickwick Papers*, and walk with them into the shade of the walled apple-orchard, on the gentle slope below the house. There the children would settle happily in the shade, while she read to them.

On a mid-morning late in September, Jane was completely caught up in the schoolroom; as she was during most hours of the day, save for the last three-quarters. She often felt as if she were a kind of academic plate-spinner, juggling and overseeing the lessons of her pupils: Emma was diagramming a compound sentence on half of the blackboard, while her brothers' heads were bent over a thick atlas, working out the answers to a series of questions written out on the other half. Jane led her other four pupils in reciting the alphabet, followed by an exercise in consonants. She had constructed a series of pasteboard cards, with a letter written on each. Now the letters were laid out in a random order upon the tabletop.

"What letter makes this sound – tee?" She asked, noting with a corner of her mind that Cody Weeks still looked baffled by the whole concept of written letters standing for specific sounds. She had begun to doubt that he would never be able to write more than his name, although he was sharp enough at numbers. Gratifyingly, Liza and 'Chita Menchaca had begun demonstrating that they understood the concept, going as far as to speak to her without Andrew Sibley's interlocution. "Now, which letter is the sound of 'cee'?" she asked, as a movement at the doorway of the schoolhouse diverted her attention.

There was a woman standing there; a handsome woman in her thirties, tall and as fashionable as Lady Isobel had always tried to appear and as elegant as Lady Caroline truly was. She was not beautiful; her face was square and strong-featured, with level dark eyebrows, but her features were animated by a formidable intelligence and character. As for her attire, Jane had not seen anything so modish since departing New York – no, since departing England. This woman was looking into Jane's schoolroom; the place Jane had taken for her own and for her oddly-assorted students with what seemed to be a coldly-appraising eye.

As soon as the woman saw that Jane was about to speak, she exclaimed, "No, no, Miss Goodacre, I do not wish to disturb you and your pupils when you are all so hard at work. I was merely curious. Might I observe for a time? I am Miss Johnson, a guest of the Beckers. We shall meet at dinner today."

"Of course," Jane answered, fearing that she might be terribly rattled, having a stranger watch. She thought the younger children might have been distracted also, although Jeff Inman and Cody Weeks were not. Cody Weeks whispered, "She's <u>that</u> Miss Johnson, Miss Goodacre, all the way from Austin!"

"<u>She</u> is the cat's mother," Jane whispered back, reprovingly. "And who is this most famous Miss Johnson, when she's at home?"

"She buys cattle and land," Jeff Inman answered, unbidden. "A lot of both, an' she's a friend of the Beckers, but that's not what everyone knows her for the most."

"And what would that be?" Jane cast a worried glance at the door, but the elegant Miss Johnson remained without, a shadow out of earshot.

"She's a school-teacher." Cody Weeks spoke up. Jane could scarcely conceal her astonishment. *A school-teacher?* Jane thought that she conducted the rest of the morning's class with a good portion of her usual attention to detail but the presence of Miss Johnson was intriguing, even as her elegantly attired person remained just outside the doorway. Jane dismissed her pupils at the appointed time and they scattered, full of happy energy at being so released, although Cody Weeks and Jeff Inman did pause and respectfully greet Miss Johnson before they also scattered. Jane lingered, resettling the books on the shelf, and gathering up the scattered school slates, was aware that Miss Johnson had finally advanced from the doorway, assessing the tiny schoolroom with a thoroughly professional interest.

"This is very nice, Miss Goodacre," Miss Johnson observed at last. "Better than nice – impressive; and I should better introduce myself. I am Miss Johnson, but my friends call me Lizzie. Sam Becker and Peter Vining are friends as well as business associates. I should like to consider you as a friend also, since we all have the same vocation."

"Would that be the school-teaching, or property and cattle?" Jane asked without thinking and Miss Johnson chuckled. "Very shrewd, Jane – I may call you Jane, then? Sam told me of this enterprise and I must needs come and see for myself. He said that you have the eight pupils and half of them likely to have never seen the inside of a schoolbook before. Is this true?" Jane put on her hat and the two of them walked companionably, side by side.

"Yes, it is true. Although," Jane sighed, "I fear the two lads, having come to it so late, will never advance much beyond simple mathematics and writing their own names. I shall not give up on them," she added. "Being able to read and write opens everything else to an active mind."

"Commendable," Miss Johnson answered. "And quite true: In my experience, it is quite difficult – nay, nearly impossible to impress the joys of literacy upon young men past a certain age. Now, tell me, Jane; this is your first venture into teaching? And you were schooled yourself only until the age of twelve or so?"

"In the village school," Jane answered, obscurely pleased to see that Miss Johnson was impressed.

"So – I gather, not a wide range of subjects; but those taught to you were taught thoroughly and well, so well that you have easily moved into teaching others. You need not answer, Jane – I can see with my own eyes. Sam told me about you. He says that you are particularly gifted."

"I wouldn't know, Miss Johnson," Jane began. Miss Johnson corrected her, "Please, Jane, call me Lizzie."

"I don't know that I am gifted, as Sam says. I have nothing to compare it to. But I do take a satisfaction in it. Spending the day in the schoolroom sometimes seems as if it was only five minutes and seeing that the children are improving their knowledge – there is nothing like it that I have ever done before."

"And what had you done before?" Lizzie Johnson smiled. Jane was emboldened to honesty. "I am Mrs. Dolph Becker's personal maid. Before that, I was in service at her father's estate as an upstairs maid."

"Were you?" Lizzie Johnson's strong dark eyebrows arched in astonishment. "That was a waste of intellect and skill, no doubt about it. Teaching is a step up, I can assure you. Do you want to go on teaching after Sam's brother and Mrs. Becker return at the end of the year?"

"I don't know," Jane answered frankly. "I am attached to my lady and she depends on me. As to what I might do after this, I do not know."

"If you'd like to continue teaching," Lizzie Johnson ventured. "I suggest you consider accepting a position at my school. I have a rather nice little private academy in Austin," she explained with an air which combined becoming modesty with honest pride. "I own the building; we – that is, myself and the other teachers live upstairs. I always have need of a teacher for the junior grades. One who speaks correctly and grammatically would be received very well."

"I don't know," Jane said, "I will think about it. I have always thought that I would remain with my lady in service. She needs me, very much. I came with her from England because of that."

"Do consider it, if you are serious," Lizzie answered. "There's time between now and December."

It was not her maid that Isobel was thinking of, the morning after she had talked to Dolph about Daddy Hurst's age, as she and Daddy Hurst finished the last of the breakfast dishes and prepared to break camp. The tree root under their bedroll had annoyed her all night, whenever she woke to feel the lump underneath her. Now, while Dolph brought around the horses that pulled her wagon and prepared to hitch them up, she folded up the quilts and sheets that made up their bedding. Last to be put into the wagon was the heavy cotton-stuffed pallet they had slept upon, and the water-proof canvas ground-cloth underneath it. As Isobel folded the ground-cloth, lifting it from the grass crushed flat underneath, she made a discovery that nearly sent her shrieking, but for the necessity ingrained into her from weeks of traveling with the herd, not actually screaming for the fear of not frightening the cattle. It was no tree root under their bed, but a huge snake, with buff-grey leathery scales patterned in darker diamonds which were outlined in a paler lozenge. It laid still: a monster as thick through the body as a strong man's arm, the head a massive wedge-shape, and the full evil length of it still half-concealed under the mattress. Isobel sprang gracelessly backwards from the half-folded ground-cloth.

"Dolph!" she called, in a half-strangled whisper. "Help! There's this horrid . . ." Her voice failed her entirely. "We slept on . . ." she gasped, and her voice failed her again. Her husband leapt to her side as soon as she called for him.

"Keep back, Bell!" he commanded, his own voice perfectly steady. "The cold at night – they can't move much, but once they warm up, you ain't seen anything move so fast as a rattler."

"Not to worry!" Isobel gasped. Instead of taking out his own revolver, Dolph moved without apparent hurry to the tool-chest strapped to the other side of the kitchen-wagon, where Daddy Hurst was still stowing away the remains of the breakfast biscuits and beans for the noon meal.

"Bell found a snake in our bed," he said. Daddy Hurst answered, "You don't say!" and added something in a lower voice, at which her husband chuckled with a flash of grim humor before replying, "Don't you say that where she can hear, Daddy. I just need to borrow the shovel."

"You be careful, now – you hear?" Daddy Hurst commanded and Isobel watched as Dolph sorted out the shovel from the tool-chest and came back, carrying it across his shoulder.

"You might want to look away now, Bell." her husband warned her. He brought the shovel blade down on the horrible creature's head, chopping that narrow neck clean through, while the monstrous body writhed and the severed head snapped and snapped again at empty air. Isobel caught a glimpse of a pair of long curved teeth. Her husband bashed the head several times with the back of the shovel, until it was reduced to a bloody smear among the flattened grass. "No fear, Bell," Dolph came up and embraced her briefly with one arm, the shovel in the other, the blade still smeared and dripping with blood and ichor. The body of the snake moved, although with decreasing vigor. Shuddering with horror, she pulled the rest of the mattress and the canvas ground-cloth away, while Wash Charpentier, Daddy Hurst and several of the wranglers came to take a look at the still-feebly thrashing body.

"Somebody gonna have a damned-fine hatband," observed Wash Charpentier. He unsheathed the hunting knife at his waist and squinted up at Isobel. "You want the rattles, Miz Becker?"

"I do not," Isobel replied; she felt faint from revulsion, especially when Wash coolly sliced off the end of the snake's tail and held it towards her.

"It's a big ol' fella," Wash said and shook the disgusting thing with a brisk motion – it rattled dryly. "Might be near twenty year old." The snake had now ceased moving. With a few deft cuts, Wash slit the skin and began peeling it off the snake; it came away with a sound like tearing paper. Isobel came very close to loosing her breakfast.

"I think you should finish hitching the horses," she said to her husband, her voice sounding faint and hollow in her own ears. "India was full of snakes, so my brother told me. It was one reason I did not want to go there and I do not think I wish to remain here a moment longer."

"I don't believe you do," Dolph answered, although he did sound rather more amused than Isobel thought the situation called for. "But it will make a funny story to tell your folks, the next time you write."

Once having gotten over the horror, of which she was reminded often, since Wash nailed the snake skin to the side of the cook-wagon to dry, Isobel added the incident to the long letter she was writing to Fa. She added to this letter every few days, a compilation of the incidents of the journey, the accidental wounding of Gawain excepted. *The dried skin of the snake measures a full five feet long,* she wrote several days later, after she and Daddy Hurst finished setting up camp for the night. *I sincerely hope that I shall never see its like again or sleep on a mattress with such a specimen hibernating underneath throughout a cold night. We are very close to the end of this journey. . .*

She paused to re-ink her pen. She sat the wagon-seat, with the ink-pot on the wagon-set beside her and her letter-paper laid out on a short length of smooth plank which served as a temporary writing desk. The horses were unharnessed and left to graze nearby, tethered to picket-pins pounded middling-deep into the turf. Daddy Hurst had already built up the evening cook-fire. Although she had spread out the cotton-stuffed mattress and their bedding next to the wagon, Isobel chose to sit up there, so she could watch for the cattle. The ground was level all the way around, but for the shallow canyon to the south which they had crossed in mid-afternoon and a low northerly eminence shaped like current bun, studded with small round boulders, which made a handy land-mark. Dolph had marked the night bed-ground in the lee of that little hill. Although she and Daddy Hurst had crossed without any difficulty, the canyon vexed them all, for reasons that Isobel did not wish to articulate in her letter. They had traveled only a short distance that day. In mid-afternoon, her husband came riding back from scouting the trail ahead. He gestured for hers and Daddy Hurst's wagons to halt side-by side for a brief parley.

"We're coming up on an arroyo, a dry canyon, two or three miles ahead," he said, squinting up at her as his pony shifted restlessly. "Full of brush and mesquite, some good-sized trees, too. No running water though – too long since a good rain, not to worry about crossing. There's a good-sized draw down and up again, lots of cattle and wagon-tracks. It's a well-used trail. Looks like the best way across but that place gives me a bad feeling. Like there's an ambush set, waiting on the right moment. I keep feeling that there is someone watching."

"What are we going to do, then?" Isobel asked, as Daddy Hurst wrapped the reins around one fist and felt around underneath the wagon-seat with the other hand. He came up with a double-barreled shotgun, which he propped on the seat next to him, the barrel pointing up at the sky.

"Be on guard more than the usual," Dolph answered with a short laugh. "Keep a tight rein on the teams. I'm going to cross through the canyon with you, just to make sure, after I let the boys know."

Isobel's heart sank. There had been little disruption of the drive since they had begun; the rattlesnake and the wounding of Gawain being exceptions. They were all but alone out here; no higher law to appeal to. Only themselves and what Wash Charpentier had jestingly referred to as the 'six statutes of Colt.' Dolph explained that reference to her; it meant the six chambers of the revolver strapped at her waist. Now Dolph brought the tips of his fingers to his lips, blew a kiss in her direction. "I'll catch up, Bell, darlin'. Let the dogs down off the wagon and keep your eyes open."

He rode on, at a purposeful trot. Isobel looked across at Daddy Hurst, who said stoutly, "Don' you worry, Miz Becker, dis ol' Parker is triple-loaded wid buckshot, both barrels. You jes' keep dat team in line; we'll be through dat canyon in two shakes of a lamb's tail." He slapped the reins on his teams' backs and whistled; the cook-wagon rolled on. Isobel followed closely, squinting against the dust that rose up from its wheels. Gawain and Sorsha trotted alongside, questing now a little way into the grass and scattered small shrubs, never far and always returning at Isobel's call. It relieved Isobel to have the dogs close to her wagon, their heads up as they bounded gracefully along. If there were anyone about, lurking in the taller coverts within the canyon, the dogs would give warning. Her own revolver was loaded and there was another Parker charged with buckshot underneath her own wagon seat. Still, she had been relieved to hear the regular hoof beats of her husband's pony catching up from behind, just as they approached the line of darker trees and scrub which filled the canyon. Her eyes now accustomed to the wilderness, Isobel saw what Dolph had noted before; many cattle and horses had passed this way. The ground was much chopped for some distance with hoof-prints . . . which had gone in many directions. Isobel felt the skin on the back of her neck prickle. There was something not right about this crossing, yet nothing was obviously out of place. A hawk circled high overhead, wings outspread dark and motionless; no overt sign of danger, but Isobel sensed what her husband had felt. There should have been scattered bird-song coming from the dense thickets that filled the canyon. Instead there was only a muffled cheeping, which barely broke the oppressive silence.

"I wish you had brought more of the hands to guard us, if you thought this passage so perilous," she said. Dolph reined in alongside the wagon. Ahead, the cover on the cook wagon bellied like a sail filled with wind, as the trail slanted downwards into the shallow canyon.

"Bell, darlin', you are dear to me and Daddy an' the chuck-wagon are dear to the hands, but you ain't the most valuable part of this company," Dolph answered. "It's the cattle. If someone wanted to set off a stampede, here's the place they would do it. Right here where there's cover in the canyon, and send them running in all directions."

"I see," Isobel said. Now she could. An ordinary brigand might think of robbing the wagons, but to steal cattle by setting off a panic among them and then rounding up the strays? Of course her husband would see them through and then ride back to convey the cattle safely. She and Daddy could well look after themselves with the aid of the dogs and the statutes of Colt.

The cook wagon pulled ahead, the un-sprung wagon rocking as the iron-shod wheels rolled over rocks and ruts at the bottom of the canyon, where intermittent floods had gouged a stream-bed. The way up and down that tangled, dry streambed was clear for just one moment. As Isobel looked, her attention was attracted by a half-sensed stirring in the brush that could not be accounted for by wind. She saw Gawain lift his head, his purposeful trot arrested and every muscle tense. He was looking in the direction of where she had seen that movement; a thicket on the far lip of the canyon, underneath a line of scraggly and half-dead trees. She halted the wagon, and pointed towards the thicket.

"Stay, Gawain – sit! There!" she said to Dolph. "There's something – someone there!" In the sudden quiet, she heard the rattle of pebbles and a puff of dust rose from within the distant thicket. Dolph un-holstered his own revolver and snapped off a quick single shot into the place where the brush grew thickest, a shot which echoed like a cannon-shell exploding in the shallow canyon. The branches within the thicket were violently agitated, as someone burst from within that shelter and vanished over the far rim. Dolph fired again; Sorsha and Gawain both snarled and would have lunged in pursuit, but for Isobel calling them back. It would have been fruitless in any case; a horse briefly whinnied and then there was nothing but the sounds of hoof-beats at a fast gallop vanishing into the distance. Isobel hastily fumbled underneath the wagon-seat for the brass and Morocco spy-glass. No, the man and his horse were gone from sight, over the edge of the canyon. Her husband's face was set in grim lines, as he wheeled his own mount around.

"Whatever he was up to, he's gone," he called to Isobel. "I've marked the bed-ground for tonight a little way on. We'll camp early tonight."

Now, Isobel set aside her pen and took up the spyglass again, looking back along the trail towards that line of dark-green. She could see nothing but a faint haze of dust, marring the clear blue of the sky; the cattle, of course. She swept the spyglass in a half-circle, scanning the horizon. Nothing moved save an occasional hawk and a few puffy clouds sailing across the sky, where the sun had already began to sink. Shadows stretched across the distant prairie, revealing by their presence that the land was not quite as flat as it appeared at high noon. The sun dipped closer, touching the slight eminence of that little hill which had marked their camping place in this otherwise featureless country. The youngest calf bawled disconsolately from the back of her wagon; the poor thing likely wanting its mother and a bit of freedom from the wagon.

"Seen 'em yet, Miz Becker?" Daddy Hurst called from below.

"No, not yet," Isobel answered. It was nearly time to punch down the sourdough for the evening's bread, form it into small loaves, and set it to rise again, in the iron oven that the bread would bake in, now that the fire had burned to red-hot coals. Supper for the hands should be ready and piping hot, when they arrived and settled the cattle for the night. She raised the spyglass to her eye for one last look at the range of spindly trees marking the trail where the cattle would come into sight. She thought that she could hear the distant lowing of the herd, the shouts of the hands and wranglers; they must very close, just beyond the shallow canyon and commencing their descent into it.

Again she was startled by a sudden movement in those distant trees. She hastily trained the spyglass on it, hardly daring to believe what she saw; something large and black in the largest tree; a black flapping shape like a gigantic crow. It moved as if on strings manipulated by some gigantic puppeteer. Isobel knew instinctively that it was not natural. The faint sounds of the cattle herd had changed; louder and louder, with a frantic undertone to them. The first of them burst over the edge of the canyon, not in the contained column, accustomed to plod steadily and slowly on, but in a panicked undisciplined rush, pouring over the prairie like water from a broken pot, heedless, dangerous and unstoppable.

"Hurst!" she screamed. "Hurst – they've stampeded the cattle!"

"Stay in yo' wagon, Miz Becker!" He shouted in reply and Isobel screamed back, "No – they're coming this way! The horses!"

"Nebber you mind de horses!" Daddy Hurst had already dropped his long cooking fork, hobbling towards where the six horses were picketed to graze. "I got 'dem!"

Isobel flung aside the plank with her letter, calling to the dogs. Sorsha and Gawain had already sensed something wrong, something baffling. They came leaping up onto the wagon, whining low in their throats, pressing against each other and against her. "Stay!" Isobel commanded and scrambled down from the wagon. She could already feel, more than hear, the drumming of a thousand hoofs, louder and louder.

Chapter 15 – *Palo Duro*

The main body of stampeding cattle ran straight for the the cookfire and the wagons. The draft horses stamped uneasily at the ends of the picket ropes. Isobel cast another glance over her shoulder; tossing horns amid a cloud of dust, rolling inexorably towards them. She caught a brief glimpse of a man at the edge of the herd, crouched low on the neck of his galloping horse, attempting to ride ahead of them, but in another second that sight was lost. The horses – the cattle would panic the draft horses. The picket ropes would never hold; already they had caught the contagion of panic as Daddy Hurst ran towards them. Isobel knew instantly what the old man intended: to calm the horses, lead them closer into camp and a fragile shelter behind the wagons. Another instinct told her it was not going to work; six fractious horses would be too much for the old man's strength. She would have to help him. She caught up a blanket from hers' and Dolph's bed-roll, with a mad hope of covering one of the horses' heads with it. That's what Mr. Arkwright had always said. '*Cover their eyes, Miss Isobel – if they can no' see, then they must trust you.*' Now the onrush of cattle sounded like an endless roll of thunder – worse than thunder, since she could feel the ground under her feet trembling. She ran towards the horses, while Daddy Hurst struggled with the picket ropes; he had two, three freed from the picket-pins screwed deep into the ground . . . and then one reared, neighing so loudly that it sounded like a scream, jerking the rope out of the old man's hand. Isobel had never in her life before heard a horse make a noise like that. In the midst of that horror, Daddy Hurst fell. Isobel did not see clearly what caused him to fall; she was certain that he was not kicked by the struggling horses. He simply fell, the picket ropes falling from his slack hands and the terrified horses dashed away.

No time, no time – the cattle were nearly upon them. Isobel shook out the blanket, remembering how the hands had talked of other such stampedes, how they would wave their jackets in the face of panic-stricken cattle. She ran a short way towards them from the wagons, hardly aware that she was screaming, shaking the folds of the blanket as if she were shaking dust from its folds. Her heart pounded in her chest, but was it her heart or the earth pulsating underneath her feet? She must keep them from running through the camp, running over where Daddy Hurst lay helpless. Now the dogs were howling behind her and she shook the blanket again, hardly considering her own peril. The cattle would wash over the camp, a wave of them, as unrelenting as an ocean tide sweeping all before, but in a flick of an instant, the tide broke and parted. They thundered past, some to one side of Isobel and the wagons, some to the other. She was enveloped in a choking cloud of dust and sank to her knees. From the buzzing in her ears she thought she might faint from sheer terror. But she did not. Slowly, she stood on legs that trembled violently. The main body of running cattle was beyond the wagons. They had gone in all directions, gone as abruptly from her sight as they had appeared from the canyon. The three horses which Daddy Hurst tried to lead to safety were gone. The other three remained, nervous and stamping uneasily at the end of their picket lines. One had managed to loosen a picket-pin halfway from the ground. Isobel dropped the blanket from her nerveless hands and stumbled towards that horse. She caught the rope just as the horse jerked away. The coarse grass rope ripped at the flesh of her hands and the picket pin slipped all the way out of the ground. The pin flew up, the sharpened end slashing the side of her face. Isobel cried out from the sudden pain in her palms and cheek. She held on, gasping out soothing endearments to the frightened horse. The rope slackened, as the horse calmed and stopped pulling away from her hands, now slick with her own blood. She could never drive the picket pin in solidly enough to hold fast. She led the horse to the cook-wagon and tied the picket rope securely to one of the straps that secured the water-barrel. Now to see to Daddy Hurst.

He lay very still, just as he had fallen, his eyes half-open to the sky overhead. There was no wound that Isobel could see, no disarrangement of his clothing signifying injury to the flesh underneath. She took up his hand, unnaturally limp in hers. She could find no pulse in his wrist; no steady beat of a living heart in his chest. Isobel sank back on her heels, stunned with the feeling of being completely alone. The hands, her husband, and the wranglers – they were chasing the cattle. They would eventually return . . . but when?

She was not entirely sure how long she knelt with Daddy Hurst's hand in hers, but eventually she was made aware of Sorsha and Gawain, crouching on either side of her. Gawain nosed at her other hand, whining piteously. That recalled her to herself; no, she was not entirely alone. There were the dogs. She laid Daddy Hurst's hands on his chest, and straightened his limbs, knowing she had been right to worry about him. Where were his family; would they know that he would likely be buried in a lonely grave?

The dust settled quietly. It had all happened in the blink of an eye. The fire burned unharmed, although some of the iron pots around it were upset and scattered. Daddy Hurst had just set a covered iron kettle of sourdough rolls on the fire. The kettle stood where he had put it down, although the passage of a cow had tipped it sideways and farther into the coals than it should have been. The long cooking fork he had dropped at the moment of going to rescue the horses lay on the ground. Isobel rescued the fork and the kettle, wrapping a fold of her skirt around her bleeding hand and setting the kettle on the edge of the fire. The pot of beans was upset, scattered beyond redemption. She would have to begin another pot . . . surely the hands would be hungry, when they returned? The little calf bawled piteously from her wagon. She let down the gate. The calf jumped down readily and looked around, obviously quite puzzled at the absence of its mother.

A quick shadow passed overhead and Isobel started; a bird, gliding on dark, outstretched wings. It landed on the ground near to where Daddy Hurst lay. The bird was large, almost the size of a goose, but with black feathers, an ugly naked head, and a hooked beak. It hobbled purposefully towards the old man and Isobel cried out in horror as it was joined by another. Vultures – that's what they were! She had noted them, gathered by some dead thing close by the trail, or scavenging whenever Daddy Hurst had butchered some game for the evening meal and thrown away the scraps and innards. She bent and grasped his body by the shoulders of his shirt and waistcoat, while the dogs darted towards the scavenger-birds. Isobel dragged him a short way, closer to the shelter of her wagon. His body was pitifully light; she moved it quite easily. She covered him tenderly with a blanket, while the birds flew away, flapping their wings heavily. They went but a short distance, apparently content to wait until Isobel's attention was distracted.

Those horrible birds would certainly return. Digging a grave herself was out of the question. Covering the body and standing guard would be the best for now, with dusk falling. Perhaps the men would return soon. She should build up the fire, with wood that Daddy Hurst had gathered. The men would be hungry and they would be looking for the fire, after dark. She lit the lantern that usually hung from the back of the cook-wagon – something else that the men would see, and busied herself with assembling another pot of beans, feeling all the while that Daddy Hurst was lingering at her elbow, directing her efforts, instead of a quiet still shape some twenty feet distant.

She was not in the least bit hungry, but her hands hurt and she was thirsty. Recalling what Anna Vining said of the medicinal properties of sage tea, she set a pan of water to boil and made a decoction of sage leaves to wash the wounds on her hands and face, and to drink with a little sugar in it. She pulled the cotton-stuffed mattress closer to the fire, where she could sit and guard both the meager evening meal and the still, blanket-swathed body of Daddy Hurst. She sat with a tin cup of sage tea warming her abused hands, the dogs pressing close against her for mutual comfort, and waited . . . waited for what? She was not quite sure. What would happen in the morning? She was not quite sure of that, either. *What if no one comes? What should I do then?* If it came to that, she could hitch two of the remaining horses to her wagon and return south by the way they had come. But Cuz Peter Vining was two or three days journey behind, with a second herd of RB cattle. It might be better to wait here.

That was what she should do, Isobel concluded. Wait for Peter Vining; but what if someone lay in wait to stampede that herd, as they had the first? She had definitely seen that black, kite-shaped thing through the spyglass. Yes, of course; now it came clear. That was a place where someone deliberately set out to stampede any herd of cattle passing by. The way that a man departed on a fast horse when Dolph shot into the thicket argued a guilty conscience. Isobel resolved that if her husband and the other hands did not appear within two days, she would hitch two horses to the wagon and set off south to warn Peter Vining of the hazard presented by the shallow canyon.

She felt rather more tranquil, having arrived at a course of action, and poured another cup of herb tea; nothing to do but wait. The sun set, a dark red orb in a smear of red sky, wreathed with cloud-shreds that briefly flamed in tints of purple and gold. Isobel roused from an exhausted stupor to add more wood to the fire and take the oven of bread from it. The lantern burned brightly at first, then faded against the moon; a full moon which burned with a cold silver light. Isobel dozed, comforted by the presence of the dogs and the weight of the revolver at her waist. Once, she woke from a dream of calling on the Home Farm and passing the cows in the field; the gentle tinkling of a bell from her dream merged with the present world. In the dark, a large creature came to the campfire and a gusty breath stirred her hair. At her side, Sorsha growled. Isobel opened her eyes to see Old Blue looking down at her, interrogatively.

"Sorry, old thing – nothing tonight," she said. Old Blue clomped heavily away, although she thought he remained close at hand, for she heard the bell tinkling as he grazed for a little.

She slept and dreamed again. Such was the nature of the dream that she was not sure if she were waking or dreaming when she opened her eyes again. The stars in the east had begun to fade; so had the moon. In the queer directionless light of early dawn, there was a strange creature romping just beyond the cook-fire, which had died down to a bed of pulsing red coals. The creature appeared something like a dog, but smaller than Sorsha and Gawain, lean and with shaggy fur and ears that pricked upwards – not a wolf or a coyote. The edges of its ears, tip of the tail and the long hairs of its coat shimmered with the look of the moon reflected in rippling water. Isobel watched, intrigued. Sorsha and Gawain slept at her side undisturbed as the dog-wolf creature pounced and pirouetted; as if it chased something small, catching and then letting it go, all for its own pleasure and amusement. Isobel watched, feeling no particular threat from the creature. After some minutes of play, the creature sat down on its haunches, across the fire from her. It scratched the back of one ear with a hind-foot and regarded Isobel with curiosity.

"This is a strange place for you, isn't it?" the creature observed. Isobel was so caught in this waking dream that she didn't think it the least odd that a dog-wolf thing should be talking to her in a voice that sounded as chiding as Lady Caroline's. Curiously, the creature's mouth didn't move when it spoke. What it said was communicated directly to Isobel's mind. It was another aspect of the dream that this did not seem odd in the least.

"It is," Isobel agreed.

"Is there a reason for you being here, if I might ask?"

"You may," Isobel answered. "The cattle were panicked and ran away. My husband and the men followed after . . . to catch them, if they can. I am waiting for them to return."

"I didn't mean that," the creature regarded Isobel. Its voice was tinged with impatience. "I meant you. Why are you here? Where are you going – and what did you come here to find?'

"I don't know." Isobel said. "Quivera, perhaps. I really don't know." The creature's eyes fixed on hers. They were curiously human eyes, glowing with an odd, golden light. "That's a lie," the dog-wolf said, as if it were self-evident. "You do know. Just as you do not know your husband, whom you married without love."

"I wanted to escape." Isobel thought about it for a brief moment. "I was in a trap and he was the only way out. I thought I might come to love him. And I have." Her voice trailed off, uncertainly. "I hoped that he might come to love me, but of that I am unsure."

"Ah. You looked at him and thought he was the perfect gentle knight in splendid armor. But if not him, any other would do. Was that it?"

"Yes," Isobel admitted, struck anew with the old sense of shame and worthlessness. "I have always wondered why he would want to marry me." There it was; the worm at the core of the apple, the doubt that ate away at her, even as she danced in his arms, lay with him in bed at night, or when he teased her at the dressing-table. *Why her, indeed?*

"You are not without gifts or appeal," The dog-wolf observed, in such dry and clinical tones that Isobel derived little satisfaction from that mild degree of approval.

"I am clumsy and fat and tactless," Isobel answered, in bitter self-recrimination. "My mother has always said so. I never can think of the right thing to say or to wear and I hate Society and everything to do with it. I hate those to whom I must be polite and their spiteful daughters presumed to be my equals and confidants. All I ever wanted was to be left alone, to have a respectable husband and a dear little house of my own to look after. Children, too. Those awful people – I was made to marry a perfect stranger in order that I might gain that and get away." Tears wobbled on the edge of her eyelids, and she concluded, "Now I am all alone in this horrid wilderness of a country, keeping the vultures from eating the corpse of a dead man."

"You did not mention your greatest failing," answered the wolf-dog. "You allowed others to tell you what you are and taken such counsel to heart. You allowed them power over you, which you should not have permitted. You should be stronger than that."

I am not," Isobel felt the tears now spilling out of her eyes and trailing down her cheeks. "I don't know how I can be!"

"Ridiculous girl!" the dog-wolf snorted, suddenly sounding very human in mild exasperation. It stood and walked around the fire, to stand before her not an arm's reach away from Isobel, regarding her with those unfathomably knowing eyes. The dog-wolf's pale fur shimmered with an unearthly luminescence. "No one made you do anything. You can be who you wish to be here and now. You married freely – unless oaths mean nothing. He asked you and you said yes."

"I still don't know why he asked." Isobel sniffed and wiped her face with the back of her dirty hand. At her side, Gawain shifted and settled into a comfortable position, still pressed close against her.

"Although you have no firm belief in yourself, you still have courage," The dog-wolf explained patiently. Now it sounded uncomfortably like Anna Vining. "This counts for much with him; that and decency towards beings which have no other defender. He is a knight-errant to his soul – he lives for rescuing the weak and helpless. People, too. Perhaps he will see you as a fit mate. Your children will bind you together, tighter than you can imagine."

"Children?" Isobel gulped. "Do you know for a certainty that we will have children?"

"You already have them," the dog-wolf replied cryptically. It lifted its pointed nose and sniffed the air. "Dawn comes," it added as it turned and trotted away. Isobel called after it, or thought she did, so very real was this dream. "Wait! Children? How many children?"

"Two for now," answered the dog-wolf over her shoulder and Isobel saw a pair of cubs, with the same pale luminescent fur, rising out of the short grass, hardly an arm's-reach away from where she sat with Sorsha and Gawain. The cubs both looked at her, although one was timid and looked away almost at once. The other held Isobel's gaze for a long bold moment; it had blue eyes, the same sky-blue eyes as her husband and Lottie. Isobel held her breath, as they trotted briskly away after their mother.

Sorsha and Gawain had hardly been disturbed from their sleep. Isobel blinked; her face felt itchy, from the tracks of tears dried on her cheeks. The sky was now well-alight with the fire of the sun, just showing a thread of itself on the eastern horizon. Was she still dreaming, or had she been awake, during that strange interlude? Isobel stretched her cramped limbs and looked around. The remaining horses and Old Blue, with the bell around his neck occasionally chiming as he moved, were grazing peacefully a short distance away. A scattering of cattle bearing the RB brands had joined him and the forlorn calf was greedily nuzzling at its mother's udder. Some of the cattle had returned. Isobel was reassured by that sight. The fire had burned down to a heap of ash. She uncurled her legs – so stiff that it was acutely painful to straighten then – and tried to stand. There was a man on horseback in the distance, casting a long and moving shadow. Isobel staggered to her wagon and climbed up into the seat, to where she could retrieve the spy-glass.

Not her husband, but Wash Charpentier; even at a distance she could not mistake his hat, with the brim turned up and the mop of curly hair falling on his shoulders. The sense of relief left her breathless. She was not entirely alone. Perhaps Wash Charpentier could give her news of her husband, perhaps he and the other hands had retrieved the scattered cattle.

"Miz Becker!" he called, when he was within earshot, with a grin of relief that almost split his countenance in two and which she did not need the spyglass to see. "Yo' alive, an' doin' fairly, I see?"

"I am," Isobel answered, her voice and her person trembling with relief. "What of my husband, the other men? Where are they – surely there was no one injured. I was certain that someone would come. I had set some beans to cook last night and Hurst . . ." Her throat closed. She must tell him of poor Hurst. The dogs romped to meet him, as he swung easily down from the saddle.

"Mister Becker, he an' young Seb an' all, they're in mighty fine fettle," Wash exclaimed. "Dey is all fine, but dat Trotter kid, he's likely scared out of a year's growth. Mister Becker, he say for me to tell you, he'll be returning wid dey cattle by noon – dat dey could find. He tol' me to tell you an' Daddy we would camp here some days, while de fellers look for more of our cattle, an' take care o' some bidness. Miz Becker, has Daddy fired up the coffee pot yet? I would kill fo' some o' dat coffee." He cast a brief look around at the campsite. The merriment fled his face the instant his gaze fell upon that long, blanket-covered form, even as Isobel answered, "It happened without warning last night just as the cattle overran us. He fell, as he was trying to calm the horses. I believe his heart failed. There was no injury on him and his face was quite calm. I do not think he felt any pain at all. He just fell."

Wash had already doffed his hat. Now he hunkered on his heels next to the blanket-covered form of Hurst, turning back a corner so that he could gaze upon the old man's still face for a long moment. When he covered Hurst again with the blanket, tenderly tucking it in as if he were putting a sleeping child to bed, he turned towards Isobel. "If that ain't a discouragement, Miz Becker," he remarked. The expression of desolation on his face belied the casual tone of his voice. "Miz Hetty, at de ol' Vining place, she will be that grieved. She called him an ol' fool but he was boun' an' determined. The RB outfit surely will miss him."

"I am sorry also. I shall miss him," Isobel confessed. "I liked him very well. He served the RB trail drives with such devotion and efficiency. And he was teaching me to cook!"

"That he did," Wash Charpentier agreed and looked searchingly at Isobel. "Miz Becker, when the boys return with the cattle, they're gonna want grub, an' want it soon."

"I can manage, well enough," Isobel answered with odd confidence. She didn't quite know where it came from. Yes, she could cook for the hands, simple, plain food and nothing like for a hundred guests and royalty too! "There is another matter, Mr. Charpentier; the cattle were deliberately frightened. I saw through the spyglass. There was a black shape in the trees, that suddenly emerged and spread itself and that was what started it all. I saw – I was watching."

Wash Charpentier slowly nodded. "Dat's what it looked like to me, too. Mister Becker had us all on guard. He thought dat fellow that ran away when he shot into dat thicket; he thought dat fellow was gone. Guess he sneaked hisself back. A couple a hunnerd head o' RB cattle, too much to let pass by. What you want me to do, Miz Becker?" He looked at her with an earnest expression, reminding Isobel of what Anna Vining said about the ordinary hands would looking to her authority. Isobel took a deep breath. "You must ride south at once and warn Mr. Vining about the danger of this particular passage. I do not think that this enterprise can risk a second herd of cattle being scattered. You need not have a particular care for me. I am well-armed and guarded by the dogs. In time my husband and the other hands will return here. But it is imperative that you warn Mr. Vining and tell of him of what has happened."

"I surely will indeed, Miz Becker," Wash turned his hat in his hands, reluctant to leave. "I don't like leavin' you here alone. It ain't fittin' an' I sure ain't looking forward to give Mister Vining that news 'bout Daddy."

"Was Hurst related to you?" Isobel asked, feeling at once guilty for not having offered her condolences. "I am terribly sorry. He was a comrade of many years to the other men and to my husband."

Wash Charpentier shook his head. "No, he warn't no kin, but I knew him mos' my life. He and my mama both b'longed to Old Marse Burnett in slavery days. Daddy hired himself out to Ol' Miz Vining – all the colored folk in Austin knew Daddy, an' all de white folk, too. Everyone thought well of Daddy Hurst."

"I am certain that he will be greatly missed," Isobel ventured, squaring her shoulders. "But he is beyond pain. The care of the cattle is important. My husband said so. I will be safe." She patted the butt of the revolver at her side. "The six statues of Colt will see to that."

"It shore will, Miz Becker. You can depend on that!" Wash clapped his hat upon his head once more, his face set in lines of determination, and what Isobel suspected was relief at being given a definite order when he might otherwise have felt torn between several different proposals of action. He fairly leaped into the saddle of his horse and galloped off towards the line of trees that lined the margin of that shallow canyon, as if personally determined to bear the good news from Aix to Ghent.

Although his departure left Isobel alone once more, she did not feel particularly disheartened. No, she was cheered by the news that he brought. Her husband and all the other men had survived the cattle stampede, and were on a good way to recovering most of the cattle. The sun was well-up in the sky and there was a task for her to perform. She wondered briefly about the vivid dream of the wolf-dog. Might she already be with child? Isobel counted back the days and weeks. What a ridiculous notion. She had the usual monthly course not three weeks ago. Such an inconvenience it was to do with the usual rags; soaking and washing them out of sight of the men. It might not be so much an inconvenience to be with child, if it meant that the monthlies were banished for some nine months, save for the danger and the pain of delivering a child at the end of that time. Although dogs and cattle didn't seem to be too much inconvenienced by the process. Isobel firmly set that possibility aside. Unto the day of it were the evils thereof. She must prepare a meal for the returning men. Last night's bread was probably too dried to be eaten, so she might make a pudding of it! Yes, of course. Isobel's thoughts went along a comfortable track. A pudding, of raisins and sugar, of preserved condensed milk, to mix with the bread; the men would find it a sweet reward after their exertions in searching for and retrieving the panicked cattle. She went to ransack the store of goods in the back of the cook-wagon, grateful for the distraction that it provided.

Just as Wash Charpentier said, when the sun stood high overhead, her husband and a handful of the other hands appeared on the distant horizon, driving a much-diminished herd of cattle ahead of them. She saw them coming from a distance, and heard them as well – the faint whoops and cries from the men, the areole of dust rising from the passage of many hooves, although the horses and men looked as small as ants in the distance. She was as much relieved by seeing the proof of Wash Charpentier's assurances as she was in knowing that from her own efforts she had provided a good meal for them. Dolph would be proud of her, she was certain, as proud as Hurst would have been. Maybe Lady Caroline might bring herself to admit that her younger daughter could be of use.

The faint drumming of hoofs from another direction drew her attention. A horse at a gallop burst from the canyon; that place which had provided a hiding place from which to stampede the cattle the day before. Two more horses followed at a more sedate pace, one riderless and on a lead-rope lead by the other. Isobel's breath caught in her throat. The first rider was hatless and his hair was the same wheat-pale fairness as Dolph. It must be Peter Vining. Isobel wiped her hands on her apron and nervously ran them over her hair. She had gathered from casual remarks made by her husband and Wash Charpentier that the Vinings held Hurst in particular fondness. Now Peter Vining's very haste towards the camp where Hurst's body lay gave indication of how deep that affection ran.

Peter Vining reined in his horse as he came to the camp. He flung himself from the saddle of his panting horse, letting the long reins fall to the ground, rushing past Isobel without a word to acknowledge her presence. He went to his knees as Wash had done, next to the still and blanket swathed form of the old trail cook. Just as Wash had, he folded back the blanket to look at the face underneath. To Isobel's secret horror, Peter wept openly, unashamedly; a grief so profound that his shoulders shook with the force of it. There was nothing that Isobel could think of that might offer comfort in this moment, no words, no sisterly embrace. She did seek out the cleanest of her own calico kerchiefs from her luggage in the wagon and pressed it into his hand. Otherwise, there was nothing to be done save wait for the worst of that storm of sorrow to pass over.

Isobel withdrew to attend to her business of setting out the plates and tin forks and spoons for the men, oddly reassured that Hurst would not go into a lonely grave, unmarked and mourned only in the most perfunctory manner. What family that the old man had could not have been any more grieved over him. Isobel was reassured that Peter Vining would see that they were informed. Both Sorsha and Gawain were made uneasy by his all-to-obvious sorrow. Presently Isobel called them to her. The men were coming with the cattle; best that the meal be ready. She did hope that the worst of Peter's grief would have passed by the time they did. There was little privacy on the cattle trail, more the result of a silent and mutually-agreed upon arrangement to look away, as when she had need to relieve herself a little distance from her wagon. There was almost a palpable wall, as solid as if there were an actual one; solid and made of brick, or the native stone that Dolph's family home had been built from. Wash Charpentier followed at some distance, leading another horse. Isobel saw that the second horse was laden with a number of wide milled planks, a bundle of boards tied on each side of the saddle. The horse did not seem to appreciate being used as a pack-beast. With sudden insight, Isobel realized that they were for – a coffin, of course. Everyone said that the second herd would be accompanied by a wagon of lumber and those items necessary to build a simple ranch house.

"I have made coffee," Isobel said to Wash Charpentier, as he unsaddled his own horse and loosed it to graze with the scattering of cattle and horses in the meadow that Dolph had marked for the evening bed-ground for the herd only yesterday. It seemed to have been an age.

"Bless you, ma'am," Wash Charpentier smiled gratefully over his shoulder, as he went to relive the second horse of the burden of planks. "An' thank you. I think that Mr. Vining will thank you for a cup an' some consideration. He is sore grieving," Wash added, as he loosed the ropes that held the planks fast. They tumbled to the ground with a clatter. "I would not have guessed," Isobel replied, instantly regretting such levity. "Thank you for the boards. I would not have thought of it."

"Don't seem right, Miz Becker, puttin' a man straight in the ground," Was Charpentier agreed, softly. "Ol' Hurst done plenty o' coffin buildin' in his time. I reckon it's only right to pay him back. Them tools be where they allus are?"

"They are," Isobel answered. Wash Charpentier nodded. "You bes' see to Mr. Vining, then – I'll start work."

"You know carpentry?" Isobel was startled. Wash Charpentier chuckled. "Miz Becker, when I ain't on the trail, I work at mos' anything that pays; carpentry, painting, digging ditches. Don' matter much what, so long as it pays. I'll get right to work," he added hastily.

Now Peter Vining was silent, although he still knelt by Hurst's body. As Isobel cast a worried glance in his direction, he blew his nose into the handkerchief in his hand and rose awkwardly to his feet. Isobel already had a tin mug of coffee poured and sweetened with molasses, the way that the hands liked it. Upon consideration, she had also added a dollop of the harsh whiskey, several bottles of which were secreted away in the cook-wagon for medicinal purposes, reasoning that the man whom her husband fondly called 'Cuz' likely needed a bit of restorative. He took it from her hands, with a forced smile on his face. He looked composed now, although his eyes were reddened. He so resembled Dolph. Her own heart was wrung with sympathy.

"Bless you, Cuz Isobel," he said. Isobel answered, "I did put some whiskey in it; I hope you don't mind. I'll give you another cup, if you do."

"It's what I need, I think," he admitted. His expression was desolate. Isobel ventured, "If it is any comfort, I do not believe he suffered and it was very sudden. I told Mr. Charpentier that I believe his heart failed, under the stress and terror of the cattle stampeding through the camp. It was very frightening," she added. No, she should not sound as if she were excusing herself. "He meant much to you? Everyone says so. Had he been one of your family's . . . people for a very long time?"

"I cannot recall a time when Hurst was not there," Peter Vining answered, with a slightly crooked smile. "But he was not ever owned by our family. My mother did not believe in owning a human being, as you would own a horse or a cow. She paid wages to Hurst for years." He took a long drink of the coffee. His voice remained steady, although there was still an expression of desolation in his eyes. "I do not remember my father – Hurst stood in stead for him in most ways. When I came home after the settlement at Appomattox – all of my family was gone. Mama, my stepfather, my brothers; all gone save Daddy Hurst and Miss Hetty. Everyone else whom I knew and loved – all dead. Daddy brought me to myself. He advised me to seek out out Mama's brother or his family." Another one of those crooked smiles crossed Peter Vining's scarred countenance. "I went to the Hill Country . . . those hills that

restoreth the soul. It was excellent advice, since it returned a part of my family
to me and brought me my wife. There was nothing better than Daddy's advice.
I shall miss him more than words can say. He always seemed to be
indestructible. Is your own father in the living world, Cuz Isobel?"

"He is," Isobel answered. "I love him very much – I believe there is
nothing that can happen to you which will leave any mark, as long as there is
a loving father to come to your aid and give proof of love everlasting, no
matter how far away he might be."

"No doubt," Peter Vining answered. "And now my father in spirit is gone.
He did more for me than mine in blood ever did."

Isobel was briefly fearful that he might begin to weep again – but Peter
Vining did not. As her husband rode into the camp, Peter Vining was assisting
Wash Charpentier in construction of a coffin for Daddy Hurst.

Chapter 16 – *The Hanging Tree*

When her husband finally slid down from the back of his weary horse, Isobel knew at a glance that Dolph had passed a night as exhausting and likely as frightening as hers. He looked years older, his clothing and person coated with dust. He walked like an old man stiffened with rheumatics. His face was a mask of more dust and perspiration, which once mixed together, had caked over the stubble of his unshaven beard. His eyes, vividly blue against the dirt, were bloodshot. Still, he smiled when he saw her with a large and much-abused dish-cloth tucked into her waistband, and her skirts looped up and close to keep them from brushing the fire.

"I don't know why I worried so," he said, as he embraced her. She could feel the bone-deep weariness in him, the way that his knees trembled with the effort to keep standing. "I was sure you'd get through, Bell darlin'. God, what are we going to do without Daddy Hurst?" Her arms went about him and she returned his embrace with fierce affection. It felt as if he leaned on her for support and that gratified her. She could indeed carry out her part and be a true and able wife to him.

"We will do what we need to do," she answered. "It was but a little trial and I had the dogs. As for Mr. Hurst; he had taught me to cook well enough that I can carry on, if one of the boys will drive the cook wagon."

"Oh, god," he said only. "Poor Cuz." He released his embrace of her and she stepped back. Enough of married pleasantries, especially in front of the hand who had returned with him, driving a much-diminished herd. Now they were unsaddling their own horses and watching the two of them with undisguised interest, all as filthy and exhausted as her husband.

Isobel said briskly, "When Mr. Charpentier came and gave me the news, I began fixing supper for everyone. I knew that the men would be hungry. You might wish to scrape off the worst of the dirt, so that I may be certain that you are indeed my husband."

"You're a treasure, Bell." He smiled, a crooked smile. Isobel answered, "Sit and rest for a few moments. You've almost become an Englishman, with such a fine gift for understatement."

Nothing lent such contentment to Isobel's soul, to see how the drovers assembled, one by one, pausing by where Daddy Hurst lay, with expressions of deep sorrow. Some ventured a few words of consolation. The Mexican horse-wranglers crossed themselves in the manner of Catholics. They were all so very young, Isobel realized yet again; most only a year or two older than

Seb Bertrand and the transported Cockney, Alf Trotter. A bare few were the age of Dolph and his cousin. They came to the cook wagon in ones and twos, as their custom, to take a battered tin plate and accept a scoop of bean stew and help themselves to a slab of cornbread. They ate with such appetite, which relieved Isobel's mind until she realized that they were so desperately hungry that anything at all would have tasted good. The bread-pudding was a rousing success. The iron pot that she baked it in was scraped clean of every crumb and sweet morsel. She hugged that satisfaction to her. She could cook over an open fire in the middle of the wild and desolate prairie – a method and a menu which assuredly Mrs. Huckaby had never attempted.

Towards the end of that peculiar and scattered meal, which Dolph gobbled as if nearly starving, Peter Vining joined them, hunkering down on his heels near to where they sat on the cotton-bedroll, their backs against the wagon-wheel. "Wash and I finished the wood-working," he said. "Daddy is all settled in it. In the morning, I'll take some of the boys to the top of this hill and dig a good deep grave. Best to make it where we can mark and find it again."

Dolph nodded, in perfect agreement. "We'll stay here for two, maybe three more days, Cuz. We're still missing at least sixty head an' it will take at least that many days to round them up, get 'em to settle down, some. I sent two of the boys with young Bertrand, searching east. I've a good idea that's where our missing cows are; somewhere in a deep side canyon, out of sight."

Peter Vining whistled softly under his breath. "You certain, Cuz?"

"As sure as I am that they were stampeded deliberate," Dolph's expression was set as if in stone and his voice just as hard. "I know what I saw and I saw a man running away from that big tree with that kite-thing in it. He went east along the arroyo, on a fast horse."

"Ah." Peter Vining's scarred countenance now held the same expression. "We'll have to do something about that."

"In the morning," Dolph answered obliquely. "Before first light, I think." He suddenly recollected that Isobel was listening. His voice turned lighter. "Bell, darlin', can you rustle up a good breakfast first thing tomorrow morning for the hands? We'll have a lot of work in front of us."

"Certainly," Isobel agreed. "But we will need more wood, soon."

"I'll take one of the hands in a while," Dolph yawned. "We'll go down to the arroyo and cut us some wood – seeing as we'll be scouting out a good tree," he added with a significant look at his cousin. "I want to rest a bit, first." He yawned again and Isobel took the tin plate and fork from him. His eyes were closing before she even turned away. "We'll need water, too," she added. He was already deep asleep, his head slumping against the wagon wheel at his back.

She saw to her own meal from the remains of the stew; unexpectedly, Alf Trotter brought a bucket of clean water and insisted on washing the dishes for her. "Miss G – she'd tell me to do it," he said by way of explanation. It struck Isobel that Alf did not sound quite as much a Cockney as he had before. Now she realized Alf conscientiously mimicked his fellow drovers in manner and way of speech. There was healthy flesh on his gutter-sparrow bones and a better color to his face, even under the dirt. He still worshipped Dolph, following him with much the same devotion as the dogs did, all during those long days of moving the cattle.

"What do you think of this cattle-droving business, Alf?" she asked, genuinely curious. There couldn't possibly be anything in the world more different than this place and the grimy slums of Whitechapel.

"I loike it fine, ma'am," he answered and Isobel stifled a laugh. He was trying so hard to sound like the others! "Sir promised me 'orses, so 'e did. It ain't no harder to earn a bob – a buck – punchin' cattle than it is blacking' boots."

"What do you want to do when the drive is done?" Isobel asked, supposing that Alf would go back being a general errand-boy and attendant on her husband.

"This," Alf answered fervently. "Not scrubbing dishes, ma'am. I want to be a real cowboy, a top han' like Mr. Charpentier; a real champeen w' a rope, a wild, bronc-bustin' buckaroo. He says he'll teach me to shoot. Soon as we get back to Santone, I'm gonna buy me a reg'lar Colt six-shooter, too." He continued expanding on his ambition in a scrambled patois of Cockney and Texas, while Isobel sorted out the other remnants of the meal just past. The rest of the hands slept with their hats over their faces, unrolling blankets and ground cloths in the meager shade of the wagon. They, like Dolph, were filthy and completely exhausted. The remnant of the herd grazed contentedly, kept from wandering very far by two of the hands, who had snatched a few bites of the pudding and climbed wearily into their saddles again to patrol the herd.

Isobel wondered who had deliberately stampeded the cattle and if that malevolent someone were watching the camp, waiting for a chance when everyone's guard was relaxed. Her husband and his cousin had spoken of doing something in the morning at first light. Isobel considered their brief words about firewood and looking for a tree. That must be it; cutting wood for the fire. She fed the remainder of the stew and broken breads to Sorsha and Gawain, who snapped it up eagerly. Isobel wiped her gravy-dabbled fingers on the towel at her waist and thought that she was more content at this moment than she would ever have thought possible.

In mid-afternoon, Seb Bertrand and the last two drovers returned from ranging east along the banks of the dry canyon. Isobel was taking advantage of the pause in their journey by heating a pan of water to wash her clothes. Seb and the drovers rode hard, at a fast trot. There were no cattle; their passage raised a brief plume of dust which settled slowly after. Isobel saw by the way they held themselves and the grim expressions on their faces when they conferred briefly with her husband and Peter Vining, that they had seen something which concerned them. Young Seb looked angry.

She overheard a snatch or two of the conversation. "Thirty head and more with our brand on them, in a little draw away down the arroyo."

"Certain sure?" That was Peter Vining. The drover nodded. "Looked like they corralled 'em up there pretty regular." He was one of the oldest, a man perhaps in his late twenties, but so weathered he looked even older than that. He chewed a grass stem, wedged in the corner of his mouth. "Looked like they had a fire there. Handy."

"They held guns on me!" Seb Bertrand's voice was raised, indignant. The older drover drawled, "Easy, hoss; we kinda thought they would. But your pony didn't have an RB brand on it."

"They were up to no good, I am certain!" Seb exclaimed. The two drovers exchanged a look. "Nothin' much gets past you, hoss, does it?" The younger observed mildly. Seb blushed beet-red. "Those are clearly our cattle!" He answered, "Our property – my property! Do we allow those those brigands to get away with stealing them?"

"Matter of fact, no, we don't." Dolph answered, in even and level tones. He and his cousin exchanged a look freighted with meaning. "We'll take care of it, Seb – in the morning." He turned towards the older drover. "You spotted their dug-out?"

The man chewed the straw through a turn or two. "Yep."

"Find it again? In the dark?"

"Yep."

"Good." Dolph and his cousin exchanged a nod, the two drovers – dismissed with some kind of invisible understanding that Isobel could not fathom – went and got their bedrolls out of the cook wagon. Seb trailed after them, his expression one of anger at war with mystification.

"What has happened, Mr. Bertrand?" Isobel asked and the young man looked at her distractedly. "What has happened to Hurst?" He asked in return. The anger drained from his sun-scoured face when she explained what had happened. "That poor old fellow!" he exclaimed. "My god – Lady Isobel, you must have been terrified!"

"Not so much," Isobel answered with serene conviction. "Perhaps at first. Mr. Vining came with some lumber from the freight-wagon. We are to bury him at the top of this hill tomorrow, so my husband says. It is a shame that we cannot send for an ordained minister. It seems so unfitting. I suppose there is not a church of any sort for hundreds of miles."

Seb Bertrand's face brightened a little. "No, I don't suppose there is," he answered. "But I do have a *Common Book of Prayer* with me. I can read the Service for Burial out of it. Will that suit, Lady Isobel?"

"I think it would," Isobel answered. "Hurst was a Christian, although I don't know of what particular sect. I believe he would be appreciative. It would also be of comfort to his friends; Mr. Vining especially, since he had known him from childhood."

"Very well, Lady Isobel – I will be happy to oblige."

Late in the afternoon Dolph and several hands went to cut firewood from the brushwood along the dry canyon, returning with a large quantity piled onto a stout ground-cloth, and pulled by ropes attached to the leading corners, dragged along as if it were a kind of sledge by two horsemen. Isobel received it with gratitude; enough dry firewood for several meals. She strung a clothesline between the wheels of her wagon, on the side away from the general camp, hung her dripping small garments to dry overnight, and went to prepare the evening meal for the drovers and wranglers. They were all cheered that some of the cattle and horses panicked in the stampede had wandered back to their fellows on their own. More had been retrieved by ones and twos as Dolph's men had found them straying and chivvied them back to the bed-ground overlooked by the low hill; a mere pimple of a hillock, but a veritable Matterhorn when compared to the flat country around. Peter Vining and Wash Charpentier went to the top of it with a pick, a pair of shovels, and a couple of buckets. From the top of the little hill, the faint sounds of metal ringing on hard earth and the rattle of stones floated down all that afternoon as the shadows lengthened and the small ridges and shallows in the vast prairie revealed themselves. Isobel reflected upon this capacity for ordinary labor, as she set about preparing another meal: Peter Vining and her husband were part-owners of the herd, ranchers and men of substance but they did not stand aside from the work to be done. Peter Vining was working side by side with a former slave, digging a grave for another former slave and her husband gathered wood. No one thought this the least out of the ordinary, save perhaps

Seb Bertrand, who was himself taking a turn at guarding and soothing the reassembled herd.

That would appear very strange to Fa and Martyn, she thought, *considering how things were so different in India!* According to Martyn, a proper sahib hardly had to lift a hand to anything at all, for there were so many servants. Every one of them and all observers would be shocked and offended beyond measure to see a sahib doing their work; but that was the custom of that country. It would also be incomprehensible to her mother; Lady Caroline contemplating the spectacle of her daughter standing in as trail-cook for these grubby and uncouth drovers. How Mama would berate Fa and Isobel herself for agreeing to a marriage which put her youngest daughter in such a disgraceful situation. It amused Isobel to envision her mother's face and probable remarks. She set to work chopping onions, to flavor the evening's inevitable bean stew. When Alf Trotter, detailed as her assistant in the preparation of meals, saw the tears on her cheeks, he exclaimed, "'ere, you ain't weeping for ol' Hurst, are you, Miss?"

"No," Isobel wiped her cheeks with the cleanest corner of the dishcloth. "These are tears for the onions, Alf, and the comedy of imagining my mothers' face if she could see me at this moment. My mother was one of Her Majesty's ladies . . . a bridesmaid at her wedding, even." Isobel began to laugh, until she gasped for breath. "Imagine the contrast, Alf; my mother in her court gown and myself at this moment!"

"If you say so, Miss," Alf answered with a sideways look of wary skepticism. "You certain you ain't been out in the sun too long?"

"Of course I've been out in the sun! I haven't had a roof over my head in two months, Alf!" Isobel gasped and laughed so long and deeply that she had to hang onto the edge of the folding tabletop.

When she recovered herself, she continued with supper preparations, feeling oddly refreshed. In spite of the terror, the sorrow, and the uncertainty of the day before, as night swept in across the prairie like the wings of an immense black bird, she also had a curious feeling of contentment. She curled up under the blankets of their shared bed, grateful beyond words for the comfort of her husband's presence, the gentle rise and fall of his breathing, and the silent wheeling of the stars overhead, every bit as spectacular as Jack Sutcliffe had promised they would be.

The stars were still bright; the eastern horizon held not even a hint of dawn, when the night-guard drover wakened her with a respectful touch on her blanket-covered foot and a whisper. "Miz Becker, it's half-past four. Mister Becker said I should wake you now."

"Where is he – my husband?" Isobel demanded, jolted from half-sleep to wakefulness upon realizing that the place in bed next to her was empty, although there was still some fleeting warmth where he had lain. How long had he been gone and how had he managed to slip from their bed without waking her? And for what purpose?

"He said he had some trail business to attend to," the drover answered; he sounded honestly perplexed. "He an' Mister Vining went about half an hour ago. Them and Wash Charpentier, an' Jim Holt . . . one or two of the other boys, all in a body together."

"What manner of business?" Isobel wondered aloud. The drover shook his head. "Ma'am, I don't know. They wouldn't say and I dassn't ask."

"What orders did my husband give otherwise?" Isobel sat up, pushing the covering blankets from her. She didn't fear being immodest in front of drovers, servants, or anyone else; she had slept in her clothes, only removing her stout laced boots.

"Only that we continue as before," the boy answered. "He would return after sunrise and that we would bury Daddy then."

"Very well," Isobel retrieved her boots, shaking them vigorously as her husband had advised her to do every morning, in order to ensure that nothing with a stinger or fangs had taken refuge in them overnight. "Thank you – I will have breakfast ready very shortly."

"Yes, ma'am," the young drover answered. He and his horse vanished into the dark, the grass muffling the noises that the horses' hoofs made. Isobel laced up her boots and went to light the lantern that sat on the top chest that made the cook-wagon. She added more wood onto the fire, which burned in sullen red coals under a haze of ash. Yellow flames danced among the logs, casting writhing shadows of themselves on the wagon wheels, and on the sleeping figures of the drovers, wrapped in blankets and quilts with their heads pillowed on their saddles. By lantern and firelight, Isobel set about the work of making breakfast, utterly content – but with a small niggle of worry in the back of her mind. *What business would take Dolph and Peter Vining and a handful of men away from camp, hours before sunrise?*

They returned with a small herd of cattle driven before them, as the bright sun rose at their backs. Isobel set another pot coffee to brew, as soon as she saw them in the distance, and verified through the spy-glass that it was, indeed, her husband and his men. "They have got the missing cattle back!" she said merrily to Seb Bertrand. "You see, there was nothing to worry about!"

"Save those men who were guarding them," Seb sounded morose. "There were at at least three. They did not welcome claims of ownership or assist us in retrieving our cattle in any fashion."

"I may only assume that my husband made a convincing argument," Isobel answered.

"I am certain that he did," Seb Bertrand scowled. Isobel thought that he looked like Martyn at the age of fourteen or so, unfairly reproved and simmering with resentment. "I saw our brands upon the cattle, and insisted upon ownership. I demanded that they release our property, but to no effect. They were ruffians of the worst kind, Milady . . . Mrs. Becker. They had no notion of their place – or the proper respect due to a gentleman."

"Oh, Seb," Isobel sighed, concealing a smile. "Haven't you noticed? The meanest ragged working-man assumes he is the equal of a duke. It might be better to just treat with strangers as if they are."

"Those men," Seb answered, still scowling like a thundercloud, "were rough and ill-spoken. One of them drew his pistol and threatened me, Mrs. Becker. Those two that I was with? They did nothing to assist me. They stayed out of sight and did nothing! I can't think what they were about!"

"It was about the brands," Isobel explained. "Your horse does not have a brand upon it connected with the RB, but theirs did. It is one thing that my husband has made clear to me. Sometimes a brand is like one of those Highland plaids in the days of the wars between the clans. To have the wrong one spells death, if you meet up with one from an enemy clan. They sent you ahead to treat with the men who held our cattle, whilst they remained out of sight. Perhaps they feared for their own safety, but I am certain they meant to conduct a careful survey of the land around. You must forgive them for using you as a stalking goat. He talked long with your comrades of yesterday and they went with him this morning." Isobel thought for a moment. "Yes – they were scouting, while you distracted those men. That is a good job finished, Mr. Bertrand, so now I expect that we will attend to our next duty. You have your *Book of Common Prayer* at hand, I trust?"

"I do," Seb Bertrand's expression went from sullen to somber. "It is a tragedy for a man of such years, but as you said, it will be a comfort for his family to know that the proper obsequies were observed."

"They will be grateful, I am certain of it." Isobel pulled the towel from her waistband, and smoothed her hair. "Honestly – I should try to put on some cleaner clothes. It is unsuitable to wear every-day clothes to a funeral."

"Most of the lads have only that and maybe a good shirt for town," Seb answered, a smile briefly lighting his countenance. "But I'll put on my best, for old Hurst. Best do the done thing and hold up one's standards. Just because we are out here, no reason to let down the side."

"Exactly," Isobel nodded agreement. It gratified her to see that most of the hands thought the same. At the very least they had made an attempt to wash, if unable to change into their best clothes, tucked away among the baggage and bedrolls carried in the cook wagon. The cattle retrieved by the light of stars were added to the herd. To Isobel's eyes it now looked the size it had been before the stampede. How much work retrieving them had entailed for all the drovers, for her husband, too! Isobel silently hoped that whatever her husband said to the ruffians who had held that portion of the RB's cattle had a lasting effect. It would be horrible for another cattle herd passing this way to be put though so much needless labor.

Dolph and his cousin arrived in camp with what Isobel thought were exceedingly somber faces; she assumed that it was because of the funeral rites to be performed. No one of decency and feeling truly relished a funeral, especially not one for an old friend and loyal family retainer. Dolph kissed her cheek briefly, saying, "All done, Bell; I guess we better see to the burying, now."

"Seb has volunteered to read the service for Hurst," Isobel returned the kiss. "He has a prayer book – It's not right for someone to go into a grave without the words being said. I hope you agree."

"I do, Bell," he answered. Isobel wondered why then did he seem so grim and distant; so did Cousin Peter. Dolph unsaddled his own horse, as did the other men and his cousin and he added over his shoulder, "For the next order of business… Has Seb unlimbered his prayer-book?"

"Yes, he has," Isobel answered. Her husband nodded. "Let's get on with it, then," he said. "It's been a day and a half in warm weather; well past time to do the needful."

Isobel was faintly shocked at the tone of grim practicality in his voice. But she recollected that her husband had been a soldier, hardened in the field against natural sentiments and so had Peter Vining. The the two of them, with Wash Charpentier and three of the other hands took up the rough plank-built coffin, bearing it awkwardly but with tenderness upon their shoulders. They climbed the low hill, the other drovers and wranglers following with Isobel and Seb Bertrand in the lead, arranging themselves in two lines of mourners. The sun was well-up in the sky, now the perfect cerulean blue of her engagement-ring. Those few clouds in it floated as pure-white as thistle-blossom, or the tufts of cotton growing here and there in the fields around the old town of San Antonio. The wind blew fresh and clear from the north, the barest hit of coolness in it. Isobel looked around; this was perfect – the view of the plain around and the distant thread of the arroyo and fringe of trees were unobstructed.

The pallbearers silently let down their burden next to the yawning hole, and Seb Bertrand stepped forward. He opened his book with nervous attention and began to read from it. His voice sounded reedy and uncertain at first, but then gained in confidence. "I am the resurrection and the life, saith the Lord; he that believeth in me, though he were dead, yet shall he live; and whosoever liveth and believeth in me shall never die."

The drovers and wranglers hastily uncovered their heads and Seb read on. Isobel stood next to her husband and sought his hand for the comfort that human contact might offer. He stared straight ahead, his jaw tight-clenched and expression unreadable; perhaps he was not as hardened against misfortunate death as she had assumed. "Oh, God, whose mercies cannot be numbered," Seb continued. "Accept our prayers on behalf of thy servant –" he hesitated and shot a panicky look towards Peter Vining and Wash Charpentier, who stood side by side.

Wash cleared his throat and answered the unspoken plea. "Burnett. Leastwise, that was his ol' Massa's name. I ain't ever heard Daddy wanted to call hisself anything else."

"Hurst Burnett," Seb continued gratefully. "And grant him an entrance into the land of light and joy, in the fellowship of thy saints; through Jesus Christ thy Son our Lord, who liveth and reigneth with thee and the Holy Spirit." Isobel closed her eyes briefly against the sudden tears springing up into them. It had all been so sudden, so horribly final, the end of a life and an odd kind of friendship. Now Hurst was gone and there were so many questions that she wished that she had asked him. She had a sense of something left unfinished and now never to be finished.

Of the appropriate psalms, Seb lighted on the 23rd – a fortunate choice, since many of the men knew it well enough to recite along with his reading. Isobel took almost as much comfort from her husband's closeness, as she did from the familiar words and cadence, read in familiar accents. Seb Bertrand was doing quite well, his confidence increasing as he continued. Really, he managed to sound quite authoritative. *It was a pity that he has no vocation for the Church,* Isobel thought. As far as it went, Seb was doing quite well with the ritual. Perhaps this was why people had rituals; performing it was a comfort in itself. Even that dreadful, hollow sound of handfuls of earth, falling in single handfuls was a comfort, too, for it was Hurst's friends performing the required ritual, with somber and yet resigned faces. When it was done, all but Wash Charpentier and Peter Vining trailed silently down from the top of the little hill. The sound of the earth falling by the shovel-full into the open grave followed them for quite some way. With a few quiet words from her husband, the hands and wranglers resumed their duties; Isobel gathered that quite a few cattle and a dozen horses were still missing. The men having scattered, Isobel and Dolph were all but alone in the camp, when Wash Charpentier and Peter Vining returned, shovels over their shoulders.

"That's done," Peter said as he returned the shovel to the tool-box bolted to the side of the cook-wagon. He was quite dry-eyed. Dolph clapped him on the shoulder; Isobel thought there was another of those wordless exchanges between the two. "I'd best be getting back to my own herd. Another week's journey north, you say?"

"About so," Dolph answered. "Onkel's surveyor marked the center of the property with a flag-pole and the boundary markets with stone cairns and arrows pointing to the next ones, each way."

"I'll be glad to get this range settled," Peter smiled – more for Isobel than anyone else, she thought. "And the other matter, Cuz . . ."

"I don't regret the decision," Dolph cut him off. Peter frowned.

"I hope there'll be no repercussions," he began, and Dolph said, "There shouldn't be . . . he was only a boy."

"So were you, once," Peter said. "So was I. Nits make lice, Cuz."

Isobel wondered, *Who was only a boy?* Dolph and his cousin said nothing more. Peter Vining saddled a pony from the remuda and ride away towards the south, a single dark-coated figure, diminishing in the distance towards the line of dusty green scrub trees which marked the dry canyon. Something moved among the trees; not only the dark angular shape of the kite, which had been deployed to frighten the cattle into stampeding . . . was it now only two days ago? It was a curious shape. Now there were two more shapes, side by side. Isobel was frankly puzzled. They had not been there when last she peered through the spyglass. She scrambled up to the seat of her wagon and retrieved the red-morocco case which held the spyglass. She held it to her eye, and followed the dark shape of Peter Vining, along the faint trail which let to the track that crossed the canyon . . . there! That was the tree which the dark kite-shape hung from. On another branch . . . Isobel adjusted the focus of the old spyglass, disbelieving at first the evidence of her own eyes. Two men . . . now she was certain – boots, clothing and all, their faces obscured by some bag-like fabric which looked uncommonly like flour-sacks. She gazed, appalled and astonished. They hung from ropes around their necks, tied to the branch above, a still burden, even as the kite-shape swayed in the lightest breeze. They had not been there previously, when she looked in that direction through the glass. She raised it again, seeing Peter Vining ride past. He reined in his own horse and turned his head to look towards the tree with that ugly unnatural burden hanging from the lower branches, before he vanished below the canyon rim and was lost to her sight through the glass. She looked once more through the glass, as if to assure herself that she really saw what was there. When she climbed down from her wagon, her husband was still sitting on their bed, his back against the wheel, and writing in the little book which served as his aid-de-memoir and account of brands.

Isobel took a deep breath. "There are two dead men, hanging in the tree by the trail. Did you know of this?"

"I hope so," Dolph replied, not raising his gaze from the page. "Since we put them there – Cuz and I. They were the ones who stampeded our cattle, Bell – and likely many others. It was a regular scheme. They had done it before. This time, it killed killed Hurst. I won't stand for killing out of hand while breaking the law."

"You executed them," Isobel felt breathless, as if she had fallen from a great height. "Out of hand and without the benefit of law!"

"No," Dolph corrected her, his countenance set and stern. "We carried out a proper sentence. Stock-stealing is a hanging offence and there wasn't any doubt about what they were doing. Not a doubt in the world. We found a couple of running irons in their dugout, they had thirty head of RB cattle, and they ran off Seb when he asked nicely for their return."

"But what about a proper magistrate, an officer of the law!" Isobel pleaded, icy with horror and revulsion. Dolph lifted his gaze from the page, and explained with great patience. "Bell, darlin' – there ain't no law any closer than six days hard riding and no federal judge any closer than Fort Smith – another two days beyond that. All the law out here is what we make ourselves. I sure as hell didn't want to waste time taking the Whitmire boys all the way to Fort Smith, just to have the Judge do exactly what Cuz and I did. It's the way things are done here, Bell – this isn't England."

"So I was informed." The horror that she felt still must have shown in her face. Dolph put away his book and pencil and rose to his feet.

"Bell, we did justice proper," he said, a note of pleading in his voice. "We only hanged the two men. We let the boy go, as soon as it was finished. We gave him a horse and five dollars in gold and told him never to set foot on Becker land or look cross-eyed at RB cattle, ever again."

"A boy?" Isobel looked at him, not quite believing her own ears. Dolph nodded, "'Bout thirteen or fourteen . . . didn't seem right, since he didn't have a chance to say no to what the others were up to. There were things I saw in the War, Bell. I didn't want to think I was a man who could do them. So I let him go. Cuz thought I was a fool – he said we should hang the lot of them while we had a chance."

"I'm glad of that," Isobel answered, oddly reassured until another horrible possibility occurred to her. "But won't you be prosecuted for hanging those men yourself?"

"By whom, Bell?" He laughed, embracing her and she felt the rumble of his amusement deep in his chest. "It was my right and our cattle. There's not a jurisdiction in the whole of Texas would prosecute or convict me. Matter of fact, I'd most likely get a reward for cleaning up a nest of bandits."

With that, Isobel had to be content. This was not England, and her husband was better versed in the way things were done in Texas.

Chapter 17 – *The Turning of the Year*

The autumn season came came as a mild shock to Jane; harvest time, when the apple trees in the walled orchard below the Becker home ranch hung heavy with ripe fruit – russet and ruby and a yellow-splotched pink – and the term of her school year came to an end. The months and weeks passed as swift and sweet as the hours and days. She knew her tenure as a schoolteacher was to end when the family went to Austin to spend the Christmas holidays with their Vining cousins, but in Jane's mind, Christmas meant frost, cold, snow and dark evenings which descended in the late afternoon. When the weather remained summer-mild, even as the oak leaves turned from green to bronze, Jane remained serenely detached from the calendar. The happy dream lasted until one morning where a pale layer of frost veiled the ground and the remnants of summer grass crunched underfoot. A fire burned in the parlor fireplace that evening. When Sam Becker came in from riding his pastures and paddocks, he shed his coat in the hall and came into the parlor rubbing his hands.

"About time," he observed. "There's never a good crop the next year, without there's a good hard freeze about now. Miss Jane, are your pupils nearly ready for the Christmas holidays?" Jane felt as if the comfortable parlor had shuddered underneath her, as if in some kind of earthquake. She stared at Sam, mildly horrified. How the time had passed so swiftly! She had forgotten, or managed to put it all from her mind. At Christmas Lady Isobel would return from the Palo Duro ranch with Mr. Becker, and she herself would be a simple ladies' maid once more. Her first unbidden reaction was of horror and distaste. She had never in her life been so happy and content as those weeks and days spend in that makeshift classroom; her oddly-assorted pupils were advancing – and now all was to be snatched away? The prospect was like being put in prison. Jane chided herself for that selfish thought. She owed so much to Lady Isobel. After all, she was not really a teacher. To continue as such was beyond her station, and Lady Isobel needed her. And yet . . .

"I had forgotten," Jane allowed, honestly. "They are all doing so very well. I will miss them very much."

"You will miss teaching them, Miss Jane?" Sam asked, with an unexpectedly shrewd expression on his face.

"I will," Jane confessed. "I had not thought that work – for it is truly work – could be such a pleasure. I took pride in serving my lady … but not nearly as much as I did in teaching these children."

"It made more of a difference," Sam answered. "That's why." Jane thought he would say more, but Lottie exclaimed, "You will love Austin, and Cousin Peter's house, Jane! There are so many amusements and parties. It is especially lively when the Legislature meets. Everyone who is everyone knows the Vinings . . . because of Aunt Margaret, you know. They used to say that if you came to supper at her house every night for a month you would meet simply everyone of importance in Texas."

I am not sure that I want to meet everyone, Jane thought to herself. *But I would like to return with my lady to this place. Surely she would permit me to continue with the school. Society is so very, very different; it can't be that I must wait upon her every moment of the day, and she has always been dedicated to the welfare of the tenants. I might be able to convince her of lending me to that service.*

That was a happy inspiration, recalling how Lady Isobel had done the rounds of calls to Sir Robert's tenants. Surely her ladyship could be brought to see the usefulness of that, even if Lady Isobel returned to the Palo Duro, rather than the Becker home ranch. Jane thought Sam was looking at her as if he were thinking about her, but he did not speak again about the school, until the morning came for their departure, a fortnight later. Her trunk was packed again with her clothing and few possessions, loaded with Lottie's and Mrs. Becker's trunk, along with another trunk of Lady Isobel's into the back of the odd-looking two-horse spring conveyance that the family used for their long trips.

As Sam handed her her up into it, he said very softly, "Miss Jane, if you should want to return and open your school again, I would do what I could to see that happen. I would talk to my brother."

"I would like that," Jane answered in the same quiet tone. "But my duty is to milady. Her wishes are my first consideration."

"Whatever you would like, Jane," Sam answered. "I promise I will always do what I can." He closed the little door at the rear of the conveyance. Jane took her place, wistfully thinking that she would miss his company at least as much as she would miss her school and pupils, if Lady Isobel's plans returned them all to the Palo Duro, once the Christmas celebrations were done.

It was a two-day-long journey. They spent the first night in the quaint little town of Fredericksburg; in a timber-and-plaster house on the edge of a vast open market square which reminded Jane irresistibly of the shop in Didcot. This was not so much American as the Becker's stone ranch house, or the mansion in San Antonio, although the street upon which it sat was broad but unpaved. This shop and house were kept by yet another Richter cousin and his young family, who welcomed them with rapturously generous hospitality. Jane was tired enough from the day's journey to appreciate the consideration. Lottie and Sam were as much at home in the quaint half-timber house as in any other. Jane gathered that the two had spent a large part of their childhood years there. Early the following morning, they set out again; this second day's journey was a long one. It lasted until well past sundown, ending in a city of some size, to judge from the golden-glowing lights that were strewn the length and width of a valley between velvet-dark hills. To reach it, they crossed over a wide river, flowing silent and with hardly a ripple in it to disturb the silver reflection of the moon.

"Almost there, Miss Jane," Sam looked over his shoulder to smile at her. Mrs. Becker had long since lain down on one of the folding wooden seats and gone to sleep. Lottie was so quiet that Jane thought she had gone to sleep as well. Even the horses were weary, drawing the spring-wagon up that last long hill. Through the bare branches of the trees which surrounded it, Jane could see the lights of a house – a tall house with wide covered verandahs that reached out in warm welcome.

Two figures waited to greet them, as the wagon crunched to a halt – Mr. Vining's pale hair and height made him instantly recognizable, with his tiny, doll-like wife at his side.

Lottie scrambled down from the wagon, her energy revived at once. "Cuz!" she embraced him rapturously, "How good to see you – did Seb come with you, or is he still playing the cattle rancher?"

"He is, Lottchen," Peter Vining returned her embrace, lifting her off her feet as she squealed, begging to be put down. "He's coming next week, with Cuz and his missus. You should not demand much of him. He has worked very hard all summer and a man needs a rest. Marm!" he turned to Mrs. Becker, kissing her cheek with equal affection, while Lottie and Anna chattered in German. Jane hung back in the shadows, uncertain of her own standing or welcome. A groom appeared for the horses. Sam took her elbow to guide her up the stairs – such a reassuring presence.

"Cuz, you remember Miss Goodacre," he exclaimed to the Vinings. "She was sick with the age and couldn't go with Dolph and Sister Isobel, so she stayed with us – teaching school at the ranch. We set up a school for Inman's children. It worked out so well, I'm going to tell Dolph we should keep it."

"I do remember Miss Jane," Peter Vining took Jane's hand in his, as Lottie and Mrs. Becker vanished into the house with Anna Vining. "I'll never forget anyone who can make Harry and Christian behave. Welcome to Austin!" He added in a lower voice. "Good to have you here, Sam. Amelia has decided to bless us with her presence for Christmas this year." Mr. Vining's expression and voice were studiously neutral. Not Sam's response. "The devil, you say! Well, I have planned a great painting to work on, so that will be my excuse for making myself scarce."

"Coward," Peter Vining returned equably. "I thought I would be able to depend on you."

"Amelia is enough to make me consider retreating to the wilderness in a hair shirt and taking vows of eternal bachelorhood. How is Horrie managing his dear Ma-ma?"

"At a brisk trot, usually," Peter Vining answered with a wry grimace. "Rope him into your project. The boy will do anything at all to escape; she still treats him as if he were five years old and feeble-minded."

"That's Cousin Amelia," Sam replied, looking down at Jane with a smile. "Miss Jane, we are being rude in talking about another lady in this way, but consider yourself to be fairly warned. Cousin Amelia Vining is the very proper widow of Peter's older brother Horace and charming in the way that only a belle of the south can be, but above all else she prefers to be the only woman at the ball." He took her arm again and Jane felt that sense of attraction to him, an attraction that she also suspected that she had in common with many other women. He was kind, gallant, and appealing in his features, if not handsome in the way that his brother was. "Or in the parlor, which makes other women simply furious. Never fear, Jane – we shall see you protected from Cousin Amelia."

"Hetty has promised to take her under her wing," Peter Vining added, over Jane's head. Sam squeezed her hand, comfortingly. "There you see, Jane? Hetty is a stalwart friend to any woman who must earn her own living. She was my mother's dearest support and confidant. You could ask for no better friend in the world."

Jane was escorted through the door into the Vining's house; not near as grand as the Hall, or the London residence, but exuding an air of comfort. There was a woman waiting for her in that hall, a white-haired crone clad all in black with a heavy stick that she hardly needed, as she stood as straight as a rule.

"Miss Hetty," Peter made as if to take her arm protectively. "I thought you would wait upstairs and I would show Miss Goodacre to to your sitting room."

"Sauce!" exclaimed the old woman and batted his hand away. Her eyes were still sharp, although her hair had thinned so much that Jane could see her pale-pink scalp. Her aged voice retained a strong musical Irish accent, which

Jane found quite comforting. "I'm no' an invalid yet, young Peter-me-lad. They're waiting for ye in the old boarder's parlor. I'll see the girl to her room, then and we'll have a supper upstairs." She took Jane's hand briefly. "So, Miss Goodacre, you've been in service to a proper noble house, the young mistress said? I wanted to hear m'self all about it! I've always tried to keep th' same sort here, since m'sister and I came to work w' Herself, thirty years and more ago it was! You'd not have recognized the place, so ye would!" As she talked, she pulled Jane along with her. Miss Hetty still had considerable strength in those fragile-appearing hands, thin and worn with toil, with the knotted joints caused by age and arthritis. The stick was more for effect, although she used it as a support when she climbed the stairs. Jane followed her obediently, up that generous staircase and down a side corridor on the upper floor. As much as Jane could see by lamp and candle-light, the place was swept clean, the woodwork gleamed with polish and smelt faintly of beeswax and lavender. "I'll have the boys bring up your trunk to your room," Miss Hetty added. She paused to peer into Jane's face. "You're not tired from the journey? I'd like not to tire ye even more, but y'see," the old woman added in a burst of frankness, "I've a mind to talk about the old ways an' the grand houses an' all. I dinna sleep at night until late, y'see."

"No, I am not tired at all," Jane assured her, although she was aching in every bone. Miss Hetty had said something having supper upstairs. Perhaps this was like Aunt Lydia having a quiet meal on a tray in her parlor, apart from the other servants at the Hall. Jane's spirits rose. In one regard the Vining's house was familiar; the upper floors were as random and rambling as the Hall, with odd turns in the corridors and sometimes a step up or down.

Miss Hetty paused at one of these, and opened a door. "I have set aside this room for ye. When you have put off your bonnet and mantle and refreshed yourself, then come to my sitting-room. Down the hall at the left, three doors . . . I shall leave mine ajar."

Miss Hetty courteously left Jane to take possession of the room which would be hers for at least a few weeks. Grateful to the old woman – who appeared as a familiar refuge in a strange and curious land – she divested herself of her outer garments and bonnet, noting that the room was small, but scrupulously clean and replete with comforts. A new fire already burned on the hearth and the water in the jug was hot. Miss Hetty might be old, but obviously she still held the reins of housekeeping authority in a commanding grip. Refreshed from a brief washing of her face and hands, Jane followed Miss Hetty's instructions. The door to Miss Hetty's room spilled a wedge of warm golden lamplight into the darkened hallway; a comfortable room, spotlessly clean as everything else, if a little over-crowded with mementos. A number of framed daguerreotypes vied for space on the mantelpiece. There was a small table drawn close to the fire, with a pair of comfortable overstuffed chairs on either side. A covered tray sat on the table. Miss Hetty uncovered it to reveal the dishes underneath.

"Sit yourself down, Miss Goodacre, 'tis starving you must be, but when I heard of young Master Becker marrying the daughter of a noble lord and that herself had brought her own ladies' maid from the Old Country, me own curiosity was too great. Y'see, this is a grand establishment," Miss Hetty waved a careless hand, a gesture which encompassed not only the room but the house of which it was a part, and the tree-crowned height from where it had sprung and grown. "Marm herself – that is Mrs. Williamson-and-Mrs.Vining-who-was – had the building of it from the beginning. I was there at her side of course. 'Hetty,' she said once to me, 'if this is a great house, then you had no small part in the making of it! And so I did," Miss Hetty added, with an expression that was pride and sorrow mixed. "I gave Marm the best advice that I could. Our own Mam worked in a grand house and the tales that she told! Sure, and I would hear of how 'tis to live and serve in such a house, if you would not mind."

"No, I would not," Jane answered. As she ate, she answered Miss Hetty's keen questions. Without being aware of how swiftly time passed, between mouthfuls of a very good supper of beef ragout, with dishes of pickled vegetables, of sweets and preserves, and a pie of apples with a tender crust that broke at the touch of a fork, Jane talked of the Hall and the management of it, the doings of the Family, and those bits of wisdom that Aunt Lydia had vouchsafed to her. She told – perhaps unwisely, she thought upon later reflection – how she had been chosen to be Lady Isobel's chief attendant and how Auntie Lydia thought it advancement in station. But Miss Hetty was intrigued and approving, even while apologizing once again for her curiosity.

"Oh, it sounds grand, so it does! A staff of how many? More than a hundred i' the house, an' another hundred for the stables an' grounds! Well, that would have astonished our Mam, but her old lordship was only an Irish peer an' kept no state at all. But here," Miss Hetty's pride was unmistakable. "We kept as grand a state as enny, even when bats roosted in the President's house an' we feared to go out at night in the full moon for fear o' them Comanche Indians. But I dinna think we ever had more than ten or fifteen girls to do the work and old Hurst, god rest him," she reflexively crossed herself in the old fashion, "to drive Herself and do the outside work. But to look around now, ye'd never ha' believed it!"

"It is a very fine house," Jane offered with unfeigned approval. Miss Hetty chuckled. "Ye should ha' seen it when Morag – that's me sister – an' I first came here. Just a plain log house of two-three rooms! The boarding gentlemen, they slept out on the back verandah. Herself, she would hae' better! She saw to th' buildin' of this, ye know. Aye," and there was a reminiscent shine in the old woman's eyes. "Four wee boys, an' their father sick w' the consumption. It finally carried him off, but in the meantime, he could nae work. Young Peter, he was just a babe in arms then. What could she do, but take in boarders, an' then enlarge the house for more rooms! So it came to be; any who was anyone at all boarded here, or came to sup. Ivry man who was President of Texas sat down at that very table an' more than once, I tell ye, and ivery governor, too." The animation fled from Miss Hetty's face, as she sat back with a sigh. "Aye, we have important guests now and again, but it is no' the same. The young master an' Missus Anna, they live in style, but it is no' as it was before the War, when Herself was alive." The expression of desolation on the old woman's face was plain, even in the firelight. "Aye, I miss her still. She was a good mistress. She had it in her will that I would have wages for me life an' live here as long as I pleased."

"That was very kind and foresighted of her," Jane ventured. Miss Hetty nodded. "Aye, I oversee the household still, as Herself would have had it. Missus Anna manages very well," she admitted grudgingly. "But its no' as it once was."

Seeking to change the subject from memories which saddened the old woman, Jane ventured, "It must have been a happy home for children and so many of them, I see."

"Aye," Miss Hetty agreed. "But these are Morag's children, in the main. Seven she had, six still living. Her oldest boy was killed in the War. Such a toll that took on our boys. All of Herself's sons but Peter and the Old Sir as well. It's a sad thing indade, to outlive the little ones, Miss Jane. When young Peter married Missus Anna that filled the house with children, so it did. Next week, your Ladyship is expected. An' Morag's eldest daughter will come calling, I am certain. You would like her – she is a schoolteacher. Did I not hear that you are in a way of being a teacher yourself?"

"Briefly," Jane admitted wistfully. "It was something that I enjoyed doing. Were it not for what I owe to milady, I would happily continue."

"Aye so," the old woman answered in a voice intended to be comforting. "But keeping a grand establishment – that is no such a bad thing for a woman, if she chooses not to marry an' works into old age." She looked around at her comfortable room, the shelves laden with mementos, ornaments and framed daguerreotypes. "No, no' such a bad thing at all." Miss Hetty repeated in a voice of satisfaction and deep content; a privileged servant after a lifetime of service rendered.

"My aunt always believed so," Jane replied. "She hoped that I would take the same position for my lady." In her own mind, Jane had secretly begun to feel reservations; was the life of Aunt Lydia and Miss Hetty one which she truly wished for? This room struck Jane as being a mausoleum for a living occupant. Other women's children, another woman's house, an adjunct to another woman's life; was that all that there would be for her? Jane had little inclination for more talk – or perhaps it was the exhaustion of the day's journey telling on her at last. She excused herself by pleading that weariness. Miss Hetty accepted her excuses, although obviously still eager to hear more of life at Acton. Jane retreated to her own room and slept as if dead well into the following morning.

As had been at the Becker home ranch, Jane at first searched for a task to fill the hours at hand. Besides Miss Hetty, the Vinings had a hired cook and several girls to do the heavy work of housekeeping. Mrs. Becker and Lottie had only occasional need of her, in readying themselves for some special occasion. Amelia Vining, the visiting cousin, had no need of a maid at all, as she had brought her own with her; a smooth-faced colored woman who spoke little to anyone and to Jane not at all. Mrs. Amelia set her teeth on edge, although the woman was a picture of elegance, in spite of favoring the black of mourning. She barely noticed the presence of Jane anyway. Finally Jane offered to tutor Harry and Christian during the afternoons.

Anna Vining fell upon the suggestion with happy gratitude. "Oh, would you? Harry is the plague of his teachers; he will argue with them. We despair of a school which will endure him! You may use the private parlor for a schoolroom. There is a desk and a big table and all of my husband's father's old books." Anna conducted Jane and the momentarily disconsolate boys to a small, cozy room in the older part of the house. Jane looked around with approval. Yes, this would do very nicely; a table and chairs, a desk with a shelf of worn ledger-books over it, a day-bed piled with pillows, and a round rug stitched out of braided rags. There was an old parlor piano in the corner, draped with a fringed silk shawl. "My mother-in-law used this as her office," Anna Vining explained. "Behave for Miss Goodacre!" she added a sharp remark in German to her two sons, whose feelings about lessons were decidedly mixed. Even if the prospect of lessons was not relished, time spent in Jane's company was welcomed with enthusiasm. Harry and Christian had not forgotten the days spent in the palace car parlor with her. Jane settled in happily. Christian was only four, but clever. Harry could already read simple words and the old office proved to be an ideal schoolroom. Once, Jane looked up from a large atlas spread out on the table. She and Harry were tracing the course of the Nile River and Mr. Vining was in the doorway, observing them wistfully.

"My mother used to give us our lessons here in the afternoons," he explained, in a voice husky with emotion. "There wasn't a school of any sort, until much later. Brings back memories, Miss Jane – Harry, you mind Miss Goodacre, you hear?"

One Tuesday afternoon, the day on which the Vining ladies were 'at home' to receive calls, Harry appeared from tea in the elegant main parlor with his mother and the other ladies of the household, looking unnaturally glum; Jane asked him what the matter was. "It's a stupid Christmas party for children. Mama says I have to go and I have to dance with girls, too! Stupid party. Stupid girls! And I don't know how to dance!"

Jane barely managed to hide her amusement. Harry was fair like his father, big for his age, and brash in a way that Jane was certain would never have been tolerated by an English nanny. But he was exuberant in his affections – and he had taken to Jane. Now Jane said, "I can teach you to dance well enough that the girls won't be laughing at you."

"Stupid girls," Harry scowled. Jane reproved him. "I'm a girl, Harry and I am most assuredly not stupid. Besides, when you are a little older, you will want girls to like you. The best ways to get them to like you is to be a good dancer. Lady Isobel told me once, that she began to like Mr. Becker very much at a Christmas ball because he danced with her so very well." Harry mumbled an ungracious assent. His face fell even farther when Jane continued, "Christian will have to pretend to be a girl. Can you do that, Christian? No, you won't have to put on a baby-dress." Christian was Harry's loyal aide and follower, whatever the older boy proposed, Christian agreed. Jane told them both to stand in the middle of the parlor, facing each other. "Now you should bow just a little bit, Harry, and say, 'May I have the pleasure of this dance with you, Miss' whatever her name is. And then you take her hand, like so. And she will put her other hand on your shoulder, yes, Christian, go ahead. Look straight ahead, not at your feet."

"Whatever are you doing, Miss Jane?" Peter Vining spoke from the doorway, much amused. Harry answered, sturdily. "Teaching me to dance proper, Papa."

"You'll need music for that," Peter answered with a broad smile. "I think I will rescue Horrie, so that he can play the piano for your lesson." Before Jane could protest, he had gone, returning in a few minutes with Horrie and Sam who was stealthily wiping paint from his fingers with a turpentine-reeking handkerchief. Horrie sat down at the little parlor piano and opened the cover over the worn ivory keys. He started with a lively schottische, but Jane begged for a country dance; something simpler, as the boys were already baffled enough.

"You'll have to demonstrate for them," Peter settled himself on the day-bed. "Sam, do your gentlemanly duty!"

"My pleasure!" Sam stuffed the paint-smeared handkerchief into his trouser pocket. "Miss Jane, may I accompany you in this dance?"

"Certainly," Jane answered. Their hands met, she rested her left on his shoulder and he put his on her waist. "Now, see, Harry? Watch how we move our feet – in time to the music, one, two, three and four!" The two of them stepped demurely around the tiny space, while Harry and Christian attempted to copy them. It rather surprised Jane that she felt so very comfortable, standing so close to Sam, their bodies linked by their hands, their faces closer than they had ever stood so before. She could see that his chin and cheeks were a little rough, as he had neglected to barber himself that morning. His calico shirt smelled of oil paints and turpentine. She thought she would have felt some apprehension, being so very close – since he was a man and strong, so much stronger than her, yet he held her with such restraint and gentleness, as if she were something fragile that might break. Jane found this quite reassuring. It would be pleasant to dance at a grand ball with Sam Becker – as if that was something that would ever happen! He was above her station, and out of her reach, the younger brother of her lady's husband. But still . . .

Peter Vining watched with approval, encouraging his sons. Horrie looked over his shoulder, grinning. They did the country dance twice more, as Harry and Christian gained confidence in their abilities.

"Try this now!" Horrie exclaimed, his hands flying over the keys in a merry waltz.

"One, two and three!" Sam grinned widely at Jane and whirled her away with such irresistible energy that her heart and her feet could only follow. There was not room in the parlor for those sweeping circles and turns that the waltz demanded. Before Jane could protest, Sam swooped out of the little parlor door and into the corridor, where he led her to the end of the corridor and back again – no carpet or furniture to impede their feet. Jane gave herself up to the pure pleasure of the music. The boys followed, galumphing in clumsy enthusiasm, while their father watched from the door.

"What on earth are you doing?" Amelia Vining appeared at the turn of the corridor; a beautiful and severely disapproving shadow, as the music came to an abrupt halt.

"Teaching Harry to dance," Sam answered in blithe high spirits, and he would have gone on dancing, but for Jane stepping back, suddenly apprehensive.

Amelia frowned. "The noise! We could hear the thumping in the parlor. I don't know what the ladies think of it!"

"That someone, somewhere in the house might be having fun!" Sam replied. Amelia looked even more displeased. "Really, Sam – have you no consideration for other people? As for Miss . . . Goodpasture, is it? I didn't think your duties in the house extended to such antics as this."

Jane's heart sank; she had been certain that until that moment Amelia Vining had barely noticed her. This was how one survived in a strange house: attending to one's duties and not being noticed.

Peter Vining saved her from making any reply or explanation by apologizing, "Sorry for the noise, 'Melia – the whole thing was my idea. We'll try to be quieter."

Amelia's lovely features instantly held an expression of hurt disappointment. "I do wish you would. I feel one of my headaches coming on. You and my son should be present in the parlor for receiving guests, Peter. It's not seemly, playing with the servants and children."

"Sorry, 'Melia," Sam added and he whispered to Jane. "Well, I have a better idea, anyway." Amelia sniffed and absented herself – although her very skirts and petticoats sounded indignant. The merriment of dancing with Sam seeped away from the afternoon. Peter and Horrie exchanged looks of commiseration and followed, leaving Jane and Sam with the boys in the schoolroom.

"What was your idea?" Jane asked. The boys wouldn't relish settling down to lessons again, not after the fun of dancing, but Sam answered readily. "A lesson in sketching. Peter let me set up a studio upstairs, where I can work while I'm here. And," he added with a speculative look at Jane. "There's something you can help me with. I asked Cousin Anna, but she laughed and told me she was too busy. Could you pose for me, in a costume? It wouldn't take more than a few hours and it would keep us all away from Cousin Amelia for a good long while."

"I'll consider it," Jane answered, but Sam begged, "Oh, please, Miss Jane – favor me? It's simple. All you need do is to hold still. The costume is as plain as anything – an Indian woman's dress. Colonel Ford loaned it to me, along with some other things from his collection."

"Then I'll do it," Jane yielded. How could she not? She and the boys followed Sam up to the very top of the house, to a large room in the garret, which boasted an immense window in the gable end. This window being un-curtained, it let the afternoon sunshine spill in without hindrance. Jane looked around. So this was where Sam had spent his time in Austin. It looked as she had always imagined an artists' workroom should look; canvas on wooden stretchers leaning against the slanting walls, stacks of paper and paint-brushes lined in array, and a large easel in the center of the room. Three or four flat-topped trunks were pushed together in the center of the room and draped with a brilliantly patterned blanket woven of coarse wool. Every corner of the garret had things pushed into it higgledy-piggledy; chairs, baskets, a large painted clay pot, a dresser with all the drawers hanging open, a saddle and bridle, a long rifle and a couple of old revolving pistols. The whole place smelt strongly of turpentine.

"It looks as if no one has swept and straightened up in a hundred years." Jane observed. Sam answered, "It's not been that long. This place isn't near a hundred years old. Miss Hetty doesn't let anyone in here to clean, ever. Here, go put these on." He conjured up a bundle of pale cured leather out of the dresser. "Take the pins out of your hair and let it loose. Take your shoes off, too – here's a pair of moccasins."

Jane accepted the bundle with some trepidation; already this did not seem as good an idea as before. She retreated to her own room and unrolled the bundle, which jingled faintly; a plain straight buckskin shift, trimmed at hem, neckline and short sleeves with deep fringe and sewn all over with tiny bells. She must take off her dress, all but her shift and corset. The dress fit loosely, as did the moccasin slippers. She took down her hair and combed through it with her fingers. *What would Auntie Lydia think, seeing her now? What would her ladyship think?* Jane looked at what she could see of herself in the tiny mirror over the wash-stand; she did not look anything like herself at all, in the leather dress which left her neck and part of her shoulders bare, her long hair flowing down her back. She suspected that she had already begun to change from the girl who had left England on the Wayland, almost nine months ago – but what she had begun to change into, Jane could hardly begin to fathom.

Chapter 18 – *The High Wide Lonesome*

The matter of hanging the two cattle thieves was not mentioned by anyone – not Isobel, or her husband, not after the morning of the funeral for Daddy Hurst. Isobel worried for days that her husband and Peter Vining and the hands who knew of it might be prosecuted by the law. She was haunted by a vision of a very proper English constable in his blue coat and peaked helmet, miraculously appearing in the middle of the prairie, saying that there had been an incident and would Dolph be so kind as to answer some questions. But it never happened. Some seven or eight days later the two wagons and the herd arrived at the site of the as-yet-to-be-established ranch.

To Isobel the place for the new ranch looked like many another that her husband had selected as a night-camp during their journey, save that this one was somewhat sheltered from the north by a line of flat-topped hills – hills that in certain lights were striped like ribbon candy in shades of rose, honey and rust. The new ranch was to be built on a level stretch of high ground ground, sprinkled like a current bun with rocks of all sizes. It afforded a commanding view over the tumbled canyons to a distant thread of green which Isobel knew meant a watercourse of some sort, fringed by grassy meadows. There were few trees taller than a man on horseback and those were gnarled and misshapen things, their leaves the grey-green color of furze. As promised, there was a tall cairn of stones piled up around a tall pole bearing a banner of yellow cloth. They reached it at midday, having seen the yellow cloth from a considerable distance; the clearness of the air deceiving them into thinking it was closer. Seb Bertrand and Dolph rode next to the wagons for the last few miles.

When Dolph remarked laconically, "This is it, Seb. Home, sweet home," Seb looked around with an expression of dismay and horror.

"There's nothing here at all," he exclaimed. "Surely Mr. Richter's surveyors were misinformed! This must be some kind of mistake."

"No mistake, Seb," Dolph reached up to assist Isobel down from the light wagon. "Of course there's nothing here. There won't be, until we build it." He held one arm around Isobel's waist to steady her and buffeted Seb on the shoulder. "Put a smile on your face, Seb – or are you having second thoughts about starting a ranch in the West?"

"Not so much," Seb answered, but Isobel could see the effort that it took for him to put a pretense of good cheer on his young face, even through the set of scruffy whiskers adorning it. "How far is it from here to the nearest outpost of civilization?'

"Six day's journey on a good horse," Dolph pointed to the southeast. "Fort Worth, on the Clear Fork of the Trinity River. Don't you worry, Seb. Cuz is bringing some of Uncle Hansi's wagons, loaded with everything we'll need. It won't be the Langham Hotel," he tightened his embrace of Isobel, "But it will be home – an' better than a bedroll under the stars. By the time winter sets in, we'll be under a good roof, and a deep well dug. Uncle even sent the parts for a patent Halladay windmill pump. Over the winter, all those heifers we brought up from the RB will be making themselves a whole lot of little calves. You'll be a richer man before you know it, Seb."

"There will be much work involved for us, though," Seb observed, and Dolph chuckled. "Seb, your arms and legs ain't painted on!"

Isobel thought of how her husband and his cousin worked alongside the men. In India, even at home, this would have been thought unseemly. Here it was only right and proper. That night, and for several nights thereafter, they did spread their beds under the stars, in the sketchy shelter of canvas strung between the wagons, but within a very short time the space around the wagons looked less like a trail camp and more like a building site. On the first day, she and Seb had worked out where the proposed house was to be – in a place which would offer the most striking views from its windows. They marked the corners with small piles of stones and the walls with lines drawn in the dirt with stout stick. Isobel felt as if she were a child at the seashore, outlining sand-castles. A cook-house, a bunk-house for the hands, and a stable for the horses were established by similar methods. The cattle scattered into the meadows and lowlands. As Dolph explained it to her, he and the hands, and the other ranchers would round them up in the spring and brand the new calves.

"How many other ranches are there in the vicinity?" Isobel asked. She had seen no one but their own people in months.

"Mr. Goodnight at the JA is the main one," Dolph answered. "On the other side of the Palo. He has a partner – some Englishman, so I hear. Seb might feel right at home. You and Mrs. Goodnight are the only white women within three hundred miles of this place. If you see a white woman coming to call, Bell darlin', you'll know it's her."

"I have no parlor in which to receive callers," Isobel answered, demurely. Strangely, the prospect seemed of no moment. She was as free as one of the circling hawks, as the dog-wolf of her vision the night after the stampede. If this Mrs. Goodnight appeared, Isobel would simply invite her to sit on the cotton-stuffed mattress by the wagon, and that would do very well. But such would not do for long. Ten days after their arrival, the second herd arrived, scattering like their fellows to the meadows in the lowlands. More importantly, they arrived with Peter Vining. In his charge were no less than four freight wagons heavily laden with lumber and supplies. The teamsters, their wagons and horses would have to return as soon as was possible, so the crates of goods and stacks of lumber were piled up here and there so that they might return south. Peter Vining and those hands who had only been hired for the long drive itself would go with them. Only a dozen would remain at the new ranch over winter. To Isobel's relief one of them was Wash Charpentier.

"Your Uncle Hansi has thought of everything," Isobel marveled, awe-stricken at the variety of useful goods and supplies, even a few luxuries, which had been crated carefully and stowed in the wagons for the journey. "Stoves and furnishings, even windows, ready-made!"

"No, that was Onkel Fredi," Dolph answered, scratching his jaw. "He worked as a freight-driver on the overland to California, among other things. He's a man of all trades and master of most of them. One of the things he knows best is what would be needed out in a place like this. Cuz and I laughed at him once, because of his everlasting lists of necessaries. But he was right. You'll note, Bell, I do not laugh at him now. If there's a requirement for ten chamber pots at this ranch of Seb's, Onkel Fredi will have packed fifteen, with a note to trade the extra five to whoever might have a need and be willing to exchange something you value for them."

"Chamber pots! He didn't really, did he?" Isobel exclaimed and her husband laughed. "Onkel Fredi has a head for trade out here. Odd folk wander through, he says. You never know."

The cook-house went up first with a rapidity which astonished Isobel. It was a simple shed of milled planks, roofed with canvas and tarpaper, and the largest of the iron stoves installed within it. To her vague disappointment, the trail cook who had come with Peter Vining's party was established as the cook for the hands. 'Cookie' Benson was what they called him; an unkempt and uncouth little man, who always had a chaw of tobacco in his bulging cheek. Isobel couldn't see how anyone could have sufficient faith in his cooking, not to mention his standards of cleanliness, to eat it with any relish, especially after she saw him methodically pounding cutlets of beef to tenderness with the butt of a revolver.

"They care that it is hot, tastes familiar and there is plenty," Peter Vining explained, when she mentioned this to him. "And they do not puke their guts out after one of his meals. Sorry, Cuz Isobel. That's just the way of it. The hands have simple tastes, after all. But," he added, after a moment. "They still talk of that pudding of yours – the dried-apple and bread thing you dished up after the stampede. They would relish that for a special occasion. If you fix it for them sometime, you'll have their devotion and Old Cookie would not gripe too much about having his cooking overruled by your recipes, now and again." Her husband added, "Seb and I would prefer yours, though. Just one of our peculiarities. You did very well, Bell, filling in for Daddy."

"How long will it take for the house, then?" Isobel asked, a little nostalgic for the evenings spent as they were doing now, the men smoking their pipes as they lounged by the fire, while Sorsha and Gawain slept curled up next to Isobel, now and again twitching as if they dreamed of a hunt. Still, it would be good to sleep under a roof once and have a place to sit other than on the ground or a wagon-seat.

"Another week or so," Dolph answered, yawning. "Digging the well . . . that will take weeks longer. I hope we find water soon. We're down thirty feet already and it's as dry as a bone." They began that task even before the cookhouse was done; chipping away with shovels and pickaxes. The nearest water was in the creek bottom; rain-fed and seasonal. They sent the light wagon with empty barrels every other day or so, to fill them from the creek. At the height of summer, Dolph and Peter feared that it would dry up entirely, so the well was necessary. Only one man could work at the bottom, sending buckets of dirt and stones up in buckets by a windlass erected over the well-shaft.

It did take longer to finish the well than the house, although Isobel was certain that her family and the servants at Acton Hall would consider it the meanest patchwork shanty, not even fit for the dogs to live in. "I should like to call it Acton," Isobel confessed on the day that it was finished enough that she, Dolph and Seb could move in. Seb agreed; Isobel thought that Fa would be pleased to know that his beloved Hall had a namesake, half a world away. This new Acton had three rooms only, of thin wooden planks and a floor of canvas pegged down over packed and leveled earth. To Isobel's amusement, every scrap of the sawn lumber left over, even that which had been used to make crates for the stoves and the glass windows was put to use in making crude tables, chairs and bedsteads. What a contrast to the Green Parlor, the Yellow Salon, and the gallery. *'Why,'* Isobel thought, *'you could put it all, the bunkhouse and the cook-house, too, into the Great Hall and have room left over!'* But all the rooms had glass windows, and a stove stood in the largest, which served as parlor and kitchen. When winter came, that stove would warm the entire house. Two smaller rooms on either side were bedrooms; one for Isobel and Dolph, the other for Seb. Isobel owned it a relief to actually unpack her trunk. Both Seb and Dolph shaved off the beards they had cultivated along the trail, even if Seb's was a sparse affair. Both resumed the regular habit of of clean shirts. Seb even went to the extent of a cravat in the evenings – a gesture to the custom of dressing properly for the evening meal.

However plain and rough, Isobel took great pride in the little house, adorning it inside with bunches of wildflowers in tin cups, and planting whole plants themselves outside. She studied *Mrs. Beeton's* with great attention. That was about all that she could do, as little of Mrs. Beeton's advice for household management applied. She kept the the floor swept clean, the window glass polished, and the little stove clean of ash and cinders.

The bunk-house took about the same amount of time to build as the house; one large room to house the remaining hands and a small lean-to room against one side as private quarters for Jim Holt, now the foreman of the ranch. Late in summer, the well-diggers struck water, to their infinite relief and that of Dolph. That did not mean that well-work ceased; they moved on to erecting a timber tower for the windmill pump over the well shaft, and a cistern of stone, sealed with pitch and plastered on the inside with Portland cement. Isobel found time hanging heavily on her hands, with the various buildings completed and freed from the labor of cooking for all the hands and wranglers. Care of a little house was not all that much of a burden, so she decided to amuse herself taking long rides and exploring the deep canyon.

She unpacked her black riding habit, which now was an exceedingly tight fit around her waist. She had to draw her corset very tightly to be able to fasten the skirt waistband – but dressed so, in the elegant English-cut habit, she explored the ranges of hills and canyons, the rolling prairie which made up this new-world Acton with delight and wonder. The effects of wind and water carved certain canyons and cliffs into the most amazing, vividly-colored towers and palisades. The streambeds which still contained water were often lined with tall cotton-wood trees, whose leaves the slightest breeze set a-tremble. Often there were wild deer, browsing peacefully in the mornings. Once or twice she saw the native bison; huge, hairy-humped creatures they were. Dolph said regretfully that once they had been more common, in herds of thousands; Onkel Fredi had seen such on the plains to the far, far north. But the Indians depended on them, just as the white men depended on their cattle so it became policy for the buffalo to be reduced. Usually, she went alone with the dogs, although sometimes Seb Bertrand or Alf Trotter accompanied her. She never perceived any danger in these expeditions, although her husband insisted that she take her revolver, just the same.

On one of those days when Seb rode with her, Isobel suggested that they ride out to where an abrupt bend in the watercourse had eroded the cliff into a free-standing tower the shape of a lighthouse. Isobel wanted to show it to him; she had never seen the like before, and was certain that he had not, either. They set off at mid-morning, soon leaving the sight of the new rooftops, pale and un-weathered fresh-cut wood far behind them. The turning blades of the windmill remained in sight, as Isobel and Seb's horses picked a careful way down-hill. Sorsha and Gawain romped alongside them, with occasional forays into the low brush.

"I think that autumn is here, at last," Seb observed. "Some of those aspen-trees are taking on a golden color to their leaves. I wonder; will it be as cold here as it is in England during the winter?"

"It might," Isobel answered. Dolph had expounded on this topic several times. "We are a good way north of the Hill Country and there is nothing to break the winter storms coming down from the north. My husband says that this land is a flat as a platter for hundreds of miles to the north and west. When the winter blizzards strike, there is nothing for the storms to break against. Only this canyon provides shelter – the only shelter for hundreds of miles in any direction. This is why the Comanche Indians used it as a winter refuge."

"With good reason," Seb answered. The flat-topped hills around them were even more spectacular today. The last of the mist rising from the deeper canyons diminished as it rose and the sunlight of mid-morning threw bars of shadow across it. "Perhaps they had an appreciation of such harsh natural beauty . . . so alien, Lady Isobel, but I begin to love it. Mr. Richter was wiser than he knew, in partnering with me and advising that we should put our joint resources into establishing this ranch here."

"And entrusting you with a share of management," Isobel added.

"After a suitable apprenticeship to an experienced master," Seb's wry expression softened into affection. "I expect that Mrs. Becker had much to do with me even being considered to such a position of trust. I am not bound to serve seven years as Isaac did for his Sarah. They have guided me well, Lady Isobel. I am more grateful than I can say."

"You are in love!" Isobel ventured and Seb laughed. "I did not think that I would in the beginning. But now I do. It is something more than love – a hold on my heart that I do not think will ever let go. Just as Lottie has such a hold on it." Seb blushed a little at that; he was still boy enough to be embarrassed by admitting such emotions. Isobel considered him as a younger brother in blood, as he would be by marriage in a few years. That they were alien transplants to this place had drawn them close over the months of the journey and the toil and isolation of building the new Acton.

"It is a splendid land," Isobel looked around, appreciating the harsh and irregular beauty once again. "And Lottie is a splendid girl." Sorsha gave voice, barking just once. At Isobel's call, she and Gawain came bounding back from where they had been exploring. The dogs had gone a little way farther down the track leading to the distant stream of water, a track worn by the hooves of Isobel's horse and the daily journey to fetch barrels of water until the well began to run. The track; a pair of wheel-ruts worn though the sketchy leaf-mast and patches of near-dead grass was the only sign that anyone had ever been there at all; that and the distant windmill, ceaselessly turning.

"There's someone coming up the track," Isobel said, as a flight of birds erupted in panic from a thicket by the side of the track. Isobel was proud that had spent long enough in the wilderness to – as her husband said – read trail-sign, even if only in the most rudimentary manner. She drew rein as did Seb, waiting for the other party to approach. The dogs watched with curiosity and a breeze rustled the leaves of the trees on either side. It did not take long; a tall man on horseback, in advance of a younger man and a lanky boy leading a heavy laden pack-horse. The boy lingered some distance behind his fellows. All three and their horses appeared tired and trail-worn.

The tall man approached to a courteous distance and removed his battered hat, evidently nominated as spokesman. "Morning, ma'am," he ventured. He was older; perhaps in his fifties, as his face was weathered to the appearance of leather. The hair that hung past his shoulders was braided into a pair of plaits and entirely snow white. The younger man also had dark hair worn in the same fashion. Isobel could not help but think that they looked as she had always imagined Indians to appear, even though all three were dressed as white men. Like many another in Texas, the old man wore a belt with two heavy pistols and a large knife in a fringed sheath hanging from it. Another long rifle-sheath hung from the saddle of his horse. Out of habit, Isobel noted that this horse was one of quality, although shaggy and unkempt. It stood several hands higher than the usual mustang ponies favored for work with cattle.

"Good morning, sir," Isobel answered, before Seb did. Plainly he would let her take command in this instance. Something about this stranger; his appearance, his fine-blooded horse, and the manner in which his younger companions held back, all aroused a sense of unease within Isobel. She was hard-put to place a finger on what caused it, precisely. There was a faint air of menace about them, especially the old man, although his manner and words remained perfectly respectful. Taking counsel of her fears, Isobel decided to be open and polite in return; firm without without giving offense. "You are on the trail to Acton ranch lands – may I know what you seek?" She watched his face carefully.

The stranger maintained an expression as bland as her own. "Me and my grandsons are looking for work," the man answered. He did not sound nearly as submissive as Isobel thought a true seeker of worthwhile labor would sound. But this was Texas. No, this was America. Even the beggars commonly behaved as the equal of propertied men.

Isobel shook her head and put the timbre of thoughtful regret in her voice. "I am sorry, my good man. We will have no work here until spring round-up. All the labor of establishing our herd and building the necessary structures has already been done. If you still desire work, come back in time for spring round-up."

"Thank you, ma'am. You are not from these parts, I take it?" Instead of turning his horse and riding down the trail, the old man looked boldly into her face.

"No, we are not," Isobel answered. "We are from England, just this year past. We came as investors in cattle and land, following the advice of men such as . . ." It was on the tip of her tongue to make mention of Mr. Richter, kinsman as well as co-investor. But what if this man, who truly looked like the veriest kind of brigand; what if he took them captive for ransom? Seb was hardly more than a boy. Both could be readily overpowered by the three who faced them on the trail; even with her revolver and Sorsha and Gawain sitting obedient to her command, flanking her horse. "Mr. Goodnight," Isobel threw in the first name which came to mind; their closest neighbor in the trackless acres, six days hard ride from the closest established town. She did not like this man; neither did Sorsha and Gawain. Every line of their shaggy bodies was tense, alert as they eyed him with wary displeasure. "Yes, Mr. Goodnight. We were well-advised. My husband told me that he was the first to see the possibilities in this place."

"Cap'n Goodnight is a sharp-eyed man, ma'am," the old man answered. To Isobel's infinite relief, he pulled on his horses' reins, making as if to turn around. Isobel let out her breath; unaware until that moment that she had been holding it. "Good day, ma'am. If me and the boys are still looking for work, come spring, we'll be back."

"We'll welcome you at Acton," Isobel answered. "I am told we will need good hands for the spring roundup."

"Thank ye kindly, ma'am," the old man answered over his shoulder. He shot an appraising look at Seb, who had been quiet and wary during their exchange. "Your man ain't got much to say for hisself, does he?"

"Good day, sir," Isobel answered, mimicking her mother's most forbidding tones. She and Seb watched as the old man and his companions vanished around a turn of the trail. "We will not welcome you and your grandsons!" she whispered under her breath. Seb fiddled with the reins of his own horse and ventured, "I did not like the looks of them either, Milady. I think that their story of seeking work was a pretext of some kind. Shouldn't we return to the ranch? I fear they may lie in wait for us."

"No," Isobel answered. "But we will take another way to the tower that I wished to show you. When we return, I will tell my husband about strange men seeking work, as if they did not know there would be none until spring! Why are you laughing, Seb?"

"Because that man assumed that we were husband and wife," Seb answered. "If I rightly understood his last words – should I fear that Mr. Becker will be jealous?"

"No more than Lottie would be, if she might infer from them that I have alienated your affections," Isobel answered. They laughed together, while the dogs fidgeted in impatience. Presently, Isobel brought to mind an alternate path towards the weather and water-carved stone tower, one which would avoid the direction in which the three strangers had ridden.

She did tell Dolph of them privately, as they were preparing for the night's rest. The weather had drastically changed that very afternoon, as her husband had warned her that it would at this time of year. She and Seb and her husband enjoyed their evening meal together, laughing over the small venison roast which Cookie had set aside for them, in an iron pot over the cookhouse fire. Isobel and Seb returned in time for Isobel to dash into the cookhouse and sprinkle a few of Mrs. Huckaby's recommended herbs over the roast while Cookie was not looking. The results were flavorful, but the meat still tough. Even so, their supper was a merry one. Seb and Dolph teased Isobel, but with affection, as they ate their plain meal. A chill wind whistled around the eaves of the little house. Even with a good few dry logs burning down to coals in the stove, the icy drafts could not be banished, merely beaten back for a few hours. A bed piled high with blankets and quilts and a heated stone wrapped in a towel at the bottom provided the only comfortable warmth for the hours of darkness. Isobel hastily shed her outer clothes, petticoats and undergarments, and washed in water warmed in a tin pitcher over the stove. Her hair hung in a simple braid down her back; she pulled on her long nightgown and blew out the flame in the single kerosene lamp that lit the tiny room. In the darkness, the bedclothes rustled as Dolph held them up long enough for her to slip between. She settled into the warmth of the bed, and of his arms around her, as they lay spoon-fashion, while the bitter-cold wind howled in the eaves. Her back was pressed against the length of his body, their feet against the warmth of the stone.

"I meant to tell you about those men that Seb and I saw," she ventured presently, as his arm curled around her, pulling him towards her under the covers. She felt his breath stirring her hair, as they lay close-curled in the shelter of bed, and his hand wandered down to her waist, cupping her belly gently.

"What men?" Dolph did not sound interested at all. Isobel answered, "Three men, who met Seb and I on the trail to the creek this morning. They said that they were looking for work but something about them did not ring true. One was old, the age of your uncle. He did not look the sort of man seeking ranch labor. Not at this time of year. The dogs did not like him and neither did Seb or I."

"All kinds of men look for work out here," Dolph answered. He did not sound very concerned. Isobel's worry lessened somewhat. It was just that the three men were strangers and one of them rode a finer horse than his circumstances could account for. She and Seb did not really know this country or the tenor of men who lived in it. Her husband continued, "If they come in spring, seeking work for the round-up, Jim Holt and I will make our own judgement." He was quiet for some time; Isobel thought that he had gone to sleep. And then he said, "I thought you had something else to tell me, Bell."

"I can't think what. "Isobel was honestly confused. What could he possibly mean – and then she felt him sigh a little.

"You're in foal, Bell. Couldn't you read the signs? I can. I thought women knew about things like that."

"I am?" Isobel's voice rose to a squeak, out of sheer astonishment. "A foal – you mean to say that I am with child? I never . . ." Her first honest indignation died away in the face of her husband's certainty and her own relative ignorance of such things. The question instantly sprang to her mind; how long had it been since her last monthly course? She couldn't recall precisely, only that it had been while they were trailing the cattle, before arriving in the Palo Duro and beginning to build the ranch. She had not had the regular spasm of bleeding since. All this time she had never contemplated what that might mean. "How could you know such a thing if I did not?" she demanded. Dolph pulled her closer into his arms.

"Bell, darlin', we've been sharing a bed ever since our wedding and I wasn't raised as a fool. There are things that I can't help noticing and one of those is that you are fatter here," his hand on her belly tightened. "And thinner in your face. I saw it in Cousin Anna and Aunt Rosalie after they wed. I was purely surprised that others couldn't see it until they were told, but there's a look to a woman with her first child that can't be mistook." He sounded faintly exasperated with her

Isobel rolled over under the covers until she faced him in the darkness. "I think that I am," She admitted, feeling a sudden stab of fear and uncertainty. What might happen now? They had been nearly four months in this place, or longer as now it was nearly mid-winter. "How very curious. I have felt amazingly well, all this time. I thought that being with child would be – almost an incapacity. I should not have gone on all those long rides, knowing now what I do."

"Oh, Bell," as she had expected, his arms embraced her again, and she felt the reassuring laughter in his chest, as she tucked her head into the curve of his chin and shoulder. In her confusion, she sought comfort from the only reliable source of it her life, aside from Fa and dear Kitty-Cat, who were so far away! "To your gentle English ladies it must be an incapacity, but not to women here. Nor to the dogs, or the heifers! You are well, so the child is well, so why not do as you wish." His voice turned serious. "But I think that you should stay with Aunt Liesel and Onkel Hansi in San Antonio, after Christmas, rather than return here with Seb and me, until the child is safely delivered."

"But I don't want to be away from you – or from here!" Isobél cried, in her horror and astonishment. "No, I have been well, why should I not continue so? I love this place, and am perfectly safe!"

"No, Bell, I will not have it," her husband answered gravely. "There is no doctor within three hundred miles and no other women that I know of, other than Mrs. Goodnight, god bless her. I don't think she has any more familiarity with delivering babies than I do and my skill largely lies with dogs and cows. I won't take that risk with my wife and my first-born. Papa made Mama stay in Fredericksburg when she was within a month of bearing me, I won't do any less for my own wife. You must stay where there is a good doctor to hand. There is none better than Dr. Herff."

"I want to stay here!" Unaccountably, Isobel burst into tears. "I don't want to be apart from you. I am not sick, why can't you let be return with you after Christmas?"

"Bell, darlin'," Dolph's voice sounded as if he was trying for patience and restraint. "<u>Now</u> you are carryin' on as if you are bearing and making up for lost time. I won't have you here alone, which is what you will be, especially during the spring round-up. It's not your decision, Bell. It's mine, and it's for your own good, and the baby's good as well. I promised your father and I promised you too; you would be safe and that I would always protect you."

And Isobel knew that once again, he had made a decision that she could not gainsay however much she might wish it. He might even be right in it, for it would be as perilous for her to return, and often be alone in the little ranch house. Still, she couldn't help wishing that he might have talked it over with her, first.

Chapter 19 - *The Green Hills of Texas*

In the end, it turned out that posing for Sam was a tedious and muscle-cramping experience for Jane, who obediently trooped upstairs in the afternoon when she had finished schooling Harry and Christian. Lottie also came upstairs to the studio and sat in the corner during the painting sessions, pleading the excuse of keeping Jane company and avoiding that of the poisonously disapproving Amelia Vining. Now Lottie fussed over the folds of the buckskin dress as Jane carefully lay on the blanket-draped platform propped on one elbow and arranged the unbound waves of Jane's dark hair to fall in the most artistic and graceful fashion.

"I'm glad it's you who agreed to pose," she exclaimed the first time. "Sam asked me but he would have the trouble of painting my hair in dark, and I don't look anything like an Indian at all! Cousin Anna just laughed at him and said she had more than enough to do than to waste her days being an Indian dressmaker's mannequin."

"I can't think that I look very much like a Red Indian either." Jane crossed her ankles, arranging her moccasin-clad feet into the same pose which Sam had specified on the day before.

"You have dark hair at least, even if you are oh so much prettier than most of the Indian women that I have ever seen," Lottie replied. "Such plain drudges, very sunburnt and worn out with work. But Mr. Iwonski – he's an old friend of Mama's in San Antonio – had some paintings of Lipan Apache girls which a friend of his did in the earlies when all the Indians were at peace with the German towns. He said they were beautiful, but the Comanche women were quite plain. Poor dears; they must do all the work, you know. Is that still true, Sam, now that they have been made to stay on the reserve?"

"I don't know," Sam answered, in a rather abstracted tone. He had his paint palette in one hand, a brush in the other. Jane had already learned that once he had begun to paint or sketch, he was absorbed in a world where no one could follow, listening to music which no one could hear.

"But you did visit Cousin Willi last year. . ." Lottie ventured, and then she stopped.

"I did," Sam replied, as if this was a matter of no interest. "I didn't see any of his Indian family. I assume he was married, but he didn't offer to introduce me to his wife. Be still, Lottie – I'm thinking."

Lottie did not remain silent for more than a few seconds, whispering to Jane as she coaxed the long strands of leather fringe into the same shape as they had been the day before, "Our Cousin Willi, Onkel Hansi's youngest boy, had no liking for commerce or cattle, so he went off to live with the Indians last year. Cousin Anna was relieved. He was a bad influence on Harry and Christian."

"I had heard that every family has a black sheep in it," Jane whispered back. Lottie giggled. "Or a red one!" Across the room at his easel, Sam cleared his throat emphatically. Lottie gave the fringe one last adjustment and went to sit with her book in a battered armchair that was the only comfortable seat in the room. Jane tilted her head at the angle that Sam had specified when he first coaxed her to pose for him. Holding very, very still was almost as exhausting as constant work. She still had no idea of what the painting looked like. Sam wouldn't show it to her or to anyone else until he was finished. As still as she must remain, Jane's mind remained active. Was Sam in his way as black a sheep as this Cousin Willi? If so, he was better at feigning interest in the family businesses. It made the Baron and his family appear to be a little more ordinary, knowing that not quite all of his sons were obedient to his drive for wealth, a cog in the great wheel of enterprise. She glanced at Sam through the veil of her eyelashes; daubed with paint, disheveled and totally absorbed in the canvas before him. Energy crackled around him like St. Elmo's fire; this was Sam truly wished to be doing. Jane wondered if any other than herself saw that. Surely his family must, or at least guess at his artistic inclinations. She was only an outsider and a visitor.

Sundays were the only day that Sam did no work on his painting, for which Jane was grateful after a week of posing every afternoon. As hard as Sam was working at it, Jane wished that he would progress a little faster. She thought to take a long walk by herself on Sunday afternoon, but a dreary cold rain, the equal of any that marked an English winter drove her to reconsider. She compromised on her intentions of exercise by briskly walking the lower verandah of the great, rambling house. This went all the way around; a covered wooden gallery offering a vista of bedraggled trees dripping rain at the front of the house, and a distant view of the city below. The most prominent hill was crowned with a small dome on pillars; itself perched on the roof of a square white building which housed the state offices and the governor. Jane felt rather kindly towards that little dome, which looked like the round temple folly in the park at Acton Hall. When she rounded to the front of the house for the second time, there was a carriage drawn by a single horse before the steps, and Peter Vining with an opened umbrella in his hand, sheltering two ladies from the drizzle as he helped them down from the carriage.

The ladies were both young and one of them familiar. Miss Lizzie Johnson appeared even more elegant in the occasion of her call on the Becker's ranch. A tiny modish confection of a hat with a tall plume skewered to her high-piled dark hair wobbled dangerously as she alighted on the ground. The other woman had not achieved the same degree of fashion; her dress and the mantle over it were simply cut and all in black. Her hat was adorned with sable ribbons and a bunch of purple silk violets, in a way that reminded Jane of Mrs. Becker. How Lottie complained to Jane of how her mother refused to wear any other color, although the late Mr. Becker had been dead and buried for fifteen years!

Upon seeing Jane, Miss Johnson smiled and hurried up the steps, catching Jane's hands in her own elegantly gloved ones and exclaiming, "My dear Miss Goodacre – how are you! I hope that you are enjoying the pleasures of Austin! I had not expected to see you here." She turned to the other young woman, negotiating the descent from the carriage, "This is my good friend, Miss Fritchie. Jemima, this is Miss Goodacre from England. She has been teaching at the Becker's ranch school. Eight pupils, half of whom had never set foot in a schoolroom before, and dear Miss Goodacre had only ever tutored small children before. She's a born teacher if ever I saw one!"

"Indeed," Miss Fritchie answered breathlessly. Mr. Vining kissed her hand and then her cheek, as if she were a relative of whom he was fond and assured her, "She is indeed. She tamed the wild maverick Harry and the elusive Christian. They have both submitted to lessons, every morning this week, without complaint."

"A miracle!" Miss Johnson acknowledged. Miss Fritchie laughed. She was a pretty woman, older than Jane; with a complexion of pure ivory color, startlingly blue eyes and hair so black that it had a bluish gleam to it like a blackbird's wing. She came up the steps on Mr. Vining's arm, saying to him, "And Auntie is well? I was worried for her, hearing of poor Hurst. They had worked together for so long."

"Miss Hetty is as well as ever," Mr. Vining closed the umbrella and shook the water from it. "Indestructible! In less gentle company, I would call her 'a tough old bird.'" Miss Fritchie laughed, in fond relief as they went into the house. Mr. Vining shut the door on the driving rain and chill wind just beginning to make itself felt.

Miss Fritchie looked around at the hall, with an expression of deep content, remarking, "I have always felt so welcome here, Peter; as if I came home, every time I visit."

"You are home, in a manner of speaking," Mr. Vining answered. A brief shadow appeared on his pleasant, scarred face." But for General Pickett and damned ill-advised orders at Gettysburg, this might truly have been your home, Jemima."

"I know," Miss Fritchie sighed. Jane thought that her eyes momentarily brightened with unshed tears. "Even though James is gone . . . I still think of you as a brother."

"Only logical, as you were born here," Mr. Vining answered, his voice most melancholy. "Jemima, you are always welcome. Should you ever wish to make a home under this roof, then you have it, without even asking. Jamie would have wanted that." *Ah,* Jane realized, *this Miss Fritchie was affianced to his brother who died in that war between North and South. She must have loved him very much, to wear black and not to have wed another since them."*

"I know," Miss Fritchie answered, in brief melancholy, which she set aside almost at once, as her face became animated by interest. "Miss Goodacre, you would be the one which Auntie spoke of on my last visit! Oh, do come with me, for I have as many questions as Auntie did."

"I wouldn't want to interfere in your visit," Jane hesitated, but Miss Fritchie's countenance lit up with a smile and she took Jane's hands into hers, as Miss Johnson had done. "Please, Auntie is often forgetful these days."

Jane allowed herself to be drawn upstairs in her wake, to Miss Hetty's overheated room. She listened to the two women, now and again answering a question as they turned to her, once Miss Fritchie had finished relating all of the doings of her parents, her younger brothers and sisters, and their friends. Such gossip as was of interest to them both, but of little import to Jane. Miss Hetty mentioned Sam Becker's painting, saying that Jane had been sitting for it, every day that week.

Miss Fritchie frowned, slightly – not in disapproval, Jane sensed, but concern. "I had heard something of that. We had a little soiree at the school this week, and the mother of one of our pupils was telling everyone who would listen. She made it sound quite indecent, as if he were painting you . . . unclothed. Austin is such a small town. Everyone knows just what everyone else had for supper the night before!"

"It is nothing of the sort," Jane exclaimed, with honest indignation. This was the kind of rumor which would paint an innocent woman as the blackest of sinners in the minds of her childhood neighbors in Didcot, and in the minds of those at the Hall, upstairs and down. *Why had she never thought to guard herself so stringently here in America, as she had in England?* "Mr. Becker is a very kind and upright gentleman. He and his mother have been most generous and I would certainly never consent to anything like that! I am posing wearing a leather Indian frock and leggings, which covers me at least as much as a ball-gown would. And Lottie – Miss Becker – she is in the studio with us, always. Do you think for a moment that Mrs. Vining would countenance that kind of indecency under her roof, especially as she and Mr. Vining have trusted me with the education of their children?"

"Aye, so it is; evil tongues will find a purchase where no evil exists," Miss Hetty answered comfortably. She looked towards her niece, raising a scant-grey eyebrow. "The Young Marm would never permit that. Tell me, Jemima-Mary, is your informant with the evil tongue an intimate of the other Mrs. Vining – Mrs. Amelia Vining?"

"I believe she is," Miss Fritchie answered, with an easing of her expression which Jane found reassuring. "Yes, I am certain. She talked to me about visiting Mayfield often. Mayfield is the grand house which Mrs. Amelia Vining's father built before the War," she added in an explanatory aside to Jane. Miss Hetty sat back in her armchair with an expression of deep satisfaction. "I thought as much. Oh, such a plague an' a curse that woman is! Poor Marm wouldn't hear any bad said of her and the Young Sir; Mr. Horace who had the ill-chance of marrying that fair-faced, spiteful jade; he believed she was the best woman who ever trod the earth. They say it's love that makes ye blind indeed, although I never thought that Marm fell into that delusion. She married him at the start o' the War and ne'er lived with her above a month or so before he and his brothers marched away with Hood's brigade. Ah, well; there would have been a foine time of it, if Young Horace had returned with his brother." Miss Hetty bent a sharp look upon her niece, "Or if you had married Jamie-my-lad before the boys marched away."

"James did not wish to burden me with the care of a cripple, or to bind me in matrimony in such an uncertain time," Miss Fritchie answered firmly, as if this was an old disagreement. "As much as I would have loved to have borne his name and cared for Miss Margaret in her last sickness, I cannot claim I would have endured sharing a house with Amelia for more than a few hours. We would have been screeching like fishwives and fighting like cats. I've never wanted to give the gossips of Austin the meat and drink such a feud would provide. I am glad to hear of Miss Goodacre's perfect innocence – and I assure you that I will take every opportunity to share with anyone inclined to think otherwise."

"Ye had better be wary of that one," Miss Hetty agreed, looking at Jane with a serious expression. "She was gifted with a venomous tongue – and not above playing spiteful turns against a woman she takes a dislike to. The prettier and the younger they are and the more favored by the gentlemen, the worse she can be, especially as she grows older herself. They say th' heaviest burden of beauty is the curse of seeing it fade with age." The old woman cackled in amusement. "Never having been a prize for looks m'self, or a saint, either, I'll have my satisfaction watching Miss Amelia see herself turning into a hag, when 'ere she looks into th' glass." Hetty's expression turned serious. "I dinna think that Miss Amelia will be any kinder to your lady, though she will veil her malice in a show o' fair affection. You should warn y'r ladyship, since she trusts ye."

"Lady Isobel has had a Season in London," Jane answered, "Among the very highest in Society there. I am certain that she would be able to defend herself against a spiteful, trouble-making woman." Even as she said those words with assurance, in her heart Jane was not so certain. Amelia Vining was exactly the sort who would shred every particle of Lady Isobel's confidence, as easily as a sharp-clawed cat ripping apart a net-lace shawl.

The week before Christmas, Mr. Vining received a telegram. Jane, during her afternoon walk through the orchard and the meadows which hemmed the edge of the Vining's hilltop mansion, intercepted the messenger bearing the telegram from town and took it directly to Mr. Vining. He and his father-in-law, the Baron – as Jane still thought of him – were playing billiards in a room which had been set aside for that purpose. Miss Hetty told her that the billiards-parlor had once been two rooms at the end of a wing, which Mr. Vining's doctor step-father used as an office and consulting room. There was still a tall old-fashioned desk in the corner, with many shelves and niches in it. This had once belonged to the doctor and Mr. Vining had taken over.

"It was the first change made to the house, after the war, and when the Young Sir began to prosper in cattle and a good thing that room is so far away from the rest of the house, with the smell of th' gentlemen smoking," Miss Hetty said about it. "The gentlemen will take their pleasure and ought I to be used to it, now!" Jane thought that the old woman was revived by the clamor of guests in the house. Mr. Richter was accompanied by his plump and fussy little wren of a wife, their youngest daughter and several of his sons, with their wives, and children. "Oh, ye may think it's o'er much with all the families here," she said that very morning to Jane, leaning on her cane and inspecting the freshly-made beds in the guest rooms with a gimlet eye. "It's not a bit like it was, when Marm was alive, an' this house full of boarding gentlemen. Fifty at supper every night! You have never seen the like, Miss Goodacre, I am certain."

"I have seen the like," Jane demurred, trying her best to keep her respectful expression. "Last Christmas at Acton, there were more than a hundred and fifty for supper and many staying at the Hall. There are more than a hundred guest rooms, although ordinarily most of them are closed up during the year."

"As many as that?" Miss Hetty managed to sound envious, yet unimpressed. "'Tis glad I am never to have had to make up that many beds!"

Now Jane, with the little telegraph office envelope in her hand, knocked on the door to the billiards parlor. At a preemptory command from within, she opened the door to a cloud of aromatic tobacco smoke and the gentle click of billiards on the green-felt surface.

"Ah-ha!" Exclaimed the Baron, with an avuncular expression of pleasure and surprise on his bearded face, a billiards cue in one hand and his smoke-trickling pipe in the other. "It is the little maid Jane and still a maid! I loose faith hereby in the good taste of the gallants of Austin, and their eyesight as well."

Jane blushed ferociously, for she caught the whole meaning, even if he meant to be teasing. "I've brought a telegram for Mr. Vining," she said. "The messenger from the telegraph office brought it to the bottom of the garden and gave it to me, as he didn't want to go all the way up the hill." She held out the little yellow envelope, and Mr. Vining took it from her.

"Thank you, Miss Goodacre," he said, and added. "Onkel, you have embarrassed the poor girl. Were I were her brother I would either hit you or call you out."

"My apologies, dear little Miss Goodacre," answered the Baron at once, while Mr. Vining tore open the envelope and absorbed the few words printed on a narrow strip of paper and glued to the single sheet within. "I am devoted to my dear wife, but I am not myself blind to the charms of the ladies, as I encounter them."

Jane had no idea what to say in reply to this, other than to bob a respectful curtsy as she fled in the general direction of the door, but Mr. Vining said, "They'll be here tomorrow, Onkel. Miss Goodacre, you should know as well. I imagine Mrs. Becker will want to be returned to her accustomed habits and state, after eight months of roughing it."

"Thank you, sir," Jane stammered. As she fled, the Baron growled something which might have been humorous, for Mr. Vining laughed.

Instead of going to the rooms which had been set aside for her lady and Mr. Becker; rooms which she had carefully dusted and tended since arriving in Austin, Jane found herself climbing the narrow flight of stairs to the attic studio. She had a melancholy sense of something ending, something which she cherished. It was not yet the hour when Sam preferred to begin painting, yet he was there already. He sat at ease in the battered armchair, contemplating the painting. For the first time it was turned away from the wall. Jane saw that it was finished, or as near to finished as she could see. She was struck with wonder and a little thrill; did she really appear that beautiful, even in that strange leather garment, with her hair falling in a dark cloud around her face? Sam had painted her as an Indian girl, resting on her side and propped on one elbow, idly toying with a horsehair whisk, against the backdrop of a length of hide painted with primitive patterns. He leaped up from the chair, as soon as he heard her footsteps in the doorway.

"Is it entirely finished?" Jane breathed. Sam nodded. "As finished it can be," he answered. "If I add any more, it will be as cluttered as Auntie Liesel's parlor. I still don't know what I will do with it – keep it here, I suppose. Onkel Hansi might like it."

"I think that he might," Jane answered, quailing inwardly at the thought of men, especially the Baron, looking at the painting and seeing her in that outlandish costume. "But you should sell it to him, rather than give it away. You've worked very hard on it. People don't value something that they're just given."

"I don't know if I can," Sam pleasant countenance bore on it an unaccustomed expression of discouragement. "Ask for money for my paintings, that is. I've never been properly schooled in painting. I only dabble in it, like a lady making watercolors to amuse her friends. I really wish …"

"Wish for what?" Jane asked, although she had an inkling.

"I want to go to Europe – Italy for certain and see all the famous paintings in museums. I want to go to Paris and apply to study at the School for Fine Arts. Even if I didn't get in, I'll bet I can find good teachers. Better than I can find here. I've already learnt everything I can from Mr. Iwonski. I have to do that, Jane – I can't make a living at painting just as I am. Anyone can hang out a shingle and call themselves a painter, but they don't take you serious, until you can say that you've studied in Europe."

"Is that what you really want to do?" Jane came closer, and studied the painting. Sam began to pace the floor. "Go to Paris and study painting? Will they let you?"

"I do and they'll have to," Sam answered firmly. "I've wanted to do it all my life. Well, ever since I was a boy. Opa – our grandfather in Fredericksburg – he thought I could. As for Onkel Hansi and Dolph, all they think about is cattle, the land and the business, and I worked in it because I had to. The family and all; it puts food on the table, but the longer I go on doing it, the more it galls me raw, like a wrinkle in a saddle-blanket. I can't spend the whole of my life at this, Jane." The words spilled out of him in a torrent as he paced the studio floor, and Jane listened. "Surely Dolph can spare me for a time – I ran the whole ranch for almost two years myself, went up the trail to Kansas three times, while he went to Europe with Onkel and fiddled around with courting in England. Onkel willingly funds whatever business enterprise his boys wish to take up. I've worked at least as hard as any of us, so why can't I do the same?"

"Why not?" Jane ventured. "You're not afraid to ask for it, are you?"

"A little bit," Sam agreed, sighing.

"The worst they could do would be to say no," Jane pointed out. "Would you go ahead anyway?"

"I think I would," he answered. Determination came up like sunrise in his expression, as if he had never considered the question before. "Yes, I definitely would."

"Then, why don't you?" Jane said. "You're a man. Men can do anything that they want. Not like women; there's only a few things that women may do and still be thought respectable. Mr. Vining just had a telegram. Your brother will be here tomorrow, with Seb and milady. Perhaps you may ask him then."

"I will, Jane. I will. Thank you." To her mild surprise, he took her right hand in his, and raising it to his lips, briefly kissed it. "Thank you for everything – including this." He nodded toward the painting. "If you ask, I will put it away so that no one outside of the family will ever see it and thereby embarrass you. It's a good thing it is finished," he added. "I expect you will have to go back to being Sister Isobel's maid tomorrow."

"I expect that I will," Jane agreed, overtaken by a sudden feeling of desolation, as she had felt when the brief school term at the Becker home ranch came to an end. As happy as she would be to see Lady Isobel again, the thought of returning to the duties expected of her felt like returning to an iron-barred dungeon, and hearing the door clang shut behind her.

The light spring wagon bearing the travelers did not arrive until late in the afternoon, although Jane and everyone else had been anticipating it since breakfast. Jane dismissed Harry and Christian for the day, saying that she must return to attending on Isobel. Feeling at a loss, Jane set herself to unpacking the last trunk of Isobel's clothing which had been brought to Austin from the ranch. Here at Christmas, Lady Isobel might have better excuse to wear some of the the fine day costumes and ball gowns from her trousseau. Jane shook out the tissue paper in which they had been packed. She busied herself in those tasks which had given her so much contentment a year ago, and wondered why she felt only impatience. When the wagon finally drew up the hill and stopped before the front door, practically everyone in the household gathered on the verandah and front steps to welcome the travelers, even the elegant Amelia Vining, who stood a little aside with Anna Vining and the baby, with an expression on her face which suggested she smelled something bad. Jane hung back behind them, waiting for a word from her lady. She bit back a startled gasp when Isobel emerged from the wagon, followed by the shaggy forms of the dogs; *Dear heaven, was that truly her ladyship?* The only familiar aspect was her hair, woven into an untidy thick braid and hanging down her back like a school-girl. Her complexion had been roughened by sun and wind, her cheeks ruddy and her lips chapped. Obviously her hat had been of little use – and her clothes! She had no shape at all, dressed as the roughest kind of scullery-maid; Lady Caroline would have have been shocked beyond words. Even Aunt Lydia would have been taken back.

Amelia Vining looked down her beautiful nose and whispered to her sister-in-law, "And that creature is the daughter of a lord? The Duke of the Dung-heap is more like it!"

"You would know dung-heaps, my dear," Anna Vining shot back, unperturbed. It sounded even more cutting, spoken in her accented English. Amelia only sniffed contemptuously, while Jane recollected Miss Hetty's warning. Lady Isobel did look a perfect fright. She was looking around now, while the dogs competed in fawning around the feet of the grownups and licking the faces of Harry and Christian, who squealed in mock-revulsion and sheer excitement.

Isobel's eyes lighted on Jane, and she cried, "Dearest Jane! I have missed you so much! You simply would not believe the splendid times we had! The rides, the excitement with the cattle, and the lovely new ranch! Such a beautiful location! I am simply bursting to tell you all about it!"

"I did promise you cows," Mr. Becker drawled, taking her arm. "Lots of cows."

Once inside, Lady Isobel shrugged off the shawl wrapped around her shoulders like a peasant woman, and the shapeless coat she had on under it. Jane took them from her, recoiling from the coarse feel of the fabric and the grubbiness which they had taken on, along with a smell of horses and dogs. Promising herself silently that she would set them to air outside and for a thorough laundering before she consented to see Isobel put them on again, Jane at first did not notice the other significant change in her lady, until Isobel put her hands to the small of her back, as if she were stiff and wished to stretch.

"Jane, I am absolutely perishing for a good hot bath. I never thought that I would miss one so much. And I must lie down for a while; my husband insists on it. He and dear Uncle Hansi have much of import to discuss, although I do not know why it can't wait."

"I will draw a bath for you at once," Jane promised, and then her eyes widened. "Milady . . . you are . . ."

"Yes, I am, indeed! With child, Jane – isn't it marvelous?" Lady Isobel laughed, as merry as if she had not a care in the world, while Jane wondered how long it would take her to let out the waist of a dress which Lady Isobel could wear at supper.

"Right then, lads," Hansi Richter demanded as soon as the door to the billiard parlor closed. "I want to know what it was that you couldn't tell me in a letter – about what happened on the day that you buried old Hurst."

The two cousins looked at each other, warily. Dolph spoke first. "What have you told him, Cuz?"

"Nothing," Peter answered. "Other than our cattle were stampeded deliberate. We found out it was an organized gang doing it. We dealt with the matter and the men responsible; all but one."

"He was just a boy, Cuz." Dolph said softly. "We let him go with a warning, Onkel. I reckon he fell into bad company."

"Alas for your good intention," Hansi answered, the words in English clipped short in irritation. "That boy just didn't fall into bad company. He was born into it. He is the grandson of Randall Whitmire of the Cherokee Nation, born to a white woman and so bearing her name. The other two men were his uncles – two of Randall Whitmire's many sons." Hansi tapped a small pile of letters on his desk. "This I had from Judge Parker's chief marshal in Fort Smith. The whole Whitmire clan are very bad news."

"Ah." Peter shook his head, sadly. "Cuz, they say to be kind to the cruel is eventually to be cruel to the kind."

"Who are these Whitmires?" That was a new voice, and unexpected. Magda Vogel Becker had taken a quiet place in an armchair, invisible in her widow-black, a shadow in the corner. All three of the men started; Hansi Becker spoke first. "Magda, what do you do here? This is a business that you should have no part in. You should not know of such things."

Magda spoke a very harsh, contemptuous word and switched into German. "Do not take me for a fool, Hansi, or you, my son. I know of the doings of men. I know them very well, of what they do in the darkness, with ropes and guns. Yes, I know very well! What have you done? And who are these Whitmires of whom the law in Fort Smith should be concerned? What threat do they pose to ours – to my son and our family?"

"The Whitmires," Peter Vining answered carefully, after it became clear the other men hesitated to answer. "Are a clan who live in the wilder parts of the Oklahoma Territory. They are of the Cherokee affiliation, although not of the worthy part of their tribe. Even so, they have the protection of their Indian blood on that account. White lawmen cannot touch them, regardless of the crime or complaint against them. They have the reputation of being lawless, brawling and immoral, saturated with every vice common to both races; drunkenness, brutality, and criminal as the day is long. Their reputation is for horse and cattle thievery, of being ingenious and persistent in that pursuit, and vengeful towards those who have resisted their depredations. Now it seems that their collective ire might have landed upon us, Ma'am Becker. I am sorry indeed. Cuz has altogether too soft a heart."

Magda Becker fixed her son with a stern eye. "And how did you deal with this matter, Dolphchen? Do not mince words with me."

"We hanged the two rustlers," Dolph answered bluntly. "From the same tree where they had set their device to panic the herd. We caught them with running irons, thirty head of RB cattle, and ten of our remuda horses. They said nothing about being Whitmires but we did not ask."

"Who knows of you having done this?" Hansi Richter demanded. "Will they talk out of turn?" Peter shook his head. Dolph answered, "The foreman, Jim Holt – a good trusty man. Wash Charpentier, Bob Beckwith, Orry Karnes. They were there, but they won't talk. Seb doesn't know a thing about it. Isobel does, because I told her. Some of the other hands might have seen the bodies afterwards and guessed, but they won't know anything for certain."

"Whether they talk or no, may not make any difference," Hansi Richter's countenance was dark. "Understand this, lads; I would have approved your actions. Our property is to be protected in any case, but now we have a vendetta upon our heads. I have been advised to hire hands for the Palo Duro ranch who are more skilled with a gun than they are with cattle. In this letter from Fort Smith, the chief marshal says that to the best of his knowledge, Randall Whitmire and some of his gang have gone from their usual haunts. No one knows where they have gone. If they know, they do not say, only that he had talked about vengeance and departed for the west."

"That is curious," Dolph said at last. "Isobel and Seb told me they had encountered three men, last month who said they were looking for work. Bell did not like their looks and sent them away, but if they were the Whitmire gang, they might still be around."

"Show them this," Hansi Richter took out a folded sheet of paper from one of the envelopes at hand. "See if they recognize him, but do not alarm them unduly."

Dolph took the paper from him. He tore a long strip from the bottom, observing as he did so, "They needn't see the bit about what he's wanted for. Guess it's a good thing that Bell will stay in Santone with you, Onkel – I wouldn't want her back at the Palo Duro, knowing that the Whitmires are saving up for a range war."

Chapter 20 – *A Parting of Ways*

It gratified Jane that Isobel greeted her with such exuberant affection. Both her husband, and the Baron's plump and overdressed wife insisted that Isobel go upstairs at once and rest from the ardors of the journey. Jane went to drag in the tin slipper bath. On returning from arranging for one of Mrs. Vining's other housemaids to bring up bucket after bucket of hot water, she was taken back to discover that Isobel had divested herself of her outer clothing and stout laced boots with no assistance whatsoever.

"Milady, you should have waited for me!" Jane protested, gathering up the discarded garments from the floor where Isobel had left them. Isobel laughed. "I so wanted out of those clothes. I couldn't bear them on me for another minute! I have been doing very well without a maid for months."

"Not as well as all that," Jane chided her. "Your complexion is ruined – and your hair is a perfect fright of tangles.

"Now that we are back together," Isobel answered with a happy sigh, "you may do as you wish in seeing me turned out for the cold eyes of Society, just as you always have done." She had assumed the ruffled and beribboned loose wrapper which Jane had laid out, and sat in the chair in front of the dressing table, with a half-sigh, half-groan of relief. "I am so tired, Jane. You should take care that I do not fall asleep in the bath. Being with child is so very strange. Most times I feel quite well and strong, as if I could climb mountains and then suddenly I feel completely exhausted!" Silently, Jane took up her hairbrush and began coaxing the tangles out of Isobel's hair, while her lady talked. Might as well do something, while they waited for the kitchen-maid to bring up the cans of hot water for her ladyships' bath. "I was distraught when my husband told me that I must stay with Aunt and Uncle Richter for my confinement . . . did I tell you that Seb and I decided to name the ranch Acton – after the Hall? Fa would be so pleased. After jolting all that way in the wagon. I think now I love my husband very much, for being so thoughtful and provident, insisting on this in spite of how I begged to return. He wanted to name the new ranch 'Quivera' – but then he only told me so afterwards. Quivera – such a strange name, and story! It was supposed to be one of the golden cities sought by the Spanish conquistadors, so long ago. A city of towers and riches, where the natives drank from cups of gold, hanging from the trees by a crystal-clear river, somewhere to the north. They looked for it, the conquistadors did, but they never found it. Or perhaps when they did find it, it was only an Indian village of mud and thatch, by the side of a river. The new ranch . . . oh, Jane dear, the house is very plain, but the lands surrounding it – they are enchanting! Such spectacular canyons, carved by the river! I could look on them a thousand times throughout the day and each time, they would appear different! And the house . . . at last I could say that I had my own dear little house, Jane. All my own . . . although my husband and Seb lived in it also, and I could arrange it all to my own satisfaction! I cooked, too. I did write about that to you, did I not?" She chattered disjointedly, while Jane silently worked on untangling the mass of her hair and considered her own thoughts. Her lady was happy, Jane conceded at last; she had gained a good husband and an independent household, no matter how unconventional they were by the standards of Society – and now blessed with a baby of her own? Who would have guessed that Lady Isobel would have had all three, barely a year after their visit to young Mrs. Wright at Dale Farm?

The girl who worked in the kitchen appeared in several relays, with water to fill the slipper-bath. Jane laid out towels, a clean shift and nightgown, and eyed Isobel's waistline. "While you rest, I will work on altering a gown for you to wear downstairs for supper tonight, Milady," she offered.

"Jane – that will be perfect! I will leave everything to you, of course. I suppose that I can't wear my trail clothing here. I wish that I could have supper on a tray, for I feel quite exhausted now." she stifled a yawn. "But everyone is expecting me. I confess that after so many months without the company of my own sex, to be among other ladies again will be sheer bliss! Mrs. Anna has such refreshing opinions and Lottie is such a sweet child! Even Mrs. Becker, for all her strange attitudes – I find her a very worthy woman. She is inexpressibly thrilled regarding our child, Jane! Did I tell you how Aunt Richter promised to see to arranging all the baby-linen? Such a comic figure she cuts, but she is a kindly woman at heart. I promise that I will not make fun of her when we are together." She stifled another yawn, as Jane cast one look over the bath with the screen around it, the towels, and delicately-scented soap all laid out invitingly. "I shall sleep for hours, I fear – but Jane, do not fail to wake me in time to dress for supper."

"I will, Milady," Jane answered, with a niggle of rancor in the back of her mind. Lady Isobel had not asked a single question about what Jane had been doing all summer, although Jane had dutifully written to her about the school, the visits to Comfort, and other such curiosities had struck her fancy and which she thought might excite interest. This was most unlike her lady; she had always taken a lively interest in Jane's tales of the doings downstairs at Acton, or at the London house, or even of Jane's childhood in Didcot. Marriage and the journey north had changed Lady Isobel, Jane thought with some resentment, and in some ways not for the better. She did remember, as she sat by the window of her room, picking out stitches in the waistband of the simplest of Lady Isobel's evening dresses, that she had not had a chance to pass on Miss Hetty's warning about Amelia Vining. *Oh, well,* she told herself. *Lady Isobel will know at once, I am sure. That Mrs. Vining minds me of Lady Caroline; an icicle of a woman, dressed all in silk and lace.*

Jane simply forgot about that matter that evening when she came to wake Lady Isobel and assist her in dressing for supper and even later, when – yawning – she came to the Becker's suite of rooms to help her ladyship prepare for bed. When she raised her hand to tap on the door, she heard Mr. Becker laughing within, and Lady Isobel giggling.

"Milady, I've come to assist you with your gown!" she called, and Lady Isobel replied, breathlessly, "Oh, Jane, you need not have waited up! Dolph – my husband . . . he is undoing my buttons and pulling out my hairpins!"

"Oh," Jane answered in some dismay. "But I have completed work on letting out a dress for you to wear tomorrow."

"Oh, very well," Lady Isobel answered, and spoke to her husband in a voice too low for Jane to hear. When she opened the door, it was to see Mr. Becker in his shirtsleeves, and Lady Isobel, very pink of cheek, clutching her wrapper around her as she sat on the edge of the bed, barefoot. Mr. Becker held one of her shoes in his hand, and a stocking in the other; he also looked rather flushed. Obviously, Jane had interrupted a pleasurable moment between them. This lack of restraint annoyed her.

"I've let out the waist of the blue day-dress, while you were at supper," Jane laid the dress across the blanket-chest at the foot of the bed. "And the purple challis wrapper is sufficiently loose-fitting to be comfortable without any alteration, Milady." She had little idea of what to say; only that she had never felt so awkward in coming into the presence of her lady as a married woman. "I shall come in the morning to assist you, Milady."

"Yes, thank you, Jane. It looks quite lovely – I am so grateful that you are thinking ahead." But her eyes went towards her husband, and it was clear that she was not thinking of the blue dress or the other garments that would have to be altered. Jane bobbed a brief curtsy and closed the door firmly after herself. She couldn't mistake the sound of soft laughter in the room.

Mr. Becker was already gone from their rooms when Jane returned in the morning; which cheered Jane. Perhaps this was a step on the way back to the happy companionship they had formed before Lady Isobel's marriage; lady and maid, sharing every confidence and dream imaginable. She noted that her lady looked happy and rosy-cheeked, still drowsy from a long and comfortable sleep in a good bed. The morning was chill. Jane built up the fire and opened the curtains over the long windows. This room looked out over the city, veiled with mist, half-hidden behind the leafless trees which ringed the height on which the Vining mansion sat.

"I have brought you some coffee, Milady," Jane said, in an encouraging tone, as she set down the tray which she had brought. "Breakfast is in twenty minutes downstairs. Miss Hetty has consented to prepare a batch of her savory biscuits. She was famous for preparing them, when this house took in boarders. Now she prepares them for special occasions. Everyone says they are best when hot from the oven." She brought Lady Isobel's wrapper, holding it so that her lady could easily don the garment.

"Bliss! Thank you, Jane – you are always a treasure!" Lady Isobel wrapped her fingers around the coffee-cup. "I have come to be at least as fond of coffee as I am of tea. Hurst would prepare it by the gallon. Now I prefer it of a morning. Do you suppose that I am becoming an American?" She sat down in front of the dressing table. Jane began to unravel her braided hair.

"Since you have married an American, that would only be logical, Milady, but what will Sir Robert and Lady Caroline think of that?"

"As long as I behaved with perfect refinement and proper rectitude, I do not think Mama will mind. As for Fa, he thinks that everything I do is perfection itself." Lady Isobel set down her coffee on the dressing table, and frowned slightly. "There is a matter which I . . . it's my responsibility, Jane, as it touches on your good name and mine; that is the matter of you posing for a painting. I can't imagine what would lead you to consent to such a thing. There would be a most awful scandal if anyone were to hear of it. Women who do such reckless things are not respectable. It's almost as bad as being an actress or a dancing girl and Mrs. Vining assures me that it is the same here in America."

"It was for Sam – for Sam Becker," Jane replied, in indignation, which was further roused when Lady Isobel chided her, "Don't interrupt me, Jane. It was thoughtless and inconsiderate of him to even ask you! Such women are not respectable. It's nearly as bad as selling your body."

"Mrs. Vining – Mrs. Anna Vining – she knew of this and had no objection and Lottie sat with us, every day."

"Jane, you should speak of her as Miss Lottie," Isobel answered. "And it's Mr. Becker to you, whether it is my husband or his younger brother. I fear you have become altogether too familiar with your betters. It's most unseemly; Mrs. Kittredge would never have allowed this manner of speech from servants at Acton, and I cannot permit it here."

Jane stared at her in the mirror, stung with sudden anger at being chided unfairly in this way. "He . . . Mr. Becker treated me perfectly respectfully," she answered, in a voice that shook with suppressed fury. "And it was no more intimate than if he had chosen to make a pencil sketch of me at a public gathering. He has been very kind to me, he encouraged me to make myself of use. His mother nursed me when I was ill and cared for me as if I were one of their own by blood! In accusing me of impropriety, Milady, you imply insult to them as well!"

"Jane," Isobel's eyes met Jane's in the mirror. Jane saw without caring that Isobel was angry at this rebuff, although she managed to keep her voice steady and cold, in a way which reminded Jane of Lady Caroline. "You forget your place. I will not have a servant thoughtless of her position and mine."

"Then you will not!" Jane's anger flamed up, struck the dry kindling of her resentment and uncertainties and exploded. She slammed the hairbrush down on the dressing-table top and snapped, "I give my notice to you, Milady, and bid you good-day. You have done very well without me for more than half this year; I dare say you may get along without me from now on!"

Jane saw, before she turned on her heel and stalked out of the room, that Lady Isobel's continence had an expression of shocked horror upon it, her mouth rounded into an 'o' of disbelief. She flung the door closed behind her, not caring that the sound it made was quite loud. The anger carried her along the corridors, the many jogs and up-and-down steps in it, until she came to her own room and realized with horror what she had done. She had cast herself off, burned the bridge behind her to the world that she knew so well; the safe and well-known world of service, of Acton Hall, the assurance that her lady would always be there. What would she do now? Despair overwhelmed her, despair and horror at what she had done. She had spoken with intemperate anger to Lady Isobel with words which likely would never be forgiven.

Isobel blindly took up the silver-backed hair brush which Jane had flung down. What had happened, what had she said, which had sent Jane – dear, faithful Jane – into such an ill-temper? What was she to do about this, upon being deserted by her sweet friend and companion? Isobel could think of nothing better than to seek the advice and counsel of her husband. She braided her hair loosely, and buttoned the wrapper around herself; now that she was decent, she went to find him. But he was not at breakfast in the dining room, that room with the long, white-covered table in it; only the women and children of the household were there, with Sam and Seb Bertrand. Mr. Vining,

Mr. Richter and her husband were not present. Anna Vining looked up, startled, as Isobel stood in the doorway demanding breathlessly, "My husband – Mr. Becker – where is he? He has – I mean, I have a question for him."

"They have gone to the billiards-room. A messenger came with some news." Anna replied. "They are there now. Do sit down and have some breakfast. I am certain they will not be very long. The men are hungry also."

"I must speak to him at once," Isobel shook her head, although she was hungry, so hungry that she felt a trifle nauseated from the smell of bacon and sausages and the hot cornmeal cakes waiting on the sideboard. She knew the twisting hallways and odd corridors of the Vining's mansion as well as she did the far more extensive ramble of Acton. The door to the billiards room was closed. A man with a plain derby hat resting in his lap sat in a chair beside it, as if on watch, or waiting to be summoned within; a Negro man in a neat dark suit, whom Isobel did not recognize at first.

"Mr. Charpentier!" she exclaimed, as he sprang out of the chair upon seeing her. "I did not know you in these clothes! I thought you were at the ranch! What are you doing here in Austin? Mrs. Vining spoke to me of a messenger; is that you, then? What is this news? Did Cookie succeed in poisoning everyone with his food?"

"No, Miz Isobel," Wash Charpentier's dark face broke into his usual smile, but one which faded quickly. No wonder that she had not recognized him at first; his hair clipped close to his head, not the wild shoulder-length mob. The swaggering top-hand was diminished into an ordinary man in a dapper city suit of clothes. "They're all well, all but Jim Holt. We buried him a week ago tomorrow."

"What happened?" Isobel demanded, with swift concern. "Who is in charge, now?"

Wash named one of the older hands who had remained and then he looked at the floor. "Jim an' me . . . we was out one morning on the north boundary, setting out a site for a line camp. We was riding along, about thirty yards apart, an' someone dry-gulched Jim from behind. He fell like a sack o'flour, dead before he hit the ground. They shot at me, too – bunch of shots, sounded like two, mebbe three men. Killed m' horse. I was throwed a piece, when he went down. Guess they thought I was dead, too, at first." He turned his hat in his hands, a nervous gesture that Isobel had never seen in him before. "Jim's horse got the reins tangled in a bit o'brush – kept him from running very far. I caught ol' Jim's horse an' high-tailed it out o' there. Miz Isobel, I rode like the Devil hisself was after me. We came back for to bury Jim the next day, four o' the boys an' me. We foun' tracks o' their horses, an' it was murder done, Miz Isobel. There ain't no doubt about that; an' they were sightin' on us deliberate, Jim an' me."

"How can you be certain of that?" Isobel asked. Wash turned his hat once more. "When we came to bury Jim," he answered slowly, "there was a six o'spades card in his hand. 'S if someone had but it there, sendin' a message, like. Spades, Miz Isobel – that's for diggin' graves with. An' there was six of us, when we hanged those rustlers' an' left the third one go. Jim an' me, Mr. Vining, Mr. Becker, Ol' Bob Beckwith an' Orry Karnes. Now. Mister Richter, he tol' me dat those good-for-nothin' cow thieves were Whitmires, an' mebbe now dey on a man-hunt fo' us?" He shook his head, sadly. "Me, I got de message. I was 'bout ready to hang up my spurs anyways, an' take on some steadier line o' work. So's I said I'd take de message 'bout poor ol' Jim an' get my pay. Dat's why I'm waitin'. Mister Becker said if I would wait a bit, he's see I had breakfast an' a little extra fo' my trouble."

"You've given your notice?" Isobel exclaimed. *What fateful day was this? Jane and Wash both departing their service?* Wash Charpentier might have a much better reason, yet Isobel was still disappointed. "What will you do, now?" she asked; indeed, she would miss him from the ranch. He had been so so very considerate of her, that day after the awful stampede. Now he smiled again, a more lasting expression and one more heart-felt. "Me? I'm gonna work on de railroad, Miz Isobel. My sister's husband, he's a porter for those Pullman cars, an' he already got me on! I allus liked to travel, an' de pay, it's regular. I been thinkin' 'bout settlin' down. Ain't no future in ridin' de range; dat's a young man's game, an' I ain't no young man no more. Miz Isobel, I don' want you thinkin' that Wash Charpentier ain't got no sand, that I'm a coward, leavin' y'all like this. But I hired out as a hand, not one o'dem gunslingers. I got my mama an' ol daddy to support an' I cain't do that iffen I'm daid."

"No one thinks any the worse of you," Isobel answered, with some heat, for she had been thinking exactly that. "You are right. It is a hard life, only ameliorated if one can work up to owning a ranch and a herd of fine cows yourself. You'll be a good a porter and you'll care for your passengers ever so much more than you cared for our cows."

"Ain't that de truth!" Wash Charpentier answered laughing, while Isobel also laughed. She had a picture in her mind of him, dressed as a train porter, with a lariat and a six-shooter, chivvying cows and travelers into line. At that moment, Seb Bertrand appeared in the corridor. "Lady Isobel, we were wondering what was taking you. Wash, old man, what are you doing here? I never thought . . ."

"Mr. Charpentier came with a message," Isobel explained. "And a warning. It seems there are lives in danger." She explained in a few words about the two rustlers, hanged by the neck with their kite contraption. Seb's face sobered. "I did wonder about that. It seemed most providential. No one would say anything to me. I had begun to wonder if Mr. Becker truly trusted me."

"I think my husband wished to keep knowledge of the matter from you for your own protection. If any questions were ever asked, you wouldn't be forced into telling a lie." Isobel explained. Wash Charpentier nodded in agreement. "It's a bad business, Mr. Bertrand."

"That it is," Seb answered, "I'll not argue. But I wish Mr. Becker had shared this intelligence with me, or permitted me to have taken part."

"You would have done so?" Isobel was genuinely shocked. Seb Bertrand was the finest kind of English gentleman. To wish now that he had taken full part in that dark deed . . . but perhaps he had come the same distance from England that Isobel herself had. His countenance was stern, grim and unboyish. "Certainly I would have. The Acton ranch is half-mine, since I have invested my inheritance from Uncle Rollie in it. Half the cattle are mine as well. While I would not grudge one of them to a man with a starving family, I object most strenuously to being robbed blind and laughed at by the robbers. If there is no law, than what can a man do who respects law, than to administer justice accordingly?"

At that moment, the door at their backs opened. Uncle Richter appeared, with an envelope in his hand. He did not seem startled to see the three of them in the hallway. "Good that you are present. It is most convenient. Mr. Charpentier, thank you for waiting. This is for you, with our thanks and best wishes. I have written a letter for your future employer, testifying to your good character. You should go around to the kitchen for breakfast. Tell Mrs. Briggs I said that you should be fed. You – Sebastian, Miss Isobel, come in, please. We have a question for you both."

Isobel entered rather timidly. This was the retreat and abode of men; dim, with the windows heavily draped against the morning sunlight, and smelling of tobacco. A scattering of ivory billiard balls were left on the felt table, as if a game had been interrupted. Uncle Richter showed her to the most comfortable chair in the room, one of a half-dozen arranged in a half-circle in the same corner as the tall-front desk. Puzzled, she looked towards Dolph, who had taken up a heavy piece of paper from the desk; a crudely printed sketch of a man's head and shoulders; an older man with a scowling face, and long hair, hanging below his shoulders. The picture made him look brutish, with wrinkles carved so deeply that they looked like scars.

"Why, that is the man that I told you about!" Isobel exclaimed at once, "He was with another man and a boy, looking for work, he said. Seb – that is the man, isn't it?"

"Yes," Seb answered slowly, while Dolph, his cousin and Uncle Richter exchanged a long look. Uncle Richter swore softly in German. "Yes. I am certain of it. The picture does not flatter him, but it is an excellent likeness. This is the man we saw, out riding to see Lady Isobel's wondrous tower." Seb examined the faces of the three older men with the same care that he had looked at the crude sketch. "So, who is this man – someone dangerous to us all, I deduce."

"No flies on you, Seb," Dolph answered. "I should have paid more mind, when Isobel told me of how you encountered him and his kin on our lands. He's Old Randall Whitmire, of the Cherokee; head of a clan of brigands as vicious as they are ingenious." He paused, as if searching for the right words, and Peter Vining explained, in a more blunt fashion. "Because Cuz here has a soft heart, Old Randall is out for blood revenge on those RB folk who hanged his sons for stampeding our herd. He's as mean as a snake and it won't end soon or easily. Wash came to tell us that Holt was killed from ambush a week ago, and he was nearly done for as well. Wash doesn't have a stomach for this, so we've given him passport to leave and put crowns in his purse for convoy. I don't blame him in the least. It's not his fight in the same way that it's mine and Cuz's."

"Mine also, is it not?" Seb Bertrand observed with a shrewdness that Isobel had not thought him capable of, before this morning. The gentle, mannerly English schoolboy had become a harder man in the last six months. The cattle drive, the wilderness, the hardships; although relatively minor, had conspired to shape him into something else. Isobel could not decide if this was a change for the better, and if the experience had also worked something upon herself as well.

"It is, Seb. I'm sorry for that." Dolph answered and Seb laughed, a curt and grim chuckle. "Don't be. Do you know what my family pretends is their motto? *Quod habemus tenere*. Probably scavenged it from a Latin phrase-book; it means "what is mine, I hold." Damned if I'd let any half-breed bandits take anything of mine, as I told Lady Isobel. So, what are we planning to do about all this?"

"Onkel is planning to put a reward out," Peter Vining answered. "And I'm going to carry a pistol with me, at all times, although Austin has been a relatively civilized place for the past ten years. Cuz is going to return to the ranch and take charge in Jim Holt's place. Sorry, Cuz Isobel. One other thing: it seems that when Old Randall's band is balked of their prey, they take it out on the women and kinder. It fair made me sick to read of what they did in the Territories. "

"There was a man whom Ol' Randall had a grudge against. And he couldn't catch that man, he and his boys went to that man's house." Dolph looked as if he didn't want to say anything more, but he did. "It was a log house, Bell, with only small windows and one door. They blocked the door and windows, threw kerosene all around, and lit it on fire. Two women and a bunch of children burned alive. Ol' Randall boasted about it later, sayin' the law couldn't touch him."

Isobel felt faint with shock; yes, now she knew she had good reason to dislike the old man who asked for work. To have done such evil must have lent an aura to such a man, one that she could sense. Her face must have turned pale, for Uncle Richter reached for her hand, and her husband moved to stand at her shoulder.

"Bell, I promised once that I'd keep you safe – always!" he whispered. "This is why we have decided you should go with Auntie Liesel and Onkel to San Antonio and stay until it is all over. This isn't the Territory, where the Whitmires can do as they please. We got law here. You'll be safe in Santone. It's . . . well, it's close to the best doctors anyway. And I won't have you and the baby in danger . . . not until Ol' Ran'll is dealt with – by law, or the six statutes of Colt, I don't care much, either way."

"I wish you had asked me what I thought!" Isobel spoke through dry lips. Jane leaving her was a small thing, against this horror. For nearly the first time in half a year, she regretted leaving England. If she might only take refuge in her room in the ancient Hall, curl up in the window seat, and look out over the tranquil garden and grounds, where nothing vile or violent ever happened. "I trust you, my dearest – but I wish that you would tell me of your thinking on matters which touch on the both of us!"

"I couldn't, not without explaining." Dolph answered, resolute and expressionless as always. "It was just too complicated, Bell. I didn't want you involved, not when you have our child to consider."

"Children; they change everything," Uncle Hansi rumbled. "Six sons had I; two more gained in wedding my daughters. But I would not have ventured knowingly into any enterprise which would have harmed them. Alas, that two were harmed regardless of intent!"

"But you will return to the Palo Duro ranch!" Isobel was newly outraged at how this was all connived. No, she could not bear the thought of being alone without the presence and affection of her husband. This was too much to bear, especially since it was being conducted under the interested eyes of Peter Vining, Uncle Richter and Seb Bertrand. This was too much. Her humiliation was complete, as she began to cry. "I will not consent to this! You promised that we would be together until spring!"

"You must, Bell." Her husband's voice was calm, implacable. "I am sorry at how it worked out, but I would have had to go back to the Palo Duro for round-up anyway."

"I'll be all alone!" Isobel wept; truly desolate, without the support of Jane and the comforting presence of her husband, whose unhappiness mirrored her own. In part of her mind, she wondered why she was weeping like this, as if a stranger spirit had taken over her mind and self. Dolph felt in the front of his coat, but it was Uncle Richter who produced a vast, clean linen handkerchief and pressed it into her hands.

"There, Liebchen," Uncle Richter didn't seem to be the least discomfited by her tears. Over her head, he said something in German to Dolph. I sounded like an explanation. "Women when they are bearing, they will do this. It's expected. This business with Whitmire . . . she has something to cry about, not so?" Now he patted Isobel's shoulder. "You shall not be alone. You will be a guest in my house, and my dearest Liesel will care for you as one of ours. You will lack for nothing, until Dolph deals with this matter. We could do no less; besides, she loves babies dearly." He spoke over her head to Dolph. "Ach, lad, call for that pretty maid of hers. Take her upstairs until she can compose herself." Isobel knew the men regarded her with fresh exasperation as she was taken with renewed grief.

"Jane has given notice," she gasped. "There is no one that I may depend on now."

Dolph said a very short, exasperated word. "She's picked a fine time. Bell, darlin' you did without Jane all this summer, I believe that you'll be able to get along without her now. " Uncle Hansi chuckled.

"Alas, too pretty a maid to be a maid for long. Go on, lad – take your wife upstairs. Don't take to long about it. Get Lise or your mother to sit with her. We have business to attend."

Chapter 21 – *Schooled to Endure*

Jane sat on the edge of her bed, hardly daring to contemplate the last five minutes. Panic – she felt as if she were about to choke. What had she done? In a flash of temper, she had thrown away all of her future; the hope which Aunt Lydia had invested in her were gone for naught, just because she was annoyed with Lady Isobel. What would she do now? Jane closed her eyes briefly, feeling as if a bottomless abyss had opened before her feet. Obviously, she could not remain with the Beckers and she hesitated to ask them for help, even Sam. What of Anna Vining? Surely, she could appeal to them. Jane took a deep breath, consciously willing her hands to un-clench. Yes – Mrs. Vining. And Miss Hetty, Miss Hetty was her friend as well. She had money; all that she had saved, since coming to America. She had spent very sparingly of what she had from Lady Isobel and nothing of what Sam Becker had paid her for teaching. Surely there was enough for a room in a respectable boarding-house somewhere within Austin. She could take in sewing; perhaps she might find work as a governess for small children. Before she had thought much farther than that, someone tapped on her door.

"Jane, are you there? I cannot make my hair stay in the pins the way that I want it. Can you help me?" It was Lottie. Jane must have made a sound; Lottie opened the door, appearing with half of her hair pinned up and the other half in wheat-pale fan hanging to her waist. "I went to Isobel's room, but no one was there," she began and something in Jane's attitude and expression gave warning. "Jane, is there something wrong?"

"I have told milady . . . Mrs. Becker that I am leaving her service."

"You have?" Lottie's mouth gaped in astonishment but only for a moment. "Then, what are you going to do?" She came and sat next to Jane on the bed, waiting patiently for Jane's answer.

"I don't know," Jane said at last. "I'm still thinking." Lottie reached for her hand and Jane was briefly comforted. Lottie was little more than a child herself, but she was a friend.

"What happened? What did Isobel say to you?"

"We had words. She had heard about the painting – someone had said it was indecent, and she chided me, and I was angry."

"Well, I just know who told her about it!" Now Lottie sounded angry. "Amelia – that snake in the grass! Now I know why she looked like a cat who's been at the cream this morning!" She sprang up from the bed, with a look of determination on her young face which momentarily made her look like her oldest brother. "She's never that content unless she has made trouble for someone. I could snatch out her hair by the roots! I'll go and tell Isobel – I just know she'll understand."

"No," Jane begged but Lottie had already gone, her impatient footsteps diminishing down the uncarpeted hallway. Sighing, Jane dragged her small trunk out from under the bed and opened the lid. No matter what Lottie did, Jane felt obliged to begin packing.

She had nearly done with her trunk and begun with the carpetbag, when Lottie returned, beaming. "Oh, that was fast," she observed, upon seeing Jane's neatly folded garments vanishing into the maw of the carpetbag. "I couldn't find Isobel or Seb; they're not in the dining room. But I did find Sam and I explained it all to him. He is the best of brothers. He put on his coat and hat and he went out but he told me to tell you, don't do anything until he returns and speaks to you."

"What is he doing?" Jane asked, her heart sinking. "Where did he go?"

"I don't know," Lottie answered, perfectly tranquil. "But he has a plan. I am certain it will be all right."

Touched by her concern and of Sam's evident care of her, Jane finished with the last of her things. Lottie insisted on helping her and of fetching three or four books from her own room as a parting gift. With difficulty, Jane wedged them into the bulging carpetbag. She felt rather breathless, as she had on the day when Lady Isobel had married, waiting for the coach which would take them all away and upon boarding the *Wieland* at Southampton. Here was the unknown and she was about to take a step into it. Presently there came a heavier tread on the stairs; a man's booted steps and a tap on the door. It was Sam, breathless and grinning ear to ear. He had a neat white envelope in hand.

"Good," he said, upon seeing Jane's luggage ready and her mantle and bonnet set aside on the neatly-remade bed, ready for her departure. "This is for you." Jane took the envelope, addressed to her in a woman's hand. She opened it with haste, tearing it open across the wax seal, aware that both Sam and Lottie watched her impatiently, and read the note inside.

My dear Miss Goodacre – I would be grateful, if you can come at once. Miss S--- who taught the First and Second Readers has been called away without warning by sickness in her family.

E. Johnson

PS. Wages are $18 monthly, board and bed provided.

"Well?" Sam's grin broadened. "Coming? I've got Cousin Anna's trap waiting downstairs. No one keeps Miss Lizzie waiting."

"Oh, yes!" Jane answered joyfully.

* * *

Letter, to Mrs. Lydia Kittredge
Acton Hall, Oxfordshire
January 22nd, 1877

Dearest Auntie, please do not reproach yourself for my leaving service with Lady Isobel, once having been so privileged and entrusted by his Lordship so as to rise to a higher position. Should her marriage have kept her in England – or should she have gone to India to marry there – I believe I would have remained happily with her until the end of our days. But our situation here is so very different, as you had once warned me – and so different for her Ladyship as well. Her husband's manner of life left little room or need for a maid entirely dedicated to her service and so I have been encouraged by friends to take my future into my own hands. I assure you, dearest Auntie, Lady Isobel and I parted as friends, bound through ties of affection for each other, and to mutual friends whom we also hold dear . . .

* * *

Sam carried down Jane's trunk; to Jane's embarrassment, Lottie took one handle of her carpetbag so they could carry it between them. They went down the back staircase, a steep passageway in the oldest part of the house, which led past the kitchen. Only old Hetty noticed them, propped on her cane as the three of them passed by the door which led into the kitchen.

"An' where are ye off to, this foine morning?" She fixed them with a gimlet eye. "An' Miss Jane with her trunk all packed? Aye, I did no' think you would last, not with Miss Amelia takin' agin ye."

"To Miss Johnson's, Hetty," Sam answered. The old woman looked enormously pleased.

"Well, that will be a black eye for Miss Amelia – but here, ye have no' had breakfast. Take sommat to eat, it'll never do to start a new day and new work on an empty stomach!"

"Yes, but hurry about it!" Sam commanded. "We'll be outside." He led the two girls out through the arbor which led to the old summer kitchen to a small trap with a single horse in the shafts. The yard at the back of the house was rimmed with a large garden plot, now plowed over for the winter, a small corral and stable, and a row of tiny and rather ramshackle houses which Jane had been told were for the colored servants, of whom only Mrs. Amelia's maid remained. There was a mound of fresh horse dung, where a single horse might have been tied to the corral railing, but no sign of the horse which had left it. Sam loaded the trunk and carpetbag into the back of the wagon, and looked around, frowning slightly. "Odd – it's very quiet today. I think something must be going on. Onkel and Dolph have been holed up with Cousin Peter in the billiards room all morning."

"I thought Isobel would make more of a fuss," Lottie observed. "Jane came all the way from England with her, and to leave now . . ."

"It's a riddle, sure enough," Sam handed Jane up into the trap, just as Miss Hetty tottered out from the house, carrying a small basket covered with a clean white napkin. "But we cannot wait to find out the answer, not if it keeps Miss Lizzie waiting! Miss Hetty, we're only going over to the Johnsons', not to Bastrop."

"Niver mind," Miss Hetty replied. "I'll not let it be said that anyone came away hungry from this house."

* * *

Miss Lizzie Johnson is a lady of refinement, much respected for her enterprise and education. She owns a large house which serves as our home and day-school and is of very comfortable means, owing to proprietorship of the school. She also writes, Auntie – for a respectable weekly illustrated paper, can you believe that? She is received socially by the best families in this place and no blue-stocking for she is energetically courted by men of means. On my very first day, she greeted me on arrival with wonderful courtesy, explaining that my need of work agreed most comfortably with her sudden need of a teacher. She already had an excellent opinion of me, seconded by Miss Fritchie, who is connected to the Vining family and confessed that Lady Isobel's bad fortune was to her gain and she thanked the Almighty for it. She bade me to come downstairs as soon as I could, as the school day was set to commence in twenty minutes! Auntie – I am very comfortably settled, at a work which daily pleases me greatly. My pupils are dear and biddable children in the main, although sometimes more high-spirited than I recollect English children being and some have the most horrid way of speaking. (I am endeavoring to correct both of these tendencies.) In the late afternoon when the children are dismissed to their homes, my time is my own, although Miss Johnson attempts to remedy the lapses in my own education by teaching me bookkeeping, which she insists is a skill most suited to a woman and much more remunerative than sewing.

The young Mr. Becker – who had helped me to gain my current fortunate position – called on me last Sunday to assure himself that I was happily settled. His own future, alas, is not so fortunate; it seems that his uncle and brother do not wish to consider fostering his artistic ambitions for at least another year. He was much disappointed in this, but made fair to mention that my pleasure and happiness are some recompense . . .

* * *

Some weeks into the New Year, Jane had just dismissed her class for the day, when Jemima Fritchie put her head around the doorway of the classroom.

"Jane, dear; there is a caller for you in the parlor – a lady." Jane and Jemima had moved into calling each other by first names on the first day, when Jemima exclaimed that it was just too ridiculous to go on with such formality, when they lived and ate their meals every day together.

"A mother?" Jane gathered up her books, assuming that it might be the mother of one of her pupils. Jemima's eyes twinkled merrily. "No, not yet. It's Mrs. Becker – young Mrs. Becker."

"Oh!" Jane exclaimed, firmly resisting her first impulse, which was to hurry towards the comfortable book-lined parlor. That room overlooked a pleasant garden planted with rose bushes at the side of Miss Johnson's establishment. Instead, she ran upstairs to her own room, washed her fingers of chalk-dust and smoothed her hair into place after a quick glance into the glass. Lizzie Johnson encouraged her to dress plainly but well; there was no fault in the day dress she wore today, a cast-off from Lady Isobel's wardrobe which Jane had altered to suit herself. She had no idea of what to expect from Lady Isobel; certainly not that Isobel should rise from the settee and rush to embrace her with a look of affection on her face. She was wearing a plain dark dress, high-waisted and with a looped apron-overskirt generously cut to disguise that she was with child.

"Jane! You look so well and happy! I can't tell you how much I regret the things that I said! Can you forgive me?"

"Milady, I . . ." in that moment Jane did forgive her; easily enough, for apart from writing to Auntie Lydia and fearing that Lord Robert would be dreadfully disappointed in her, she had buried such regrets under the distraction of teaching a dozen lively little boys and girls every day. "I am sorry to have caused you a moment of distress." Jane returned the embrace fondly. "You did not worry unduly. You have not been inconvenienced, being without me?"

"Oh, no!" Isobel answered, as her eyes spilled over. "Well, only a little! I am so sorry, Jane, I am crying over the silliest things. It has to do with being with child. Lottie told me where you had gone, even before I realized you had rushed away. My husband has been very plain-spoken with me. I had thought to beg you to return, but I see what your new situation is and you are sublimely happy in it; I cannot bring myself to that. Is that my poplin day dress from last season? It suits you so much more than it did me!" She hiccupped and Jane feared that Lady Isobel would begin weeping again."

"Come, sit down, Milady – tell me of what has been happening. Lottie and Mrs. Becker told me of how Christmas is celebrated at the Vining house? Was it grand – everything you expected?"

"It was!" Isobel exclaimed, "And the children were ecstatic! Uncle Richter dressed as Father Christmas to hand out the presents – it is one of their family traditions, you see. Did you pass a pleasant holiday, Jane?"

"I did," Jane replied. She had reveled in her new independence as a prisoner newly released from a dungeon. Still, she felt some pangs of guilty concern; Isobel's eyes were hollow, ringed with shadows of worry. "We had a lovely meal and went for a carriage ride with one of Miss Johnson's beaux. I had a parcel from Auntie Lydia and every day since then has passed most agreeably for me. But of you, Milady? Do you remain in Austin, or to the Becker ranch?"

"Neither!" A fat tear rolled down each of Isobel's cheeks. "There has been an awful occurrence, Jane. The foreman of the new ranch – he was murdered, Jane! Uncle Richter has intelligence of a gang of criminals threatening my husband and his cousin . . . indeed, almost all those who work for the family interests may be at risk of murder by this gang in their quest for vengeance against us. These horrible feuds, Jane; some of them go on for years and leave all the men of a family in hiding for fear of their lives or buried in an untimely grave! I cannot bear the thought of my child being an orphan – or inheriting such hate along with the family name!"

"That is horrible, Milady!" Jane captured one of Isobel's hands in hers. "I am sorry indeed to hear it! What is the Baron – your Uncle Richter planning to do? Lottie says that he is a man bold and sagacious and one who does not allow an enemy to strike at him! And," Jane added as Isobel nodded tearfully, "The men that I know and have met are so gentlemanly and chivalrous. But I do not believe an enemy would catch them unawares. Times were lately hard here, within memory of all those not much older than Miss Lottie or myself. I do not think any enemy will catch them unawares. Surely, you will be kept safe? Certainly your husband will not ask you to return to the new place, if there are such brigands prowling about?"

"No," Isobel sniffed and wiped her cheeks with the back of her hand. Jane sighed inwardly and produced a clean handkerchief from the sleeve of her dress. Isobel murmured her thanks and continued. "I am to take refuge with Uncle Richter and his good lady in San Antonio, until it is all resolved for the better, I hope. My husband and Uncle Richter assure me of it. You recall, Jane; such a lovely new house with gardens, by the river and in the best part of town! We depart tomorrow, Lottie and Mrs. Becker and all, while my husband and Seb Bertrand wend their way north. There is a doctor-surgeon in San Antonio; Doctor Herff, who is most wonderfully skilled, being trained in Germany. His patients are also most fortunate; it seems that nearly all survive his ministrations. He is a most accomplished physician; Uncle Richter and my husband all insist that he attend on me in confinement and Aunt Richter has been so very affectionate. Such a funny woman to look at; my mother and the ladies of Society would think her so very crude and vulgar, but she has been kindness itself. She has born nine children and supervised the confinement of at least twice that many grandchildren, although she does not like to travel; she has been, " Isobel blushed pink, "What I wish my lady mother had been, instead of being so severe. Do not worry for me, dear Jane. I will be well-looked-after. Are we to part as friends? May we exchange letters? Yours would be such a comfort to me, recollecting Acton and London and all."

"I will, Milady," Jane answered, feeling a tide of warm affection that nearly sent her weeping like Isobel. "I promise. I will send a letter by post, ever week, without fail – even if there is nothing of event to write about."

"Jane, dear," Isobel sighed. Now her tears were truly mastered, as she held Jane's hand in her own. "Your friend – Miss Fritchie, who saw me in today? She called you Jane, as if you were equal in the eyes of all. I wish now that you would call me Isobel, as if we were true companions and voyagers in this peculiar new world. You are not in my employ as a maid any longer; here you are the equal of any other woman of good birth and respectable position. I have always liked you, Jane, for your good sense and care of me. I did not assume such was my due only because my father paid your wages and custom commanded. I believed we were friends; indeed, you were my one true friend in the world. If such is the case as you see it, then I wish that you would address me as Isobel, and not 'my lady.' Can you set aside custom and do that? Then I would know that we are truly friends."

"I can, m – I think I can. Isobel," Jane tasted the word experimentally. "Although I fear that I may slip once and again. May we talk honestly, on any matter which fancy brings to mind?"

"Of course," Isobel's face glowed with happiness. "Ask me anything you wish."

"Where did you get that dress?" Jane had been wondering; it had not been among Lady Isobel's – Isobel's wardrobe. She was genuinely curious, for it was well-cut and flattered Isobel even with the bulge of the unborn child.

Isobel pealed with laughter, "You'd never believe it," she answered. "Aunt Richter made it! She is an accomplished seamstress. It gives her pleasure to create garments for those of whom she is fond."

"Then I am certain that you would not be better cared for, if you were in England," Jane assured her and Isobel was content. "When are you leaving for San Antonio?"

"Tomorrow," Isobel answered. She rose from the settee, still with Jane's hand in hers. "I had put off paying this call, dear Jane – until I simply had to do it. Suddenly I have become such a coward about things. Aunt Richter says it is a perfectly natural moodiness. I am looking forward to the journey – Sam will accompany us as far as Comfort, and he is always such cheerful company."

"I am glad of that," Jane said, although she doubted that Sam was much in the mood to be cheerful. He had been deeply disappointed when his desire to study art in Paris had been refused; he had not said why his uncle and brother had refused his request, although now Jane suspected why. It must have something to do with the threat of brigands, although that danger was not mentioned again, as Isobel took her affectionate leave.

The next morning, both the younger and the older Mrs. Beckers departed from Austin, with Aunt Richter, Sam and Lottie, and the Richter's near-silent youngest daughter, Grete. Seb, Dolph and Alf Trotter accompanied them on horseback, as far as the swaying bridge which led the road south over the wide silver river. Winter fog hung in the trees and rose like smoke from the river, so heavy that Isobel could not see the other side. They waved a final farewell on the riverbank, before the three riders wheeled their horses around and headed north; back to the empty country of the Palo Duro, to the stunted trees, and the amazingly-tinted cliffs, to the scattering of sawn-plank buildings that marked the new Acton and perhaps the deadly peril which waited for them there. Isobel looked after them wistfully, thinking of that freedom she had enjoyed, as if she wheeled high in the pale-blue sky, as free as a hawk, on motionless outspread wings, and wished that she could trade the comfort – the luxury, even – afforded by her condition, for the freedom of the sky, the endlessly-rolling prairie, and the water-carved cliffs of the Palo Duro.

For Isobel, time hung suspended after the Richters and Beckers returned to San Antonio, that garden-jeweled town spreading out on either side of the green-glass river which threaded through it like a tangled length of ribbon. The oldest parts of the town felt as old to her as anything in England, although with a Continental aspect; walls of white-washed unbaked brick, with deep doorways and small shuttered windows which hinted at the medieval thickness of walls, topped with rust-red roof tiles. Those oldest roofs sagged most quaintly – the very oldest of them suffering the most pronounced sagging. Many houses boasted interior courtyards, spangled with vivid magenta bougainvillea vines and oleander bushes spiked with scarlet flowers. The lacy grey campanile towers of the San Fernando Cathedral punctuated the skyline, and at the hours of the holy offices, the chiming of church bells echoed in narrow, muddy streets. But that was in the old part of San Antonio, clustered around two or three streets which intersected in several plazas, which opened most unexpectedly. At every hour of the day and night, the plazas were filled with life; with men in black suits trimmed with silver buttons and women who wore long veils draped over tall combs in their hair, instead of hats or bonnets. The newer part, spreading out in the meadows to the south was also a place of gardens, of elegant modern villas trimmed with wooden lace and tall windows open to the spring breeze. At first, Isobel reveled in the mild spring days, especially as the grassy meadows on the outskirts of town were starred by wildflowers; great sweeps of red, pale pink, lavender and dark blue, tossing among the grass and temporarily overpowering the green. Early in her stay, she and Lottie loved to go for drives in the Richter's open landau, with Sorsha and Gawain trotting after, to the San Pedro springs on the west of town. There in a garden shaded with majestic oak trees, the water created a splendid fountain, gushing up from the ground, sparkling clear and cold.

Isobel enjoyed those weeks, cossetted and fussed over by Aunt Richter and Lottie, but eventually the growing weight of the child pinned her in place, confined within limits which slowly narrowed to the Richter's house and garden. To sit upright for very long in one position sent pains shooting up her back and legs, and that put an end to the carriage rides. Her belly swelled to enormous dimensions. To her horror, so did her breasts. Walking very far in the Richter's garden became a great trial and so did Isobel's embarrassment about her awkward shape. She felt as fat and clumsy as a cow, lumbering from bed to chaise to commode on clumsy feet. Her hands were swollen as well; at last she had to take off her rings, as they cut into the flesh of her fingers. Aunt Richter banished Sorsha and Gawain to the downstairs of the house, although they whined piteously about that.

"I feel as fat as a sow about to farrow!" she moaned one morning to Lottie. "Surely that cannot be natural, to be this . . . this huge! Sometimes I think that I will burst! And ugly! I think myself fortunate that your brother is not here to see me the way that I am."

"I think you look very pretty," Lottie answered stoutly. Isobel was still faintly shocked that American girls of Lottie's age should know about babies and where they came from; yet another difference in the upbringing of children. Lottie, having lived on the ranch and associating with her Richter cousins – of course she would know. "You glow – and I do not think you are fat, not in the least. Cousin Marie was simply huge when she had her baby. I heard Auntie Liesel talking to Dr. Herff yesterday; she was asking if he thought there was a chance of two babies. There are twins in Mama's family – Onkel Fredi is a twin. Are there twins among your ancestors?"

"I don't believe so, but I will ask Fa in my next letter." Isobel groaned. "Two babies – how could this happen to me?"

"I don't know and if I did, I don't think it would be polite to say," Lottie answered. "But if it is, Auntie will be ecstatic, save for making another set of baby linen."

She wrote to Fa, and then another letter to Dolph, but entertained little hope that he would be able to return to be with her, as the baby was due at the time of the spring round-up, when his presence would most be needed, especially if the Whitmires were still looking for their vengeance. Isobel knew that Uncle Richter had offered a reward; an amount sufficient to excite any bounty-hunter to commence the hunt. She had no answer from either, on the day that that her world and her own body finally up-ended themselves. She ate a good dinner that evening – on a tray in her own room, brought by one of Aunt Richter's maids and retired early. Aunt Richter, plump, sweet-smelling and rustling in the bronze-silk evening gown she had worn for supper with guests appeared early in the evening as Isobel wearily swung her feet into bed. Isobel's ankles were swollen; she had not dressed that morning. Indeed, she remained in her nightgown and wrapper for the whole day. Since she had not risen from bed until nearly mid-day it was hardly worth the trouble of dressing at all. Aunt Richter's bronze-dyed feather head-dress drooped hectically over one eye, as she settled the covers over Isobel's grossly-swollen form, but the expression in them was unexpectedly shrewd.

"Rest tonight, Liebchen," she bade Isobel. "Tomorrow you work." She patted Isobel's belly through the covers. "The babies come, I t'ink."

"Do you think so?" Isobel groaned. She was tired of the whole thing, of being clumsy, of being fat beyond Lady Caroline's most vicious observations, of having to use the convenience every twenty minutes and constantly feeling sharp little elbows and knees punching against her inward parts. It was only the prospect of the pain which held her back from wishing it to be over now and all at once.

"I t'ink so," Aunt Richter assured her. She brushed Isobel's brow with a brief and fond kiss." Sleep now." She assessed Isobel with another one of those shrewd, motherly looks. "While you can. My maid – she will sleep in your dressing room tonight. She will fetch me, when you have need, *hein*?"

"Thank you," Isobel answered, with a pang for the absence of Jane – dear Jane, whose future did not seem to lie in service to a great household after all. She had not missed Jane nearly as much as she feared that she would, but her presence this evening was one of those times when she most sincerely did.

She was tired – as bone weary as any of the days on the trail, when she had crawled under the quilts next to her husband, the stars glittering overhead and fallen asleep almost before she found a comfortable position. She thought she might fall into slumber tonight as readily as she had before, but no. Something kept her from that restful sleep; she tossed and turned, and supper rested most uneasily. The clock downstairs in the parlor chimed a musical half-hour; sleep still eluded her, as if it were an untamed thing seeking escape. At last, she rise from her nest of tangled bidding; may as well turn up the flame on her bedside lamp and read for a while. Hardly had she found the little wheel which raised the wick when she must hastily search out the chamber pot in order to be violently sick into it. She had hardly done with that, when the connecting door to her dressing room opened, and Aunt Richter entered, drawing her frilliest wrapper around herself.

"So I thought!" she exclaimed triumphantly. "You will want peppermint tea now . . . for the stomach to settle."

"My back aches," Isobel complained. Aunt Richter clicked her tongue. "So. The babies come. It is best to walk now."

"Shouldn't you send for Dr. Herff?" Isobel ventured and Aunt Richter laughed. "Oh, no. It is hours yet, Liebchen."

Isobel sought her slippers, left neatly at the side of the bed. *This isn't so bad,* she thought; although the funny tightening across her belly – which came and went at irregular intervals – was like nothing she had ever experienced before. It was a curious, cramp-like feeling which went from the point of one hip-bone to the point of the other which left her feeling quite breathless, and her belly rock-hard.

"I think I can endure this for some hours yet, Auntie," she observed jauntily, but it should have been a warning to her that Aunt Richter wasn't smiling as she answered, "Good."

In the end of it all, Isobel did loose track of time, only that dawn flushed the sky outside the curtains of her room, and Mrs. Becker and Anna Vining eventually spelled Aunt Richter. The sun set in grand smears of purple and gold, which slanted in bars though a crack in the curtains, and still the doctor did not come. This did not seem to worry anyone but Isobel, wracked by pains that tightened and tightened across her middle, until she bit her lips bloody with the effort not to cry out.

No matter what happens, I will not scream. Isobel held onto that determination like a talisman. She would not scream, she would not cry out. Mrs. Becker, Anna, Aunt Richter – she would not make a sound in front of them. The fancy took her that she was being tortured in the dungeons of the Spanish Inquisition; she must show the Inquisitor that she was a loyal Englishwoman, she would not beg for mercy. She retained enough presence of mind at first to thank Aunt Richter for the sips of peppermint tea, or the chips of ice which they gave her to suck upon, which provided a tiny sliver of bodily comfort, before the world of pain spun the room around and drew her down again into its depths.

She was very briefly aware at the last, of lying wrung-out and exhausted, while the two older women talked over her in German. Aunt Richter and Mrs. Becker's voices were hushed. They whispered, but their faces bore identical expressions of worry. Isobel struggled to comprehend. *Was she dying? Was there something wrong with the baby? Why wouldn't they speak so that she might understand?* She wished hopelessly for Fa . . . dearest Fa. Surely he might make the pain stop, make these women talk so that she could understand them. Silent tears slid out of the corners of Isobel's eyes, tears which mingled and spread into the perspiration which matted her hair. There was someone else in the room – a man, and Isobel's heart rose. Fa! No, it was a man his age, with a heavy beard. Dr. Herff, speaking gruffly in German over his shoulder to someone she could not see. Now he was bending over the bed where Isobel lay helpless. Isobel blinked, the room wavered . . . much like the prairie, shimmering in the heat of summer, the air dancing in waves. Dr. Herff had blood on his hands; with a queerly distant sense of horror, Isobel knew that blood was hers. She must be dying, then. Someone leaned over her, holding something like a tea-strainer over her mouth and nose.

"Breathe now," Aunt Richter commanded firmly and Isobel obeyed. A strange, sweet smell caught at her throat; she almost wanted to cough, but then the feeling went away, and she didn't mind, for the pain went with it, pulled down into pillowy clouds of grey nothingness.

Chapter 22 – *Daughters and Sons*

Isobel drifted up from the grey depths to just below the surface of wakefulness, aware of the sound of a woman's voice, a sweet cracked voice, singing in words that she didn't understand . . . because she was so tired. She would have gone all the way up, opened her eyes and came awake, but for the awareness that her body pained her, or that it would, if she came entirely awake. So she lay quiet, soothed by the song and the voice, content to float in the grey world and keep the knowledge that she ached in every bone at a distance. Gradually, she became aware that she was alone in her body again; that the almost incessant twitch and flutter of the baby within her belly had ceased. This saddened her; now she felt quite empty and alone, but also relieved her immensely, as this meant that the birthing was done. The last thing she could recall was someone lowering a gauze tea-strainer over her mouth and nose and a sickly-sweet odor, which mercifully wiped out the sight of the heavy-set bearded man in shirtsleeves, standing at the foot of the bed brandishing a heavy, gleaming metal instrument and telling Aunt Richter to have it boiled. The man also had blood on his hands and wrists, and Isobel knew without a possibility of doubt that it was her own blood.

That was over. Isobel listened drowsily to the woman singing and was comforted. She floated a little farther away from the surface, covering herself like a cozy quilt with the grey unthinkingness, and when she floated up again the woman was no longer singing. The bedroom was flooded with the golden light of late afternoon. No longer could she pull that blissful greyness around herself; her mouth tasted like a cast iron pot boiled dry and she was aware of an urgent need to use the chamber pot. She opened her eyes; yes, she was still lying in the bed of that room which Aunt Richter had allocated to her, with a smaller one adjacent which Aunt Richter had seen fitted out as a nursery. Someone stood by the window, watching the sunset; Anna Vining. Isobel must have made a sound, because Anna turned around; she had a baby in her arms, a bundle swathed all in white and too large to be Anna's own little daughter.

"Ah, you are awake at last," Anna observed without any surprise. "How do you feel? I need not ask, but it is considered courteous to do so. Three times have I done this, although not for two at once. I assume the discomfort was not doubled."

"Two?" Isobel croaked. Well, Dr. Herff had said something about twins, once Aunt Richter had suggested the possibility.

"Twin girls," Anna answered. "You would like to see them, I think. They are very well. This one was born first. See where Dr. Herff's patent forceps made a little bruise on her forehead?" She brought the child to Isobel's bedside. "The other is not marked but Mama said we should tie colored ribbons on their wrists, so that we may learn to tell them apart." Isobel sat up, wincing as she did so. Below her belly, she felt that she had been ripped into tattered rags of flesh. Anna laid the baby in her lap, and capably settled some pillows behind her so that she could rest against them. Isobel and the infant regarded each other with no particular sentiments at all. Her daughter was a pink-faced mite with a wide-open, unfocused blue gaze, regarding Isobel solemnly over a pink fist balled against her mouth. There was a narrow length of yellow ribbon tied around her wrist, and a faint blue bruise in the center of her forehead. Anna went to a cradle at the foot of the bed and bent over it, drawing out another white-wrapped baby; this one was not awake, but sleeping with brief pale eyebrows drawn in an accusing scowl. Anna laid the second baby next to Isobel on the bed, where it stirred and then settled into sleep again. This one had a pink ribbon. "They have been fed. Mama engaged a wet-nurse for them, one of Dr. Herff's recommending. What had you thought to name them?"

"In my last letter to my husband, we had agreed; a boy should have our father's names, a girl our mother's."

"So . . . a name for each." Anna sounded pleased. "Auntie Magda would like that. Her name in English is Margaret, which would honor my husband's mother also. What is your mother's name, then?"

"Caroline," Isobel answered. "I think the oldest should be Margaret and this one should be Caroline." It must have been a trick of the light, or of familial blood, but the sleeping infant's unformed features looked so like Lady Caroline when she was most displeased with her youngest daughter. Isobel hoped that wouldn't prove an omen. It was bad enough knowing that her mother was unhappy with her; having a daughter similarly disproving would be unendurably horrible.

"I should write to my husband," Isobel ventured at last. Anna answered briskly, "Yes – about what you have named them. Papa sent a messenger once they were safely delivered. Dolph will be most pleased, I am certain. Children of his own instead of dogs, or those orphan boys. That pleases Auntie Magda."

"I hope he will be happy with the news." Isobel looked at the faces of her children and wondered why she felt so bleak. Empty, as if she could not feel any emotions at all. These were her children, mothers were supposed to love their children dearly. *Was there something else wrong with her that she didn't?*

"Of course. He will be overjoyed." Anna answered. Well, at least she was acting if everything were perfectly straight-forward, and nothing at all was wrong with Isobel's cool reaction to hers' and Dolph's children. "You look tired, still. When you have had enough of admiring your daughters, I will return them to their cradle and tell Mama and Aunt Magda that you are awake. Doubtless, they will want to pay a call, *hein*?"

"Yes," Isobel agreed. It was too much trouble not to. She wished that Anna would just take the children away. She wanted to wrap that grey unthinkingness around her and sleep, to dream of the blue sky over the steep carved canyons of the Palo Duro, or of hunting in the green hills around Acton; anywhere but here, any time but now. Eventually Anna took the babies back, laying them each in the cradle with a casual familiarity which Isobel only hoped she could manage in time. They were so tiny, as helpless as puppies – and so fragile!

"I go downstairs," Anna announced. "To tell Mama and Auntie Magda that you are awake – do you wish to see them, or would you rather rest more?"

"I need to wash," Isobel answered miserably, having made the unfortunate discovery that the necessary rag was saturated. Without turning a hair, Anna pointed out where the fresh rags were, and brought out a clean nightgown. There was something bracing about her very matter-of-factness, but Isobel was apprehensive all over again when Anna said, "Ten minutes. I can only restrain Mama for that long."

Isobel couldn't think of anything other than to thank her for her consideration, and then wonder if Anna didn't think she was responding to kindness by being rude. There were moments when she didn't know how to talk to her husbands' relatives, even the ones who spoke English well.

Ten minutes was just barely long enough to wash and refresh herself, before there was a brief knock on the door. Aunt Richter opened it unbidden, her pleasant plump countenance beaming with happiness. She embraced Isobel in a flurry of flower-scented ruffles, exclaiming in her usual affectionate muddle of languages, of which Isobel could only understand, 'darling' and 'sweet girl.' For some inexplicable reason, such frank and unfettered approval moved Isobel beyond speaking. To her humiliation, she found herself weeping uncontrollably. She sank onto the edge of the bed and cried a fountain, a veritable river of tears on Aunt Richter's shoulder. Aunt Richter patted her and held her as if she were as small and in as much need of comfort as one of the babies, completely heedless of Isobel's tears spotting her silk afternoon gown. When Isobel finally hiccupped, realizing that she had cried her eyes entirely dry, Aunt Richter dabbed her cheeks with a tiny embroidered handkerchief and observed fondly, "Ach – no wonder. It is one of those t'ings, *Liebchen*. It is over now and you are still tired. The little ones – they are beautiful, not so? Little Dolph, he will be so proud!" Isobel felt like crying again. Aunt Richter, funny and vulgar and over-dressed, yet such a dear! Her affection encompassed the world; she did not judge, she only loved unstintingly. More than anything, Isobel wished that Lady Caroline could have been like her, devoid of harsh judgments on her children. With a mother like Aunt Richter, Isobel would never have left England to marry a foreigner, bear children to a man that she still hardly knew and move in a society so strange and violent. She envied Anna for having the unreserved affections of such a mother.

By degrees, Aunt Richter soothed Isobel, making her feel as if all that storm of emotions, and acute bodily discomfort were only normal and to be expected. Isobel reclined against the high-piled pillows; she already felt tired again, but she was buoyed up by the interest of the older women. Mrs. Becker was soberly admiring the children in their cradle; she demonstrated little in the way of Aunt Richter's overflowing emotions, but she also glowed with satisfaction.

"To have children together," she remarked with simple honesty, "and to see that they are part of you, and part of your husband, yet are a person of themselves – that is to complete and bless a marriage. You and Dolphchen are now truly married."

"I suppose we are," Isobel answered. She certainly did not feel that anything between herself and Dolph had been completed – in fact, rather the reverse. After the honeymoon journey and those brief blissful months in the Palo Duro, she had been set aside like a toy too fragile for ordinary play, while Dolph went about his own business. It felt, Isobel thought resentfully, like being a breeding cow; the bull did his duty and the heifer retired to the home paddock to produce a calf or two. Dolph's letters were regular in their arrival but it was plain to Isobel, scrutinizing every word as if it were a lover's Valentine, that the interests in his life lay elsewhere. His inquiries as to her wellbeing and the doings of his family were perfunctory and he never seemed to recall her answers to them from one letter to the next. He was a man, Isobel concluded with some resentment; no poet like Browning, who could make a woman fall in love with him through the medium of words, ink and paper. Whatever his father had in character which could make his wife love him with such devotion that she was disinclined to ever marry again – that quality had not devolved upon his son. Would she have ever consented to marry him, if she had not been desperate to marry anyone and escape the humiliation of India and the fishing fleet? Oh, for a proposal from some solid country squire with a small estate, as Mrs. Kittredge had envisioned. She would never have had to face such a situation as this. Would that Fa would come to her rescue, as he had when she was in such dire need. But Fa was far away in England and she was here, wed to a man whom she was not sure she loved at all, even though she might be cosseted in the bosom of his family! She thought she might commence weeping again, but that would distress Aunt Richter and Mrs. Becker. She pleaded exhaustion and promised she would call for the wet-nurse and Aunt Richter's maid if and when she thought that the babies required attention. The senior ladies departed with some hesitancy. They were plainly worried at leaving Isobel alone, but Isobel didn't mind at all. She rested against the pillows, wondering yet again if there were something wrong with her. She ought to feel something more than indifference after birthing two children. She thought about this until she fell asleep.

Within a few days, Isobel found herself able to dress, by dint of pulling her corsets very tight, and venture downstairs and into the garden once again. She rejoiced at the fact that her feet and ankles were no longer swollen, and her belly was beginning to retreat from a grotesquely huge form, though alas, she was not as shapely as she had been, even if she had never been a stick-thin ivory doll like her sister Victoria. Lottie attended on her in the afternoons after school, charmed and excited by the presence of the babies. To her relief, Isobel also began feeling a proprietary interest in them. They were not very much different from puppies or foals; helpless, small and trusting. On that account she was becoming rather fond of them.

"You forgot their ribbons!" Lottie exclaimed one afternoon, as they sat with the children on the deep and shaded verandah which overlooked the lawn and the cypress trees which framed the riverbank beyond. "How can we tell them apart now?"

"I can," Isobel answered. She held small Caroline in her lap, while Lottie cuddled her sister. "Caro's face is not so round as Maggie's, and her hair is browner, while Maggie's is so fair that you'd think she had no hair at all."

"They are still twins enough," Lottie lifted the ruffle of Maggie's cap to peer at the head underneath it. "Oh, you are right. They will not look anything alike when they are older."

"They re different in temperament, too," Isobel pointed out. "Maggie cries often and loudly, but she is always readily soothed. Caro cries rarely, but when she does, I must hold her for hours. Don't I, little Miss Fussy?" Isobel added to the baby, who lay in her arms with her head tilted sideways to look up at her mother's face. The baby had such a look of intense trust and adoration in her infant features that Isobel's heart turned over in her breast. *How could anyone ever ignore or mistreat a tiny being, who looked at one with such worship?* In that instant, Isobel fell deeply in love with her children, especially Caro. Now she experienced that intense mother-love which she had not felt on the night they were born and it relieved her. She was not an unnatural mother, after all. She knew without a doubt that she would put herself in the way of any danger which threatened Maggie and Caro, defend them with any weapon at all, even if only her own bare hands. The strength of that conviction unsettled her a little, being so sudden and so strong, so like an animal – a bitch with her litter, a tigress with her kittens.

She was privately rather glad that being a new mother excused her from obligatory participation in Aunt Richter's exhausting social rounds. She could pick and choose among those occasions which truly engaged her interest, much as her mother-in-law did. There was a performance by a traveling Shakespeare troop at the German 'casino', a concert by the singing society, and an afternoon garden party at the home of Aunt Richter's friends, the Guenthers. They were in trade. The older Mr. Guenther owned a prosperous flour mill. They had a lovely house in the most modern taste, situated on the banks of the river a short way from the Richter mansion. To Isobel's relief, most of the younger Guenthers and their friends spoke English well, and she enjoyed that outing very much. They were old and dear friends of Aunt and Uncle Richter. They admired and cherished Caro and Maggie as if they were kin – which, given the close ties among the Germans of San Antonio could hardly come as a surprise.

"They all came over from the Old Country at the same time," Lottie explained carelessly, when Isobel remarked on this. "Mama and Auntie Liesel were young, and Onkel Fredi and Onkel Johann were just little boys. They came on a sailing ship and it was horrid. They were put ashore at Indianola, but it was just a camp on the seashore. Can you imagine? Mama says it was even more awful; people were dying there in the hundreds, even thousands. Our old Opa and the rest of the family came to Friedrichsburg, but it wasn't built, it was just a clearing among the trees between two creeks. And then the War came," Lottie's earnest young face turned even more serious, between the two schoolgirl plaits of hair the color of pale wheat. "We – Opa and Papa and Onkel Hansi – were all for the Union. All the older folk here remember the hard times they suffered together and they remember how things were back in Germany, so they are inclined to trust each other rather more than someone from outside. It's different for Dolph and Sam and I. We're Americans. We've never lived anywhere else. Germany is just the old country. Everyone else here came from another country, even if their families came over so long ago that they don't remember." Abruptly, she changed the subject, tossing her braids back over her shoulders. "Are you going to come to the Casino with us tonight? Mr. Steves is talking about his grand new house. Onkel says he may give us a tour of what has been built so far."

"It sounds exhausting," Isobel answered. Mr. Steves was another one of Onkel Richter's good friends, an old neighbor of the Beckers from Comfort. He was a lumber magnate, frenetically active in various German clubs and societies. "No, I think I shall stay in tonight, pleading that Maggie has the colic."

"Does she?" Lottie asked, in swift concern. Isobel giggled. "No, she does not, but I had never considered what a grand excuse children are for not doing something that one really doesn't want to do."

That evening, Isobel waved from the verandah to the Richter's open barouche as it rolled away down the gravel drive, filled as if it were a basket of flowers by the ladies' dresses; Aunt Richter, her daughters and Lottie. Uncle Richter sat next to the driver; Isobel did not doubt that he would take the reins himself, if the notion took him. Only the elder Mrs. Becker's plain black dress ruined the flower vision. Isobel recalled again how she had mistaken Lottie and Dolph's mother for the governess on that first meeting in Galveston. Heavens, could that have been a year ago? Isobel supposed that it must be. The red-bud trees were in flower, just exactly as they had been. She was tired, as Anna had said she would be – adding with a cheerfully cynical laugh that a mother would be tired until her children were of an age to go to school at least. Aunt Richter's cook, a stern and precise woman who sometimes reminded Isobel of her mother-in-law, provided a bounteous supper on a tray for Isobel. On nights like this, she preferred withdrawing to her own room to contemplate the pink perfection of her daughters, and read in bed until it was time to nurse them. That done, Isobel laid them in the cradle at her bedside and fell asleep, although it was only mid-evening. In England at this hour, she would have still been at the dining table, somewhere between the third course and the fourth. Now she could luxuriate in freedom and Aunt Richter's crisp cotton sheets, the cradle with her baby daughters in it close at hand, and Sorsha and Gawain – allowed to return from exile once the babies were born – asleep in their beds in the corner of her room.

Perfectly content, Isobel fell asleep and slept soundly . . . so soundly that in the deep of the night, she had no idea of what had roused her from it. Downstairs the parlor clock chimed faintly; a musical quarter-hour. But something had wakened her; no, not the clock. The children! Isobel came entirely awake. She rolled over in the bed and made as if to reach for the cradle where they slept, at the side of the big bed, but there was a presence in the bed with her, a long solid bulwark of human warmth. Isobel sat bolt-upright, and in the dim light of the spirit lamp on the bedside table, she recognized her husband's tousle of fair hair on the pillow next to her own. Isobel was dumbfounded; How had be come to be in San Antonio and how had he managed to slip into their bed without waking her? She slept lightly, the slightest noise woke her from slumber, especially now with the children. Dolph stirred as Caro began to fuss in the cradle, and opened his eyes. He smiled impishly, upon seeing Isobel awake, staring at him with astonished disbelief.

"Hullo, Bell," he drawled. "I thought I'd surprise you."

"You have," Isobel whispered, still not quite certain she was entirely awake and his presence was real. "Surprised me, I mean. You were not expected until August. I thought you had gone to . . . where is it you were taking the herd this year."

"Dodge City," Her husband yawned. "As soon as we got a good price, I turned over matters to Seb and hopped on the train east. Onkel was still awake – he let me in." Caro's wailing achieved a more urgent note. "Hell! Do they make that noise all the time?" He added, as Isobel sat up, plumping the pillows behind her. "No, sometimes they are even louder. Hand her to me, Dolph. I'd best nurse her before . . . botheration, now they're both awake."

"Here," Dolph pushed back the blankets over him and reached into the cradle. With casual tenderness, he gathered up Caro and handed her to Isobel, who hastily unbuttoned the front of her nightgown. This was no time to waken the wet-nurse. In any case, Isobel didn't want to have anyone else present. This would be her husband's first encounter with his children. Caro's unhappy cries ceased immediately as soon as she latched onto Isobel's breast. Isobel sank back onto her pillows, cradling the now-silent child, barely aware of her husband's approving regard.

"Which one is this?" Dolph asked presently. Isobel smiled. He was holding Maggie, propped against his knees, gently bouncing her while she made happy gurgling noises. "That's Margaret," Isobel answered. "Maggie, I call her. She's the happy little one. This is Caroline – Caro for short. She's over-sensitive – ow!" She added, as Caro suckled a little too vigorously.

"They're beautiful, anyway," Dolph remarked, the emotion in his voice belying the casual tones in which he said it. "My daughters."

"I'm told that most men want sons, above all else." Isobel said, for she had rather feared him saying so, as if that would put all the miseries of pregnancy and delivering them at naught. Dolph shook his head. "Most men might," he answered. "But Opa and Papa and Onkel Hansi thought as much of their daughters as of their sons. Looking at Mama and Cousin Anna, you can see why. Maggie here; she'll be sitting a horse as soon as she can walk. They'll ride and learn cattle and manage a ranch. They'll have to, 'cause they'll be older than any brothers they might have an' I sure as hell don't want my daughters to be helpless little fools at the mercy of whomever they marry. No you won't, Maggie-pumpkin," he added to the infant, which elicited another gurgle. Isobel giggled. "My mother will be thoroughly shocked, hearing that plan," she said. "She will consider it terribly unseemly."

"That's her problem," Dolph answered, abruptly curt. "I know she's your mother, Bell – but she's the last woman on earth that I would take advice from on how to bring up my daughters. Look," his voice softened. "Bell, darlin', weren't you happier last year with Seb and I in the Palo Duro than you were the year before that, dragged around through all those society doings with your mother?"

"I was, of course," Isobel answered, without a second thought. "Happier than I ever was before. I had a purpose to the day, and the cut of my dress and color of my hat didn't matter to anyone at all." She cuddled the now-content Caro close to her. Her husband continued, in his calm remorseless voice. "Well then, you see. Our girls – my daughters – they're born Americans. They'll want a life with a purpose, like Cousin Anna, not one where they'll sit around the parlor being ornamental, like Cousin Amelia." Isobel snorted and ventured a rude word about Cousin Amelia. Dolph laughed. "She is that, isn't she? I'd have said vicious, as well, after how she told tales about your little Miss Jane."

"You did read my letters," Isobel sighed, much contented after the fact. "I am glad. I sometimes thought you had not read them at all."

"Every word," Dolph answered. "Let's trade. I b'lieve Maggie is hungry now. She's making faces at me."

"She is," Isobel replied, with all the assurance those ten weeks of motherhood had given her. "Here, take Caro. You manage very well," she added as they exchanged babies and her husband settled the now-somnolent Caro between them. "I was afraid for simply days to pick them up. They were so tiny I thought I might hurt them in some way."

"I had years of little cousins," Dolph answered. "Not to mention calves and puppies. Onkel Fredi said once they were all very alike when they are small. Keep them warm, dry, fed and safe . . . and love them, of course."

In the dim light of the spirit lamp, Isobel could see the expression on his face, more fond and frank than she had seen in months, even on the trail with the cattle, even more than on their wedding night. It was only logical, she thought. He loved Caro and Maggie dearly and it was only right and fitting that he would also. At moment, she was lapped in contentment and quiet happiness; her children and her husband, together and close. She wondered briefly about the danger from the Whitmires; Dolph had written nothing of them in his letters over the last four or five months, and Uncle Richter hadn't been forthcoming, either. Isobel wondered if she were being particularly sheltered from the knowledge of what might be going on, because of the babies. Very likely she was, she concluded. She ought to ask her husband now. No. This moment of utter content was too precious to mar.

But the next morning, and the morning after that, Isobel refrained from asking. She reasoned that if there were some renewed or particular danger from the Whitmires, Dolph or Uncle Richter would tell her. It would be her business to know. Both her husband and Uncle Richter reposed considerable trust in the women of the family. Perhaps the generous rewards which Uncle Richter authorized in the Territory had gained results, and the most dangerous Whitmires were restrained by arrest or a hasty grave. Isobel resolved to defer any worries about the threat to her husband, his family and to Seb and Acton in the Palo Duro country. Dolph was with her; she had borne him two healthy daughters and survived the experience. He told her that he must return north in a few months to prepare for the spring round-up and drive to the cattle markets, but that he would spend days at the home ranch in Comfort now and again.

"What of Sam?" she asked, when he informed her of this. "I know that he wishes to go to France and Italy for a year, to study art . . . can you let him go now?"

"Oh, that's just Sam," Dolph answered her carelessly. "He's always talking about his little dabs. It's just a thing to amuse his friends. He's too good at managing the ranch to be serious about anything else. Besides, the family needs him."

"But he is really good at those dabs," Isobel answered. "He showed me one of his paintings. It was magnificent and I ought to be a fair judge. There were enough paintings at Acton, never mind the first showings at the

Academy that Mama made me attend. He is serious about studying. Jane wrote to me; he wants to set up a professional studio."

Dolph laughed heartily and deep. "My little brother thinks that he does and he is as good as most. But I don't think he can expect to keep himself and a family on his little dabs, unless he lives in a shanty or an attic somewhere. There's not a market for pictures the way there is for cattle. Uncle and his friends pay him a pittance now and again, because they want an oil-painting of a prize cow or their children to hang on the wall to fill in the space. There's no money in art, Bell. My little brother will find it out the hard way, and it will be a waste of time and money. Onkel says he will let him go as soon as he can spare him. He'll get all that nonsense out of his system and settle down."

"I don't think Sam will disappoint you," Isobel answered. Privately, she thought Sam's paintings were as lively and enchanting as anything she had ever seen hung on the walls at Acton or the Academy, but she did not want to argue over it with Dolph. They were about to set out on a Sunday afternoon excursion to the spring-fed pools and gardens of the city park, acres bountifully adorned with ornamental plantings, pavilions, and game-fields. Aunt Richter planned a lavish picnic and invited several friends of the family, so it was quite a merry party which set out that day. After thinking and worrying over it, Isobel decided to bring Caro and Maggie. The distance was not that far and the day promised fair and temperate. And of course Dolph would be with them. Mrs. Becker and Lottie, too; what could be the harm? If her husband had his way, little Caro and Maggie would be learning to ride very shortly, so Isobel thought she may as well become accustomed to living with that cold knot of fear at her heart and an expression of calm reserve on her countenance. The babies were carried to the picnic grounds in a large padded basket, perfectly content. It reassured Isobel no end that the park was a treasure of beautifully-planted grounds.

"At least this is not as hot as India is said to be!" she remarked to her husband and Lottie. "There it is said that no one can endure venturing out at this time of day."

They were reclining on coarse Mexican blankets, spread out here and there on the greensward, although Aunt Richter had seen that a number of folding chairs and tables were brought along for the use of those whose bones were not up to going down to the ground or easily getting up from it again. Dolph lay on his back, with Maggie on his chest, peacefully asleep for the moment. It reassured Isobel to a degree that she had not previously realized; her husband had taken Maggie and Caro into fierce affection, and the girls instinctively adored him in return. Just so she loved and trusted Fa. "You'll spoil them, for when you must go to the Palo Duro again," Isobel remarked. "They will miss you and be inconsolable. You have no idea of how awful they can be, when they are inconsolable."

"I don't think that I'll need go many more times," her husband smiled, and Isobel saw a trace of mockery in his expression. Oh, he was going to tease his little sister. "In my judgement, Seb is perfectly able now to manage that ranch. He has taken to heart all that I had to teach him. But, Lottchen – do not assume from this that he is perfectly approved as a suitor. I have every confidence in him as a ranch manager, but to marry you? I have higher standards. Slay a dragon or two, bring home the treasures of the Indies, feed the starving, and make peace between the Russians and the Turks . . ."

"You are horrible!" Lottie responded, and struck a mock-blow with her fan. "Seb is the very perfect gentleman, and has done every task set for him!"

"But one," Dolph drawled, as Isobel observed, much amused. Yes, Dolph was teasing his little sister. This was all very familiar. Her husband sat up, handing the sleeping Maggie all of a lump to Lottie. "Here; take care of her while Bell and I go for a walk." He helped Isobel up from the blanket and offered her his arm. "This reminds me a little of the garden in Belgrave Square," he observed, as they strolled along one of the curved walkways. "A bit of an English garden in Texas."

"Nothing could be less like the Palo Duro," Isobel agreed wistfully. "I suppose that we might visit now and again, even though Seb has taken charge."

"We might," Dolph answered, in a noncommittal manner. "But we'll be at the home ranch, most times. You won't mind that, will you Bell? Being away from the city and all?"

"Not at all. I will miss Aunt Richter very much, but nothing of her social whirl. Was she always like this?"

"No, but she had very some bad times after the war; she and Onkel both. Hers' and Mama's younger sister Rosalie and her husband were murdered by Indians. They had just been married. Auntie took that ... and some other things very hard. For a long while, she stayed in her room all the time. When Onkel and I made enough from trailing cattle, he decided to settle in San Antonio for her sake. One of the reasons that we all went back to Germany two years ago was for her to take a water-cure at Baden-Baden. She's been much better, ever since . . . "

"It's difficult to picture Aunt Richter as a recluse," Isobel said. Dolph grinned. "Up on the highest tower, or down in the deepest cellar; that's what our Opa used to say. She's been on the tower since we came home, mostly." He paused to tip his hat in response to an approaching gentleman, a wiry young man who was at first sight familiar, for he was smiling at them both.

"Why, Becker! Just the man I was looking for," he drawled, as if he was really pleased to see them. Isobel lifted her hand, out of habit and the young man bowed over it. "And a pleasant afternoon, Ma'am," he added, and made as if to raise it to his lips, but for Dolph's scowl. The smile broadened. "Becker, that's a cool welcome for a man about to do you a favor."

"I don't care for being beholden to you, Wes," Dolph answered, as Isobel recalled why he was so familiar. He was the dangerous gallant who had brought a pitcher of iced water to the ladies, as they all waited for Uncle Richter's palace car in the Houston railway station. He had called himself James Swain, although Dolph, Sam, and Cuz had all known him by another.

"You will when you hear what I have to say," Wes – or James Swain was entirely serious, now. With a sideways look at Isobel, he added, "Is there a place where we can discuss this in private?"

"Whatever you have to say to me, you may say in front of my wife," Dolph answered, and Wes – or James Swain merely appeared amused.

"Well, don't ever say I didn't warn you," he drawled. Dolph snapped, "Out with it, then."

"Since you insist; Ol' Ran'll Whitmire hired me to kill you."

Chapter 23 – *Of Letters and Arts*

Isobel gasped, speechless with shock and horror. This could not be happening. The man Wes grinned as if he had said something amusing. Her husband stood stock still in the path, his face pleasant and expressionless as he absorbed the import of those words. Finally he replied in the mildest of tones, "I hope you didn't sign a legal contract, Wes, since it seems you have no intent to carry it out."

"No, seh," Wes – or Swain, or whatever his name was replied. "It was put to me as a favor. Then I found out who was doing the asking, an' it just didn't sit right. Walk with me; I'll tell you the whole story."

Silent, Dolph nodded an assent. Isobel clung to his arm, and they strolled in the most elaborately casual manner in the speckled shade, although Isobel was not too shaken to note that the men kept silent when within hearing of others on the path or that Dolph had let his coat fall open so that the dark-polished hilt of the revolver at his waist showed now and again as they walked.

"Can't say I wasn't all that surprised," Dolph observed. "Ol' Ran'll and his kin are the only dangerous party I have annoyed of late."

"Let this be a lesson to you, Becker," Wes – Mr. Swain drawled. "Don't leave no witnesses afterwards. Saves trouble in the long run."

"Your story," Dolph said only. Isobel remembered how Cuz Peter Vining had chided him, over leaving one of the rustlers un-hung, and her heart turned cold. In the midst of all that cruelty, her husband had it in him to be merciful. Now that mercy was turned against him.

"I was . . . asked," Mr. Swain began, although he kept a careful eye on all others, as they sauntered along, Isobel making a pretense of admiring the plantings of trees and shrubs, the inviting vistas of greenswards and rock-lined pools. "Through someone I decline to name – for their peace of mind, you'll know – if I would kill you and your Vining cousin, for a certain amount of money, which I also decline to state. The offer was for an interesting amount and I'm a family man. You know how these things go." Mr. Swain's grin widened into a brief unpleasant leer. "I asked for details and my messenger told me that it was tendered on behalf of the Whitmires. Whom I know by repute. It pays to keep track of this kind of matter."

"It does," and Dolph's tone of voice sounded carefully neutral. "They're your kind of folk, aren't they? Birds of a feather and all."

"No," and Isobel saw that Mr. Swain's countenance had taken on a hard aspect. "They ain't the kind I would risk a capital sentence for. I purely don't hold with taking the side of a red nigra against a white man and the RB outfit never gave me cause to hold a grudge."

"Grateful for the consideration," Dolph answered, his tone very dry. "You could have written a letter."

"Between you an' me, I wouldn't risk putting this to paper. Might be used against me, sometime. Anyways, I thought you'd take it more serious if I brought it in person. One more thing." Mr. Swain brought two slips of pasteboard from his vest-pocket; playing cards.

"Three and four of spades," Dolph took the two, looking them over, back to front. "You were supposed to leave this on my body . . . and one on Cuz Vining's as well?" Mr. Swain nodded, and Isobel's blood went cold. Yes, there was a playing card left on Bill Holt's body; Wash Charpentier had said so, when he brought the news to the Vining house at Christmas. "So, how long will take the Whitmires to figure out they have been dreadfully disappointed in you, Wes, and hire another gunslinger?"

"Not long," Mr. Swain answered, his voice almost cheerful. "They may already know that I thought better of their request and declined, but they ain't in a position to do nothin' 'bout it. Two, three days after meeting with my messenger, Ol' Randall and most of his boys were rounded up, quiet-like by the marshals from Fort Smith. I think they've been warming one o' Judge Parker's jail cells for a good few weeks. Judge Parker's boys have enough on the Whitmires and enough witnesses to swear to it in court to hang most of 'em twice over and Ol' Randall three times or more. I think, and it's purely my opinion, that you're safe from the Whitmires for a good long time. Perhaps forever. The rewards posted for their arrest and conviction," Mr. Swain added with professional envy, "was enough to tempt any man, even one in mortal fear of the Whitmires."

"Uncle Hansi doesn't mince words, or spare expense," Dolph answered. "Not when it comes to the RB's cattle, or employees."

"Mr. Richter is famous for his generosity to the deserving," Mr. Swain scratched his jaw. "Since I have taken care in bringing this message, besides the cost of train fare and lodgings, I see myself as deserving. It would be kind if you can convince your uncle of it."

"Right," Dolph sighed. With a touch of deliberate malice, he added, "What name shall I tell him to put on the bank draft? You have so many, it's easy to loose track."

"Cash would be sufficient," Mr. Swain answered blandly. "And gold preferable. I'm staying at the Menger until . . . until later. Good day, Becker. Ma'am." He touched the brim of his hat once more, nodded to Isobel and sauntered away, soon lost among the other men in dark suits spending a Sunday afternoon in the pleasure-grounds of San Pedro Park.

"Does that mean you are safe now?" Isobel ventured after a long moment, as they turned and began the long stroll back along towards where the family had gathered.

"From the Whitmires? Likely," Dolph answered with a quick smile. "Can't say that wasn't a relief. It's wearing on the nerves, wondering if you're about to be dry-gulched, every minute of the last six months."

"We should tell Uncle Richter the good news," Isobel suggested, but her husband hastened to add, "Not with Auntie Liesel in hearing. She doesn't need to know, even if it is all over. Things like this always worried her, put her down in that dark cellar again. There is one good thing," he added, as they approached the clump of shade trees where Aunt Richter and the servants had set up the picnic. "Sam can go spend his time in Europe, playing with his dabs and paints, now. We can spare him for a year – but a year only. As for us," he turned to smile down at her. Isobel could sense the easing of tension in him. "We can take the girls home to the house my father built for the family. You didn't stay there long enough before to really see it as a home."

"I'd like that so very much," Isobel replied, entirely content with the prospect. "You promised me dogs and horses and cows, after all."

* * *

14 September 1877
Becker Ranch, Near Comfort,
Kendall County, Texas

Dearest Fa;
I have received yours of the 20th and am happy to say that we are all well, and the little ones are thriving. They are now seven months old and very active; Maggie in particular is attempting to rise on her hands and knees in an effort to creep across the floor. I think that they are both very intelligent, for they have both myself and my dear husband wound around their littlest finger.

I am sorry to hear about your persistent cough. I will consult with our housekeeper, Madame Benavidez, who has a splendid command of herbal remedies – regarding those native remedies of which she may have particular knowledge. On many occasions she has provided me with simple draughts and teas which have proved effective, especially for the little ones. I care for them so much, Fa – and am simply paralyzed with fear upon every sniffle or fever!

The air in the Hills is so much cooler and refreshing in the summer just lately past, although I miss the scenic splendors of last summer in the Palo Duro region, establishing the new property. This is a gentler country, Fa – gentle, green and rolling. It would, I think, remind you of the wilder parts of Somerset, or perhaps the Lake District or the Pennines, all green hills and oaks and low cliffs of limestone. My husband's late father settled on this tract some thirty years past, and built the original stone house, which is so quaint and perfect. It calls the Home Farm to mind and already looks as old as the hills. So there is not much required for it, although D. finds many small means to improve the property. This summer he has amused me very much by searching out and transplanting more small saplings to line the drive from the main gates to the property, all the way to the house, so that in future decades we will have a splendid avenue of trees. He does this work himself, Fa – not wishing to burden – or shame the hands – by requiring them to do such labor. I tease him, calling him a new-world Capability Brown in his efforts to shape and refine the landscape. I shall ask Sam, my young brother-in-law, to do some sketches of the house, and of the gardens and orchards for your amusement. I will send them in my next letter, or have him bring his sketchbook when he calls upon you next year – as I so hope he will!

Tell all that I am well, happy beyond all my dreams and that I have gained everything that I wished for when I first consented to wed. And next year, our family circle will be blessed by a new addition. I hope for a son, to carry on the work that my husband's father began here, but when I say so to D., he laughs and says that he has younger brothers and cousins enough, and even that young Mr. Bertrand and Alf Trotter – who came to Texas with us from London and took to the strenuous life of cattle-herding as if he had never done anything else – are sons enough to him for now.

My love to you all, to Mama and all at Home.
Your loving daughter,

Isobel

* * *

From Jane Goodacre,
Johnson Select Academy, Austin, Texas
November 22, 1877

Dear Auntie,

Thank you for your parcel of English magazines and books, and for the
tin of marmalade and the cake, which arrived only a little crumbled on one
side, thanks to the many layers of newspapers that it was wrapped in. I must
confess that my fellow teachers here were almost more interested in the
newspaper wrapping then the cake itself. We had a little slice each, with tea
yesterday afternoon, which much gratified Miss Johnson, as the weather has
been so cold and dreary of late! She says that if the weather in England is so
constantly like it has been here of late, no wonder that the English race takes
such comfort in constantly partaking of hot tea! She has been invited to visit
with friends in San Antonio at Christmas, and having business to do with her
cattle interests in that city, says she is inclined to accept, hoping that the
weather there – although it is winter still – may be more enjoyable. She is
urging me to accompany her, for the company of another respectable woman
and my own benefit. She is encouraging me to invest what I have saved from
my wages in property. She insists that is a means for a woman – any woman
– to maintain a happy degree of independence, rather than marry in haste to
the first man who asks and thereafter be subject to her husband's wishes in all
things, or to spend a life as an unhappy spinster, toiling away for mere pennies
required for survival. I have considered her advice quite carefully, Auntie.
While I do not share her interests in livestock, I can see that property in a
commercial district would be to my taste as well as my pocketbook.

Should I accompany Miss Johnson to San Antonio, I will likely enjoy
only a brief reunion with Lady Isobel. Mr. Becker's family usually spends the
Christmas holiday with their cousins in Austin. We have exchanged many
letters though, assuring each other of our happiness and contentment with our
varied lot. The children sound so very dear, and she is happy beyond all words
– as am I, although our situations differ in details. The only marring of this
contentment is hearing of Sir Robert's continued ill-health. In his letters to
Lady Isobel, he insists that he is fit and only a little discommoded by his
condition, but Lady Isobel notes that his most recent letters do not contain
very much about local matters, and nothing about the hunt – which was ever
one of his dearest pleasures. Auntie, should you confide in me regarding the
truth of Sir Robert's condition and if it be more serious than has been alluded
to previously, I will not share that with Lady Isobel. She is in a delicate

condition once more, the child to be born in mid-summer, and I will not communicate anything which may distress her. Do this for mine own peace of mind, dearest Auntie? Sir Robert was always so kind to me. In elevating me to the position of attendance on Lady Isobel – a situation well beyond my years and experience – he did me a great honor, which I will likely never be able to repay in kind.

Convey my best wishes to my mother and brothers, and to all at Acton who remember me,

> With affection always,
> Your Jane

* * *

"Dear Jane, it is warm!" Lizzie exclaimed, stretching out her arms in exultation. "Oh, I can hardly believe it is December and only days ago we were shivering under cloudy skies – and now we can smell lemon trees in bloom!"

"I don't think it is lemon trees," Jane answered, seriously. "It's more like verbena, and it is lovely."

Lizzie's friends were a young couple, Will and Ellen Lockhart; distant kin of her family, Lizzie had explained. They were staying as guests, in a dear little house with wide verandas on either side, trimmed along the eaves and roof-edges with a superfluity of modern wood lacework, in a pleasant block along Pecan Street. This house was, as Jane understood it, rather to the north and east of the town, and some distance of where the Richter's property lay. Still, it had a pretty garden, shaded with pecan trees, and was but a short walk or drive from the newer part of town.

"Enjoy a good night's sleep, Jane," Lizzie advised her, "For tomorrow, we have been invited to dine with Captain King at the Menger Hotel . . . the dining room is splendid beyond words, and the food there is legend."

The following day, Will Lockhart had hired a horse and buggy for them from a nearby livery stable. Lizzie took the reins in her own capable hands, and drove along a series of fine, wide avenues, as straight as if drawn by a ruler. The houses which lined those roads were far-scattered at first, interspersed with orchards, and small gardens. When they reached the long and irregular plaza where the grand edifice of the Menger Hotel stood, Jane saw that the plaza itself was solidly lined with buildings, many of them fronted with deep boardwalks and shaded by overhanging roofs. Most were new; brightly painted or whitewashed clean – all but the limestone of one façade which looked like a church, with empty niches where four statues had once been, supported by elaborately twisted columns on either side.

"It's the old garrison chapel," Lizzie explained, as they drove past, negotiating their way past a gaudy storefront, adorned with galleries and wooden towers at the corners, and banners advertising the goods for sale to the commercial trade within. "That was the convent, although Mr. Grenet's establishment has taken it over since the federal Army has moved out of the city. It's much improved now that their wagons aren't parked here, day and night."

"Wasn't this was the place where the Mexicans overwhelmed the garrison and killed them all at the start of the war for independence?" Jane asked, and Lizzie nodded.

"Yes, it was – it was rather ghastly. It was ruinous for a long while afterwards. They say that when the federal soldiers began clearing out the rooms and rebuilding the walls, they found skeletons, buried where they fell among the rubble. Their poor families. . ." Lizzie sighed. "Never to know. It's tragic – my brother John was a soldier during the late war. Such hardships he suffered wrecked his health, even though he lived through it. At least I know where he is buried, not like Jemima's beloved!"

"It's very small, for a fort," Jane observed and Lizzie corrected her. "No, it was too big! This plaza encompasses the whole of it; the buildings along the sides stand over where the outer fortifications once were. It was once the largest military fort west of the Mississippi and north of the Nueces."

"You'd hardly think that to look at it now," Jane said, as the buggy drew up to the front of the Menger, a whole elegant two stories and a bit, with a row of trees planted out front.

"Well, it was almost fifty years ago," Lizzie answered, laughing. "I know; hardly any time in England, but for us, fifty years is an age!"

Lizzie tied up the horse to one of the empty hitching posts; she was as capable as a man, in most things, Jane reflected with a trace of envy. She did as she pleased, and no one thought her to be the least unladylike. Or they might have but Lizzie didn't care two pins. Lizzie sailed into the black and white tile-floored lobby of the Menger as if she owned the place herself. It wouldn't have surprised Jane a bit to find out that she did. In a way, this was a little like attending on Lady Isobel but no one expected Jane to be self-effacing when she was with Lizzie, even if Lizzie paid her wages. There was a small party of people waiting for them; men and women both. Among them, to Jane's astonishment, was Sam Becker.

"I thought you were in Austin!" she exclaimed, as Sam kissed her hands and looked with admiration on her fashionable turn-out. He laughed merrily, answering, "So did I, Miss Jane, so did I!" That's where I sent my letter. I thought you would be pleased to know that Onkel Hansi and my brother are letting me go at last!"

"To Paris!" Jane gasped. "This is marvelous news."

"I'm sailing from Galveston in two weeks," Sam explained. "I didn't want to waste time, not even for Christmas, so I wrote you to explain. I truly would have missed seeing you then." He looked embarrassed, while Lizzie's friends regarded Sam and Jane with fond indulgence, as if they were particularly winsome children.

Lizzie interjected, "Why don't you go walk in the garden and explain to her?" Sam looked relieved and offered Jane his arm, saying over his shoulder, "I will owe you a painting for that, Miss Lizzie – once I come back from Europe."

"I will hold you to that," Lizzie answered. "As I have a wall in my parlor which simply begs for a spectacular landscape."

"Slave-driver!" Sam murmured, as he and Jane stepped out into the garden at the back of the hotel, filled with tidy beds of late-blooming roses and sheltered from the wind, so that the scent hung in the air like perfume. "I will paint her something grand, something that will fill up that wall to the exclusion of anything else. And, no," he looked down at Jane and smiled. "A landscape; you will not have to dress up and pose for it."

"You are too kind," Jane's voice was demure, although she felt a sudden rush of overwhelming affection for Sam. They had written now and again during the year past, just as friends and Jane often and wistfully recalled that summer spent at the Becker ranch. Sam had paid a single call on her in Austin, assuring himself, so Jane assumed, of her contentment and safety at Lizzie's school. "I thought that your uncle and your brother were adamant regarding a year abroad in Paris. Did you talk them around, somehow?"

"There was a situation which unexpectedly resolved itself," Sam said. He smiled again, so carefree and happy that Jane felt as if her heart had just turned to warm butter. "They decided that they could spare me after all. I ran away as soon as I could, before their minds changed and they could haul me back. Do you think me a coward, Jane? The door opened, I saw freedom and the bright air outside, and so I ran for it."

"Never!" Jane exclaimed. "I felt the same at being offered employment by Miss Johnson. That was your doing and I have been more grateful than I can ever say. You offered me a chance to become what I dearly wished to be;

a teacher, a woman with a good income of her own, and so I ran for it, too. Oh, Sam – Mr. Becker, never feel that I would think you a coward! A life of work at tasks which you do not embrace with a whole heart will turn your whole soul sour. It would not matter if one has no ambition or knowledge of anything else, but when you do, existence becomes a torment! It is as if one is ill-fed, but a banquet of good things is just out of reach!"

"Exactly, Miss Jane – you have put it into words most fittingly." Sam took her hands in his and kissed her fingers, a butterfly-brush of his lips. In that instant Jane knew that she loved him, loved him with a whole and pure heart. It didn't matter if he only thought her a friend; she loved him and could live with him within reach, even should he court and marry another girl. Still, she thought with a touch of wistfulness; it would be very pleasant to fall into his embrace, hold him close, even to kiss each other. Something of this must have shown in her face, for he was looking at her with sudden concern. "Miss Jane, is there something the matter?"

"No," she answered, feeling breathless as if she had fallen from a great height. "I just wish . . . it was so pleasant, that day when we were teaching Harry and Christian to dance. I wish we could dance together, just once."

"Why, we can!" He answered, with a smile so brilliant that Jane thought it must rival the sun in the sky over their heads. "Miss Jane, do you want to come to a real fandango? This friend of ours . . . he's as much of an uncle as Onkel Hansi . . . he is throwing a grand *baile* – that's a ball in Spanish – tonight. One of his nieces has gotten married or engaged or something and Tio Porfirio is throwing a grand celebration. We'll have enough dancing in one night to last for a year! I have an invite – do you and Lizzie wish to shake the chalk-dust off you? Tio Porfirio is quite respectable," Sam added hastily. "He's about the richest Mexican around. Everyone knows him, and there ain't many Anglos wouldn't say no to an invitation of his, or pass up a chance to invite him to their parties. Come and dance with me tonight, Jane. You won't regret it. Say that you will?"

"Of course," Jane answered. *No, how could she refuse Sam anything?*

Lizzie was agreeable, as soon as Sam relayed the invitation to her, when they rejoined her friends around a beautifully set table in one of the Menger's private dining rooms.

"At Don Porfirio's? How splendid and what fun!" She clapped her hands in glee. "I have seen his house from the outside and a little of the garden. It's old-fashioned, very Spanish, so they say. Very like Mr. Irving's *Spanish Sketchbook*, but not so many fantastical Moorish elements. Señor Menchaca de Lugo," she explained to Mrs. King, who sat across from her, "is from one of the old families. He has properties on either side of the border and interests in commerce and horse-breeding, which he inherited from his grandfather and the family of his wife – who is so old-fashioned she is hardly ever seen in public."

"I promised Miss Jane some dancing," Sam added, as Jane wondered if she had gotten herself in deep water by even suggesting it. He promised to come for them that evening at sunset, and convey them to Don Porfirio's mansion.

"I wish that I had thought to bring something fitting for a ball like this," Lizzie exclaimed that evening, as she and Jane fussed with each other's hair, and Ellen Lockhart sat on the bed, giving judgement when appealed to. "You are so clever with a needle, Jane. I am green with envy." In the few hours of afternoon and early evening, Jane had altered the bodice of a sky-blue silk taffeta summer dress that she had brought with her to San Antonio; removing the sleeves and lowering the neckline. She trimmed the bodice with ribbons, silk ribbon flowers and lengths of cream-colored Honiton lace, carefully removed from a petticoat which had been the fashion three years ago in England, now looped up to form short sleeves, and adorn the lowered neckline. The dress and the petticoat had been gifts of Lady Isobel, both items dropping from fashion in the year following her disastrous debut. Jane was inordinately fond of both of them, especially the petticoat – but she wished to appear at her best, this evening. After all, she could always reattach the lace. Her hands were rough with needle pricks. It had been a year since she had done this kind of last-minute and frantic sewing, but she felt a small shiver of satisfaction, regarding herself in the pier glass mirror of the guest bedroom of the house on Pecan Street. She looked like a lady of fashion; a lady with the more modest requirements of a colonial outpost in mind. Lizzie said that Don Porfirio's family was old-fashioned, so showing off her shoulders to the level of her breasts and much of her arms above the elbow would probably not be appreciated by the ladies of Don Porfiro's household. She so wanted to reflect well on Sam, to look her best for him.

"I have spent hours and hours with a needle and thread," Jane explained. "So I would hope to be good with them."

"We are ready at last," Lizzie answered, gathering up the velvet evening mantle which she had borrowed from Ellen. They could hear the crunch of carriage wheels coming along Pecan Street, and stopping before the Lockhart's house. "We're off, dear – don't stay up waiting for us."

"Indeed not," Ellen answered, tartly. "We understand these fandangos continue until sunrise – as long as the musicians can play and the men and women dance."

"I think I could dance until dawn!" Jane wrapped herself in the warmest garment she had brought; a bright-patterned challis shawl – again, an inheritance from Lady Isobel.

Sam waited for them downstairs; talking to Will Lockhart and leaning against one of the porch pillars. But he straightened as soon as Jane and Lizzie emerged. He hastily stuffed his sketchbook and pencil into his coat and the expression on his face warmed Jane as if by a fire.

The home of Don Porfirio and his family was one of those lining a narrow street leading off of the Military Plaza, in the very oldest part of town. The Casa Menchaca turned a plain and unremarkable face to the street, a low and squat building, with a few narrow windows, shuttered and barred to the outside. It was unadorned, save for a tall pair of ornate wooden and metalwork doors in the very center; doors which would have done credit to a castle. The sound of music floated on the night air. Tonight the doors stood wide open, spilling light and color into the street. A groom sprang out of the shadows when Sam's conveyance drew close; Sam gave the reins over to him, handed Jane and Lizzie down, walked between them through the doorway and into another world. A woman all in black came to relieve Jane and Lizzie of their outer garments as soon as they entered a kind of vestibule. The brief silence and looks of admiration at Jane left her feeling well-recompensed for the long afternoon of sewing.

The inside of Casa Menchaca was quite plain, with plastered walls turned honey-gold by the light of candles and lanterns. The floors were of ordinary, rust-colored tiles, faintly irregular, as if in places the soil had shifted or risen a little out of level. Those few pieces of furniture were heavy, medieval-appearing things of dark wood; chairs and chests and tables. But the music and light, and the other guests filled it all with movement and color. From the garden beyond, through another set of double doors, the heavy scent of jasmine perfumed the night air. A stout Mexican gentleman stood in the foyer, greeting guests. Jane recognized him almost at once; last year he had partnered with old Mrs. Becker on the night of the ball at the Richter's. Now he beamed with delight, upon catching sight of Sam and the ladies.

"Samuel! *Mi hijo*! And the beautiful ladies – welcome, welcome!"

"Tio 'Firio," Samuel returned the stout gentleman's hearty embrace. "This is Miss Jane Goodacre. Miss Johnson you know already, of course."

"You do us honor, and grace this house with your presence," Don Porfirio bowed very correctly over each of their hands, his expression one of frank admiration, but he was so very honest and good-humored in it that Jane could not help but be charmed. Don Porfirio was dressed in black, as were most of the other men present; a short jacket trimmed with braid and many silver buttons and a brilliantly colored silk sash around his waist. Jane thought it quite exotic, so very different from the drab and ordinary dark suits of Englishmen. Only regimentals came close to it for color.

"I have promised Miss Jane that we will dance," Sam explained and Don Porfirio waved a dismissing hand. "Go then, *mi hijo*. I would not see you break a promise to such a beautiful lady. I ask only that I may ask for a chance to dance with her myself, after I dance with the magnificent Miss Johnson," he added suavely. Laughing, Lizzie swept him a deep curtsey, saying, "But certainly – I would be honored."

"Shall we?" Sam offered Jane his arm, and escorted her into the next room; a long salon where half a dozen musicians gathered at the end, playing a lively reel. Long windows along one side of the salon opened into a cloister-like gallery with a garden beyond; all lit with lanterns. The women's dresses swirled like the petals of a peony flower as they danced in the arms of their gallants; the music pulled Jane into it, ravishing her senses. Most of Don Porfirio's guests at the *baile* were Mexican; dark of hair and eye, but otherwise as fair of skin as any Anglo. Only their manner of dress marked them out; the men in short-cut jackets, and colorful sashes, the ladies wearing tall combs in their dark hair with a fine lace mantilla depending from it. It was a delirious feeling to be so close to Sam, to see the tiniest smile, experiencing the touch of his hands on hers and at her waist, to catch the slight scent of bay-laurel pomade that he must have used earlier that evening.

They danced without speaking, the room was noisy and the music was loud, until they were both breathless. Finally, Sam put his mouth close to her ear, saying, "Let's go out into the veranda. Tio 'Firio always has the refreshments laid out there, and it's quieter."

Whatever Sam wished tonight, Jane was agreeable; the verandah and the garden was cooler than the salon, but no less well lit; a pebble-paved courtyard with a low fountain in the center, and tubs of flowers and small shrubs adorning the margins. A gate in the wall opposite the house stood open, affording a glimpse of the rush-fringed riverbank beyond. A simple timber pergola sheltered a number of benches and a table where had been spread with many good things. It made a kind of outdoor dining room. Jane thought that it must be very pleasant to dine there, especially on a warm day, listening to the gentle splashing of the fountain and the bustle of the city at a distance behind the tall walls surrounding the courtyard. Sam found a bowl of iced lemon punch, and procured a glass for each of them. They found a place on a stone bench side by side and savored it all; the tart punch, the evening, with the wind rustling the branches of the trees in the courtyard, the music and the graceful forms of the dancers, seen through the tall open windows of the salon.

"How did you come to know Don Porfirio so very well?" Jane mused. It had been her limited experience that the native-born Americans did not mix with the Mexicans, socially or otherwise.

"Our families go back a very long way," Sam said, after a moment. "You would not know it to look at him but Tio 'Firio is a bit of a rogue. He had – still has – an eye for the ladies, he's just not so reckless about it now. But when he was just a lad, that got him into trouble – bad trouble; that kind of trouble that maybe leaves a man in an alley, bleeding from a great many knife wounds, or at the very least, brought before the magistrates. I don't know the ins and outs of it all, but it was Papa who rescued him. This was before he and Mama married, or even knew each other. Back then, Papa was one of Captain Hays' ranger company here; not a man to start a fight with, at any rate. All Tio 'Firio ever said was that Papa came to his aid and stood by him when every other hand was against him, even his own grandfather. Tio 'Firio came and lived at Papa's ranch for a good few years, waiting for the hue and cry to die down. When it did and Tio 'Firio's grandfather died, that's when he went back to San Antonio. I was about five or six then. It was a long time ago," Sam added, as if it really had been. "Later, when Papa was killed and his property confiscated, Tio 'Firio sent money to Mama. He was there when we buried Papa and he promised Mama on his mos' solemn word that he would see that the man who killed Papa would pay. I've since wondered if he did have anything to do with . . ." Abruptly, Sam pulled himself from the past. "That's one of the reasons all of the Mexican folk at the ranch are connections of his; cousins and nephews and such. He also invested in the first herd that Dolph an' Cuz took up to Kansas. He's as close as kin, no matter what everyone else thinks of it."

"That is loyalty such as books written about," Jane ventured at last. She was trying to see the stout little man with a sash about his middle as a heedless boy and ladies' delight. She couldn't see it, but the affection for him was plain in what Sam said. Now he took her hand in his. "You've been busy," he remarked. "I can tell – you've little needle marks all over your fingers."

"I wanted to look my best tonight," Jane answered, startled at his perception. "And I had not brought the right sort of gown with me."

"Jane, you would be perfection to me in anything and I don't think Tio 'Firio cares, much beyond a pretty face and a shapely form, no matter how it is clad. But I swear, the effort was well worth it, especially since he can admire your bosom with advantages."

"So, who is the rogue now?" Jane asked, laughing.

Sam answered with uncharacteristic gravity, "Me. I think we should get married, Jane."

Chapter 24 – *A Married Woman*

"What did you say?" Jane was startled into unsuitable bluntness – she simply did not believe what she heard. The music now sounded tinny, distant in her ears as she stared at Sam. The dancing in the salon now spilled out onto the arcade, even to the courtyard; young men and girls laughing flirtatiously. The wings of months flickered in the golden lamplight, as pale as the colors of the ladies' dresses. "I thought we might get married," Sam answered. A slight shadow fell on his face. "If you wanted to marry me, that is. Do you?"

"Yes, I would," Jane answered, without thinking. "I do, very much."

"That's it, then." Sam's pleasant countenance was ablaze with renewed happiness. "I was hoping you would, Jane. Tio 'Firio will arrange it all. I'd like to tie the knot right away, Jane. And . . ." he began rooting through his coat and vest pockets with one hand as he held one of hers in the other.

"Why would that be? You're going to Europe in a fortnight?" Jane was still boggled. It had happened all at once, in the space of mere seconds. She had always thought that a proposal of marriage would be a momentous event. A suitor would be kneeling on one knee and he would have said a little more by way of asking for her hand.

"Well, that's the thing." Unaccountably, Sam was flustered. Jane found it endearing; he looked like a small boy caught out. "I thought I'd have more time, but I didn't want to go away for a whole year without saying something. I know how it is here in Texas. You might be courted by any fellow, any time and say 'yes' to him. Onkel Hansi says he can't figure out why you haven't been already; he thinks the men of Austin must all be gel – or something," he added in haste. "Jane; you're the cleverest and prettiest girl I know. I need you in my corner, so to speak. More than anything, even over the chance to study in Paris. You're the one person who really believes I can make a living from painting. Mama says she does, but she is my mother. Lottie too, but Lottie is my sister. Everyone else says I'm a fool and wasting my time. I need someone on my side, Jane. Besides," he drew a deep breath. "If I must support a wife and mebbe a family, then I *have* to make a success of it. We can go together, man and wife. Have you ever been to Paris, Jane?"

"Oh, no, I couldn't," Jane answered at once. "I'd be letting Miss Johnson down and I'd have to give up teaching. A year," she straightened her shoulders and frowned thoughtfully. "I couldn't go with you, Sam, but I can save enough so that we'd have a place to live, afterwards. You don't have to go back to your uncle with your cap in your hand."

"A year is a mighty long time, Jane." He sounded regretful. He had finally found the thing in his pockets that he had been searching for; a ring, a slender band of gold set with tiny red stones and a single pearl. "But I have a ring. I bought it with the money that Colonel Ford paid me for doing a painting to his order," he added proudly.

"I think that a very good omen," Jane said. "I'll wear it for tonight, as a promise and put it to my other hand as a marriage ring."

With an uncharacteristically solemn face, Sam put the ring on Jane's hand; he kissed her and Jane thought how miraculous this was; a dream from which she hoped never to awake. "We can be wed tomorrow," he said. "If you wish it. Tio 'Firio can arrange it, if I ask."

"I would like that," Jane answered, her voice barely steady. She wanted him to kiss her again, to hold her even more closely than he held her in dancing. She wanted more than anything to share a bed with him, as Lady Isobel had shared one with his brother, to laugh together, and to make plans for a future. All other considerations were swept aside in the intensity of her desire – or very nearly all. "Very much, but I think we should keep it a secret at first. It's not thought seemly for a wedded wife to work and it would ruin everything. When someone holds the purse-strings, they can make you dance to any tune they choose for you."

"You're practical, too," Sam's expression was wholly admiring. "Like Cousin Anna and Miss Lizzie. I like that in a woman." He put his arm around her. She leaned into his shoulder, reveling in the closeness. The stone bench at their backs still radiated faint warmth from the day.

"I can cook," Jane answered. "And keep accounts. We'll never starve."

"Thought that was what artists did," Sam laughed and Jane giggled. "You'll be the first not to, then," she assured him, and then they were silent for a long moment. Jane contemplated the upending of her future with relative equanimity. She had wistfully assumed she might marry someday, as a matter of course. It was what women did, unless they chose to remain a spinster forever. Jane did not think she meant to teach for the rest of her life but she had not expected a proposal, or to accept it instantly. It just felt 'right' to her, as it had felt 'right' to being Lady Isobel's personal maid. "I will have to tell Miss Lizzie, too," she ventured at last. "But I think she will approve. Married or not, she thinks women should be more independent. How long a time do we have before you must go to Galveston?"

"A week," Sam answered.

"Will that be time enough?" Jane ventured. Sam chuckled, "It will, if Tio 'Firio has a hand in it," he assured her. At that moment, Lizzie appeared in the courtyard, laughing and breathless.

"There you are," she exclaimed. "The pair of you look as if you have been up to no good! What has Mr. Becker been asking of you, Jane?"

"He asked me to marry and I have said yes," Jane answered. Lizzie's eyebrows arched only slightly. "You are not surprised?"

"Not in the least," Lizzie answered. "Only that it took him so long."

* * *

To Jane, her wedding passed in the blink of an eye, in a queer unreal dream-state. Mid-afternoon of the day after Don Porfirio's ball, she and Sam stood up before a justice of the peace in a dusty little office off Main Plaza. The sounds of horse-teams outside in the square and the rough voices of teamsters blended with the chiming of the bells from the cathedral. Don Porfirio, his mustaches shining with brilliantine, stood as witness with Lizzie Johnson as Ellen and Will Lockhart watched. The voice of the justice, of Sam repeating the solemn vows and her own voice, low yet firm; all that was real, and the feel of the little ring sliding onto the third finger of her left hand – that was real, too. It was a hundred times removed from the elaborate ceremony of Lady Isobel's nuptials. Jane wore the best of the day dresses that she had brought with her, and carried a tiny posy of flowers which Ellen picked from her garden. When it was done, she and Sam signed the ledger, Lizzie and Ellen embraced her, teasingly addressing her as 'Mrs. Becker' and Don Porfirio kissed her hand. *Oh,* thought Jane, for the first time, *My lady and I have married brothers. That will make it very strange. What will Auntie Lydia make of this? What will Sir Robert and Lady Caroline think?*

Don Porfirio, who seemed to fancy himself as a father to them both, invited everyone to a celebratory meal at his house – including the Justice in that invitation – who answered, "I don't mind if I do," as he closed his desk and took up his hat from a stand in the corner. Don Porfirio's home was only a short distance away. They all walked, Sam with Jane's hand tucked safely into his. She stole a sideways glance at Sam's – her husband's face. He looked so proud, so pleased, although she had overheard Will Lockhart teasing him, saying that his happy bachelor days were over. *No,* Sam answered, as if he had been quoting something: *The best is yet to be.*

Jane hugged that thought to herself. *The best was yet to be,* and she would do her very best to make it so.

* * *

10 January, 1878
From Jane Becker, Austin, Texas
To Lydia Kittredge, Acton Hall, Oxfordshire

Dearest Auntie;
You will see from the return address that I have married. Is this what you had expected when you bid me a fond farewell and told me that things might be very different, in that country that service to my lady might lead me? I cannot help but think that you did, having knowledge of the world that was not vouchsafed to me! I was such a child, such an innocent! I am certain that you would see my marriage as difficult, even an embarrassment, since it establishes me on the same plane as kin by marriage to the Family! This will be very awkward indeed. Lady Isobel and I have married brothers but our prospects will be as varied as the brothers are themselves in character and in perspective upon the world! Lady Isobel's husband, the senior Mr. Becker, is the very picture of prosperity; his future and his life as well-settled as any man of property in England. But my husband is a younger son and his unhappiness with the same prospect has led him to strike out on a different path, which he does with my confident support. We could be as well-settled as his brother but the family business of cattle commerce is not to his liking. He is passionately drawn to art and the life of the mind. I believe with all my heart that together we might make a comfortable living from his painting, as long as we do this together. I have some skill in domestic management and sufficient in savings to invest in some small establishment where we may live together while he practices his art. He has been painting for friends in a small way. His family and connections are widely known and much respected. I believe that once he has achieved the laurels bestowed upon an artist known to have studied 'abroad,' my dearest husband may draw sufficient in painting commissions that we might live very comfortably, once established. We are not friendless, even now. Miss Johnson has taken our part very decidedly and Don Porfirio was kind enough to lend us a small house in the old Spanish part of town, that we might spend the first days of our marriage peacefully together.

Dearest Auntie, I wish that you might meet him. He promises that should his journey take him to Oxfordshire, he will visit under the pretense of bearing personal messages and gifts from Lady Isobel to her family. When he does, contrive somehow to meet privately with him and treat him kindly as I am certain that you will, as you stand in my own mother's place. I have not written to her with the news of my marriage. I may, when I return to Austin, or entrust a message to you to forward to her. It pains me to have so harsh a judgment with regards to my living parent but your words to me and your actions upon assessing our true situation have remained ever with me. My mother was no more a true and loving parent to me than my lady's was to her. I suppose I might seem harsh, unloving, and ungrateful in this judgement, but it is a true one nevertheless. Mine and my lady's mothers thought very little of us and little considered our content and happiness, as I believe a true mother should. Be kind to my husband, dearest Aunt. He is the dearest and most gallant of gentlemen, and those qualities of his which I most value were apparent to me as a friend – and dare I say, those of mine to him – and as such we were, long before we ever considered each other as partners of the heart.

> Your very loving,
> Jane – now Becker

* * *

"I should paint you, as you look to me now," Sam murmured. It was the last night they would spend together in the little house in the old village, and they lay close-knit together, with Jane's hair spread across the pillow. A small fire burned in the tiny masonry fireplace in the corner of the room.

"Oh, you wouldn't!" Jane exclaimed, covering herself hastily with bedclothes. "It wouldn't be decent."

"Maybe not," Sam agreed, "But you should see some of the paintings of naked nymphs in cow-town saloons in Kansas – you'd outclass them by a country mile."

"I'm sure it's because you're a better painter than anyone painting indecent pictures of . . . those women," Jane replied. Sam sighed a little, and drew her closer. The night was chill, and the shutters were drawn tightly closed over the small, deep-set windows of Don Porfirio's little house. On the afternoon of the day they married, Don Porfirio drove them there himself, through the tiny winding streets of what had once been a separate little village across the narrow river which threaded like a green ribbon through town. At the door of a certain house in a row of them, all alike and built of heavy unbaked brick with plaster over it, Don Porfirio halted his horses. Sam leaped down and took their small luggage; Don Porfirio kissed Jane on both cheeks before handing her a heavy, old-fashioned wrought-iron key.

"My children, tonight begins your life together. May God and his saints grant that it be long and sweet, and blessed with many sons and daughters!"

Jane turned the key in the door, but before she could step through, Sam had picked her up, as easily as if she weighed no more than a feather and carried her across the threshold, laughing and saying that it was an old tradition. And so they spent five nights there, the last of them tonight. Jane wished that either she could slow time and relish every moment as if it were a day of itself . . . or hasten those moments so as to get the moment of parting over and done with. For the next year, she would be going over each of these precious days and hours, like a miser counting his gold coins. Marriage agreed with Jane very much more than she had expected. It was very like assuming a brand-new – but comfortable and well-fitting garment.

"You could come with me," Sam said, one more time. "I'd telegram Onkel Hansi and tell him . . ."

"No," Jane stopped his lips with the touch of her finger. "We've already agreed on this, my dear. We can't be beholden to your family for any more than you already are. The cost of two passages on a steam-packet to Europe and back, not to mention the costs for us both to live respectably are more than we can ask, knowing that you will ask your freedom when you return. You may live in any old boarding-house or in rooms, but a man with a wife must spend ever so much more for a respectable place. It's too much to ask. You will be studying, dearest Sam, night and day. There will be no time for me. You would resent the time spent away from your precious paints and your lessons. I know this; you would, although you would never say so. No man can serve two masters – or even yet, two mistresses."

"My beloved distraction," Sam sighed and tightened his arms around her. Jane settled herself comfortably in the curve of his body, thinking how easily she had become accustomed to sleeping next to him. More – accustomed to sharing the days also; walking through the streets of town, an alfresco luncheon by the spring-fed ponds in San Pedro Park; in part such excursions were partly for the pleasure of it and part with an eye for the future; a nice piece of property where Sam could establish his studio, and they could make a home for themselves. They had dined once with Miss Lizzie and the Lockharts, once with Don Porfirio and this evening, they had dined at the Menger, just themselves. In the morning Don Porfirio would return, taking Jane to the Lockharts, and Sam to the new railroad station on Austin Street. "I know we had agreed; you would go on teaching, and finding us a place here. You're certain of here, rather than Austin?"

"It's where all the trade is," Jane answered. "Now that the railroad has arrived." Just in those twenty months since she had first come to Texas, San Antonio had become even larger. Where the station was now established, a hustle and bustle of commerce had sprang up; chop-houses, hotels, warehouses and stockyards. Street after street of modern cottages and small houses climbed the hill to the north of town, where once had been only the bare, grass-covered hills. To the south lay the districts of mansions and grounds where many of the German mercantile barons lived and now the spaces between the long avenues were steadily filled in. "Your uncle was right to come from the Hill Country to establish the seat of his empire here. I think we should benefit by following his example. I will find the perfect place, and with Lizzie's help, I will buy it."

"Oh, Jane!" his voice broke with emotion, as he cupped her chin in one hand, "I will miss you so much, but this I promise. I will write and send a letter every day that we are apart, even if it is only a line or two about what I had for supper."

"I'll do the same," Jane promised fervently. "And it will make the year pass swiftly, I am certain of it."

"For now," Sam embraced her again, "Sweeting, that is not a lark, but a nightingale. We'll use those hours that we have together to best effect."

Once returned to Austin and the familiar classroom routine, memories of those six precious, idyllic days with Sam often felt like a dream to Jane, save on those days when the post arrived for her, with a fat bundle of letters, stamped and adorned with foreign postmarks and proudly addressed to Mrs. Samuel Becker. True to his promise, he wrote a letter every day, although most often they arrived many at once at one and two week intervals. Jane saved them to read one by one, just before she went to bed of an evening, for then Sam was in her dreams. Lizzie and Jemima teased her gently whenever the post arrived. Otherwise, things went on as before; most everyone save Lizzie and Jemima still addressed her as Miss Goodacre, although there was no great secret kept regarding her married state. It was just that no one called attention to it. Jane began to think that she and Sam had succeeded in keeping the marriage a secret from anyone in the family who mattered, until a Saturday afternoon when Lizzie Johnson met Jane and Jemima as they returned from a visit to the delights offered by various mercantile establishments. Lizzie had such a grave expression on her face that Jemima paled.

"Is it Aunt Hetty?" she gasped. Old Miss Hetty had been in very poor health over the winter, although tottering out to the kitchen when she felt strongest, to make a batch of her peerless biscuits. Jane knew that Jemima feared a message from the Vining house; that her aunt had gone, or was about to fall into that final deep sleep.

"No my dear, not that news; but rather it concerns Jane," Lizzie cleared her throat, significantly. "Mrs. Carl Becker and Miss Lottie are waiting for her, in the parlor. They would not say, nor would I ask, what their call concerns. But I think, dear Jane, the cat has departed the bag, as far as the Becker ladies are concerned."

"Oh, dear!" Jane stifled a small groan. Jemima gave her a quick and affectionate squeeze of the hand. The door to the parlor was closed: Jane ran into her room and shed her outer garments hastily. She smoothed her hair in front of the mirror, and straightened the lace collar of the plain dress that she wore. A hasty inspection of her skirts revealed no smudges or smuts, especially at the hem; the streets of Austin were not paved to any degree, and the edging of filth acquired along the hems of dresses plagued the ladies mightily. She ran downstairs again, and composed herself at the door for a moment before setting her hand to the knob.

Head proudly held high, she opened it. "Good afternoon, Marm Becker," she said, in even tones. "Miss Lottie, I am so pleased that you have paid a call. This is most unexpected. I thought you would have gone to the ranch. I did not think to see you in Austin again until Christmas."

"There was no need," Mrs. Becker said, in tones as dry as dust and that accent as harsh-sounding as ever. "My son Rudolph and his family maintain their home there now. I do not wish interfering with their lives."

"I am certain that M . . . Isobel would not think the worse of you, taking an interest in the children. They must be a year and a half old now. They seem like very dear children. They are a joy to Isobel. She writes often, telling me of them."

"They are a joy to me also," Mrs. Becker answered. "But my son's children are not my reason for this call. Rather, my other son's wife." There was a shrewd grey gleam in her eyes. Jane's heart sank in her breast. *She knew*. The Baron doubtless knew also. It was common knowledge that he shared his business confidences with his sister-in-law, rather than his wife. Everything outside the confines of the mansion in what everyone had begun to call the King Wilhelm district fell into the Baron's interest. Mrs. Becker continued, "I have been told by someone I trust that in December of last year you married my son in the offices of a justice of the peace in San Antonio. My son Samuel, that is. Is this true?"

"It is," Jane confessed, with her heart hammering in her breast like a trip-hammer. "We were married in front of reliable witnesses."

"Oh, Jane!" Lottie cried, ecstatic; she sprang from where she sat beside her mother and embraced Jane with fierce affection. "How wonderful! I so hoped that rumor might be true, you have no idea!" and she whispered in Jane's ear, "Sam is the very dearest brother; how romantic that he would pick one of my fondest friends for a bride! I so wish that I had the courage to run away and marry Seb!"

"You are not of age," Mrs. Becker's ears hadn't missed a word and her voice was stern, reproving. "Lottchen, you are only sixteen. To marry before you are of age, that I would not allow. Jane is old enough to marry without the approval of a parent or guardian. This was the wish of your Opa; that girls might not be hastened to marry before they knew their own minds, and what the world offered to them."

"Oh, pooh, Mama!" Lottie answered. "I love Seb very dearly. I would marry him tomorrow, now that he has proved himself."

"When you are eighteen," Mrs. Becker's tone was final, even crushing. Lottie only pouted, brief and prettily, which reminded Jane of the summer at the ranch, when she ate at the same table and Lottie had been every bit as much of a friend as Sam. "Lottchen, this matter is not for you, but about marriage and a family keepsake." Now Mrs. Becker fumbled within the depths of her reticule; that large leather satchel which had always accompanied her, and drew something small from it. Now she was kind and perhaps a little uncertain, not as severe in her widow-black as she had first appeared. "This was a gift to me," she continued. "From a mother to the wife of her son. It came to me on my marriage, the gift of my mother-in-law, although she was long-dead when my husband gave it to me. I hesitated, making a gift of this to Rudolph's wife. She has so many jewels; it would have cut me to the heart, knowing that something I treasured would be only a paltry thing to her. I believe Samuel's wife would treasure it as I have done. I choose to make it my bride-gift to you, little Jane. You do not have any such, so I think you might treasure it also. It is trusted to you now, to give to the wife of your son, as you choose."

Jane was struck to silence; she had not expected this. Rising from the settee, Mrs. Becker took the small thing, and placed it in Jane's hand, briefly closing her own around Jane's. She ducked her head; tall for a woman, she stood a head taller than Jane, and kissed Jane's forehead. "There, little Jane – my new daughter: You are one of my family now, one such as I would have chosen as wife for either of my sons."

"Thank you," Jane stammered, quite overcome. She had not expected such a mark of affection from Sam's mother or the bestowing of a family heirloom on her, even such a small token as this. She opened her hand; yes, this was the small brooch she had often seen Mrs. Becker wear for best; an old-fashioned cameo a little larger than a three-penny bit, set in a narrow frame of gold and tiny seed pearls. "I will treasure it very dearly. I will write to Sam and tell him. I am sorry that we did not tell anyone that we married. We were afraid that you wouldn't approve."

"I have never been able to prevent any of my children from doing that which they truly wanted to do," Mrs. Becker answered dryly. "Once they became of a certain age. It is my good fortune that sometimes they inform me of afterwards of they have done. You are fortunate with Samuel. He has always been open of heart. He does not keep secrets, like his brother. Little Jane, you will always know what is in his mind. Dolphchen will always do as he thinks best, and then he will tell his wife – perhaps."

"I still can't understand why you and Sam kept it a secret," Lottie ventured. "Auntie Liesel would have had such a party for you and a proper wedding, like Cousin Marie."

"Because we . . ." Jane began. No, she could not lie to Mrs. Becker or Lottie; the two other women in the family who believed that Sam could make a living painting. "We didn't plan anything like that. He wanted to get married at once, before he left for Europe and I agreed. We decided that I should go on teaching during the year that he is away. Because we will need the money I earn. He wants to paint for his living in an atelier, a studio of his own. It is our own enterprise, you see. We do not want to owe the family anything more, after this." Jane looked at the others, miserable and ashamed. It had first been so easy to keep their secret from the family.

"Dolph will not be pleased at all," Lottie ventured at last. "He was already planning on Sam to manage the home ranch next year. Isobel is having another baby, you know. I think he wanted to take her and the children traveling." Her mother was already nodding in agreement.

"Hansi has plans also. He has been saying that this is only a year, a young man sowing his . . . how to you say, wild oats? I tried to tell him otherwise," she snorted, almost scornfully. "But men; they think they know better, always. And the longer they go on thinking so, the harder it may be to tell them otherwise."

"That's it," Lottie agreed. "Dolph will be furious that Sam kept this secret for this long. What should we do, Mama?" Lottie appeared very young and anxious. Mrs. Becker had rather more of a grim expression on her own face.

"I think it best to say that Sam and Jane have entered into an understanding," she said at last. "And say to everyone on his return, that they are now married. That Sam wishes now to pursue art? I think to say nothing to Hansi and your brother until he returns in January. There will be a storm, of course, but I would have him face it and speak for himself. But I will quietly suggest the possibility in the next months. Perhaps they may become more accustomed to the possibility."

"I do hope so!" Lottie's exuberance returned. "Jane, I am so happy for you! Promise that you will come to visit often. We missed you very much and I know Isobel did. It must be rather odd, though," and Lottie's words echoed Jane's own thoughts. "That now we are all sisters. It will seem very strange to folk in the old country, won't it?"

"Doubtless," her mother agreed. "But many things in Texas are odd to them. One more will not make a difference."

Chapter 25 – *Visitors from Abroad*

27 October, 1878
Becker Ranch, Near Comfort
Kendall County, Texas

Darling Fa;

I am so pleased that you enjoyed the visit from Samuel and that his sketches of the ranch and of his travels were well-received by all. He will be returning to Texas sometime early in the New Year. The family has missed him very much. D. looks most particularly for his return and a relief from the burdens and duties of the ranch, and of Uncle R.'s cattle enterprises. The necessity for the long trail drives which once absorbed so much time and effort have been alleviated by the advance of the railway into even the most remote parts of this country, but there still remains much to be done. D. and Uncle R. are contemplating a further investment, in ranchland in the North. There have been many English investors taking up establishments in the Sweetwater region of Wyoming, and D. is much intrigued by the project. Have you heard any of this? I know that you were confined to your bed earlier this year with a return of your old catarrhal troubles, but Samuel said you were up and about during his visit. I am so glad to hear of this, for I had been worried.

Next week, we shall all travel by gentle stages to San Antonio to prepare for the advent of – I so pray – our son. D. is insistent upon this, that I be in the care of the best doctor-surgeon in Texas, dear Doctor H., in the household of Aunt R. I shall mind confinement to indoors, although Aunt R. adores little Maggie and Caro. I can hardly believe they are eighteen months old. They both walk very well, I should tell you, and Maggie is most adventurous – a child without fear of anything. It would amuse you so much to see them lying on the floor with Sorsha and Gawain, the dogs watching over them so tenderly. D. will insist on riding with one or the other on his saddle-bow and sometimes he lets Maggie sit in the saddle by herself and astride, which frightens me terribly as well as being quite unsuitable for a girl. I think ponies for the girls would be much more suitable, but D. laughs at me. 'No,' he says, 'they'd best learn to ride on a real horse.' I vow, they could both say 'Papa' before they could say Mama. Did I tell you that Sorsha has whelped a fine litter of six pups at last? Maggie and Caro will each have their own pup, we plan to give two to Cousin P. and two to Uncle R., whose friends have all admired Sorsha and Gawain immensely.

Give my love to all at Acton, especially to Mama, Robert and dearest Kitty-Cat. In a year or two I hope that we will be able to travel to England for a visit, and so that you may meet my children. I live in hope of receiving your loving embrace once more, dearest and most loving Fa –

From your loving daughter,
Isobel

PS – I took this letter with me unsealed, to mail in San Antonio, lest there be anything else in our journey to remark upon. Just this evening, on our arrival, Lottie told me of the most astonishing news; that Samuel has entered into an arrangement to marry – to marry Jane! You remember, Jane, who came with me as my maid? In England this would be cause for a great scandal, by which we would all be mortified, but I vow that I have been here for such a time as to regard this with equanimity. The divisions of society here are so fractured that hardly anything qualifies as a mésalliance save only a marriage between the white and black race. And all other aside, Jane is a dear, sweet and loyal girl, who has improved her station in life by her own efforts. I did write to you, I think – that she had taken a position as a school-teacher in a private academy in Austin, run by a very respectable maiden lady? We have remained friends since and written often, although we have not met in some months. She did send some very handsome little dresses for the girls – dear Jane was always such an accomplished needlewoman. I know that it seems very strange to contemplate – but I hope that with this marriage, I might see her more often.

In haste – your loving I.

* * *

12 November, 1878
Johnson's Select Academy
Austin, Texas

Dearest Auntie;

Our year apart is nearly ended – and what did you think of my husband? He wrote me a long letter, telling of his visit to Acton, and of your discrete kindness. He tells me that he could see the resemblance of family in your features and bearing – and wishes me to send personal and extravagant thanks for the hospitality extended to him, both from the Family and from you. I had written to you before of how Mrs. B and Lottie have accepted our marriage with a whole heart, and agreed to a certain deception regarding it, as well as our plans for an enterprise independent of what his family has expected of him. I reflect that this is not unlike my own expectations of being in domestic service for all of my life! Just so had everyone expected of my husband that he would join in the family enterprise! We are alike, dear Auntie, in that we have chosen to defy such expectations! I trust that in so doing, our partnership may become more perfect and enduring – and lest you assume that I have no sober council to the otherwise, Miss Johnson is as wise an advisor as you would be. The property that I have purchased in Houston Street is legally in my own name. Under her guidance, I have obtained every security under law that it will remain so – since I have purchased it with funds which I have earned through honest labor. At her suggestion, our marriage included such an agreement between my husband and myself. 'The act of marital union,' so she advises me, 'ought not to make you and your children liable to impoverishment should your husband be incompetent at providing living. Consider your own security, and that of your children! Secure your own property against your husband's creditors – and your own safety thereby!' I did need to secure a loan from her for a third of the purchase price, as the street is in a fashionable and commercial district, and so was a little more than I thought to afford. She has offered the loan with very generous terms for repayment. The building is narrow but deep, with high ceilings on two floors, the lower of which houses a tenant; Mr. Gottleib Knauer who keeps a retail furniture establishment and whose rent will serve to repay a portion of the loan. Mr. Knauer lives in two rooms at the back; the situation is very fortunate, as it is on the corner of Houston Street overlooking the river and an iron bridge which crosses over it. The upper floor has a separate entrance; a stairway and landing at the top. There is a stable adjacent and a small garden. I very much love the aspect on the river which threads in lazy loops back and forth through town. The water is so clear and swift, so clean that it is transparent! The upper floor, which has very high ceilings, is divided into a suite of rooms. The first of these has fine tall windows which overlook the street; I think eventually to make this our gallery and atelier. All the other rooms have windows which look out on the garden or on a view of the river. We have a small parlor, kitchen and bedroom, and another room overlooking the back, where I think to have a skylight installed, so that the light for painting will be abundant. This room my husband will use as a studio, for not only is it well-lit, it is large enough to keep the various small items necessary for him to have. Mrs. Becker will see to transferring his motley possessions to my custody . . . many of them items of artistic merit or utility, intended to be used as artistic properties. He also had a great number of books, which I will cherish – although a great many of them are in German, a language which I cannot read, although I shall endeavor to learn it, when I have time enough and leisure. Mrs. Becker appeared on first acquaintance to be a stern and forbidding woman, but she has always been kindness itself to me; even more so now in accepting me as a daughter. She addresses me as 'Little Jane' and I call her 'Mother Magda.'

I have already tendered my resignation from Johnson's Select Academy, with Miss Johnson's consent and perfect agreement, contingent upon my husband's return. He is to take ship and arrive in Galveston sometime around the end of February. I have planned to wait for his arrival in San Antonio and spend those weeks in the interim arranging our new home to best effect. It seems to me, dearest Auntie – that I, having been born in rooms over a shop – will live the rest of my life in them, and let me add that such a prospect pleases me very well. Not for me the rural cottage and garden, or even the stately mansion in its own park, and a life of womanly leisure. Those women in my life here whom I most respect and take as a pattern for my own life – all are independent, or work in tandem with their husband or kin. They have a place of honor in society, however unconventional it might seem to you, dearest Auntie.

My next letter will be posted from San Antonio; my new address will be No. 2011 Houston Street, San Antonio. Give my love to all. I am so pleased to hear that Sir Robert has recovered somewhat and pray that he might be restored to full health. He is a dear gentleman, whom all hold in the highest regard.

Your affectionate niece,
Jane Becker

* * *

"There's visitors for ye, downstairs," said the maid, in brusk tones to Isobel. At least, she had knocked on the door of the suite of rooms which Isobel, Dolph, the children and the dogs had been allocated at the Richter's establishment. "The ma'am says you'd best come to the parlor."

"Did she say who they are?" Isobel swung her feet to the floor. She had been resting on the chaise longue in front of the window which overlooked the garden and the stretch of lawn where Lottie Becker and her colorless cousin Grete Richter were teaching Maggie and Caro how to play croquet. "It's too early for calls."

"The ma'am did no' say," the maid returned as she closed the door behind her. Isobel sighed inwardly. She was already accustomed to the erratic manners of servants in Aunt Richter's household. This one sounded Irish and looked in her person as if she was much more accustomed to carrying large burdens on her back or in her arms, although she was in no way lazy or disobliging – not if she worked in Aunt Richter's house. Mrs. Kittredge would never have allowed so rough a person to present herself upstairs at the Hall; not a girl more suited to the laundry or scullery. Isobel looked for her low-heeled shoes, glad that she was presentably arrayed in one of her best wrappers, and that Doctor Herff had assured her that she was only bearing one child. She had been spared the most extreme grotesqueries of her first essay in child-birth and felt rather the better for it. According to the doctor, she was in splendid health; the baby could be born at any time. She found her shoes and made her way downstairs. Aunt Richter took such pride in her parlor, whose long French doors opened to a stone terrace and the lawn and gardens beyond. It was filled to excess with a jumble of over-ornamented furniture, objects d'art and paintings, much of it brought from Europe. But Aunt Richter's parlor made up what it lacked in elegance by being comfortable. Isobel could never look upon the room without thinking of how it reflected the mistress of the house; fussy, vulgar, but kind-hearted and loving.

Isobel went down the stairs, holding carefully to the bannister; pregnancy made her not only tired, but clumsy. There were so many stories of dreadful falls and resulting miscarriages, whispered by Aunt Richter's kindly-meant but tactless acquaintances. There were two men in the parlor conversing with Aunt Richter, who rose from where they sat as soon as Isobel came into the parlor. She blinked; not believing her eyes. Surely Martyn and Jack Sutcliffe couldn't be here. They should be in India; Martyn with his regiment and Jack doing whatever it was that he did there. They were clad in plain dark suits, somewhat disarrayed by travel, chatting with Aunt Richter. The sounds of the girl's laughter came from outside, borne on the light breeze that fluttered Grete and Lottie's hat ribbons and the skirts of their dresses.

"Izzy!" Martyn swept her into a warm embrace. "How splendidly well you look!"

"I do not – I'm as large as a cow," Isobel answered. "But thank you for the comforting compliment! What are you doing here in Texas? I had no idea. Jack . . ." Jack Sutcliffe grinned and bowed over her hand. "Are you making a return to cattle-trailing?"

"Alas, tempting as the thought might be, no. Nor have I been tempted to invest in cattle. Although," Jack cast an assessing eye around the parlor, "it does seem to be profitable in the long run. It didn't seem so in the beginning, dear little cousin."

"Everything has changed with the railway," Isobel assured them. "You simply must visit the home ranch; Dolph is traveling back and forth between there, because of the baby, you know. But he will take you for a visit . . ."

"We can't stay for long, Izzy," Martyn answered. "You'd best sit down. Jack and I aren't travelling for pleasure. We're on our way Home; we came this way for you, so that you might travel with us."

"For me?" Isobel looked from Martyn to Jack, puzzled. There was something wrong; all the merriment had fled from Martyn's face and Aunt Richter's suddenly-alert gaze went between them. "I'm in no fit condition to travel anywhere. What is happening, that you should both take leave and travel Home. It's Fa, isn't it?" She felt a cold clutch of fear in her chest as her brother nodded.

"He's not been well, Izzy. No, he's been gravely ill. They kept this from us for as long as they could – you, especially. The doctors all hoped that would recover, but now it seems," Martyn's jaw tightened. "It seems that he only has months. Maybe weeks. We wrote to you before we departed from Calcutta, but we traveled faster than our letters. We thought that you'd still be able to accompany us. Don't cry, Izzy."

"I'm not crying," Isobel insisted but she was. Her eyes overflowed. This couldn't be; Fa was strong, hearty, and indestructible as Acton Hall itself. Her happiness in this place depended on knowing that Fa was there, would always be there. His absence took something out of her world, making it desolate, as empty and hostile as that empty land north of the Red River. Aunt Richter sat next to her on the settee, patting her hands, putting one of her own sweet-smelling handkerchiefs to Isobel's face.

Martyn sat at her other side; "You are too crying, Izzy. I am sorry. So sorry. Robert wrote me that Fa wants to see us all, one last time."

"No!" exclaimed Aunt Richter, in righteous indignation. "To travel at this time is not possible. I forbid, so will Dolphchen, and Doctor Herff will certainly not approve. Not until afterwards!" she continued, more in German than her usual scrambled German and English.

"Can you . . . is it possible to delay for some few weeks? Until I am recovered and can travel?" Isobel ventured at last, which elicited another water-spout of indignation from Aunt Richter. The baby would need her, it was dangerous traveling with an infant – here Aunt Richter began to weep herself – and exhausting to travel with the children. Dirt, discomfort, bad water, all dangerous for a new mother, a baby, small children; no, Aunt Richter insisted again that Dolph would forbid such a journey.

Now Jack Sutcliffe sighed, and pulled one of the light little side chairs so that he could sit, facing them all. "Little Cousin Isobel," he said patiently, "We can delay only a little. Even if . . ." he cleared his throat, "your foal drops tonight, we must still be in New York in a fortnight to catch the packet steamer. I don't think it will be possible or advisable for you to accompany us now. Later, perhaps; all of you, or just your husband and yourself; yes, that is a possibility. Look to travel in a month's time. Uncle Robert is as stubborn as a commissariat mule. He'll make it his duty to hold on. It's not that far a journey, these days." Jack's calm and reasonable tones were more comforting than anything. At last Isobel dried her eyes on Aunt Richter's sodden handkerchief. "I'll speak to my husband," she said. "And will you stay long in San Antonio? At least a few days, long enough for you to meet the girls. I so want to show them off to Fa! We had thought of visiting England next year." That reminder nearly sent her weeping again; Fa was the best part of Acton. Their older brother Robert was only a pale shadow of him. Without Fa, there existed no real reason to return, other than her own sentimental fondness for the folk of Acton and the fields around Upton. "We will sort something out," she said at last, resolving to speak to Dolph as soon as he returned from the ranch. Surely he would see the urgency.

Martyn and Jack stayed but a few days, long enough for Maggie and Caro to become guardedly acquainted with their young uncle. But the urgency of returning to England drew them; within three days they had taken the train to Galveston, not waiting for Dolph to come from the ranch. Isobel took her leave from them in the hallway of the Richter's mansion, already feeling the pangs of childbirth, while Aunt Richter fluttered around her like a nervous nursemaid.

It went much more easily this time; which relieved Isobel no end. Dr. Herff, when summoned had no need of his metal instruments, and the child came easily; not a boy, to Isobel's disappointment, but another girl. The baby was of a good size, pink and healthy, with hair that curled in loose pale-brown ringlets.

Aunt Richter beamed with fond pleasure. "She looks like my little Grete," she observed. "What shall you call her?"

"I'm not sure," Isobel answered. "I was certain this one was a boy, so we never considered any girl's names. I so wanted a son for Dolph." Aunt Richter patted her cheek, with her lavishly be-ringed fingers. "Matters little," she answered. "There will be more. I will send Dolphchen to you. He has been smoking in the study with Hansi for many hours, waiting for the dear little one."

When he came to her, bearing the faint scent of pipe-tobacco smoke on his clothes, she was too wearied to say very much. The baby slept in her arms, blissfully content. Dolph already knew of Martyn's visit and purpose for it; Aunt and Uncle Richter had probably told him everything.

"We must go to England, at once that I am recovered," she whispered. "I must see Fa, this once and last time." She thought that a tremor of grief or something like it passed over his features. "We'll see what can be done," he said in a manner meant to be soothing, but which she later realized was calculated not to promise anything. "Go to sleep, Bell. We'll work out something in the morning."

Impatient to begin the journey, Isobel thought of nothing else for days, but there did not seem to be a good time to talk to Dolph about departing for

England, although she discussed it with Lottie, Aunt Richter and Mrs. Becker. The ladies were sympathetic, Aunt Richter especially; but all three were horrified at the thought of her traveling with a new baby and the girls, all the way to England in the winter. She did go as far as to study the train and steamship schedules, and consider what to pack for herself and the children, assuming that her husband would readily agree to a departure in the first week of December. She put it to Dolph over breakfast, the first morning that she could rise from bed and come downstairs unaided. He heard her out, frowning slightly and crumbling the biscuit that he had been spreading with jam. They were alone in the dining room; everyone else had already gone on with the business of the day. The baby slept peacefully in her cradle and her sisters were with Lottie and Mrs. Becker in the guest cottage at the bottom of the garden.

"No. I can't leave now, not until Sam returns. It's a serious business, Bell. I would if I could, but it's not possible until March at least."

"We can't wait until March," Isobel was taken back. "Martyn and Jack told me that Fa is most desperately ill. He's my father, Dolph! I have to see him one last time."

"Why?" Dolph's biscuit dissolved into crumbs. His countenance was as stern and hard as a soldier. Likely he had the same expression when he and Cuz Peter hanged the Whitmire rustlers. "Do you think you especially privileged, Bell – to make a long journey only to say goodbye to a father? Do you think he loved you any less or more, that you will bid farewell in the same room or from half the world away? Death doesn't always come with a warning, Bell!"

"As you were not so privileged as to bid farewell, I am to be deprived of my own chance?" Isobel snapped, utterly overwrought by nerves. "I'll take the girls, hire a companion and go myself!"

"No, you will not," her husband's voice was low but absolute in determination. "I'll not have my children under the authority of your mother in that damned great barracks of a house for god knows how many months. She had her wretched claws stuck so deep into you, but I'm damned if let her have anything to do with Maggie and Caro, let alone the baby. Your mother is a venomous snake but if you like the taste of poison, that's your business."

"I'll go alone!" Isobel cried. "I'll leave the girls with Aunt Richter!"

"Then don't bother to come back to Texas," Dolph answered, in a tone so cold that it felt to Isobel as if he had struck her with his open hand. She dropped into her chair, staring at him in breathless disbelief.

"You can't mean that," she gasped.

"Every word." He took another biscuit and began spreading butter on it. His very composure provoked Isobel to higher fury.

"I despise you!" Her voice shook. "I wish that we had never married, that I had never come here, that Fa had withheld his permission!"

"Well, he didn't and you did," Dolph answered evenly. "Bit late for regrets now." He crammed half a biscuit into his mouth and rose from the table. "Do what you like, Bell. I have to meet someone at the Menger." The door of the dining room closed on him. Isobel burst into tears. *What has just happened? Why did I say such perfectly horrible things to him*? Why is he so adamant about the children and Mama's influence? He had never liked Lady Caroline; he had certainly dropped several mild remarks to that effect during the time they had been married. Isobel didn't much like her mother either, especially compared to Aunt Richter. She mopped her eyes on the table napkin in her hand, and composed herself. Upstairs, the baby slept quietly in the old cradle, her pink little fists curled like the petals of Aunt Richter's chrysanthemums. For lack of any other ideas for a name, Mrs. Becker had suggested Elizabeth Helene, after some dear friends of hers. After some consideration, Isobel thought the names fitted her youngest daughter as if especially woven for her, so Lizzie Helene it would be. Contemplating the sleeping infant, Isobel felt like bursting into tears again. No, she couldn't leave her children, not for love of Fa, or anyone. They held her heart in their dear, chubby little hands.

"Goodbye, Fa," she whispered, and fell onto the bed. "Dearest darling Fa – forgive me. I cannot come to your side. My husband made the choice plain." Memories of her childhood flooded over her, of those precious times spent with her father, in the hunting field, the stables and the kennels. She saw herself; a plump child with skinned knees and often rather grubbier than a young lady should be, following after her father – who had never in all of his life spoken a harsh word to his youngest daughter. She wept into the pillow for a long time, until exhaustion pulled her into sleep again.

She did not go downstairs for supper that evening, but pled exhaustion to retire to bed early. When Dolph came up to bed, she pretended to be asleep, although he touched her shoulder gently and whispered, "Bell, darlin' – are you awake?" She held still and didn't answer. She remained awake long after his breathing settled into the quiet rhythm of sleep. In the morning she didn't speak to him; her resentment and grief still slumbering like a volcano underneath a placid surface. It was easy enough to avoid speaking to him at all, save when he spoke to her directly, since the baby Lizzie Helene absorbed so much of her interest. And on the second day, he went back to the ranch, saying nothing of his reasons. His kiss on her cheek felt cold, a mere formality and a show.

"I'll go straight from there to Cuz's for Christmas," he said quietly. "Will you be there, Bell?"

"I don't know," she answered, curt and cold – thinking that such an indefinite answer would be a torment to him. She wished to savage his assurance and his peace of mind at least as much as hers had been made a misery.

"Do whatever you wish, Bell darlin'," was all he said, as he put on his hat and strode out of the entryway. She heard the hoof beats of his horse diminishing on the gravel drive and felt nothing in particular – but old Mrs. Becker was looking at her from the parlor doorway with an expression of shrewd sympathy on her face.

"Tell me, Isobel; what has happened between you and my son?"

"Nothing," Isobel replied. Her mother-in-law only looked skeptical and snorted. "Nothing? Yes, I can see that. I am not a fool; you have been stepping around each other like two dogs about to begin fighting. What has my son said or done which has set such a barrier between you?"

"He forbade me to leave for England with my daughters," Isobel said. To her secret horror, her voice choked. She feared she might burst into tears again. This was not the time. "To see my father, likely on his deathbed; it is Fa's wish to see us all. Your son forbade it; why I don't know. He won't permit the children to go with me. He said if I go alone, I should not bother with coming back. Then I said some cruel things to him. Why cannot I see my father one last time? To go to my own home . . ."

"It is not your home, Daughter Isobel," Mrs. Becker's tone was as dry as dust. "Your home is, if not the ranch, then wherever your husband is. Your father is dear to you. That is plain and also right, but there are things that you should know about my son, things that he would not have told you. He doesn't. That is his way. Which is sad for you, but to understand would perhaps help you." She came to a swift decision. "Come; sit with me in the parlor . . . no, not this one. Mine, in the cottage."

Obediently, Isobel followed her mother-in-law out onto the terrace, down the wide stone stairs and across the sweep of lawn to the cottage. This was the bright-painted guest house where Mrs. Becker and Lottie often stayed; a tiny refuge of their own. Next to the Richter mansion, it looked like a children's play house, perched among the trees at the edge of the green and rush-lined river. Isobel had visited often, usually only as far as the parlor or Lottie's bedroom next to it. Now Mrs. Becker courteously gestured Isobel to a chair. For a brief moment, she vanished into an adjoining room, returning in a moment with a framed daguerreotype in her hands. She held it carefully, as if it were something precious. "Did my son ever say anything of his father to you?" She asked and gave the daguerreotype into Isobel's hands. "This is he as he was, when first we met."

Isobel looked down at the faded sepia features; a young man with hair so fair that it looked almost white, who sat stiffly with a long rifle across his lap. He wore a fringed leather coat, over an old-fashioned high collar and stock; his features eerily resembled Dolph's, but there was an elusive sweetness in the pictured expression.

"The resemblance is very marked," Isobel ventured at last. "Knowing nothing else, I would have said they were twins. My husband said little of him; only that he was a soldier and killed during the war."

"He was a soldier, yes," Mrs. Becker nodded. "But not in that war." She took daguerreotype back and looked at the pictured face with sorrowful affection. "So many battles he fought in and survived! I know the names of some, but they do not make any sense to me, nor would they to you. And many – against the wild Comanche – have no name at all, although they were hard-fought and valorous. When I married him, he had forsworn war, having had enough of it. He took the land that he had for service, we married, and the fates allowed us fourteen years of happiness in which our children, all but the last, were born. But when the War Between the States came upon us – he chose to stand aside. It broke his heart in some way, I think. He could not countenance defending slavery, but he had many dear friends on either side, and in any case," Mrs. Becker chuckled with a complete lack of humor, "Our ranch was then on the frontier! The wild Indians raided as they pleased, not heeding the peace treaty that Mr. Meusebach had arranged with them, with my husband's assistance, I may add. He saw that it was his proper place to stay and do what he could to protect us. And so they came for us one night."

"Who came?" Isobel asked, hardly daring to breathe. She had wondered on this matter now and again. *What happened to Dolph's father? Apparently it was not a simple matter of death in battle like Cousin Peter Vining's brothers, but something more complicated.*

"The hanging band," Dolph's mother answered. Her countenance was for one moment a Niobe, weeping in an unceasing fountain for her children. This woman's tears were for a husband and Isobel recalled those gravestones in a tiny corner of the orchard below the ranch house. Yes, the folk of the distant ranches were buried on the property, a circumstance which she had considered only a local peculiarity until now. "They came on an evening and my husband opened the door to them, thinking that it was a friend who knocked, but they took him away after ransacking the house. Dolphchen was the age of thirteen; Sam was nine. They took my husband prisoner. They said he was under arrest for the crime of being a Union man, but they did not allow him to say a private farewell to us. He bid me to be happy and look after our children. Then they took him away. Their leader," Mrs. Becker added in stoic tones, "then struck me on the face with his fist, which had a pistol in it. I was rendered senseless for many hours. When I came too . . . Dolphchen had gone on one of our horses to get help from our nearest neighbors and seek out where his father had been taken. Sam took a pistol and sat in the window, guarding us all through that long night while Dolphchen went in search of his father."

"What happened then?" Isobel whispered, although she knew very well how this had turned out; a loving father dead, his children scarred with memories. Her mother-in-law's countenance remained stoic, as a Roman matron contemplating the ruin of all.

"The body of my husband was brought back to us the next day in the back of a wagon," Mrs. Becker replied. "He freed his hands and attempted to escape but was shot for this temerity. My son was never the same after this. He loved his father. From then on, he took no counsel but his own. Two years later, without a word said to us, he joined with Colonel Ford's border regiment . . . a secession man, fighting for the Confederates!"

"But wasn't Dolph also for the Union?" Isobel asked, much puzzled. Mrs. Becker chuckled again, short and humorless as before. "It was a complicated matter, Daughter Isobel. Any man of an age to fight had choices to make, all of them bad. It is a matter best not spoken of now. We must live together and do business with all of those who made other choices. If it is not on our lips, the memory is in our heart always. I believe that my son is deeply grieved by the news of your father but that is something he would never tell you."

"But if he truly understands, he would allow me to travel to England," Isobel answered, and her mother-in-law shook her head.

"No, he will not – nor will he explain his reasons. It is not his way. But I believe he thinks he is protecting you and the children."

"I don't understand," Isobel was honestly baffled. "I believed that he liked and respected my father. He encouraged us to marry, although my mother –" She recalled Dolph's angry words about Lady Caroline being a venomous snake. *Might that be it?* "My mother was exceeding cold towards him . . . although his manner towards her gave no grounds for reproach. I did not think he held a dislike for my mother."

"He does not," Mrs. Becker's answer was crisp, assured. "He merely despises her. He thinks her cruel and unnatural. He told me once, of how she permitted your governess beat you so that you still have scars. Oh, yes – I have seen them and I could not stop myself from sharing his feelings. He told me how he swore to you that he would keep you safe . . . and I believe he means to keep that promise. He treasures the children above all. No," Mrs. Becker shook her head. "He will not permit your children to have anything to do with your mother – even if it costs your affection towards him."

Chapter 26 – *News of a Distressing Nature*

The fatal telegram arrived two days before Christmas, at Cousin Peter's sprawling house in Austin. Isobel had begun to fret guiltily because her husband had not yet arrived – while she and the whole Richter ménage had come safely and comfortably by train, some ten days before Christmas. They had traveled in the luxury of Uncle Richter's parlor car with Aunt Richter in affectionate attendance on the girls.

"She has been most eager to travel this year," Lottie whispered, as they entrained at the Austin Street main station. "Once there were days, months even, when she could not be coaxed to set foot outside, or even come from her room. But she does love your daughters – she adores children."

"Children are small and biddable," Isobel answered. "Auntie Richter spoils them with affection – and they adore her. She would never consider a harsh punishment, no matter what."

It comforted Isobel to wrap herself in Aunt Richter's unquestioning affection, after her talk with Mrs. Becker on the morning that Dolph had taken himself off. There was someone in the world, not judging her harshly or telling her of matters that she had no idea of how to reckon with. When Anna Vining tapped on the door of her room that morning, Isobel thought first that it was because there was a message from Dolph.

"You should come downstairs to the parlor," Anna's face was unnaturally grave. "There is a telegram for you. From England. I think it is bad news."

"It would be, if it's a telegram," Isobel gasped. She gathered her skirts in one one hand and fairly ran down the stairs, heedless of ladylike dignity. In the Vining's comfortable, elegant parlor, her mother-in-law waited for her with Aunt and Uncle Richter hovering protectively.

"This was just been delivered to the house," Uncle Richter's voice was heavy, as if he already knew the contents of the little brown telegraph office's envelope. Aunt Richters' eyes were already welling up with tears. "You had best sit down." He guided her to the divan where Aunt Richter already sat and put the envelope into her hand; it was not sealed. She opened it with shaking fingers and read the few words printed neatly on the slip of paper within.

FA PASSED TO GLORY ETERNAL 22 INST STOP. LETTER FOLLOWS STOP. SO SORRY STOP M STOP.

Isobel had steeled herself against such news for weeks. Having it incontrovertibly in her hand still came as a hard blow. She handed the paper silently to her mother-in-law. "I could not have journeyed there in time," she said; her voice sounding flat and dull in her own ears. "Even if I had gone when I wished to."

"I am sorry, Daughter Isobel. I know your presence would have meant much to you and a comfort to your father. But it was not possible." Mrs. Becker's voice was as kind as always. Isobel wondered if they were humoring her. She was numb at the thought of Fa, no longer in this world but passed to glory eternal. It didn't seem right, somehow. She could still hear his voice in her ears, close her eyes and see him in his scruffy, smoke-aged study, or out and about on horseback, trailed by his favorite wolfhounds. She wrung her hands together. "I wish now that my husband would be here. He said that his business would not permit us to travel to England at this time, and . . ." Abruptly, she was aware of Uncle Richter and Mrs. Becker exchanging a look and Uncle Richter looking perfectly thunderous. "What is the matter? Has something happened to him?" She demanded in sudden alarm. Uncle Richter made an effort to banish the dark expression from his countenance. "No, nothing has happened to Dolphchen, but that scamp young Samuel, has decided that the cattle business is not good enough for him. He has written us, saying that he wishes to be an artist! Such ideas as he got for himself now, I wish that we had never consented to his studying in Paris. Now he fancies that he can make a living at it."

"I think he can," Isobel moved to defend Sam, in spite of Uncle Richter's scowl and a quick warning shake-of-the-head from Mrs. Becker. "He is a very talented painter."

"Talent doesn't put food on the table," Uncle Richter rumbled, at his most magisterial. "I knew some of those artistic fellows, back before the war in Live Oak. Poor chaps; couldn't make a living at anything. Finally had to go back to trade. I thought Sam had more sense," he added to the senior Mrs. Becker. "More fool him. But this leaves Dolphchen with much more responsibilities . . . he may not be able to join us here for another week or so. He writes that thinks of going to Galveston to meet Sam and try and talk him out of this nonsense."

Isobel opened her mouth; no, Sam likely wouldn't be talked out of it, but it was useless to try and convince Uncle Richter of this. Instead she said, "I would that my husband were here now."

"I am sure that he thinks of you often," Uncle Richter answered. "And wishes to be at your side but it cannot be helped. Cows, weather and hired men take no care for what a wife may say."

"I thought he had married me, not the cows and hired men!" Isobel's tears spilled over. Aunt Richter put an arm around her and snapped something in angry German to her husband. "I said some horrible things to him," Isobel added, between sobs. "Things that I am sorry for saying now. I don't blame him for staying away from us!"

"Then you should write to him," Mrs. Becker advised and Isobel thought again with remorse of how she had spoken to Dolph and turned coldly away from. How terribly childish of her; it would serve her right, if he had decided to end any kind of intimacy and to be married to her in name only, like any number of Society couples in England that she had heard rumors about. *But he loves Maggie and Caro*, she thought – *Surely he would not stay away for long! How long could Dolph spin out the excuse of business matters?*

"I will do that," she said at last, wishing wretchedly that it could all have been again as it was in summer at the Becker ranch. What an idyll that had been! She made her excuses to Aunt Richter and Mrs. Becker, and went upstairs to write that letter.

Austin, Texas
December 22, 1878

My dear husband . . . I have begun this letter several times over, so please excuse any blots or crossed out words and lines. First I must tell you that we received a telegram this morning from my brother Martyn, informing me that my most dear father has entered that eternal sleep, so there is now no need of a long journey to be at his side and receive his final blessing. My brother promised a letter to follow, containing all the particulars. I presume that according to custom, the final rites will be held at the church in Upton, which you may well remember from the celebration of our nuptials. I do not feel any particular need to travel Home, knowing that all will be done as custom dictates long before we would ever arrive. For now, I would sooner keep my memories of Acton simple and unaltered, with dearest Fa a living presence within its walls.

I must also apologize from the bottom of my heart for those thoughtless words spoken to you in hasty inconsideration. I was in such distress at the news received from my brother and Major Sutcliffe that I could give no thought to your feelings, or indeed to your fears for myself and for our children, and so spoke so rashly. I was often chided for speaking so impetuously as a child and I fear that the years have made no improvement to my tongue. I would give nearly anything to have unsaid them, for your sake and for the sake of our children.

Caro and Maggie long for your return; they will need your presence as their father far more than I had reason to be with my dear Fa in his last hours. Please say that you forgive me,

Isobel

* * *

Isobel labored over that letter and mailed it the following day, wondering when and where it would finally reach her husband, and if it would have any effect in the least upon him. When her feelings of remorse became too heavy to bear in silence, she sought reassurance from Lottie and Mrs. Becker, some days after a rather somber Christmas celebration.

"He has not answered my letter, or came to Austin as he promised he would," she confessed, wretchedly. "I don't know what to think. Might he still be so angry with me that he will not consider any apology at all?"

"Dolph – oh, never!" Lottie answered in perfect confidence. "He is the kindest of brothers – he would never carry a grudge, not for hasty words, anyway." Her mother frowned, deep in consideration.

"I do not like to think that he would," she ventured. "He is my son, after all. But as I said before; he does not speak of those matters closest to his heart, or even set them to paper. All the time that he was with Colonel Ford, I think we had three letters. To be fair," she added, "He might have written – just that everything was so unsettled by war and letters were few for lack of paper."

"I never had more than a brief note, several times, when we were courting," Isobel admitted and Lottie giggled. "That would be my brother! Now Seb wrote to me once a week, sometimes more – although there isn't anything new in most of his letters. 'Three strayed cows found today,' 'weather most threatening,' and 'burgoo again for supper, not quite as vile as usual.'"

"Dolphchen does not waste paper with trivialities," Mrs. Becker said, as if in austere disapproval. "No, Daughter Isobel – I think there may be more to bother my son than a grudge held over hasty words. It was in the paper some days ago. Lottie, this may be of concern to Sebastian, so I share this news with you . . . there was an escape from the prison in Fort Smith some weeks ago. The men who escaped were all convicted of crimes. One eluded capture for a long time. There was a body found later, much decayed in the river which they thought might be his . . . Randall Whitmire. But they could not be entirely certain."

"The old man?" Isobel gasped; she still shivered to recall the grey-haired man she and Seb met by chance, riding along the road to the Palo Duro ranch. She had been right to sense menace in him. Mrs. Becker nodded, while Lottie looked grave.

"Seb mentioned a rustler gang in one of his letters; that there might be a danger to Dolph and Cuz, while they were at large."

"Yes, that was the Whitmire gang," Isobel answered, with another shiver, remembering the warning brought to them by the mysterious Mr. Swain. "The old man was a criminal with a reputation of darkest hue. I don't think there was a law of God or man which he had not broken. Is there a chance he might be alive?"

"He is only one man and old," Lottie said, much relieved. "How much can one man do, alone?"

"You would not want to know what a single man full of malice is capable of doing." Mrs. Becker looked as bleak as she had on the day when she told Isobel what had really happened to Dolph's father. "Dolphchen, Cousin Peter, even your Seb, may need to guard themselves and walk warily. But if Randall Whitmire is still alive, he will need to walk warily also. Hansi has sent out inquiries to Fort Smith in an effort to find an answer. If you have no letter from your husband, or from Seb," she nodded at each of them. "It may be they have matters of more immediate concern."

"I hope so," Isobel answered. She still felt wretchedly ashamed of her coldness towards her husband and hoped for any sign or word of forgiveness from him. "I shall return to San Antonio with you and Aunt Richter. Such a wretched tangle, I hardly know what to think."

"Then that is your proper welcome to Texas," Mrs. Becker replied dryly. Lottie exclaimed, "Mama, you should not say such things!"

"Why not – since they are the truth?" Mrs. Becker reposted. Isobel wondered if she were correct. *What would Fa have thought of all this?*

Not having received any word from Dolph, she returned with the Richters to San Antonio after Christmas. She hoped that he might be waiting for here there, but instead there was a thick letter with English stamps and postmarks, addressed to her in handwriting that was familiar, but not Fa's or Martyn's. After a moment, she decided that it must be Mr. Aubrey's hand; Fa's estate agent, secretary, and man of business. She opened it carefully, wishing that it had been from Fa – which it was, in a way.

December 19th, 1878
Acton Hall, Oxfordshire

Dear madam; I have taken down this communication from Sir Robert, as he was too enfeebled by illness to write to you himself. His final decline came with little warning, but he knew before any of us attending on him that his mortal end was near. He regretted very much that he could not take pen in hand himself, or live to witness your eventual happy return to Acton with your children, as he had hoped upon your marriage. Receipt of your letters and daguerreotypes of your infant daughters provided him with much pleasure during his final months, a circumstance which he remarked upon frequently. Let me take this opportunity to convey to you my own deepest condolences. Sir Robert was not only a generous patron and employer; I flatter myself that he was a friend as well. The following was dictated to me on the afternoon of the 19th instant, when I visited at his request.

Darling Pet; Martyn and Jack arrived this morning, bearing news of their call on you at Richter's abode in San Antonio, whilst on their way home to England to attend on this old and decrepit builder of bridges and roads. Do not regret for a moment that you were unable to accompany them; your duty is to your children, to all of them – little Caro and Margaret and the one whose name is yet unknown to me. My prayer is that you have the pleasure of seeing them grow to a womanly estate; women of spirit, accomplished and beloved by all – the very same pleasure which I derived as your father from observing you. However it cannot be denied that your mother partook little of that pleasure, for which I feel more regret than I can ever express. Your mother possesses many fine qualities and never failed to bring honor to my name and title, in every sphere save one. She took less and less joy in children, suffering increasingly in every confinement and for some months afterwards. She was most particularly afflicted following your birth. So wretched was her condition that doctors advised that you be given over entirely to the care of wet-nurses, while your mother recovered her health. To this day I believe this was the reason for her oft-demonstrated coldness towards you, which I did my best to alleviate. Pet, my sole regret is that I did not do more to repair the misery which I know this lack of proper motherly affection caused for you. I am content to know that at least I managed to secure you some portion of happiness in permitting you to marry, when all others expressed doubts of Mr. Becker's fitness and sincerity. Indeed, I thought it fortunate that this marriage would remove you from England and afford a means of escaping the demands which our family's station pressed upon you. Each of your many letters confirmed to me that you had attained such happiness and content as I had hoped that you would on your wedding day.

Darling Pet, farewell for now. Do not torment yourself with regrets.

Your loving Fa

Through her tears, Isobel could barely make out Sir Robert's barely legible scrawl of a signature. Mr. Aubrey had appended a brief note.

Sir Robert also directed me to amend his final will and testament, which included a behest to you in the form of the freehold of a small residence near Upton, with grounds and outbuildings, etc., so that in the event that you wish a return to England, you will have the means of maintaining an independent establishment for yourself, your husband and the children. There are tenants in it at present, so under the terms of his will, rents for that property will accrue to you. Until you desire to take up residence yourself, or I am in receipt of other instructions I am most happy to continuing as your agent with regard to this property. Again, my own deepest condolences, etc., etc.

Thomas Aubrey, Esq.

Isobel wiped her streaming eyes and read it over several times more, with a taste like ashes in her mouth. A little residence of her own, near Upton . . . well, she had it, but she couldn't really say that she wanted it. This would give her a place to go with the children, if she chose to leave Texas entirely – but doing so would feel like defeat.

The wagon dray dispatched from Comfort by Mrs. Becker – from Mutti Magda, as Jane called her – arrived in Houston Street on a mid-week in January; Jane hurried from the Lockhart's little house on Pecan Street, where she had been staying with Will and Ellen, on receipt of a message from the driver. The upstairs rooms over Mr. Knauer's workroom and furniture shop had been scoured and swept clean, made ready for those small items of furniture and Sam's own possessions. Jane could not yet move in; Houston Street was a busy and commercial part of town and she had already been warned that a respectable woman could not live there alone without harm to her reputation. Jane was sensitive to those opinions, having skated so close to danger in posing for Sam to paint and thereby earning Mrs. Amelia's spiteful regard. She waited on Sam's return and in lieu of rent had accepted some tables and chairs, a dresser and a bedstead from the downstairs tenant; items which Mr. Knauer had readily admitted had been either slow to sell, or bespoke and subsequently refused or refused payment for. The upstairs rooms so sparsely furnished, still appeared airy and open to Jane, long accustomed to servant's quarters and the tiny rooms over the shop in Didcot. *I must not have been so long in America, that this place would seem grand to me,* she thought to herself.

The drayman grumbled when she told him that all the contents of the wagon must be carried upstairs to count as truly delivered. There was space in the big room at the front to unload the crates, open them and to take out the smaller things. Mr. Knauer detailed one of his apprentices to assist; Jane decided that it must have been from courtesy and not that he was expecting another deduction from the rent.

The drayman brought several boxes of books and a trunk of clothes. Jane took particular pleasure in sorting them out and putting them away. They smelled faintly of verbena, camphor, and lavender, and now and again of the bay balm that she particularly associated with Sam. By the time she finished, afternoon sunlight sent long golden fingers across the city. In the room that would be Sam's studio, Jane sat before the wide un-curtained windows that looked one way towards to the back of the city lot; and the other to the stand of rushes and cottonwood saplings marking the river-edge. There would be plenty of light in this room, all the day long, for Sam to paint. She hoped he would like the building and the situation. His latest letter crackled in the pocket of her apron. He had written it from Cherbourg, waiting for the weekly steam packet; by now he would be nearly to New York. Another week would see him in Galveston where his Richter cousins would meet him on the dock. Jane felt quite overwhelmed; their long separation was nearly over. Sam did not plan to linger there, but come straight away on the train. Jane already planned what she would wear to meet him. The only fly in the ointment was that upon arrival, Sam must make clear his intention of independence from the family business. Jane dreaded the fireworks which would erupt from the Baron and Sam's brother.

At last, she took off her apron, hanging it in the kitchen with a feeling of proud possession. She took down her hat and settled it on her head for the walk back across town towards Pecan Street. She locked the outside door and stayed for a moment, looking down at the busy, dusty street outside; wagons, men on horseback passing up and down. The bustle pleased her very much.

She started down the stairway to the sidewalk, when someone called out to her from the street.

"Oi! Miss G!" Jane looked around, confused; that could be no other voice but Alf Trotter, but no one there on the street looked in the least like him. One of the horsemen took off his hat, waving at her. "Over 'ere, Miss G!" Jane was rendered speechless with disbelief. Could that wiry, sun-burnt cowhand possibly be the skinny and feral street urchin that Mr. Becker had brought from London? He was dressed in the rough working clothes of a wrangler or a drover, with the customary open-collared shirt and bright handkerchief tied around his throat . . . also the customary adornment of a pair of revolvers on his belt. Now he slid down from the saddle of his horse with the grace of an otter sliding down a creek bank, an ear-to-ear grin lighting up his face. "I thought it was you, Miss G! Put 'er here!" He bowed over her hand, plainly happy beyond all measuring to see her. "I didn' think to see yer in Santone – thought you was school-teachering in Austin."

"I was," Jane answered, "but I got married."

"O-er!" he exclaimed. "No surprise, Miss G; oo's the lucky chap?" Jane hesitated for a brief moment; may as well reveal it now. "Mr. Samuel Becker."

Alf's eyes rounded, for once rendered quite speechless. "Sir's brother – Miss G, that's a turn-up an' no mistake."

Jane thought she might as well give away the rest of it. "He's going to set up as an artist when as he returns. This is where we're going to live." Alf whistled in wordless astonishment. "I heard summat. Sir ain't happy."

"No, I don't suppose that he is," Jane agreed. "But this is what my husband and I have planned and agreed upon to do together."

Alf squinted at her. Jane realized that he had grown taller since departing from England with her on the *Wieland*; healthier and filled out from eating better food and hard work in the open air. But he still looked young for his age; likely he would always remain undersized.

"Serious, Miss G? Good fortune you came wi' 'er ladyship, innit?"

"Yes it was, Alf," she answered. Alf frowned. "I don't go by that now, Miss G. Them as are my friends call me Tom. I were baptized Thomas Alfred. A bit ago, I ast Sir would he mind if I called myself Becker, too. Everyone said I was like a shadow to Sir; all roun' the RB, they call me Becker's boy, 'r that Becker kid an' all."

"What did he say to that?" Jane thought it sounded dreadfully presumptuous of Alf, but apparently Americans took a more indulgent view towards those who wished to cast off the rags of their old selves. Alf – no, Tom – appeared as worshipful as he always did at the mention of the 'Sir.'

"He smiled a bit an' he said I might as well, but that name did have enemies on that account, an' I might want to think again. But I said, any enemy of theirs' was mine as well, an' Trotter weren't nuffink to be proud of, any roads. That's why I came wi' Sir to Santone. There's maybe a man 'scaped from prison in Fort Smith, with a grudge 'gainst Sir. I been Sir's Pinkerton all this while."

"You certainly seem prepared for anything." Jane remarked, and Alf – no, Tom – proudly squared his narrow shoulders. "I am, Miss G, I am. Wash Charpentier, 'e taught me to shoot – said I had a dead-eye. They taught me some other prime tricks, too. I could be a champeen buckeroo, iff'n I wanted to practice it regular. I might at that, Miss G – Miz Becker! They were right, them as said the streets were paved w' gold! "

"It's been your good fortune too," Jane said. The boy clapped his hat on his head again and grinned. "Adios, Miz Becker – time t' mosey 'long."

"Adios, Mr. Becker," Jane returned with equal formality. "Tell . . . your 'Sir' that we shall be at home and receiving calls sometime early in March." He nodded an acknowledgement, then swung up onto his horse and rode away down Houston Street towards the plaza of the old citadel with an outlandish whoop and at a fast trot. Jane looked after him until he was lost in the crowd.

Isobel put the letter from Mr. Aubrey with Fa's dictation away in her jewel-case, along with the papers concerning the freehold which Mr. Aubrey enclosed. She was not entirely certain what she ought to do now, although Aunt Richter was blissfully incurious and un-judgmental about Isobel and her daughters remaining with them. Little Elizabeth Helene was a love of a baby; rosy, placid and plumb, but her sisters were loudly disappointed in her. They wanted ready playmate and missed the company of their cousin Rose, Peter and Anna's youngest.

"She is only a baby, yet," Isobel explained one morning, which dawned fair and pleasant, not a bit like February in England. Maggie's expression reflected crushing disappointment. "But we want to play now!" Maggie said and Isobel sighed.

"Darling, then I will show you how to play at hoops on the lawn." Maggie's expression brightened instantly. Isobel fetched out the bent ash-wood hoops and sticks from among the tangle of children's toys left here and there on the verandah overlooking the lawn between the mansion and the play-house wooden gingerbread of the cottage by the river-bank. She left Elizabeth Helene sleeping in her pram in the shade of the rose arbor that was the centerpiece of Aunt Richter's garden, and began showing the girls how to trundle the hoop, urging it along with deft use of the stick. They shrieked happily, romping up and down the lawn, trying to keep the hoops rolling. Isobel ran with them until she was breathless, feeling unaccountably happy. She loved watching Caro and Maggie run, their neatly-shod feet in high-buttoned shoes twinkling through the grass, their sashes coming undone and trailing after them. They soon lost their hats. Maggie's pale straight locks and Caro's light brown curls escaped their hair ribbons. No matter what clouded Isobel's thoughts, none of that shadow fell on the girls. This realization gratified Isobel enormously. Children ought to be happy, kept safe from every peril, far from distressful imaginings and hurtful people . . . people like their grandmother, Lady Caroline. That was what Fa had tried to do, Isobel realized, but he had come about it too late. *What would my life been if Mama was affectionate and loving; everything that Aunt Richter was?* Isobel wondered. No, it didn't matter any more; the past was past and she cared not a jot. This realization gave her an enormous sense of relief, as if she had set down something too heavy for her to carry.

She collected Caro's abandoned hat from where it lay on the grass. Caro and Maggie had gotten their hoops to roll straight, almost to the border of rose bushes that lined the gravel drive. She shaded her eyes against the sun; there was a man standing there, a man in a dark town suit and wide-brimmed hat, watching the girls. Caro shrieked joyously, "Papa!" and immediately abandoned her hoop. She and Maggie raced towards their father, holding up their arms to him. Maggie reached him first; he swung her up to his shoulder laughing, while Caro launched herself at his knees. Isobel followed more sedately, her heart in her throat. The girls were ecstatic. With an effort, Isobel kept her own expression serene. Over her daughter's small fair heads, she met his level gaze. She didn't know what to say, but he spared her the effort.

"So you stayed," he remarked with mild surprise.

"Of course," she answered. "Shouldn't I have? This is our home." She took Caro from him, and balanced the child on her hip. "Well, not here, exactly – I meant the ranch."

"I did wonder," he observed and kissed her very gently on the cheek. Inside, Isobel went limp with relief.

"I sent you a letter to explain," she said and he looked puzzled.

"I never got it. Guess I was moving around too much."

"I wrote that I was sorry," Isobel began. He smiled, lifting Maggie to his shoulder as she squealed with excitement at being up so high.

"It doesn't matter," he said. "I spoke too hasty myself, Bell."

From Hansi Richter's study window, unseen from outside, Hansi Richter and Magda Becker silently observed the familial reunion. Magda blew out her breath, hardly aware that she had been holding it. "That's a relief," she observed.

Hansi nodded agreement. "Lise was beside herself with worry. Every day she was afraid that little Isobel would pack herself and the children back to England. Dolphchen would have let them go without a murmur, too. Stubborn lad!"

"The problem is that they did it all backwards," Magda said.

Her brother-in-law looked at her with an eyebrow raised in puzzlement. "Explain."

"They married," Magda answered. "The usual thing is that a young lady and gentleman meet and over time become interested in each other. Like your lads, like Anna and Marie; as you and Liesel did. Then they fall in love, or begin to court, and think then of marriage. Then, poof! They marry; all else follows after that. But my son and his wife married first. I think my Dolphchen felt sorry for her at first, poor girl; a sad little songbird in a jeweled cage. And she was desperate to escape. A pity that among the Firsts, marriage is the only way to do it. Then they came to know each other and finally to fall in love, I think – I hope!"

"They'd better," Hansi observed. "There's the little ones to think of. But they look happy enough.

Chapter 27 – *The Day of Reckoning*

By dint of saying very little to the Lockharts regarding Samuel's expected arrival, Jane contrived to be alone at the G H & SA station when the afternoon train arrived. She took special care with her dress and her person that morning, fastening the little pink cameo at her throat with a feeling like butterflies fluttering in her stomach. *This is the day.* She looked at herself in the mirror, as she pinned her hat to her carefully-arranged hair and saw that her eyes looked huge in a pale face. That wouldn't do – she pinched her cheeks to bring out a shade of pink to them and bit her lips to the same effect. There, that was better. She told Ellen Lockhart that she was going to the station to wait for the train, for Samuel was supposed to be on it.

"Give me a moment to put on my hat and I'll come as far as the station with you," Ellen offered. Jane acquiesced; she would be glad of the company. *What if Sam was not on the train today? What if?* Jane firmly disciplined her unruly doubts, those skittering thoughts which went everywhere. Of course Sam would return; he would be on the train today, although sometimes in the dead of night, Jane worried that it couldn't be true that she was married and Sam might want to remain in Paris. No, of course not; she had the letter from Cherbourg in her reticule. Perhaps Ellen sensed some of Jane's disquiet and worry, for she chattered cheerfully about other things; about the many wagons in the street, and how that part of town had grown. Once a stretch of rolling green meadows north-east of town, now it was called the Levee because of the great earthen embankment constructed to make the tracks run level. Even with the Army moving their warehouses and stores out of the city altogether, the Alamo plaza was still crowded, and lively. She and Ellen took the mule-drawn street car from the plaza in front of the crumbling old citadel chapel – another new thing which had happened in the city since Sam had gone to France. The new depot building was on Austin Street, a vast timber barn two stories tall, with a deep open veranda at the front for travelers to wait in the shade.

"Will, he says the railway is the wonder of the age!" she exclaimed. "His old grandfather came to Texas in an ox-cart, years ago – he can hardly believe it as well. Oh, the stories he tells of when he was a young man, you can hardly believe it, for many of them are so indecent. I expect that you will set up housekeeping very shortly. Which reminds me, unless you plan to keep your own cow, find a reputable dairyman to purchase milk from. Whatever you do, don't patronize that awful Bean person. He waters the milk and is quite shameless about it. There were minnows in the last pail that I had from him! When I said so, he had the gall to tell me that he'd just have to stop letting the cows drink from the river . . . well, here we are, Jane dear." she took Jane's hands in hers, very briefly and kissed her cheek. "If he is not on the train from Harrisburg today, promise me you come straight back to the house. We will take the streetcar to San Pedro Springs Park and avail ourselves of this fine day – just the two of us."

"He will be on the train," Jane insisted, realizing Ellen meant to comfort and divert her against a possible disappointment.

"Of course he will, dear girl. Bring him to the house for dinner after you show him your new home. Listen," Ellen turned her ear towards the east and listened intently for something foreign to the regular street hubble-bubble. "There's the steam whistle. The train will be here in a few minutes. I'll see you in a little while; both of you." Ellen turned and swiftly walked away. The distant train whistle shrilled again. Jane swallowed, trying to quell the butterflies, lifted her skirts against the dust and hurried toward the rambling wooden pile. She looked for a place to stand where she might be apart from the crowd, and still observe the passengers as they debarked. She pretended a calm that she did not feel, neat in a walking costume of dark blue Melton cloth that was not, for once, a hand-me-down from Lady Isobel, but purchased out of her earnings as a teacher. The noise of the engine, the screeching of iron wheels on rails drowned out all the noise from the waiting crowd on the platform – porters with barrows, small children screaming with excitement, officers in smart blue uniforms and gold braid frowning importantly as they strode back and forth.

Jane stood very still, her white-gloved hands clasped together; a cloud of dust rose from the tracks, steam leaked in spurts from every part of the huge engine. Now the passenger car doors clanged open, and men – mostly men – began emerging. None of them so far were Sam. Her heart sank a little. *Oh, this is torturous! Where is he?* She blinked away a sudden stinging in her eyes, telling herself it was only a cinder. One more man emerged from the train. Jane's heart instantly turned feather-light; Sam, dapper in European-cut clothes, his hat in one hand and a bulging carpetbag in the other. He was looking around as if searching for her. Jane moved a step or two towards the platform edge and waved – she did not dare trust her voice, but his face lit up in a blaze of happiness. She was in his arms, he in hers in the next ecstatic instant, with his carpetbag abandoned at their feet.

"Welcome home, Mr. Becker," Jane gasped when she could speak again. She drank in the sight of his face, lively, open, and affectionate and was moved to kiss him on the lips.

"That welcome is worth the whole journey," he answered, in deliberately grave tones, but there was laughter trying to escape the mock-sobriety. "I can't say how much I have missed you, Jane. Paris is a marvel. You would have loved it all."

"I think not," Jane answered. "They eat strange things there and perfectly respectable married women think nothing of taking lovers. Anyway, I had to see to a place for us to live."

"That is true," Sam sighed and kissed her again. Jane shivered at the touch of his lips on hers, the feel of his cheek; slightly bristly, as his most recent barbering had begun to wear off. She marveled again at the comfortable way that their bodies molded together. "You wrote about the building you and Miss Lizzie bought; when do I get to see it?"

"Now," Jane answered. "This very minute."

He took her hand and settled it into his elbow. "Lead on, Mrs. Becker. Was anyone else coming to the station to meet me?"

"I don't think so," Jane said, with fierce affection. "I am the only one who knew which train you would be on and I wanted you to myself just for a time and not to share you with anyone else. The Lockharts have invited us for supper tonight, though."

"We're putting off the inevitable a little longer, Jane," Sam replied with a wry smile. "I'll have to have it out with Dolph and Uncle Hansi soon. There's my trunk. Let me hire a wagon and we'll go see this place you bought for us."

"Well, what do you think of it?" Jane asked, some time later, although she knew the answer from the moment that they climbed the outside stairs and she unlocked the door. Sam dropped the carpetbag just inside the door, as she removed her hat and set it on the elaborate rack just inside the door – another bit of unsellable merchandise from Mr. Knauer.

"The show room and gallery," he said at once. This was the large and empty room which looked out over the bustle of Houston Street. Outside, the stairs creaked under the weight of the drayman and Sam's trunk, melded with some muffled curses. "Just leave it inside the door," Sam called to the drayman. "Now, show me the rest." Jane took his hand. Like children they went from room to room, with Sam's pleased approval warming Jane's heart more than any fire could on this mild spring day. His books and a few of his paintings already hung on the walls, the bed made up with clean linen sheets and covered with a fancy pieced quilt which Lizzie had pressed upon her as a bride-gift. All was clean, airy, and welcoming – and their own. As they went out into the sunny back room which overlooked the lush green riverbank and the crystal-clear depths beyond, the drayman dropped the trunk with a sullen thump and they heard the outside door slam after him. Jane paid little mind, for Sam stood before the tall un-curtained windows, the golden afternoon sunlight slanting through them and painting wavering pools of light on the floor.

"I'd almost forgotten how blue the sky is," he said presently. "And how bright the sunlight can be. I can see the back of the old Veramendi place from here. What have they done with it now – looks like a beer garden." He turned around and Jane went to his arms once more. "It's perfect, Jane, and I'm the luckiest man and most fortunate husband in the world."

"When you have a commission for a painting as big as one of those in that Louvre-place that you wrote me of," Jane said and kissed him. "Then you may call yourself a fortunate husband."

"Until then, I'll consider myself still a fortunate husband," Sam mused, his hands engaged in removing the pins from Jane's hair. "Once we give that lovely bed a try."

"It's only afternoon!" Jane demurred, although she was also thinking on that possibility and made no effort to resist. "Ellen and Will are expecting us for supper tonight."

"I'm an artist," her husband answered, as Jane's hair tumbled out of the careful arrangement she had made of it, an ink-dark cloud falling past her shoulders. "Our hours and rules are different."

As much as Jane dreaded it, she knew that she and Sam must present themselves to the Family very soon; they had a day of grace and a night of ecstatic reunion under the roof that they had every reason to call their own. They sent a message to Hansi Richter before setting off to Lockharts' that evening. They returned to the apartment on Houston Street very late, when the hustle and bustle of the street had died down. The music and merriment from Main Plaza, a short few blocks away, was just a faint and rather pleasant tantalization. They found an envelope tacked to the door. Once inside, Jane lit the parlor lamp and quietly watched for her husband to finish reading the brief note Jane recognized the handwriting; Sam's brother.

"Uncle Hansi will send a carriage for us, tomorrow afternoon at two," Sam said at last, setting down the note. His expression reflected unaccustomed unhappiness and dread. "I fear it will be rather an unpleasant interview. If you don't want to accompany me, Jane, you need not. This is between Dolph and Onkel Hansi and I."

"Certainly I will go with you,'" Jane replied. "'Entreat me not to leave you … where you go, I go also; your people are now mine and that includes your uncle."

"Good," Sam's face brightened with relief. Jane realized once again how uncomfortable it must be for him to go against his brother and his uncle; they who had been everything to him, generous and kindly in all things but one. It was easier for herself or Alf Trotter to break ties which were gossamer thin in any case.

She put on the blue walking costume again for the call on the Baron and the family. It was her best. Jane reasoned that she must have every advantage of her own confidence for herself and for her husband. If Sam needed a stiffening to his backbone, Jane would serve and gladly, too. Promptly at two, as the chimes of a nearby church rang the hour, there came a tap on the outside door. Jane already had her hat and reticule in hand.

She exchanged a brief smile with her husband and opened the door to Dolph Becker, whose brief expression of surprise was swiftly quenched. "Good afternoon, Miss Jane – and Sam. You are ready?"

"We are," Jane smiled brightly to cover the awkwardness. "You were not put to any trouble in finding our home? We mean to have a sign painted."

"You mean, Sam can't see to it?" Mr. Becker grinned and Jane answered firmly, "My husband is not that kind of painter. If all he was fit to do was paint signs, then why go to Paris?"

"I am rebuked," Mr. Becker still grinned. "And Onkel would have wasted his money. You could have stayed here and painted signs for a living, little brother." Jane thought that her husband formed some rather rude words with his lips, as if the two of them were still schoolboys. She took Sam's elbow, and they followed Dolph down the wooden staircase to the sidewalk, where a single horse buggy stood hitched to a rail, guarded by Alf Trotter – Tom, as he wanted to be called now. Tom had the reins of his own horse in hand, leaning against the post that held up the roof over the sidewalk. He watched the busy street, his young features set in grim lines, eyeing every wagon, every horseman or man on the sidewalk with suspicion.

As Sam handed Jane into the buggy, Dolph said, "Tom, you didn't have to follow. Santone is a law-abiding place and I'm safe enough."

"If you say so," Tom answered, in a tone which just missed being insubordinate. "But I say, there's many 'oos last words were, 'I'm safe

enough.'" Dolph made no answer to that, save to slap the reins on the horse's
back, and they bowled away down Houston Street in a cloud of dust.

The Richter mansion didn't look much different from the last time Jane
had been there, save that the gardens had become more extensive, almost
English in their colors and arrangements of flowering plants. Under the *porte
cochère* at the side, the Baron waited impatiently as the buggy drew in.
"Little Miss Jane!" He exclaimed gleefully, hurrying forward to assist her
down. "You return to us again and my faith in young manhood is restored!
You and young Sam, married already! My dearest Lise is distraught, deprived
of the opportunity to plan a grand wedding. She is waiting to see you in the
parlor." He kissed her on both cheeks with a great deal of relish; behind him
in the doorway, Jane saw the elder Mrs. Becker; a pale face in the shadows
and the darkness of her dress blending with it. She cast a look over her
shoulder at her husband. Thus were they being separated at the very doorway,
yet Sam looked resolute, calm.
"Go on, join the ladies, sweetheart," he murmured and Jane obeyed. She
was certain that Sam would hold his own, once he proved to his uncle's
satisfaction that he and Jane had established a means of making an
independent living; there was nothing the Baron could do or say to dissuade
them from that purpose. But Dolph might; that prospect worried Jane until
she recalled that the formidable senior Mrs. Becker held their part.
Now the older lady took her hands in hers and also kissed her with
affection. "Dear little Jane, we did not know that Sam had returned until we
received your note last night. Josef sent a telegram from Galveston, but said
nothing of Samuel's travel. That was deliberate, was it not?"
"Yes, Mutti Magda," Jane answered. "We wanted to see each other after
so long apart." Mrs. Becker led Jane into the hallway, their footsteps muffled
by the fine Turkey carpets laid on the polished wooden floor. These were parts
of the house that Jane had never spend any time in, other than briefly attending
on Isobel, two years ago.
"It is written that a man should leave his parents and having taken a wife
they should therefore be as one," Mrs. Becker observed dryly. She glanced at
Jane's dress. Seeing the cameo pinned there, she added. "I see that you have
taken the family brooch as your own also."
"It is dear to me as a token of affection from from you," Jane replied. Her
mother-in-law smiled with wintry approval. "Have no fear, little Jane," she
whispered as they went into the parlor, which was empty of people but full of
things. "We are all women here – of a family, but women." The long windows

to the verandah overlooking the lawn and garden stood open. As in that house in Galveston, the shaded verandah was transformed into a comfortable outdoor parlor, with willow-work chairs, a table, and pots of flowering geraniums lending their spicy scent to the air. Lottie was there, dandling an infant in her lap. So was her pallid cousin, the youngest Richter daughter whose name Jane always forgot, the Baron's lady in her fussy afternoon gown and hair tortured into impossibly elaborate curls . . . and Isobel.

She sprang up from a settee, abandoning the storybook and the two little girls that she had been reading it to and embraced Jane without reserve or hesitation, crying, "Jane, you have been the naughtiest and dearest girl in the world, never telling us what you and that scapegrace Samuel had done! My husband is positively distraught and Uncle Richter – well never mind! Aunt Richter is simply furious, deprived of the opportunity to host a splendid affair! I suffered through a wedding, why shouldn't you!"

"I did suffer through it," Jane answered, practically choking on her own relief and a sudden surge of affection. "I was there, remember?" Isobel pealed with laughter. "That's not what I meant, you ninny! Your own wedding; the dress, the endless plans, the horror of it all, and being afraid you would have a fainting fit, or a sudden attack of hiccups . . ."

"I was there for all of that," Jane said again. "And once was quite enough for me; all that fuss and expense. We chose to be sensible." Isobel kissed her on the cheek and embraced her again. "You ran away," she said, still laughing. "From the obligations of your class and putting on the proper display; Jane, you will never be a proper aristocrat."

"Just as well I don't want to be," Jane observed and Isobel giggled again. "Jane, you simply must pay mind to the duties of your new station . . . such as meeting my children and being a proper auntie. Girls," she added, "Come meet your Aunt Jane; she knows all about you, my darlings, although you have never met her."

The two little girls – who looked nothing alike, for all that they were the same age and dressed identically – slid down from the settee and approached cautiously. One had a bold look to her and straight fair hair, so pale it was nearly white, while her sister had a rounder face and light brown curls. Isobel must have looked like her, at the age of two or so; Jane knelt so as to see them on eye-level. "You are Margaret," she said to the fair twin. "And you are Caroline," she said to the other. "I have married your father's brother." Both girls' eyes rounded in astonishment, but only Margaret – Maggie – was bold enough to speak, while her sister looked as if she would like to suck her thumb. "You're pretty," Maggie lisped. "You have Oma's pin."

"I do," Jane agreed. "Your Oma gave it to me as a bride present."

"I like presents," Maggie confided. "We had a birfday. Onkel Hansi gave us a goat cart, but the goat ate Tante's roses."

"Bad goat," Caro whispered. Aunt Richter said something indignant in German and Lottie laughed. "Well, it was funny to see! And this is Maggie and Caro's little sister, Lizzie Helene. She's a dear little baby; I can hardly wait to have one of my own. Auntie Liesel says you have been a sly little thing, marrying Samuel in secret, but it wasn't a secret at all, since Mama and I knew. She is so angry that she won't throw one of her grand balls for you," Lottie added, impishly. Jane replied, "I thank her for her kind consideration." The Baroness laughed, so Jane knew that she wasn't really angered. She enveloped Jane in a sweet-smelling froth of ruffles, but had lost all of her English once again.

A maid brought a tray of cakes, little sandwiches, and coffee and presently Jane was sitting next to Isobel, each with a twin in her lap. Isobel and Lottie had a hundred questions about Sam's gallery and how Jane had purchased the building on Houston Street, with the assistance of Lizzie Johnson. It was as if hardly any time had passed, until Sam and Dolph appeared on the verandah, followed by the Baron. Jane did not ask what had gone on, during the meeting with his uncle and brother. As old Mrs. Becker advised, Sam would likely tell her unbidden. At least she had not heard raised voices from the Baron's study, so that was all to the good. Both Sam and his brother were in good and social spirits; Sam must have persuaded his uncle and brother of his intentions and held his own. Old Mrs. Becker had prepared the ground well. Now Jane made space on the settee for Sam to sit beside her and Maggie insisted on squeezing between them.

Presently Lottie exclaimed, "We should go and see your atelier, Sam; you must show it to us. I think I know the building, but I have never been farther down Houston Street than the Turner Hall Theater since all those new buildings went up."

"Oh, let us!" Isobel agreed. "Would you mind at all, Jane? I am simply eaten up with curiosity!"

"Not at all," Jane assured them, confident that she had left the upstairs rooms in apple-pie order. In fact, she now owned to a certain eagerness to show off the home which she had made of the tall-ceilinged rooms over the furniture store to the Becker ladies and especially for Isobel. It was time for baby Lizzie Helene's afternoon nap. The Baron and his lady declined the excursion, as did their daughter, but Mrs. Becker and Lottie eagerly agreed. The day was fair, the sky over their head speckled with cotton-white clouds;

a fine day for an excursion. They set out in the buggy; Lottie, Jane and Isobel with Caro in her lap and Mrs. Becker at the reins. Sam and his brother saddled horses from the Baron's stable, Sam laughing because he had not ridden above two or three times during his year away. Sorsha and Gawain paced regally after the buggy. Maggie, to her inexpressible delight, rode on her father's saddle bow, her hat hanging by ribbons from her neck. Isobel shook her head, laughing fondly at the sight, as they followed. "The girls adore him, Jane. I have been fortunate – although at times I doubted it."

"I was so sorry to hear of Sir Robert," Jane said. Isobel's eyes shown bright with sudden tears, until she mastered herself. "He was a very great man."

"Yes, he was," Isobel agreed. "I will go on missing his letters for a very long time. I wish that I could have taken the girls to England to meet him before the end. But I could not."

"Sam says that he took such an interest in your letters," Jane answered. "He told me that when he visited Acton, they talked for simply hours. Everything interested him, Sam says – so everyone he met thought the world of him. Perhaps you may take the children home to England when they are older."

"If my husband permits," Isobel answered. There was momentarily such a bleak expression in her eyes that Jane knew at once there was something distressing to her in mentioning the matter. She looked over her shoulder at the dogs, as they turned from the drive from the Baron's property onto the road. Another horseman followed at a little distance; young Tom, still in his self-appointed duty as Mr. Becker's 'Pinkerton' guard. Jane thought it was curious that he was still at it; surely the danger of that madman from the Oklahoma Territory must be past.

Presently, they joined the current of traffic along Commerce Street – still the main avenue into the main part of town. They crossed into the busy Alamo plaza, before the galleried façade of the Menger, the enormous dogs following close upon the buggy often being stared at with fear or admiration by those passing by in the street or on the stone and timber sidewalks. Old Mrs. Becker handled the reins deftly amidst the wheeled traffic on Houston Street. Being a newer part of town, it had been laid out by the surveyors to be much wider than the close-packed lanes around the old plazas where the square campanile towers of the San Fernando cathedral reached up above the rust-red roof-tiles huddled around it.

"This is it," Jane said as they approached the iron bridge over the river. "Upstairs from Knauer's Cabinetry." Her mother-in-law brought the buggy close to the rail for horses, before the sidewalk which connected all the storefronts along that block. She was the first from the buggy, without any assistance.

"Very nice," The senior Mrs. Becker observed, glancing into the large window which admitted light into the shop and where several of the most ornamented chairs were displayed. She stepped closer to the windows, peering inside. Over her shoulder, she asked, "Is this Knauer person acquainted with Mr. Tatsch in Fredericksburg? He does much the same kind of fine cabinetry."

"I have never asked," Jane answered, as Sam dismounted from his own horse and went to assist her and Lottie from the carriage. Dolph made as if to tie up his own horses' reins to the hitching rail, leaving Maggie perched in the saddle by herself, gleefully laughing at being up so far above the ground.

"That little one, she fears nothing," Mrs. Becker observed.

"I know," Isobel shuddered. "And I will have grey hair myself before very long. If there is a wild animal, or deep water, an untamed horse, Maggie is running straight towards –"

Jane was never entirely sure about the order of what happened next; she had turned towards the buggy, lifting up her arms to take Caro from Isobel. Out in in the street the dogs waited patiently, watching while Tom approached the furniture store and the little group of women and children with the buggy. The hoofs of his horse clip-clopped gently in the dust and a strange male voice shouted harshly from quite near at hand, "Becker – you're chose!"

It was so sudden, so unexpected; Jane whirled around and caught a glimpse of the shouter as he appeared from around the corner of the building. He was a tall old man in ragged workmen's clothing, with long gray hair done in Indian plaits falling past his shoulder. His face was contorted with maniacal rage, a face engorged and red with it. He had a huge pistol in his hand, a thing that looked as large as a cannon, his fingers curling around the grip, a finger through the trigger – and he was pulling, pulling it. A woman's scream rent the air – Isobel's voice and a man shouting in the street. Instinctively, Jane hugged Caro to her and crouched against the buggy-wheel, sheltering the child with her own body, aware in a corner of her mind that Sam had done the same for Isobel as the bullet firing crashed with an explosion like that of a cannon. Something kicked up dust by the buggy-wheel, a sudden spurt like a small burrowing animal diving down into a safe refuge.

Everything happened all at once, yet very slowly. Jane looked to where the shot had come from the man's pistol, but it wasn't in his hand any more, but spinning on the boards at his feet, while Mrs. Becker swung that heavy valise in a vicious half-circle. She must have spoiled his aim by striking his gun-hand down with it. Now the old man was snarling obscenities at them all, but mostly at Mrs. Becker as he scrabbled to retrieve his side-arm.

"Whitmire!" That was Dolph shouting, even as his horse reared in fright, throwing small Maggie screaming from the saddle. Her father caught her with one arm as the child slipped sideways; grasping the loose reins with his other hand. Even as he did, his horse reared again, pulling the leather from his hand as it went up, and up, an angry horse and tossing mane all black against the bright sky, the steel shoes flashing bright sparks. Jane screamed. She only knew afterwards that she had, because that scream scraped her throat raw. One of those flashing hoofs struck Dolph Becker on the head as the horse came down, a sickening soft thud, like a hammer striking a ripe melon. He crumpled to the ground with Maggie half under his body. A pool of blood widened in a dark red tide around his head. From Jane's side, Sam launched himself at the panicky horse, snatching the reins in both hands, dragging the creature's head down by sheer weight, pulling those slashing feet away from the man and child dropped in the dust, even as three – four more shots crashed over their heads.

The old man with the white Indian braids lay slack and loose, his hands not two inches from his lost pistol, with two bloody smears of gore in his chest. His face was entirely gone and the back of his skull looked to have exploded onto the lower wall of Knauer's shop in a smear of blood, bits of white bone and teeth, along with spongy masses of brain. The dogs barked in deep booming chorus that would have drawn attention on Houston Street even if the gunfire had not. Alf Trotter – no, he was Tom Becker now – cried out, "Oh, sir – sir, didn't I warn you! That villain – he was lookin' f'r, ye, I tol' ye so, over an' over I did!" Tom held his own pistols, both still smoking slightly. He was as white as a sheet and looked as if he were about to be sick.

Maggie wailed disconsolately from beside her father, crying, "Papa – Papa!" Tom holstered his six-shooters, looked once more at the bullet-smashed body of the old man, at the mess splattered on the wall, and vomited. Jane was momentarily paralyzed with horror. To whom should she go to first, with Caro sobbing in her arms; Dolph and Maggie, Mrs. Becker, or to Isobel? Isobel stumbled from where she had crouched by the buggy wheel, fierce and fearless, as composed in the face of disaster as any of her storied ancestors. She knelt at her husband's side, careless of the dirt or the blood on her hands and skirts, drawing Maggie into her arms, turning the child's face towards her breast to spare her the sight of the horrors all around her.

"Jane dear," her voice was faint, but perfectly steady. "We need to call Doctor Herff. He is the best in this country. Will you take the children and

Mother Becker inside? They do not need to see any more of this sight. Sam –
do you know his place of business, can you find him quickly?"

"Unless he's gone to the Hills or to another patient," Sam answered, so
deathly pale that he looked hardly more alive than his brother. Jane saw that
Dolph's chest still rose and fell regularly, even with that horrible, gory
crescent-shaped wound smashed into the top of his skull above his left
eyebrow. In a distant part of her mind, Jane also noted with satisfaction that
the expensive glass windows at the front of her property had not been
damaged. It would have been a great trouble and expense to replace them if
they had been. Suddenly the length of sidewalk before Knauer's was full of
people; Mr. Knauer and his two apprentices erupted from the door; one of the
apprentices held a long stick of wood, and Mr. Knauer himself had a pistol.
There were men running from the other stores on Houston Street and others
from across the street, the sounds of their boots ringing on the iron footbridge.

"Fetch him, at once," Isobel commanded, her voice gaining strength and
authority. "And . . . a man of the law, Sam." Her eyes fell on young Tom, now
kneeling next to her. He still looked very green, as if he might be sick again.
"You shall have to talk with him, Tom – explain what happened. If you would
be so good as to go in with Mrs. Sam, I'm sure she will fix you a good cup of
tea."

"Help me with the girls, Lottie," Jane whispered to the girl, who was ashen
with horror, her cheeks smeared with tears. "Take Caro. Don't let her look at
anything until we are upstairs. I think your mother should come with us, too.
She does not look well. Take Caro, Lottie; there's a good girl." Lottie obeyed,
while Jane worried that Mrs. Becker might faint away entirely; she trembled
like a leaf. Maggie went obediently to Jane, as Isobel whispered comforting
endearments to her daughter. They trailed up the wooden staircase to the
upstairs apartment, stepping carefully around the dusty boots of the dead man
sprawled in their path.

The sudden silence inside enfolded them all – the clamor from outside
remote, nothing to do with them, nothing to do with the sudden violent horror
springing on them, striking as swiftly as a lightening bolt. Jane sent Tom to
build up the fire in the little kitchen stove, while she settled Mrs. Becker into
the largest parlor chair; her hands were icy cold. Jane gently chafed them
between hers. Her mother-in-law's hazel-grey eyes were wide with horror.
She was temporarily incapable of speaking and did not answer to anything
that Lottie said for many minutes. The little girls clung to each other and to
Lottie. They were too small to even comprehend the least part of this horror.

"I think – after a bit, you should take the girls and your mother and go to the Richters'," Jane said at last. Lottie nodded mutely. "Can you drive, or shall I ask one of Mr. Knauer's apprentices?"

"I can drive," Lottie had found her voice. "Likely, Uncle Hansi will come for us anyway." Now her tears overflowed. "Jane, what shall we do?"

"Have a cup of tea, first" Jane answered, accepting that her duty now was to remain calm, to reassure Lottie, and to be a sturdy support to Isobel – just as she had been from the very first. It felt familiar, comfortable, as if putting on a well-worn garment. "Be brave and sort out what we are to do. Since Dolph is so badly hurt – don't cry, Lottie, it frightens the children – they will likely bring him here. There's a day-bed in the back room. There's enough light for the doctor to do his work there."

Chapter 28 – *The Door Between Life and Death*

Jane set out her little array of tea-cups; it had amused Sam very much that she had never become accustomed to coffee. Tom stood by the the stove, his hands hanging awkwardly. Jane thought he must be horribly shaken; he looked shrunken inside of his clothes, as if a boy had dressed in a man's garb. Tom worshipped the ground that Dolph Becker walked upon. It must be a hard thing to kill a man and perhaps not been able to save the life of the one that he revered.

"Tom, will you be so good as to bring some more water?" Jane suggested gently. "There is a well by Mr. Knauer's back door."

"Yes, Miss G." Tom gulped. He still looked very green. As she handed him the buckets, she contrived to pat him on the shoulder, by way of comfort and approval. "You did very well," she said. "You kept your head and shot well and true. Whitmire was a very wicked man. He may have meant to hurt the children or Lottie; any of us. If Mrs. Becker not caused him to miss his aim and if he had gotten his pistol back again, we might have been killed. He was that close to all of us and that kind of villain. You're a true hero, Tom, stopping him as you did. I am sure that Sir would – will be proud of you."

"I didna think there'd be such a right mess of it," Tom mumbled. Jane swallowed a little of her own revulsion. "Mess or no, it was, bravely done. There – the water now, Tom." She pushed him gently in the direction of the door, but as she did, it opened from the outside. A man stood there, a diffident and courteous man of middle age who asked, in a softly husky Irish voice as he took off his hat, "May I come into th' house, Marm? They are bringing the poor gentleman upstairs, with every care. Is there a bed where he might be put to rest?"

"Yes," Jane answered swiftly, "Through this door. The bed is made already. Go fetch the water, Tom," she added again.

"I would speak with you all, then," the man continued, "As to what you saw of this unfortunate event. I am Thomas McCall, with the duty of sheriff in this county. I was doing business at the Turner Theater and came as soon as I heard the ruckus."

"Jane Becker," Jane answered. "And this is Tom, who is Mr. Becker's – that is, Mr. Rudolph Becker' ward. He protected us all against that madman after Mrs. Becker – my mother-in-law – struck his pistol out of his hands."

"Indade?" Mr. McCall's mild gaze held a look of respect. "A very brave and composed lady and excellent shooting, lad, excellent; I will have some questions for you, after I pay respects to the ladies."

"They are in the parlor, Mr. McCall," Jane said, unaccountably feeling rather shaky in the knees herself. "Tom, you should join us there, when you have fetched the water. They are composing themselves and seeing to the children," she added to the sheriff. "I hope that your questions will not take long. This horrible event happened so suddenly!"

"Ah, the poor wee mites," Mr. McCall shook his head. "'Tis a sad thing to happen, on such a fine day! Y'r good man has already gone for the doctor; I saw Dr. Herff his very self, as I was passing by the Menger this morning, an' certain I am that he was still there." There was a trampling off feet on the stairs, as if a number of men bearing a burden and Mr. McCall added, "That will be the poor gentleman. He breathes still, an' that is a good sign. I have seen w' my own eyes the good doctor working miracles. There are men as good as dead, today walking around hale an' hearty, thanks to him. When Mr. Rudolph comes 'round, you must send for me at once, day or night."

Jane noticed that he said 'when', not 'if'; that confidence expressed was bracing. Likely it was bracing for Isobel, too; her face was as pale as the sheets that Jane had dressed the day bed in the corner of the studio with. Isobel followed Mr. Knauer, his apprentices and a stranger. Each man bore a corner of a window shutter, hastily pressed into service as a litter. On it lay Dolph, his head roughly bound in a strip of calico cloth; someone's handkerchief and already soaked through with gore. Jane hoped that Isobel did not notice the erratic trail of blood droplets spattering across the floor. Isobel herself was composed, although her eyes looked bruised.

"Through here," Jane told Mr. Knauer and Isobel and ran for another armful of coarse huck towels – clean ones, which she could sacrifice to bloodstains. When she carried them into the studio room, Isobel knelt by the day bed, Dolph's slack hand in hers. "The doctor is on his way, I am certain. I think we should clean the wound, as best we can. I have sent Tom for more water. And I've a pot of tea brewing, then," Jane added. As hoped, that elicited a faint smile from Isobel.

"The sovereign remedy, Jane?" For a moment, Isobel's composure nearly broke. "He has neither moved nor opened his eyes, after that horrible blow! How cruel this is! What shall I tell my children – whatever will I do?"

"What you can," Jane answered, firm and kind. "A single thing at a time; then another. Lottie and Mrs. Becker are in the parlor with the children. I told

Lottie that she ought to take them all home, if Mr. Richter does not come for them at once. Here is Tom with the buckets. I'll bring in some warm water."

"Thank you, Jane. Your hospitality is bountiful, even in emergencies, and so appreciated." Isobel's resolve firmed and steadied. "I am more grateful than I can say. When Sam returns, I will need him to take some messages to the Western Union office. That old man – he was a veritable bandit king, Jane. I will not let whoever survived him prey on our properties. They all must be warned at once – Seb, Uncle Fredi, and Mr. Inman. Uncle Richter must know of this, also."

"Of course." Jane was heartened; Isobel was thinking with her mind, not merely following the erratic dictates of her heart. She hurried to the kitchen, found the kettle purring on the stove. The tea she had set to seep was a good color; in this case, the stronger the better. She poured a basin of warm water for Isobel and hurried into the parlor with the pot and a tray of cups. There she found Lottie, the children curled up beside her like kittens seeking the warmth and reassurance of the mother cat. Maggie and Caro were quiet, no longer crying; Lottie had recovered color to her face, although the pale freckles across her nose still stood out. Jane took a cup and wrapped her mother-in-law's cold fingers around it, saying, "There now – this will do you good, Mutti Magda." She didn't answer, but at least there was some life in her eyes.

Sheriff McCall took a cup with a nod of absent thanks; he was listening with deep attention to Tom explain how Old Randall Whitmire had threatened the Becker cousins over the hanging of his kin for stealing cattle in the Palo Duro all those months ago. To Jane's vague surprise, McCall did not appear to think this of particular moment, or even that Tom had been nominated himself as a body-guard all this time. He asked a deft question or two, in that soothing Irish-tinged voice, so mild and fatherly as to put Tom entirely at ease. Finally he observed,

"It sounds like a clear case of self defense, lady; so I dinna think you'll hear any more about it from the city marshal or meself, although I will look to Mr. Richter to confirm what you have said. Ran'll Whitmire was a wanted man, several times over; I've no doubt there is a bit o' reward in the offing, for the removin' of a public nuisance. An' speaking o' public nuisance, the fellows from the undertakers will be along presently for the remains o' the late Mr. Whitmire. The city pays for buryin' th' indigent, y'know. Dr. Herff will take a moment, I am certain, to certify the death."

Tom moistened his lips, looking more of his usual self. "Thank'ye, Sheriff. It's not an easy thing in my mind, knowing I have killed a man."

"Aye, but knowing he was well-deserving should make it aisier, then?" Sheriff McCall answered. From her chair, Mrs. Becker spoke for the first time. "He was an evil man. Justice was done," she said. "Perhaps not as customary and as a judge would have allowed. But it has been done. You were its instrument."

"Just so, lad," Sheriff McCall agreed. "Just so; I'll take m 'leave of you all, then. 'Tis sorry I am that this happened in our city, to as foine a man as young Becker. You'll have as many as know him wishing well, lightin' a candle and sending up a prayer." Jane saw him to the door, hearing through the part-opened window in the parlor that someone else was coming up the wooden steps. It was Sam, taking them two at a time, gasping. "I found Dr. Herff, thank God. He is on the way. He said that we should take care in moving Dolph and not to do so any more than necessary. I told him what had happened. He said that he may have to operate at once."

Jane's heart sank. "Here? In the studio?" Sam nodded. "He does his cutting and bone-setting wherever he happens to find himself and someone in need. Dolph couldn't be in better hands."

"Isobel is with him now," Jane was braced by Sam's confidence. "Everyone else is in the parlor; your mother, Lottie and the children. Isobel wants you to send some telegrams and to fetch your uncle."

In the studio the afternoon light fell softly across the floor, moved by the shadows of the feathery branches of the cypress trees which dotted the river bank. Isobel knelt by the day bed in a pool of her skirts spread around her, gently sponging the bloody gash on Dolph's head. The only sounds within the room were the sound of his hoarse breathing and the gentle dripping of water as Isobel rinsed the towel and wrung it out.

"*Mein gott!*" Sam whispered, as they looked from the doorway. Jane saw that he was nearly as pale as his brother. This was the first time in her memory that Sam had slipped into his childhood language in speaking to her. He looked at her, stricken. "It is like when they brought our father's body home. Mama fainted dead away when she saw. I had not thought of that in years. We built the coffin; Tio 'Firio, Mr. Brown, Dolph, and I. Mrs. Brown washed and dressed him for the grave." He turned away from the door way, as if he could no longer bear the sight or the memory that it recalled so vividly. The door to the bedroom closed behind him. Jane thought of the day that her own father died, a day now cushioned and cob-webbed with the passing of many years. She recalled the desolate incomprehension, the stab of grief like a knife to the heart, how she had climbed into lower branches of the gnarled plum tree at the foot of the garden behind the store in Didcot and remained for many hours, while her mother called for her. Within the studio, Isobel lifted her head from the task. "Is Dr. Herff come?" She asked, her eyes desperate with hope. Isobel closed the studio door at her back and answered with careful calm. "Sam says he is on his way. He may have to perform an operation. But he will do it here. He is said to be the very best doctor surgeon in the district."

"I know that!" Isobel choked on a brief laugh. "He was sent to attend to me, in my confinements. He is a very gruff man, but a most excellent doctor."

"Has … Dolph shown any sign of returning to sensibility?" Jane asked. Isobel shook her head. "I thought that he groaned once. I just don't know."

"Perhaps he can hear you, just a little," Jane said. "My aunt told me once of a man having been so ill as to be thought beyond this world – but when he recovered at last, he recalled perfectly those words that had been said in his presence, in spite of not being sensible. Perhaps you should speak to your husband; your voice may hold him with us."

"I will do that, Jane," Isobel answered; Jane sensed she was in such desperate hope that she would indeed. "I will tell Sam to carry the message to the telegraph office," Jane continued. "And then to the Richters' – to tell them of what has happened, if they do not already know. This is a small town, and the hue and cry will be very great. Is there any one else that Sam should send a telegram to?"

"No," Isobel answered. "Thank you, Jane." She swallowed bravely, conquering her fears and uncertainty all over again. "You have been so steady and composed. I do not know how we would manage, without you, as a friend . . . and a sister."

"It is my duty to the family," Jane answered, "And to those in it who have done the like for me, since they held me in affection and esteem – and whom I also love."

"Sometimes I fear I am not worthy of such devotion and friendship," Isobel answered. "Please tell me when Dr. Herff arrives. Bring him here to this room immediately."

Jane closed the studio door, already hearing Isobel's low voice. In the bedroom, Sam sat on the side of the bed. He was already struggling to regain his composure. By his eyes, Jane knew that he had been weeping as well. "There are times, Jane – when I hate this place," he said. "Times when I wish that Opa had taken all our family to the North, instead of accepting the offer of the Verein."

"So many wherefores and there-byes," Jane answered. "What might you have been for this chance? A clerk in a shop in Cincinnati, or not even having been born at all? Your brother might never have come to England, married a lord's daughter. So many perhapses! There is no way to chart them all. In the end, it makes no difference, anyway. Isobel wants you to send telegrams; to Mr. Inman at the Comfort ranch, to Seb, and to your Uncle Fredi; she is afraid that any of the Whitmire gang might strike at the cattle herds – or even at the ranches. You probably ought also to inform Mr. Vining in Austin. He and your brother are so very close. When that is done, fetch your uncle." She sat for a moment next to her husband and set her arm around him for comfort. Had it only been a single day since they were reunited at the train station, after a year apart? And only half an hour by the chiming of church bells, since they had come up Houston Street? In the space of those few moments, every assumption and assurance of their lives had been upended. Now Sam leaned a little against her; there was no need for further words. At last he laughed, short and hollow, like a man facing the gallows.

"A good reason to pray for Dolph and for Doctor Herff's skills . . . if my brother dies, I'll have to set aside the painting ambitions and take his place with Uncle."

No – Jane wanted to cry. *No; think of yourself, of your skills and talent, my dear!* But she knew better than to say so. Duty bound Sam to his family and their interests, more than it had ever constrained her, even when it appeared as if she would spend the rest of her life as Isobel's shadow. Anna Vining and Lizzie Johnson talked sometimes of the duty that bound women in chains of silk – but their chains were as nothing compared to those which bound a man of honor.

Isobel folded a clean towel into a pad and dabbed carefully at the blood-oozing wound; she could not bear using any but the lightest pressure for fear of causing more harm. The darkening gore matted Dolph's wheat-pale hair together in a way horrible to look at, almost more horrible than the perceptible dent in the top of his skull.

"I cannot bear this, Dolph," Isobel whispered. "I cannot bear that you would be taken from us like this. Not after loosing dear, darling Fa. It's simply too cruel – and your mother; she can't be asked to endure this again. Don't you dare give up; not when Caro and Maggie are so little . . . and Lizzie might never know you at all? She will make up stories in her head, to make up for never having known her father, just like Lottie does. Don't you dare die like this, Dolph! I won't have it and Uncle Richter will be furious. He will storm in here and order you to stop this nonsense when you have the ranch to run and important matters to see to. Listen to me, Dolph. Come back from wherever you have gone. Stay with us, we love you so dearly. . ."

She went on talking in this vein, coaxing or ordering in a whisper; Dolph lay silent, unresponsive and marmoreal-pale, save for the unnatural blue shadows around his eyes. The minutes ticked past, without change. When Jane opened the door without any ceremony at all, Isobel's heart near leaped from her breast from relief; behind Jane loomed Dr. Herff, burly and reassuring by his mere presence. His beard was as untidy as a windblown dark haystack strewn across his magnificent waistcoat.

"The doctor's here," Jane announced unnecessarily, as Dr. Herff strode into the room without a glance at any but his patient.

He set down his bulging satchel next to the bed. "How long has be been in this condition?"

"Since it happened . . . half an hour? No forty minutes past," Isobel answered and the doctor grunted noncommittally. He lifted Dolph's eyelids, first one and then the other, studying each eye for some moments, then parted the front of his shirt, and listened to his heart with an oddly shaped ivory cone, with an earpiece connected to the top of the cone by a length of rubber wrapped in silk braid. His findings appeared to satisfy him.

"Has there been any sign of returning consciousness?" Dr. Herff demanded, and Isobel shook her head. "Can you do anything for him, Doctor?" she asked.

"I will operate, of course," he answered gruffly. "There is a piece of the skull bone, you see – pressing upon the brain. Not good, of course – and there is probably hematomeous materiel also pressing against the brain; such pressure must be relieved promptly. Otherwise . . ." the Doctor recalled himself. "Recovery may be impaired significantly. I have called on two colleagues to assist me; they are military surgeons . . . eminently qualified but somewhat lacking in experience in performing surgery of this degree. I feel that your husband will have the benefit with persons of some skill assisting me and they will gain some experience in observing."

"Certainly, Doctor – whatever you need to do that will restore my husband," Isobel agreed. "What will you need of us?"

"I think that you should leave the room during the operation," Dr. Herff answered, still gruff but kindly. "I cannot risk a moment of distraction from what I must do and I fear that you may become distressed. I have become accustomed – indeed, hardened – to the most revolting sights and think nothing of them, but to allow a gentle lady to witness them . . . no, no, consideration for tender sensibilities urges me to take such care."

"I believe I am made of sterner stuff," Isobel protested, but the doctor shook his head. "No, Mrs. Becker – comfort your children while I do my utmost for your husband."

"Come away, Isobel," Jane urged, helping her to her feet, and led her from the studio. "I have already promised the doctor my own assistance. He thinks me merely the wife of the householder and thus proof against any megrims and hysterics," she added in a whisper. "Come away to the parlor; you look nearly as unwell as Dolph."

Isobel consented to being led away from the studio, now that Dr. Herff had arrived, tut-tutting under his breath as he continued his examination. The doctor's very assurance was heartening. In the parlor Jane settled her onto the settee and put a cup of tea in her hands. "I sent the boy with Lottie and the girls, to see them safely back to the Richters'," she whispered. "But Mrs. Becker would not go with them."

"I would not," the older woman answered, clearly composed and recovered from the shock which had taken her. "I am well accustomed to nursing the sick and injured and this is my son. My place is here."

"Yes, Mutti Magda," Jane answered. With a corner of her mind, Isobel wondered where and how by what talent Jane had come to be on such good and familiar terms with the wholly intimidating elder lady. Thinking on it, though – it was obvious; once Isobel considered it for a moment. In that same moment she envied Jane; so much better suited by background to meld seamlessly into their husbands' family and to be more comfortable there already than Isobel had ever been in months of seeking her way to it. Certainly, Isobel had never considered calling her mother-in-law 'Mutti Magda.' Mama would be horrified. Isobel reproached herself for even caring a rap what Lady Caroline thought. *There was England, and Mama's world; I never wanted it, so why should I still care, but from old habit? Should my husband not survive* – and Isobel considered this with a twist of grief in her breast – *I will not return Home, and take up residence in that place that Fa left for me, against expectation of an accident like this. I cannot possibly crawl back into the strait-jacket of Society and their expectations. Not even for love of Upton and the folk there. Dolph did not want that for his girls – and where would I ever feel so free and happy again?*

Jane hastily excused herself, upon hearing someone coming up the steps; Sam, breathless and panting from the run and the exertion of his errand. "Onkel Hansi is on his way," he gasped. "The telegrams are sent. Is Dr. Herff here? What does he say?"

"He will have to operate," Jane answered. "But I think that he is confident – he sent for two of his doctor friends to assist. I don't know why they delay."

"Likely they have to come all the way from the new fort, with all of their traps and gear," Sam answered. "I see that the buggy is gone – did you manage to send all to Onkel Hansi's?"

"All but your mother," Jane replied, and Sam sighed in resignation. "No, Mama would remain regardless – if not to nurse Dolph herself, then to see to you and Isobel."

They sat in the parlor with Isobel and Mrs. Becker for some time; a restless wait for word from Dr. Herff. Sam paced, unable to settle at anything, while Isobel made a pretense of occasionally sipping at a cup of tea, hardly noticing that it was stone cold. Mrs. Becker sat contemplating her own thoughts, the calmest among them. Jane took refuge in pattering back and forth between parlor and kitchen. Dr. Herff had requested that his surgical instruments have the metal parts of them dipped into boiling water, and then laid out in tidy order, on a tray lined with a clean towel. Jane couldn't even begin to guess, thinking that it must have something to do with the doctor's well-known fastidiousness in dealing with his patients, although to her own eyes the things looked clean enough. It was almost a relief to hear heavy footsteps on the staircase; thus warned Jane reached the door and opened it, even as the first man had raised his hand to rap upon the door panels; two men, neither of them young, nor absolutely old. After a moment – so used was she to summoning up people – she saw they were actually young, not very much above the age of Sam and his brother, but they looked older, as if several lifetimes had gone past while they held a surgical knife and the power of life against death in their hands. They were both clad alike, in blue uniform frock coats. Two other men in similar blue uniforms followed after, carrying an odd contraption of wood and metal between them. The first two, who had rather much more gold braid about their persons, especially on their shoulders, swiftly doffed their hats.

"Beg pardon, ma'am – is this where Dr. Herff is attending on the gentleman suffering a depressed fracture of the skull?"

"It is," Jane answered, "And he has been waiting impatiently on your arrival . . . with – whatever is that?"

"Portable operating table, ma'am," answered the first man, "If you will show us to Dr. Herff, we can get it set up in two shakes,"

"Spares us having to use your kitchen table," the second officer explained.

"I am grateful for the consideration," Jane answered, not being entirely certain that they weren't making sport of her. "The best-lighted room is this way."

Dr. Herff looked up from where he sat at the bedside; he was in his shirtsleeves and barely spared a glance aside. Apparently he had been examining the wound, touching Dolph's skull with careful fingers, for his own hands were now dabbled with smears of blood. "Ah, there you are. Have your orderlies set up your marvelous contraption, gentlemen and let's get to work; there's a life of a man to be saved and returned to the full usage of his limbs and intellect. The longer we delay, the more damage will be done." He briskly outlined the nature of the injury to the two younger men, who hovered over the day-bed, utterly fascinated. "I would trouble you for the use of a pair of scissors," he added in an aside to Jane. When she produced them, he began clipping Dolph's hair from around the clotted gash. That done, the orderlies had unfolded the narrow, metal-legged table and set it it before the windows, where the light was best. Dr. Herff directed the other men to carry Dolph from the daybed to the table, "We will begin, as soon as we wash our hands. It may seem to you gentlemen to be an action, of little practical use – but I have long found that scrupulous cleanliness of the surgeon's hands and instruments reduces the occurrence of wound fever in surgical patients. I am uncertain as to why this would be so, but the practice does no harm and in my own experience there is a positive correlation."

Dutifully, the two Army surgeons followed Dr. Herff's example. Jane brought the tray of cleaned instruments to the table. Standing at Dolph's head, Dr. Herff took up the first of them – a long-handled razor with a shining steel blade. When he began to slice calmly into the edge of the wound, Jane felt a high-pitched kind of buzzing in her ears. The metallic smell of blood in the room was oppressive; she hastily excused herself and stumbled to the door. She rather thought no one noticed, so complete was the absorption of all those hovering around that tall narrow table in what Dr. Herff was doing.

In the parlor, the Baron sprang up from the best chair. Jane had not heard him arrive. Sam, pacing up and down, was still the closest to her. Jane gratefully allowed him to steer her to the settee, next to Isobel.

"They have begun the operation," Jane said. "I thought I could bear to stay and be of assistance, but then I began to feel quite faint."

"He would not allow me to remain for much the same reason," Isobel observed. "I am just grateful that he has begun. Do you know how long it will take?"

"I don't know," Jane answered, frowning in concentration. "He was telling the other doctors that he must lift out a broken piece of skull pressing in on the brain inside and that there was likely blood underneath that must be allowed to drain. Once the blood drained, and the broken piece was no longer pressing down . . . that Mr. Becker might very well awake with nothing more than an awful headache. The doctor seemed quite cheerful . . . as if he did not anticipate anything but success. He also said that Mr. Becker should not be moved, until the broken bone begins to knit together again. " Jane added. She took Isobel's hands within her own. "What must we do now?" Isobel asked: her voice remarkably steady.

"Wait. Until they are done . . . and then wait some more." Jane answered. It was already late afternoon. When the sun dropped behind the cypress trees. Dr. Herff would no longer be able to see as well as he needed to. The birds were already gathering in the cypress branches, swooping back and forth. chattering carelessly together. Across the room, the Baron nodded in grave agreement.

Twilight had fallen when Dr. Herff finally emerged from the studio. settling his good coat over his shoulders. Beyond the windows of the parlor. lights were lit in the buildings across the river, their reflections dancing in the water like the stars which would emerge later. The sun was setting in a bank of purple cloud. Jane was wondering what she should fix for a meal, or if everyone was too worried about Dolph to even consider having an appetite. Mrs. Becker had dozed off, but Isobel sat up from where she had been laying on the settee, the words from her, "What has happened – is my husband awake?" before her feet even met the floor.

"We are finished," Dr. Herff said; his mien was not one of cheer, but not sunk in gloom either. "We have found and removed some small bone fragments that were pressing upon the brain matter and successfully drained the hematoma which had formed. Mr. Becker has not yet recovered consciousness, but he has made some small involuntary movements. He should be watched carefully for the next twelve hours, lest he injure himself in violent movement. And," Doctor Herff added in magisterial tones. "It is possible that he may suffer lingering effects in the form of headaches, or spells of dizziness. Great care should be taken in moving him from this place to your home," he nodded at Uncle Richter." I will pay a call tomorrow, and judge his fitness for even a brief journey. I would also recommend against resuming an active life until the bones have knitted well-together."

"Dolph will hate being an invalid," Sam observed, with a spark of good humor lightening his own expression. "Once he begins feeling better, you'll be hard pressed to make him rest, Isobel. You'll have to have Onkel Hansi or Cuz or I to sit on him, just to keep him in one place."

"Do what you must to enforce rest for my patient," Dr. Herff nodded, utterly un-amused, as Uncle Richter shook his hand. "Expect me at about mid-morning – if I am delayed, I will send word. And good night to you all . . . ladies," he nodded, but Isobel had slipped into the studio. With the sun gone from the sky, leaving only a pale glow cut across with a smear of purple cloud edged in gold, the studio was dim, lit only by a single lamp. Isobel spared barely a nod and some breathless words of thanks for the two Army doctors. Their marvelous folding operating table was already disassembled, the orderlies lifting the compact thing between them to carry it away. Isobel only had eyes for Dolph, returned to the day bed with a wide swath of snow-white bandage covering his head. Considerately, someone had thought to divest him of his boots and outer clothing – but inconsiderately leaving them on the chair by the day bed. Isobel swept them aside, and contemplated her husband, hardly daring to hope. Yes, as near as she could see, his color was better, and he breathed more as if asleep. *Wake*, she begged silently, *open your eyes and recognize me, recognize our children.* She recollected what Jane had said, about talking to him. Perhaps some part of Dolph could hear her voice, follow her from that particular Hades, in some strange reversal of Orpheus and Eurydice. She took his hand in hers – how horribly slack it was!

"I think we should go to the ranch, as soon as we can," she said. "It will be summer soon, and so hot . . . although I think I have become accustomed to the heat. If . . . I should ever return to England, I am certain that it will seem very cold and dim to me." She talked on and on, as the sky darkened outside, as if he could really hear her, speaking of homely matters, of the children, sometimes reminiscing about the journey to the Palo Duro. "I would countenance you teaching the girls to ride, if we could find ponies for them. Maggie is completely fearless – she would ride the largest horse, even at her age, but you must be tender with Caro; she is not as bold as her sister."

She heard a light step behind her, and the quiet rustle of a woman's skirts. "He looks much better," Jane whispered. "I have prevailed on Mr. Richter to take Mutti Magda home. She will return in the morning, to take her turn as nurse. Sam is going with them, but he is going to bring you a nightgown and a change of clothing for you and a cot to set up in here. I expect you will want to lie down and rest for a little time. Sam will bring us some supper as well. Does it not seem to you that this day will ever end?"

"It seemed most endless as we were waiting for Doctor Herff to finish his good work," Jane answered. She bent down to look more closely at Dolph. "I believe that he is coming around. His eyes are moving, although they are still closed. The doctor said that he might come around tonight; tomorrow at the very latest." Dolph's hand suddenly closed on Isobel's, startlingly strong, and his lips moved, very slightly. "I believe he is trying to tell you something!" Jane exclaimed. Isobel's own eyes overflowed. She felt as if she might faint from the easing of that terror which had laid hold of her from the very moment that Old Randall Whitmire came around the corner, brandishing his pistol, and then from the long grinding fear that Dolph might die.

"What are you trying to say, my dearest love?" she whispered, bending low and close. His lips moved again; two words only and so faint that only she could hear them, but Isobel began to laugh.

"What did he say?" Jane breathed.

"Damned horse!" Isobel answered, crying with relief amidst the laughter. When she recovered control of herself, she kissed him very gently. "Rest now, dearest – we are all safe. Your boy Tom did the work of saving us from Whitmire. Dr. Herff has been and gone. We are at Sam and Jane's. Rest now . . . as soon as you are well, we will go back to the ranch."

His hand in hers closed briefly. It looked as if he was truly sleeping. Isobel laid down his hand, overcome with relief. She fell into Jane's embrace, now weeping openly. To her everlasting gratitude, Jane had a clean handkerchief on her person. She could always depend on Jane, as dear and sweet a sister as she had been a friend, when she was just the upstairs sewing maid at Acton.

"Now, you see?" Jane whispered, "He will recover and it will be all that you wished for on your wedding day. You remember – you cried then, too. And his Lordship your father, he told you that you might call it off, if you wanted to. Did you ever wish to have taken him at his word – to remain as you were; your mother's daughter?"

"No," Isobel hiccupped. "I did not – although sometimes I had doubts. But there was . . . a something . . . a someone, who told me once that my greatest failing was that I allowed everyone else to tell me who I was and who I ought to be, when I should have been telling and deciding myself. Sometimes I felt as if I were in chains, Jane."

"Or a cage," Jane nodded. "Miss Johnson, my dearest friend apart from you, has often said the same thing. We are enslaved by taking too much to heart other people's expectations expectations, especially when those expectations have the capacity to do harm." Isobel laughed a little in self-deprecation. "And for all of that, I came to love and contentment almost accidentally. The ways of the human heart are mysterious, Jane, and sometimes the purpose of life cannot be easily discerned. All the same, I am glad of the choices I made and that Fa, and you, and my dear husband saw what I was capable of, long before I realized it myself. "

"And now that you know it," Jane said briskly. "You should live happily ever after, just like those romantic stories. You know, I think I should make a fresh pot of tea."

"Yes for the tea," Isobel answered, "I don't know about the happy ever after, Jane – but we will live, and often be happy."

Postscript – *In Sickness and in Health*

Letter, San Antonio, March 3, 1910
To Mrs. Lydia Kittredge

Dearest Auntie, yesterday we had the most exciting day imaginable; there was to be a demonstration of a flying machine at Fort Sam Houston! My husband was most excited, enough to tear himself away from his latest painting. (Which is a most strange visualization, in style very like to the so-called impressionistic works, where more is suggested than actually shown. It is in tones of white and green, representing Native women butchering a buffalo by moonlight in the snow. It is not the least to my taste . . . and yet I find myself looking at it again and again, when I bring messages or a bite of something to eat in the studio.) Anyway, there was much to-do in the newspaper, that one rash young officer, Lieutenant Foulois of the Signal Corps would demonstrate the Army's Wright flying machine. Just two weeks ago there was a demonstration of a similar machine in Houston, which attracted much public interest – being billed as the greatest invention of the present era.

Which it may truly be, Auntie – but it seemed a gossamer thing, a dragon-fly or a kite made of canvas, wire and bamboo, and the engine stuttered and halted as it climbed into the sky. Sam took Lottie and Seb's youngest, Mutti Magda, and such of our children and grandchildren who were at leisure and could fit into the touring car. We packed a picnic lunch and set off. The day was pure and clear, the winds light, and the grass of the loveliest emerald green. The parade ground is a long oval, lined with trees and substantial brick officer's residences – almost dwarfing the crowd. My husband roved everywhere with his sketchbook. He was allowed by consideration of his stature as an artist to approach the marvelous invention and sketch the aviator; a thin young man, slight of build and most particularly trained in the art of making maps.

Lt. Foulois essayed four flights, to the delight of the crowds, taking off from the ground and vaulting into the sky, circling the parade ground and the crowds watching from below. Alas, the final flight ended, not in a gentle settling to the ground, but in a splintering crash, in which fortunately he was not injured greatly. The drama of the crash excited the crowd at least as much as anything else. So I have seen the marvelous flying machine, Auntie. By way of proof I enclose several of my husband's hasty sketches.

Our children continue well, as well as our grandchildren, although small Lydia is much afflicted with a bad tooth. I fear it will have to be extracted, but such is the advancement of Science and the medical arts these days, I am assured this can be done without pain to your dear little namesake. We did see Maggie at the flying exhibition; she has been visiting her Richter cousins and came in a smart little motor runabout. I told her that I don't know what their father was thinking, buying such a thing for her, but Maggie insists she is an expert driver, and bought the runabout herself. She represents herself to be a journalist; I would say that she is an old maid, but my friend Lizzie Johnson married when she pleased herself and at an age of several years older than Maggie is at present. I would have thought this distresses Isobel very much, but she appears to pay no mind. In this, she and her husband might be wiser than I. They have allowed all their daughters every latitude to pursue where interest and ambition takes them. For Caro and Lizzie, it was marriage, at a time of their own choosing, but it appears that Maggie has not chosen yet.

With my love and good wishes from all the dearest ones,

Your devoted niece, Jane

* * *

October, 1918

"We should have taken the train at once upon receiving Dolph's telegram," Jane said, as the powerful engine of the Hudson labored up the gradual climbing slope towards Comfort. It was late afternoon, and the winter sun low in the sky over the western hills. Samuel disliked driving after sundown, as the headlamps illuminated very little. "We would have been in Boerne by now and sent a message to the ranch for someone to fetch us."

"There are quarantines everywhere," Sam answered mildly. "Because of this horrible epidemic. We might not have even been able to find a messenger or Dolph to find anyone brave enough to come for us." His eyes, protected by thick motoring goggles, were set upon the road unfurling before them, a pale ribbon from which the fine dust rose in a gale under the wheels of the touring car. "Better to come ourselves, all the way. It's only another thirty miles and I filled up the auxiliary tanks. We'll be there before dark."

Following several more dusty miles, Jane remarked, "I hope that we are in time. He only said that we should come, as soon as we could." Sam replied,

"My brother is what he is; a stoic. This dreadful grippe has afflicted the young and strong most dreadfully. It cannot be said that we are now in that cohort," he looked aside at Jane, wrapped in a canvas motoring coat and many veils, sitting next to him. "Which curiously, lends me hope."

"It's just that he sent a telegram," Jane answered. Sam kept his eyes steady on the windshield "He would not have done that, if it weren't a matter of urgency. Isobel has been my dearest friend since the day that we met . . . since the day that we came here together."

"We've made good time, Jane. Coming in the motor was better than killing a horse or two in our hurry." Sam answered. Jane thought again of how they fitted together so finely in their long marriage together. When she was agitated, he was calm, steady, reassuring. When he worried incessantly about some matter of art and aspects of his respected and mildly profitable career as a painter in the Western genre, Jane was there to steady and reassure. This was what a marriage was, Jane had often thought; each steadied the other, a partnership and shield-wall against the vagaries of fate. She had been the business-oriented one, the manager who allowed Sam's flights of artistic fancy and extracted a good price from those who loved his visions of the West well enough to pay that price which Jane had calmly set for possessing them. But her worry over Isobel had grown since receiving the telegram in the dark hours of that morning. Isobel had never been one to to enjoy ill-health. After some miles more of the road unreeling beneath the fat rubber tires of the Hudson, Sam announced, "Comfort, Jane – only a few miles more."

The lights behind the windows of the shops on Main Street flashed past. As the Hudson swept around a gentle curve, the headlamps briefly illuminated the white marble obelisk at the edge of town marking the graves of the Union men of the locality. Jane had heard the tale from Mutti Magda and those older friends who remembered those grim days; that war fought by men who were tottering elders now – not like the strong and young, arrayed in dust-colored modern uniforms. She wondered, in an irreverent aside, what those old men thought of it all and what that reckless young lieutenant of Signals was doing now. Those fragile canvas and bamboo kite toys were tools of serious war, in this depressing present day. Of motorcars such as the one that Sam now drove . . . that was a grief to recent to consider without tears. Isobel's daughter Maggie had gone as a volunteer to drive a Red Cross motor-ambulance in the first years of the war. A woman in her forties should not be so impetuous; yet she was and did. There was a rough grave for Maggie somewhere near Arras, with the shrieking of artillery shells overhead to mark the passing of Dolph and Isobel's stubborn and adventurous oldest daughter.

Jane wrenched her thoughts from that grief. Her mind lighted instead on the picture she had at home of Isobel's girls; a guest of the Beckers for the spring round-up one year had indulged everyone by making an extensive photographic record of it. Maggie and Caro would have been about eighteen, Lizzie a year younger. Prim in their ruffled dresses and near-to ankle length skirts, neatly hatted against the sun, they stood in the middle of a corral. Caro and Lizzie each held a lariat taut, a calf stretched on on the ground at their feet, while Maggie administered a branding iron. Yes, Dolph had seen to it that his girls could ride, rope, and shoot as well as any young man, and better than most.

"I wonder if he sent a telegram to Tom as well." Jane ventured.

Sam shook his head. "Even if he did, California is a sight farther than San Antonio."

"Tom would still drop everything – even if he was in the middle of shooting another movie – and ride the fastest express train that he could. He worships the ground that Dolph walks on and he adores Isobel." Sam nodded in agreement. Suddenly he laughed and Jane demanded, "What is so amusing?"

"All those tall tales put out about Tom; the Bandera Kid, King of the West and hero of the nickelodeon serials. Born in a log cabin, the youngest-ever deputy sheriff in Dodge City, kidnapped by the Comanche as a boy and adopted by a chief, capturing the whole Whitmire gang, single-handed! Every one of them a made-up story from whole cloth." Sam shook his head in amused wonderment. "It was our Cousin Willi kidnapped by the Comanche and adopted by a chief, by the way – but none of Tom's worshippers would ever believe that the Bandera Kid was a Cockney guttersnipe who never laid eyes on a longhorn or a six-shooter until he was twelve years old. Scrappy little devil. I don't believe Tom thinks himself anything other than a natural American."

"It would be good to have him with us," Jane observed. "I wish that Lottie would have come."

"Too busy nursing her sick soldiers," Sam answered. "And we would have had to explain to Mama. Mama would insist on coming with us, which would do her no good at all and Lottie would be furious with us for endangering Mama's health. I'd rather . . . I'd rather just quietly make the journey and not alarm anyone else. It's just another few miles."

Now the Hudson was on the road which ran alongside the riverside towards Kerrville. Very shortly they would come to the monumental gateposts which marked the start of the RB home ranch property – those tall gateposts marked in pale limestone, the avenue of spring-flowering trees which led among the fields and gated pastures. *If this was England,* Jane thought, *there would be a gatehouse, with a tenant in it, who would greet them as they passed, and send word to the main house.* Only this was Texas, no gatehouse and no messenger who would travel as swiftly as themselves.

"There is a crepe wreath on the gatepost," Jane said, as they turned in at the place which marked the main drive.

"It may be old – for Maggie," Sam said. Jane kept to herself the observation in the brief sweep of headlamps that the wreath was new and un-faded. Dusk had fallen. The headlamps of the Hudson flashed on the trunks of the redbud trees which lined the drive at precise intervals. Dolph had begun planting them upon returning from Europe in the year of the Centennial; they were mature trees now, their branches lacing overhead. In the spring, the drive was an avenue of dark pink, leading up to the main house. Isobel had expanded the gardens, remaking them in spectacular English fashion; terraces, walls and pergolas lined with roses, several spring-fed ponds filled with lilies ... but it was winter now and after sunset in any case. There were lighted windows in the main house and the door opened as Sam drove the Hudson around to what had once been the farmyard, but was now an expanse of cobbles set in sand, adorned with a marble fountain brought all the way from Spain. He turned off the engine, set the hand-brake, and hopped nimbly down from the driver's seat. The open door and the isinglass curtain admitted a gust of cold air. In the sudden quiet, Jane could hear the ticking of the metal engine parts, as the engine cooled.

Dolph stood in the open doorway, a man-shaped indistinct shadow against the pale yellow glow from within. Jane hardly needed the assistance of her husband, climbing down; the modern fashion for shorter and narrower skirts really made it easier for women to debark from an automobile. Dolph stood silent, waiting for them. Jane felt a sudden chill at her heart which had nothing to do with winter in the Hills. Dolph had grown craggy with age, but still handsome, tall and broad of shoulder, although his hairline had retreated far back enough to show the old crescent-shaped indentation in his skull, still marked with scar tissue. Even so, he could still do the same work of the ranch as well as any of the hands.

"Dolph, we came as soon and as rapidly as we could," she gasped, as she ran up the stairs. Tell me that we are not too late!" Her brother-in-law was dry-eyed, as stoic as he had always been, the set expression which gave nothing away to strangers. But Jane was not a stranger. She said only, "When?"

"Around noon today," he answered. Sam took her hand, saying, "I'm so sorry, Dolph. This damnable Spanish influenza. We thought you would be safe from infection out in the country."

"Pneumonia," Dolph was tight-lipped, as he closed the door behind them. "The influenza first, then pneumonia. That's what the sawbones from Comfort said. We thought she was getting better, but she just got weaker and weaker. Don't think she suffered any. I was glad of that. She said to me, 'I think I would like to go for a ride on Thistle today,' and then after a long while, she said, 'Don't worry about Maggie, Dolph. I have seen her and she is very well.' Then," he shrugged. "It was like a draft blowing out a candle. I have been thinking all day of what I should do. Just didn't feel like doing any of it."

"I am so very sorry," Jane said again. "I would that we had been here. May I see her? Perhaps we might help you now, in seeing all that needs seeing to."

"Suit yourself," Dolph answered; from any other man it would have sounded curt to the point of rudeness, but Jane intuited that it came from the depths of a grief so profound that any other man would have been shouting curses at the sky, at God, at the influenza. Jane divested herself of her veils and motoring coat, unpinned the wide-brimmed hat, and abandoned them on the hall stand. She straightened her shoulders and walked quickly up the stairs; herself a maid again this one last time, ready to attend on her lady.

Becker – Vining Family

Maria Bloch
b. ? - 1836

Alois Becker
b. ? - 1844

Rudolph "Rudi"
1814-1836

Margaret
1812-1865

Carl
1819-1862

Margaretha
"Magda" Vogel
1823-1918

Hannah (2)
Sr. Mary Dolores
1855-1900

Jane Goodacre
1850-1961

Samuel "Sam"
1854-1950

Hannah (1)
1851

Rudolph "Dolph"
1849-1928

Elizabeth
1878-1970

Margaret
1877-1917

Isobel Carey-Groves
1857-1918

James Vining
1838-1863

John Vining
1834-1863

Caroline "Caro"
1877-1965

Horace Vining (1)
b. ? - 1841

Horace Vining
1831-1863

Peter Vining
1839-1910

Rose
1876-1959

Henry Williamson (2)
1843? - 1862

Amelia Stoddard
1840-1883

Horace "Horrie"
Vining
1861-1937

Anna Richter
1843-1925

Christian
1872-1964

Henry "Harry"
1870-1945

Charlotte "Lottie"
1862-1938

Sebastian Bertrand
1860-1930

Steinmetz – Richter Family

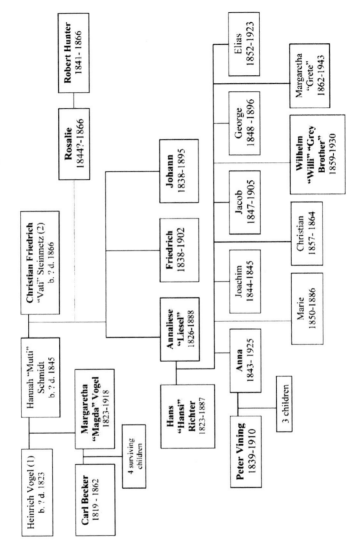

Notes on Texas, the Railway, and the Quivera Trail

This book came about because readers wanted to know what happened to the Becker and Richter families after the *Trilogy* – especially to Dolph and his English bride, Isobel – and eventually, so did I. It became a small running joke in the last volume of the *Trilogy*, that Dolph resisted most attempts to match him with a nice girl and that his usual excuse would be that when he found one who liked dogs and horses, he would consider it. The chance meeting with Isobel in the last chapters of *The Harvesting* was an attempt to match him with a nice girl who did like dogs and horses – a lot – and moreover, one who was deeply unhappy in her current mode and station in life, and just desperate enough to marry a foreign stranger.

Until I came around to working out what I would write about next – I didn't really consider how Isobel's side of it all could be expanded upon, in a mad homage to about every classic romance novel I ever read (starting with *Jane Eyre*) and in collision with every classical western that I also read, such as Owen Wister's *The Virginian*, which set the tone for the western rancher/cowboy hero for all time. I actually hadn't read that many of either, preferring sturdier fare. A little of typical romance authors, like marshmallow fluff, goes a long way. But I had also mapped out another trilogy, after completing *Adelsverein*, and commenced writing. The first prospective novel followed Margaret Becker's life in the early years in Texas, and during the Republic of Texas, the second being this volume, and the third (and next) being the adventures of teen-aged Fredi Steinmetz in Gold Rush-era California. For a good few months, I was writing this and *Daughter of Texas/Deep in the Heart* in alternate chapters. Whenever I got stuck, or bored of one, I'd scribble away on the other – until I got to about halfway through Chapter 7, and then I had to go full-tilt on *Daughter*. Nothing is as inspiring as a deadline, although the viewpoints of female main characters tend to be a trifle limiting.

I came back to the draft of *The Quivera Trail*, already certain that I would tell the story alternately from Isobel and Jane's perspective. Jane came about as a character as I roughed out Chapter 1. Of course a lady would have a personal maid, and that maid would be someone who would have a very close relationship with her, yet would have had completely different life experiences and expectations. A ladies' maid of that time was privy to her mistresses' most intimate life and since the clothing of the time was intricate and high-maintenance, they would be thrown together often. Isobel and Jane escaped from their limited circumstances and explored their new lives and opportunities; wouldn't it be interesting, seeing the experience and each other – through their eyes? And wouldn't it be interesting to see how they fashioned those new lives for themselves, just as most 19th century immigrants to America did?

Just as an aside, I drew on Nancy Bradfield's *Costume in Detail 1730-1930* (1983 edition) for details of Isobel's dresses and outfits, especially for her wedding dress, which is the dress described on pages 225-226. This is a beautiful volume of mainly line drawings, showing details of construction, ornament, fastenings and fine details, as well as the general appearance of authentic period garments.

Isobel's experiences on the cattle drive are loosely based on those of Cornelia Adair, Mollie Bunton, and other daring wives of cattlemen and investors who followed their husbands on the cattle trails, as related in a collection of brief biographies edited by Sara Massey, *Texas Women on the Cattle Trails*. It was Mollie Bunton who discovered the skunk kittens and the somnolent rattlesnake underneath her mattress one morning. Historically, Charles Goodnight was the first rancher to realize the fortunate situation of the canyon complex and take advantage in establishing the vast JA ranch there. Cornelia Adair's husband John was Goodnight's 'angel investor' in the ranch.

1876 was also a miraculous year for Texas ranchers and citizens; the Comanche and Kiowa, whose raids into Texas for loot, captives and horses had scourged Texans from the earliest days, had finally been decisively defeated – and by coincidence, at Palo Duro two years previously, by Colonel Ranald McKenzie, who raided into the Comanche camps there. He destroyed their stores and more importantly, their horse herds. As cruel as this action appears; it was no crueler than the results of Comanche war parties raiding into Texas and Mexico for decades. The plains above the Hill Country were finally safe for settlement, when the desperate and starving Comanche survivors were forced onto the reservations in Indian Territory. One cannot stress how much this was a relief to those settlers who had been on the receiving end of Comanche depredations. Contemporary Texans like Anna Richter Vining could find very little sympathy in their hearts for the Comanche, after having seen loved ones kidnapped, tortured, and slaughtered by Comanche war parties.

Those three years covered in this volume also turned out to be interesting for two other reasons. 1876 was that Centennial year; the United (and occasionally dis-united) States observed a hundred years of existence. Citizens looked back on the last hundred years and were generally pleased and satisfied with what had been accomplished. Here was an independent country, a democratic republic, based on the active participation of engaged and responsible citizens; no hereditary ruling class, no established nobility or royalty, just a from-the-bottom-up administration drawn from the local and state level, feeding into a relatively restrained federal establishment! And it had managed to last a hundred years! It had succeeded politically, militarily, socially, and technologically, establishing dominion over a large swath of the American continent, from sea to shining sea.

Lastly, 1877 was the year that San Antonio was finally connected by railway ties to the rest of Texas and the greater U.S. – the very last major city left un-served by a railway. The change which the railway brought to San Antonio is most evident in comparing a pair of birds-eye view city maps of San Antonio; the first by Augustus Koch from 1873; a tight cluster of buildings around Main and Military Plazas, along a couple of blocks of Soledad and Flores Streets, and the length of Commerce Street between the Alamo and Main Plazas. All the rest of town is a scattering of small houses scattered among gardens, small pastures and orchards of trees. When Koch returned to the city in 1886 for another birds-eye map, the railway had arrived – so had a streetcar system. The Army had removed to a new establishment, Fort Sam Houston, on the uplands to the north, and many of the open spaces in the 1873 map had been filled in by taller and more modern structures. The railway revived what had been previously a sleepy and remote backwater, served by stages and freight wagons. This made San Antonio an especially fascinating backdrop for Isobel and Jane's experiences – and I have taken full advantage.

Of the actual historical figures wandering in and out, there are only a handful in comparison to *Daughter of Texas* and *Deep in the Heart*. Lizzie Johnson, or Elizabeth Johnson Williams is the most prominent of them. (Her biography is one of those in *Texas Women on the Cattle Trail*.) She was a formidable woman well ahead of her time; a resourceful businesswoman and entrepreneur who parlayed teaching school, working as a bookkeeper and writing for *Leslies' Illustrated Weekly* into a fortune in real estate and cattle – about which she was startlingly knowledgeable for a maiden lady school teacher. Another astonishingly modern touch – she married well beyond the age that a woman was expected to have committed in matrimony, and it was not for lack of serious suitors. Lizzie was, to judge from contemporary formal daguerreotype portraits of her, dark-haired and handsome rather than the conventional Victorian ideal of beauty, although she dressed elegantly and in the latest fashion. She was also courted assiduously by any number of prosperous men and eligible bachelors, every one of whom knew her as a woman of property and exactly how she came by it. Brains, beauty and business sense apparently had considerable allure. When she did finally marry, at the age of 39, to a handsome and rather raffish widower, Hezekiah Williams, it was with the equivalent of a prenuptial agreement in place. She controlled her own property acquired before the marriage, as well as anything she acquired in her own name after it. When she died in the 1920s, her neighbors and family were astounded to discover that she owned property worth about a quarter of a million dollars.

James Swain is an alias. So was the name Wesley Clemmons and "Little Arkansas"; all were used by John Wesley Hardin, who at the time of this story was living in relative hiding with his family in Florida, although he may have traveled back and forth several times and kept in touch with his parents and family network. He was a fugitive from the law in Texas and the post-Civil War reconstruction administration several times over, for his part in killing several lawmen in various confrontations, his involvement in the Sutton-Taylor feud, and for escaping from custody on at least two occasions. He left a large number of bodies in his wake although the exact total is in dispute. He claimed a tally of 42, beginning when he was but a callow youth of fifteen or so, but contemporary newspapers could actually confirm only 27. Finally captured by Texas Rangers, sentenced and convicted shortly after his second appearance in this story, he spent seventeen years in prison, where he studied law. He was released early, passed the Texas bar and practiced law in El Paso, Texas. Unfortunately, prison had not mellowed his violent impulses very much and his deadly reputation followed him. After an angry encounter with a local lawman, Hardin was ambushed and killed by the lawman's father while playing dice in a saloon. After Hardin's death a local citizen is supposed to have rendered the following judgement: *"If he shot Wes Hardin face to face, he was a brave man – if he shot him in the back, he was a wise one."*

Dr. Ferdinand Herff was also a real person; an experienced and well-trained surgeon who arrived with the first wave of Adelsverein-sponsored settlers in 1847. He was initially a founding member of an idealistic commune called 'The Forty' – who had a jolly adventure for a year or two in their little settlement-utopia called Bettina, near present-day Castell. The Forty were long on ideals, enthusiasm, and funds, but short on relish for back-breaking agricultural labor. The community foundered on the rocks of human nature and self-interest, but not before Doctor Herff performed a single amazing feat of surgery; the first ever operation in Texas to remove cataracts . . . and the patient was a Comanche warrior. Dr. Herff practiced medicine tirelessly for most of the next sixty years. He established San Antonio's first hospital, several medical associations and served on the Texas Board of Medical Examiners. He operated anywhere, quite often out in the open, and sometimes with a large audience watching. Generally, if there is a surgical "first" anywhere in Texas during the last half of the 19th century, he was the surgeon responsible for it. A historical marker on the Riverwalk at Soledad Street marks the site of one of his homes and another on a hill outside the little town of Boerne, where Dr. Herff and his family later spent the summers. He was noted for being scrupulous when it came to cleanliness of his instruments and hands well before antiseptic practice became the norm. Very likely, as I have noted, he was aware of a strong correlation between his practices and the survival rates of his patients following what was pretty invasive surgery.

Sheriff Tomas McCall was a law officer in San Antonio at the time. Gottleib Knauer was a cabinetmaker, but his premise was not on Houston Street, downstairs from Sam and Jane's atelier and home. With regard to Jane and Sam's atelier, the building on Houston Street by the iron bridge crossing over the river to St. Mary's Street was an office, a tailor shop and two auction houses, according to the Sanborn Fire Insurance map of a decade later – but the 1873 map clearly shows an earlier building on that site, by the iron bridge and overlooking the river and the backs of houses along Saint Mary's and Soledad Streets.

The 'awful Bean person' briefly mentioned to Jane, as a dubious source of fresh milk is the infamous Roy Bean, later the infamous 'only law west of the Pecos.' Roy Bean was at this time scraping a living in San Antonio in a number of enterprises – including vending milk adulterated with water, and firewood poached from other people's wood-lots.

Of invented characters, some are based on real people: Wash Charpentier, the champion cowboy-turned-Pullman porter, was based on the flamboyant Nat Love; wrangler and top hand, an early rodeo champion and Western personality, who did indeed walk away from the open rage in early middle age to embark on a long and relatively secure second career as a Pullman porter.

Sam Becker's career as a painter was very loosely based on his slightly younger contemporary Charles M. Russell. The Missouri-born Russell's works were grounded in and inspired by his work as a cowhand in Montana, some decades after the glory days of the long-trail drives from Texas to the Kansas railheads. Unlike Sam, Russell did not study in Europe, but was almost entirely self-taught. It is noted that he did not settle down to become a professional painter until he married in his early thirties, to a strong-minded young woman named Nancy Cooper, who is usually given considerable credit for managing his business affairs and publicity. Russell did a charming full-length portrait of Nancy, dressed in a buckskin Indian costume, reclining in front of a panel of painted buckskin, leaning on her elbow, and toying with a horsehair whisk.

The Whitmire gang are complete inventions, although loosely based on the Cherokee Starr clan, notorious because one of their number married Myra Maybelle Shirley, later known as Belle Starr. There were a number of dangerous – not to mention vicious criminal gangs – who found a safe refuge in the Indian Territories of present-day Oklahoma; gangs who specialized in bank and train robberies, in stealing horses, cattle, and everything else not nailed down with foot-long rail spikes. This degree of lawlessness continued well into the 20th century.

Alf Trotter, or Tom Becker, the Bandera Kid is also an invention, inspired by several elements. One of them is the life of a celebrity who came from England at a relatively young age and yet merged more or less seamlessly into an American persona: Bob Hope. Another are the careers of a handful of performers who gravitated from having actually worked as cowboys and wranglers in their youth in the late 19th century to performing in Wild West shows, and finally in silent movie serials. Alf/Tom is not based on anyone in particular – but I thought how interesting it was that someone who had actually experienced the real life of the western frontier could have gone from that to playing it in the movies and helping to create the legendary Wild West.

CPSIA information can be obtained at www.ICGtesting.com
Printed in the USA
LVOW11s2353190614

390763LV00002B/119/P